Great Ghost Stories

Great Ghost Stories

34 Classic Tales of the Supernatural

Compiled by
Robin Brockman

Illustrations by
Barrington Barber

GRAMERCY BOOKS
NEW YORK

Copyright © 2000 by Arcturus Publishing Limited
All rights reserved under International and Pan-American Copyright Conventions.

This 2002 edition is published by Gramercy Books, an imprint of Random House Value Publishing, Inc., 280 Park Avenue, New York, NY 10017, by arrangement with Arcturus Publishing Limited.

Gramercy is a registered trademark and the colophon is a trademark of Random House, Inc.

Random House
New York • Toronto • London • Sydney • Auckland
www.randomhouse.com

Printed and bound in the United States of America

[Previously published as *Classic Tales of the Supernatural*.]

Library of Congress Cataloging-in-Publication Data

Classic tales of the supernatural.
    Great ghost stories : 34 classic tales of the supernatural / compiled by Robin Brockman;
    illustrations by Barrington Barber.
        p. cm.
    Previously published as: Classic tales of the supernatural.
    ISBN 0-517-22095-4
        1. Ghost stories, English. 2. Ghost stories, American. I. Brockman, Robin. II. Title.

PR1309.G5 C55 2002
823'.0873308--dc21

                                                        2002022398

10 9 8 7 6 5 4 3 2

For Jane

Contents

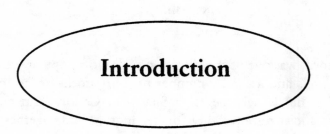

Introduction

The tales in this volume are the work of some of the most noted writers of the last two centuries. A number of names will be unfamiliar to modern readers, although they would have been recognised in their own time. We have to confess to knowing virtually nothing about two of the writers represented here: Sir Thomas Gordon Jackson, author of an atmospheric tale of possession, 'The Lady of Rosemount', and the mysterious 'S. B. T.', author of 'The Case of the Reverend Toomey'. The latter's reluctance to proclaim ownership may be symptomatic of the negative view of commercial writers taken by 'polite' society in the 19th century, when this story was probably written. A person with social pretensions looking to supplement their income might have been too embarrassed to put their real name to a story that would in all probability have been published in a popular magazine. An alternative explanation might be sensitivity about the subject matter. A professional man – especially in the sciences – would probably not have wished to be associated with this particular horror tale, which is narrated as though it were true; the protagonist, we are told, was educated by Jesuits and subsequently lost to science, namely the Royal College of Surgeons.

The lack of private means could be as much of a handicap to recognition as misplaced social pretensions. Nathaniel Hawthorne had to wait years – until 1850 and publication of his masterpiece *The Scarlet Letter* – before the proceeds from his writing provided enough for him and his family to live on. Others who came from the professional classes were better placed to make the break sooner. Among our authors the most popular occupation for abandonment was the law – Sheridan Le Fanu, R.L. Stevenson, William Thackeray, Henry James and Wilkie Collins left its certainties for the precarious career of the professional writer. These men at least had a skill to fall back on. Many of our writers wrote because it was the only means of making a living open to them.

Charlotte Riddell (1832–1906), who also wrote under the name

F. G. Trafford, was one of the Victorian era's most popular writers, with over 40 novels and a similar number of short stories to her name. On the death of her father, the High Sheriff of County Antrim, she had assumed financial responsibility for her mother and together they had moved to London where Charlotte established herself as a writer. Her success, though, did not ward off further financial misfortune. In 1880, her husband, Joseph Hadley Riddell, a civil engineer, died heavily indebted and she spent the rest of her life paying off this legacy. She was the first writer to receive a pension from the Society of Authors.

Amelia Edwards (1831–92) was as well known as Charlotte Riddell, though as a journalist and self-taught Egyptologist as well as a novelist. She had published poems and short stories from an early age and gone on to write a number of novels, including the very popular *Lord Brackenbury* (1880). The example of her work included here, 'The Phantom Coach', contains excellent descriptions of ghostly manifestations and a convincing argument, put by one of the characters, supporting the existence of the supernatural.

Both Edwards and Riddell chose male characters as their protagonists, as did Edith Nesbit (1858–1924), who is best remembered today for *The Railway Children*. Her stories often contain both humour and magical elements and she obviously relished the supernatural genre (see her collection *Tales Told in the Twilight*). 'Man-Size in Marble' belongs in the line of cautionary tales: if usually sensible people warn you about something weird, it pays to listen.

All of these women became commercial writers out of financial necessity. Two of the stories in this collection, however, are from the pens of people who are better remembered for their success in other forms of artistic endeavour. The actress Sarah Bernhardt is one; the other is the decorative artist and social reformer William Morris (1834-96). 'The Story of the Unknown Church' – first published in the *Oxford & Cambridge Magazine* and later in book form (1904) – is an evocative reminder of his primary artistic talent. The founder of the Arts and Crafts movement in England and practitioner of the neo-Gothic style, Morris shared the Pre-Raphaelites' fascination with the medieval, which is the setting for this story. This is not so much a ghost story as a ghost's story told in a Pre-Raphaelite word painting.

Morris's vivid descriptions and the unique point of view presented by the medieval stone-mason in his story would have struck some chords in Thomas Hardy (1840-1928). At about the same time as Morris was embarking on a career in architecture, Hardy was starting his apprenticeship with a church restorer who would train him in the architecture of the Gothic revival, the style with which Morris himself would later become so closely associated. Although Hardy gave up architecture to pursue a writing career, he did not lose his interest in the subject and especially his deep appreciation of stonework.

'The Withered Arm' is representative of much of Hardy's fiction in its tone, style and situation. The supernatural element arises from the dark thoughts of an embittered country-woman and is presented as just another of the tribulations which Hardy's Wessex characters had to endure.

Female malevolence is also at work in Nathaniel Hawthorne's 'The Hollow of the Three Hills' (originally published in 1830 in the *Salem Gazette*). It shares other similarities with Hardy's tale as well, eschewing the usual form of a horror or ghost story and depicting the supernatural very much as Hardy does, as a fact of life.

A large number of 'spooky' tales were penned because, as Jerome K. Jerome points out so charmingly, the ghost story, especially the Christmas ghost story, became a traditional part of Anglo-American culture, almost an institution. His contribution to this collection, 'The Haunted Mill or The Ruined House', is not set at Christmas, but is typically Jeromian in its main thrust – that a ghost should not be expected to behave better than he did when he was alive.

One writer who cashed in on the popularity of the Christmas story was Charles Dickens (1812–70). Few writers were as successful or as 'professional' in their approach to their craft as Dickens. We have included two of his tales, 'The Bagman's Story' and 'The Goblins Who Stole A Sexton', both of which are taken from *The Pickwick Papers* (1836–37). The latter is reminiscent of 'A Christmas Carol'. Written seven years earlier, its harder edge has greater appeal for the modern reader. The story's protagonist, Gabriel Grub, is not dissimilar to Ebeneezer Scrooge in character, but his deliverance from his worst instincts is handled in a less cloying manner.

Dickens was a cultivator of talent, largely through the periodicals he edited. Wilkie Collins (1824–89), who is best remembered for *The*

Woman in White (1860) and for penning the first English detective novel, *The Moonstone* (1868), was among the young writers he helped. He contributed many stories to Dickens' publications and the two men became close friends as well as literary collaborators. 'Miss Jéromette and the Clergyman' has many of the ingredients of a good mystery story and displays Collins' strength as a master of plot. His sympathetic depiction of the unenviable situation of the young Frenchwoman Jéromette may have been based on personal experience. Collins sinned against Victorian morals by living with a widow and keeping another mistress by whom he had several children.

It is also thanks to Dickens that one of the most remarkable tales in this collection was published. Although she was already an established name when she sat down to write 'The Old Nurse's Story', Mrs Gaskell (1810–65) – or Elizabeth Cleghorn as she really was – had not previously attempted anything in the genre of supernatural fiction. The result greatly impressed Dickens, who asked her to contribute it to the 1852 extra Christmas issue of his weekly magazine *Household Words*. The story contains the quintessential features of classic ghost literature, in its setting, structure, deft characterisations and mixing of horror and tragedy. It was published in book form in 1865, in a collection entitled *Cousin Phyllis and Other Tales*.

The subject of Mrs Gaskell's only biography, Charlotte Brontë (1816– 55), is also represented in this collection, by 'Napoleon and the Spectre', an oddity extracted from a manuscript tale entitled 'The Green Dwarf' and first published in 1919.

Dickens, Collins and to a lesser extent Mrs Gaskell are rare exceptions among the authors represented here. Few of them prospered, died comfortably, in funds, and highly praised, or even with living spouses and surviving children.

If not penury, then personal tragedy dogged their existence. This is true to life on earth as we know it, and exactly how a select number of our writers chose to depict it. Two who famously did were the American Edgar Allan Poe and the French writer Guy de Maupassant.

Edgar Allan Poe (1808–49) particularly is as much remembered today for the misery of his life as his work. An orphan, then a failure in the army, from which he was drummed out for neglect of his duties, he struggled constantly against poverty, alcohol and depression. After the death of his child-bride, Virginia, in 1847, guilt overtook him, closely followed by madness. 'The Oval Portrait' was written in 1842 and first published some three years later in the *Broadway Journal*. Short and atmospheric, it is in the form of a prose poem with a singularly harrowing effect at the end. In its central idea – that of a portrait becoming imbued with the essence of the living – it is strikingly similar to Wilde's classic story *The Portrait of Dorian Gray*.

In some respects Guy de Maupassant (1850–93) took up the flame which was extinguished at Poe's death. His horror fiction is razor sharp and resonates starkly against the backdrop of his personal circumstances. De Maupassant ended his days a victim of insanity (like Poe), and died at his own hand.

In a letter to a friend, Paul Bourget, de Maupassant confided something of his inner state:

'Every other time I come home, I see my double. I open my door, and I see him in my armchair. I know it for a hallucination, even while experiencing it. Curious! If I didn't have a little common sense, I'd be afraid.'

Bear these words in mind when you read de Maupassant's contribution to our collection, 'The Horla' (originally published in French in 1887), in which the reader is left with the impression that the narrator's sanity is in question.

While writers such as Poe and de Maupassant chose to reflect their own sense of reality in their writing, others chose to use their work as a means of escape or perhaps as a palliative.

The Reverend Richard Barham managed to keep on the plus side of sanity despite unhappy personal circumstances. Four of his five children died prematurely, and from middle age both he and his wife suffered severely from depression. Around 1837 his stories began to find favour with the better magazines of the day and were eventually published in book form, in 1844, as *The Ingoldsby Legends* (subtitled 'Or Mirth and Marvels'), under his pen-name Thomas Ingoldsby. 'The Spectre of Tappington' is set in his native Kent and is full of invention and good humour, as is his second contribution, 'Grey Dolphin', in which he pokes fun at the Catholic clergy as they wrestle with the problems that ensue when the ghost of St Bridget protests at the burying of a reprobate too close to her resting place.

Conell Cearnach, the pen-name of Frederick O'Connell (1876–1925), was also a man of the cloth. Educated at Trinity College, Dublin, he was ordained into the Church of Ireland in 1902 and was appointed Rector of Achonry in 1907. Subsequently, he lectured in Celtic at Queen's University, Belfast, and became Assistant Director of Radio Eireann. 'The Homing Bone' is about the disquieting consequences that follow the removal from consecrated ground of a seemingly insignificant part of a corpse. Cearnach clearly intended his readers to enjoy the spectacle of an eminent man of science being hoisted with his own petard. The protagonist is so well drawn, one wonders if the author did not have a subject in mind. Another tale in which the unthinkingly confident are made to look foolish is 'Teiuge of the Lee' by T. Crofton Croker (1798–1854), who is principally remembered today as the first collector of Irish folklore.

The infamous Burke and Hare case must have been in the thoughts of R. L. Stevenson (1854–94) when he wrote 'The Body-Snatcher', which was not published until after his death, in 1904. Burke and Hare operated at the extreme end of a practice that had flourished for almost a century, murdering people in order to sell their bodies to an Edinburgh surgeon. There was a public outcry when the duo's activities and details of the trade in corpses were brought to light. The case resulted in a change in the law, which had hitherto classified the taking of a naked corpse merely as a misdemeanour. 'The Body Snatcher' is a very modern piece, in that at its spine-chilling heart it is about moral ambiguity.

As in all good literature, motivation is a key element in these stories of the restless dead, of monsters, vampires, elemental spirits, evil enchantment, possession by demons, out-of-body experiences and murder by mysterious and unnatural means. In the best of them the human psyche is unpicked and opened up for us to view. Few writers do this more stylishly than Henry James (1843–1916). In 'The Romance of Certain Old Cloths' (1885), which has a satisfyingly appropriate dénouement, the acuity of his observations on human behaviour is delivered with wry humour.

James's fellow countryman, Kentuckian Ambrose Bierce (1842–1913?), was similarly clear-eyed about human nature. In 'The Moonlit Road' he presents as pessimistic a view of the realm that might be available to us as he does of the one that undeniably is. By 1907, the date of the story's first publication, Bierce had experienced enough – of his parents, marriage, fatherhood, and life in the army – to form his generally unflattering view of humanity. In the 1890s he established his reputation as a master of supernatural and psychological horror stories, notably with the collection *Can Such Things Be?* (1893), and as the author of the delightfully wicked *Devil's Dictionary*. The exact date of 'Bitter' Bierce's death is not known. He disappeared in Mexico during one of that country's most violent civil wars.

The worldview of William Makepeace Thackeray (1811–63) was as cynical as Bierce's but made more palatable by the wit he used to put it across. In Thackeray's time the watch-word for literature was 'edification' and he, more than most among British writers, strained against this limiting ideal. 'The Devil's Wager' is one of the many miscellaneous pieces he produced in addition to his novels. In this spoof on Goethe's revered *Faust* the central character, the black-hearted Sir Roger de Rollo, is snatched at death by Mercurius, the messenger of demons, who bets him that they will be unable to find anyone willing to pray for him and thus save his soul.

Thackeray was an early contributor to the satirical magazine *Punch*, which was co-founded and, from 1843, edited by the multi-skilled Mark Lemon (1809–70), who almost single-handedly kept the magazine afloat in its early years. Lemon wrote numerous stories and over 60 plays in addition to editing magazines, such as the *London Journal*, *Family Herald*, *London Illustrated News* and *The Field*, of which he was founder-editor. The protagonist of 'The Ghost Detective' is a forerunner of later fictional investigators, a highly sceptical fellow who plays – or perhaps is – the devil's advocate. The odd happenings in the story are explained in various arguments put forward by the characters, leaving the reader to judge their validity for himself.

O. Henry (1862-1910) takes a similar line in 'The Furnished Room' (1904), leaving us to decide how the events which come through the voices, thoughts, and deeds of his characters should be explained. Although the story is untypical of his output, in that it is not intended to amuse and it does not have a tricky ending, it shows his fatalistic side. Henry, whose real name was William Sidney Porter, had a deep pool of life-experiences to draw from. Virtually orphaned at birth in North

Carolina and the recipient of little formal schooling, he worked in his uncle's drugstore until he was old enough to make his way in the world. He took a series of unskilled jobs, writing in his spare time and in 1894 launching a humour magazine, *Rolling Stone*. This soon failed, and he began writing a column for the *Houston Daily Post*. An accusation of embezzlement was then made against him by a bank for which he had worked years earlier. He fled to Central America, hiding out there until news that his wife was dying forced him to return and start the long prison sentence that awaited him. He began to write in earnest from his cell in the Federal Penitentiary, Columbus, Ohio. On his release Henry settled in New York and made himself familiar with every aspect of city life. International acclaim for his masterly short stories eventually came and with it a contract to *World* magazine. 'The Furnished Room' is one of these New York tales, written when he was at the height of his popularity and turning out stories at the rate of one a week to satisfy demand. Described as generous and unassuming by those who knew him, Henry did not manage to hold on to the material rewards of his success, and died an alcoholic.

Any connection between the supernatural and religious belief is incidental in most of the stories included here. Belief in an after-life of sorts was once almost universal, although then, as now, church-going was a minority activity. In the comparatively rare instances when religion puts in an appearance, it is always in the guise of the old faith and usually the object of humour. Writers did not, it seems, lightly poke fun at their own faith, though it was acceptable to do so at somebody else's. Even those who were clergymen in real life – such as Thomas Ingoldsby and Conell Cearnach – do not write from an obviously religious perspective. Ironically, the one writer who does is the actress Sarah Bernhardt (1845–1923). In 'The Last Drop' she paints a very Romish, very personal picture of the after-life and spiritual redemption. The Divine Sarah, whose real name was Rosine Bernard, was fascinated by the supernatural and possessed a large library of material on this and related subjects. 'The Last Drop' was first published in 1893, during one of Bernhardt's world tours.

J. Sheridan Le Fanu (1814–73) also had an interest in the supernatural which extended beyond mere curiosity and the desire to explore as wide a range of human experience as his imagination could embrace. He had become obsessed with other-worldly matters as only the grief-stricken can be, in his case on the death of his wife, Susan, in 1858. Although childless, their 14-year union had been a very happy one, and without her he is said to have virtually dwelt with death. Nevertheless, he managed his business affairs well for the remaining 15 years of his life, the period in which he produced his best work. A few days after finishing his last book, *Willing to Die*, he passed away at his home in Dublin.

Unlike Le Fanu, Arthur Conan Doyle (1859–1930) rarely wrote fiction which dealt with the supernatural, although he was deeply interested in the subject, especially after the death of his son in the First World War. Certainly, Conan Doyle's most famous creations, Sherlock Holmes and Doctor Watson, never encountered anything of the sort, having their hands full, as the author once remarked, with ordinary mysteries. The story we have chosen, 'The Captain of the Pole-Star' (1890), can be read in several ways: as a tale of the supernatural, a depiction of mental breakdown or as a synthesis of both elements. (For those who are interested, there is evidence that Doyle kept his promise to return in spirit and reveal what is on the other side of death. His correspondence with mediums is well documented and has been written about by Ian Cooke in his book *The Return of Arthur Conan Doyle*.)

Our selection involves just about every form of supernatural phenomenon known to man. Even the tales which fall into the general category of ghost story take many forms, from those whose other-worldly nature may be put down to pure and harmless imagination (such as Dickens' 'The Bagman's Story'), to full-blown, full-frontal supernatural horror, such as 'The Case of the Reverend Mr. Toomey'.

In this collection the truly frightening or weird may be bracketed by the amusing on one side and the hilarious on the other, or you may be hit with something ghoulish, macabre or insidiously haunting. Above all there is variety, for that is the nature of the literature of things that go bump in the night – there are so very many things that can and will go bump. Such is the way of life and the stranger aspects of existence.

The modern reader might also do well to keep two points in mind as he or she approaches these gems of a past age. First, many of the stories were written with the spoken voice in mind, as dramatic pieces. In those pre-radio, pre-television days, family or group entertainment at home often entailed someone reading aloud, with expression. As anyone who has ever been a Boy Scout or Brownie knows, scary stories shared with others are the most rewarding of all. A good example of the kind of tale that would have come across as powerfully in that other great story-telling venue, the country pub, is 'The Ghost Ship'. Its author, Richard Middleton (1882–1911), was related to Richard Barham, creator of *The Ingoldsby Legends*, and would appear to have shared his depressive tendencies, committing suicide at the age of 29. A year after his death, a collection of Middleton's stories appeared in print for the first time, largely due to the support of the respected writer of fantasy stories, Arthur Machen. Ironically, they received the acclaim that Middleton must have dreamt of and which might have encouraged him to believe that his life was worth living.

Secondly, from this distance in history it is easy to forget how fundamentally different life was in the 19th century, when most of these stories were written. Until Thomas Edison designed his complete electrical distribution system for lighting and power, the world was a very different place after dark. Prior to the late 1880s – and in most places much later than this – live flame in the form of candles and gaslight was all our ancestors could depend on for illumination. Relative gloom after sundown was a given for the original readers of most of our stories, in town as well as country. This world of shadows and dark corners, smoky rooms and easily extinguished light did things for, and to, the imagination.

Coupled with this literal gloom was the knowledge that life would in all probability be short and uncomfortable. It is little wonder that the supernatural should have been of interest to so many writers. Life not only looked scary, it was scary. There were few ways of escaping this knowledge. Most people spent their entire lives in the area where they were born, imbibing the local wisdom. Dwellings were often used by succeeding generations of the same family, and memories were long. Every ill-timed death or odd occurrence in the community was remembered, and its location pointed out and frequently encountered. Some of our stories take the form of traditional knowledge passed on orally to those who are prepared to listen.

Le Fanu's 'An Account of the Strange Disturbances at Aungier Street', touches on several of these elements. In this chilling example of his work the scene of the 'disturbances' is a house that 'had seen years and changes enough to have contracted all that mysterious and saddened air, at once exciting and depressing, which belongs to most old mansions.' Evil has imprinted itself in the atmosphere of this place. Both the narrator, who confesses to having 'a superstitious weakness', and the other principal character, the sceptical Tom, are deeply affected by their experiences. The reader could be either of these two individuals. The choice is his, the outcome irresistible.

The goings-on in Sir Walter Scott's (1771–1832) 'The Tapestried Chamber' owe more to romantic literature than the full-blooded horror that was Le Fanu's forte. In supernatural fiction haunted houses are as varied as the stories of the ghosts that populate them. The stately home with resident ghost that puts the fear of God into unsuspecting guests became a cliché of the genre. We have included only as many stories as it takes to give you an idea of the different treatments meted out to the theme.

By the end of the 19th century the ancestral home had figured in just about every type of haunting and supernatural happening that literary minds could devise. Exhausted of possibilities as a venue for 'serious' ghosts, it was taken up by the wags and, in a couple of instances at least, used as a backdrop for a humorous exploration of the differences between the British and their American cousins. Oscar Wilde (1854–1900) presents a delightfully subtle and witty Anglo-Irish perspective on this in 'The Canterville Ghost' (1904), an Old World spook which finds itself at a loss when trying to deal with New World attitudes and methods.

American writers also took up the challenge of undermining the convention of taking literary ghosts seriously. In the humorously fanciful 'Ghosts That Have Haunted Me', published in 1896 in *Harper's Weekly*, John Kendrick Bangs (1862–1922) treats 'visitants from other worlds' with refreshing nonchalence.

By and large, it is doubtful whether our ancestors took paranormal matters any more or less seriously than we do. It would also be wrong to suppose that people then were necessarily more superstitious than we are, although they may have been more credulous. They were certainly less dependent on science when it came to what was accepted as fact, simply because there was less science to depend on. In our time we still execute or imprison people on eyewitness testimony, yet if science insists something cannot be repeated and verified, the most honourable and reliable folks alive can see and report the seemingly incredible and still be laughed at as fools or liars.

Familiarity with the stories we present here brings home the extent to which film and television has relied on this genre of fiction for plots and story-lines. Many of these films and programmes, themselves classics now, largely owe their success to these original works. Without 'The Canterville Ghost', for example, there would have been no *Beetlejuice* or countless similar movies of recent times. And how different would such a cult favourite as *The X Files* be without the creation of psychic investigator Flaxman Low? He and others like him are the ancestors of – and in some cases models for – the archetypal heroes and indispensable villains who appear on our screens. Described as the Sherlock Holmes of the supernatural, Low was dreamt up by mother- and-son writing team Kate (1851–1913) and Hesketh Pritchard (1876–1922), who wrote under the pen-name E. and H. Heron. 'The Story of the Moor Road' first appeared in *Pearson's Magazine* in 1898 and 1899, as one of their '12 Real Ghost Stories'. Hesketh, a noted sportsman and big game hunter, also authored tales of a bandit named Don Q, who was as popular with readers as Conan Doyle's Holmes.

The turn of the millennium has spawned increasing interest in the supernatural, along with a search for spiritual contentment in a society that has largely rejected organized religion, yet grown suspicious of materialism run rampant. Our forebears went through much the same thing, as the passage of time, new inventions and terrible wars changed their lives forever. These stories reflect those seismic shifts, and despite the gulf in years between our time and the age when the stories were written, there is no corresponding gap in our understanding or belief in them. There is little in this book that could not happen, or be supposed to happen, today.

The non-fiction literature of the supernatural, old and new, reads exactly like these tales. Indeed, some of them were purported as truth. Anyone familiar with recent tales of modern ghost hunters and paranormal investigators will remark on this at once. They will also know that we scare as easily, react much the same, and deal no differently with fictional or real phenomena than did past generations. Amusing ghost stories come as sheer relief, as surely they must have done to previous generations of readers.

Their simple approach to the spirits of dead humans is instructive. When all is said and done, ghosts are dead humans, and no more dangerous, indeed less so, and no less foolish. It is, again referring to contemporary paranormal literature and investigation, the comic ghost writer who knows best how to handle apparitions. For the sake of your peace of mind, if you should see a ghost of any kind, let Wilde, Bangs, Jerome and Middleton be your guides, not Stevenson, Scott or Poe.

The Furnished Room

by O. Henry

RESTLESS, shifting, fugacious as time itself, is a certain vast bulk of the population of the red-brick district of the lower West Side. Homeless, they have a hundred homes. They flit from furnished room to furnished room, transients for ever – transients in abode, transients in heart and mind. They sing "Home Sweet Home" in ragtime; they carry their *lares et penates* in a bandbox; their vine is entwined about a picture hat; a rubber plant is their fig tree.

Hence the houses of this district, having had a thousand dwellers, should have a thousand tales to tell, mostly dull ones, no doubt; but it would be strange if there could not be found a ghost or two in the wake of all these vagrant ghosts.

One evening after dark a young man prowled among these crumbling red mansions, ringing their bells. At the twelfth he rested his lean hand-baggage upon the step and wiped the dust from his hat-band and forehead. The bell sounded faint and far away in some remote, hollow depths.

To the door of this, the twelfth house whose bell he had rung, came a housekeeper who made him think of an unwholesome, surfeited worm that had eaten its nut to a hollow shell and now sought to fill the vacancy with edible lodgers.

He asked if there was a room to let.

"Come in," said the housekeeper. Her voice came from her throat; her throat seemed lined with fur. "I have the third floor back, vacant since a week back. Should you wish to look at it?"

The young man followed her up the stairs. A faint light from no particular source mitigated the shadows of the halls. They trod noiselessly upon a stair carpet that its own loom would have forsworn. It seemed to have become vegetable; to have degenerated in that rank, sunless air to lush lichen or spreading moss that grew in patches to the staircase and was viscid under the foot like organic matter. At each turn of the stairs were vacant niches in the wall. Perhaps plants had once been set within them. If so they had died in that foul and tainted air. It may be that statues of the saints had stood there but it was not difficult to conceive that imps and devils had dragged them forth in the darkness and down to the unholy depths of some furnished pit below

"This is the room," said the housekeeper, from her furry throat. "It's a nice room. It ain't often vacant. I had some most elegant people in it last summer – no trouble at all, and paid in advance to the minute. The water's at the end of the hall. Sprowls and Mooney kept it three months. They done a vaudeville sketch. Miss B'retta Sprowls – you may have heard of her – Oh, that was just the stage names – right there over the dresser is where the marriage certificate hung, framed. The gas is here, and you see there is plenty of closet room. It's a room everybody likes. It never stays idle long."

"Do you have many theatrical people rooming here?" asked the young man.

"They comes and goes. A good proportion of my lodgers is connected with the theatres. Yes, sir, this is the theatrical district. Actor people never stays long anywhere. I get my share. Yes, they comes and they goes."

He engaged the room, paying for a week in advance. He was tired, he said, and would take possession at once. He counted out the money. The room had been made ready, she said, even to towels and water. As the housekeeper moved away he put, for the thousandth time, the question that he carried at the end of his tongue.

"A young girl – Miss Vashner – Miss Eloise Vashner – do you remember such a one among your lodgers? She would be singing on the stage, most likely. A fair girl, of medium height and slender, with reddish gold hair and a dark mole near her left eyebrow."

"No, I don't remember the name. Them stage people has names they change as often as their rooms. They comes and they goes. No, I don't call that one to mind."

No. Always no. Five months of ceaseless interrogation and the inevitable negative. So much time spent by day in questioning managers, agents, schools and choruses; by night among the audiences of theatres from all-star casts down to music-halls so low that he dreaded to find what he most hoped for. He who had loved her best had tried to find her. He was sure that since her disappearance from home this great water-girt city held her somewhere, but it was like a monstrous quicksand, shifting its particles constantly, with no foundation, its upper granules of to-day buried to-morrow in ooze and slime.

The furnished room received its latest guest with a first glow of pseudo-hospitality, a hectic, haggard, perfunctory welcome like the specious smile of a demirep. The sophistical comfort came in reflected gleams from the decayed furniture, the ragged brocade upholstery of a couch and two chairs, a foot-wide cheap pier glass between the two windows, from one or two gilt picture frames and a brass bedstead in a corner.

The guest reclined, inert, upon a chair, while the room, confused in speech as though it were an apartment in Babel, tried to discourse to him of its divers tenantry.

A polychromatic rug like some brilliant-flowered, rectangular, tropical islet lay surrounded by a billowy sea of soiled matting. Upon the gay-papered wall were those pictures that pursue the homeless one from house to house – The Huguenot Lovers, The First Quarrel, The Wedding Breakfast, Psyche at the Fountain. The mantel's chastely severe outline was ingloriously veiled behind some pert drapery drawn rakishly askew like the sashes of the Amazonian ballet. Upon it was some desolate flotsam cast aside by the room's marooned when a lucky sail had borne them to a fresh port – a trifling vase or two, pictures of actresses, a medicine bottle, some stray cards out of a deck.

One by one, as the characters of a cryptograph become explicit, the little signs left by the furnished room's procession of guests developed a significance. The threadbare space in the rug in front of the dresser told that lovely women had marched in the throng. Tiny finger-prints on the wall spoke of little prisoners trying to feel their way to sun and air. A splattered stain, raying like the shadow of a bursting bomb, witnessed where a hurled glass or bottle had splintered with its contents against the wall. Across the pier glass had been scrawled with a diamond in staggering letters the name "Marie". It seemed that the succession of dwellers in the furnished room had turned in fury – perhaps tempted beyond forbearance by its garish coldness – and wreaked upon it their passions. The furniture was chipped and bruised; the couch, distorted by bursting springs, seemed a horrible monster that had been slain during the stress of some grotesque convulsion. Some more potent upheaval had cloven a great slice from the marble mantel. Each plank in the floor owned its particular cant and shriek as from a separate and individual agony. It seemed incredible that all this malice and injury had been wrought upon the room by those who had called it for a time their home; and yet it may have been the cheated home instinct surviving blindly, the resentful rage at false household gods that had kindled their wrath. A hut that is our own we can sweep and adorn and cherish.

The young tenant in the chair allowed these thoughts to file, soft-shod, through his mind, while there drifted into the room furnished sounds and furnished scents. He heard in one room a tittering and incontinent, slack laughter; in others the monologue of a scold, the rattling of dice, a lullaby, and one crying dully; above him a banjo tinkled with spirit. Doors banged somewhere; the elevated trains roared intermittently; a cat yowled miserably upon a back fence. And he breathed the breath of the house – a dank savour rather than a smell – a cold, musty effluvium as from underground vaults mingled with the reeking exhalations of linoleum and mildewed and rotten woodwork.

Then, suddenly, as he rested there, the room was filled with the strong, sweet odour of mignonette. It came as upon a single buffet of wind with such sureness and fragrance and emphasis that it almost seemed a living visitant. And the man cried aloud, "What, dear?" as if he had been called, and sprang up and faced about. The rich odour clung to him and wrapped him about. He reached out his arms for it, all his senses for the time confused and commingled. How could one be peremptorily called by an odour? Surely it must have been a sound. But, was it not the sound that had touched, that had caressed him?

"She has been in this room," he cried, and he sprang to wrest from it a token, for he knew he would recognize the smallest thing that had belonged to her or that she had touched. This enveloping scent of mignonette, the odour that she had loved and made her own – whence came it?

The room had been but carelessly set in order. Scattered upon the flimsy dresser scarf were half a dozen hairpins – those discreet, indistinguishable friends of womankind, feminine of gender, infinite of mood and uncommunicative of tense. These he ignored, conscious of their triumphant lack of identity. Ransacking the drawers of the dresser he came upon a discarded, tiny, ragged handkerchief. He pressed it to his face. It was racy and insolent with heliotrope; he hurled it to the floor. In another drawer he found odd buttons, a theatre programme, a pawnbroker's card, two lost marshmallows, a book on the divination of dreams. In the last was a woman's black satin hair-bow, which halted him, poised between ice and fire. But the black satin hair-bow also is femininity's demure, impersonal, common ornament, and tells no tales.

And then he traversed the room like a hound on the scent, skimming the walls, considering the corners of the bulging matting on his hands and knees, rummaging mantel and tables, the curtains and hangings, the drunken cabinet in the corner, for a visible sign unable to perceive that she was there beside, around, against, within, above him, clinging to him, wooing him, calling him so poignantly through the finer senses that even his grosser ones became cognizant of the call. Once again he answered loudly, "Yes, dear!" and turned, wild-eyed, to gaze on vacancy, for he could not yet discern form and colour and love and outstretched arms in the odour of mignonette. Oh, God! whence that odour, and since when have odours had a voice to call? Thus he groped.

He burrowed in crevices and corners, and found corks and cigarettes. These he passed in passive contempt. But once he found in a fold of the matting a half-smoked cigar, and this he ground beneath his heel with a green and trenchant oath. He sifted the room from end to end. He found dreary and ignoble small records of many a peripatetic tenant; but of her whom he sought, and who may have lodged there, and whose spirit seemed to hover there, he found no trace.

And then he thought of the housekeeper.

He ran from the haunted room downstairs and to a door that showed a crack of light. She came out to his knock. He smothered his excitement as best he could.

"Will you tell me, madam," he besought her, "who occupied the room I have before I came?"

"Yes, sir. I can tell you again. 'Twas Sprowls and Mooney, as I said. Miss B'retta Sprowls it was in the theatres, but Missis Mooney she was. My house is well known for respectability. The marriage certificate hung, framed, on a nail over – "

"What kind of a lady was Miss Sprowls – in looks, I mean?"

"Why, black-haired, sir, short and stout, with a comical face. They left a week ago Tuesday."

"And before they occupied it?"

"Why, there was a single gentleman connected with the draying business. He left owing me a week. Before him was Missis Crowder and her two children, that stayed four months; and back of them was old Mr. Doyle, whose sons paid for him. He kept the room six months. That goes back a year, sir, and further I do not remember."

He thanked her and crept back to his room. The room was dead. The essence that had vivified it was gone. The perfume of mignonette had departed. In its place was the old, stale odour of mouldy house furniture, of atmosphere in storage.

The ebbing of his hope drained his faith. He sat staring at the yellow, singing gaslight. Soon he walked to the bed and began to tear the sheets into strips. With the blade of his knife he drove them tightly into every crevice around windows and door. When all was snug and taut he turned out the light, turned the gas full on again and laid himself gratefully upon the bed.

It was Mrs. McCool's night to go with the can for beer. So she fetched it and sat with Mrs. Purdy in one of those subterranean retreats where housekeepers foregather and the worm dieth seldom.

"I rented out my third floor back, this evening," said Mrs. Purdy, across a fine circle of foam. "A young man took it. He went up to bed two hours ago."

"Now, did ye, Mrs. Purdy, ma'am?" said Mrs McCool, with intense admiration. "You do be a wonder for rentin' rooms of that kind. And did ye tell him, then?" she concluded in a husky whisper, laden with mystery.

"Rooms," said Mrs. Purdy, in her furriest tones, "are furnished for to rent. I did not tell him, Mrs McCool."

"'Tis right ye are, ma'am; 'tis by renting rooms we kape alive. Ye have the rale sense for business, ma'am. There be many people will rayjict the rentin' of a room if they be tould a suicide has been after dyin' in the bed of it."

"As you say, we has our living to be making," remarked Mrs. Purdy.

"Yis, ma'am; 'tis true. 'Tis just one wake ago this day I helped ye lay out the third floor back. A pretty slip of a colleen she was to be killin' herself wid the gas – a swate little face she had, Mrs. Purdy, ma'am ."

"She'd a-been called handsome, as you say," said Mrs. Purdy, assenting but critical, "but for that mole she had a-growin' by her left eyebrow. Do fill up your glass again, Mrs. McCool."

The Canterville Ghost

Oscar Wilde

When Mr Hiram B. Otis, the American Minister, bought Canterville Chase, everyone told him he was doing a very foolish thing, as there was no doubt at all that the place was haunted. Indeed, Lord Canterville himself, who was a man of the most punctilious honour, had felt it his duty to mention the fact to Mr Otis when they came to discuss terms.

'We have not cared to live in the place ourselves,' said Lord Canterville, 'since my grand-aunt, the Dowager Duchess of Bolton, was frightened into a fit, from which she never really recovered, by two skeleton hands being placed on her shoulders as she was dressing for dinner, and I feel bound to tell you, Mr Otis, that the ghost has been seen by several living members of my family, as well as by the rector of the parish, the Rev Augustus Dampier, who is a Fellow of King's College, Cambridge. After the unfortunate accident to the Duchess, none of our younger servants would stay with us, and Lady Canterville often got very little sleep at night, in consequence of the mysterious noises that came from the corridor and the library.'

'My Lord,' answered the Minister, 'I will take the furniture and the ghost at a valuation. I come from a modern country, where we have everything that money can buy; and with all our spry young fellows painting the Old World red, and carrying off your best actresses and prima-donnas, I reckon that if there were such a thing as a ghost in Europe, we'd have it at home in a very short time in one of our public museums, or on the road as a show.'

'I fear that the ghost exists,' said Lord Canterville smiling, 'though it may have resisted the overtures of your enterprising impresarios. It has been well known for three centuries, since 1584 in fact, and always makes its appearance before the death of any member of our family.'

'Well, so does the family doctor, for that matter, Lord Canterville. But there is no such thing, sir, as a ghost, and I guess the laws of Nature are not going to be suspended for the British aristocracy.'

'You are certainly very natural in America,' answered Lord Canterville, who did not quite understand Mr Otis's last observation, 'and if you don't mind a ghost in the house, it is all right. Only you must remember I warned you.'

A few weeks after this the purchase was completed, and at the close of the season the Minister and his family went down to Canterville Chase. Mrs Otis, who, as Miss Lucretia R. Tappan, of West 53rd Street, had been a celebrated New York belle, was now a very handsome, middle-aged woman, with fine eyes, and a superb profile. Many American ladies, on leaving their native land, adopt an appearance of chronic ill-health, under the impression that it is a form of European refinement, but Mrs Otis had never fallen into this error. She had a magnificent constitution, and a really wonderful amount of animal spirits. Indeed, in many respects, she was quite English, and was an excellent example of the fact that we have really everything in common with America nowadays, except, of course, language. Her eldest son, christened Washington by his parents in a moment of patriotism, which he never ceased to regret, was a fair-haired, rather good-looking young man, who had qualified himself for American diplomacy by leading the German at the Newport Casino for three successive seasons, and even in London was well known as an excellent dancer. Gardenias and the peerage were his only weaknesses. Otherwise he was extremely sensible. Miss Virginia E. Otis was a little girl of fifteen, lithe and lovely as a fawn, and with a fine freedom in her large, blue eyes. She was a wonderful amazon, and had once raced old Lord Bilton on her pony twice round the park, winning by a length and a half, just in front of the Achilles statue, to the huge delight of the young Duke of Cheshire, who proposed for her on the spot, and was sent back to Eton that very night by his guardians, in floods of tears. After Virginia came the twins, who were usually called 'The Stars and Stripes', as they were always getting swished. They were delightful boys, and, with the exception of the worthy Minister, the only true republicans of the family.

As Canterville Chase is seven miles from Ascot, the nearest railway station, Mr Otis had telegraphed for a wagonette to meet them, and they started on their drive in high spirits. It was a lovely July evening, and the air was delicate with the scent of the pinewoods. Now and then they heard a wood-pigeon brooding over its own sweet voice, or saw, deep in the rustling fern, the burnished breast of the pheasant. Little squirrels peered at them from the beech trees as they went by, and the rabbits scudded away through the brushwood and over the mossy knolls, with their white tails in the air. As they entered the avenue of Canterville Chase, however, the sky became suddenly overcast with clouds, a curious stillness seemed to hold the atmosphere, a great flight of rooks passed silently over their heads, and before they reached the house, some big drops of rain had fallen.

Standing on the steps to receive them was an old woman, neatly dressed in black silk, with a white cap and apron. This was Mrs Umney, the housekeeper, whom Mrs Otis, at Lady Canterville's earnest request, had consented to keep on in her former position. She made them each a low curtsy as they alighted, and said in a quaint, old-fashioned manner, 'I bid you welcome to Canterville Chase.' Following her, they passed through the fine Tudor hall into the library, a long, low room panelled in black oak, at the end of which was a large stained-glass window. Here they found tea laid out for them, and, after taking off their wraps, they sat down and began to look round, while Mrs Umney waited on them.

Suddenly Mrs Otis caught sight of a dull red stain on the floor just by the fireplace and, quite unconscious of what it really signified, said to Mrs Umney, 'I am afraid something has been spilt there.'

'Yes, madam,' replied the old housekeeper in a low voice, 'blood has been spilt on that spot.'

'How horrid,' cried Mrs Otis; 'I don't at all care for bloodstains in a sitting-room. It must be removed at once.'

The old woman smiled, and answered in the same low, mysterious voice, 'It is the blood of Lady Eleanore de Canterville, who was murdered on that very spot by her own husband, Sir Simon de Canterville, in 1575. Sir Simon survived her nine years, and disappeared suddenly under very mysterious circumstances. His body has never been discovered, but his guilty spirit still haunts the Chase. The blood-stain has been much admired by tourists and others, and cannot be removed.'

'This is all nonsense,' cried Washington Otis; 'Pinkerton's Champion Stain Remover and Paragon Detergent will clean it up in no time,' and before the terrified housekeeper could interfere he had fallen upon his knees, and was rapidly scouring the floor with a small stick of what looked like a black cosmetic. In a few moments no trace of the blood-stain could be seen.

'I knew Pinkerton would do it,' he exclaimed triumphantly, as he looked round at his admiring family; but no sooner had he said these words than a terrible flash of lightning lit up the sombre room, and fearful peal of thunder made them all start to their feet, and Mrs Umney fainted.

'What a monstrous climate!' said the American Minister calmly, as he lit a long cheroot. 'I guess the old country is so over-populated that they have not enough decent weather for everybody. I have always been of the opinion that emigration is the only thing for England.'

'My dear Hiram,' cried Mrs Otis, 'what can we do with a woman who faints?'

'Charge it to her, like breakages,' answered the Minister; 'she won't faint after that'; and in a few moments Mrs Umney certainly came to. There was no doubt, however, that she was extremely upset, and she sternly warned Mr Otis to beware of some trouble coming to the house.

'I have seen things with my own eyes, sir,' she said, 'that would make any Christian's hair stand on end, and many and many a night I have not closed my eyes in sleep for the awful things that are done here.' Mr Otis, however, and his wife warmly assured the honest soul that they were not afraid of ghosts, and, after invoking the blessings of Providence on her new master and mistress, and making arrangements for an increase of salary, the old housekeeper tottered off to her own room.

The storm raged fiercely all that night, but nothing of particular note occurred. The next morning, however, when they came down to breakfast, they found the terrible stain of blood once again on the floor. 'I don't think it can be the fault of the Paragon Detergent,' said Washington, 'for I have tried it with everything. It must be the ghost.' He accordingly rubbed out the stain a second time, but the second morning it appeared again. The third morning also it was there, though the library had been locked up at night by Mr Otis himself, and the key carried upstairs. The whole family were now quite interested; Mr Otis began to suspect that he had gone too dogmatic in his denial of the existence of ghosts, Mrs Otis expressed her intention of joining the Psychical Society, and Washington prepared a long letter to Messrs

Myers and Podmore on the subject of the Permanence of Sanguineous Stains when connected with Crime. That night all doubts about the objective existence of phantasmata were removed for ever.

The day had been warm and sunny; and, in the cool of the evening, the whole family went out for a drive. They did not return home till nine o'clock, when they had a light supper. The conversation in no way turned upon ghosts, so there were not even those primary conditions of receptive expectation which so often precede the presentation of psychical phenomena. The subjects discussed, as I have since learned from Mr Otis, were merely such as form the ordinary conversation of cultured Americans of the better class, such as the immense superiority of Miss Fanny Davenport over Sarah Bernhardt as an actress; the difficulty of obtaining green corn, buckwheat cakes, and hominy, even in the best English houses; the importance of Boston in the development of the world-soul; the advantages of the baggage check system in railway travelling; and the sweetness of the New York accent as compared to the London drawl. No mention at all was made of the supernatural, nor was Sir Simon de Canterville alluded to in any way. At eleven o'clock the family retired, and by half-past all the lights were out. Some time after, Mr Otis was awakened by a curious noise in the corridor, outside his room. It sounded like the clank of metal, and seemed to be coming nearer every moment. He got up at once, struck a match, and looked at the time. It was exactly one o'clock. He was quite calm, and felt his pulse, which was not at all feverish. The strange noise still continued, and with it he heard distinctly the sound of footsteps. He put on his slippers, took a small oblong phial out of his dressing-case, and opened the door. Right in front of him he saw, in the wan moonlight, an old man of terrible aspect. His eyes were as red burning coals; long grey hair fell over his shoulders in matted coils; his garments, which were of antique cut, were soiled and ragged and from his wrist and ankles hung heavy manacles and rusty gyves.

'My dear sir,' said Mr Otis, 'I really must insist on your oiling those chains, and have brought you for that purpose a small bottle of the Tammany Rising Sun Lubricator. It is said to be completely efficacious upon one application, and there are several testimonials to that effect on the wrapper from some of our most eminent native divines. I shall leave it here for you by the bedroom candles, and will be happy to supply you with more should you require it.' With these words the United States Minister laid the bottle down on a marble table, and, closing his door, retired to rest.

For a moment the Canterville ghost stood quite motionless in natural indignation; then, dashing the bottle violently upon the polished floor, he fled down the corridor uttering hollow groans, and emitting a ghastly green light. Just, however, as he reached the top of the great oak staircase, a door was flung open, two little white-robed figures appeared, and a large pillow whizzed past his head! There was evidently no time to be lost, so, hastily adopting the Fourth Dimension of Space as a means of escape, he vanished through the wainscoting, and the house became quite quiet.

On reaching a small, secret chamber in the left wing, he leaned up again a moonbeam to recover his breath, and began to try and realise his position. Never, in a brilliant and uninterrupted career of three hundred years, had he been so grossly insulted. He thought of the Dowager Duchess, whom he had frightened into a fit as she stood before the glass in her lace and diamonds; of the four housemaids, who had gone off into hysterics when he merely grinned at them through the curtain of one of the spare bedrooms; of the rector of the parish, whose candle he had blown out as he was coming late one night from the library, and who had been under the care of Sir William Gull ever since, a perfect martyr to nervous disorders; and of old Madame de Tremouillac, who, having wakened up one morning early and seen a skeleton seated in an arm-chair by the fire reading her diary, had been confined to her bed for six weeks with an attack of brain fever, and, on her recovery, had become reconciled to the Church, and broken off her connection with that notorious sceptic Monsieur de Voltaire. He remembered the terrible night when the wicked Lord Canterville was found choking in his dressing-room, with a knave of diamonds halfway down his throat, and confessed, just before he died, that he had cheated Charles James Fox out of £50,000 at Crockford's by means of that very card, and swore that the ghost had made him swallow it. All his great achievements came back to him again, from the butler who had shot himself in the pantry because he had seen a green hand tapping at the window pane, to the beautiful Lady Stutfield, who was always obliged to wear a black velvet band round her throat to hide the mark of five fingers burnt upon her white skin, and who drowned herself at last in the carp-pond at the end of the King's Walk. With the enthusiastic egotism of the true artist he went over his most celebrated performances, and smiled bitterly to himself as he recalled to mind his last appearance as 'Red Ruben, or the Strangled Babe,' his debut as 'Gaunt Gideon, the Bloodsucker of Bexley Moor,' and the furore he had excited, one lovely June evening, by merely playing nine-pins with his own bones upon the lawn-tennis ground. And after all this, some wretched modern Americans were to come and offer him the Rising Sun Lubricator, and throw pillows at his head! It was quite unbearable. Besides, no ghosts in history had ever been treated in this manner. Accordingly, he determined to have vengeance, and remained till daylight in an attitude of deep thought.

The next morning when the Otis family met at breakfast, they discussed the ghost at some length. The United States Minister was naturally a little annoyed to find that his present had not been accepted. 'I have no wish,' he said, 'to do the ghost any personal injury, and I must say that, considering the length of time he has been in the house, I don't think it is at all polite to throw pillows at him' – a very just remark, at which, I am sorry to say, the twins burst into shouts of laughter. 'Upon the other hand,' he continued, 'if he really declines to use the Rising Sun Lubricator, we shall have to take his chains from him. It would be quite impossible to sleep with such a noise going on outside the bedrooms.'

For the rest of the week, however, they were undisturbed, the only thing that excited any attention being the continual renewal of the blood-stain on the library floor. This certainly was very strange, as the door was always locked at night by Mr Otis, and the window kept closely barred. The chameleon-like colour, also, of the stain excited a good deal of comment. Some mornings it was a dull (almost Indian) red, then it would be vermilion, then a rich purple, and once when they came down for family prayers, according to the simple rites of the Free American Reformed Episcopalian Church, they found it a bright emerald-green. These kaleidoscopic changes naturally amused the party very much, and bets on the subject were freely made every evening. The only person who did not enter into the joke was little Virginia, who, for some unexplained reason, was always a good deal distressed at the sight of the blood-stain, and very nearly cried the morning it was emerald-green.

The second appearance of the ghost was on Sunday night. Shortly after they had gone to bed they were suddenly alarmed by a fearful crash in the hall. Rushing downstairs, they found that a large suit of old armour had become detached from its stand, and had fallen on the stone floor, while seated in a high-backed chair was the Canterville ghost, rubbing his knees with an expression of acute agony on his face. The twins, having brought their pea-shooters with them, at once discharged two pellets on him with that accuracy of aim which can only be attained by long and careful practice on a writing-master, while the United States Minister covered him with his revolver, and called upon him, in accordance with Californian etiquette, to hold up his hands! The ghost started up with a wild shriek of rage, and swept through them like a mist, extinguishing Washington Otis's candle as he passed, and so leaving them all in total darkness. On reaching the top of the staircase he recovered himself, and determined to give his celebrated peal of demoniac laughter. This he had on more than one occasion found extremely useful. It was said to have turned Lord Raker's wig grey in a single night, and had certainly made three of Lady Canterville's French governesses give warning before their month was up. He accordingly laughed his most horrible laugh, till the old vaulted roof rang and rang again, but hardly had the fearful echo died away when a door opened, and Mrs Otis came out in a light blue dressing-gown. 'I am afraid you are far from well,' she said, 'and I have brought you a bottle of Dr Dobell's tincture. If it is indigestion, you will find it a most excellent remedy.' The ghost glared at her in fury, and began at once to make preparations for turning himself into a large black dog, an accomplishment for which he was justly renowned, and to which the family doctor always attributed the permanent idiocy of Lord Canterville's uncle, the Hon Thomas Horton. The sound of approaching footsteps, however, made him hesitate in his fell purpose, so he contented himself with becoming faintly phosphorescent, and vanished with a deep, churchyard groan, just as the twins had come up to him.

On reaching his room he entirely broke down, and became a prey to the most violent agitation. The vulgarity of the twins, and the gross materialism of Mrs Otis, were naturally extremely annoying, but what really distressed him most was, that he had been unable to wear the suit of mail. He had hoped that even modern Americans would be thrilled by the sight of a Spectre In Armour, if for no more sensible reason, at least out of respect for their national poet, Longfellow, over whose graceful and attractive poetry he himself had whiled away many a weary hour when the Cantervilles were up in town. Besides, it was his own suit. He had worn it with great success at the Kenilworth tournament, and had been highly complimented on it by no less a person than the Virgin Queen herself. Yet when he had put it on he had been completely overpowered by the weight of the huge breastplate and steel casque, and had fallen heavily on the stone pavement, barking both his knees severely, and bruising the knuckles of his right hand.

For some days after this he was extremely ill, and hardly stirred out of his room at all, except to keep the blood-stain in proper repair. However, by taking great care of himself, he recovered, and resolved to make a third attempt to frighten the United States Minister and his family. He selected Friday, the 17th of August, for his appearance, and spent most of that day in looking over his wardrobe, ultimately deciding in favour of a large slouched hat with a red feather, a winding-sheet frilled at the wrists and neck, and a rusty dagger. Towards evening a violent storm of rain came on, and the wind was so high that all the windows and doors in the old house shook and rattled. In fact, it was just such weather as he loved. His plan of action was this. He was to make his way quietly to Washington Otis's room, gibber at him from the foot of the bed, and stab himself three times in the throat to the sound of slow music. He bore Washington a special grudge, being quite aware that it was he who was in the habit of removing the famous Canterville blood-stain by means of Pinkerton's Paragon Detergent. Having reduced the reckless and foolhardy youth to a condition of abject terror, he was then to proceed to the room occupied by the United States Minister and his wife, and there to place a clammy hand on Mrs Otis's forehead, while he hissed into her trembling husband's ear the awful secrets of the charnel-house. With regard to little Virginia, he had not quite made up his mind. She had never insulted him in any way, and was pretty and gentle. A few hollow groans from the wardrobe, he thought, would be more than sufficient, or, if that failed to wake her, he might grabble at the counterpane with palsy-twitching fingers. As for the twins, he was quite determined to teach them a lesson. The first thing to be done was, of course, to sit upon their chests, so as to produce the stifling sensation of nightmare. Then, as their beds were quite close to each other, to stand between them in the form of a green, icy-cold corpse, till they became paralysed with fear, and finally, to throw off the winding-sheet, and crawl round the room, with white, bleached bones and one rolling eyeball, in the character of 'Dumb Daniel, or the Suicide's Skeleton,' a role in which he had on more than one occasion produced a great effect, and which he considered quite equal to his famous part of 'Martin the Maniac, or the Masked Mystery.'

At half-past ten he heard the family going to bed. For some time he was disturbed by wild shrieks of laughter from the twins, who, with the light-hearted gaiety of schoolboys, were evidently amusing themselves before they retired to rest, but at a quarter past eleven all was still, and, as midnight sounded, he sallied forth. The owl beat against the window panes, the raven croaked from the old yew tree, and the wind wandered moaning round the house like a lost soul; but the Otis family slept unconscious of their doom, and high above the rain and storm he could hear the steady snoring of the Minister for the United States. He stepped stealthily out of the wainscoting, with an evil smile on his cruel, wrinkled mouth, and the moon hid her face in a cloud as he stole past the great oriel window, where his own arms and those of his murdered wife were blazoned in azure and gold. On and on he glided, like an evil shadow, the very darkness seeming to loathe him as he passed. Once he thought he heard something call, and stopped; but it was only the baying of a dog from the Red Farm, and he went on, muttering strange sixteenth-century curses, and ever and anon brandishing the rusty dagger in the midnight air. Finally he reached the corner of the passage that led to luckless Washington's room. For a moment he paused there, the wind blowing his long grey locks about his head, and twisting into grotesque and fantastic folds the nameless horror of the dead man's shroud. Then the clock struck the quarter, and he felt the time was come. He chuckled to himself, and turned the corner; but no sooner had he done so, than, with a piteous wail of terror, he fell back, and hid his blanched face in his long, bony hands. Right in front of him was standing a horrible spectre, motionless as a carven image, and monstrous as a madman's dream! Its head was bald and burnished; its face round, and fat, and white; and hideous laughter seemed to have writhed its features into an eternal grin. From the eyes streamed rays of scarlet light, the mouth was a wide well of fire, and a hideous garment, like to his own, swathed with its silent snows the Titan form. On its breast was a placard with strange writing in antique characters, some scroll of shame it seemed, some record of wild sins, some awful calendar of crime, and, with its right hand, it bore aloft a falchion of gleaming steel.

Never having seen a ghost before, he naturally was terribly frightened, and, after a second hasty glance at the awful phantom, he fled back to his room, tripping up in his long winding-sheet as he sped down the corridor, and finally dropping the rusty dagger into the Minister's jack-boots, where it was found in the morning by the butler. Once in the privacy of his own apartment, he flung himself down on a small pallet-bed, and hid his face under the clothes. After a time, however, the brave old Canterville spirit asserted itself, and he determined to go and speak to the other ghost as soon as it was daylight. Accordingly, just as the dawn was touching the hills with silver, he returned towards the spot where he had first laid eyes on the grisly phantom, feeling that, after all, two ghosts were better than one, and that, by the aid of his new friend, he might safely grapple with the twins. On reaching the spot, however, a terrible sight met his gaze. Something had evidently happened to the spectre, for the light had entirely faded from its hollow eyes, the gleaming falchion had fallen from its hand, and it was leaning up against the wall in a strained and uncomfortable attitude. He rushed forward and seized it in his arms, when, to his horror, the head slipped off and rolled on the floor, the body assumed a recumbent posture, and he found himself clasping a white dimity bed-curtain, with a sweeping-brush, a kitchen cleaver and a hollow turnip lying at his feet! Unable to understand this curious transformation, he clutched the placard with feverish haste, and there, in the grey morning light, he read these fearful words:

YE OTIS GHOST
Ye Onlie True and Originale Spook,
BEWARE OF YE IMITATIONES.
ALL OTHERS ARE COUNTERFEITS.

The whole thing flashed across him. He had been tricked, foiled and outwitted! The old Canterville look came into his eyes; he ground his toothless gums together; and, raising his withered hands high above his head, swore, according to the picturesque phraseology of the antique school, that when Chanticleer had sounded twice his merry horn, deeds of blood would be wrought, and Murder walk abroad with silent feet.

Hardly had he finished this awful oath when, from the red-tiled roof of a distant homestead, a cock crew. He laughed a long, low, bitter laugh, and waited. Hour after hour he waited, but the cock, for some strange reason, did not crow again. Finally, at half-past seven, the arrival of the housemaids made him give up his fearful vigil, and he stalked back to his room, thinking of his vain hope and baffled purpose. There he consulted several books on ancient chivalry, of which he was exceedingly fond, and found that, on every occasion on which his oath had been used, Chanticleer had always crowed a second time. 'Perdition seize the naughty fowl,' he muttered. 'I have seen the day when, with my stout spear, I would have run him through the gorge, and made him crow for me as 'twere in death!' He then retired to a comfortable lead coffin, and stayed there till evening.

The next day the ghost was very weak and tired. The terrible excitement of the last four weeks was beginning to have its effect. His nerves were completely shattered, and he started at the slightest noise. For five days he kept his room, and at last made up his mind to give up the point of the blood-stain on the library floor. If the Otis family did not want it, they clearly did not deserve it. They were evidently people on a low, material plane of existence, and quite incapable of appreciating the symbolic value of sensuous phenomena. The question of phantasmic apparitions, and the development of astral bodies, was, of course, quite a different matter, and really not under his control. It was his solemn duty to appear in the corridor once a week, and to gibber from the large oriel window on the first and third Wednesday in every month, and he did not see how he could honourably escape from his obligations. It is quite true that his life had been very evil, but, upon the other hand, he was most conscientious in all things connected with the supernatural. For the next three Saturdays, accordingly, he traversed the corridor as usual between midnight and three o'clock, taking every possible precaution against being either heard or seen. He removed his boots, trod as lightly as possible on the old, worm-eaten boards, wore a large black velvet cloak, and was careful to use the Rising Sun Lubricator for oiling his chains. I am bound to acknowledge that it was with a good deal of difficulty that he brought himself to adopt this last mode of protection.

However, one night, while the family were at dinner, he slipped into Mr Otis's bedroom and carried off the bottle. He felt a little humiliated at first, but afterwards was sensible enough to see that there was a great deal to be said for the invention, and, to a certain degree, it served his purpose. Still, in spite of everything, he was not left unmolested. Strings were continually being stretched across the corridor, over which he tripped in the dark, and on one occasion, while dressed for the part of 'Black Isaac, or the Huntsman of Hogley Woods,' he met with a severe fall, through treading on a butter-slide, which the twins had constructed from the entrance of the Tapestry Chamber to the top of the oak staircase. This last insult so enraged him that he resolved to make one final effort to assert his dignity and social position, and determined to visit the insolent young Etonians the next night in his celebrated character of 'Reckless Rupert, or the Headless Earl.'

He had not appeared in this disguise for more than seventy years; in fact, not since he had so frightened pretty Lady Barbara Modish by means of it that she suddenly broke off her engagement with the present Lord Canterville's grandfather, and ran away to Gretna Green with handsome Jack Castleton, declaring that nothing in the world would induce her to marry into a family that allowed such a horrible phantom to walk up and down the terrace at twilight. Poor Jack was afterwards shot in a duel by Lord Canterville on Wandsworth Common, and Lady Barbara died of a broken heart at Tunbridge Wells before the year was out, so, in every way, it had been a great success. It was, however, an extremely difficult 'make-up,' if I may use such a theatrical expression in connection with one of the greatest mysteries of the supernatural, or, to employ a more scientific term, the highernatural world, and it took him fully three hours to make his preparations. At last everything was ready, and he was very pleased with his appearance. The big leather riding-boots that went with the dress were just a little too large for him, and he could only find one of the two horse-pistols, but, on the whole, he was quite satisfied, and at a quarter past one he glided out of the wainscoting and crept down the corridor. On reaching the room occupied by the twins, which I should mention was called the Blue Bed Chamber, on account of the colour of its hangings, he found the door just ajar. Wishing to make an effective entrance, he flung it wide open, when a heavy jug of water fell right down on him, wetting him to the skin, and just missing his left shoulder by a couple of inches. At the same moment he heard stifled shrieks of laughter, proceeding from the four-post bed. The shock to his nervous system was so great that he fled back to his room as hard as he could go, and the next day he was laid up with a severe cold. The only thing that at all consoled him in the whole affair was the fact that he had not brought his head with him, for, had he done so, the consequences might have been very serious.

He now gave up all hope of ever frightening this rude American family, and contented himself, as a rule, with creeping about the passages in list slippers, with a thick red muffler round his throat for fear of draughts, and a small arquebus, in case he should be attacked by the twins. The final blow he received occurred on the 19th of September. He had gone downstairs to the great entrance-hall, feeling sure that there, at any rate, he would be quite unmolested, and was amusing himself by making satirical remarks on the large Saroni photographs of the United States Minister and his wife, which had now taken the place of the Canterville family pictures. He was simply but neatly clad in a long shroud, spotted with churchyard mould, had tied up his jaw with a strip of yellow linen, and carried a small lantern and a sexton's spade. In fact he was dressed for the character of 'Jonas the Graveless, or the Corpse-Snatcher of Chertsey Barn,' one of his most remarkable impersonations, and one which the Cantervilles had every reason to remember, as it was the real origin of their quarrel with their neighbour, Lord Rufford. It was about a quarter past two o'clock in the morning, and, as far as he could ascertain, no one was stirring. As he was strolling towards the library, however, to see if there were any traces left of the blood-stain, suddenly there leaped out on him from a dark corner two figures, who waved their arms wildly above their heads, and shrieked out 'BOO!' in his ear.

Seized with a panic, which, under the circumstances, was only natural, he rushed for the staircase, but found Washington Otis waiting for him there with the big garden-syringe; and being thus hemmed in by his enemies on every side, and driven almost to bay, he vanished into the great iron stove, which, fortunately for him, was not lit, and had to make his way home through the flues and chimneys, arriving at his own room in a terrible state of dirt, disorder and despair.

After this he was not seen again on any nocturnal expedition. The twins lay in wait for him on several occasions, and strewed the passages with nutshells every night, to the great annoyance of their parents and the servants, but it was of no avail. It was quite evident that his feelings were so wounded that he would not appear. Mr Otis consequently resumed his great work on the history of the Democratic Party, on which he had been engaged for some years; Mrs Otis organised a wonderful clam-bake, which amazed the whole county; the boys took to lacrosse, euchre, poker and other American national games; and Virginia rode about the lanes on her pony, accompanied by the young Duke of Cheshire, who had come to spend the last week of his holidays at Canterville Chase. It was generally assumed that the ghost had gone away, and, in fact, Mr Otis wrote a letter to that effect to Lord Canterville, who, in reply, expressed his great pleasure at the news, and sent his best congratulations to the Minister's worthy wife.

The Otises, however, were deceived, for the ghost was still in the house, and, though now almost an invalid, was by no means ready to let matters rest, particularly as he heard that among the guests was the young Duke of Cheshire, whose grand-uncle, Lord Francis Stilton, had once bet a hundred guineas with Colonel Carbury that he would play dice with the Canterville ghost, and was found the next morning lying on the floor of the card-room in such a helpless paralytic state, that though he lived on to a great age, he was never able to say anything again but 'Double Sixes.' The story was well known at the time, though, of course, out of respect to the feelings of the two noble families, every attempt was made to hush it up; and a full acount of all the circumstances connected with it will be found in the third volume of Lord Tattle's *Recollections of the Prince Regent and his Friends*. The ghost, then, was naturally very anxious to show that he had not lost his influence over the Stiltons, with whom, indeed, he was distantly connected, his own first cousin having been married *en secondes noces* to the Sieur de Bulkeley, from whom, as everyone knows, the Dukes of Cheshire are lineally descended. Accordingly, he made arrangements for appearing to Virginia's little lover in his celebrated impersonation of 'The Vampire Monk, or the Bloodless Benedictine,' a performance so horrible that when old Lady Startup saw it, which she did on one fatal New Year's Eve, in the year 1764, she went off into the most piercing shrieks, which culminated in violent apoplexy, and died in three days, after disinheriting the Cantervilles, who were her nearest relations, and leaving all her money to her London apothecary. At the last moment, however, his terror of the twins prevented his leaving his room, and the little Duke slept in peace under the great feathered canopy in the Royal Bedchamber, and dreamed of Virginia.

A few days after this, Virginia and her curly-haired cavalier went out riding on Brockley meadows, where she tore her habit so badly in getting through a hedge, that, on her return home, she made up her mind to go up by the back staircase so as not to be seen. As she was running past the Tapestry Chamber, the door of which happened to be open, she fancied she saw someone inside, and thinking it was her mother's maid who sometimes used to bring her work there, looked in to ask her to mend her habit. To her immense surprise, however, it was the Canterville Ghost himself! He was sitting by the window, watching the ruined gold of the yellowing trees fly through the air, and the red leaves dancing madly down the long avenue. His head was leaning on his hand, and his whole attitude was one of extreme depression. Indeed, so forlorn, and so much out of repair did he look, that little Virginia, whose first idea had been to run away and lock herself in her room, was filled with pity, and determined to try to comfort him. So light was her footfall, and so deep his melancholy, that he was not aware of her presence till she spoke to him.

'I am so sorry for you,' she said, 'but my brothers are going back to Eton tomorrow, and then, if you behave yourself, no one will annoy you.'

'It is absurd asking me to behave myself,' he answered, looking round in astonishment at the pretty little girl who had ventured to address him, 'quite absurd. I must rattle my chains, and groan through keyholes, and walk about at night, if that is what you mean. It is my only reason for existing.'

'It is no reason at all for existing, and you know you have been very wicked. Mrs Umney told us, the first day we arrived here, that you had killed your wife.'

'Well, I quite admit it,' said the Ghost petulantly, 'but it was a purely family matter, and concerned no one else.'

'It is very wrong to kill anyone,' said Virginia, who at times had a sweet Puritan gravity, caught from some old New England ancestor.

'Oh, I hate the cheap severity of abstract ethics! My wife was very plain, never had my ruffs properly starched, and knew nothing about cookery. Why, there was a buck I had shot in Hogley Woods, a magnificent pricket, and do you know how she had it sent up to the table? However, it is no matter now, for it is all over, and I don't think it was very nice of her brothers to starve me to death, though I did kill her.'

'Starve you to death? Oh, Mr Ghost, I mean Sir Simon, are you hungry? I have a sandwich in my case. Would you like it?'

'No, thank you, I never eat anything now; but it is very kind of you, all the same, and you are much nicer than the rest of your horrid, rude, vulgar, dishonest family.'

'Stop,' cried Virginia, stamping her foot, 'it is you who are rude, and horrid, and vulgar, and as for dishonesty, you know you stole the paints out of my box to try and furbish up that ridiculous blood-stain in the library. First you took all my reds, including the vermilion, and I couldn't do any more sunsets, then you took the emerald-green and the chrome-yellow, and finally I had nothing left but indigo and Chinese white, and could only do moonlight scenes, which are always depressing to look at, and not at all easy to paint. I never told on you, though I was very much annoyed, and it was most ridiculous, the whole thing; for who ever heard of emerald-green blood?'

'Well, really,' said the Ghost, rather meekly, 'What was I to do? It is a very difficult thing to get real blood nowadays, and, as your brother began it all with his Paragon Detergent, I certainly saw no reason why I should not have your paints. As for colour, that is always a matter of taste; the Cantervilles have blue blood, for instance, the very bluest in England; but I know you Americans don't care for things of this kind.'

'You know nothing about it, and the best thing you can do is to emigrate and improve your mind. My father will be only too happy to give you a free passage, and though there is a heavy duty on spirits of every kind, there will be no difficulty about the Custom House, as the officers are all Democrats. Once in New York, you are sure to be a great success. I know lots of people there who would give a hundred thousand dollars to have a grandfather, and much more than that to have a family Ghost.'

'I don't think I should like America.'

'I suppose because we have no ruins and no curiosities,' said Virginia satirically.

'No ruins! no curiosities!' answered the Ghost; 'you have your navy and your manners.'

'Good evening; I will go and ask papa to get the twins an extra week's holiday.'

'Please don't go, Miss Virginia,' he cried; 'I am so lonely and so unhappy, and I really don't know what to do. I want to go to sleep and I cannot.'

'That's quite absurd! You have merely to go to bed and blow out the candle. It is very difficult sometimes, to keep awake, especially at church, but there is no difficulty at all about sleeping. Why, even babies know how to do that, and they are not very clever.'

'I have not slept for three hundred years,' he said sadly, and Virginia's beautiful blue eyes opened in wonder; 'for three hundred years I have not slept, and I am so tired.' Virginia grew quite grave, and her little lips trembled like rose-leaves. She came towards him, and kneeling down at his side, looked up into his old, withered face.

'Poor, poor Ghost,' she murmured; 'have you no place where you can sleep?'

'Far away beyond the pine-woods,' he answered, in a low dreamy voice, 'there is a little garden. There the grass grows long and deep, there are the great white stars of the hemlock flower, there the nightingale sings all night long. All night long he sings, and the cold, crystal moon looks down, and the yew tree spreads out its giant arms over the sleepers.'

Virginia's eyes grew dim with tears, and she hid her face in her hands.

'You mean the Garden of Death,' she whispered.

'Yes, Death. Death must be so beautiful. To lie in the soft, brown earth, with the grasses waving above one's head, and listen to silence. To have no yesterday, and no tomorrow. To forget time, to forgive life, to be at peace. You can help me. You can open for me the portals of Death's house, for Love is always with you, and Love is stronger than Death is.'

Virginia trembled, a cold shudder ran through her, and for a few moments there was silence. She felt as if she was in a terrible dream.

Then the Ghost spoke again, and his voice sounded like the sighing of the wind.

'Have you ever read the old prophecy on the library window?'

'Oh, often,' cried the little girl, looking up; 'I know it quite well. It is painted in curious black letters, and it is difficult to read. There are only six lines:

> When a golden girl can win
> Prayer from out the lips of sin,
> When the barren almond bears,
> And a little child gives away its tears,
> Then shall all the house be still
> And peace come to Canterville.

'But I don't know what they mean.'

'They mean,' he said sadly, 'that you must weep for me for my sins, because I have no tears, and pray with me for my soul, because I have no faith, and then, if you have always been sweet, and good, and gentle, the Angel of Death will have mercy on me. You will see fearful shapes in darkness, and wicked voices will whisper in your ear, but they will not harm you, for against the purity of a little child the powers of Hell cannot prevail.'

Virginia made no answer, and the Ghost wrung his hands in wild despair as he looked down at her bowed golden head. Suddenly she stood up, very pale, and with a strange light in her eyes. 'I am not afraid,' she said firmly, 'and I will ask the Angel to have mercy on you.'

He rose from his seat with a faint cry of joy, and taking her hand bent over it with old-fashioned grace and kissed it. His fingers were as cold as ice, and his lips burned like fire, but Virginia did not falter, as he led her across the dusky room. On the faded green tapestry were broidered little huntsmen. They blew their tasselled horns, and, with their tiny hands waved to her to go back. 'Go back! little Virginia,' they cried, 'go back!' but the Ghost clutched her hand more tightly, and she shut her eyes against them. Horrible animals with lizard tails, and goggle eyes, blinked at her from the carven chimneypiece, and murmured, 'Beware! little Virginia, beware! we may never see you again,' but the Ghost glided on more swiftly, and Virginia did not listen. When they reached the end of the room he stopped, and muttered some words she could not understand. She opened her eyes, and saw the wall slowly fading away like a mist, and a great black cavern in front of her. A bitter cold wind swept round them, and she felt something pulling at her dress. 'Quick, quick,' cried the Ghost, 'or it will be too late,' and, in a moment, the wainscoting had closed behind them, and the Tapestry Chamber was empty.

About ten minutes later the bell rang for tea, and, as Virginia did not come down, Mrs Otis sent up one of the footmen to tell her. After a little time he returned and said that he could not find Miss Virginia anywhere. As she was in the habit of going out to the garden every evening to get flowers for the dinner-table, Mrs Otis was not at all alarmed at first, but when six o'clock struck, and Virginia did not appear, she became really agitated, and sent the boys out to look for her while she herself and Mr Otis searched every room in the house. At half-past six the boys came back and said that they could find no trace of their sister anywhere. They were all now in the greatest state of excitement, and did not know what to do, when Mr Otis suddenly remembered that, some few days before, he had given a band of gypsies permission to camp in the park. He accordingly at once set off for Blackfell Hollow, where he knew they were, accompanied by his eldest son and two of the farm-servants. The little Duke of Cheshire, who was perfectly frantic with anxiety, begged hard to be allowed to go too, but Mr Otis would not allow him, as he was afraid there might be a scuffle. On arriving at the spot, however, he found that the gypsies had gone, and it was evident that their departure had been rather sudden, as the fire was still burning, and some plates were lying on the grass. Having sent off Washington and the two men to scour the district, he ran home, and despatched telegrams to all the police inspectors in the county, telling them to look out for a little girl who had been kidnapped by tramps or gypsies. He then ordered his horse to be brought round, and, after insisting on his wife and the three boys sitting down to dinner, rode off down the Ascot Road with a groom. He had hardly, however, gone a couple of miles when he heard somebody galloping after him, and, looking round, saw the little Duke coming up on his pony, with his face very flushed and no hat. 'I'm awfully sorry, Mr Otis,' gasped out the boy, 'but I can't eat dinner as long as Virginia is lost. Please, don't be angry with me; if you had let us be engaged last year there would never have been all this trouble. You won't send me back, will you? I can't go! I won't go!'

The Minister could not help smiling at the handsome young scapegrace, and was a good deal touched at his devotion to Virginia, so leaning down from his horse, he patted him kindly on the shoulders, and said, 'Well, Cecil, if you won't go back I suppose you must come with me, but I must get you a hat at Ascot.'

'Oh, bother my hat! I want Virginia!' cried the little Duke, laughing, and they galloped on to the railway station. There Mr Otis inquired of the stationmaster if anyone answering the description of Virginia had been seen on the platform, but could get no news of her. The stationmaster, however, wired up and down the line, and assured him that a strict watch would be kept for her, and, after having bought a hat for the little Duke from a linen draper, who was just putting up his shutters, Mr Otis rode off to Bexley, a village about four miles away, which he was told was a well-known haunt of the gypsies, as there was a large common next to it. Here they roused up the rural policeman, but could get no information from him, and, after riding all over the common, they turned their horses' heads homewards, and reached the Chase about eleven o'clock, dead-tired and almost heart-broken. They found Washington and the twins waiting for them at the gate-house with lanterns, as the avenue was very dark. Not the slightest trace of Virginia had been discovered. The gypsies had been caught on Brockley meadows, but she was not with them, and they had explained their sudden departure by saying that they had mistaken the date of Chorton Fair, and had gone off in a hurry for fear they might be late. Indeed, they had been quite distressed at hearing of Virginia's disappearance, as they were very grateful to Mr Otis for having allowed them to camp in his park, and four of their number had stayed behind to help in the search. The carp-pond had been dragged, and the whole Chase thoroughly gone over, but without any result. It was evident that, for that night, at any rate, Virginia was lost to them; and it was in a state of the deepest depression that Mr Otis and the boys walked up to the house, the groom following behind with the two horses and the pony. In the hall they found a group of frightened servants, and lying on a sofa in the library was poor Mrs Otis, almost out of her mind with terror and anxiety, and having her forehead bathed with eau-de-Cologne by the old housekeeper. Mr Otis at once insisted on her having something to eat, and ordered up supper for the whole party. It was a melancholy meal, as hardly anyone spoke, and even the twins were awestruck, and subdued, as they were very fond of their sister. When they had finished, Mr Otis, in spite of the entreaties of the little Duke, ordered them all to bed, saying that nothing more could be done that night, and that he would telegraph in the morning to Scotland Yard for some detectives to be sent down immediately. Just as they were passing out of the dining-room, midnight began to boom from the clock tower, and when the last stroke sounded they heard a crash and a sudden shrill cry; a dreadful peal of thunder shook the house, a strain of unearthly music floated through the air, a panel at the top of the staircase flew back with a loud noise, and out on the landing, looking very pale and white, with a little casket in her hand, stepped Virginia. In a moment they had all rushed up to her. Mrs Otis clasped her passionately in her arms, the Duke smothered her with violent kisses, and the twins executed a wild war-dance round the group.

'Good heavens! child, where have you been?' said Mr Otis, rather angrily, thinking that she had been playing some foolish trick on them. 'Cecil and I have been riding all over the country looking for you, and your mother has been frightened to death. You must never play these practical jokes any more.'

'Except on the Ghost! except on the Ghost!' shrieked the twins, as they capered about.

'My own darling, thank God you are found; you must never leave my side again,' murmured Mrs Otis, as she kissed the trembling child, and smoothed the tangled gold of her hair.

'Papa,' said Virginia quietly, 'I have been with the Ghost. He is dead, and you must come and see him. He had been very wicked, but he was really sorry for all that he had done, and he gave me this box of beautiful jewels before he died.'

The whole family gazed at her in mute amazement, but she was quite grave and serious; and, turning round, she led them through the opening in the wainscoting down a narrow secret corridor, Washington following with a lighted candle, which he had caught up from the table. Finally, they came to a great oak door, studded with rusty nails. When Virginia touched it, it swung back on its heavy hinges, and they found themselves in a little, low room, with a vaulted ceiling, and one tiny grated window. Imbedded in the wall was a huge iron ring, and chained to it was a gaunt skeleton, that was stretched out at full length on the stone floor, and seemed to be trying to grasp with its long, fleshless fingers an old-fashioned trencher and ewer, that were placed just out of its reach. The jug had evidently been once filled with water, as it was covered inside with a green mould. There was nothing on the trencher but a pile of dust. Virginia knelt down beside the skeleton, and, folding her little hands together, began to pray silently, while the rest of the party looked on in wonder at the terrible tragedy whose secret was now disclosed to them.

'Hallo!' suddenly exclaimed one of the twins, who had been looking out of the window to try to discover in what wing of the house the room was situated. 'Hallo! the old withered almond-tree has blossomed. I can see the flowers quite plainly in the moonlight.'

'God has forgiven him,' said Virginia gravely, as she rose to her feet, and a beautiful light seemed to illumine her face.

'What an angel you are!' cried the young Duke, and he put his arm round her neck and kissed her.

Four days after these curious incidents a funeral started from Canterville Chase at about eleven o'clock at night. The hearse was drawn by eight black horses, each of which carried on its head a great tuft of nodding ostrich-plumes, and the leaden coffin was covered by a rich purple pall, on which was embroidered in gold the Canterville coat-of-arms. By the side of the hearse and the coaches walked the servants with lighted torches, and the whole procession was wonderfully impressive. Lord Canterville was the chief mourner, having come up specially from Wales to attend the funeral, and sat in the first carriage along with little Virginia. Then came the United States Minister and his wife, then Washington and the three boys, and in the last carriage was Mrs Umney. It was generally felt that, as she had been frightened by the ghost for more than fifty years of her life, she had a right to see the last of him. A deep grave had been dug in the corner of the churchyard, just under the old yew tree, and the service was read in the most impressive manner by the Rev Augustus Dampier. When the ceremony was over, the servants according to an old custom observed in the Canterville family, extinguished their torches, and, as the coffin was being lowered into the grave, Virginia stepped forward and laid on it a large cross made of white and pink almond-blossoms. As she did so, the moon came out from behind a cloud, and flooded with its silent silver the little churchyard, and from a distant copse a nightingale began to sing. She thought of the ghost's description of the Garden of Death, her eyes became dim with tears, and she hardly spoke a word during the drive home.

The next morning, before Lord Canterville went up to town, Mr Otis had an interview with him on the subject of the jewels the ghost had given to Virginia. They were perfectly magnificent, especially a certain ruby necklace with an old Venetian setting, which was really a superb specimen of sixteenth-century work, and their value was so great that Mr Otis felt considerable scruples about allowing his daughter to accept them.

'My Lord,' he said, 'I know that in this country mortmain is held to apply to trinkets as well as to land, and it is quite clear to me that these jewels are, or should be, heirlooms in your family. I must beg you, accordingly, to take them to London with you, and to regard them simply as a portion of your property which has been restored to you under certain strange conditions. As for my daughter, she is merely a child, and has, as yet, I am glad to say, but little interest in such appurtenances of idle luxury. I am also informed by Mrs Otis, who, I may say, is no mean authority upon Art – having had the privilege of spending several winters in Boston when she was a girl – that these gems are of great monetary worth, and if offered for sale would fetch a tall price. Under these circumstances, Lord Canterville, I feel sure that you will recognise how impossible it would be for me to allow them to remain in the possession of any member of my family; and, indeed, all such vain gauds and toys, however suitable or necessary to the dignity of the British aristocracy, would be completely out of place among those who have been brought up on the severe, and I believe immortal, principles of republican simplicity. Perhaps I should mention that Virginia is very anxious that you should allow her to retain the box as a memento of your unfortunate but misguided ancestor. As it is extremely old, and consequently a good deal out of repair, you may perhaps think fit to comply with her request. For my own part, I confess I am a good deal surprised to find a child of mine expressing sympathy with mediaevalism in any form, and can only account for it by the fact that

Virginia was born in one of your London surburbs shortly after Mrs Otis had returned from a trip to Athens.'

Lord Canterville listened very gravely to the worthy Minister's speech, pulling his grey moustache now and then to hide an involuntary smile, and, when Mr Otis had ended, he shook him cordially by the hand, and said, 'My dear sir, your charming little daughter rendered my unlucky ancestor, Sir Simon, a very important service, and I and my family are much indebted to her for her marvellous courage and pluck. The jewels are clearly hers, and, egad, I believe that if I were heartless enough to take them from her the wicked old fellow would be out of his grave in a fortnight, leading me the devil of a life. As for their being heirlooms, nothing is an heirloom that is not so mentioned in a will or legal document, and the existence of these jewels had been quite unknown. I assure you I have no more claim on them than your butler, and when Miss Virginia grows up I daresay she will be pleased to have pretty things to wear. Besides, you forget, Mr Otis, that you took the furniture and the ghost at a valuation, and anything that belonged to the ghost passed at once into your possession, as, whatever activity Sir Simon may have shown in the corridor at night, in point of law he was really dead, and you acquired his property by purchase.'

Mr Otis was a good deal distressed at Lord Canterville's refusal, and begged him to reconsider his decision, but the good-natured peer was quite firm, and finally induced the Minister to allow his daughter to retain the present the ghost had given her, and when, in the spring of 1890, the young Duchess of Cheshire was presented at the Queen's first drawing-room on the occasion of her marriage, her jewels were the universal theme of admiration. For Virginia received the coronet, which is the reward for all good little American girls, and was married to her boy-lover as soon as he came of age. They were both so charming, and they loved each other so much, that everyone was delighted at the match, except the old Marchioness of Dumbleton, who had tried to catch the Duke for one of her seven unmarried daughters, and had given no less than three expensive dinner-parties for that purpose; and, strange to say, Mr Otis himself. Mr Otis was extremely fond of the young Duke personally, but, theoretically, he objected to titles, and, to use his own words, 'was not without apprehension lest, amid the enervating influences of a pleasure-loving aristocracy, the true principles of republican simplicity should be forgotten.' His objections, however, were completely overruled, and I believe that when he walked up the aisle of St George's, Hanover Square, with his daughter leaning on his arm, there was not a prouder man in the whole length and breadth of England.

The Duke and Duchess, after the honeymoon was over, went down to Canterville Chase, and on the day after their arrival they walked over in the afternoon to the lonely churchyard by the pine-woods. There had been a great deal of difficulty, at first, about the inscription on Sir Simon's tombstone, but finally it had been decided to engrave on it simply the initials of the old gentleman's name, and the verse from the library window. The Duchess had brought with her some lovely roses, which she strewed upon the grave, and after they had stood by it for some time they strolled into the ruined chancel of the old abbey. There the Duchess sat down on a fallen pillar, while her husband lay at her feet smoking a cigarette and looking up at her beautiful eyes. Suddenly he threw his cigarette away, took hold of her hand, and said to her, 'Virginia, a wife should have no secrets from her husband.'

'Dear Cecil, I have no secrets from you.'

'Yes, you have,' he answered, smiling, 'you have never told me what happened to you when you were locked up with the ghost.'

'I have never told anyone, Cecil,' said Virginia gravely.

'I know that, but you might tell me.'

'Please don't ask me, Cecil, I cannot tell you. Poor Sir Simon! I owe him a great deal. Yes, don't laugh, Cecil, I really do. He made me see what Life is, and what Death signifies, and why Love is stronger than both.'

The Duke rose and kissed his wife lovingly.

'You can have your secret as long as I have your heart,' he murmured.

'You have always had that, Cecil.'

'And you will tell our children some day, won't you?'
Virginia blushed.

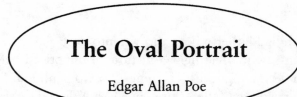

The Oval Portrait

Edgar Allan Poe

The château into which my valet had ventured to make forcible entrance, rather than permit me, in my desperately wounded condition, to pass a night in the open air, was one of those piles of commingled gloom and grandeur which have so long frowned among the Apennines, not less in fact than in the fancy of Mrs Radcliffe. To all appearance it had been temporarily and very lately abandoned. We established ourselves in one of the smallest and least sumptuously furnished apartments. It lay in a remote turret of the building. Its decorations were rich, yet tattered and antique. Its walls were hung with tapestry and bedecked with manifold and multiform armorial trophies, together with an unusually great number of very spirited modern paintings in frames of rich golden arabesque. In these paintings, which depended from the walls not only in their main surfaces, but in very many nooks which the bizarre architecture of the château rendered necessary – in these paintings my incipient delirium, perhaps, had caused me to take deep interest; so that I bade Pedro to close the heavy shutters of the room – since it was already night, – to light the tongues of a tall candelabrum which stood by the head of my bed, and to throw open far and wide the fringed curtains of black velvet which enveloped the bed itself. I wished all this done that I might resign myself, if not to sleep, at least alternately to the contemplation of these pictures, and the perusal of a small volume which had been found upon the pillow, and which purported to criticise and describe them.

Long, long I read – and devoutly, devoutly I gazed. Rapidly and gloriously the hours flew by and the deep midnight came. The position of the candelabrum displeased me, and outreaching my hand with difficulty, rather than disturb my slumbering valet, l placed it so as to throw its rays more fully upon the book.

But the action produced an effect altogether unanticipated. The rays of the numerous candles (for there were many) now fell within a niche of the room which had hitherto been thrown into deep shade by one of the bedposts. I thus saw in vivid light a picture all unnoticed before. It was the portrait of a young girl just ripening into womanhood. I glanced at the painting hurriedly, and then closed my eyes. Why I did this was not at first apparent even to my own perception. But while my lids remained thus shut, I ran over in my mind my reason for so shutting them. It was an impulsive movement to gain time for thought – to make sure that my vision had not deceived me – to calm and subdue my fancy for a more sober and more certain gaze. In a very few moments I again looked fixedly at the painting.

That I now saw aright I could not and would not doubt; for the first flashing of the candles upon that canvas had seemed to dissipate the dreamy stupor which was stealing over my senses, and to startle me at once into waking life.

The portrait, I have already said, was that of a young girl. It was a mere head and shoulders, done in what is technically termed a *vignette* manner; much in the style of the favorite heads of Sully. The arms, the bosom, and even the ends of the radiant hair melted imperceptibly into the vague yet deep shadow which formed the background of the whole. The frame was oval, richly gilded and filigreed in *Moresque*. As a thing of art nothing could be more admirable than the painting itself. But it could have been neither the execution of the work, nor the immortal beauty of the countenance which had so suddenly and so vehemently moved me. Least of all, could it have been that my fancy, shaken from its half slumber, had mistaken the head for that of a living person. I saw at once that the peculiarities of the design, of the *vignetting*, and of the frame, must have instantly dispelled such idea – must have prevented even its momentary entertainment. Thinking earnestly upon these points, I remained, for an hour perhaps, half sitting, half reclining, with my vision riveted upon the portrait. At length, satisfied with the true secret of its effect, I fell back within the bed. I had found the spell of the picture in an absolute *lifelikeliness* of expression, which, at first startling, finally confounded, subdued, and appalled me. With deep and reverent awe I replaced the candelabrum in its former position. The cause of my deep agitation being thus shut from view, I sought eagerly the volume which discussed the paintings and their histories. Turning to the number which designated the oval portrait, I there read the vague and quaint words which follow:

"She was a maiden of rarest beauty, and not more lovely than full of glee. And evil was the hour when she saw, and loved, and wedded the painter. He, passionate, studious, austere, and having already a bride in his Art: she a maiden of rarest beauty, and not more lovely than full of glee; all light and smiles, and frolicsome as the young fawn; loving and cherishing all things; hating only the Art which was her rival; dreading only the pallet and brushes and other untoward instruments which deprived her of the countenance of her lover. It was thus a terrible thing for this lady to hear the painter speak of his desire to portray even his young bride. But she was humble and obedient, and sat meekly for many weeks in the dark high turret-chamber where the light dripped upon the pale canvas only from overhead. But he, the painter, took glory in his work, which went on from hour to hour, and from day to day. And he was a passionate, and wild, and moody man, who became lost in reveries; so that he *would* not see that the light which fell so ghastly in that lone turret withered the health and the spirits of his bride, who pined visibly to all but him. Yet she smiled on and still on, uncomplainingly, because she saw that the painter (who had high renown) took a fervid and burning pleasure in his task, and wrought day and night to depict her who so loved him, yet who grew daily more dispirited and weak. And in sooth some who beheld the portrait spoke of its resemblance in low words, as of a mighty marvel, and a proof not less of the power of the painter than of his deep love for her whom he depicted so surpassingly well. But at length, as the labor drew nearer to its conclusion, there were admitted none into the turret; for the painter had grown wild with the ardor of his work, and turned his eyes from the canvas rarely, even to regard the countenance of his wife. And he *would* not see that the tints which he spread upon the canvas were drawn from the cheeks of her who sat beside him. And when many weeks had passed, and but little remained to do, save one brush upon the mouth and one tint upon the eye, the spirit of the lady again flickered up as the flame within the socket of the lamp. And then the brush was given, and then the tint was placed; and, for one moment, the painter stood entranced before the work which he had wrought; but in the next, while he yet gazed, he grew tremulous and very pallid, and aghast, and crying with a loud voice, 'This is indeed *Life* itself!' turned suddenly to regard his beloved: – *She was dead*!"

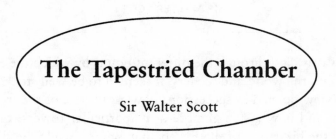

The Tapestried Chamber

Sir Walter Scott

About the end of the American war, when the officers of Lord Cornwallis's army which surrendered at York-town, and others, who had been made prisoners during the impolitic and ill-fated controversy, were returning to their own country, to relate their adventures and repose themselves after their fatigues, there was amongst them a general officer of name of Browne. He was an officer of merit, as well as a gentleman of high consideration for family and attainments.

Some business had carried General Browne upon a tour through the western counties, when, in the conclusion of a morning stage, he found himself in the vicinity of a small country town, which presented a scene of uncommon beauty and of a character peculiarly English.

The little town, with its stately old church whose tower bore testimony to the devotion of ages long past, lay amidst pasture and corn-fields of small extent, but bounded and divided with hedge-row timber of great age and size. There were few marks of modern improvement. The environs of the place intimated neither the solitude of decay, nor the bustle of novelty; the houses were old, but in good repair; and the beautiful little river murmured freely on its way to the left of the town, neither restrained by a dam, nor bordered by a towing-path.

Upon a gentle eminence, nearly a mile to the southward of the town, were seen amongst many venerable oaks and tangled thickets the turrets of a castle, as old as the wars of York and Lancaster, but which seemed to have received important alterations during the age of Elizabeth and her successors. It had not been a place of great size; but whatever accommodation it formerly afforded, was, it must be supposed, still to be obtained within its walls; at least, such was the inference which General Browne drew from observing the smoke arise merrily from several of the ancient wreathed and carved chimney-stalks. The wall of the park ran alongside of the highway for two or three hundred yards; and through the different points by which the eye found glimpses into the woodland scenery, it seemed to be well stocked. Other points of view opened in succession; now a full one, of the front of the old castle, and now a side glimpse at its particular towers; the former rich in all the bizarrerie of the Elizabethan school, while the simple and solid strength of other parts of the building seemed to show that they had been raised more for defence than ostentation.

Delighted with the partial glimpses which he obtained of the castle through the woods and glades by which this ancient feudal fortress was surrounded, our military traveller was determined to inquire whether it might not deserve a nearer view, and whether it contained family pictures or other objects of curiosity worthy of a stranger's visit; when, leaving the vicinity of the park, he rolled through a clean and well-paved street, and stopped at the door of a well-frequented inn.

Before ordering horses to proceed on his journey, General Browne made inquiries concerning the proprietor of the chateau which had so attracted his admiration, and was equally surprised and pleased at hearing in reply a nobleman named whom we shall call Lord Woodville. How fortunate! Much of Browne's early recollections, both at school and at college, had been connected with young Woodville, whom, by a few questions, he now ascertained to be the same with the owner of this fair domain. He had been raised to the peerage by the decease of his father a few months before, and, as the general learned from the landlord, the term of mourning being ended, was now taking possession of his paternal estate in the jovial season of merry autumn, accompanied by a select party of friends to enjoy the sports of a country famous for game.

This was delightful news to our traveller. Frank Woodville had been Richard Browne's fag at Eton, and his chosen intimate at Christ Church; their pleasures and their tasks had been the same; and the honest soldier's heart warmed to find his early friend in possession of so delightful a residence, and of an estate, as the landlord assured him with a nod and a wink, fully adequate to maintain and add to his dignity. Nothing was more natural than that the traveller should suspend a journey, which there was nothing to render hurried, to pay a visit to an old friend under such agreeable circumstances.

The fresh horses, therefore, had only the brief task of conveying the general's travelling carriage to Woodville Castle. A porter admitted them at a modern Gothic Lodge, built in that style to correspond with the castle itself, and at the same time rang a bell to give warning of the approach of visitors. Apparently the sound of the bell had suspended the separation of the company, bent on the various amusements of the morning; for, on entering the court of the chateau, several young men were lounging about in their sporting dresses, looking at, and criticizing, the dogs which the keepers held in readiness to attend their pastime. As General Browne alighted, the young lord came to the gate of the hall, and for an instant gazed, as at a stranger, upon the countenance of his friend, on which war, with its fatigues and its wounds, had made a great alteration. But the uncertainty lasted no longer than till the visitor had spoken, and the hearty greeting which followed was such as can only be exchanged betwixt those who have passed together merry days of careless boyhood or early youth.

"If I could have formed a wish, my dear Browne," said Lord Woodville, "it would have been to have you here, of all men, upon this occasion, which my friends are good enough to hold as a sort of holiday. Do not think you have been unwatched during the years you have been absent from us. I have traced you through your dangers, your triumphs, your misfortunes, and was delighted to see that, whether in victory or defeat, the name of my old friend was always distinguished with applause."

The general made a suitable reply, and congratulated his friend on his new dignities, and the possession of a place and domain so beautiful.

"Nay, you have seen nothing of it as yet," said Lord Woodville, "and I trust you do not mean to leave us till you are better acquainted with it. It is true, I confess, that my present party is pretty large, and the old house, like other places of the kind, does not possess so much accommodation as the extent of the outward walls appears to promise. But we can give you a comfortable old-fashioned room; and I venture to suppose that your campaigns have taught you to be glad of worse quarters."

The general shrugged his shoulders, and laughed. "I presume," he said, "the worst apartment in your château is considerably superior to the old tobacco-cask, in which I was fain to take up my night's lodging when I was in the Bush, as the Virginians call it, with the light corps.

There I lay, like Diogenes himself, so delighted with my covering from the elements, that I made a vain attempt to have it rolled on to my next quarters; but my commander for the time would give way to no such luxurious provision, and I took farewell of my beloved cask with tears in my eyes."

"Well, then, since you do not fear your quarters," said Lord Woodville, "you will stay with me a week at least. Of guns, dogs, fishing-rods, flies, and means of sport by sea and land, we have enough and to spare: you cannot pitch on an amusement, but we will pitch on the means of pursuing it. But if you prefer the gun and pointers, I will go with you myself, and see whether you have mended your shooting since you have been amongst the Indians of the back settlements."

The general gladly accepted his friendly host's proposal in all its points. After a morning of manly exercise, the company met at dinner, where it was the delight of Lord Woodville to conduce to the display of the high properties of his recovered friend, so as to recommend him to his guests, most of whom were persons of distinction. He led General Browne to speak of the scenes he had witnessed; and as every word marked alike the brave officer and the sensible man, who retained possession of his cool judgement under the most imminent dangers, the company looked upon the soldier with general respect, as on one who had proved himself possessed of an uncommon portion of personal courage – that attribute, of all others, of which everybody desires to be thought possessed.

The day at Woodville Castle ended as usual in such mansions. The hospitality stopped within the limits of good order; music, in which the young lord was a proficient, succeeded to the circulation of the bottle: cards and billiards, for those who preferred such amusements, were in readiness but the exercise of the morning required early hours, and not long after eleven o'clock the guests began to retire to their several apartments.

The young lord himself conducted his friend, General Browne, to the chamber destined for him, which answered the description he had given of it, being comfortable, but old-fashioned. The bed was of the massive form used in the end of the seventeenth century, and the curtains of faded silk, heavily trimmed with tarnished gold. But then the sheets, pillows, and blankets looked delightful to the campaigner, when he thought of his mansion, the cask. There was an air of gloom in the tapestry hangings, which, with their worn-out graces, curtained the walls of the little chamber, and gently undulated as the autumnal breeze found its way through the ancient lattice-window, which pattered and whistled as the air gained entrance. The toilet too, with its mirror, turbaned, after the manner of the beginning of the century, with a coiffure of murrey-coloured silk, and its hundred strange-shaped boxes, providing for arrangements which had been obsolete for more than fifty years, had an antique, and in so far a melancholy, aspect. But nothing could blaze more brightly and cheerfully than the two large wax candles; or if aught could rival them, it was the flaming bickering faggots in the chimney, that sent at once their gleam and their warmth through the snug apartment; which, notwithstanding the general antiquity of its appearance, was not wanting in the least convenience that modern habits rendered either necessary or desirable.

"This is an old-fashioned sleeping apartment, General," said the young lord; "but I hope you will find nothing that makes you envy your old tobacco-cask."

"I am not particular respecting my lodgings," replied the general; "yet were I to make any choice, I would prefer this chamber by many degrees, to the gayer and more modern rooms of your family mansion. Believe me that when I unite its modern air of comfort with its venerable antiquity, and recollect that it is your lordship's property, I shall feel in better quarters here, than if I were in the best hotel London could afford."

"I trust – I have no doubt – that you will find yourself as comfortable as I wish you, my dear General," said the young nobleman; and once more bidding his guest good night, he shook him by the hand and withdrew.

The general again looked round him, and internally congratulating himself on his return to peaceful life, the comforts of which were endeared by the recollection of the hardships and dangers he had lately sustained, undressed himself, and prepared himself for a luxurious night's rest.

Here, contrary to the custom of this species of tale, we leave the general in possession of his apartment until the next morning.

The company assembled for breakfast at an early hour, but without the appearance of General Browne, who seemed the guest that Lord Woodville was desirous of honouring above all whom his hospitality had assembled around him. He more than once expressed surprise at the general's absence, and at length sent a servant to make inquiry after him. The man brought back information that General Browne had been walking abroad since an early hour of the morning, in defiance of the weather, which was misty and ungenial.

"The custom of a soldier," – said the young nobleman to his friends; "many of them acquire habitual vigilance, and cannot sleep after the early hour at which their duty usually commands them to be alert."

Yet the explanation which Lord Woodville thus offered to the company seemed hardly satisfactory to his own mind, and it was in a fit of silence and abstraction that he awaited the return of the general. It took place near an hour after the breakfast bell had rung. He looked fatigued and feverish. His hair, the powdering and arrangement of which was at this time one of the most important occupations of a man's whole day, and marked his fashion as much as, in the present time, the tying of a cravat or the want of one, was dishevelled, uncurled, void of powder, and dank with dew. His clothes were huddled on with a careless negligence, remarkable in a military man, whose real or supposed duties are usually held to include some attention to the toilet; and his looks were haggard and ghastly in a peculiar degree.

"So you have stolen a march upon us this morning, my dear General," said Lord Woodville; "or you have not found your bed so much to your mind as I had hoped and you seemed to expect. How did you rest last night?"

"Oh, excellently well! remarkably well! never better in my life." – said General Browne rapidly, and yet with an air of embarrassment which was obvious to his friend. He then hastily swallowed a cup of tea, and neglecting or refusing whatever else was offered, seemed to fall into a fit of abstraction.

"You will take the gun today, General," said his friend and host, but had to repeat the question twice ere he received the abrupt answer, "No, my Lord; I am sorry I cannot have the honour of spending another day with your lordship; my post-horses are ordered, and will be here directly."

All who were present showed surprise, and Lord Woodville

immediately replied, "Post-horses, my good friend! what can you possibly want with them, when you promised to stay with me quietly for at least a week?"

"I believe," said the general, obviously much embarrassed, "that I might, in the pleasure of my first meeting with your lordship, have said something about stopping here a few days; but I have since found it altogether impossible."

"That is very extraordinary," answered the young nobleman. "You seemed quite disengaged yesterday, and you cannot have had a summons today; for our post has not come up from the town, and therefore you cannot have received any letters."

General Browne, without giving any further explanation, muttered something of indispensable business, and insisted on the absolute necessity of his departure in a manner which silenced all opposition on the part of his host, who saw that his resolution was taken, and forbore further importunity.

"At least, however," he said, "permit me, my dear Browne, since go you will or must, to show you the view from the terrace, which the mist that is now rising will soon display."

He threw open a sash window, and stepped down upon the terrace as he spoke. The general followed him mechanically, but seemed little to attend to what his host was saying, as, looking across an extended and rich prospect, he pointed out the different objects worthy of observation. Thus they moved on till Lord Woodville had attained his purpose of drawing his guest entirely apart from the rest of the company, when, turning round upon him with an air of great solemnity, he addressed him thus:

"Richard Browne, my old and very dear friend, we are now alone. Let me conjure you to answer me upon the word of a friend, and the honour of a soldier. How did you in reality rest during last night?"

"Most wretchedly indeed, my lord," answered the general, in the same tone of solemnity; – "so miserably, that I would not run the risk of such a second night, not only for all the lands belonging to this castle, but for all the country which I see from this elevated point of view."

"This is most extraordinary," said the young lord, as if speaking to himself; "then there must be something in the reports concerning that apartment." Again turning to the general, he said, "For God's sake, my dear friend, be candid with me, and let me know the disagreeable particulars which have befallen you under a roof, where, with consent of the owner, you should have met nothing save comfort."

The general seemed distressed by this appeal, and paused a moment before he replied. "My dear lord," he at length said, "what happened to me last night is of nature so peculiar and so unpleasant, that I could hardly bring myself to detail it even to your lordship, were it not that, independent of my wish to gratify any request of yours, I think that sincerity on my part may lead to some explanation about a circumstance equally painful and mysterious. To others, the communications I am about to make, might place me in the light of a weak-minded, superstitious fool who suffered his own imagination to delude and bewilder him; but you have known me in childhood and youth, and will not suspect me of having adopted in manhood the feelings and frailties from which my early years were free." Here he paused, and his friend replied:

"Do not doubt my perfect confidence in the truth of your communication, however strange it may be," replied Lord Woodville; "I know your firmness of disposition too well, to suspect you could be made the object of imposition, and am aware that your honour and your friendship will equally deter you from exaggerating whatever you may have witnessed."

"Well then," said the general, "I will proceed with my story as well as I can, relying upon your candour; and yet distinctly feeling that I would rather face a battery than recall to my mind the odious recollections of last night."

He paused a second time, and then perceiving that Lord Woodville remained silent and in an attitude of attention, he commenced, though not without obvious reluctance, the history of his night's adventures in the Tapestried Chamber.

"I undressed and went to bed, so soon as your lordship left me yesterday evening; but the wood in the chimney, which nearly fronted my bed, blazed brightly and cheerfully, and, aided by a hundred exciting recollections of my childhood and youth which had been recalled by the unexpected pleasure of meeting your lordship, prevented me from falling immediately asleep. I ought, however, to say, that these reflections were all of a pleasant and agreeable kind, grounded on a sense of having for a time exchanged the labour, fatigues, and dangers of my profession, for the enjoyments of a peaceful life, and the reunion of those friendly and affectionate ties which I had torn asunder at the rude summons of war.

"While such pleasing reflections were stealing over my mind, and gradually lulling me to slumber, I was suddenly aroused by a sound like that of the rustling of a silken gown, and the tapping of a pair of high-heeled shoes, as if a woman were walking in the apartment. Ere I could draw the curtain to see what the matter was, the figure of a little woman passed between the bed and the fire. The back of this form was turned to me, and I could observe, from the shoulders and neck, it was that of an old woman, whose dress was an old-fashioned gown which, I think, ladies call a sacque; that is, a sort of robe, completely loose in the body, but gathered into broad plaits upon the neck and shoulders, which fall down to the ground, and terminate in a species of train.

"I thought the intrusion singular enough, but never harboured for a moment the idea that what I saw was anything more than the mortal form of some old woman about the establishment, who had a fancy to dress like her grandmother, and who, having perhaps (as your lordship mentioned that you were rather straitened for room) been dislodged from her chamber for my accommodation, had forgotten the circumstance, and returned by twelve to her old haunt. Under this persuasion I moved myself in bed and coughed a little, to make the intruder sensible of my being in possession of the premises. – She turned slowly round, but gracious heaven! my lord, what a countenance did she display to me! There was no longer any question what she was, or any thought of her being a living being. Upon a face which wore the fixed features of a corpse, were imprinted the traces of the vilest and most hideous passions which had animated her while she lived. The body of some atrocious criminal seemed to have been given up from the grave, and the soul restored from the penal fire, in order to form, for a space, a union with the ancient accomplice of its guilt. I started up in bed, and sat upright, supporting myself on my palms, as I gazed on this horrible spectre. The hag made, as it seemed, a single and swift stride to the bed where I lay, and squatted herself down upon it, in precisely the same attitude which I had assumed in the extremity of horror, advancing her diabolical countenance within half a yard of mine, with a grin which seemed to intimate the malice and the derision of an incarnate fiend."

Here General Browne stopped, and wiped from his brow the cold perspiration with which the recollection of his horrible vision had covered it.

"My lord," he said, "I am no coward. I have been in all the mortal dangers incidental to my profession, and I may truly boast that no man ever knew Richard Browne dishonour the sword he wears; but in these horrible circumstances, under the eyes, and as it seemed, almost in the grasp of an incarnation of an evil spirit, all firmness forsook me, all manhood melted from me like wax in the furnace, and I felt my hair individually bristle. The current of my life-blood ceased to flow, and I sank back in a swoon, as very a victim to panic terror as ever was a village girl or a child of ten years old. How long I lay in this condition I cannot pretend to guess.

"But I was roused by the castle clock striking one, so loud that it seemed as if it were in the very room. It was some time before I dared open my eyes, lest they should again encounter the horrible spectacle. When, however, I summoned courage to look up, she was no longer visible. My first idea was to pull my bell, wake the servants, and remove to a garret or a hay-loft, to be ensured against a second visitation. Nay, I will confess the truth, that my resolution was altered, not by the shame of exposing myself, but by the very fear that, as the bell-cord hung by the chimney, I might, in making my way to it, be again crossed by the fiendish hag, who, I figured to myself, might be still lurking about some corner of the apartment.

"I will not pretend to describe what hot and cold fever-fits tormented me for the rest of the night, through broken sleep, weary vigils, and that dubious state which forms the neutral ground between them. A hundred terrible objects appeared to haunt me; but there was the great difference betwixt the vision which I have described, and those which followed, that I knew the last to be deceptions of my own fancy and over-excited nerves.

"Day at last appeared, and I rose from my bed ill in health, and humiliated in mind. I was ashamed of myself as a man and a soldier, and still more so, at feeling my own extreme desire to escape from the haunted apartment, which, however, conquered all other considerations; so that, huddling on my clothes with the most careless haste, I made my escape from your lordship's mansion, to seek in the open air some relief to my nervous system, shaken as it was by this horrible rencounter with a visitant, for such I must believe her, from the other world. Your lordship has now heard the cause of my discomposure, and of my sudden desire to leave your hospitable castle. In other places I trust we may often meet; but God protect me from ever spending a second night under that roof!"

Strange as the general's tale was, he spoke with such a deep air of conviction, that it cut short all the usual commentaries which are made on such stories. Lord Woodville never once asked him if he was sure he did not dream of the apparition, or suggested any of the possibilities by which it is fashionable to explain supernatural appearances, as wild vagaries of the fancy or deceptions of the optic nerves. On the contrary he seemed deeply impressed with the truth and reality of what he had heard; and, after a considerable pause, regretted, with much appearance of sincerity, that his early friend should in his house have suffered so severely.

"I am the more sorry for your pain, my dear Browne," he continued, that it is the unhappy, though most unexpected, result of an experiment of my own! You must know, that for my father and grandfather's time, at least, the apartment which was assigned to you last night had been shut on account of reports that it was disturbed by supernatural sights and noises. When I came, a few weeks since, into possession of the estate, I thought the accommodation which the castle afforded for my friends was not extensive enough to permit the inhabitants of the invisible world to retain possession of a comfortable sleeping apartment. I therefore caused the Tapestried Chamber, as we call it, to be opened; and without destroying its air of antiquity, I had such new articles of furniture placed in it as became the modern times. Yet as the opinion that the room was haunted very strongly prevailed among the domestics, and was also known in the neighbourhood and to many of my friends, I feared some prejudice might be entertained by the first occupant of the Tapestried Chamber, which might tend to revive the evil report which it had laboured under, and so disappoint my purpose of rendering it a useful part of the house. I must confess, my dear Browne, that your arrival yesterday, agreeable to me for a thousand reasons besides, seemed the most favourable opportunity of removing the unpleasant rumours which attached to the room, since your courage was indubitable and your mind free of any preoccupation on the subject. I could not, therefore, have chosen a more fitting subject for my experiment."

"Upon my life," said General Browne, somewhat hastily, "I am infinitely obliged to your lordship – very particularly indebted indeed. I am likely to remember for some time the consequences of the experiment, as your lordship is pleased to call it."

"Nay, now you are unjust, my dear friend," said Lord Woodville. "You have only to reflect for a single moment, in order to be convinced that I could not augur the possibility of the pain to which you have been so unhappily exposed. I was yesterday morning a complete sceptic on the subject of supernatural appearances. Nay, I am sure that had I told you what was said about that room, those very reports would have induced you, by your own choice, to select it for your accommodation. It was my misfortune, perhaps my error, but really cannot be termed my fault, that you have been afflicted so strangely."

"Strangely indeed!" said the general, resuming his good temper; "and I acknowledge that I have no right to be offended with your lordship for treating me like what I used to think myself – a man of some firmness and courage. – But I see my post-horses are arrived, and I must not detain your lordship from your amusement."

"Nay, my old friend," said Lord Woodville, "since you cannot stay with us another day, which, indeed, I can no longer urge, give me at least half an hour more. You used to love pictures, and I have a gallery of portraits, some of them by Vandyke, representing ancestry to whom this property and castle formerly belonged. I think that several of them will strike you as possessing merit."

General Browne accepted the invitation, though somewhat unwillingly. It was evident he was not to breathe freely or at ease until he left Woodville Castle far behind him. He could not refuse his friend's invitation, however; and the less so, that he was a little ashamed of the peevishness which he had displayed towards his well-meaning entertainer.

The general, therefore, followed Lord Woodville through several rooms, into a long gallery hung with pictures, which the latter pointed out to his guest, telling the names, and giving some account of the personages whose portraits presented themselves in progression. General Browne was but little interested in the details which these accounts conveyed to him. They were, indeed, of the kind which are usually found in the old family gallery. Here was a cavalier who had ruined the estate in the royal cause; there a fine lady who had reinstated it by contracting a match with a wealthy Roundhead. There hung a gallant who had been in danger for corresponding with the exiled Court of St Germain's; here one who had taken arms for William at the Revolution; and there a third that had thrown his weight alternately into the scale of Whig and Tory.

While Lord Woodville was cramming these words into his guest's ear, 'against the stomach of his sense', they gained the middle of the gallery, when he beheld General Browne suddenly start, and assume an attitude of the utmost surprise, not unmixed with fear, as his eyes were caught and suddenly riveted by a portrait of an old lady in a sacque, the fashionable dress of the end of the seventeenth century.

"There she is!" he exclaimed; "there she is, in form and features, though inferior in demoniac expression to the accursed hag who visited me last night!"

"If that be the case," said the young nobleman, "there can remain no longer any doubt of the horrible reality of your apparition. That is the picture of a wretched ancestress of mine, of whose crimes a black and fearful catalogue is recorded in a family history in my charter-chest. The recital of them would be too horrible; it is enough to say, that in yon fatal apartment incest and unnatural murder were committed. I will restore it to the solitude to which the better judgement of those who preceded me had consigned it; and never shall any one, so long as I can prevent it, be exposed to a repetition of the supernatural horrors which could shake such courage as yours."

Thus the friends, who had met with such glee, parted in a very different mood; Lord Woodville to command the Tapestried Chamber to be unmantled and the door built up; and General Browne to seek in some less beautiful country, and with some less dignified friend, forgetfulness of the painful night which he had passed in Woodville Castle.

An Account
of the Strange Disturbances
at Aungier Street

J. Sheridan Le Fanu

My cousin (Tom Ludlow) and I studied medicine together. I think he would have succeeded, had he stuck to the profession; but he preferred the Church, poor fellow, and died early, a sacrifice to contagion, contracted in the noble discharge of his duties. For my present purpose, I say enough of his character when I mention that he was of a sedate but frank and cheerful nature; very exact in his observance of truth, and not by any means like myself – of an excitable or nervous temperament.

My Uncle Ludlow – Tom's father – while we were attending lectures, purchased three or four old houses in Aungier Street, one of which was unoccupied. He resided in the country, and Tom proposed that we should take up our abode in the untenanted house, so long as it should continue unlet; a move which would accomplish the double end of settling us nearer alike to our lecture-rooms and to our amusements, and of relieving us from the weekly charge of rent for our lodgings.

Our furniture was very scant – our whole equipage remarkably modest and primitive; and, in short, our arrangements pretty nearly as simple as those of a bivouac. Our new plan was, therefore, executed almost as soon as conceived. The front drawing-room was our sitting-room. I had the bedroom over it, and Tom the back bedroom on the same floor, which nothing could have induced me to occupy

The house, to begin with, was a very old one. It had been, I believe, newly fronted about fifty years before; but with this exception, it had nothing modern about it. The agent who bought it and looked up the titles for my uncle, told me that it was sold, along with much older forfeited property, at Chichester House, I think, in 1702; and had belonged to Sir Thomas Hackett, who was Lord Mayor of Dublin in

James II's time. How old it was then, I can't say; but, at all events, it had seen years and changes enough to have contracted all that mysterious and saddened air, at once exciting and depressing, which belongs to most old mansions.

There had been very little done in the way of modernising details; and, perhaps, it was better so; for there was something queer and by-gone in the very walls and ceilings – in the shape of doors and windows – in the odd diagonal site of the chimney-pieces – in the beams and ponderous cornices – not to mention the singular solidity of all the woodwork, from the banisters to the window-frames, which hopelessly defied disguise, and would have emphatically proclaimed their antiquity through any conceivable amount of modern finery and varnish.

An effort had, indeed, been made, to the extent of papering the drawing-rooms; but, somehow the paper looked raw and out of keeping; and the old woman, who kept a little dirt-pie of a shop in the lane, and whose daughter – a girl of two and fifty – was our solitary handmaid, coming in at sunrise, and chastely receding again as soon as she had made all ready for tea in our state apartment; – this woman, I say, remembered it, when old Judge Horrocks (who, having earned the reputation of a particularly "hanging judge," ended by hanging himself, as the coroner's jury found, under an impulse of "temporary insanity," with a child's skipping-rope, over the massive old banisters) resided there, entertaining good company, with fine venison and rare old port. In those halycon days, the drawing-rooms were hung with gilded leather, and I dare say, cut a good figure, for they were really spacious rooms.

The bedrooms were wainscoted, but the front one was not gloomy; and in it the cosiness of antiquity quite overcame its sombre associations. But the back bedroom, with its two queerly-placed melancholy windows, staring vacantly at the foot of the bed, and with the shadowy recess to be found in most old houses in Dublin, like a large ghostly closet, which, from congeniality of temperament, had amalgamated with the bedchamber, and dissolved the partition. At night-time, this "alcove" – as our "maid" was wont to call it – had, in my eyes, a specially sinister and suggestive character. Tom's distant and solitary candle glimmered vainly into its darkness. There it was always overlooking him – always itself impenetrable. But this was only part of the effect. The whole room was, I can't tell how, repulsive to me. There was, I suppose, in its proportions and features, a latent discord – a certain mysterious and indescribable relation, which jarred indistinctly upon some secret sense of the fitting and the safe, and raised indefinable suspicions and apprehensions of the imagination. On the whole, as I began by saying, nothing could have induced me to pass a night alone in it.

I had never pretended to conceal from poor Tom my superstitious weakness; and he, on the other hand, most unaffectedly ridiculed my tremors. The sceptic was, however, destined to receive a lesson, as you shall hear.

We had not been very long in occupation of our respective dormitories, when I began to complain of uneasy nights and disturbed sleep. I was, I suppose, the more impatient under this annoyance, as I was usually a sound sleeper, and by no means prone to nightmares. It was now, however, my destiny, instead of enjoying my customary repose, every night to "sup full of horrors." After a preliminary course of disagreeable and frightful dreams, my troubles took a definite form, and the same vision, without an appreciable variation in a single detail, visited me at least (on an average) every second night in the week.

Now, this dream, nightmare, or infernal illusion – which you please – of which I was the miserable sport, was on this wise:

I saw, or thought I saw, with the most abominable distinctness, although at the time in profound darkness, every article of furniture and accidental arrangement of the chamber in which I lay. This, as you know, is incidental to ordinary nightmare. Well, while in this clairvoyant condition, which seemed but the lighting up of the theatre in which was to be exhibited the monotonous tableau of horror, which made my nights insupportable, my attention invariably became, I know not why, fixed upon the windows opposite the foot of my bed; and, uniformly with the same effect, a sense of dreadful anticipation always took slow but sure possession of me. I became somehow conscious of a sort of horrid but undefined preparation going forward in some unknown quarter, and by some unknown agency, for my torment; and, after an interval, which always seemed to me of the same length, a picture suddenly flew up to the window, where it remained fixed, as if by an electrical attraction, and my discipline of horror then commenced, to last perhaps for hours. The picture thus mysteriously glued to the window-panes, was the portrait of an old man, in a crimson-flowered silk dressing-gown, the folds of which I could now describe, with a countenance embodying a strange mixture of intellect, sensuality, and power, but withal sinister and full of malignant omen. His nose was hooked, like the beak of a vulture; his eyes large, grey and prominent, and lighted up with a more than mortal cruelty and coldness. These features were surmounted by a crimson velvet cap, the hair that peeped from under which was white with age, while the eyebrows retained their original blackness. Well, I remember every line, hue, and shadow of that stony countenance, and well I may! The gaze of this hellish visage was fixed upon me, and mine returned it with the inexplicable fascination of nightmare, for what appeared to me to be hours of agony. At last –

"The cock he crew, away then flew"

the fiend who had enslaved me through the awful watches of the night; and, harrassed and nervous, I rose to the duties of the day.

I had – I can't say exactly why, but it may have been from the exquisite anguish and profound impressions of unearthly horror, with which this strange phantasmagoria was associated – an insurmountable antipathy to describing the exact nature of my nightly troubles to my friend and comrade. Generally, however, I told him that I was haunted by abominable dreams; and, true to the imputed materialism of medicine, we put our heads together to dispel my horrors, not by exorcism, but by a tonic.

I will do this tonic justice, and frankly admit that the accursed portrait began to intermit its visits under its influence. What of that? Was this singular apparition – as full of character as of terror – therefore the creature of my fancy, or the invention of my poor stomach? Was it, in short, subjective (to borrow the technical slang of the day) and not the palpable aggression and intrusion of an external agent? That, good friend, as we will both admit, by no means follows. The evil spirit, who enthralled my senses in the shape of that portrait, may have been just as near me, just as energetic, just as malignant, though I saw him not. What means the whole moral code of revealed religion regarding the due keeping of our own bodies, soberness, temperance, etc.? Here is an obvious connexion between the material and the invisible; the healthy tone of the system, and its unimpaired energy, may, for aught we can tell, guard us against influences which would otherwise render life itself terrific. The mesmerist and the electro-biologist will fail upon an average with nine patients out of ten – so may the evil spirit. Special conditions of the corporal system are indispensable to the production of certain spiritual phenomena. The operation succeeds sometimes – sometimes fails – that is all.

I found afterwards that my would-be sceptical companion had his troubles too. But of these I knew nothing yet. One night, for a wonder, I was sleeping soundly, when I was roused by a step on the lobby outside my room, followed by the loud clang of what turned out to be a large brass candlestick, flung with all his force by poor Tom Ludlow over the banisters, and rattling with a rebound down the second flight of stairs; and almost concurrently with this, Tom burst open my door, and bounced into my room backwards, in a state of extraordinary agitation.

I had jumped out of bed and clutched him by the arm before I had any distinct idea of my own whereabouts. There we were – in our shirts – standing before the open door – staring through the great old banister opposite, at the lobby window, through which the sickly light of a clouded moon was gleaming.

"What's the matter, Tom? What's the matter with you? What the devil's the matter with you, Tom?" I demanded, shaking him with nervous impatience.

He took a long breath before he answered me, and then it was not very coherently.

"It's nothing, nothing at all – did I speak? – what did I say? – where's the candle, Richard? It's dark; I – I had a candle !"

"Yes, dark enough," I said; "but what's the matter? – what is it? – why don't you speak, Tom? – have you lost your wits? What is the matter?"

"The matter? Oh, it is all over. It must have been a dream – nothing at all but a dream – don't you think so? It could not be anything more than a dream."

"Of course," said I, feeling uncommonly nervous, "it was a dream."

"I thought," he said, "there was a man in my room, and – and I jumped out of bed; and – and – where's the candle?"

"In your room, most likely," I said, "shall I go and bring it?"

"No; stay here – don't go; it's no matter – don't, I tell you; it was all a dream. Bolt the door, Dick; I'll stay here with you – I feel nervous. So, Dick, like a good fellow, light your candle and open the window – I am in a shocking state."

I did as he asked me, and robing himself like Granuaile in one of my blankets, he seated himself close beside my bed.

Everybody knows how contagious is fear of all sorts, but more especially that particular kind of fear under which poor Tom was at that moment labouring. I would not have heard, nor I believe would he have recapitulated, just at that moment, for half the world, the details of the hideous vision which had so unmanned him.

"Don't mind telling me anything about your nonsensical dream, Tom," said I, affecting contempt, really in a panic; "let us talk about something else; but it is quite plain that this dirty old house disagrees with us both, and hang me if I stay here any longer, to be pestered with indigestion and – and – bad nights, so we may as well look out for lodgings, don't you think so? – at once."

Tom agreed, and, after an interval, said –

"I have been thinking, Richard, that it is a long time since I saw my father, and I have made up my mind to go down tomorrow and return in a day or two, and you can take rooms for us in the meantime."

I fancied that this resolution, obviously the result of the vision which had so profoundly scared him, would probably vanish next morning with the damps and shadows of night. But I was mistaken. Off went Tom at peep of day to the country, having agreed that so soon as I had secured suitable lodgings, I was to recall him by letter from his visit to my Uncle Ludlow.

Now, anxious as I was to change my quarters, it so happened, owing to a series of petty procrastinations and accidents, that nearly a week elapsed before my bargain was made and my letter of recall on the wing to Tom; and, in the meantime, a trifling adventure or two had occurred to your humble servant, which, absurd as they now appear, diminished by distance, did certainly at the time serve to whet my appetite for change considerably.

A night or two after the departure of my comrade, I was sitting by my bedroom fire, the door locked, and the ingredients of a tumbler of hot whisky-punch upon the crazy spider-table; for, as the best mode of keeping the

"Black spirits and white,
Blue spirits and grey,"

with which I was environed, at bay, I had adopted the practice recommended by the wisdom of my ancestors, and "kept my spirits up by pouring spirits down." I had thrown aside my volume of Anatomy, and was treating myself by way of a tonic, preparatory to my punch and bed, to half-a-dozen pages of the *Spectator*, when I heard a step on the flight of stairs descending from the attics. It was two o'clock, and the streets were as silent as a church-yard – the sounds were, therefore, perfectly distinct. There was a slow, heavy tread, characterised by the emphasis and deliberation of age, descending by the narrow staircase from above; and, what made the sound more singular, it was plain that the feet which produced it were perfectly bare, measuring the descent with something between a pound and a flop, very ugly to hear.

I knew quite well that my attendant had gone away many hours before, and that nobody but myself had any business in the house. It was quite plain also that the person who was coming downstairs had no intention whatever of concealing his movements; but, on the contrary, appeared disposed to make even more noise, and proceed more deliberately, than was at all necessary. When the step reached the foot of the stairs outside my room, it seemed to stop; and I expected every moment to see my door open spontaneously, and give admission to the original of my detested portrait. I was, however, relieved in a few seconds by hearing the descent renewed, just in the same manner, upon the staircase leading down to the drawing-rooms, and thence, after another pause, down the next flight, and so on to the hall, whence I heard no more.

Now, by the time the sound had ceased, I was wound up, as they say, to a very unpleasant pitch of excitement. I listened, but there was not a stir. I screwed up my courage to a decisive experiment – opened my door, and in a stentorian voice bawled over the banisters, "Who's there?" There was no answer, but the ringing of my own voice through the empty old house, – no renewal of the movement; nothing, in short, to give my unpleasant sensations a definite direction. There is, I think, something most disagreeably disenchanting in the sound of one's own voice under such circumstances, exerted in solitude and in vain. It redoubled my sense of isolation, and my misgivings increased on perceiving that the door, which I certainly thought I had left open, was closed behind me; in a vague alarm, lest my retreat should be cut off, I got again into my room as quickly as I could, where I remained in a state of imaginary blockade, and very uncomfortable indeed, till morning.

Next night brought no return of my barefooted fellow-lodger; but the night following, being in my bed, and in the dark – somewhere, I suppose, about the same hour as before, I distinctly heard the old fellow again descending from the garrets.

This time I had had my punch, and the *morale* of the garrison was consequently excellent. I jumped out of bed, clutched the poker as I passed the expiring fire, and in a moment was upon the lobby. The sound had ceased by this time – the dark and chill were discouraging; and, guess my horror, when I saw, or thought I saw, a black monster, whether in the shape of a man or a bear I could not say, standing, with its back to the wall, on the lobby, facing me, with a pair of great greenish eyes shining dimly out. Now, I must be frank, and confess that the cupboard which displayed our plates and cups stood just there, though at the moment I did not recollect it. At the same time I must honestly say, that making every allowance for an excited imagination, I never could satisfy myself that I was made the dupe of my own fancy in this matter; for this apparition, after one or two shiftings of shape, as if in the act of incipient transformation, began, as it seemed on second thoughts, to advance upon me in its original form.

From an instinct of terror rather than of courage, I hurled the poker, with all my force, at its head; and to the music of a horrid crash made my way into my room, and double-locked the door. Then, in a minute more, I heard the horrid bare feet walk down the stairs, till the sound ceased in the hall, as on the former occasion.

If the apparition of the night before was an ocular delusion of my fancy sporting with the dark outlines of our cupboard, and if its horrid eyes were nothing but a pair of inverted teacups, I had, at all events, the satisfaction of having launched the poker with admirable effect, and in true "fancy" phrase, "knocked its two daylights into one," as the commingled fragments of my tea-service testified. I did my best to gather comfort and courage from these evidences; but it would not do. And then what could I say of those horrid bare feet, and the regular tramp, tramp, tramp, which measured the distance of the entire staircase through the solitude of my haunted dwelling, and at an hour when no good influence was stirring? Confound it! – the whole affair was abominable. I was out of spirits, and dreaded the approach of night.

It came, ushered ominously in with a thunder-storm and dull torrents of depressing rain. Earlier than usual, the streets grew silent; and by twelve o'clock nothing but the comfortless pattering of the rain was to be heard.

I made myself as snug as I could. I lighted *two* candles instead of one. I foreswore bed, and held myself in readiness for a sally, candle in hand; for, *coute qui coute*, I was resolved to see the being, if visible at all, who troubled the nightly stillness of my mansion. I was fidgety and nervous and tried in vain to interest myself with my books. I walked up and down my room, whistling in turn martial and hilarious music, and listening ever and anon for the dreaded noise. I sat down and stared at the square label on the solemn and reserved-looking black bottle, until "Flanagan & Co's Best Old Malt Whisky" grew into a sort of subdued accompaniment to all the fantastic and horrible speculations which chased one another through my brain.

Silence, meanwhile, grew more silent, and darkness darker. I listened in vain for the rumble of a vehicle, or the dull clamour of a distant row. There was nothing but the sound of a rising wind, which had succeeded the thunder-storm that had travelled over the Dublin mountains quite out of hearing. In the middle of this great city I began to feel myself alone with nature, and Heaven knows what beside. My courage was ebbing. Punch, however, which makes beasts of so many, made a man of me again – just in time to hear with tolerable nerve and firmness the lumpy, flabby, naked feet deliberately descending the stairs again.

I took a candle, not without a tremor. As I crossed the floor I tried to extemporise a prayer, but stopped short to listen, and never finished it. The steps continued. I confess I hesitated for some seconds at the door before I took heart of grace and opened it. When I peeped out the lobby was perfectly empty – there was no monster standing on the staircase; and as the detested sound ceased, I was reassured enough to venture forward nearly to the banisters. Horror of horrors! within a stair or two beneath the spot where I stood the unearthly tread smote the floor. My eye caught something in motion; it was about the size of a Goliath's foot – it was grey, heavy, and flapped with a dead weight from one step to another. As I am alive, it was the most monstrous grey rat I ever beheld or imagined.

Shakespeare says – "Some men there are cannot abide a gaping pig, and some that are mad if they behold a cat." I went well-nigh out of my wits when I beheld this *rat*; for, laugh at me as you may, it fixed upon me, I thought, a perfectly human expression of malice; and, as it shuffled about and looked up into my face almost from between my feet, I saw, I could swear it – I felt it then, and know it now, the infernal gaze and the accursed countenance of my old friend in the portrait, transfused into the visage of the bloated vermin before me.

I bounced into my room again with a feeling of loathing and horror I cannot describe, and locked and bolted my door as if a lion had been at the other side. D—n him or *it*; curse the portrait and its original! I felt in my soul that the rat – yes, the *rat*, the RAT I had just seen, was that evil being in masquerade, and rambling through the house upon some infernal night lark.

Next morning I was early trudging through the miry streets; and, among other transactions, posted a peremptory note recalling Tom. On my return, however, I found a note from my absent "chum," announcing his intended return next day. I was doubly rejoiced at this, because I had succeeded in getting rooms; and because the change of scene and return of my comrade were rendered specially pleasant by the last night's half ridiculous, half horrible adventure.

I slept extemporaneously in my new quarters in Digges' Street that night, and next morning returned for breakfast to the haunted mansion, where I was certain Tom would call immediately on his arrival.

I was quite right – he came; and almost his first question referred to the primary object of our change of residence.

"Thank God," he said with genuine fervour, on hearing that all was arranged. "On *your* account I am delighted. As to myself, I assure you that no earthly consideration could have induced me ever again to pass a night in this disastrous old house."

"Confound the house!" I ejaculated, with a genuine mixture of fear and detestation, "we have not had a pleasant hour since we came to live here"; and so I went on, and related incidentally my adventure with the plethoric old rat.

"Well, if that were *all*," said my cousin, affecting to make light of the matter, "I don't think I should have minded it very much."

"Ay, but its eye – its countenance, my dear Tom," urged I; "if you had seen *that*, you would have felt it might be *anything* but what it seemed."

"I am inclined to think the best conjurer in such a case would be an able-bodied cat," he said, with a provoking chuckle.

"But let us hear your own adventure," I said tartly.

At this challenge he looked uneasily round him. I had poked up a very unpleasant recollection.

"You shall hear it, Dick; I'll tell it to you," he said.

"Begad, sir, I should feel quite queer, though, telling it *here*, though we are too strong a body for ghosts to meddle with just now."

Though he spoke this like a joke, I think it was serious calculation. Our Hebe was in a corner of the room, packing our cracked delf tea and dinner-services in a basket. She soon suspended operations, and with mouth and eyes wide open became an absorbed listener. Tom's experiences were told nearly in these words:

"I saw it three times, Dick – three distinct times; and I am perfectly certain it meant me some infernal harm. I was, I say, in danger – in *extreme* danger; for, if nothing else had happened, my reason would most certainly have failed me, unless I had escaped so soon. Thank God, I *did* escape.

"The first night of this hateful disturbance, I was lying in the attitude of sleep, in that lumbering old bed. I hate to think of it. I was really wide awake, though I had put out my candle, and was lying as quietly as if I had been asleep; and although accidentally restless, my thoughts were running in a cheerful and agreeable channel.

"I think it must have been two o'clock at least when I thought I heard a sound in that – that odious dark recess at the far end of the bedroom. It was as if someone was drawing a piece of cord slowly along the floor, lifting it up, and dropping it softly down again in coils. I sat up once or twice in my bed, but could see nothing, so I concluded it must be mice in the wainscot. I felt no emotion graver than curiosity, and after a few minutes ceased to observe it.

"While lying in this state, strange to say, without at first a suspicion of anything supernatural, on a sudden I saw an old man, rather stout and square, in a sort of roan-red dressing-gown, and with a black cap on his head, moving stiffly and slowly in a diagonal direction, from the recess, across the floor of the bedroom, passing my bed at the foot, and entering the lumber-closet at the left. He had something under his arm; his head hung a little at one side; and merciful God! when I saw his face."

Tom stopped for a while, and then said –

"That awful countenance, which living or dying I never can forget, disclosed what he was. Without turning to the right or left, he passed beside me, and entered the closet by the bed's head.

"While this fearful and indescribable type of death and guilt was passing, I felt that I had no more power to speak or stir than if I had been myself a corpse. For hours after it had disappeared, I was too terrified and weak to move. As soon as daylight came, I took courage, and examined the room, and especially the course which the frightful intruder had seemed to take, but there was not a vestige to indicate anybody's having passed there; no sign of any disturbing agency visible among the lumber that strewed the floor of the closet.

"I now began to recover a little. I was fagged and exhausted, and at last, overpowered by a feverish sleep. I came down late; and finding you out of spirits, on account of your dreams about the portrait, whose *original* I am now certain disclosed himself to me, I did not care to talk about the infernal vision. In fact, I was trying to persuade myself that the whole thing was an illusion, and I did not like to revive in their intensity the hated impressions of the past night – or, to risk the constancy of my scepticism, by recounting the tale of my sufferings.

"It required some nerve, I can tell you, to go to my haunted chamber next night, and lie down quietly in the same bed," continued Tom. "I did so with a degree of trepidation, which, I am not ashamed to say, a very little matter would have sufficed to stimulate to downright panic. This night, however, passed off quietly enough, as also the next; and so too did two or three more. I grew more confident, and began to fancy that I believed in the theories of spectral illusions, with which I had at first vainly tried to impose upon my convictions.

"The apparition had been, indeed, altogether anomalous. It had crossed the room without any recognition of my presence: I had not disturbed *it*, and *it* had no mission to *me*. What, then, was the imaginable use of its crossing the room in a visible shape at all? Of course it might have been in the closet instead of *going* there, as easily as it introduced itself into the recess without entering the chamber in a shape discernible by the senses. Besides, how the deuce *had* I seen it? It was a dark night; I had no candle; there was no fire; and yet I saw it as distinctly, in colouring and outline, as ever I beheld human form! A cataleptic dream would explain it all; and I was determined that a dream it should be.

"One of the most remarkable phenomena connected with the practice of mendacity is the vast number of deliberate lies we tell ourselves, whom, of all persons, we can least expect to deceive. In all this, I need hardly tell you, Dick, I was simply lying to myself, and did not believe one word of the wretched humbug. Yet I went on, as men will do, like persevering charlatans and impostors, who tire people into credulity by the mere force of reiteration; so I hoped to win myself over at last to a comfortable scepticism about the ghost.

"He had not appeared a second time – that certainly was a comfort; and what, after all, did I care for him, and his queer old toggery and strange looks? Not a fig! I was nothing the worse for having seen him, and a good story the better. So I tumbled into bed, put out my candle, and, cheered by a loud drunken quarrel in the back lane, went fast asleep.

"From this deep slumber I awoke with a start. I knew I had had a horrible dream; but what it was I could not remember. My heart was thumping furiously; I felt bewildered and feverish; I sat up in the bed and looked about the room. A broad flood of moonlight came in through the curtainless window; everything was as I had last seen it; and though the domestic squabble in the back lane was, unhappily for me, allayed, I yet could hear a pleasant fellow singing, on his way home, the then popular comic ditty called, "Murphy Delany". Taking advantage of this diversion I lay down again, with my face towards the fireplace, and closing my eyes, did my best to think of nothing else but the song, which was every moment growing fainter in the distance: –

" *'Twas Murphy Delany, so funny and frisky,*
Stept into a shebeen shop to get his skin full;
He reeled out again pretty well lined with whiskey,
As fresh as a shamrock, as blind as a bull."

"The singer, whose condition I dare say resembled that of his hero, was soon too far off to regale my ears any more; and as his music died away, I myself sank into a doze, neither sound nor refreshing. Somehow the song had got into my head, and I went meandering on through the adventures of my respectable fellow-countryman, who, on emerging from the "shebeen shop," fell into a river, from which he was fished up to be "sat upon" by a coroner's jury, who having learned from a "horse-doctor" that he was "dead as a door-nail, so there was an end," returned their verdict accordingly, just as he returned to his senses, when an angry altercation and a pitched battle between the body and the coroner winds up the lay with due spirit and pleasantry.

"Through this ballad I continued with a weary monotony to plod, down to the very last line, and then *da capo*, and so on, in my uncomfortable half-sleep, for how long, I can't conjecture. I found myself at last, however, muttering, "*dead* as a door-nail, so there was an end"; and something like another voice within me, seemed to say, very faintly, but sharply, "dead! dead! *dead*! and may the Lord have mercy on your soul!" and instantaneously I was wide awake, and staring right before me from the pillow.

"Now – will you believe it, Dick? – I saw the same accursed figure standing full front, and gazing at me with its stony and fiendish countenance, not two yards from the bedside."

Tom stopped here, and wiped the perspiration from his face. I felt very queer. The girl was as pale as Tom; and, assembled as we were in the very scene of these adventures, we were all, I dare say, equally grateful for the clear daylight and the resuming bustle out of doors.

"For about three seconds only I saw it plainly; then it grew indistinct; but, for a long time, there was something like a column of dark vapour where it had been standing between me and the wall; and I felt sure that he was still there. After a good while, this appearance went too. I took my clothes downstairs to the hall, and dressed there, with the door half open; then went out into the street, and walked about the town till morning, when I came back, in a miserable state of nervousness and exhaustion. I was such a fool, Dick, as to be ashamed to tell you how I came to be so upset. I thought you would laugh at me; especially as I had always talked philosophy, and treated *your* ghosts with contempt. I concluded you would give me no quarter; and so kept my tale of horror to myself.

"Now, Dick, you will hardly believe me, when I assure you, that for many nights after this last experience, I did not go to my room at all. I used to sit up for a while in the drawing-room after you had gone up to your bed; and then steal down softly to the hall-door, let myself out, and sit in the "Robin Hood" tavern until the last guest went off; and then I got through the night like a sentry, pacing the streets till morning.

"For more than a week I never slept in bed. I sometimes had a snooze on a form in the "Robin Hood," and sometimes a nap in a chair during the day; but regular sleep I had absolutely none.

"I was quite resolved that we should get into another house; but I could not bring myself to tell you the reason, and I somehow put it off from day to day, and because my life was, during every hour of this procrastination, rendered as miserable as that of a felon with the constables on his track, I was growing absolutely ill from this wretched mode of life.

"One afternoon I determined to enjoy an hour's sleep upon your bed. I hated mine; so that I had never, except in a stealthy visit every day to unmake it, lest Martha should discover the secret of my nightly absence, entered the ill-omened chamber.

"As ill-luck would have it, you had locked your bedroom, and taken away the key. I went into my own to unsettle the bedclothes, as usual, and give the bed the appearance of having been slept in. Now a variety of circumstances concurred to bring about the dreadful scene through which I was that night to pass. In the first place, I was literally overpowered with fatigue, and longing for sleep; in the next place, the effect of this extreme exhaustion upon my nerves resembled that of a narcotic, and rendered me less susceptible than, perhaps I should in any other condition have been, of the exciting fears which had become habitual to me. Then again, a little bit of the window was open, a pleasant freshness pervaded the room, and, to crown all, the cheerful sun of day was making the room quite pleasant. What was to prevent me enjoying an hour's nap *here*? The whole air was resonant with the cheerful hum of life, and the broad matter-of-fact light of day filled every corner of the room.

"I yielded – stifling my qualms – to the almost overpowering temptation; and merely throwing off my coat, and loosening my cravat, I lay down, limiting myself to *half*-an-hour's doze in the unwonted enjoyment of a feather bed, a coverlet, and a bolster.

"It was horribly insidious; and the demon, no doubt, marked my infatuated preparations. Dolt that I was, I fancied, with mind and body worn out for want of sleep, and an arrear of a full week's rest to my credit, that such measure as *half*-an-hour's sleep, in such a situation, was possible. My sleep was death-like, long, and dreamless.

Without a start or fearful sensation of any kind, I waked gently, but completely. It was, as you have good reason to remember, long past midnight – I believe, about two o'clock. When sleep has been deep and long enough to satisfy nature thoroughly, one often wakens in this way, suddenly, tranquilly, and completely.

"There was a figure seated in that lumbering, old sofa-chair, near the fireplace. Its back was towards me, but I could not be mistaken; it turned slowly round, and, merciful heavens! there was the stony face, with its infernal lineaments of malignity and despair, gloating on me. There was now no doubt as to its consciousness of my presence, and the hellish malice with which it was animated, for it arose, and drew close to the bedside. There was a rope about its neck, and the other end, coiled up, it held stiffly in its hand.

"My good angel nerved me for this horrible crisis. I remained for some seconds transfixed by the gaze of this tremendous phantom. He came close to the bed, and appeared on the point of mounting upon it. The next instant I was upon the floor at the far side, and in a moment more was, I don't know how, upon the lobby.

"But the spell was not yet broken; the valley of the shadow of death was not yet traversed. The abhorred phantom was before me there; it was standing near the banisters, stooping a little, and with one end of the rope around its own neck, was poising a noose at the other, as if to throw over mine; and while engaged in this baleful pantomine, it wore a smile so sensual, so unspeakably dreadful, that my senses were nearly overpowered. I saw and remembered nothing more, until I found myself in your room.

"I had a wonderful escape, Dick – there is no disputing *that* – an escape for which, while I live, I shall bless the mercy of heaven. No one can conceive or imagine what it is for flesh and blood to stand in the presence of such a thing, but one who has had the terrific experience. Dick, Dick, a shadow has passed over me – a chill has crossed my blood and marrow, and I will never be the same again – never, Dick – never!"

Our handmaid, a mature girl of two-and-fifty, as I have said, stayed her hand, as Tom's story proceeded, and by little and little drew near to

us, with open mouth, and her brows contracted over her little, beady black eyes, till stealing a glance over her shoulder now and then, she established herself close behind us. During the relation, she had made various earnest comments, in an undertone; but these and her ejaculations, for the sake of brevity and simplicity, I have omitted in my narration.

"It's often I heard tell of it," she now said, "but I never believed it rightly till now – though, indeed, why should not I? Does not my mother, down there in the lane, know quare stories, God bless us, beyant telling about it? But you ought not to have slept in the back bedroom. She was loath to let me be going in and out of that room even in the day time, let alone for any Christian to spend the night in it; for sure she says it was his own bedroom."

"*Whose* own bedroom?" we asked, in a breath.

"Why, *his* – the ould Judge's – Judge Horrock's, to be sure, God rest his sowl"; and she looked fearfully round.

"Amen!" I muttered. "But did he die there?"

"Die there! No, not quite *there*," she said. "Shure, was not it over the banisters he hung himself, the ould sinner, God be merciful to us all? and was not it in the alcove they found the handles of the skipping-rope cut off, and the knife where he was settling the cord, God bless us, to hang himself with? It was his housekeeper's daughter owned the rope, my mother often told me, and the child never throve after, and used to be starting up out of her sleep, and screeching in the night time, wid dhrames and frights that cum on her; and they said how it was the speerit of the ould Judge that was tormentin' her; and she used to be roaring and yelling out to hould back the big ould fellow with the crooked neck; and then she'd screech 'Oh, the master! the master! he's stampin' at me, and beckoning to me! Mother, darling, don't let me go!' And so the poor crathure died at last, and the docthers said it was wather on the brain, for it was all they could say."

"How long ago was all this?" I asked.

"Oh, then, how would I know?" she answered. "But it must be a wondherful long time ago, for the housekeeper was an ould woman, with a pipe in her moth, and not a tooth left, and better nor eighty years ould when my mother was first married; and they said she was a rale buxom, fine-dressed woman when the ould Judge come to his end; an', indeed, my mother's not far from eighty years ould herself this day; and what made it worse for the unnatural ould villain, God rest his soul, to frighten the little girl out of the world the way he did, was what was mostly thought and believed by everyone. My mother says how the poor little crathure was his own child; for he was by all accounts an ould villain every way, an' the hangin'est judge that ever was known in Ireland's ground."

"From what you said about the danger of sleeping in that bedroom," said I, "I suppose there were stories about the ghost having appeared there to others."

"Well, there *was* things said – quare things, surely," she answered, as it seemed, with some reluctance. "And why would not there? Sure was it not up in that same room he slept for more than twenty years? and was it not in the alcove he got the rope ready that done his own business at last, the way he done many a betther man's in his lifetime? – and was not the body lying in the same bed after death, and put in the coffin there, too, and carried out to his grave from it in Pether's churchyard, after the coroner was done? But there was quare stories – my mother has them all – about how one Nicholas Spaight got into trouble on the head of it."

"And what did they say of this Nicholas Spaight?" I asked.

"Oh, for that matther, it's soon told," she answered.

And she certainly did relate a very strange story, which so piqued my curiosity, that I took occasion to visit the ancient lady, her mother, from whom I learned many very curious particulars. Indeed, I am tempted to tell the tale, but my fingers are weary, and I must defer it. But if you wish to hear it another time, I shall do my best.

When we had heard the strange tale I have not told you, we put one or two further questions to her about the alleged special visitations, to which the house had, ever since the death of the wicked old Judge, been subjected.

"No one ever had luck in it," she told us. "There was always cross accidents, sudden deaths, and short times in it. The first that tuck it was a family – I forget their name – but at any rate there were two young ladies and their papa. He was about sixty, and a stout healthy gentleman as you'd wish to see at that age. Well, he slept in that unlucky back bedroom; and, God between us an' all harm! sure enough he was found dead one morning, half out of the bed, and his head as black as a sloe, an swelled like a puddin', hanging down near the floor. It was a fit, they said. He was as dead as a mackerel, and so *he* could not say what it was;

but the ould people was all sure that it was nothing at all but the ould Judge, God bless us! that frightened him out of his senses and his life together.

"Some time after there was a rich old maiden lady took the house. I don't know which room *she* slept in, but she lived alone; and at any rate, one morning, the servants going down early to their work, found her sitting on the passage-stairs, shivering and talkin' to herself, quite mad; and never a word more could any of *them* or her friends get from her ever afterwards but, 'Don't ask me to go, for I promised to wait for him.' They never made out from her who it was she meant by *him*, but of course those that knew all about the ould house were at no loss for the meaning of all that happened to her.

"Then afterwards, when the house was let out in lodgings, there was Micky Byrne that took the same room, with his wife and three little children; and sure I heard Mrs Byrne myself telling how the children used to be lifted up in the bed at night, she could not see by what mains; and how they were starting and screeching every hour, just all as one as the housekeeper's little girl that died, till at last one night poor Mickey had a dhrop in him, the way he used now and again; and what do you think, in the middle of the night he thought he heard a noise on the stairs, and being in liquor, nothing less id do him but out he must go himself to see what was wrong. Well, after that, all she ever heard of him was himself sayin', 'Oh, God!' and a tumble that shook the very house; and there, sure enough, he was lying on the lower stairs, under the lobby, with his neck smashed double undher him, where he was flung over the banisters."

Then the handmaiden added –

"I'll go down to the lane, and send up Joe Garvey to pack up the rest of the taythings, and bring all the things across to your new lodgings."

And so we all sallied out together, each of us breathing more freely, I have no doubt, as we crossed that ill-omened threshold for the last time.

Now, I may add this much, in compliance with the immemorial usage of the realm of fiction, which sees the hero not only through his adventures, but fairly out of the world. You must have perceived that what the flesh, blood and bone hero of romance proper is to the regular compounder of fiction, this old house of brick, wood, and mortar is to the humble recorder of this true tale. I, therefore, relate, as in duty bound, the catastrophe which ultimately befell it, which was simply this – that about two years subsequent to my story it was taken by a quack doctor, who called himself Baron Duhlstoerf, and filled the parlour windows with bottles of indescribable horrors preserved in brandy, and the newspapers with the usual grandiloquent and mendacious advertisements. This gentleman among his virtues did not reckon sobriety, and one night, being overcome with much wine, he set fire to his bed curtains, partially burned himself, and totally consumed the house. It was afterwards rebuilt, and for a time an undertaker established himself in the premises.

I have now told you my own and Tom's adventures, together with some valuable collateral particulars; and having acquitted myself of my engagements, I wish you a very good night, and pleasant dreams.

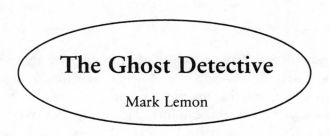

The Ghost Detective

Mark Lemon

'You take an interest in Christmas legends, I believe?' said my friend Carraway, passing the claret.

'Yes, I think they are as good as any other,' I replied.

'And have faith in ghosts?'

'Well, I must answer that question with an equivocation. Yes – no.'

'Then if you care to listen, I can, I fancy, remove your scepticism,' said Carraway.

I professed my willingness to be converted, provided I might smoke whilst my friend talked, and the conditions being agreed to, Carraway commenced:

'When I first came into the City – now some thirty years ago – I formed an intimacy with a young man in the wine trade, and we passed most of our leisure time together. He was much liked by his employers, whose principal business was with publicans and tavern-keepers, and after a time my friend became their town traveller – a position of trust and fair emolument. This advancement enabled my friend, James Loxley, to carry out a long-cherished desire, and that was to marry a fair cousin to whom he had been attached from his boyhood. The girl was one of those pretty *blondes* that are so attractive to young fellows with a turn for the sentimental, and a tendency to sing about violet eyes and golden hair and all that. I was never given that way myself, and I confess Loxley's cousin would not have been the woman I should have chosen for a wife had I ever thought of taking to myself an encumbrance. I had had a step-mother, and she cured me of any matrimonial inclinations which I might have had at one time. Well, Loxley thought differently to me, and his marriage with his cousin, Martha Lovett, was settled, and I was appointed best man upon the occasion.

'The bride certainly looked very pretty in her plain white dress – very pretty, though somewhat paler than usual, and that perhaps made me think more than ever that Martha was not the wife my friend James should have selected, knowing as I did that they would only have his salary to live upon, and that much would depend upon her to make his means sufficient for decent comfort. However, they were sincerely attached to each other, and that, I was told, was worth one or two hundred a year, which I did not believe. Martha was greatly agitated at the altar, and at one time I thought she would have fainted before the ceremony, as they call it, had finished. As it was, she had a slight attack of hysteria in the vestry, but the pew-opener told me that was nothing unusual with brides, especially with those who had been widows.

'The wedding-breakfast was a quiet affair – nothing like the sacrificial feasts of the present day – and we were all merry enough until the happy pair were to leave for their own home, and the poor little Martha hung about her mother's neck and sobbed – much more than I thought was complimentary to her new husband – but then I was not a fair judge of the sex, having been worried all my life by a step-mother.

'When Loxley and his wife were fairly settled in their new home I used frequently to pop in for a game at cribbage or a chat with my old friend, and a more loving couple I never saw in my life. Not being by any means rich, they had babies, of course, and in less than three years, there were two most charming creatures – when they didn't cry or poke out their eyes with tea-spoons, or perform any other of those antics which are the delight of parents, but can only be designated as inflictions to unattached spectators.

'I have thought it only fair to mention these little matters; you will see wherefore by and by.

'Loxley had invited me to take my Christmas dinner with him, and a pleasant day we had! He was partial to keeping Christmas with all the honours, and his little dining-room – it was his drawing-room also – was sprigged about with holly, even to the picture frames. He had only two oil paintings – portraits of his father and mother, both long deceased, but the likenesses, he said, were so good, that he could always fancy his parents were present.

'Well, as I have mentioned, we passed a happy day and night; Loxley had arranged to go with me for a couple of days into the Country, on a visit to a good old uncle of mine, as an atonement for keeping me away from the family dinner.

'The visit was paid; but I was rather annoyed at the effort which Loxley evidently made to appear entertained, and I thought he was home-sick, or vexed that I had not invited his wife to join us, as there were lady visitors at my uncle's. Whatever was the cause of his frequent abstractions, I could only regret it, as I had given him such a good character for cheerfulness and pleasant companionship, that one of my cousins twitted me, with rural delicacy, for having brought a thorough wet blanket from London.

'During our journey back to town Loxley was silent and thoughtful, and I longed to ask if anything troubled him. But we had passed such a jovial Christmas Day together that I could not suppose he had any other anxiety than what the restoration to the arms of his Martha would remove. We parted, however, without any explanation being asked or volunteered.

'On the second day after our return, I was astounded at receiving a message from Loxley to come to him at the Mansion House. The officer who brought the note told me that Loxley was in custody, charged, he believed, by his employer with no less an offence than embezzlement.

'Such an accusation seemed at first to me, who had known Loxley so long, so intimately, preposterous – impossible. As I walked to the Mansion House a cold sweat seized me, and for a moment I thought I should have fallen, as the strange conduct of my friend during the past two days came to my recollection. Had he found his means too small for his home requirements ? Had he been tempted, and yielded as good men had done before him? No, no! – a thousand times, no! – if I knew James Loxley rightly.

'He was standing at the prisoners' bar when I reached the Mansion House, and I was not permitted to speak to him. He saw me, however, and knew his friend was with him.

'The junior principal, who had recently joined the firm of X and Co – by the by, he had for some reason never taken kindly to Loxley – was giving his evidence. He said: "That John Rogers, a customer of the house, had caused a great deal of trouble with his overdue account, and that it was thought he would prove a defaulter. Mr X (the prosecutor) had heard accidentally that Rogers had received a large sum of money, and as Mr Loxley was away from business Mr X had called upon the debtor to demand payment of his debt. Mr X was received with much insolence by Rogers; and his conduct was accounted for subsequently by the production of Loxley's receipt for the money, dated the 24th of December. The man had paid £40 by a cheque to Loxley, and no such amount was credited in the books of X and Co. Rogers produced his banker's book, and the cheque with Loxley's signature on the back. It was found, also, that a person answering by description to Loxley had received two notes of £20 each, one of which had been paid at the Bank of England in gold early on the morning after Christmas Day."

'This evidence was confirmed by John Rogers, who had given the cheque; by the banker's cashier, who had paid it; and by the Bank of England clerk, who had given gold for the note.

'Loxley was asked – having received the usual caution – if he wished to say anything.

'He answered:

' "Yes;" and he thought he had been hardly used by his employers, that an explanation of the matter had not been required from him by them before he had been taken into custody as a thief. He had also heard of Rogers' accession to money; and having the interests of his employers in view, went at once to the man and with great difficulty succeeded in obtaining payment of the debt. He received the cheque, but, fearing that Rogers might stop the payment of it at his banker's, he, Loxley, cashed it immediately, placing the notes he received, as he believed, in his pocket-book. As it was Christmas Eve, he did not return to X and Co's, the house being closed, but walked home with a friend he had met in the banking house when he received the money for Rogers' cheque. On the morning of the 26th he had intended calling at X and Co's on his way to his appointment with me; but, finding he was late, he attached no consequence to the omission, having a holiday. When he was at his journey's end and in his bedroom, he was looking in his pocket-book for some matter or the other, and for the first time missed the banknotes he had received for the cheque. He was completely perplexed, being certain that he had placed the notes in the case, and that he had never lost possession of them. He had employed the morning of his return to town in searching – vainly, he knew – all conceivable places at home for the missing notes, and of course without success. Before he could go to X and Co's offices he was taken into custody."

' "One of the notes was cashed at the Bank of England early on the morning of the 26th, was it not?" asked the Lord Mayor.

'The bank clerk who cashed the note said "Yes, it appeared so, but he could not remember exactly whether it was presented by a man or a woman. He thought it was not paid to the prisoner."

' "But it was paid, and in gold," said the Lord Mayor. "The embezzlement of employers' money is one of the gravest offences against the law, and must be severely punished and put a stop to. The statement of the prisoner is very plausible — very feasible, perhaps I should say – but I cannot feel it my duty to decide upon its truth or falsehood. He must be committed for trial."

'Loxley bowed his head and remained immovable, until a shriek in the passage of the court reached him, and he started as from a dream. He instantly looked to where I had been standing, and I understood his meaning. He was right. He had recognized the voice of his wife, who, having heard where they had taken her husband, had followed after. I found her as I had seen her on her wedding day – hysterical, but the attack was very violent; it was with great difficulty I conveyed her to her mother's, and thence to her own home.

'I said all I could to comfort her. I told her my own conviction of Loxley's innocence, my full belief in the explanation which he had given, and the certainty of his speedy liberation. But I spoke to a stricken woman, to a distracted wife, a half mad mother. She sat for some time with her children in her lap, rocking to and fro, and sobbing as though her heart would burst. She cried to me to succour her husband, to bring him home, if not for her sake, for that of her innocent children. She would not let her mother speak, but continued to appeal to me until – yes, I own it – until I fairly broke down and could not answer her. And all this while the green holly garnishing the room, and the faces of the father and mother looking on placidly from the walls.'

The recollection of the painful scene he had been describing made Carraway silent for a time, and I remarked that he had the satisfaction of knowing he had done his duty to his friend, whether he proved guilty or innocent.

'Yes,' continued Carraway. 'I had that satisfaction, though I did not desire to blow my own trumpet in what I have said. Well, when the elder X, who had been away from town, heard of the matter he was inclined to believe Loxley's statement, and blamed his son for his precipitancy. The matter, however, was beyond his control now, and the law had to vindicate its supremacy.

'The trial came on, and the gentleman whose professional business it was to prove Loxley guilty necessarily did all that was possible to show the weakness of the defence. He asked why Loxley had not instantly returned to town when he had discovered the loss of the notes? Why had he not written to his employers? Why had he not mentioned his loss to me – the friend who he had called to speak of his character? No satisfactory answer could be given for such omissions. What had become of the other note? If a dishonest person had found the notes – supposing them to have been lost – would they not have changed both of them for gold? The most favourable construction which could be placed upon the case was the supposition that the prisoner had need of twenty pounds and had taken his employer's money, intending, very likely, to replace it. That was no uncommon case. The pressure of what seemed to be only a temporary difficulty had often led well-meaning men into such unpardonable breaches of trust. And now, having placed the case as fairly as he could before the jury, his duty was done, and it rested with the twelve intelligent men in the box to pronounce their verdict.

' "Embezzlement," the judge said, very properly, "was a serious crime, and must be repressed by the punishment of offenders. The jury had heard the prosecutor's statement – proved by highly respectable witnesses; and the prisoner's defence – unsupported by any corroborative evidence. The jury had to judge between them."

'Without leaving their box the jury, after a brief consultation, pronounced a verdict of "Guilty," and my friend – my dear friend James Loxley – was sentenced to transportation.

'This terrible sentence was almost fatal to Mrs Loxley. Her delicate constitution would have given way under her excess of grief had not – well, had not I set before her the duty she owed to her children, who had a right to a share in her affection. Poor thing! she struggled bravely to overcome her great sorrow, but I doubt much if she would have succeeded but for what I am now about to relate to you. Stay – I must mention one or two matters before I tell you that portion of my story.

'The Loxleys occupied only part of the house in which they lived. They had their own furniture, but the landlady of the house provided servants, excepting a little girl who acted as nurse.

'The general servant who waited upon the Loxleys was one of those patient drudges often found in lodging-houses. Her name was Susan, but Loxley had given her the sobriquet of "Dormouse," as she was a drowsy, stupid – perhaps sullen is the better word – girl, who moved about more like a piece of machinery than a living being. She never showed any feeling, either of displeasure or gratification, excepting in her strong attachment to Loxley's children. That arose, perhaps, from her womanly instinct. But when Mrs Loxley's great trouble came, when the girl had come to understand what had befallen Mr Loxley, and that misery and ruin had overtaken them and their children, Susan's whole nature appeared to undergo a change. She seemed to watch every want, every movement of Mrs Loxley. More than once she was found sitting on the stairs near Mrs Loxley's door, when the poor lady was in her paroxysms of grief, as though desirous to lend what aid she could in subduing them. I was so struck by the devotion and sympathy of this poor, stupid creature that I could not help noticing her, and on one occasion offered her money. She refused to take it.

' "No, thank'ee, sir," she said; "that's not what I want; but I should like to be of use to poor missus, if I could, sir."

'I told her she had been of great use, great comfort, to Mrs Loxley, who had seen, as I had, how much she felt for her misfortunes.

' "Yes, sir, that's true enough. And what will they do to Mr Loxley, sir?" she asked.

' "He will have to suffer a great deal, Susan – great misery; but neither you nor I can help him."

'The girl burst into tears, and cried so bitterly that Mrs Loxley overheard her, and I have no doubt questioned her when I was gone.

'Mrs Loxley's mother was staying with her, the elder Mr X having insisted upon making a temporary provision for the unhappy wife of the man he still believed to be innocent – I say Mrs Loxley's mother was staying with her daughter. She had gone to bed in an adjoining room, as Mrs Loxley frequently begged to be allowed to sit alone, as she found it difficult to sleep. I have reason to believe that after her mother had gone to rest, Mrs Loxley had an interview with Susan; but, for reasons which will appear, I never questioned her on that point. It was past midnight, according to Mrs Loxley's statement, when, sitting with her head resting on her hands, she saw the door of her room open, and her husband enter; saw him as plainly and like himself as she had ever seen him. She rose up; but the figure motioned her to remain where she was. She complied; now conscious that it was not her husband in the flesh upon which she looked. The figure sat down in his accustomed place, and then appeared to gaze steadfastly on the portrait of his father, still ornamented with the faded holly twigs which had been placed there at Christmas-time. This continued for some minutes. The figure then rose up and, looking towards Mrs Loxley with a most loving expression on its face, walked from the room, opening and closing the door after it.

'Mrs Loxley tried to follow, but could not. She was not asleep, she had not been even dozing – she was sure of that, but had seen with her waking senses the apparition of her husband, then lying in Newgate prison.

'What followed seemed equally inexplicable to me, who had more than once witnessed her tendency to hysteria and fainting. She said she had felt no alarm at what she had seen. She was stupefied for a few moments, but not alarmed. She went to her mother; but finding her quietly sleeping Mrs Loxley lay down beside her without disturbing her. In the morning she narrated to her mother what she had witnessed during the past night, and subsequently repeated her story – word for word, her mother said – to me, in the presence of her landlady and the maid Susan.

'The effect upon the poor, dull-witted servant was very remarkable. She fixed her eyes on the portrait which had attracted the notice of the apparition as though she were fascinated by it. She then asked Mrs Loxley, with a voice and look of terror, "Did you speak to the ghost, missus?" And when Mrs Loxley replied "No," Susan inquired, "And didn't the ghost speak to you?"

'Mrs Loxley answered that she had told all that had occurred, adding nothing, keeping back nothing; and this assurance seemed to have a consolatory effect upon the girl, who then busied herself with her work. I had made inquiries at the prison, as Mrs Loxley foreboded illness or death to her husband, and learned that my unfortunate friend was in health, and had become more resigned to the cruel future which awaited him. Mrs Loxley appeared to be satisfied with this account of her husband.

'The night which succeeded Mrs Loxley proposed to pass in the same manner; but her mother insisted upon remaining with her, and that night no apparition came.

'Mrs Loxley was disappointed, and attributed the absence of the spirit to the presence of her mother, and it was now her turn to insist. Mrs Lovett went to her room, having promised to go to bed and not seek to watch or return to her daughter. It was impossible, however, for the old lady to sleep, and she listened to every noise in the street, and to those unaccountable sounds which we have all heard in our lonely rooms.

'It was again past midnight, and Mrs Loxley had, she admitted, worked herself into a high state of expectancy, when, without the opening of the door, the figure of her husband stood in the room. Again it regarded her most tenderly for a few seconds, and then fixed its gaze on the portrait of Loxley's father. It had not seated itself, as on the former visitation, but stood, with its hands folded, as though in supplication. It then turned its face to Mrs Loxley and opened its arms, as if inviting her to its embrace. Without a moment's hesitation she rose, and almost rushed to the bosom of the shadow. But the impalpable figure offering no resistance, she dashed herself against the panelling of the room, and the withered holly sprigs in the frame of the picture above her fell rustling to the ground. The shade was gone!

'Mrs Lovett, hearing the noise against the panel and the scratching of the falling holly, immediately went to her daughter. Mrs Loxley had not borne the second visitation so bravely as she had done the former one, and it was necessary to call for assistance, as a violent attack of hysteria succeeded the vision.

'The "Dormouse", usually most difficult to arouse, was the first to hear the calling of Mrs Lovett and to go to her assistance.

' "Has she seen it again?" asked Susan, almost directly she had entered.

' "Yes."

' "And did he speak to her this time, missus?" asked Susan. Mrs Lovett could not satisfy the girl's curiosity, but when Mrs Loxley revived sufficiently to tell what she had seen, Susan repeated her inquiries and appeared to be relieved when she heard that the ghost had been silent.

'I was sent for early in the morning, and, having dispatched what pressing business matters I had, I went to Mrs Loxley. She was, as before, perfectly circumstantial in her account of what she had seen, not varying in the least from her first statement; and she and her mother believed that she had seen with her corporeal eyes the spirit of her living husband. I could not bring myself quite to this conclusion. I therefore suggested that it was possibly the association of the portrait with her husband, acting upon her over-taxed brain, that had conjured up these shadows. Mrs Loxley admitted the possibility of such a solution and readily acceded to my proposal to take down the portrait which had attracted, as it seemed, the attention of the figure, and then to abide the result of another night, if Mrs Loxley felt equal to courting the return of the vision.

'I rang the bell for the maid, and requested her to bring the steps.'

' "What for?" she asked quickly.

' "To take down one of the pictures," I replied.

' "There ain't no steps," she said firmly.

'I could have sworn I had seen a pair in the passage as I entered, but I might have been mistaken, and I did not press the request. The picture was easily removed by my standing on a chair.

'As I turned to place the picture on the floor I was perfectly thunderstruck to see the change which had come over Susan. She stood transfixed as it were, her mouth and eyes distended to the full, her hands stretched out, as though she were looking upon the ghost which had disturbed us all.

' "What is the matter with the girl?" I exclaimed, and all eyes were directed to her.

'Susan fell upon her knees and hid her face almost on the ground and screamed out, "I'm guilty, missus! I'm found out! I knowed why the ghost come! I'm guilty!"

'We were all astounded! After a few moments, as I stood on the chair with the face of the portrait towards me, Mrs Loxley uttered a shrill cry and rushed to the picture. From the inside of the frame to which the canvas was attached she took out a note for £20 – the note which Loxley had received and had lost so mysteriously!

'There was no doubt who had been the thief. Susan had already confessed herself guilty, and I did not hesitate to obtain what other confession I could from her. It seemed that Loxley had been mistaken in supposing he had placed the notes in his pocket-hook. Owing to his surprise at meeting the friend he had spoken to at the banker's he had placed the notes in his trousers-pocket, and the force of habit had induced him to think he had otherwise disposed of them. These notes, so carelessly placed, he had drawn forth with his hand whilst ascending his own stairs, and Susan had found them. The half-witted creature showed her prize to an old man employed to clean shoes and knives, and he counselled the changing of one of the notes, with what success we know. Susan received none of the money, as the old scoundrel declared himself a partner in the waif, and told Susan she might keep the other note. But what Susan saw and heard subsequently had so terrified her and filled her with remorse, that she dared not dispose of her ill-gotten money, but, strangely enough, concealed it behind the portrait of Loxley's father.

'My friend, by the exertions of X's, was soon liberated, and by the honourable conduct of the same gentleman, who did all he could to repair the wrong unwittingly done to Loxley, an excellent appointment was found in Australia. There James and Martha and their progeny are now, and thriving, I am glad to say.

'I'll trouble you for the claret,' added Carraway. 'And now do you believe in ghosts?'

'I must make the answer I did before,' I replied. 'Yes – no. I think the apparition was provoked by the cause you at first suggested – namely, the association of Loxley's with his father's portrait and Mrs Loxley's over-taxed brain. You have heard, no doubt, of the well-known case of M Nikolai, the Berlin banker, who, according to his own account, having experienced several unpleasant circumstances, saw phantasms of the living and the dead by dozens, and was yet convinced they were not ghosts. Mrs Loxley might have also been dreaming, without being aware of it, as others have done; and it is rather against the ghost, if he appeared only to discover the lost note, that he came not when Mrs Lovett was present.'

'But the note was found behind the portrait at which the ghost looked so earnestly. How can you account for that?' asked Carraway.

'Well, I am so much a doubter of spiritual manifestation that I can satisfy myself, though not you, perhaps, on that particular. Suppose this stupid Dormouse had taken it into her silly head that Mr Loxley's ghost had come for Mr Loxley's money, and under that impression had placed the note behind the picture after she had heard Mrs Loxley's account of the first visitation, in order to get rid of the money which the ghost wanted?'

'I don't believe that!' said Carraway. 'I believe it was a real, actual ghost!'

'I don't,' I replied, 'and so we end as we began. I'll thank you for the cigars.'

The Horla

Guy de Maupassant

MAY 8. What a lovely day! I have spent all the morning lying in the grass in front of my house, under the enormous plane tree that shades the whole of it. I like this part of the country and I like to live here because I am attached to it by old associations, by those deep and delicate roots which attach a man to the soil on which his ancestors were born and died, which attach him to the ideas and usages of the place as well as to the food, to local expressions, to the peculiar twang of the peasants, to the smell of the soil, of the villages and of the atmosphere itself.

I love my house in which I grew up. From my windows I can see the Seine which flows alongside my garden, on the other side of the high road, almost through my grounds, the great and wide Seine, which goes to Rouen and Havre, and is covered with boats passing to and fro.

On the left, down yonder, lies Rouen, that large town, with its blue roofs, under its pointed Gothic towers. These are innumerable, slender or broad, dominated by the spire of the cathedral, and full of bells which sound through the blue air on fine mornings, sending their sweet and distant iron clang even as far as my home; that song of the metal, which the breeze wafts in my direction, now stronger and now weaker, according as the wind is stronger or lighter.

What a delicious morning it was!

About eleven o'clock, a long line of boats drawn by a steam tug as big as a fly, and which scarcely puffed while emitting its thick smoke, passed my gate.

After two English schooners, whose red flag fluttered in space, there came a magnificent Brazilian three-master; it was perfectly white, and wonderfully clean and shining. I saluted it, I hardly knew why, except that the sight of the vessel gave me great pleasure.

May 12. I have had a slight feverish attack for the last few days, and I feel ill, or rather I feel low-spirited.

Whence come those mysterious influences which change our happiness into discouragement, and our self-confidence into diffidence? One might almost say that the air, the invisible air, is full of unknowable Powers, whose mysterious presence we have to endure. I wake up in the best spirits, with an inclination to sing. Why? I go down to the edge of the water, and suddenly, after walking a short distance, I return home wretched, as if some misfortune were awaiting me there. Why? Is it a cold shiver which, passing over my skin, has upset my nerves and given me low spirits? Is it the form of the clouds, the colour of the sky, or the colour of the surrounding objects which is so changeable, that has troubled my thoughts as they passed before my eyes? Who can tell? Everything that surrounds us, everything that we see, without looking at it, everything that we touch, without knowing it, everything that we handle, without feeling it, all that we meet, without clearly distinguishing it, has a rapid, surprising and inexplicable effect upon us and upon our senses, and, through them, on our ideas and on our heart itself.

How profound that mystery of the Invisible is! We cannot fathom it with our miserable senses, with our eyes which are unable to perceive what is either too small or too great, too near to us, or too far from us – neither the inhabitants of a star nor of a drop of water; nor with our ears that deceive us, for they transmit to us the vibrations of the air in sonorous notes. They are fairies who work the miracle of changing these vibrations into sound, and by that metamorphosis give birth to music, which makes the silent motion of nature musical . . . with our sense of smell which is less keen than that of a dog . . . with our sense of taste which can scarcely distinguish the age of a wine!

Oh! If we only had other organs which would work other miracles in our favour, what a number of fresh things we might discover around us!

May 16. I am ill, decidedly! I was so well last month! I am feverish, horribly feverish, or rather I am in a state of feverish enervation, which makes my mind suffer as much as my body. I have, continually, that horrible sensation of some impending danger, that apprehension of some coming misfortune, or of approaching death; that presentiment which is, no doubt, an attack of some illness which is still unknown, which germinates in the flesh and in the blood

May 17. I have just come from consulting my physician, for I could no longer get any sleep. He said my pulse was rapid, my eyes dilated, my nerves highly strung, but there were no alarming symptoms. I must take a course of shower baths and of bromide of potassium.

May 25. No change! My condition is really very peculiar. As the evening comes on, an incomprehensible feeling of disquietude seizes me, just as if night concealed some threatening disaster. I dine hurriedly, and then try to read, but I do not understand the words, and can scarcely distinguish the letters. Then I walk up and down my drawing-room, oppressed by a feeling of confused and irresistible fear, the fear of sleep and fear of my bed.

About ten o'clock I go up to my room. As soon as I enter it I double-lock and bolt the door; I am afraid . . . of what? Up to the present time I have been afraid of nothing . . . I open my cupboards, and look under my bed; I listen . . . to what? How strange it is that a simple feeling of discomfort, impeded or heightened circulation, perhaps the irritation of a nerve filament, a slight congestion, a small disturbance in the imperfect delicate functioning of our living machinery, may turn the most light-hearted of men into a melancholy one, and make a coward of the bravest? Then, I go to bed, and wait for sleep as a man might wait for the executioner. I wait for its coming with dread, and my heart beats and my legs tremble, while my whole body shivers beneath the warmth of the bedclothes, until all at once I fall asleep, as though one should plunge into a pool of stagnant water in order to drown. I do not feel it coming on as I did formerly, this perfidious sleep which is close to me and watching me, which is going to seize me by the head, to close my eyes and annihilate me.

I sleep – a long time – two or three hours perhaps – then a dream – no – a nightmare lays hold on me. I feel that I am in bed and asleep . . . I feel it and I know it . . . and I feel also that somebody is coming close to me, is looking at me, touching me, is getting on to my bed, is kneeling on my chest, is taking my neck between his hands and squeezing it . . . squeezing it with all his might in order to strangle me.

I struggle, bound by that terrible sense of powerlessness which paralyzes us in our dreams; I try to cry out – but I cannot; I want to move – I cannot do so; I try, with the most violent efforts and breathing hard, to turn over and throw off this being who is crushing and suffocating me – I cannot!

And then, suddenly, I wake up, trembling and bathed in perspiration; I light a candle and find that I am alone, and after that crisis, which occurs every night, I at length fall asleep and slumber tranquilly till morning.

June 2. My condition has grown worse. What is the matter with me? The bromide does me no good, and the shower baths have no effect. Sometimes, in order to tire myself thoroughly, though I am fatigued enough already, I go for a walk in the forest of Roumare. I used to think at first that the fresh light and soft air, impregnated with the odour of herbs and leaves, would instil new blood into my veins and impart fresh energy to my heart. I turned into a broad hunting road, and then turned toward La Bouille, through a narrow path, between two rows of exceedingly tall trees, which placed a thick green, almost black, roof between the sky and me.

A sudden shiver ran through me, not a cold shiver, but a strange shiver of agony, and I hastened my steps, uneasy at being alone in the forest, afraid, stupidly and without reason, of the profound solitude. Suddenly it seemed to me as if I were being followed, that somebody was walking at my heels, close, quite close to me, near enough to touch me.

I turned round suddenly, but I was alone. I saw nothing behind me except the straight, broad path, empty and bordered by high trees, horribly empty; before me it also extended until it was lost in the distance, and looked just the same, terrible.

I closed my eyes. Why? And then I began to turn round on one heel very quickly, just like a top. I nearly fell down, and opened my eyes; the trees were dancing round me and the earth heaved; I was obliged to sit down. Then, ah! I no longer remembered how I had come! What a strange idea! What a strange, strange idea! I did not the least know. I started off to the right, and got back into the avenue which had led me into the middle of the forest.

June 3. I have had a terrible night. I shall go away for a few weeks, for no doubt a journey will set me up again.

July 2. I have come back, quite cured, and have had a most delightful trip into the bargain. I have been to Mont Saint-Michel, which I had not seen before.

What a sight, when one arrives as I did, at Avranches toward the end of the day! The town stands on a hill, and I was taken into the public garden at the extremity of the town. I uttered a cry of astonishment. An extraordinarily large bay lay extended before me, as far as my eyes could reach, between two hills which were lost to sight in the mist; and in the middle of this immense yellow bay, under a clear, golden sky, a peculiar hill rose up, sombre and pointed in the midst of the sand. The sun had just disappeared, and under the still flaming sky appeared the outline of that fantastic rock which bears on its summit a fantastic monument.

At daybreak I went out to it. The tide was low, as it had been the night before, and I saw that wonderful abbey rise up before me as I approached it. After several hours' walking, I reached the enormous mass of rocks which supports the little town, dominated by the great church. Having climbed the steep and narrow street, I entered the most wonderful Gothic building that has ever been built to God on earth, as large as a town, full of low rooms which seem buried beneath vaulted roofs, and lofty galleries supported by delicate columns.

I entered this gigantic granite gem, which is as light as a bit of lace, covered with towers, with slender belfries with spiral staircases, which raise their strange heads that bristle with chimeras, with devils, with fantastic animals, with monstrous flowers, to the blue sky by day, and to the black sky by night, and are connected by finely carved arches.

When I had reached the summit I said to the monk who accompanied me: "Father, how happy you must be here!" And he replied: "It is very windy here, monsieur"; and so we began to talk while watching the rising tide, which ran over the sand and covered it as with a steel cuirass.

And then the monk told me stories, all the old stories belonging to the place, legends, nothing but legends.

One of them struck me forcibly. The country people, those belonging to the Mount, declare that at night one can hear voices talking on the sands, and then that one hears two goats bleating, one with a strong, the other with a weak voice. Incredulous people declare that it is nothing but the cry of the sea birds, which occasionally resembles bleatings, and occasionally, human lamentations; but belated fishermen swear that they have met an old shepherd wandering between tides on the sands around the little town. His head is completely concealed by his cloak and he is followed by a billy goat with a man's face, and a nanny goat with a woman's face, both having long, white hair and talking incessantly and quarrelling in an unknown tongue. Then suddenly they cease and begin to bleat with all their might.

"Do you believe it?" I asked the monk. "I scarcely know," he replied, and I continued: "If there are other beings besides ourselves on this earth, how comes it that we have not known it long since, or why have *you* not seen them? How is it that *I* have not seen them?" He replied: "Do we see the hundred-thousandth part of what exists? Look here; there is the wind, which is the strongest force in nature, which knocks down men, and blows down buildings, uproots trees, raises the sea into mountains of water, destroys cliffs and casts great ships on the rocks; the wind which kills, which whistles, which sighs, which roars – have you ever seen it, and can you see it? It exists for all that, however."

I was silent before this simple reasoning. That man was a philosopher, or perhaps a fool; I could not say which exactly, so I held my tongue. What he had said had often been in my own thoughts.

July 3. I have slept badly; certainly there is some feverish influence here, for my coachman is suffering in the same way as I am. When I went back home yesterday, I noticed his singular paleness, and I asked him: "What is the matter with you, Jean?" "The matter is that I never get any rest, and my nights devour my days. Since your departure, monsieur, there has been a spell over me."

However, the other servants are all well, but I am very much afraid of having another attack myself.

July 4. I am decidedly ill again; for my old nightmares have returned. Last night I felt somebody leaning on me and sucking my life from between my lips. Yes, he was sucking it out of my throat, like a leech. Then he got up, satiated, and I woke up, so exhausted, crushed and weak that I could not move. If this continues for a few days, I shall certainly go away again.

July 5. Have I lost my reason? What happened last night is so strange that my head wanders when I think of it!

I had locked my door, as I do now every evening, and then, being thirsty, I drank half a glass of water, and accidentally noticed that the water bottle was full up to the cut-glass stopper.

Then I went to bed and fell into one of my terrible sleeps, from which I was aroused in about two hours by a still more frightful shock.

Picture to yourself a sleeping man who is being murdered and who wakes up with a knife in his lung, and whose breath rattles, who is covered with blood, and who can no longer breathe and is about to die, and does not understand – there you have it.

Having recovered my senses, I was thirsty again, so I lit a candle and went to the table on which stood my water bottle. I lifted it up and tilted it over my glass, but nothing came out. It was empty! It was completely empty! At first I could not understand it at all, and then suddenly I was seized by such a terrible feeling that I had to sit down, or rather I fell into a chair! Then I sprang up suddenly to look about me; then I sat down again, overcome by astonishment and fear, in front of the transparent glass bottle! I looked at it with fixed eyes, trying to conjecture, and my hands trembled! Somebody had drunk the water, but who? I? I without any doubt. It could surely only be I. In that case I was a somnambulist; I lived, without knowing it, that mysterious double life which makes us doubt whether there are not two beings in us, or whether a strange, unknowable and invisible being does not at such moments, when our soul is in a state of torpor, animate our captive body, which obeys this other being, as it obeys us, and more than it obeys ourselves.

Oh! Who will understand my horrible agony? Who will understand the emotion of a man who is sound in mind, wide awake, full of common sense, who looks in horror through the glass of a water bottle for a little water that disappeared while he was asleep? I remained thus until it was daylight, without venturing to go to bed again.

July 6. I am going mad. Again all the contents of my water bottle have been drunk during the night – or rather, I have drunk it!

But is it I? Is it I? Who could it be? Who? Oh! God! Am I going mad? Who will save me?

July 10. I have just been through some surprising ordeals. Decidedly I am mad! And yet! . . .

On July 6, before going to bed, I put some wine, milk, water, bread and strawberries on my table. Somebody drank – I drank – all the water and a little of the milk, but neither the wine, bread, nor the strawberries were touched

On the seventh of July I renewed the same experiment, with the same results, and on July 8, I left out the water and the milk, and nothing was touched.

Lastly, on July 9, I put only water and milk on my table, taking care to wrap up the bottles in white muslin and to tie down the stoppers. Then I rubbed my lips, my beard and my hands with pencil lead, and went to bed.

Irresistible sleep seized me, which was soon followed by a terrible awakening. I had not moved, and there was no mark of lead on the sheets. I rushed to the table. The muslin round the bottles remained intact; I undid the string, trembling with fear. All the water had been drunk, and so had the milk! Ah! Great God! . . .

I must start for Paris immediately.

July 12. Paris. I must have lost my head during the last few days! I must be the plaything of my enervated imagination, unless I am really a somnambulist, or that I have been under the power of one of those hitherto unexplained influences which are called suggestions. In any case, my mental state bordered on madness, and twenty-four hours of Paris sufficed to restore my equilibrium.

Yesterday, after doing some business and paying some visits which instilled fresh and invigorating air into my soul, I wound up the evening at the *Théâtre-Français*. A play by Alexandre Dumas the younger was being acted, and his active and powerful imagination completed my cure. Certainly solitude is dangerous for active minds. We require around us men who can think and talk. When we are alone for a long time, we people space with phantoms.

I returned along the boulevards to my hotel in excellent spirits. Amid the jostling of the crowd I thought, not without irony, of my terrors and surmises of the previous week, because I had believed – yes, I had believed – that an invisible being lived beneath my roof. How weak our brains are, and how quickly they are terrified and led into error by a small incomprehensible fact.

Instead of saying simply: "I do not understand because I do not know the cause," we immediately imagine terrible mysteries and supernatural powers.

July 14. Fête of the Republic. I walked through the streets, amused as a child at the firecrackers and flags. Still it is very foolish to be merry on a fixed date, by Government decree. The populace is an imbecile flock of sheep, now stupidly patient, and now in ferocious revolt. Say to it: "Amuse yourself," and it amuses itself. Say to it: "Go and fight with your neighbour," and it goes and fights. Say to it: "Vote for the Emperor," and it votes for the Emperor, and then say to it: "Vote for the Republic," and it votes for the Republic.

Those who direct it are also stupid; only, instead of obeying men, they obey principles which can only be stupid, sterile, and false, for the very reason that they are principles, that is to say, ideas which are considered as certain and unchangeable, in this world where one is certain of nothing, since light is an illusion and noise is an illusion.

July 16. I saw some things yesterday that troubled me very much.

I was dining at the house of my cousin, Madame Sablé, whose husband is colonel of the 76th Chasseurs at Limoges. There were two young women there, one of whom had married a medical man, Dr. Parent, who devotes much attention to nervous diseases and to the remarkable manifestations taking place at this moment under the influence of hypnotism and suggestion.

He related to us at some length the wonderful results obtained by English scientists and by the doctors of the Nancy school; and the facts which he adduced appeared to me so strange that I declared that I was altogether incredulous.

"We are," he declared, "on the point of discovering one of the most important secrets of nature; I mean to say, one of its most important secrets on this earth, for there are certainly others of a different kind of importance up in the stars, yonder. Ever since man has thought, ever since he has been able to express and write down his thoughts, he has felt himself close to a mystery which is impenetrable to his gross and imperfect senses, and he endeavors to supplement through his intellect the inefficiency of his senses. As long as that intellect remained in its elementary stage, these apparitions of invisible spirits assumed forms that were commonplace, though terrifying. Thence sprang the popular belief in the supernatural, the legends of wandering spirits, of fairies, of gnomes, ghosts, I might even say the legend of God; for our conceptions of the workman-creator, from whatever religion they may have come down to us, are certainly the most mediocre, the most stupid and the most incredible inventions that ever sprang from the terrified brain of any human beings. Nothing is truer than what Voltaire says: 'God made man in His own image, but man has certainly paid Him back in his own coin.'

"However, for rather more than a century men seem to have had a presentiment of something new. Mesmer and some others have put us on an unexpected track, and, especially within the last two or three years, we have arrived at really surprising results."

My cousin, who is also very incredulous, smiled, and Dr. Parent said to her: "Would you like me to try and send you to sleep, madame?" "Yes, certainly."

She sat down in an easy chair, and he began to look at her fixedly, so as to fascinate her. I suddenly felt myself growing uncomfortable, my heart beating rapidly and a choking sensation in my throat. I saw Madame Sablé's eyes becoming heavy, her mouth twitching and her bosom heaving, and at the end of ten minutes she was asleep.

"Go behind her," the doctor said to me, and I took a seat behind her. He put a visiting card into her hands, and said to her: "This is a looking-glass; what do you see in it?" And she replied: "I see my cousin." "What is he doing?" "He is twisting his moustache." "And now?" "He is taking a photograph out of his pocket." "Whose photograph is it?" "His own."

That was true, and the photograph had been given me that same evening at the hotel.

"What is his attitude in this portrait?" "He is standing up with his hat in his hand."

She saw, therefore, on that card, on that piece of white pasteboard, as if she had seen it in a mirror.

The young women were frightened, and exclaimed: "That is enough! Quite, quite enough!"

But the doctor said to Madame Sablé authoritatively: "You will rise at eight o'clock to-morrow morning; then you will go and call on your cousin at his hotel and ask him to lend you five thousand francs which your husband demands of you, and which he will ask for when he sets out on his coming journey."

Then he woke her up.

On returning to my hotel, I thought over this curious séance, and I was assailed by doubts, not as to my cousin's absolute and undoubted good faith, for I had known her as well as if she were my own sister ever since she was a child, but as to a possible trick on the doctor's part. Had he not, perhaps, kept a glass hidden in his hand, which he showed to the young woman in her sleep, at the same time as he did the card? Professional conjurors do things that are just as singular.

So I went home and to bed, and this morning, at about half-past eight, I was awakened by my valet, who said to me: "Madame Sablé has asked to see you immediately, monsieur." I dressed hastily and went to her.

She sat down in some agitation, with her eyes on the floor, and without raising her veil she said to me: "My dear cousin, I am going to ask a great favour of you." "What is it, cousin?" "I do not like to tell you, and yet I must. I am in absolute need of five thousand francs." "What, you?" "Yes, I, or rather my husband, who has asked me to procure them for him."

I was so thunderstruck that I stammered out my answers. I asked myself whether she had not really been making fun of me with Dr. Parent, if it was not merely a very well-acted farce which had been rehearsed beforehand. On looking at her attentively, however, all my doubts disappeared. She was trembling with grief, so painful was this step to her, and I was convinced that her throat was full of sobs.

I knew that she was very rich and I continued: "What! Has not your husband five thousand francs at his disposal? Come, think. Are you sure that he commissioned you to ask me for them?"

She hesitated for a few seconds, as if she were making a great effort to search her memory, and then she replied: "Yes . . . yes, I am quite sure of it." "He has written to you?"

She hesitated again and reflected, and I guessed the torture of her thoughts. She did not know. She only knew that she was to borrow five thousand francs of me for her husband. So she told a lie. "Yes, he has written to me." "When, pray? You did not mention it to me yesterday." "I received his letter this morning." "Can you show it me?" "No; no . . . no . . . it contained private matters . . . things too personal to ourselves . . . . I burned it." "So your husband runs into debt?"

She hesitated again, and then murmured: "I do not know." Thereupon I said bluntly: "I have not five thousand francs at my disposal at this moment, my dear cousin."

She uttered a kind of cry as if she were in pain and said: "Oh! oh! I beseech you, I beseech you to get them for me . . . ."

She got excited and clasped her hands as if she were praying to me! I heard her voice change its tone; she wept and stammered, harassed and dominated by the irresistible order that she had received.

"Oh! oh! I beg you to . . . if you knew what I am suffering . . . I want them to-day."

I had pity on her: "You shall have them by and by, I swear to you." "Oh! thank you! thank you! How kind you are."

I continued: "Do you remember what took place at your house last night?" "Yes." "Do you remember that Dr. Parent sent you to sleep?" "Yes." "Oh! Very well, then; he ordered you to come to me this morning to borrow five thousand francs, and at this moment you are obeying that suggestion."

She considered for a few moments, and then replied: "But as it is my husband who wants them –"

For a whole hour I tried to convince her, but could not succeed, and when she had gone I went to the doctor. He was just going out, and he listened to me with a smile, and said: "Do you believe now?" "Yes, I cannot help it." "Let us go to your cousin's."

She was already half asleep on a reclining chair, overcome with fatigue. The doctor felt her pulse, looked at her for some time with one hand raised toward her eyes, which she closed by degrees under the irresistible power of this magnetic influence, and when she was asleep, he said:

"Your husband does not require the five thousand francs any longer! You must, therefore, forget that you asked your cousin to lend them to you, and, if he speaks to you about it, you will not understand him."

Then he woke her up, and I took out a pocketbook and said: "Here is what you asked me for this morning, my dear cousin." But she was so surprised that I did not venture to persist; nevertheless, I tried to recall the circumstance to her, but she denied it vigorously, thought I was making fun of her, and, in the end, very nearly lost her temper.

There! I have just come back, and I have not been able to eat any lunch, for this experiment has altogether upset me.

July 19. Many people to whom I told the adventure laughed at me. I no longer know what to think. The wise man says: "It may be!"

July 21. I dined at Bougival, and then I spent the evening at a boatmen's ball. Decidedly everything depends on place and surroundings. It would be the height of folly to believe in the supernatural on the Ile de la Grenouillière . . . but on the top of Mont Saint-Michel? . . . and in India? We are terribly influenced by our surroundings. I shall return home next week.

July 30. I came back to my own house yesterday. Everything is going on well.

August 2. Nothing new; it is splendid weather, and I spend my days in watching the Seine flowing past.

August 4. Quarrels among my servants. They declare that the glasses are broken in the cupboards at night. The footman accuses the cook, who accuses the seamstress, who accuses the other two. Who is the culprit? It is a clever person who can tell.

August 6. This time I am not mad. I have seen . . . I have seen . . . I have seen! . . . I can doubt no longer . . . I have seen it! . . .

I was walking at two o'clock among my rose trees, in the full sunlight . . . in the walk bordered by autumn roses which are beginning to fall. As I stopped to look at a Géant de Bataille, which had three splendid blossoms, I distinctly saw the stalk of one of the roses near me bend, as if an invisible hand had bent it, and then break, as if that hand had picked it! Then the flower raised itself, following the curve which a hand would have described in carrying it toward a mouth, and it remained suspended in the transparent air, all alone and motionless, a terrible red spot, three yards from my eyes. In desperation I rushed at it to take it! I found nothing; it had disappeared. Then I was seized with furious rage against myself, for a reasonable and serious man should not have such hallucinations.

But was it an hallucination? I turned round to look for the stalk, and I found it at once, on the bush, freshly broken, between two other roses which remained on the branch. I returned home then, my mind greatly disturbed; for I am certain now, as certain as I am of the alternation of day and night, that there exists close to me an invisible being that lives on milk and water, that can touch objects, take them and change their places; that is, consequently, endowed with a material nature, although it is imperceptible to our senses, and that lives as I do, under my roof –

August 7. I slept tranquilly. He drank the water out of my decanter, but did not disturb my sleep.

I wonder if I am mad. As I was walking just now in the sun by the river side, doubts as to my sanity arose in me; not vague doubts such as I have had hitherto, but definite, absolute doubts. I have seen mad people, and I have known some who have been quite intelligent, lucid, even clear-sighted in every concern of life, except on one point. They spoke clearly, readily, profoundly on everything, when suddenly their mind struck upon the shoals of their madness and broke to pieces there, and scattered and floundered in that furious and terrible sea, full of rolling waves, fogs and squalls, which is called *madness*.

I certainly should think that I was mad, absolutely mad, if I were not conscious, did not perfectly know my condition, did not fathom it by analyzing it with the most complete lucidity. I should, in fact, be only a rational man who was labouring under an hallucination. Some unknown disturbance must have arisen in my brain, one of those disturbances which physiologists of the present day try to note and to verify; and that disturbance must have caused a deep gap in my mind and in the sequence and logic of my ideas. Similar phenomena occur in dreams which lead us among the most unlikely phantasmagoria, without causing us any surprise, because our verifying apparatus and our organ of control are asleep, while our imaginative faculty is awake and active. Is it not possible that one of the imperceptible notes of the cerebral keyboard has been paralyzed in me? Some men lose the recollection of proper names, of verbs, or of numbers, or merely of dates, in consequence of an accident. The localization of all the variations of thought has been established nowadays; why, then, should it be surprising if my faculty of controlling the unreality of certain hallucinations were dormant in me for the time being?

I thought of all this as I walked by the side of the water. The sun shone brightly on the river and made earth delightful, while it filled me with a love for life, for the swallows, whose agility always delights my eye, for the plants by the river side, the rustle of whose leaves is a pleasure to my ears.

By degrees, however, an inexplicable feeling of discomfort seized me. It seemed as if some unknown force were numbing and stopping me, were preventing me from going further, and were calling me back.

I felt that painful wish to return which oppresses you when you have left a beloved invalid at home, and when you are seized with a presentiment that he is worse.

I, therefore, returned in spite of myself, feeling certain that I should find some bad news awaiting me, a letter or a telegram. There was nothing, however, and I was more surprised and uneasy than if I had had another fantastic vision.

8 August. I spent a terrible evening yesterday. He does not show himself any more, but I feel that he is near me, watching me, looking at me, penetrating me, dominating me, and more redoubtable when he hides himself thus than if he were to manifest his constant and invisible presence by supernatural phenomena. However, I slept.

August 9. Nothing, but I am afraid.

August 10. Nothing; what will happen to-morrow?

August 11. Still nothing; I cannot stop at home with this fear hanging over me and these thoughts in my mind; I shall go away.

August 12. Ten o'clock at night. All day long I have been trying to get away, and have not been able. I wished to accomplish this simple and easy act of freedom – to go out – to get into my carriage in order to go to Rouen – and I have not been able to do it. What is the reason?

August 13. When one is attacked by certain maladies, all the springs of our physical being appear to be broken, all our energies destroyed, all our muscles relaxed; our bones, too, have become as soft as flesh, and our blood as liquid as water. I am experiencing these sensations in my moral being in a strange and distressing manner. I have no longer any strength, any courage, any self-control, not even any power to set my own will in motion. I have no power left to will anything; but some one does it for me and I obey.

August 14. I am lost! Somebody possesses my soul and dominates it. Somebody orders all my acts, all my movements, all my thoughts. I am no longer anything in myself, nothing except an enslaved and terrified spectator of all the things I do. I wish to go out; I cannot. He does not wish to, and so I remain, trembling and distracted, in the armchair in which he keeps me sitting. I merely wish to get up and to rouse myself; I cannot! I am riveted to my chair, and my chair adheres to the ground in such a manner that no power could move us.

Then, suddenly, I must, I must go to the bottom of my garden to pick some strawberries and eat them, and I go there. I pick the strawberries and eat them! Oh, my God! My God! Is there a God? If there be one, deliver me! Save me! Succour me! Pardon! Pity! Mercy! Save me! Oh, what sufferings! What torture! What horror!

August 15. This is certainly the way in which my poor cousin was possessed and controlled when she came to borrow five thousand francs of me. She was under the power of a strange will which had entered into her, like another soul, like another parasitic and dominating soul. Is the world coming to an end?

But who is he, this invisible being that rules me? This unknowable being, this rover of a supernatural race?

Invisible beings exist, then! How is it, then, that since the beginning of the world they have never manifested themselves precisely as they do to me? I have never read of anything that resembles what goes on in my house. Oh, if I could only leave it, if I could only go away, escape, and never return! I should be saved, but I cannot.

August 16. I managed to escape to-day for two hours, like a prisoner who finds the door of his dungeon accidentally open. I suddenly felt that I was free and that he was far away, and so I gave orders to harness the horses as quickly as possible, and I drove to Rouen. Oh, how delightful to be able to say to a man who obeys you: "Go to Rouen!"

I made him pull up before the library, and I begged them to lend me Dr. Herrmann Herestauss' treatise on the unknown inhabitants of the ancient and modern world.

Then, as I was getting into my carriage, I intended to say: "To the railway station!" but instead of this I shouted – I did not say, but I shouted – in such a loud voice that all the passers-by turned round: "Home!" and I fell back on the cushion of my carriage, overcome by mental agony. He had found me again and regained possession of me.

August 17. Oh, what a night! What a night! And yet it seems to me that I ought to rejoice. I read until one o'clock in the morning! Herestauss, doctor of philosophy and theogony, wrote the history of the manifestation of all those invisible beings which hover around man, or of whom he dreams. He describes their origin, their domain, their power; but none of them resembles the one which haunts me. One might say that man, ever since he began to think, has had a foreboding fear of a new being, stronger than himself, his successor in this world, and that, feeling his presence, and not being able to foresee the nature of that master, he has, in his terror, created the whole race of occult beings, of vague phantoms born of fear.

Having, therefore, read until one o'clock in the morning, I went and sat down at the open window, in order to cool my forehead and my thoughts, in the calm night air. It was very pleasant and warm! How I should have enjoyed such a night formerly!

There was no moon, but the stars darted out their rays in the dark heavens. Who inhabits those worlds? What forms, what living beings, what animals are there yonder? What do the thinkers in those distant worlds know more than we do? What can they do more than we can? What do they see which we do not know? Will not one of them, some day or other, traversing space, appear on our earth to conquer it, just as the Norsemen formerly crossed the sea in order to subjugate nations more feeble than themselves?

We are so weak, so defenceless, so ignorant, so small, we who live on this particle of mud which revolves in a drop of water.

I fell asleep, dreaming thus in the cool night air, and when I had slept for about three-quarters of an hour, I opened my eyes without moving, awakened by I know not what confused and strange sensation. At first I saw nothing, and then suddenly it appeared to me as if a page of a book which had remained open on my table turned over of its own accord. Not a breath of air had come in at my window, and I was surprised, and waited. In about four minutes, I saw, I saw, yes, I saw with my own eyes, another page lift itself up and fall down on the others, as if a finger had turned it over. My armchair was empty, appeared empty, but I knew that he was there, he, and sitting in my place, and that he was reading. With a furious bound, the bound of an enraged wild beast that springs at its tamer, I crossed my room to seize him, to strangle him, to kill him! But before I could reach it, the chair fell over as if somebody had run away from me – my table rocked, my lamp fell and went out, and my window closed as if some thief had been surprised and had fled out into the night, shutting it behind him.

So he had run away; he had been afraid; he, afraid of me!

But – but – to-morrow – or later – some day or other – I should be able to hold him in my clutches and crush him against the ground! Do not dogs occasionally bite and strangle their masters?

August 18. I have been thinking the whole day long. Oh, yes, I will obey him, follow his impulses, fulfil all his wishes, show myself humble, submissive, a coward. He is the stronger; but the hour will come –

August 19. I know – I know – I know all! I have just read the following in the *Revue du Monde Scientifique*: "A curious piece of news comes to us from Rio de Janeiro. Madness, an epidemic of madness, which may be compared to that contagious madness which attacked the people of Europe in the Middle Ages, is at this moment raging in the Province of San-Paolo. The terrified inhabitants are leaving their houses, saying that they are pursued, possessed, dominated like human cattle by invisible, though tangible beings, a species of vampire, which feed on their life while they are asleep, and who, besides, drink water and milk without appearing to touch any other nourishment.

"Professor Don Pedro Henriques, accompanied by several medical savants, has gone to the Province of San-Paolo, in order to study the origin and the manifestations of this surprising madness on the spot, and to propose such measures to the Emperor as may appear to him to be most fitted to restore the mad population to reason."

Ah! Ah! I remember now that fine Brazilian three-master which passed in front of my windows as it was going up the Seine, on the 8th day of last May! I thought it looked so pretty; so white and bright! That Being was on board of her, coming from there, where its race originated. And it saw me! It saw my house which was also white, and it sprang from the ship on to the land. Oh, merciful heaven!

Now I know, I can divine. The reign of man is over, and he has come. He who was feared by primitive man; whom disquieted priests exorcised; whom sorcerers evoked on dark nights, without having seen him appear, to whom the imagination of the transient masters of the world lent all the monstrous or graceful forms of gnomes, spirits, genii, fairies and familiar spirits. After the coarse conceptions of primitive fear, more clear-sighted men foresaw it more clearly. Mesmer divined it, and ten years ago physicians accurately discovered the nature of his power, even before he exercised it himself. They played with this new weapon of the Lord, the sway of a mysterious will over the human soul, which had become a slave. They called it magnetism, hypnotism, suggestion – what do I know? I have seen them amusing themselves like rash children

with this horrible power! Woe to us! Woe to man! He has come, the –
the – what does he call himself – the – I fancy that he is shouting out his
name to me and I do not hear him – the – yes – he is shouting it out – I
am listening – I cannot – he repeats it – the – Horla – I hear – the Horla
– it is he – the Horla – he has come!

Ah! the vulture has eaten the pigeon; the wolf has eaten the lamb;
the lion has devoured the sharp-horned buffalo; man has killed the lion
with an arrow, with a sword, with gunpowder; but the Horla will make
of man what we have made of the horse and of the ox; his chattel, his
slave and his food, by the mere power of his will. Woe to us!

But, nevertheless, the animal sometimes revolts and kills the man
who has subjugated it. I should also like – I shall be able to – but I must
know him, touch him, see him! Scientists say that animals' eyes, being
different from ours, do not distinguish objects as ours do. And my eye
cannot distinguish this newcomer who is oppressing me.

Why? Oh, now I remember the words of the monk at Mont Saint-
Michel: "Can we see the hundred-thousandth part of what exists? See
here; there is the wind, which is the strongest force in nature, which
knocks down men, and blows down buildings, uproots trees, raises the
sea into mountains of water, destroys cliffs and casts great ships on the
breakers; the wind which kills, which whistles, which sighs, which roars
– have you ever seen it, and can you see it? It exists for all that, however!"

And I went on thinking; my eyes are so weak, so imperfect, that
they do not even distinguish hard bodies, if they are as transparent as
glass! If a glass without tinfoil behind it were to bar my way, I should
run into it, just as a bird which has flown into a room breaks its head
against the window-panes. A thousand things, moreover, deceive man
and lead him astray. Why should it then be surprising that he cannot
perceive an unknown body through which the light passes?

A new being! Why not? It was assuredly bound to come! Why
should we be the last? We do not distinguish it any more than all the
others created before us! The reason is, that its nature is more perfect,
its body finer and more finished than ours, that ours is so weak, so
awkwardly constructed, encumbered with organs that are always tired,
always on the strain like machinery that is too complicated, which lives
like a plant and like a beast, nourishing itself with difficulty on air, herbs
and flesh, an animal machine which is a prey to maladies, to

malformations, to decay; broken-winded, badly regulated, simple and eccentric, ingeniously badly made, at once a coarse and a delicate piece of workmanship, the rough sketch of a being that might become intelligent and grand.

We are only a few, so few in this world, from the oyster up to man. Why should there not be one more, once that period is passed which separates the successive apparitions from all the different species?

Why not one more? Why not, also, other trees with immense, splendid flowers, perfuming whole regions? Why not other elements besides fire, air, earth and water? There are four, only four, those nursing fathers of various beings! What a pity! Why are there not forty, four hundred, four thousand? How poor everything is, how mean and wretched! grudgingly produced, roughly constructed, clumsily made! Ah, the elephant and the hippopotamus, what grace! And the camel, what elegance!

But the butterfly, you will say, a flying flower! I dream of one that should be as large as a hundred worlds, with wings whose shape, beauty, colours and motion I cannot even express. But I see it – it flutters from star to star, refreshing them and perfuming them with the light and harmonious breath of its flight! And the people up there look at it as it passes in an ecstasy of delight!

What is the matter with me? It is he, the Horla, who haunts me, and who makes me think of these foolish things! He is within me, he is becoming my soul; I shall kill him!

August 19. I shall kill him. I have seen him! Yesterday I sat down at my table and pretended to write very assiduously. I knew quite well that he would come prowling round me, quite close to me, so close that I might perhaps be able to touch him, to seize him. And then – then I should have the strength of desperation; I should have my hands, my knees, my chest, my forehead, my teeth to strangle him, to crush him, to bite him, to tear him to pieces. And I watched for him with all my over-excited senses.

I had lighted my two lamps and the eight wax candles on my mantelpiece, as if with this light I could discover him.

My bedstead, my old oak post bedstead, stood opposite to me; on my right was the fireplace; on my left, the door which was carefully closed, after I had left it open for some time in order to attract him, behind me was a very high wardrobe with a looking-glass in it, before which I stood to shave and dress every day, and in which I was in the habit of glancing at myself from head to foot every time I passed it.

I pretended to be writing in order to deceive him, for he also was watching me, and suddenly I felt – I was certain that he was reading over my shoulder, that he was there, touching my ear.

I got up, my hands extended, and turned round so quickly that I almost fell. Eh! well? It was as bright as at midday, but I did not see my reflection in the mirror! It was empty, clear, profound, full of light! But my figure was not reflected in it – and I, I was opposite to it! I saw the large, clear glass from top to bottom, and I looked at it with unsteady eyes; and I did not dare to advance; I did not venture to make a movement, feeling that he was there, but that he would escape me again, he whose imperceptible body had absorbed my reflection.

How frightened I was! And then, suddenly, I began to see myself in a mist in the depths of the looking-glass, in a mist as it were a sheet of water; and it seemed to me as if this water were flowing clearer every moment. It was like the end of an eclipse. Whatever it was that hid me did not appear to possess any clearly defined outlines, but a sort of opaque transparency which gradually grew clearer.

At last I was able to distinguish myself completely, as I do every day when I look at myself.

I had seen it! And the horror of it remained with me, and makes me shudder even now.

August 20. How could I kill it, as I could not get hold of it? Poison? But it would see me mix it with the water; and then, would our poisons have any effect on its impalpable body? No – no – no doubt about the matter then – then? –

August 21. I sent for a blacksmith from Rouen, and ordered iron shutters for my room, such as some private hotels in Paris have on the ground floor, for fear of burglars, and he is going to make me an iron door as well. I have made myself out a coward, but I do not care about that!

September 10. – Rouen, Hotel Continental. It is done – it is done – but is he dead? My mind is thoroughly upset by what I have seen.

Well then, yesterday, the locksmith having put on the iron shutters and door, I left everything open until midnight, although it was getting cold.

Suddenly I felt that he was there, and joy, mad joy, took possession

of me. I got up softly, and walked up and down for some time, so that he might not suspect anything; then I took off my boots and put on my slippers carelessly; then I fastened the iron shutters, and, going back to the door, quickly double-locked it with a padlock, putting the key into my pocket.

Suddenly I noticed that he was moving restlessly round me, that in his turn he was frightened and was ordering me to let him out. I nearly yielded; I did not, however, but, putting my back to the door, I half opened it, just enough to allow me to go out backward, and as I am very tall my head touched the casing. I was sure that he had not been able to escape, and I shut him up quite alone, quite alone. What happiness! I had him fast. Then I ran downstairs; in the drawing-room, which was under my bed-room, I took the two lamps and I poured all the oil on the carpet, the furniture, everywhere; then I set fire to it and made my escape, after having carefully double-locked the door.

I went and hid myself at the bottom of the garden, in a clump of laurel bushes. How long it seemed! How long it seemed! Everything was dark, silent, motionless, not a breath of air and not a star, but heavy banks of clouds which one could not see, but which weighed, oh, so heavily on my soul.

I looked at my house and waited. How long it was! I already began to think that the fire had gone out of its own accord, or that he had extinguished it, when one of the lower windows gave way under the violence of the flames, and a long, soft, caressing sheet of red flame mounted up the white wall, and enveloped it as far as the roof. The light fell on the trees, the branches, and the leaves, and a shiver of fear pervaded them also! The birds awoke, a dog began to howl, and it seemed to me as if the day were breaking! Almost immediately two other windows flew into fragments, and I saw that the whole of the lower part of my house was nothing but a terrible furnace. But a cry, a horrible, shrill, heartrending cry, a woman's cry sounded through the night, and two garret windows were opened! I had forgotten the servants! I saw their terror-stricken faces, and their arms waving frantically.

Then, overwhelmed with horror, I set off to run to the village, shouting: "Help! help! fire! fire!" I met some people who were already coming to the scene, and I returned with them.

By this time the house was nothing but a horrible and magnificent funeral pile, a monstrous funeral pile which lit up the whole country, a funeral pile where men were burning, and where he was burning also, He, He, my prisoner, that new Being, the new master, the Horla!

Suddenly the whole roof fell in between the walls, and a volcano of flames darted up to the sky. Through all the windows which opened on that furnace, I saw the flames darting, and I thought that he was there, in that kiln, dead.

Dead? Perhaps? – His body? Was not his body, which was transparent, indestructible by such means as would kill ours?

If he were not dead? – Perhaps time alone has power over that Invisible and Redoubtable Being. Why this transparent, unrecognizable body, this body belonging to a spirit, if it also has to fear ills, infirmities and premature destruction?

Premature destruction? All human terror springs from that! After man, the Horla. After him who can die every day, at any hour, at any moment, by any accident, came the one who would die only at his own proper hour, day, and minute, because he had touched the limits of his existence!

No – no – without any doubt – he is not dead – Then – then – I suppose I must kill myself! . . .

The Story of the Unknown Church

William Morris

I was the master-mason of a church that was built more than six hundred years ago; it is now two hundred years since that church vanished from the face of the earth; it was destroyed utterly – no fragment of it was left; not even the great pillars that bore up the tower at the cross, where the choir used to join the nave. No one knows now even where it stood, only in this very autumn-tide, if you knew the place, you would see the heaps made by the earth-covered ruins heaving the yellow corn into glorious waves, so that the place where my church used to be is as beautiful now as when it stood in all its splendour. I do not remember very much about the land where my church was; I have quite forgotten the name of it, but I know it was very beautiful, and even now, while I am thinking of it, comes a flood of old memories, and I almost seem to see it again – that old beautiful land! only dimly do I see it in spring and summer and winter, but I see it in autumn-tide clearly now; yes, clearer, clearer, oh! so bright and glorious! yet it was beautiful too in spring, when the brown earth began to grow green: beautiful in summer, when the blue sky looked so much bluer, if you could hem a piece of it in between the new white carving; beautiful in the solemn starry nights, so solemn that it almost reached agony - the awe and joy one had in their great beauty. But of all these beautiful times I remember the whole only of autumn-tide; the others come in bits to me; I can think only of parts of them, but all of autumn; and of all days and nights in autumn I remember one more particularly. That autumn day the church was nearly finished, and the monks, for whom we were building the church, and the people, who lived in the town hard by, crowded round us oftentimes to watch us carving.

Now the great church, and the buildings of the Abbey where the monks lived, were about three miles from the town, and the town stood on a hill overlooking the rich autumn country: it was girt about with great walls that had overhanging battlements, and towers at certain places all along the walls, and often we could see from the churchyard or the Abbey garden the flash of helmets and spears, and the dim shadowy waving of banners, as the knights and lords and men-at-arms passed to and fro along the battlements; and we could see too in the town the three spires of the three churches; and the spire of the Cathedral, which was the tallest of the three, was gilt all over with gold, and always at night-time a great lamp shone from it that hung in the spire midway between the roof of the church and the cross at the top of the spire. The Abbey where we built the church was not girt by stone walls, but by a circle of poplar trees, and whenever a wind passed over them, were it ever so little a breath, it set them all a-ripple; and when the wind was high they bowed and swayed very low, and the wind, as it lifted the leaves and showed their silvery white sides, or as again in the lulls of it, it let them drop, kept on changing the trees from green to white, and white to green; moreover, through the boughs and trunks of the poplars, we caught glimpses of the great golden corn sea; waving, waving, waving for leagues and leagues; and among the corn grew burning scarlet poppies and blue cornflowers; and the cornflowers were so blue that they gleamed, and seemed to burn with a steady light, as they grew beside the poppies among the gold of the wheat. Through the corn sea ran a blue river, and always green meadows and lines of tall poplars followed its windings. The old church had been burned and that was the reason why the monks caused me to build the new one; the buildings of the Abbey were built at the same time as the burned-down church, more than a hundred years before I was born, and they were on the north side of the church, and joined to it by a cloister of round arches, and in the midst of the cloister was a lawn, and in the midst of that lawn a fountain of marble, carved round about with flowers and strange beasts; and at the edge of the lawn, near the round arches, were a great many sunflowers that were all in blossom on that autumn day; and up many of the pillars of the cloister crept passion-flowers and roses. Then farther from the church, and past the cloister and its buildings, were many detached buildings, and a great garden round them, all within the circle of the poplar trees; in the garden were trellises covered over with roses and convolvulus and the great-leaved fiery nasturtium; and specially all along by the poplar trees were there trellises, but on these grew nothing but deep crimson roses; the hollyhocks too were all out in blossom at that time, great spires of pink, and orange, and red, and white, with their soft downy leaves. I said that nothing grew on the trellises by the poplars but crimson roses, but I was not quite right, for in many places the wild flowers had crept into the garden from without; lush green briny, with green-white blossoms that grows so fast, one could almost think that we see it grow, and deadly nightshade, La bella donna. Oh! so beautiful; red berry, and purple, yellow-spiked flower, and deadly, cruel-looking, dark green leaf, all growing together in the glorious days of early autumn. And in the midst of the great garden was a conduit, with its sides carved with histories from the Bible, and there was on it too, as on the fountain in the cloister, much carving of flowers and strange beasts. Now the church itself was surrounded on every side but the north by the cemetery, and there were many graves there, both of monks and of laymen, and often the friends of those, whose bodies lay there, had planted towers about the graves of those they loved. I remember one such particularly, for at the head of it was a cross of carved wood, and at the foot of it, facing the cross, three tall sunflowers; then in the midst of the cemetery was a cross of stone, carved on one side with the Crucifixion of our Lord Jesus Christ, and on the other with Our Lady holding the Divine Child. So that day that I specially remember in autumn-tide, when the church was nearly finished, I was carving in the central porch of the west front (for I carved all those bas-reliefs in the west front with my own hand); beneath me my sister Margaret was carving at the flower-work, and the little quatrefoils that carry the sign of the zodiac and emblems of the months; now my sister Margaret was rather more than twenty years old at that time, and she was very beautiful, with dark brown hair and deep calm violet eyes. I had lived with her all my life, lived with her almost alone latterly, for our father and mother died when she was quite young, and I loved her very much, though I was not thinking of her just then, as she stood beneath me carving. Now the central porch was carved with a bas-relief of the Last Judgment and it was divided into three parts by horizontal bands of deep lower-work. In the lowest division, just over the doors, was carved The Rising of the Dead; above were angels blowing long trumpets, and Michael the Archangel weighing the souls, and the blessed led into heaven by angels, and the lost into hell by the devil; and in the topmost division was the Judge of the world.

All the figures in the porch were finished except one, and I remember when I woke that morning my exultation at the thought of my church being so nearly finished. I remember, too, how a kind of misgiving mingled with the exultation, which, try all I could, I was unable to shake off; I thought then it was a rebuke for my pride; well, perhaps it was. The figure I had to carve was Abraham, sitting with a blossoming tree on each side of him, holding in his two hands the corners of his great robe, so that it made a mighty fold, wherein, with their hands crossed over their breasts, were the souls of the faithful, of whom he was called Father: I stood on the scaffolding for some time, while Margaret's chisel worked on bravely down below. I took mine in my hand, and stood so, listening to the noise of the masons inside, and two monks of the Abbey came and stood below me, and a knight, holding his little daughter by the hand, who every now and then looked up at him, and asked him strange questions. I did not think of these long, but began to think of Abraham, yet I could not think of him sitting there, quiet and solemn, while the Judgment-Trumpet was being blown; I rather thought of him as he looked when he chased those kings so far; riding far ahead of any of his company, with his mailhood off his head, and lying in grim folds down his back, with the strong west wind blowing his wild black hair far out behind him, with the wind rippling the long scarlet pennon of his lance; riding there amid the rocks and the sands alone; with the last gleam of the armour of the beaten kings disappearing behind the winding of the pass; with his company a long, long way behind, quite out of sight, though their trumpets sounded faintly among the clefts of the rocks; and so I thought I saw him, till on his fierce chase he leapt, horse and man, into a deep river, quiet, swift, and smooth; and there was something in the moving of the water-lilies as the breast of the horse swept them aside, that suddenly took away the thought of Abraham and brought a strange dream of lands I had never seen; and the first was of a place where I was quite alone, standing by the side of a river, and there was the sound of singing a very long way off, but no living thing of any kind could be seen, and the land was quite flat, quite without hills, and quite without trees too, and the river wound very much, making all kinds of quaint curves, and on the side where I stood there grew nothing but long grass, but on the other side grew, quite on to the horizon, a great sea of red corn-poppies, only paths of white lilies wound all among them, with here and there a great golden sunflower. So I looked down at the river by my feet, and saw how blue it was, and how, as the stream went swiftly by, it swayed to and fro the long green weeds, and I stood and looked at the river for long, till at last I felt someone touch me on the shoulder, and, looking round, I saw standing by me my friend Amyot, whom I love better than anyone else in the world, but I thought in my dream that I was frightened when I saw him, for his face had changed so, it was so bright and almost transparent, and his eyes gleamed and shone as I had never seen them do before. Oh! he was so wondrously beautiful, so fearfully beautiful! and as I looked at him the distant music swelled, and seemed to come close up to me, and then swept by us, and fainted away, at last died off entirely; and then I felt sick at heart, and faint, and parched, and I stooped to drink of the water of the river, and as soon as the water touched my lips, lo! the river vanished, and the flat country with its poppies and lilies, and I dreamed that I was in a boat by myself again, floating in an almost land-locked bay of the northern sea, under a cliff of dark basalt. I was lying on my back in the boat, looking up at the intensely blue sky, and a long low swell from the outer sea lifted the boat up and let it fall again and carried it gradually nearer and nearer towards the dark cliff; and as I moved on, I saw at last, on the top of the cliff, a castle, with many towers, and on the highest tower of the castle there was a great white banner floating, with a red chevron on it, and three golden stars on the chevron; presently I saw too on one of the towers, growing in a cranny of the worn stones, a great bunch of golden and blood-red wallflowers, and I watched the wallflowers and banner for long; when suddenly I heard a trumpet blow from the castle, and saw a rush of armed men on to the battlements, and there was a fierce fight, till at last it was ended, and one went to the banner and pulled it down and cast it over the cliff into the sea, and it came down in long sweeps, with the wind making little ripples in it – slowly, slowly it came, till at last it fell over me and covered me from my feet till over my breast, and I let it stay there and looked again at the castle, and then I saw that there was an amber-coloured banner floating over the castle in place of the red chevron, and it was much larger than the other: also now, a man stood on the battlements, looking towards me; he had a tilting helmet on, with the visor down, and an amber-coloured surcoat over his armour; his right hand was ungauntleted, and he held it high above his head, and in his hand was the bunch of wallflowers that I had seen growing on the wall; and his hand was white and small, like a woman's, for in my dream I could see even very far-off things much clearer than we see real material things on the earth: presently he threw the wallflowers over the cliff, and they fell in the boat just behind my head, and then I saw, looking down from the battlements of the castle, Amyot. He looked down towards me very sorrowfully, I thought, but, even as in the other dream, said nothing; so I thought in my dream that I wept for very pity, and for love of him, for he looked as a man just risen from a long illness, and who will carry till he dies a dull pain about with him. He was very thin, and his long black hair drooped all about his face as he leaned over the battlements looking at me; he was quite pale, and his cheeks were hollow, but his eyes large, and soft, and sad. So I reached out my arms to him, and suddenly I was walking with him in a lovely garden, and we said nothing, for the music which I had heard at first was sounding close to us now, and there were many birds in the boughs of the trees; oh, such birds! gold and ruby and emerald, but they sung not at all, but were quite silent, as though they too were listening to the music. Now all this time Amyot and I had been looking at each other, but just then I turned my head away from him, and as soon as I did so, the music ended with a long wail, and when I turned again Amyot was gone; then I felt even more sad and sick at heart than I had been before when I was by the river, and I leaned against a tree, and put my hands before my eyes. When I looked again the garden was gone, and I knew not where I was, and presently all my dreams were gone. The chips were flying bravely from the stone under my chisel at last, and all my thoughts now were in my carving, when I heard my name, 'Walter', called, and when I looked down I saw one standing below me, whom I had seen in my dreams just before – Amyot. I had no hopes of seeing him for a long time, perhaps I might never see him again, I thought, for he was away (as I thought) fighting in the holy wars, and it made me almost beside myself to see him standing close by me in the flesh. I got down from my scaffolding as soon as I could, and all thoughts else were soon drowned in the joy of having him by me; Margaret, too, how glad she must have been, for she had been betrothed to him for some time before he went to the wars and he had been five years away; five years! and how we had thought of him through those many weary days! how often his face had come before me! his brave, honest face, the most beautiful among all the faces of men and women I have ever seen. Yes, I remember how five years ago I held his hand as we came together out of the cathedral of that great, far-off city, whose name I forget now; and then I remember the stamping of the horses' feet; I remember how his hand left mine at last, and then, someone looking back at me earnestly as they all rode on together looking back, with his hand on the saddle behind him, while the trumpets sang in long solemn peals as they all rode on together, with the glimmer of arms and the fluttering of banners, and the clinking of the rings of the mail, that sounded like the falling of many drops of water into the deep, still waters of some pool that the rocks nearly meet over; and the gleam and flash of the swords, and the glimmer of the lance-heads and the flutter of the rippled banners, that streamed out from them, swept past me and were gone, and they seemed like a pageant in a dream, whose meaning we know not; and those sounds too, the trumpets, and the clink of the mail, and the thunder of the horse-hoofs, they seemed dream-like too – and it was all like a dream that he should leave me, for we had said that we should always be together; but he went away, and now he is come back again.

We were by his bedside, Margaret and I; I stood and leaned over him, and my hair fell sideways over my face and touched his face; Margaret kneeled beside me, quivering in every limb, not with pain, I think, but rather shaken by a passion of earnest prayer. After some time (I know not how long) I looked up from his face to the window underneath which he lay. I do not know what time of the day it was, but I know that it was a glorious autumn day, a day soft with melting, golden haze: a vine and a rose grew together, and trailed half across the window, so that I could not see much of the beautiful blue sky, and nothing of town or country beyond; the vine leaves were touched with red here and there, and three overblown roses, light pink roses, hung amongst them. I remember dwelling on the strange lines the autumn had made in red on one of the gold-green vine leaves, and watching one leaf of one of the overblown roses, expecting it to fall every minute; but as I gazed, and felt disappointed that the rose leaf had not fallen yet, I felt my pain suddenly shoot through me, and I remembered what I had lost;

and then came bitter, bitter dreams – dreams which had once made me happy – dreams of the things I had hoped would be, of the things that would never be now; they came between the fair vine leaves and rose blossoms and that which lay before the window; they came as before, perfect in colour and form, sweet sounds and shapes. But now in every one was something unutterably miserable; they would not go away, they put out the steady glow of the golden haze, the sweet light of the sun through the vine leaves, the soft leaning of the full-blown roses. I wandered in them for a long time; at last I felt a hand put me aside gently, for I was standing at the head of – of the bed; then someone kissed my forehead, and words were spoken – I know not what words. The bitter dreams left me for the bitter reality at last; for I had found him that morning lying dead, only the morning after I had seen him when he had come back from his long absence – I had found him lying dead, with his hands crossed downwards, with his eyes closed, as though the angels had done that for him; and now when I looked at him he still lay there, and Margaret knelt by him with her face touching his; she was not quivering now, her lips moved not at all as they had done just before; and so, suddenly those words came to my mind which she had spoken when she kissed me, and which at the time I had only heard with my outward hearing, for she had said, 'Walter, farewell, and Christ keep you; but for me, I must be with him, for so I promised him last night that I would never leave him any more, and God will let me go.' And verily Margaret and Amyot did go, and left me very lonely and sad.

It was just beneath the westernmost arch of the nave, there I carved their tomb: I was a long time carving it; I did not think I should be so long at first, and I said, 'I shall die when I have finished carving it', thinking that would be a very short time. But so it happened after I had carved those two whom I loved, lying with clasped hands like husband and wife above their tomb, that I could not yet leave carving it; and so that I might be near them I became a monk, and used to sit in the choir and sing, thinking of the time when we should be all together again. And as I had time I used to go to the westernmost arch of the nave and work at the tomb that was there under the great, sweeping arch; and in process of time I raised a marble canopy that reached quite up to the top of the arch, and I painted it too as fair as I could, and carved it all about with many flowers and histories, and in them I carved the faces of those

I had known on earth (for I was not as one on earth now, but seemed quite away out of the world). And as I carved sometimes the monks and other people too would come and gaze, and watch how the flowers grew; and sometimes too as they gazed, they would weep for pity, knowing how all had been. So my life passed, and I lived in that abbey for twenty years after he died, till one morning, quite early, when they came into the church for matins, they found me lying dead, with my chisel in my hand, underneath the last lily of the tomb.

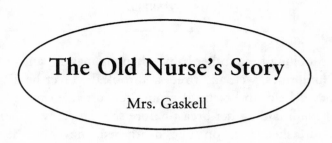

The Old Nurse's Story

Mrs. Gaskell

You know, my dears, that your mother was an orphan, and an only child; and I dare say you have heard that your grandfather was a clergyman up in Westmorland, where I come from. I was just a girl in the village school, when, one day, your grandmother came in to ask the mistress if there was any scholar there who would do for a nurse-maid; and mighty proud I was, I can tell ye, when the mistress called me up, and spoke to my being a good girl at my needle, and a steady honest girl, and one whose parents were very respectable, though they might be poor. I thought I should like nothing better than to serve the pretty young lady, who was blushing as deep as I was, as she spoke of the coming baby, and what I should have to do with it. However, I see you don't care so much for this part of my story, as for what you think is to come, so I'll tell you at once. I was engaged and settled at the parsonage before Miss Rosamond (that was the baby, who is now your mother) was born. To be sure, I had little enough to do with her when she came, for she was never out of her mother's arms, and slept by her all night long; and proud enough was I sometimes when missis trusted her to me. There never was such a baby before or since, though you've all of you been fine enough in your turns; but for sweet, winning ways, you've none of you come up to your mother. She took after her mother, who was a real lady born; a Miss Furnivall, a granddaughter of Lord Furnivall's, in Northumberland. I believe she had neither brother nor sister, and had been brought up in my lord's family till she had married your grandfather, who was just a curate, son to a shopkeeper in Carlisle – but a clever, fine gentleman as ever was – and one who was a right-down hard worker in his parish, which was very wide, and scattered all abroad over the Westmorland Fells. When your mother, little Miss Rosamond, was about four or five years old, both her parents died in a fortnight – one after the other. Ah! that was a sad time. My pretty young mistress and me was looking for another baby, when my master came home from one of his long rides, wet, and tired, and took the fever he died of; and then she never held up her head again, but just lived to see her dead baby, and have it laid on her breast before she sighed away her life. My mistress had asked me, on her death-bed, never to leave Miss Rosamond; but if she had never spoken a word, I would have gone with the little child to the end of the world.

The next thing, and before we had well stilled our sobs, the executors and guardians came to settle the affairs. They were my poor young mistress's own cousin, Lord Furnivall, and Mr Esthwaite, my master's brother, a shopkeeper in Manchester; not so well-to-do then as he was afterwards, and with a large family rising about him. Well! I don't know if it were their settling, or because of a letter my mistress wrote on her death-bed to her cousin, my lord; but somehow it was settled that Miss Rosamond and me were to go to Furnivall Manor House, in Northumberland, and my lord spoke as if it had been her mother's wish that she should live with his family, and as if he had no objections, for that one or two more or less could make no difference in so grand a household. So though that was not the way in which I should have wished the coming of my bright and pretty pet to have been looked at – who was like a sunbeam in any family, be it never so grand – I was well pleased that all the folks in the Dale should stare and admire, when they heard I was going to be young lady's maid at my Lord Furnivall's at Furnivall Manor.

But I made a mistake in thinking we were to go and live where my lord did. It turned out that the family had left Furnivall Manor House fifty years or more. I could not hear that my poor young mistress had ever been there, though she had been brought up in the family; and I was sorry for that, for I should have liked Miss Rosamond's youth to have passed where her mother's had been.

My lord's gentleman, from whom I asked so many questions as I durst, said that the Manor House was at the foot of the Cumberland Fells, and a very grand place; that an old Miss Furnivall, a great-aunt of my lord's, lived there, with only a few servants; but that it was a very healthy place, and my lord had thought that it would suit Miss Rosamond very well for a few years, and that her being there might perhaps amuse his old aunt.

I was bidden by my lord to have Miss Rosamond's things ready by a certain day. He was a stern proud man, as they say all the Lords Furnivall were; and he never spoke a word more than was necessary. Folk did say he had loved my young mistress; but that, because she knew that his father would object, she would never listen to him, and married Mr Esthwaite; but I don't know. He never married, at any rate. But he never took much notice of Miss Rosamond; which I thought he might have done if he had cared for her dead mother. He sent his gentleman with us to the Manor House, telling him to join him at Newcastle that same evening; so there was no great length of time for him to make us known to all the strangers before he, too, shook us off; and we were left, two lonely young things (I was not eighteen), in the great old Manor House. It seems like yesterday that we drove there. We had left our own dear parsonage very early, and we had both cried as if our hearts would break, though we were travelling in my lord's carriage, which I thought so much of once. And now it was long past noon on a September day, and we stopped to change horses for the last time at a little smoky town, all full of colliers and miners. Miss Rosamond had fallen asleep, but Mr Henry told me to waken her, that she might see the park and the Manor House as we drove up. I thought it rather a pity; but I did what he bade me, for fear he should complain of me to my lord. We had left all signs of a town, or even a village, and were then inside the gates of a large wild park – not like the parks here in the north, but with rocks, and the noise of running water, and gnarled thorn-trees, and old oaks, all white and peeled with age.

The road went up about two miles, and then we saw a great and stately house, with many trees close around it, so close that in some places their branches dragged against the walls when the wind blew; and some hung broken down; for no one seemed to take much charge of the place – to lop the wood, or to keep the moss-covered carriage-way in order. Only in front of the house all was clear. The great oval drive was without a weed; and neither tree nor creeper was allowed to grow over the long, many-windowed front; at both sides of which a wing projected, which were each the ends of other side fronts; for the house, although it was so desolate, was even grander than I expected. Behind it rose the Fells, which seemed unenclosed and bare enough; and on the left hand of the house, as you stood facing it, was a little, old-fashioned

flower-garden, as I found out afterwards. A door opened out upon it
from the west front; it had been scooped out of the thick dark wood for
some old lady Furnivall; but the branches of the great forest trees had
grown and overshadowed it again, and there were very few flowers that
would live there at that time.

When we drove up to the great front entrance, and went into the
hall I thought we should be lost – it was so large, and vast, and grand.
There was a chandelier all of bronze, hung down from the middle of the
ceiling; and I had never seen one before, and looked at it all in amaze.
Then, at one end of the hall, was a great fire-place, as large as the sides
of the houses in my country, with massy andirons and dogs to hold the
wood; and by it were heavy old-fashioned sofas. At the opposite end of
the hall, to the left as you went in – on the western side – was an organ
built into the wall, and so large that it filled up the best part of that end.
Beyond it, on the same side, was a door; and opposite, on each side of
the fire-place, were also doors leading to the east front; but those I never
went through as long as I stayed in the house, so I can't tell you what
lay beyond.

The afternoon was closing in, and the hall, which had no fire
lighted in it, looked dark and gloomy, but we did not stay there a
moment. The old servant, who had opened the door for us, bowed to
Mr Henry, and took us in through the door at the further side of the
great organ, and led us through several smaller halls and passages into
the west drawing-room where he said that Miss Furnivall was sitting.
Poor little Miss Rosamond held very tight to me, as if she were scared
and lost in that great place, and as for myself, I was not much better.
The west drawing-room was very cheerful-looking with a warm fire in
it, and plenty of good, comfortable furniture about. Miss Furnivall was
an old lady not far from eighty, I should think, but I do not know. She
was thin and tall, and had a face as full of fine wrinkles as if they had
been drawn all over it with a needle's point. Her eyes were very
watchful, to make up, I suppose, for her being so deaf as to be obliged
to use a trumpet. Sitting with her, working at the same great piece of
tapestry, was Mrs Stark, her maid and companion, and almost as old as
she was. She had lived with Miss Furnivall ever since they were both
young and now she seemed more like a friend than a servant; she looked
so cold and grey, and stony as if she had never loved or cared for any

one; and I don't suppose she did care for any one, except her mistress; and, owing to the great deafness of the latter, Mrs Stark treated her very much as if she were a child. Mr Henry gave some message from my lord, and then he bowed goodbye to us all – taking no notice of my sweet little Miss Rosamond's outstretched hand – and left us standing there, being looked at by the two old ladies through their spectacles.

I was right glad when they rung for the old footman who had shown us in at first, and told him to take us to our rooms. So we went out of that great drawing-room and into another sitting-room, and out of that, and then up a great flight of stairs, and along a broad gallery – which was something like a library, having books all down one side, and windows and writing-tables all down the other – till we came to our rooms, which I was not sorry to hear were just over the kitchens; for I began to think I should be lost in that wilderness of a house. There was an old nursery that had been used for all the little lords and ladies long ago, with a pleasant fire burning in the grate, and the kettle boiling on the hob, and tea-things spread out on the table; and out of that room was the night-nursery, with a little crib for Miss Rosamond close to my bed. And old James called up Dorothy, his wife, to bid us welcome; and both he and she were so hospitable and kind, that by and by Miss Rosamond and me felt quite at home; and by the time tea was over, she was sitting on Dorothy's knee, and chattering away as fast as her little tongue could go. I soon found out that Dorothy was from Westmorland, and that bound her and me together, as it were; and I would never wish to meet with kinder people than were old James and his wife. James had lived pretty nearly all his life in my lord's family, and thought there was no one so grand as they. He even looked down a little on his wife; because, till he had married her, she had never lived in any but a farmer's household. But he was very fond of her, as well he might be. They had one servant under them, to do all the rough work. Agnes they called her; and she and me, and James and Dorothy, with Miss Furnivall and Mrs Stark, made up the family; always remembering my sweet little Miss Rosamond! I used to wonder what they had done before she came, they thought so much of her now. Kitchen and drawing-room, it was all the same. The hard, sad Miss Furnivall, and the cold Mrs Stark, looked pleased when she came fluttering in like a bird, playing and pranking hither and thither, with a continual murmur, and pretty prattle of gladness. I am sure, they were sorry many a time when she flitted away into the kitchen, though they were too proud to ask her to stay with them, and were a little surprised at her taste; though to be sure, as Mrs Stark said, it was not to be wondered at, remembering what stock her father had come of. The great, old rambling house was a famous place for little Miss Rosamond. She made expeditions all over it, with me at her heels; all, except the east wing, which was never opened, and whither we never thought of going. But in the western and northern part was many a pleasant room; full of things that were curiosities to us, though they might not have been to people who had seen more. The windows were darkened by the sweeping boughs of the trees, and the ivy which had overgrown them: but, in the green gloom, we could manage to see old China jars and carved ivory boxes, and great heavy books, and, above all, the old pictures!

Once, I remember, my darling would have Dorothy go with us to tell us who they all were; for they were all portraits of some of my lord's family, though Dorothy could not tell us the names of every one. We had gone through most of the rooms, when we came to the old state drawing-room over the hall, and there was a picture of Miss Furnivall; or, as she was called in those days, Miss Grace, for she was the younger sister. Such a beauty she must have been! but with such a set, proud look, and such scorn looking out of her handsome eyes, with her eyebrows just a little raised, as if she were wondering how any one could have the impertinence to look at her; and her lip curled at us, as we stood there gazing. She had a dress on, the like of which I had never seen before, but it was all the fashion when she was young: a hat of some soft white stuff like beaver, pulled a little over her brows, and a beautiful plume of feathers sweeping round it on one side; and her gown of blue satin was open in front to a quilted white stomacher.

'Well, to be sure!' said I, when I had gazed my fill. 'Flesh is grass, they do say; but who would have thought that Miss Furnivall had been such an out-and-out beauty, to see her now?'

'Yes,' said Dorothy. 'Folks change sadly. But if what my master's father used to say was true, Miss Furnivall, the elder sister, was handsomer than Miss Grace. Her picture is here somewhere; but, if I show it you, you must never let on, even to James, that you have seen it. Can the little lady hold her tongue, think you?' asked she.

I was not so sure, for she was such a little sweet, bold, open-spoken child, so I set her to hide herself; and then I helped Dorothy to turn a great picture, that leaned with its face towards the wall, and was not hung up as the others were. To be sure, it beat Miss Grace for beauty; and, I think, for scornful pride, too, though in that matter it might be hard to choose. I could have looked at it an hour, but Dorothy seemed half frightened at having shown it to me, and hurried it back again, and bade me run and find Miss Rosamond, for that there were some ugly places about the house, where she should like ill for the child to go. I was a brave, high-spirited girl, and thought little of what the old woman said, for I liked hide-and-seek as well as any child in the parish; so off I ran to find my little one.

As winter drew on, and the days grew shorter, I was sometimes almost certain that I heard a noise as if some one was playing on the great organ in the hall. I did not hear it every evening; but, certainly, I did very often; usually when I was sitting with Miss Rosamond, after I had put her to bed, and keeping quite still and silent in the bedroom. Then I used to hear it booming and swelling away in the distance. The first night, when I went down to my supper, I asked Dorothy who had been playing music, and James said very shortly that I was a gowk to take the wind soughing among the trees for music: but I saw Dorothy look at him very fearfully, and Bessy, the kitchen-maid, said something beneath her breath, and went quite white. I saw they did not like my question, so I held my peace till I was with Dorothy alone, when I knew I could get a good deal out of her. So, the next day, I watched my time, and I coaxed and asked her who it was that played the organ: for I knew that it was the organ and not the wind well enough, for all I had kept silence before James. But Dorothy had had her lesson, I'll warrant, and never a word could I get from her. So then I tried Bessy, though I had always held my head rather above her, as I was evened to James and Dorothy, and she was little better than their servant. So she said I must never, never tell; and if I ever told, I was never to say *she* had told me; but it was a very strange noise, and she had heard it many a time, but most of all on winter nights, and before storms; and folks did say, it was the old lord playing on the great organ in the hall, just as he used to do when he was alive; but who the old lord was, or why he played, and why he played on stormy winter evenings in particular, she either could not

or would not tell me. Well! I told you I had a brave heart; and I thought
it was rather pleasant to have that grand music rolling about the house,
let who would be the player; for now it rose above the great gusts of
wind, and wailed and triumphed just like a living creature, and then it
fell to a softness most complete; only it was always music and tunes, so
it was nonsense to call it the wind. I thought at first that it might be Miss
Furnivall who played, unknown to Bessy; but one day when I was in the
hall by myself, I opened the organ and peeped all about it and around
it, as I had done to the organ in Crosthwaite Church once before, and I
saw it was all broken and destroyed inside, though it looked so brave
and fine, and then, though it was noonday, my flesh began to creep a
little, and I shut it up, and run away pretty quickly to my own bright
nursery; and I did not like hearing the music for some time after that,
any more than James and Dorothy did. All this time Miss Rosamond was
making herself more and more beloved. The old ladies liked her to dine
with them at their early dinner; James stood behind Miss Furnivall's
chair, and I behind Miss Rosamond's all in state; and, after dinner, she
would play about in a corner of the great drawing-room, as still as any
mouse, while Miss Furnivall slept, and I had my dinner ːn the kitchen.
But she was glad enough to come to me in the nursery afterwards; for,
as she said, Miss Furnivall was so sad, and Mrs Stark so dull; but she and
I were merry enough; and, by-and-by, I got not to care for that weird
rolling music, which did one no harm, if we did not know where it came
from.

That winter was very cold. In the middle of October the frosts
began, and lasted many, many weeks. I remember, one day at dinner,
Miss Furnivall lifted up her sad, heavy eyes, and said to Mrs Stark, 'I am
afraid we shall have a terrible winter,' in a strange kind of meaning way.
But Mrs Stark pretended not to hear, and talked very loud of something
else. My little lady and I did not care for the frost; not we! As long as it
was dry we climbed up the steep brows, behind the house, and went up
on the Fells, which were bleak, and bare enough, and there we ran races
in the fresh, sharp air; and once we came down by a new path that took
us past the two old gnarled holly-trees, which grew about halfway down
by the east side of the house. But the days grew shorter and shorter; and
the old lord, if it was he, played more and more stormily and sadly on
the great organ. One Sunday afternoon – it must have been towards the

end of November – I asked Dorothy to take charge of little Missey when she came out of the drawing-room, after Miss Furnivall had had her nap; for it was too cold to take her with me to church, and yet I wanted to go. And Dorothy was glad enough to promise, and was so fond of the child that all seemed well; and Bessy and I set off very briskly, though the sky hung heavy and black over the white earth, as if the night had never fully gone away; and the air, though still, was very biting and keen.

'We shall have a fall of snow,' said Bessy to me. And sure enough, even while we were in church, it came down thick, in great large flakes, so thick it almost darkened the windows. It had stopped snowing before we came out, but it lay soft, thick and deep beneath our feet, as we tramped home. Before we got to the hall the moon rose, and I think it was lighter then – what with the moon and what with the white dazzling snow – than it had been when we went to church, between two and three o'clock. I have not told you that Miss Furnivall and Mrs Stark never went to church: they used to read the prayers together, in their quiet gloomy way; they seemed to feel the Sunday very long without their tapestry-work to be busy at. So when I went to Dorothy in the kitchen, to fetch Miss Rosamond and take her upstairs with me, I did not much wonder when the old woman told me that the ladies had kept the child with them, and that she had never come to the kitchen, as I had bidden her, when she was tired of behaving pretty in the drawing-room. So I took off my things and went to find her, and bring her to her supper in the nursery. But when I went into the best drawing-room there sat the two old ladies, very still and quiet, dropping out a word now and then but looking as if nothing so bright and merry as Miss Rosamond had ever been near them. Still I thought she might be hiding from me; it was one of her pretty ways; and that she had persuaded them to look as if they knew nothing about her; so I went softly peeping under this sofa, and behind that chair, making believe I was sadly frightened at not finding her.

'What's the matter, Hester?' said Mrs Stark, sharply. I don't know if Miss Furnivall had seen me, for, as I told you, she was very deaf, and she sat quite still, idly staring into the fire, with her hopeless face. 'I'm only looking for my little Rosy-Posy,' replied I, still thinking that the child was there, and near me, though I could not see her.

'Miss Rosamond is not here,' said Mrs Stark. 'She went away more than an hour ago to find Dorothy.' And she too turned and went on looking into the fire.

My heart sank at this, and I began to wish I had never left my darling. I went back to Dorothy and told her. James was gone out for the day, but she and me and Bessy took lights and went up into the nursery first, and then we roamed over the great large house, calling and entreating Miss Rosamond to come out of her hiding-place, and not frighten us to death in that way. But there was no answer; no sound.

'Oh!' said I at last, 'Can she have got into the east wing and hidden there?'

But Dorothy said it was not possible, for that she herself had never been there; that the doors were always locked, and my lord's steward had the keys, she believed; at any rate, neither she nor James had ever seen them: so I said I would go back, and see if, after all, she was not hidden in the drawing-room, unknown to the old ladies; and if I found her there, I said, I would whip her well for the fright she had given me; but I never meant to do it. Well, I went back to the east drawing-room, and I told Mrs Stark we could not find her anywhere, and asked for leave to look all about the furniture there, for I thought now, that she might have fallen asleep in some warm hidden corner; but no! we looked, Miss Furnivall got up and looked, trembling all over, and she was nowhere there; then we set off again, every one in the house, and looked in all the places we had searched before, but we could not find her. Miss Furnivall shivered and shook so much that Mrs Stark took her back into the warm drawing-room; but not before they had made me promise to bring her to them when she was found. Well-a-day! I began to think she never would be found, when I bethought me to look out into the great front court, all covered with snow. I was upstairs when I looked out; but it was such clear moonlight, I could see, quite plain, two little footprints, which might be traced from the hall door, and round the corner of the east wing. I don't know how I got down, but I tugged open the great, stiff hall door; and, throwing the skirt of my gown over my head for a cloak, I ran out. I turned the east corner, and there a black shadow fell on the snow; but when I came again into the moonlight, there were the little footmarks going up – up to the Fells. It was bitter cold; so cold that the air almost took the skin off my face as

I ran, but I ran on, crying to think how my poor little darling must be perished, and frightened. I was within sight of the holly-trees when I saw a shepherd coming down the hill, bearing something in his arms wrapped in his maud. He shouted to me, and asked me if I had lost a bairn; and, when I could not speak for crying, he bore towards me, and I saw my wee bairnie lying still, and white, and stiff, in his arms, as if she had been dead. He told me he had been up the Fells to gather in his sheep, before the deep cold of night came on, and that under the holly-trees (black marks on the hill-side, where no other bush was for miles around) he had found my little lady – my lamb – my queen – my darling – stiff and cold, in the terrible sleep which is frost-begotten. Oh! the joy, and the tears of having her in my arms once again! for I would not let him carry her; but took her, maud and all, into my own arms, and I held her near my own warm neck and heart, and felt the life stealing slowly back again into her little gentle limbs. But she was still insensible when we reached the hall, and I had no breath for speech. We went in by the kitchen door.

'Bring the warming-pan,' said I; and I carried her upstairs and I began undressing her by the nursery fire, which Bessy had kept up. I called my little lammie all the sweet and playful names I could think of – even while my eyes were blinded by my tears; and at last, oh! at length she opened her large blue eyes. Then I put her into her warm bed, and sent Dorothy down to tell Miss Furnivall that all was well; and I made up my mind to sit by my darling's bedside the live-long night. She fell away into a soft sleep as soon as her pretty head had touched the pillow, and I watched by her until morning light; when she wakened up bright and clear – or so I thought at first – and, my dears, so I think now.

She said that she had fancied that she should like to go to Dorothy, for that both the old ladies were asleep, and it was very dull in the drawing-room; and that, as she was going through the west lobby, she saw the snow through the high window falling – falling – soft and steady; but she wanted to see it lying pretty and white on the ground; so she made her way into the great hall; and then, going to the window, she saw it bright and soft upon the drive; but while she stood there, she saw a little girl, not so old as she was, 'but so pretty,' said my darling, 'and this little girl beckoned to me to come out; and oh, she was so pretty and so sweet, I could not choose but go.' And then this other little girl had taken her by the hand, and side by side the two had gone round the east corner.

'Now you are a naughty little girl, and telling stories,' said I. 'What would your good mamma, that is in heaven, and never told a story in her life, say to her little Rosamond, if she heard her – and I dare say she does – telling stories!'

'Indeed, Hester,' sobbed out my child, 'I'm telling you true. Indeed I am.'

'Don't tell me!' said I, very stern. 'I tracked you by your footmarks through the snow; there were only yours to be seen: and if you had had a little girl to go hand-in-hand with you up the hill, don't you think the footprints would have gone along with yours?'

'I can't help it, dear, dear Hester,' said she, crying, 'if they did not; I never looked at her feet, but she held my hand fast and tight in her little one, and it was very, very cold. She took me up the Fell-path, up to the holly-trees; and there I saw a lady weeping and crying; but when she saw me, she hushed her weeping, and smiled very proud and grand, and took me on her knee, and began to lull me to sleep; and that's all, Hester – but that is true; and my dear mamma knows it is,' said she, crying. So I thought the child was in a fever, and pretended to believe her, as she went over her story – over and over again, and always the same. At last Dorothy knocked at the door with Miss Rosamond's breakfast; and she told me the old ladies were down in the eating parlour, and that they wanted to speak to me. They had both been into the night-nursery the evening before, but it was after Miss Rosamond was asleep; so they had only looked at her – not asked me any questions.

'I shall catch it,' thought I to myself, as I went along the north gallery. 'And yet,' I thought, taking courage, 'it was in their charge I left her; and it's they that's to blame for letting her steal away unknown and unwatched.' So I went in boldly, and told my story. I told it all to Miss Furnivall, shouting it close to her ear; but when I came to the mention of the other little girl out in the snow, coaxing and tempting her out, and willing her up to the grand and beautiful lady by the holly-tree, she threw her arms up – her old and withered arms – and cried aloud, 'Oh! heaven, forgive! Have mercy!'

Mrs Stark took hold of her; roughly enough, I thought; but she was past Mrs Stark's management, and spoke to me, in a kind of wild warning and authority.

'Hester! keep her from that child! It will lure her to her death! That evil child! Tell her it is a wicked, naughty child.' Then Mrs Stark hurried me out of the room; where, indeed, I was glad enough to go; but Miss Furnivall kept shrieking out, 'Oh! have mercy! Wilt Thou never forgive! It is many a long year ago' –

I was very uneasy in my mind after that. I durst never leave Miss Rosamond, night or day, for fear lest she might slip off again, after some fancy or other; and all the more because I thought I could make out that Miss Furnivall was crazy, from their odd ways about her; and I was afraid lest something of the same kind (which might be in the family, you know) hung over my darling. And the great frost never ceased all this time; and whenever it was a more stormy night than usual, between the gusts, and through the wind, we heard the old lord playing on the great organ. But, old lord, or not, wherever Miss Rosamond went, there I followed; for my love for her, pretty helpless orphan, was stronger than my fear for the grand and terrible sound. Besides, it rested with me to keep her cheerful and merry, as beseemed her age. So we played together, and wandered together, here and there, and everywhere; for I never dared to lose sight of her again in that large and rambling house. And so it happened, that one afternoon, not long before Christmas Day, we were playing together on the billiard-table in the great hall (not that we knew the way of playing, but she liked to roll the smooth ivory balls with her pretty hands, and I liked to do whatever she did); and, by-and-by, without our noticing it, it grew dusk indoors, though it was still light in the open air, and I was thinking of taking her back into the nursery, when, all of a sudden, she cried out:

'Look, Hester! look! there is my poor little girl out in the snow!'

I turned towards the long narrow windows, and there, sure enough, I saw a little girl, less than my Miss Rosamond – dressed all unfit to be out-of-doors such a bitter night – crying, and beating against the window-panes, as if she wanted to be let in. She seemed to sob and wail, till Miss Rosamond could bear it no longer, and was flying to the door to open it, when, all of a sudden, and close up upon us, the great organ pealed out so loud and thundering, it fairly made me tremble; and all the more, when I remembered me that, even in the stillness of that dead-cold weather, I had heard no sound of little battering hands upon the window-glass, although the Phantom Child had seemed to put forth all its force; and, although I had seen it wail and cry, no faintest touch of sound had fallen upon my ears. Whether I remembered all this at the very moment, I do not know; the great organ sound had so stunned me into terror; but this I know, I caught up Miss Rosamond before she got the hall-door opened, and clutched her, and carried her away, kicking and screaming, into the large bright kitchen, where Dorothy and Agnes were busy with their mince-pies.

'What is the matter with my sweet one?' cried Dorothy, as I bore in Miss Rosamond, who was sobbing as if her heart would break.

'She won't let me open the door for my little girl to come in; and she'll die if she is out on the Fells all night. Cruel, naughty Hester,' she said, slapping me; but she might have struck harder, for I had seen a look of ghastly terror on Dorothy's face, which made my very blood run cold.

'Shut the back-kitchen door fast, and bolt it well,' said she to Agnes. She said no more; she gave me raisins and almonds to quiet Miss Rosamond: but she sobbed about the little girl in the snow, and would not touch any of the good things. I was thankful when she cried herself to sleep in bed. Then I stole down to the kitchen, and told Dorothy I had made up my mind. I would carry my darling back to my father's house in Applethwaite: where, if we lived humbly, we lived at peace. I said I had been frightened enough with the old lord's organ-playing; but now that I had seen for myself this little moaning child, all decked out as no child in the neighbourhood could be, beating and battering to get in, yet always without any sound or noise – with the dark wound on its right shoulder; and that Miss Rosamond had known it again for the phantom that had nearly lured her to her death (which Dorothy knew was true); I would stand it no longer.

I saw Dorothy change colour once or twice. When I had done, she told me she did not think I could take Miss Rosamond with me, for that she was my lord's ward, and I had no right over her; and she asked me, would I leave the child that I was so fond of, just for sounds and sights that could do me no harm; and that they had all had to get used to in their turns? I was all in a hot, trembling passion; and I said it was very well for her to talk, that knew what these sights and noises betokened, and that had, perhaps, had something to do with the Spectre-Child while it was alive. And I taunted her so, that she told me all she knew, at last; and then I wished I had never been told, for it only made me afraid more than ever.

She said she had heard the tale from old neighbours, that were alive when she was first married; when folks used to come to the hall sometimes, before it had got such a bad name on the country side: it might not be true, or it might, what she had been told.

The old lord was Miss Furnivall's father – Miss Grace as Dorothy called her, for Miss Maude was the elder, and Miss Furnivall by rights. The old lord was eaten up with pride. Such a proud man was never seen or heard of; and his daughters were like him. No one was good enough to wed them, although they had choice enough; for they were the great beauties of their day, as I had seen by their portraits, where they hung in the state drawing-room. But, as the old saying is, 'Pride will have a fall'; and these two haughty beauties fell in love with the same man, and he no better than a foreign musician, whom their father had down from London to play music with him at the Manor House. For, above all things, next to his pride, the old lord loved music. He could play on nearly every instrument that ever was heard of: and it was a strange thing it did not soften him; but he was a fierce dour old man, and had broken his poor wife's heart with his cruelty, they said. He was mad after music, and would pay any money for it. So he got this foreigner to come; who made such beautiful music, that they said the very birds on the trees stopped their singing to listen. And, by degrees, this foreign gentleman got such a hold over the old lord, that nothing would serve him but that he must come every year; and it was he that had the great organ brought from Holland, and built up in the hall, where it stood now. He taught the old lord to play on it; but many and many a time, when Lord Furnivall was thinking of nothing but his fine organ, and his finer music, the dark foreigner was walking abroad in the woods with one of the young ladies; now Miss Maude, and then Miss Grace.

Miss Maude won the day and carried off the prize, such as it was; and he and she were married, all unknown to any one; and before he made his next yearly visit, she had been confined of a little girl at a farm-house on the Moors, while her father and Miss Grace thought she was away at Doncaster Races. But though she was a wife and a mother, she was not a bit softened, but as haughty and as passionate as ever; and perhaps more so, for she was jealous of Miss Grace, to whom her foreign husband paid a deal of court – by way of blinding her – as he told his wife. But Miss Grace triumphed over Miss Maude, and Miss Maude grew fiercer and fiercer, both with her husband and with her sister; and the former – who could easily shake off what was disagreeable, and hide himself in foreign countries – went away a month before his usual time that summer, and half-threatened that he would never come back again. Meanwhile, the little girl was left at the farm-house, and her mother used to have her horse saddled and gallop wildly over the hills to see her once every week, at the very least – for where she loved, she loved; and where she hated, she hated. And the old lord went on playing – playing on his organ; and the servants thought the sweet music he made had soothed down his awful temper, of which (Dorothy said) some terrible tales could be told. He grew infirm too, and had to walk with a crutch; and his son – that was the present Lord Furnivall's father – was with the army in America, and the other son at sea; so Miss Maude had it pretty much her own way, and she and Miss Grace grew colder and bitterer to each other every day; till at last they hardly ever spoke, except when the old lord was by. The foreign musician came again the next summer, but it was for the last time; for they led him such a life with their jealousy and their passions, that he grew weary, and went away, and never was heard of again. And Miss Maude, who had always meant to have her marriage acknowledged when her father should be dead, was left now a deserted wife – whom nobody knew to have been married – with a child that she dared not own, although she loved it to distraction; living with a father whom she feared, and a sister whom she hated. When the next summer passed over and the dark foreigner never came, both Miss Maude and Miss Grace grew gloomy and sad; they had a haggard look about them, though they looked handsome as ever. But by-and-by Miss Maude brightened; for her father grew more and more infirm, and more than ever carried away by his music; and she and Miss Grace lived almost entirely apart, having separate rooms, the one on the west side, Miss Maude on the east – those very rooms which were now shut up. So she thought she might have her little girl with her, and no one need ever know except those who dared not speak about it, and were bound to believe that it was, as she said, a cottager's child she had taken a fancy to. All this, Dorothy said, was pretty well known; but what came afterwards no one knew, except Miss Grace, and Mrs Stark, who was even then her maid, and much more of a friend to her than ever her sister had been. But the servants supposed, from words that were dropped, that Miss Maude had triumphed over Miss Grace, and told her that all the time the dark foreigner had been mocking her with pretended love – he was her own husband; the colour left Miss Grace's cheek and lips that very day for ever, and she was heard to say many a time that sooner or later she would have her revenge; and Mrs Stark was for ever spying about the east rooms.

One fearful night, just after the New Year had come in, when the snow was lying thick and deep, and the flakes were still falling – fast enough to blind any one who might be out and abroad – there was a great and violent noise heard, and the old lord's voice above all, cursing and swearing awfully – and the cries of a little child – and the proud defiance of a fierce woman – and the sound of a blow – and a dead stillness – and moans and wailings dying away on the hill-side! Then the old lord summoned all his servants, and told them, with terrible oaths, and words more terrible, that his daughter had disgraced herself, and that he had turned her out of doors – her, and her child – and that if ever they gave her help – or food – or shelter – he prayed that they might never enter Heaven. And, all the while, Miss Grace stood by him, white and still as any stone; and when he had ended she heaved a great sigh, as much as to say her work was done, and her end was accomplished. But the old lord never touched his organ again, and died within the year; and no wonder! for, on the morrow of that wild and fearful night, the shepherds, coming down the Fell side, found Miss Maude sitting, all crazy and smiling, under the holly-trees, nursing a dead child – with a terrible mark on its right shoulder. 'But that was not what killed it,' said Dorothy; 'it was the frost and the cold; every wild creature was in its hole, and every beast in its fold – while the child and its mother were turned out to wander on the Fells! And now you know all! and I wonder if you are less frightened now?'

I was more frightened than ever; but I said I was not. I wished Miss Rosamond and myself well out of that dreadful house for ever; but I would not leave her, and I dared not take her away. But oh! how I watched her, and guarded her! We bolted the doors and shut the window-shutters fast, an hour or more before dark, rather than leave them open five minutes too late. But my little lady still heard the weird child crying and mourning; and not all we could do or say could keep her from wanting to go to her, and let her in from the cruel wind and the snow. All this time, I kept away from Miss Furnivall and Mrs Stark, as much as ever I could; for I feared them – I knew no good could be about them, with their grey hard faces, and their dreamy eyes, looking back into the ghastly years that were gone. But, even in my fear, I had a kind of pity – for Miss Furnivall, at least. Those gone down to the pit can hardly have a more hopeless look than that which was ever on her face. At last I even got so sorry for her – who never said a word but what was quite forced from her – that I prayed for her; and I taught Miss Rosamond to pray for one who had done a deadly sin; but often when she came to those words, she would listen, and start up from her knees, and say, 'I hear my little girl plaining and crying very sad – Oh! let her in, or she will die!'

One night – just after New Year's Day had come at last, and the long winter had taken a turn, as I hoped – I heard the west drawing-room bell ring three times, which was a signal for me. I would not leave Miss Rosamond alone, for all she was asleep – for the old lord had been playing wilder than ever – and I feared lest my darling should waken to hear the spectre child; see her I knew she could not. I had fastened the windows too well for that. So I took her out of her bed and wrapped her up in such outer clothes as were most handy, and carried her down to the drawing-room, where the old ladies sat at their tapestry work as usual. They looked up when I came in, and Mrs Stark asked, quite astounded, 'Why did I bring Miss Rosamond there, out of her warm bed?' I had begun to whisper, 'Because I was afraid of her being tempted out while I was away, by the wild child in the snow,' when she stopped me short (with a glance at Miss Furnivall), and said Miss Furnivall wanted me to undo some work she had done wrong, and which neither of them could see to unpick. So I laid my pretty dear on the sofa, and sat down on a stool by them, and hardened my heart against them, as I heard the wind rising and howling.

Miss Rosamond slept on sound, for all the wind blew so; and Miss Furnivall said never a word, nor looked round when the gusts shook the windows. All at once she started up to her full height, and put up one hand, as if to bid us listen.

'I hear voices!' said she, 'I hear terrible screams – I hear my father's voice!'

Just at that moment my darling wakened with a sudden start: 'My little girl is crying, oh, how she is crying!' and she tried to get up and go to her, but she got her feet entangled in the blanket, and I caught her up; for my flesh had begun to creep at these noises, which they heard while we could catch no sound. In a minute or two the noises came, and gathered fast, and filled our ears; we, too, heard voices and screams, and no longer heard the winter's wind that raged abroad. Mrs Stark looked at me, and I at her, but we dared not speak. Suddenly Miss Furnivall went towards the door, out into the ante-room, through the west lobby, and opened the door into the great hall. Mrs Stark followed, and I durst not be left, though my heart almost stopped beating for fear. I wrapped my darling tight in my arms, and went out with them. In the hall the screams were louder than ever; they sounded to come from the east wing – nearer and nearer – close on the other side of the locked-up doors – close behind them. Then I noticed that the great bronze chandelier seemed all alight, though the hall was dim, and that a fire was blazing in the vast hearth-place, though it gave no heat; and I shuddered up with terror, and folded my darling closer to me. But as I did so, the east door shook, and she, suddenly struggling to get free from me, cried, 'Hester! I must go! My little girl is there; I hear her; she is coming! Hester, I must go!'

I held her tight with all my strength; with a set will, I held her. If I had died, my hands would have grasped her still, I was so resolved in my mind. Miss Furnivall stood listening, and paid no regard to my darling, who had got down to the ground, and whom I, upon my knees now, was holding with both my arms clasped round her neck; she still striving and crying to get free.

All at once the east door gave way with a thundering crash, as if torn open in a violent passion, and there came into that broad and mysterious light, the figure of a tall old man, with grey hair and gleaming eyes. He drove before him, with many a relentless gesture of abhorrence, a stern and beautiful woman, with a little child clinging to her dress.

'O Hester! Hester!' cried Miss Rosamond. 'It's the lady! the lady below the holly-trees; and my little girl is with her. Hester! Hester! let me go to her; they are drawing me to them. I feel them – I feel them. I must go!'

Again she was almost convulsed by her efforts to get away; but I held her tighter and tighter, till I feared I should do her a hurt; but rather that than let her go towards those terrible phantoms. They passed along towards the great hall-door, where the winds howled and ravened for their prey; but before they reached that, the lady turned; and I could see that she defied the old man with a fierce and proud defiance; but then she quailed – and then she threw up her arms wildly and piteously to save her child – her little child – from a blow from his uplifted crutch.

And Miss Rosamond was torn as by a power stronger than mine, and writhed in my arms, and sobbed (for by this time the poor darling was growing faint).

'They want me to go with them on to the Fells – they are drawing me to them. Oh, my little girl! I would come, but cruel, wicked Hester holds me very tight.' But when she saw the uplifted crutch she swooned away, and I thanked God for it. Just at this moment – when the tall old man, his hair streaming as in the blast of a furnace, was going to strike the little shrinking child – Miss Furnivall, the old woman by my side, cried out, 'Oh, father! father! spare the little innocent child!' But just then I saw – we all saw – another phantom shape itself, and grow clear out of the blue and misty light that filled the hall; we had not seen her till now, for it was another lady who stood by the old man, with a look of relentless hate and triumphant scorn. That figure was very beautiful to look upon, with a soft white hat drawn down over the proud brows and a red and curling lip. It was dressed in an open robe of blue satin. I had seen that figure before. It was the likeness of Miss Furnivall in her youth; and the terrible phantoms moved on, regardless of old Miss Furnivall's wild entreaty – and the uplifted crutch fell on the right shoulder of the little child, and the younger sister looked on, stony and deadly serene. But at that moment the dim lights, and the fire that gave no heat, went out of themselves, and Miss Furnivall lay at our feet stricken down by the palsy – death-stricken.

Yes! she was carried to her bed that night never to rise again. She lay with her face to the wall muttering low but muttering alway: 'Alas! alas! what is done in youth can never be undone in age! What is done in youth can never be undone in age!'

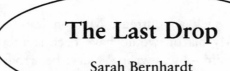

The Last Drop

Sarah Bernhardt

The Château de Ploerneuf was the terror of the Bretons. On passing it the peasants made the sign of the cross murmured under their breath: 'The Château of the Accursed!' Brambles grew about its boundary walls, which no living soul dared pass. The valets moved about within like shadows, never raising their voices. No one ever spoke to the master.

Alone, the young Comte Robert found grace before the lord of the manor, the old Duc de Kerberzoff, his uncle.

At the moment when this recital commences, Robert was at the feet of the old man, who, with livid face, glittering eyes, and marks of fear on all his features, sat in the great ducal chair, listening to what the spectre of terror said to him.

By his side, upon a porphyry column, burned a small golden lamp, ornamented with precious stones, into the flame of which a tall negro poured, minute by minute, a drop of oil. In the old man's rude hand gleamed an axe: the negro would have paid with his life the least forgetfulness of his duties.

The Duke was paler than usual. His long white hair clung to his brow, and from his eyes great tears rolled down upon his silver beard.

'My dear lord, are you in greater pain?' asked Robert, tenderly.

The Duke shuddered – listening still.

'Christmas! Christmas!' sang voices in the fields. 'Christmas! Christmas!' sounded the church bells.

Then, drawing himself up, spectre-like, he said: 'Listen, Robert, listen!'

For twenty years the old man had not spoken.

The sepulchral voice resounded in the great hall; the arms, struck by echo, gave out an iron plaint. The young Count felt frozen with fear.

'Twenty years ago, I had a son; handsome, brave, and generous. He loved a young, low-born girl, and wished to wed her; but I refused – I could not consent to such an outrage. My son implored me, but I remained inflexible. My blazon would have been shattered by such a shame! I was wrong, child – I was wrong! Never be arrogantly proud, it is a mortal sin!'

Sobs stifled the old Duke's voice. But presently he went on:

'The girl was beautiful and virtuous. I offered her gold; she refused it. Then I had her abducted and shut up in a tower of the château. Months passed; my son remained faithful to his vows, I faithful to my pride. I therefore resolved to kill the girl. To that end I sent her secretly a message, advising her to escape. A silken ladder was conveyed to her, with minutely detailed instructions as to how she was to fasten it to her window. She prepared to fly – and then I invented an infamous trap!

'Listen, Robert – listen! I caused the stones which supported the window to be loosened, so that it should give way under her and she would be dashed upon the marble pavement of the courtyard below. It was Christmas, the night of that evil deed; and ever since I have slept in fear of God.

'That same night I was transported in dreams into an immense gallery of clouds. Vaults followed upon vaults in millions – extending, ever extending. Under these vaults hung little golden lamps, swaying gently. It would have taken years to count them. Some of them burned brightly, others were extinguished suddenly. Some shone with a violent glare, others flickered and sputtered a long while before they went out.

'Some of these lamps were guarded by angels, white and beautiful as beauty itself. Other of the lamps had angels, black, ugly, and malevolent, who seemed to wait impatiently the moment when the flame should expire.

'"What does all this mean?" I asked my conductor.

'"All those lamps are human souls," he replied. Those which burn so brightly are the souls of new-born infants; stainless angels guard them. Here are the souls of those who are at the age when, some think, the Spirit of Evil and the Spirit of Good contend for them; but, at the supreme moment, the last breath almost always returns to the Spirit of Good."

'I then asked to be shown my own lamp.

'"Come with me," said the strange being; and, leading me under innumerable vaults, he made me traverse a great distance. At length, stopping me abruptly, he said: Behold! there is your soul!"

'I was petrified with terror. A single drop of oil remained in my lamp; and, above it, an angel with black wings blew upon the flame to accelerate its extinction. I was seized with dread – overtaken by cowardice – yes, cowardice!' said the Duke, trembling in every limb.

'Listen, Robert – listen! Beside me burned a flame of purest light: that lamp of gold, protected by an angel with wings of spotless white. The Spirit of Evil whispered in my ear.'

The old Duke stopped – as if the voice were speaking to him again. His eyes became bloodshot, his hair rose on his head with horror, his teeth chattered with affright, and when he continued his voice was almost a shriek.

'I went to the lamp guarded by the angel with the white wings, who looked at me sorrowfully; but the angel with the black wings still whispered in my ears. I saw nothing; I did not wish to see anything. I plucked a feather from the wing of the black angel and dipped it in the brightly flaming lamp and took from it the oil, drop by drop, and poured it into mine. My flame became glittering and red as blood; the other paled, but preserved still the brightness of a star. When but one drop of oil was left in it, the angel that guarded it spread his white wings and would have stayed me; but an angel with pearly wings and bearing a golden sword suddenly appeared.

'"Let this human being do according to his will – God will judge him!" it said.

'I took the last drop of oil! Then fear seized me. "What lamp is this?" I asked, pointing to the poor flame that was ready to expire, and the voice replied:

'"It is the soul of your beloved son."

'At the same moment the clear flame of the lamp died out: the white angel took its last breath in his wings and flew away, uttering as he went a cry of distress. The Spirit of Evil replied with a cry of triumph.

'I awoke, frozen with horror.

'In my chamber lay two bodies – crushed, unrecognizable. My son, informed by his *fiancée*, had tried to protect her in her flight, and my criminal snare had destroyed them both. It was Christmas, twenty years ago!' Saying this he made a sign to the negro tending the precious lamp to cease feeding its flame.

'I have made confession' he added, 'And can now die; but will God forgive me?'

At that moment the bells of the château pealed forth and the voices of the singers in the church were heard. The doors of the great hall opened. At the back of the chapel of the old manor, resplendent with lights, the infant Jesus, lying upon his bed of straw, appeared, radiant with celestial glory.

The old Duke fell on his knees before the infant Deity.

'Man,' said the voice of the priest, 'Jesus was born to suffer, and died for the redemption of sinners. You have sinned, you have suffered, you have repented – God forgives you. Your soul pass from you in peace.'

Then the old man turned his eyes towards the lamp, above which an angel with white wings was hovering. That angel he recognized – it was the guardian of the brilliant lamp.

The angel smiled sweetly and took within his wings the expiring flame, with which he flew heavenwards.

The Duc de Kerberzoff was dead!

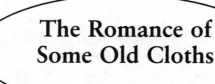

The Romance of
Some Old Cloths

Henry James

I

Towards the middle of the eighteenth century there lived in the Province of Massachusetts a widowed gentlewoman, the mother of three children, by name Mrs Veronica Wingrave. She had lost her husband early in life, and had devoted herself to the care of her progeny. These young persons grew up in manner to reward her tenderness and to gratify her highest hopes. The first-born was a son, whom she had called Bernard, after his father. The others were daughters – born at an interval of three years apart. Good looks were traditional in the family, and this youthful trio were not likely to allow the tradition to perish. The boy was of that fair and ruddy complexion and that athletic structure which in those days (as in these) were the sign of good English descent – a frank, affectionate young fellow, a deferential son, a patronizing brother, a steadfast friend. Clever, however, he was not; the wit of the family had been apportioned chiefly to his sisters. The late Mr Wingrave had been a great reader of Shakespeare, at a time when this pursuit implied more freedom of thought than at the present day, and in a community where it required much courage to patronize the drama even in the closet: and he had wished to call attention to his admiration of the great poet by calling his daughters out of his favourite plays. Upon the elder he had bestowed the romantic name of Rosalind, and the younger he had called Perdita, in memory of a little girl born between them, who had lived but a few weeks.

When Bernard Wingrave came to his sixteenth year his mother put a brave face upon it and prepared to execute her husband's last injunction. This had been a formal command that, at the proper age, his son should be sent out to England, to complete his education at the university of Oxford, where he himself had acquired his taste for elegant literature. It was Mrs Wingrave's belief that the lad's equal was not to be found in the two hemispheres, but she had the old traditions of literal obedience. She swallowed her sobs, and made up her boy's trunk and his simple provincial outfit, and sent him on his way across the seas. Bernard presented himself at his father's college, and spent five years in England, without great honour, indeed, but with a vast deal of pleasure and no discredit. On leaving the university he made the journey to France. In his twenty-fourth year he took ship for home, prepared to find poor little New England (New England was very small in those days) a very dull, unfashionable residence. But there had been changes at home, as well as in Mr Bernard's opinions. He found his mother's house quite habitable, and his sisters grown into two very charming young ladies, with all the accomplishments and graces of the young women of Britain, and a certain native-grown originality and wildness, which, if it was not an accomplishment, was certainly a grace the more. Bernard privately assured his mother that his sisters were fully a match for the most genteel young women in the old country; whereupon Mrs Wingrave, you may be sure, bade them hold up their heads. Such was Bernard's opinion, and such, in a tenfold higher degree, was the opinion of Mr Arthur Lloyd. This gentleman was a college-mate of Mr Bernard, a young man of reputable family, of a good person and a handsome inheritance; which latter appurtenance he proposed to invest in trade in the flourishing colony. He and Bernard were sworn friends; they had crossed the ocean together, and the young American had lost no time in presenting him at his mother's house, where he had made quite as good an impression as that which he had received and of which I have just given a hint.

The two sisters were at this time in all the freshness of their youthful bloom; each wearing, of course, this natural brilliancy in the manner that became her best. They were equally dissimilar in appearance and character. Rosalind, the elder – now in her twenty-seventh year – was tall and white, with calm grey eyes and auburn tresses; a very faint likeness to the Rosalind of Shakespeare's comedy, whom I imagine a brunette (if you will), but a slender, airy creature, full of the softest, quickest impulses. Miss Wingrave, with her slight lymphatic fairness, her fine arms, her majestic height, her slow utterance, was not cut out for adventures. She would never have put on a man's jacket and hose; and, indeed, being a very plump beauty, she may have had reasons apart from her natural dignity. Perdita, too, might very well have exchanged the sweet melancholy of her name against something more in consonance with her aspect and disposition. She had the cheek of a gypsy and the eye of an eager child, as well as the smallest waist and lightest foot in all the country of the Puritans. When you spoke to her she never made you wait, as her handsome sister was wont to do (while she looked at you with a cold fine eye), but gave you your choice of a dozen answers before you had uttered half your thought.

The young girls were very glad to see their brother once more; but they found themselves quite able to spare part of their attention for their brother's friend. Among the young men, their friends and neighbours, the *belle jeunesse* of the Colony, there were many excellent fellows, several devoted swains, and some two or three who enjoyed the reputation of universal charmers and conquerors. But the homebred arts and somewhat boisterous gallantry of these honest colonists were completely eclipsed by the good looks, the fine clothes, the punctilious courtesy, the perfect elegance, the immense information, of Mr Arthur Lloyd. He was in reality no paragon; he was a capable, honourable, civil youth, rich in pounds sterling, in his health and complacency and his little capital of uninvested affections. But he was a gentleman; he had a handsome person; he had studied and travelled; he spoke French, he played the flute, and he read verses aloud with very great taste. There were a dozen reasons why Miss Wingrave and her sister should have thought their other male acquaintance made but a poor figure before such a perfect man of the world. Mr Lloyd's anecdotes told our little New England maidens a great deal more of the ways and means of people of fashion in European capitals than he had any idea of doing. It was delightful to sit by and hear him and Bernard talk about the fine people and fine things they had seen. They would all gather round the fire after tea, in the little wainscoted parlour, and the two young men would remind each other, across the rug, of this, that and the other adventure. Rosalind and Perdita would often have given their ears to know exactly what adventure it was, and where it happened, and who was there, and what the ladies had on; but in those days a well-bred young woman was not expected to break into the conversation of her elders, or to ask too many questions; and the poor girls used therefore to sit fluttering behind the more languid – or more discreet – curiosity of their mother.

II

That they were both very fine girls Arthur Lloyd was not slow to discover; but it took him some time to make up his mind whether he liked the big sister or the little sister best. He had a strong presentiment – an emotion of a nature entirely too cheerful to be called a foreboding – that he was destined to stand up before the parson with one of them; yet he was unable to arrive at a preference, and for such a consummation a preference was certainly necessary, for Lloyd had too much young blood in his veins to make a choice by lot and be cheated of the satisfaction of falling in love. He resolved to take things as they came – to let his heart speak. Meanwhile he was on very pleasant footing. Mrs Wingrave showed a dignified indifference to his 'intentions', equally remote from a carelessness of her daughters' honour and from that sharp alacrity to make him come to the point, which, in his quality of young man of property, he had too often encountered in the worldly matrons of his native islands. As for Bernard, all that he asked was that his friend should treat his sisters as his own; and as for the poor girls themselves, however each may have secretly longed for that their visitor should do or say something 'marked', they kept a very modest and contented demeanour.

Towards each other, however, they were somewhat more on the offensive. They were good friends enough, and accommodating bedfellows (they shared the same four-poster), betwixt whom it would take more than a day for the seeds of jealousy to sprout and bear fruit; but they felt that the seeds had been sown on the day that Mr Lloyd came into the house. Each made up her mind that, if she should be slighted, she would bear her grief in silence, and that no one should be any the wiser; for if they had a great deal of ambition, they had also a large share of pride. But each prayed in secret, nevertheless, that upon her the selection, the distinction, might fall. They had need of a vast deal of patience, of self-control, of dissimulation. In those days a young girl of decent breeding could make no advances whatever, and barely respond, indeed, to those that were made. She was expected to sit still in her chair, with her eyes on the carpet, watching the spot where the mystic handkerchief should fall. Poor Arthur Lloyd was obliged to carry on his wooing in the little wainscoted parlour, before the eyes of Mrs

Wingrave, her son, and his prospective sister-in-law. But youth and love are so cunning that a hundred signs and tokens might travel to and fro, and not one of these three pairs of eyes detect them in their passage. The two maidens were always together, and had plenty of chances to betray themselves. That each knew she was being watched, made not a grain of difference in the little offices they mutually rendered, or in the various household tasks they performed in common. Neither flinched nor fluttered beneath the silent battery of her sister's eyes. The only apparent change in their habits was that that they had less to say to each other. It was impossible to talk about Mr Lloyd, and it was ridiculous to talk about anything else. By tacit agreement they began to wear all their choice finery, and to devise such little implements of conquest, in the way of ribbons and top-knots and kerchiefs, as were sanctioned by indubitable modesty. They executed in the same inarticulate fashion a contract of fair play in this exciting game. 'Is it better so?' Rosalind would ask, tying a bunch of ribbons on her bosom, and turning about from her glass to her sister. Perdita would look up gravely from her work and examine the decoration. 'I think you had better give it another loop,' she would say, with great solemnity, looking hard at her sister with eyes that added, 'upon my honour!' So they were for ever stitching and turning their petticoats, and pressing out their muslins, and contriving washes and ointments and cosmetics, like the ladies in the household of the vicar of Wakefield. Some three or four months went by; it grew to be midwinter, and as yet Rosalind knew that if Perdita had nothing more to boast of than she, there was not much to be feared from her rivalry. But Perdita by this time – the charming Perdita – felt that her secret had grown to be tenfold more precious than her sister's.

One afternoon Miss Wingrave sat alone – that was a rare accident – before her toilet-glass, combing out her long hair. It was getting too dark to see; she lit the two candles in their sockets, on the frame of her mirror, and then went to the window to draw her curtains. It was a grey December evening; the landscape was bare and bleak, and the sky heavy with snow-clouds. At the end of the large garden into which her window looked was a wall with a little postern door, opening into a lane. The door stood ajar, as she could vaguely see in the gathering darkness, and moved slowly to and fro, as if someone were swaying it from the lane without. It was doubtless a servant-maid who had been having a tryst with her sweetheart. But as she was about to drop her curtain Rosalind saw her sister step into the garden and hurry along the path which led to the house. She dropped the curtain, all save a little crevice for her eyes. As Perdita came up the path she seemed to be examining something in her hand, holding it close to her eyes. When she reached the house she stopped a moment, looked intently at the object, and pressed it to her lips.

Poor Rosalind slowly came back to her chair and sat down before her glass where, if she had looked at it less abstractly, she would have seen her handsome features sadly disfigured by jealousy. A moment afterwards the door opened behind her and her sister came into the room, out of breath, her cheeks aglow with the chilly air.

Perdita started. 'Ah,' said she, 'I thought you were with our mother.' The ladies were to go to a tea-party, and on such occasions it was the habit of one of the girls to help their mother to dress. Instead of coming in, Perdita lingered at the door.

'Come in, come in,' said Rosalind. 'We have more than an hour yet. I should like you very much to give a few strokes to my hair.' She knew that her sister wished to retreat, and that she could see in the glass all her movements in the room. 'Nay, just help me with my hair,' she said, 'and I will go to mamma.'

Perdita came reluctantly and took the brush. She saw her sister's eyes, in the glass, fastened hard upon her hands. She had not made three passes when Rosalind clapped her own right hand upon her sister's left, and started out of her chair. 'Whose ring is that?' she cried, passionately, drawing her towards the light.

On the young girl's third finger glistened a little gold ring, adorned with a very small sapphire. Perdita felt that she need no longer keep her secret, yet that she must put a bold face on her avowal. 'It's mine,' she said proudly.

'Who gave it to you?' cried the other.

Perdita hesitated a moment. 'Mr Lloyd.'

'Mr Lloyd is generous, all of a sudden.'

'Ah no,' cried Perdita, with spirit, 'not all of a sudden! He offered it to me a month ago.'

'And you needed a month's begging to take it?' said Rosalind, looking at the little trinket, which indeed was not especially elegant, although it was the best that the jeweller of the Province could furnish. 'I wouldn't have taken it in less than two.'

'It isn't the ring,' Perdita answered, 'it's what it means!'

'It means that you are not a modest girl!' cried Rosalind. 'Pray, does your mother know of your intrigue? does Bernard?'

'My mother has approved my "intrigue", as you call it. Mr Lloyd has asked for my hand, and mamma has given it. Would you have had him apply to you, dearest sister?'

Rosalind gave her companion a long look, full of passionate envy and sorrow. Then she dropped her lashes on her pale cheeks and turned away. Perdita felt that it had not been a pretty scene; but it was her sister's fault. However, the elder girl rapidly called back her pride, and turned herself about again. 'You have my very best wishes,' she said, with a low curtsey. 'I wish you every happiness, and a very long life.'

Perdita gave a bitter laugh. 'Don't speak in that tone!' she cried. 'I would rather you should curse me outright. Come, Rosy,' she added, 'he couldn't marry both of us.'

'I wish you very great joy,' Rosalind repeated, mechanically, sitting down to her glass again, 'and a very long life, and plenty of children.'

There was something in the sound of these words not at all to Perdita's taste. 'Will you give me a year to live at least?' she said. 'In a year I can have one little boy – or one little girl at least. If you will give me your brush again I will do your hair.'

'Thank you,' said Rosalind. 'You had better go to mamma. It isn't becoming that a young lady with a promised husband should wait on a girl with none.'

'Nay,' said Perdita, good-humouredly, 'I have Arthur to wait upon me. You need my service more than I need yours.'

But her sister motioned her away, and she left the room. When she had gone poor Rosalind fell on her knees before her dresssing-table, buried her head in her hands, and poured out a flood of tears and sobs. She felt very much the better for this effusion of sorrow. When her sister came back she insisted on helping her to dress – on her wearing her prettiest things. She forced upon her acceptance a bit of lace of her own, and declared that now that she was to be married she should do her best to appear worthy of her lover's choice. She discharged these offices in stern silence; but, such as they were, they had to do duty as an apology and an atonement; she never made any other.

Now that Lloyd was received by the family as an accepted suitor nothing remained but to fix the wedding-day. It was appointed for the following April, and in the interval preparations were diligently made for the marriage. Lloyd, on his side, was busy with his commercial arrangements, and with establishing a correspondence with the great mercantile house to which he had attached himself in England. He was therefore not so frequent a visitor at Mrs Wingrave's as during the months of his diffidence and irresolution, and poor Rosalind had less to suffer than she had feared from the sight of the mutual endearments of the young lovers. Touching his future sister-in-law he had a perfectly clear conscience. There had not been a particle of lovemaking between them, and he had not the slightest suspicion that he had dealt her a terrible blow. He was quite at his ease; life promised so well, both domestically and financially. The great revolt of the Colonies was not yet in the air, and that his connubial felicity should take a tragic turn it was absurd, it was blasphemous to apprehend. Meanwhile, at Mrs Wingrave's, there was a greater rustling of silks, a more rapid clicking of scissors and flying of needles, than ever. The good lady had determined that her daughter should carry from home the genteelest outfit that her money could buy or that the country could furnish. All the sage women in the Province were convened, and their united taste was brought to bear on Perdita's wardrobe. Rosalind's situation, at this moment, was assuredly not to be envied. The poor girl had an inordinate love of dress, and the very best taste in the world, as her sister perfectly well knew. Rosalind was tall, she was stately and sweeping, she was made to carry stiff brocade and masses of heavy lace, such as belong to the toilet of a rich man's wife. But Rosalind sat aloof, with her beautiful arms folded and her head averted, while her mother and sister and the venerable women aforesaid worried and wondered over their materials, oppressed by the multitude of their resources. One day there came in a beautiful piece of white silk, brocaded with heavenly blue and silver sent by the bridegroom himself – it not being thought amiss in those days that the husband-elect should contribute to the bride's trousseau. Perdita could think of no form or fashion which would do sufficient honour to the splendour of the material.

'Blue's your colour, sister, more than mine,' she said, with appealing eyes. 'It is a pity it's not for you. You would know what to do with it.'

Rosalind got up from her place and looked at the great shining fabric, as it lay spread over the back of a chair. Then she took it up in her hands and felt it – lovingly, as Perdita could see – and turned about towards the mirror with it. She let it roll down to her feet, and flung the other end over her shoulder, gathering it in about her waist with her white arm, which was bare to the elbow. She threw back her head, and looked at her image, and a hanging tress of her auburn hair fell upon the gorgeous surface of the silk. It made a dazzling picture. The women standing about uttered a little 'Look, look!' of admiration. 'Yes, indeed,' said Rosalind, quietly, 'blue is my colour.' But Perdita could see that her fancy had been stirred, and that she would now fall to work and solve all their silken riddles. And indeed she behaved very well, as Perdita, knowing her insatiable love of millinery, was quite ready to declare. Innumerable yards of lustrous silk and satin, of muslin, velvet and lace, passed through her cunning hands, without a jealous word coming from her lips. Thanks to her industry, when the wedding-day came Perdita was prepared to espouse more of the vanities of life than any fluttering young bride who had yet received the sacramental blessing of a New England divine.

It had been arranged that the young couple should go out and spend the first days of their wedded life at the country-house of an English gentleman – a man of rank and a very kind friend to Arthur Lloyd. He was a bachelor; he declared he should be delighted to give up the place to the influence of Hymen. After the ceremony at church – it had been performed by an English clergyman – young Mrs Lloyd hastened back to her mother's house to change her nuptial robes for a riding-dress. Rosalind helped her to effect the change, in the little homely room in which they had spent their undivided younger years. Perdita then hurried off to bid farewell to her mother, leaving Rosalind to follow. Then parting was short; the horses were at the door, and Arthur was impatient to start. But Rosalind had not followed, and Perdita hastened back to her room, opening the door abruptly. Rosalind, as usual, was before the glass, but in a position which caused the other to stand still, amazed. She had dressed herself in Perdita's cast-off wedding veil and wreath, and on her neck she had hung the full string of pearls which the young girl had received from her husband as a wedding-gift. These things had been hastily laid aside, to await their possessor's disposal on her return from the country. Bedizened by this unnatural garb Rosalind stood before the mirror, plunging a long look into its depths and reading heaven knows what audacious visions. Perdita was horrified. It was a hideous image of their old rivalry come to life again. She made a step towards her sister, as if to pull off the veil and the flowers. But catching her eyes in the glass, she stopped.

'Farewell, sweetheart,' she said. 'You might at least have waited till I had got out of the house!' And she hurried away from the room.

Mr Lloyd had purchased in Boston a house which to the taste of those days appeared as elegant as it was commodious; and here he very soon established himself with his young wife. He was thus separated by a distance of twenty miles from the residence of his mother-in-law. Twenty miles, in that primitive era of roads and conveyances, were as serious a matter as a hundred at the present day, and Mrs Wingrave saw but little of her daughter during the first twelvemonth of her marriage. She suffered in no small degree from Perdita's absence; and her affliction was not diminished by the fact that Rosalind had fallen into terribly low spirits and was not to be roused or cheered but by change of air and company. The real cause of the young lady's dejection the reader will not be slow to suspect. Mrs Wingrave and her gossips, however, deemed her complaint a mere bodily ill, and doubted not that she would obtain relief from the remedy just mentioned. Her mother accordingly proposed, on her behalf, a visit to certain relatives on the paternal side, established in New York, who had long complained that they were able to see so little of their New England cousins. Rosalind was despatched to these good people, under a suitable escort, and remained with them for several months. In the interval her brother Bernard, who had begun the practice of the law, made up his mind to take a wife. Rosalind came home to the wedding, apparently cured of her heartache, with bright roses and lilies in her face and a proud smile on her lips. Arthur Lloyd came over from Boston to see his brother-in-law married, but without his wife, who was expecting very soon to present him with an heir. It was nearly a year since Rosalind had seen him. She was glad – she hardly knew why – that Perdita had stayed at home. Arthur looked happy, but he was more grave and important than before his marriage. She thought he looked 'interesting' – for although the word, in its modern sense, was not then invented, we may be sure that the idea was. The truth is, he was simply anxious about his wife and her coming ordeal. Nevertheless, he by no means failed to observe Rosalind's beauty and splendour, and to note how she effaced the poor little bride. The allowance that Perdita had enjoyed for her dress had now been transferred to her sister, who turned it to wonderful account. On the morning after the wedding he had a lady's saddle put on the horse of the servant who had come with him from town, and went out with the young girl for a ride. It was a keen, clear morning in January; the ground was bare and hard, and the horses in good condition – to say nothing of Rosalind, who was charming in her hat and plume, and her dark blue riding coat, trimmed with fur. They rode all the morning, lost their way and were obliged to stop for dinner at a farmhouse. The early winter dusk had fallen when they got home. Mrs Wingrave met them with a long face. A messenger had arrived at noon from Mrs Lloyd; she was beginning to be ill, she desired her husband's immediate return. The young man, at the thought that he had lost several hours, and that by hard riding he might already have been with his wife, uttered a passionate oath. He barely consented to stop for a mouthful of supper, but mounted the messenger's horse and started off at a gallop.

He reached home at midnight. His wife had been delivered of a little girl. 'Ah, why weren't you with me?' she said, as he came to her bedside.

'I was out of the house when the man came. I was with Rosalind,' said Lloyd, innocently.

Mrs Lloyd made a little moan, and turned away. But she continued to do very well, and for a week her improvement was uninterrupted. Finally, however, through some indiscretion in the way of diet or exposure, it was checked, and the poor lady grew rapidly worse. Lloyd was in despair. It very soon became evident that she was breathing her last. Mrs Lloyd came to a sense of her approaching end, and declared that she was reconciled with death. On the third evening after the change took place she told her husband that she felt she should not get through the night. She dismissed her servants, and also requested her mother to withdraw – Mrs Wingrave having arrived on the preceding day. She had had her infant placed on the bed beside her, and she lay on her side, with the child against her breast, holding her husband's hands. The night-lamp was hidden behind the heavy curtains of the bed, but the room was illuminated with a red glow from the immense fire of logs on the hearth.

'It seems strange not to be warmed into life by such a fire as that,' the young woman said, feebly trying to smile. 'If I had but a little of it in my veins! But I have given all my fire to this little spark of mortality.' And she dropped her eyes on her child. Then raising them she looked at her husband with a long, penetrating gaze. The last feeling which lingered in her heart was one of suspicion. She had not recovered from the shock which Arthur had given her by telling her that in the hour of her agony he had been with Rosalind. She trusted her husband very nearly as well as she loved him; but now that she was called away forever she felt a cold horror of her sister. She felt in her soul that Rosalind had never ceased to be jealous of her good fortune; and a year of happy security had not effaced the young girl's image, dressed in her wedding-garments, and smiling with simulated triumph. Now that Arthur was to be alone, what might not Rosalind attempt? She was beautiful, she was engaging; what arts might she not use, what impression might she not make upon the young man's saddened heart? Mrs Lloyd looked at her husband in silence. It seemed hard, after all, to doubt of his constancy. His fine eyes were filled with tears; his face was convulsed with weeping; the clasp of his hands was warm and passionate. How noble he looked, how tender, how faithful and devoted! 'Nay,' thought Perdita, 'he's not for such a one as Rosalind. He'll never forget me. Nor does Rosalind truly care for him; she cares only for vanities and finery and jewels.' And she lowered her eyes on her white hands, which her husband's liberality had covered with rings, and on the lace ruffles which trimmed the edge of her night-dress. 'She covets my rings and my laces more than she covets my husband.'

At this moment the thought of her sister's rapacity seemed to cast a dark shadow between her and the helpless figure of her little girl. 'Arthur,' she said, 'You must take off my rings. I shall not be buried in them. One of these days my daughter shall wear them – my rings and my laces and silks. I had them all brought out and shown me today. It's a great wardrobe – there's not such another in the Province; I can say it without vanity, now that I have done with it. It will be a great inheritance for my daughter when she grows into a young woman. There are things there that a man never buys twice, and if they are lost you will never again see the like. So you will watch them well. Some dozen things I have left to Rosalind; I have named them to my mother. I have given her that blue and silver; it was meant for her; I wore it only once, I looked ill in it. But the rest are to be sacredly kept for this little innocent. It's such a providence that she should be my colour; she can wear my gowns; she has her mother's eyes. You know the same fashions come back every twenty years. She can wear my gowns as they are. They will lie there quietly waiting till she grows into them – wrapped in camphor and rose-leaves, and keeping their colours in the sweet-scented darkness. She shall have black hair, she shall wear my carnation satin. Do you promise me, Arthur?'

'Promise you what, dearest?'

'Promise me to keep your poor little wife's old gowns.'

'Are you afraid I shall sell them?'

'No, but that they may get scattered. My mother will have them properly wrapped up, and you shall lay them away under a double-lock. Do you know the great chest in the attic, with the iron bands? There is no end to what it will hold. You can put them all there. My mother and the housekeeper will do it, and give you the key. And you will keep the key in your secretary, and never give it to anyone but your child. Do you promise me?'

'Ah, yes, I promise you,' said Lloyd, puzzled at the intensity with which his wife appeared to cling to this idea.

'Will you swear?' repeated Perdita.

'Yes, I swear.'

'Well – I trust you – I trust you,' said the poor lady, looking into his eyes with eyes in which, if he had suspected her vague apprehensions, he might have read an appeal quite as much as an assurance.

Lloyd bore his bereavement rationally and manfully. A month after his wife's death, in the course of business, circumstances arose which offered him an opportunity of going to England. He took advantage of it, to change the current of his thoughts. He was absent nearly a year, during which his little girl was tenderly nursed and guarded by her grandmother. On his return he had his house again thrown open, and announced his intention of keeping the same state as during his wife's lifetime. It very soon came to be predicted that he would marry again, and there were at least a dozen young women of whom one may say that it was by no fault of theirs that, for six months after his return, the prediction did not come true. During this interval he still left his little daughter in Mrs Wingrave's hands, the latter assuring him that a change of residence at so tender an age would be full of danger for her health. Finally, however, he declared that his heart longed for his daughter's presence and that she must be brought up to town. He sent his coach and his housekeeper to fetch her home. Mrs Wingrave was in terror lest something should befall her on the road; and, in accordance with this feeling, Rosalind offered to accompany her. She could return the next day. So she went up to town with her little niece, and Mr Lloyd met her on the threshold of his house, overcome with her kindness and with paternal joy. Instead of returning the next day Rosalind stayed out the week; and when at last she reappeared, she had only come for her clothes. Arthur would not hear of her coming home, nor would the baby. That little person cried and choked if Rosalind left her; and at the sight of her grief Arthur lost his wits, and swore that she was going to die. In fine, nothing would suit them but that the aunt should remain until the little niece had grown used to strange faces.

It took two months to bring this consummation about; for it was not until this period had elapsed that Rosalind took leave of her brother-in-law. Mrs Wingrave had shaken her head over her daughter's absence; she had declared it was not becoming, that it was the talk of the whole country. She had reconciled herself to it only because, during the girl's visit, the household enjoyed an unwonted term of peace. Bernard Wingrave had brought his wife home to live, between whom and her sister-in-law there was as little love as you please. Rosalind was perhaps no angel; but in the daily practice of life she was a sufficiently good-natured girl, and if she quarrelled with Mrs Bernard it was not without provocation. Quarrel, however, she did, to the great annoyance not only of her antagonist, but of the two spectators of these constant altercations. Her stay in the household of her brother-in-law, therefore, would have been delightful, if only because it removed her from contact with the object of her antipathy at home. It was doubly – it was ten times – delightful, in that it kept her near the object of her early passion. Mrs Lloyd's sharp suspicions had fallen very far short of the truth. Rosalind's sentiment had been a passion at first, and a passion it remained – a passion of whose radiant heat, tempered to the delicate state of his feeling, Mr Lloyd very soon felt the influence. Lloyd, as I have hinted, was not a modern Petrarch; it was not in his nature to practise an ideal constancy. He had not been many days in the house with his sister-in-law before he began to assure himself that she was, in the language of that day, a devilish fine woman. Whether Rosalind really practised those insidious arts that her sister had been tempted to impute to her it is needless to enquire. It is enough to say that she found means to appear to the very best advantage. She used to seat herself every morning before the big fireplace in the dining-room, at work upon a piece of tapestry, with her little niece disporting herself on the carpet at her feet, or on the train of her dress, and playing with her woollen balls. Lloyd would have been a very stupid fellow if he had remained insensible to the rich suggestions of this charming picture. He was exceedingly fond of his little girl, and was never weary of taking her in his arms and tossing her up and down, and making her crow with delight. Very often, however, he would venture upon greater liberties than the young lady was yet prepared to allow, and then she would suddenly vociferate her displeasure. Rosalind, at this, would drop her tapestry, and put out her handsome hands with the serious smile of the young girl whose virgin fancy has revealed to her all a mother's healing arts. Lloyd would give up the child, their eyes would meet, their hands would touch, and Rosalind would extinguish the little girl's sobs upon the snowy folds of the kerchief that crossed her bosom. Her dignity was perfect, and nothing could be more discreet than the manner in which she accepted her brother-in-law's hospitality. It may almost be said, perhaps, that there was something harsh in her reserve. Lloyd had a provoking feeling that she was in the house and yet was unapproachable. Half-an-hour after supper, at the very outset of the long winter evenings, she would light her candle, make the young man a most respectful curtsey, and march off to bed. If these were arts, Rosalind was a great artist. But their effect was so gentle, so gradual, they were calculated to work upon the young widower's fancy with a *crescendo* so finely shaded, that, as the reader has seen, several weeks elapsed before Rosalind began to feel sure that her returns would cover her outlay. When this became morally certain she packed up her trunk and returned to her mother's house. For three days she waited: on the fourth Mr Lloyd made his appearance – a respectful but pressing suitor. Rosalind heard him to the end, with great humility, and accepted him with infinite modesty. It is hard to imagine that Mrs Lloyd would have forgiven her husband; but if anything might have disarmed her resentment it would have been the ceremonious continence of this interview. Rosalind imposed upon her lover but a short probation. They were married, as was becoming, with great privacy – almost with secrecy – in the hope perhaps, as was waggishly remarked at the time, that the late Mrs Lloyd wouldn't hear of it.

The marriage was to all appearance a happy one, and each party obtained what each had desired – Lloyd 'a devilish fine woman', and Rosalind – but Rosalind's desires, as the reader will have observed, had remained a good deal of a mystery. There were, indeed, two blots upon their felicity, but time would perhaps efface them. During the first three years of her marriage Mrs Lloyd failed to become a mother, and her husband on his side suffered heavy losses of money. This latter circumstance compelled a material retrenchment in his expenditure, and Rosalind was perforce less of a fine lady than her sister had been. She contrived, however, to carry it like a woman of considerable fashion. She had long since ascertained that her sister's copious wardrobe had been sequestrated for the benefit of her daughter, and that it lay languishing in thankless gloom in the dusty attic. It was a revolting thought that these exquisite fabrics should await the good pleasure of a little girl who sat in a high chair and ate bread-and-milk with a wooden spoon. Rosalind had the good taste, however, to say nothing about the matter until several months had expired. Then, at last, she timidly broached it to her husband. Was it not a pity that so much finery should be lost? – for lost it would be, what with colours fading, and moths eating it up, and the change of fashions. But Lloyd gave her so abrupt and peremptory a refusal, that she saw, for the present, her attempt was vain. Six months went by, however, and brought with them new needs and new visions. Rosalind's thoughts hovered lovingly about her sister's relics. She went up and looked at the chest in which they lay imprisoned. There was a sullen defiance in its three great padlocks and its iron bands which only quickened her cupidity. There was something exasperating in its incorruptible immobility. It was like a grim and grizzled old household servant, who locks his jaws over a family secret. And then there was a look of capacity in its vast extent, and a sound as of dense fullness, when Rosalind knocked its side with the toe of her little shoe, which caused her to flush with baffled longing. 'It's absurd,' she cried; 'it's improper, it's wicked'; and she forthwith resolved upon another attack upon her husband. On the following day, after dinner, when he had had his wine, she boldly began it. But he cut her short with great sternness.

'Once for all, Rosalind,' said he, 'it's out of the question. I shall be gravely displeased if you return to the matter.'

'Very good,' said Rosalind. 'I am glad to learn the esteem in which I am held. Gracious heaven,' she cried, 'I am a very happy woman! It's an agreeable thing to feel one's self sacrificed to a caprice!' And her eyes filled with tears of anger and disappointment.

Lloyd had a good-natured man's horror of a woman's sobs, and he attempted – I may say he condescended – to explain. 'It's not a caprice, dear, it's a promise,' he said – 'an oath.'

'An oath? It's a pretty matter for oaths! and to whom, pray?'

'To Perdita,' said the young man, raising his eyes for an instant, and immediately dropping them.

'Perdita – ah, Perdita!' and Rosalind's tears broke forth. Her bosom heaved with stormy sobs – sobs which were the long-deferred sequel of the violent fit of weeping in which she had indulged herself on the night when she discovered her sister's betrothal. She had hoped, in her better moments, that she had done with her jealousy; but her temper, on that occasion, had taken an ineffaceable hold. 'And pray, what right had Perdita to dispose of my future?' she cried. 'What right had she to bind you to meanness and cruelty? Ah, I occupy a dignified place, and I make a very fine figure! I am welcome to what Perdita has left! And what has she left? I never knew till now how little! Nothing, nothing, nothing.'

This was a very poor logic, but it was very good as a 'scene'. Lloyd put his arm round his wife's waist and tried to kiss her, but she shook him off with magnificent scorn. Poor fellow! he had coveted a 'devilish fine woman', and he had got one. Her scorn was intolerable. He walked away with his ears tingling – irresolute, distracted. Before him was his secretary, and in it the sacred key which with his own hand he had turned in the triple lock. He marched up and opened it, and took the key from a secret drawer, wrapped in a little packet which he had sealed with his own honest bit of glazonry. *Je garde*, said the motto – 'I keep.'

But he was ashamed to put it back. He flung it upon the table beside his wife.

'Put it back!' she cried. 'I want it not. I hate it!'

'I wash my hands of it,' cried her husband. 'God forgive me!'

Mrs Lloyd gave an indignant shrug of her shoulders, and swept out of the room, while the young man retreated by another door. Ten minutes later Mrs Lloyd returned, and found the room occupied by her little step-daughter and the nursery-maid. The key was not on the table. She glanced at the child. Her little niece was perched on a chair, with the packet in her hands. She had broken the seal with her own small fingers. Mrs Lloyd hastily took possession of the key.

At the habitual supper-hour Arthur Lloyd came back from his counting-room. It was the month of June, and supper was served by daylight. The meal was placed on the table, but Mrs Lloyd failed to make her appearance. The servant whom his master sent to call her came back with the assurance that her room was empty, and that the women informed him that she had not been seen since dinner. They had, in truth, observed her to have been in tears, and, supposing her to be shut up in her chamber, had not disturbed her. Her husband called her name in various parts of the house, but without response. At last it occurred to him that he might find her by taking the way to the attic. The thought gave him a strange feeling of discomfort, and he bade his servants remain behind, wishing no witness in his quest. He reached the foot of the staircase leading to the topmost flat, and stood with his hands on the banisters, pronouncing his wife's name. His voice trembled. He called again louder and more firmly. The only sound which disturbed the absolute silence was a faint echo of his own tones, repeating his question under the great eaves. He nevertheless felt irresistibly moved to ascend the staircase. It opened upon a wide hall, lined with wooden closets, and terminating in a window which looked westward, and admitted the last rays of the sun. Before the window stood the great chest. Before the chest, on her knees, the young man saw with amazement and horror the figure of his wife. In an instant he crossed the interval between them, bereft of utterance. The lid of the chest stood open, exposing, amid their perfumed napkins, its treasure of stuffs and jewels. Rosalind had fallen backward from a kneeling posture, with one hand supporting her on the floor and the other pressed to her heart. On her limbs was the stiffness of death, and on her face, in the fading light of the sun, the terror of something more than death. Her lips were parted in entreaty, in dismay, in agony; and on her blanched brow and cheeks there glowed the marks of ten hideous wounds from two vengeful ghostly hands.

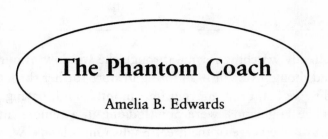

The Phantom Coach

Amelia B. Edwards

The circumstances I am about to relate to you have truth to recommend them. They happened to myself, and my recollection of them is as vivid as if they had taken place only yesterday. Twenty years, however, have gone by since that night. During those twenty years I have told the story to but one other person. I tell it now with a reluctance which I find it difficult to overcome. All I entreat, meanwhile, is that you will abstain from forcing your own conclusions upon me. I want nothing explained away. I desire no arguments. My mind on this subject is quite made up, and, having the testimony of my own senses to rely upon, I prefer to abide by it.

Well! It was just twenty years ago, and within a day or two of the end of the grouse season. I had been out all day with my gun, and had had no sport to speak of. The wind was due east; the month, December; the place, a bleak wide moor in the far north of England. And I had lost my way. It was not a pleasant place in which to lose one's way, with the first feathery flakes of a coming snowstorm just fluttering down upon the heather, and the leaden evening closing in all around. I shaded my eyes with my hand, and stared anxiously into the gathering darkness, where the purple moorland melted into a range of low hills, some ten or twelve miles distant. Not the faintest smoke-wreath, not the tiniest cultivated patch, or fence, or sheep-track, met my eyes in any direction. There was nothing for it but to walk on, and take my chance of finding what shelter I could, by the way. So I shouldered my gun again, and pushed wearily forward; for I had been on foot since an hour after daybreak, and had eaten nothing since breakfast.

Meanwhile, the snow began to come down with ominous steadiness, and the wind fell. After this, the cold became more intense, and the night came rapidly up. As for me, my prospects darkened with the darkening sky, and my heart grew heavy as I thought how my young wife was already watching for me through the window of our little inn parlour, and thought of all the suffering in store for her throughout this weary night. We had been married four months, and, having spent our autumn in the Highlands, were now lodging in a remote little village situated just on the verge of the great English moorlands. We were very much in love, and, of course, very happy. This morning, when we parted, she had implored me to return before dusk, and I had promised her that I would. What would I not have given to have kept my word!

Even now, weary as I was, I felt that with a supper, an hour's rest, and a guide, I might still get back to her before midnight, if only guide and shelter could be found.

And all this time, the snow fell and the night thickened. I stopped and shouted every now and then, but my shouts seemed only to make the silence deeper. Then a vague sense of uneasiness came upon me, and I began to remember stories of travellers who had walked on and on in the falling snow until, wearied out, they were fain to lie down and sleep their lives away. Would it be possible, I asked myself, to keep on thus through all the long dark night? Would there not come a time when my limbs must fail, and my resolution give way? When I, too, must sleep the sleep of death. Death! I shuddered. How hard to die just now, when life lay all so bright before me! How hard for my darling, whose whole loving heart – but that thought was not to be borne! To banish it, I shouted again, louder and longer, and then listened eagerly. Was my shout answered, or did I only fancy that I heard a far-off cry? I helloed again, and again the echo followed. Then a wavering speck of light came suddenly out of the dark, shifting, disappearing, growing momentarily nearer and brighter. Running towards it at full speed, I found myself, to my great joy, face to face with an old man and a lantern.

'Thank God!' was the exclamation that burst involuntarily from my lips.

Blinking and frowning, he lifted his lantern and peered into my face. 'What for?' growled he, sulkily.

'Well – for you. I began to fear I should be lost in the snow.'

'Eh, then, folks do get cast away hereabout fra time to time, an' what's to hinder you from bein' cast away likewise, if the Lord's so minded?'

'If the Lord is so minded that you and I shall be lost together, friend, we must submit,' I replied; 'but I don't mean to be lost without you. How far am I now from Dwolding?'

'A gude twenty mile, more or less.'

'And the nearest village?'

'The nearest village is Wake, an' that's twelve mile t'other side.'

'Where do you live, then?'

'Out yonder,' said he, with a vague jerk of the lantern.

'You're going home, I presume?'

'Maybe I am.'

'Then I'm going with you.'

The old man shook his head, and rubbed his nose reflectively with the handle of the lantern.

'It ain't o' no use,' growled he. 'He 'ont let you in – not he.'

'We'll see about that,' I replied, briskly. 'Who is He?'

'The master.'

'Who is the master?'

'That's nowt to you,' was the unceremonious reply.

'Well, well; you lead the way, and I'll engage that the master shall give me shelter and a supper tonight.'

'Eh, you can try him!' muttered my reluctant guide; and, still shaking his head, he hobbled, gnome-like, away through the falling snow. A large mass loomed up presently out of the darkness, and a huge dog rushed out, barking furiously.

'Is this the house?' I asked.

'Ay, it's the house. Down, Bey!' And he fumbled in his pocket for the key.

I drew up close behind him, prepared to lose no chance of entrance, and saw in the little circle of light shed by the lantern that the door was heavily studded with iron nails, like the door of a prison. In another minute he had turned the key and I had pushed past him into the house.

Once inside, I looked round with curiosity, and found myself in a great raftered hall, which served, apparently, a variety of uses. One end was piled to the roof with corn, like a barn. The other was stored with flour-sacks, agricultural implements, casks, and all kinds of miscellaneous lumber; while from the beams overhead hung rows of hams, flitches, and bunches of dried herbs for winter use. In the centre of the floor stood some huge object gauntly dressed in a dingy wrapping-cloth, and reaching half way to the rafters. Lifting a corner of this cloth, I saw, to my surprise, a telescope of very considerable size, mounted on a rude movable platform, with four small wheels. The tube was made of painted wood, bound round with bands of metal rudely fashioned; the speculum, so far as I could estimate its size in the dim light, measured at least fifteen inches in diameter. While I was yet examining the instrument, and asking myself whether it was not the work of some self-taught optician, a bell rang sharply.

'That's for you,' said my guide, with a malicious grin. 'Yonder's his room.'

He pointed to a low black door at the opposite side of the hall. I crossed over, rapped somewhat loudly, and went in, without waiting for an invitation. A huge, white-haired old man rose from a table covered with books and papers, and confronted me sternly.

'Who are you?' said he. 'How came you here? What do you want?'

'James Murray, barrister-at-law. On foot across the moor. Meat, drink, and sleep.'

He bent his bushy brows into a portentous frown.

'Mine is not a house of entertainment,' he said, haughtily. 'Jacob, how dared you admit this stranger?'

'I didn't admit him,' grumbled the old man. 'He followed me over the muir, and shouldered his way in before me. I'm no match for six foot two.'

'And pray, sir, by what right have you forced an entrance into my house?'

'The same by which I should have clung to your boat, if I were drowning. The right of self-preservation.'

'Self-preservation?'

'There's an inch of snow on the ground already,' I replied, briefly; 'and it would be deep enough to cover my body before daybreak.'

He strode to the window, pulled aside a heavy black curtain, and looked out.

'It is true,' he said. 'You can stay, if you choose, till morning. Jacob, serve the supper.'

With this he waved me to a seat, resumed his own, and became at once absorbed in the studies from which I had disturbed him.

I placed my gun in a corner, drew a chair to the hearth, and examined my quarters at leisure. Smaller and less incongruous in its arrangements than the hall, this room contained, nevertheless, much to awaken my curiosity. The floor was carpetless. The whitewashed walls were in parts scrawled over with strange diagrams, and in others covered with shelves crowded with philosophical instruments, the uses of many of which were unknown to me. On one side of the fireplace, stood a bookcase filled with dingy folios; on the other, a small organ, fantastically decorated with painted carvings of mediaeval saints and devils. Through the half-opened door of a cupboard at the further end of the room, I saw a long array of geological specimens, surgical preparations, crucibles, retorts, and jars of chemicals; while on the mantelshelf beside me, amid a number of small objects, stood a model of the solar system, a small galvanic battery, and a microscope. Every chair had its burden. Every corner was heaped high with books. The very floor was littered over with maps, casts, papers, tracings, and learned lumber of all conceivable kinds.

I stared about me with an amazement increased by every fresh object upon which my eyes chanced to rest. So strange a room I had never seen; yet seemed it stranger still, to find such a room in a lone farmhouse amid those wild and solitary moors! Over and over again, I looked from my host to his surroundings, and from his surroundings back to my host, asking myself who and what he could be? His head was singularly fine; but it was more the head of a poet than of a philosopher. Broad in the temples, prominent over the eyes, and clothed with a rough profusion of perfectly white hair, it had all the ideality and much of the ruggedness that characterises the head of Louis von Beethoven. There were the same deep lines about the mouth, and the same stern furrows in the brow. There was the same concentration of expression. While I was yet observing him, the door opened, and Jacob brought in the supper. His master then closed his book, rose, and with more courtesy of manner than he had yet shown, invited me to the table.

A dish of ham and eggs, a loaf of brown bread, and a bottle of admirable sherry, were placed before me.

'I have but the homeliest farmhouse fare to offer you, sir,' said my entertainer. 'Your appetite, I trust, will make up for the deficiencies of our larder.'

I had already fallen upon the viands, and now protested, with the enthusiasm of a starving sportsman, that I had never eaten anything so delicious.

He bowed stiffly, and sat down to his own supper, which consisted, primitively, of a jug of milk and a basin of porridge. We ate in silence, and, when we had done, Jacob removed the tray. I then drew my chair back to the fireside. My host, somewhat to my surprise, did the same, and turning abruptly towards me, said:

'Sir, I have lived here in strict retirement for three-and-twenty years. During that time, I have not seen as many strange faces, and I have not read a single newspaper. You are the first stranger who has crossed my threshold for more than four years. Will you favour me with a few words of information respecting that outer world from which I have parted company so long?'

'Pray interrogate me,' I replied. 'I am heartily at your service.'

He bent his head in acknowledgment; leaned forward, with his elbows resting on his knees and his chin supported in the palms of his hands; stared fixedly into the fire; and proceeded to question me.

His inquiries related chiefly to scientific matters, with the later progress of which, as applied to the practical purposes of life, he was almost wholly unacquainted. No student of science myself, I replied as well as my slight information permitted; but the task was far from easy, and I was much relieved when, passing from interrogation to discussion, he began pouring forth his own conclusions upon the facts which I had been attempting to place before him. He talked, and I listened spellbound. He talked till I believe he almost forgot my presence, and only thought aloud. I had never heard anything like it then; I have never heard anything like it since. Familiar with all systems of all philosophies, subtle in analysis, bold in generalisation, he poured forth his thoughts in an uninterrupted stream, and, still leaning forward in the same moody attitude with his eyes fixed upon the fire, wandered from topic to topic, from speculation to speculation, like an inspired dreamer. From practical science to mental philosophy; from electricity in the wire to electricity in the nerve; from Watts to Mesmer, from Mesmer to Reichenbach, from Reichenbach to Swedenborg, Spinoza, Condillac, Descartes, Berkeley, Aristotle, Plato, and the Magi and mystics of the East, were transitions which, however bewildering in their variety and scope, seemed easy and harmonious upon his lips as sequences in music. By-and-by – I forget now by what link of conjecture or illustration – he passed on to that field which lies beyond the boundary line of even conjectural philosophy, and reaches no man knows whither. He spoke of the soul and its aspirations; of the spirit and its powers; of second sight; of prophecy; of those phenomena which, under the names of ghosts, spectres, and supernatural appearances, have been denied by the sceptics and attested by the credulous, of all ages.

'The world,' he said, 'grows hourly more and more sceptical of all that lies beyond its own narrow radius; and our men of science foster the fatal tendency. They condemn as fable all that resists experiment. They reject as false all that cannot be brought to the test of the laboratory or the dissecting-room. Against what superstition have they waged so long and obstinate a war, as against the belief in apparitions? And yet what superstition has maintained its hold upon the minds of men so long and so firmly? Show me any fact in physics, in history, in archaeology, which is supported by testimony so wide and so various. Attested by all races of men, in all ages, and in all climates, by the soberest sages of antiquity, by the rudest savage of today, by the Christian, the Pagan, the Pantheist, the Materialist, this phenomenon is treated as a nursery tale by the philosophers of our century. Circumstantial evidence weighs with them as a feather in the balance. The comparison of causes with effects, however valuable in physical science, is put aside as worthless and unreliable. The evidence of competent witnesses, however conclusive in a court of justice, counts for nothing. He who pauses before he pronounces, is condemned as a trifler. He who believes, is a dreamer or a fool.'

He spoke with bitterness, and, having said thus, relapsed for some minutes into silence. Presently he raised his head from his hands, and added, with an altered voice and manner,

'I, sir, paused, investigated, believed, and was not ashamed to state my convictions to the world. I, too, was branded as a visionary, held up to ridicule by my contemporaries, and hooted from that field of science in which I had laboured with honour during all the best years of my life. These things happened just three-and-twenty years ago. Since then, I have lived as you see me living now, and the world has forgotten me, as

I have forgotten the world. You have my history.'

'It is a very sad one,' I murmured, scarcely knowing what to answer.

'It is a very common one,' he replied. 'I have only suffered for the truth, as many a better and wiser man has suffered before me.'

He rose, as if desirous of ending the conversation, and went over to the window.

'It has ceased snowing,' he observed, as he dropped the curtain, and came back to the fireside.

'Ceased!' I exclaimed, starting eagerly to my feet. 'Oh, if it were only possible – but no! it is hopeless. Even if I could find my way across the moor, I could not walk twenty miles tonight.'

'Walk twenty miles tonight!' repeated my host. 'What are you thinking of?'

'Of my wife,' I replied, impatiently. 'Of my young wife, who does not know that I have lost my way, and who is at this moment breaking her heart with suspense and terror.'

'Where is she?'

'At Dwolding, twenty miles away.'

'At Dwolding,' he echoed, thoughtfully. 'Yes, the distance, it is true, is twenty miles; but – are you so very anxious to save the next six or eight hours?'

'So very, very anxious, that I would give ten guineas at this moment for a guide and a horse.'

'Your wish can be gratified at a less costly rate,' said he, smiling. 'The night mail from the north, which changes horses at Dwolding, passes within five miles of this spot, and will be due at a certain cross-road in about an hour and a quarter. If Jacob were to go with you across the moor, and put you into the old coach-road, you could find your way, I suppose, to where it joins the new one?'

'Easily – gladly.'

He smiled again, rang the bell, gave the old servant his directions, and, taking a bottle of whisky and a wineglass from the cupboard in which he kept his chemicals, said:

'The snow lies deep, and it will be difficult walking tonight on the moor. A glass of usquebaugh before you start?'

I would have declined the spirit, but he pressed it on me, and I drank it. It went down my throat like liquid flame, and almost took my breath away.

'It is strong,' he said; 'but it will help to keep out the cold. And now you have no moments to spare. Good night!'

I thanked him for his hospitality, and would have shaken hands, but that he had turned away before I could finish my sentence. In another minute I had traversed the hall, Jacob had locked the outer door behind me, and we were out on the wide white moor.

Although the wind had fallen, it was still bitterly cold. Not a star glimmered in the black vault overhead. Not a sound, save the rapid crunching of the snow beneath our feet, disturbed the heavy stillness of the night. Jacob, not too well pleased with his mission, shambled on before in sullen silence, his lantern in his hand, and his shadow at his feet. I followed, with my gun over my shoulder, as little inclined for conversation as himself. My thoughts were full of my late host. His voice yet rang in my ears. His eloquence yet held my imagination captive. I remember to this day, with surprise, how my over-excited brain retained whole sentences and parts of sentences, troops of brilliant images, and fragments of splendid reasoning, in the very words in which he had uttered them. Musing thus over what I had heard, and striving to recall a lost link here and there, I strode on at the heels of my guide, absorbed and unobservant. Presently – at the end, as it seemed to me, of only a few minutes – he came to a sudden halt, and said:

'Yon's your road. Keep the stone fence to your right hand, and you can't fail of the way.'

'This, then, is the old coach-road?'

'Ay, 'tis the old coach-road.'

'And how far do I go, before I reach the cross-roads?'

'Nigh upon three mile.'

I pulled out my purse, and he became more communicative.

'The road's a fair road enough,' said he, 'for foot passengers; but 'twas over steep and narrow for the northern traffic. You'll mind where the parapet's broken away, close again the sign-post. It's never been mended since the accident.'

'What accident?'

'Eh, the night mail pitched right over into the valley below – a gude fifty feet an' more – just at the worst bit o' road in the whole county.'

'Horrible! Were many lives lost?'

'All. Four were found dead, and t'other two died next morning.'

'How long is it since this happened?'

'Just nine year.'

'Near the sign-post, you say? I will bear it in mind. Good night.'

'Gude night, sir, and thankee.' Jacob pocketed his half-crown, made a faint pretence of touching his hat, and trudged back by the way he had come.

I watched the light of his lantern till it quite disappeared, and then turned to pursue my way alone. This was no longer matter of the slightest difficulty, for, despite the dead darkness overhead, the line of stone fence showed distinctly enough against the pale gleam of the snow. How silent it seemed now, with only my footsteps to listen to; how silent and how solitary! A strange disagreeable sense of loneliness stole over me. I walked faster. I hummed a fragment of a tune. I cast up enormous sums in my head, and accumulated them at compound interest. I did my best, in short, to forget the startling speculations to which I had but just been listening, and, to some extent, I succeeded.

Meanwhile the night air seemed to become colder and colder, and though I walked fast I found it impossible to keep myself warm. My feet were like ice. I lost sensation in my hands, and grasped my gun mechanically. I even breathed with difficulty, as though, instead of traversing a quiet north country highway, I were scaling the uppermost heights of some gigantic Alp. This last symptom became presently so distressing, that I was forced to stop for a few minutes, and lean against the stone fence. As I did so, I chanced to look back up the road, and there, to my infinite relief, I saw a distant point of light, like the gleam of an approaching lantern. I at first concluded that Jacob had retraced his steps and followed me; but even as the conjecture presented itself, a second light flashed into sight – a light evidently parallel with the first, and approaching at the same rate of motion. It needed no second thought to show me that these must be the carriage-lamps of some private vehicle, though it seemed strange that any private vehicle should take a road professedly disused and dangerous.

There could be no doubt, however, of the fact, for the lamps grew larger and brighter every moment, and I even fancied I could already see the dark outline of the carriage between them. It was coming up very fast, and quite noiselessly, the snow being nearly a foot deep under the wheels.

And now the body of the vehicle became distinctly visible behind the lamps. It looked strangely lofty. A sudden suspicion flashed upon me. Was it possible that I had passed the cross-roads in the dark without observing the sign-post, and could this be the very coach which I had come to meet?

No need to ask myself that question a second time, for here it came round the bend of the road, guard and driver, one outside passenger, and four steaming greys, all wrapped in a soft haze of light, through which the lamps blazed out, like a pair of fiery meteors. I jumped forward, waved my hat, and shouted. The mail came down at full speed, and passed me. For a moment I feared that I had not been seen or heard, but it was only for a moment. The coachman pulled up; the guard, muffled to the eyes in capes and comforters, and apparently sound asleep in the rumble, neither answered my hail nor made the slightest effort to dismount; the outside passenger did not even turn his head. I opened the door for myself, and looked in. There were but three travellers inside, so I stepped in, shut the door, slipped into the vacant corner, and congratulated myself on my good fortune. The atmosphere of the coach seemed, if possible, colder than that of the outer air, and was pervaded by a singularly damp and disagreeable smell. I looked round at my fellow-passengers. They were all three, men, and all silent. They did not seem to be asleep, but each leaned back in his corner of the vehicle, as if absorbed in his own reflections. I attempted to open a conversation.

'How intensely cold it is tonight,' I said, addressing my opposite neighbour.

He lifted his head, looked at me, but made no reply.

'The winter,' I added, 'seems to have begun in earnest.'

Although the corner in which he sat was so dim that I could distinguish none of his features very clearly, I saw that his eyes were still turned full upon me. And yet he answered never a word. At any other time I should have felt, and perhaps expressed, some annoyance, but at the moment I felt too ill to do either. The icy coldness of the night air had struck a chill to my very marrow, and the strange smell inside the coach was affecting me with an intolerable nausea. I shivered from head to foot, and, turning to my left-hand neighbour, asked if he had any objection to an open window? He neither spoke nor stirred. I repeated the question somewhat more loudly, but with the same result. Then I lost patience, and let the sash down. As I did so the leather strap broke in my hand, and I observed that the glass was covered with a thick coat of mildew, the accumulation, apparently, of years. My attention being thus drawn to the condition of the coach, I examined it more narrowly, and saw by the uncertain light of the outer lamps that it was in the last stage of dilapidation. Every part of it was not only out of repair, but in a condition of decay. The sashes splintered at a touch. The leather fittings were crusted over with mould, and literally rotting from the woodwork. The floor was almost breaking away beneath my feet. The whole machine, in short, was foul with damp, and had evidently been dragged from some outhouse in which it had been mouldering away for years, to do another day or two of duty on the road.

I turned to the third passenger, whom I had not yet addressed, and hazarded one more remark.

'This coach,' I said, 'is in a deplorable condition. The regular mail, I suppose, is under repair?'

He moved his head slowly, and looked me in the face, without speaking a word. I shall never forget that look while I live. I turned cold at heart under it. I turn cold at heart even now when I recall it. His eyes glowed with a fiery unnatural lustre. His face was livid as the face of a corpse. His bloodless lips were drawn back as if in the agony of death, and showed the gleaming teeth between.

The words that I was about to utter died upon my lips, and a strange horror – a dreadful horror – came upon me. My sight had by this time become used to the gloom of the coach, and I could see with tolerable distinctness. I turned to my opposite neighbour. He, too, was looking at me, with the same startling pallor in his face, and the same stony glitter in his eyes. I passed my hand across my brow. I turned to the passenger on the seat beside my own, and saw – oh Heaven! how shall I describe what I saw? I saw that he was no living man – that none of them were living men, like myself! A pale phosphorescent light – the light of putrefaction – played upon their awful faces; upon their hair, dank with the dews of the grave; upon their clothes, earth-stained and dropping to pieces; upon their hands, which were as the hands of corpses long buried. Only their eyes, their terrible eyes, were living; and those eyes were all turned menacingly upon me!

A shriek of terror, a wild unintelligible cry for help and mercy, burst from my lips as I flung myself against the door, and strove in vain to open it.

In that single instant, brief and vivid as a landscape beheld in the flash of summer lightning, I saw the moon shining down through a rift of stormy cloud – the ghastly sign-post rearing its warning finger by the wayside – the broken parapet – the plunging horses – the black gulf below. Then, the coach reeled like a ship at sea. Then, came a mighty crash – a sense of crushing pain – and then, darkness.

It seemed as if years had gone by when I awoke one morning from a deep sleep, and found my wife watching by my bedside. I will pass over the scene that ensued, and give you, in half a dozen words, the tale she told me with tears of thanksgiving. I had fallen over a precipice, close against the junction of the old coach-road and the new, and had only been saved from certain death by lighting upon a deep snowdrift that had accumulated at the foot of the rock beneath. In this snowdrift I was discovered at daybreak, by a couple of shepherds, who carried me to the nearest shelter, and brought a surgeon to my aid. The surgeon found me in a state of raving delirium, with a broken arm and a compound fracture of the skull. The letters in my pocket-book showed my name and address; my wife was summoned to nurse me; and, thanks to youth and a fine constitution, I came out of danger at last. The place of my fall, I need scarcely say, was precisely that at which a frightful accident had happened to the north mail nine years before.

I never told my wife the fearful events which I have just related to you. I told the surgeon who attended me; but he treated the whole adventure as a mere dream born of the fever in my brain. We discussed the question over and over again, until we found that we could discuss it with temper no longer, and then we dropped it. Others may form what conclusions they please – I *know* that twenty years ago I was the fourth inside passenger in that Phantom Coach.

The Devil's Wager

William Makepeace Thackeray

It was the hour of the night when there be none stirring save churchyard ghosts – when all doors are closed except the gates of graves, and all eyes shut but the eyes of wicked men.

When there is no sound on the earth except the ticking of the grasshopper, or the croaking of obscene frogs in the pool.

And no light except that of the blinking stars, and the wicked and devilish wills-o'-the-wisp, as they gambol among the marshes, and lead good men astray.

When there is nothing moving in heaven except the owl, as he flappeth along lazily; or the magician, as he rideth on his infernal broomstick, whistling through the air like the arrows of a Yorkshire archer.

It was at this hour (namely, at twelve o'clock of the night) that two things went winging through the black clouds, and holding converse with each other.

Now the first was Mercurius, the messenger, not of gods (as the heathens feigned), but of demons; and the second, with whom he held company, was the soul of Sir Roger de Rollo, the brave knight. Sir Roger was Count of Chauchigny, in Champagne; Seigneur of Santerre, Villacerf and *autre lieux*. But the great die as well as the humble; and nothing remained of brave Roger now, but his coffin and his deathless soul.

And Mercurius, in order to keep fast the soul, his companion, had bound him round the neck with his tail; which, when the soul was stubborn, he would draw so tight as to strangle him well-nigh, sticking into him the barbed point thereof; whereat the poor soul, Sir Rollo, would groan and roar lustily.

Now they two had come together from the gates of purgatory, being bound to these regions of fire and flame where poor sinners fry and roast *in saecula saeculorum.*

'It is hard,' said the poor Sir Rollo, as they went gliding through the clouds, 'that I should thus be condemned for ever, and all for want of a single ave.'

'How, Sir Soul?' said the demon. 'You were on earth so wicked, that not one, or a million of aves, could suffice to keep from hell-flame a creature like thee; but cheer up and be merry; thou wilt be but a subject of our lord the Devil, as am I; and, perhaps, thou wilt be advanced to posts of honour, as am I also': and to show his authority, he lashed with his tail the ribs of the wretched Rollo.

'Nevertheless, sinner as I am, one more ave would have saved me; for my sister, who was Abbess of St Mary of Chauchigny, did so prevail, by her prayer and good works, for my lost and wretched soul, that every day I felt the pains of purgatory decrease; the pitchforks which, on my first entry, had never ceased to vex and torment my poor carcass, were now not applied above once a week; the roasting had ceased, the boiling had discontinued; only a certain warmth was kept up, to remind me of my situation.'

'A gentle stew,' said the demon.

'Yea, truly, I was but in a stew, and all from the effects of the prayers of my blessed sister. But yesterday, he who watched me in purgatory told me, that yet another prayer from my sister, and my bonds should be unloosed, and I, who am now a devil, should have been a blessed angel.'

'And the other ave?' said the demon.

'She died, sir - my sister died - death choked her in the middle of the prayer.' And hereat the wretched spirit began to weep and whine piteously; his salt tears falling over his beard, and scalding the tail of Mercurius the devil.

It is, in truth, a hard case,' said the demon; 'but I know of no remedy save patience, and for that you will have an excellent opportunity in your lodgings below.'

'But I have relations,' said the Earl; 'my kinsman Randal, who has inherited my lands, will he not say a prayer for his uncle?'

'Thou didst hate and oppress him when living.'

'It is true; but an ave is not much; his sister, my niece, Matilda – '

'You shut her in a convent, and hanged her lover.'

'Had I not reason? Besides, has she not others?'
'A dozen, without a doubt.'
'And my brother, the prior?'

'A liege subject of my lord the Devil: he never opens his mouth, except to utter an oath, or to swallow a cup of wine.'

'And yet, if but one of these would but say an ave for me, I should be saved.'

'Aves with them are *rarae* aves,' replied Mercurius, wagging his tail right waggishly; 'and, what is more, I will lay thee any wager that no one of these will say a prayer to save thee.'

'I would wager willingly,' responded he of Chauchigny; 'but what has a poor soul like me to stake?'

'Every evening, after the day's roasting, my lord Satan giveth a cup of cold water to his servants; I will bet thee thy water for a year, that none of the three will pray for thee.'

'Done!' said Rollo.

'Done!' said the demon; 'and here, if I mistake not, is thy castle of Chauchigny.'

Indeed, it was true. The soul, on looking down, perceived the tall towers, the courts, the stables, and the fair gardens of the castle. Although it was past midnight, there was a blaze of light in the banqueting-hall, and a lamp burning in the open window of the Lady Matilda.

'With whom shall we begin?' said the demon: 'with the baron or the lady?'

'With the lady, if you will.'

'Be it so; her window is open, let us enter.'

So they descended, and entered silently into Matilda's chamber.

The young lady's eyes were fixed so intently on a little clock, that it was no wonder that she did not perceive the entrance of her two visitors. Her fair cheek rested in her white arm, and her white arm on the cushion of a great chair in which she sat, pleasantly supported by sweet thoughts and swansdown; a lute was at her side, and a book of prayers lay under the table (for piety is always modest). Like the amorous Alexander, she sighed and looked (at the clock) – and sighed for ten minutes or more, when she softly breathed the word 'Edward!'

At this the soul of the Baron was wroth. 'The jade is at her old pranks,' said he to the devil; and then addressing Matilda: 'I pray thee, sweet niece, turn thy thoughts for a moment from that villainous page, Edward, and give them to thine affectionate uncle.'

When she heard the voice, and saw the awful apparition of her uncle (for a year's sojourn in purgatory had not increased the comeliness of his appearance), she started, screeched, and of course fainted.

But the devil Mercurius soon restored her to herself. 'What's o'clock?' said she, as soon as she had recovered from her fit: 'is he come?'

'Not thy lover, Maude, but thine uncle – that is, his soul. For the love of heaven, listen to me: I have been frying in purgatory for a year past, and should have been in heaven but for the want of a single ave.'

'I will say it for thee tomorrow, uncle.'

'Tonight, or never.'

'Well, tonight be it': and she requested the devil Mercurius to give her the prayer-book from under the table; but he had no sooner touched the holy book than he dropped it with a shriek and a yell. It was hotter, he said, than his master Sir Lucifer's own particular pitchfork. And the lady was forced to begin her ave without the aid of her missal.

At the commencement of her devotions the demon retired, and carried with him the anxious soul of poor Sir Roger de Rollo.

The lady knelt down – she sighed deeply; she looked again at the clock, and began –

'*Ave Maria.*'

When a lute was heard under the window, and a sweet voice singing –

'Hark!' said Matilda.

> Now the toils of day are over,
> And the sun hath sunk to rest,
> Seeking, like a fiery lover,
> The bosom of the blushing west –
>
> The faithful night keeps watch and ward,
> Raising the moon, her silver shield,
> And summoning the stars to guard
> The slumbers of my fair Mathilde!

'For mercy's sake!' said Sir Rollo, 'the ave first, and next the song.'

So Matilda again dutifully betook her to her devotions, and began –

'*Ave Maria gratia plena!*' but the music began again, and the prayer ceased of course.

The faithful night! Now all things lie
Hid by her mantle dark and dim,
In pious hope I hither hie,
And humbly chant mine ev'ning hymn.

Thou art my prayer, my saint, my shrine!
(For never holy pilgrim kneel'd,
Or wept at feet more pure than mine),
My virgin love, my sweet Mathilde!

'Virgin love!' said the Baron. 'Upon my soul, this is too bad!' and he thought of the lady's lover whom he had caused to be hanged.

But she only thought of him who stood singing at her window.

'Niece Matilda!' cried Sir Roger, agonizedly, 'wilt thou listen to the lies of an impudent page, whilst thine uncle is waiting but a dozen words to make him happy?'

At this Matilda grew angry: 'Edward is neither impudent nor a liar, Sir Uncle, and I will listen to the end of the song.'

'Come away,' said Mercurius; 'he hath yet got wield, field, sealed, congealed, and a dozen other rhymes beside; and after the song will come the supper.'

So the poor soul was obliged to go; while the lady listened, and the page sung away till morning.

'My virtues have been my ruin,' said poor Sir Rollo, as he and Mercurius slunk silently out of the window. 'Had I hanged that knave Edward, as I did the page his predecessor, my niece would have sung mine ave, and I should have been by this time an angel in heaven.'

'He is reserved for wiser purposes,' responded the devil: 'he will assassinate your successor, the lady Mathilde's brother; and, in consequence, will be hanged. In the love of the lady he will be succeeded by a gardener, who will be replaced by a monk, who will give way to an ostler, who will be deposed by a Jew pedlar, who shall, finally, yield to a noble earl, the future husband of the fair Mathilde. So that, you see, instead of having one poor soul a-frying, we may now look forward to a goodly harvest for our lord the Devil.'

The soul of the Baron began to think that his companion knew too much for one who would make fair bets; but there was no help for it; he would not, and he could not cry off: and he prayed inwardly that the brother might be found more pious than the sister.

But there seemed little chance of this. As they crossed the court, lackeys, with smoking dishes and full jugs, passed and repassed continually, although it was long past midnight. On entering the hall, they found Sir Randal at the head of a vast table, surrounded by a fiercer and more motley collection of individuals than had congregated there even in the time of Sir Rollo. The lord of the castle had signified that 'it was his royal pleasure to be drunk', and the gentlemen of his train had obsequiously followed their master. Mercurius was delighted with the scene, and relaxed his usually rigid countenance into a bland and benevolent smile, which became him wonderfully.

The entrance of Sir Roger, who had been dead about a year, and a person with hoofs, horns and a tail, rather disturbed the hilarity of the company. Sir Randal dropped his cup of wine; and Father Peter, the confessor, incontinently paused in the midst of a profane song, with which he was amusing the society.

'Holy Mother!' cried he, 'it is Sir Roger.'

'Alive!' screamed Sir Randal.

'No, my lord,' Mercurius said; 'Sir Roger is dead, but cometh on a matter of business; and I have the honour to act as his counsellor and attendant.'

'Nephew,' said Sir Roger, 'the demon saith justly; I am come on a trifling affair, in which thy service is essential.'

'I will do anything, uncle, in my power.'

'Thou canst give me life, if thou wilt?' But Sir Randal looked very blank at this proposition. 'I mean life spiritual, Randal,' said Sir Roger; and thereupon he explained to him the nature of the wager.

Whilst he was telling his story, his companion Mercurius was playing all sorts of antics in the hall; and, by his wit and fun, became so popular with this godless crew, that they lost all the fear which his first appearance had given them. The friar was wonderfully taken with him, and used his utmost eloquence and endeavours to convert the devil; the knights stopped drinking to listen to the argument; the men-at-arms forbore brawling; and the wicked little pages crowded round the two strange disputants, to hear their edifying discourse. The ghostly man, however, had little chance in the controversy, and certainly little learning to carry it on. Sir Randal interrupted him.

'Father Peter,' said he, 'our kinsman is condemned for ever, for want of a single ave: wilt thou say it for him?'

'Willingly, my lord,' said the monk, 'with my book'; and accordingly he produced his missal to read, without which aid it appeared that the holy father could not manage the desired prayer. But the crafty Mercurius had, by his devilish art, inserted a song in the place of the ave, so that Father Peter, instead of chanting a hymn, sang the following irreverent ditty:

> Some love the matin-chimes, which tell
> The hour of prayer to sinner:
> But better far's the midday bell,
> Which speaks the hour of dinner;
> For when I see a smoking fish,
> Or capon drowned in gravy,
> Or noble haunch on silver dish,
> Full glad I sing mine ave.
>
> My pulpit is an ale-house bench,
> Whereon I sit so jolly;
> A smiling rosy country wench
> My saint and patron holy.
> I kiss her cheek so red and sleek,
> I press her ringlets wavy.
> And in her willing ear I speak
> A most religious ave.
>
> And if I'm blind, yet heaven is kind,
> And holy saints forgiving;
> For sure he leads a right good life
> Who thus admires good living.
> Above they say, our flesh is air,
> Our blood celestial ichor:
> Oh, grant! mid all the changes there,
> They may not change our liquor!

And with this pious wish the holy confessor tumbled under the table in an agony of devout drunkenness; whilst the knights, the men-at-arms, and the wicked little pages, rang out the last verse with a most melodious and emphatic glee.

'I am sorry, fair uncle,' hiccuped Sir Randal, 'that, in the matter of the ave, we could not oblige thee in a more orthodox manner; but the holy father has failed, and there is not another man in the hall who hath an idea of a prayer.'

'It is my own fault,' said Sir Rollo; 'for I hanged the last confessor.' And he wished his nephew a surly good-night, as he prepared to quit the room.

'*Au revoir*, gentlemen,' said the devil Mercurius; and once more fixed his tail round the neck of his disappointed companion.

The spirit of poor Rollo was sadly cast down; the devil, on the contrary, was in high good humour. He wagged his tail with the most satisfied air in the world, and cut a hundred jokes at the expense of his poor associate. On they sped, cleaving swiftly through the cold night winds, frightening the birds that were roosting in the woods, and the owls that were watching in the towers.

In the twinkling of an eye, as it is known, devils can fly hundreds of miles: so that almost the same beat of the clock which left those two in Champagne found them hovering over Paris. They dropped into the court of the Lazarist Convent, and winded their way, through passage and cloister, until they reached the door of the prior's cell.

Now the prior, Rollo's brother, was a wicked and malignant sorcerer; his time was spent in conjuring devils and doing wicked deeds, instead of fasting, scourging, and singing holy psalms: this Mercurius knew; and he, therefore, was fully at ease as to the final result of his wager with poor Sir Roger.

'You seem to be well acquainted with the road,' said the knight.

'I have reason,' answered Mercurius, 'having, for a long period, had the acquaintance of his reverence, your brother; but you have little chance with him.'

'And why?' said Sir Rollo.

'He is under a bond to my master, never to say a prayer, or else his soul and his body are forfeited at once.'

'Why, thou false and traitorous devil!' said the enraged knight;

'and thou knewest this when we made our wager?'

'Undoubtedly: do you suppose I would have done so had there been any chance of losing?'

And with this they arrived at Father Ignatius's door.

'Thy cursed presence threw a spell on my niece, and stopped the tongue of my nephew's chaplain; I do believe that had I seen either of them alone, my wager had been won.'

'Certainly; therefore, I took good care to go with thee; however, thou mayest see the prior alone, if thou wilt; and lo! his door is open. I will stand without for five minutes when it will be time to commence our journey.'

It was the poor Baron's last chance: and he entered his brother's room more for the five minutes' respite than from any hope of success.

Father Ignatius, the prior, was absorbed in magic calculations: he stood in the middle of a circle of skulls, with no garment except his long white beard, which reached to his knees; he was waving a silver rod, and muttering imprecations in some horrible tongue.

But Sir Rollo came forward and interrupted his incantation. 'I am,' said he, 'the shade of thy brother Roger de Rollo; and have come, from pure brotherly love, to warn thee of thy fate.'

'Whence camest thou?'

'From the abode of the blessed in Paradise,' replied Sir Roger, who was inspired with a sudden thought; 'it was but five minutes ago that the Patron Saint of thy church told me of thy danger, and of thy wicked compact with the fiend. "Go," said he, "to thy miserable brother, and tell him there is but one way by which he may escape from paying the awful forfeit of his bond."'

'And how may that be?' said the prior; 'the false fiend hath deceived me; I have given him my soul, but have received no worldly benefit in return. Brother! dear brother! how may I escape?'

'I will tell thee. As soon as I heard the voice of blessed St Mary Lazarus' (the worthy Earl had, at a pinch, coined the name of a saint), 'I left the clouds, where, with other angels, I was seated, and sped hither to save thee. "Thy brother," said the Saint, "hath but one day more to live, when he will become for all eternity the subject of Satan; if he would escape, he must boldly break his bond, by saying an ave."'

'It is the express condition of the agreement,' said the unhappy monk, 'I must say no prayer, or that instant I become Satan's, body and soul.'

'It is the express condition of the Saint,' answered Roger, fiercely; 'pray, brother, pray, or thou art lost for ever.'

So the foolish monk knelt down, and devoutly sung out an ave. 'Amen!' said Sir Roger, devoutly.

'Amen!' said Mercurius, as, suddenly, coming behind, he seized Ignatius by his long beard, and flew up with him to the top of the church-steeple.

The monk roared, and screamed, and swore against his brother; but it was of no avail: Sir Roger smiled kindly on him, and said, 'Do not fret, brother; it must have come to this in a year or two.'

And he flew alongside of Mercurius to the steeple-top; *but this time the devil had not his tail round his neck.* 'I will let thee off thy bet,' said he to the demon; for he could afford, now, to be generous.

'I believe, my lord,' said the demon, politely, 'that our ways separate here.' Sir Roger sailed gaily upwards: while Mercurius having bound the miserable monk faster than ever, he sunk downwards to earth, and perhaps lower. Ignatius was heard roaring and screaming as the devil dashed him against the iron spikes and buttresses of the church.

Teigue of the Lee

T. Crofton Croker

"I can't stop in the house – I won't stop in it for all the money that is buried in the old castle of Carrigrohan. If ever there was such a thing in the world – to be abused to my face night and day, and nobody to the fore doing it! and then, if I'm angry, to be laughed at with a great roaring ho, ho, ho! I won't stay in the house after to-night, if there was not another place in the country to put my head under." This angry soliloquy was pronounced in the hall of the old manor-house of Carrigrohan by John Sheehan. John was a new servant; he had been only three days in the house, which had the character of being haunted, and in that short space of time he had been abused and laughed at by a voice which sounded as if a man spoke with his head in a cask; nor could he discover who was the speaker, or from whence the voice came. "I'll not stop here," said John, "and that ends the matter."

"Ho, Ho, ho! be quiet, John Sheehan, or else worse will happen to you."

John instantly ran to the hall window, as the words were evidently spoken by a person immediately outside, but no one was visible. He had scarcely placed his face at the pane of glass when he heard another loud "Ho, ho, ho!" as if behind him in the hall; as quick as lightning he turned his head, but no living thing was to be seen.

"Ho, ho, ho, John!" shouted a voice that appeared to come from the lawn before the house, "do you think you'll see Teigue? – Oh, never! as long as you live! so leave alone looking after him, and mind your business; there's plenty of company to dinner from Cork to be here to-day, and 'tis time you had the cloth laid."

"Lord bless us! there's more of it! – I'll never stay another day here," repeated John.

"Hold your tongue, and stay where you are quietly, and play no tricks on Mr Pratt, as you did on Mr Jervois about the spoons."

John Sheehan was confounded by this address from his invisible persecutor, but nevertheless he mustered courage enough to say – "Who are you? – come here, and let me see you, if you are a man"; but he received in reply only a laugh of unearthly derision, which was followed by a "Good-bye – I'll watch you at dinner, John!"

"Lord between us and harm! this beats all – I'll watch you at dinner! – maybe you will – 'tis the broad daylight, so 'tis no ghost; but this is a terrible place, and this is the last day I'll stay in it. How does he know about the spoons? – if he tells it, I'm a ruined man! – there was no living soul could tell it to him but Tim Barrett, and he's far enough off in the wilds of Botany Bay now, so how could he know it – I can't tell for the world! But what's that I see there at the corner of the wall! – 'tis not a man! – oh, what a fool I am! 'tis only the old stump of a tree! – But this is a shocking place – I'll never stop in it, for I'll leave the house to-morrow; the very look of it is enough to frighten any one."

The mansion had certainly an air of desolation; it was situated in a lawn which had nothing to break its uniform level save a few tufts of narcissuses and a couple of old trees. The house stood at a short distance from the road, it was upwards of a century old, and Time was doing his work upon it; its walls were weather-stained in all colours, its roof showed various white patches, it had no look of comfort; all was dim and dingy without, and within there was an air of gloom, of departed and departing greatness, which harmonised well with the exterior. It required all the exuberance of youth and of gaiety to remove the impression, almost amounting to awe, with which you trod the huge square hall, paced along the gallery which surrounded the hall, or explored the long rambling passages below stairs. The ballroom, as the large drawing room was called, and several other apartments, were in a state of decay; the walls were stained with damp; and I remember well the sensation of awe which I felt creeping over me when, boy as I was, and full of boyish life, and wild and ardent spirits, I descended to the vaults; all without and within me became chilled beneath their dampness and gloom – their extent, too, terrified me; nor could the merriment of my two schoolfellows, whose father, a respectable clergyman, rented the dwelling for a time, dispel the feelings of a romantic imagination until I once again ascended to the upper regions.

John had pretty well recovered himself as the dinner hour

approached, and the several guests arrived. They were all seated at table, and had begun to enjoy the excellent repast, when a voice was heard from the lawn:

"Ho, ho, ho, Mr Pratt, won't you give poor Teigue some dinner? ho, ho, a fine company you have there, and plenty of everything that's good; sure you won't forget poor Teigue?"

John dropped the glass he had in his hand.

"Who is that?" said Mr Pratt's brother, an officer of the artillery.

"That is Teigue," said Mr Pratt laughing, "whom you must often have heard me mention."

"And pray, Mr Pratt," enquired another gentleman, "who is Teigue?"

"That," he replied, "is more than I can tell. No one has ever been able to catch even a glimpse of him. I have been on the watch for a whole evening with three of my sons, yet, although his voice sometimes sounded almost in my ear, I could not see him. I fancied, indeed, that I saw a man in a white frieze jacket pass into the door from the garden to the lawn, but it could be only fancy, for I found the door locked, while the fellow, whoever he is, was laughing at our trouble. He visits us occasionally, and sometimes a long interval passes between his visits, as in the present case; it is now nearly two years since we heard that hollow voice outside the window. He has never done any injury that we know of, and once when he broke a plate, he brought one back exactly like it."

"It is very extraordinary," said several of the company.

"But," remarked a gentleman to young Mr Pratt, "your father said he broke a plate; how did he get it without your seeing him?"

"When he asks for some dinner, we put it outside the window and go away; whilst we watch he will not take it, but no sooner have we withdrawn than it is gone."

"How does he know that you are watching?"

"That's more than I can tell, but he either knows or suspects. One day my brothers Robert and James with myself were in our back parlour, which has a window into the garden, when he came outside and said, 'Ho, ho, ho! master James, and Robert, and Henry, give poor Teigue a glass of whiskey.' James went out of the room, filled a glass with whiskey, vinegar, and salt, and brought it to him. 'Here, Teigue,' said he 'come for it now.' 'Well, put it down, then, on the step outside the window.' This was done, and we stood looking at it. 'There, now, go away,' he shouted. We retired, but still watched it. 'Ho, ho! you are watching Teigue; go out of the room, now, or I won't take it.' We went outside the door and returned, the glass was gone, and a moment after we heard him roaring and cursing frightfully. He took away the glass, but the next day the glass was on the stone step under the window, and there were crumbs of bread in the inside, as if he had put it in his pocket; from that time he was not heard till to-day."

"Oh," said the colonel, "I'll get a sight of him! you are not used to these things; an old soldier has the best chance; and as I shall finish my dinner with this wing, I'll be ready for him when he speaks next. – Mr Bell, will you take a glass of wine with me?"

"Ho, ho! Mr Bell," shouted Teigue. "Ho, ho! Mr Bell, you were a Quaker long ago. Ho, ho! Mr Bell, you're a pretty boy; – a pretty Quaker you were; and now you're no Quaker, nor anything else; ho, ho! Mr Bell. And there's Mr Parkes: to be sure, Mr Parkes looks mighty fine today, with his powdered head, and his grand silk stockings, and his brand new rakish-red waistcoat. – And there's Mr Cole – did you ever see such a fellow? A pretty company you've brought together, Mr Pratt: kiln-dried Quakers, butter-buying buckeens from Mallow-lane, and a drinking exciseman from the Coal-quay, to meet the great thundering artillery-general that is come out of the Indies, and is the biggest dust of them all."

"You scoundrel!" exclaimed the Colonel. "I'll make you show yourself"; and, snatching up his sword from a corner of the room, he sprang out of the window upon the lawn. In a moment a shout of laughter, so hollow, so unlike any human sound, made him stop, as well as Mr Bell, who with a huge oak stick was close at the colonel's heels; others of the party followed on the lawn, and the remainder rose and went to the windows. "Come on, colonel," said Mr Bell; "let us catch this imprudent rascal."

"Ho, ho! Mr Bell, here I am – here's Teigue – why don't you catch him? – Ho, ho, Colonel Pratt, what a pretty soldier you are to draw your sword upon poor Teigue, that never did any body harm."

"Let us see your face, you scoundrel," said the colonel.

"Ho, ho, ho – look at me – look at me: do you see the wind, Colonel Pratt? – you'll see Teigue as soon; so go in and finish your dinner."

"If you're upon the earth I'll find you, you villain!" said the colonel, whilst the same unearthly shout of derision seemed to come from behind an angle of the building. "He's round that corner," said Mr Bell – "run, run."

They followed the sound, which was continued at intervals along the garden wall, but could discover no human being; at last both stopped to draw breath, and in an instant, almost at their ears, sounded the shout.

"Ho, ho, ho! Colonel Pratt, do you see Teigue now? – do you hear him: – Ho, ho, ho! you're a fine colonel to follow the wind."

"Not that way, Mr Bell – not that way; come here," said the colonel.

"Ho, ho, ho! what a fool you are; do you think Teigue is going to show himself to you in the field, there: But, colonel, follow me if you can: – you a soldier! ho, ho, ho!" The colonel was enraged – he followed the voice over hedge and ditch, alternately laughed at and taunted by the unseen object of his pursuit – (Mr Bell, who was heavy, was soon thrown out), until at length, after being led a weary chase, he found himself at the top of the cliff, over that part of the river Lee which, from its great depth, and the blackness of its water, has received the name of Hellhole. Here, on the edge of the cliff, stood the colonel, out of breath and mopping his forehead with his handkerchief, while the voice, which seemed close at his feet, exclaimed – "Now, Colonel Pratt – now, if you're a soldier, here's a leap for you; – now look at Teigue – why don't you look at him – Ho, ho, ho! Come along: you're warm, I'm sure, Colonel Pratt, so come in and cool yourself; Teigue is going to have a swim!" The voice seemed as descending amongst the trailing ivy and brushwood which clothes this picturesque cliff nearly from top to bottom, yet it was impossible that any human being could have found footing. "Now, colonel, have you courage to take the leap? – Ho, ho, ho! what a pretty soldier you are. Good-bye – I'll see you again in ten minutes above, at the house – look at your watch colonel: there's a dive for you"; and a heavy plunge into the water was heard. The colonel stood still, but no sound followed, and he walked slowly back to the house, not quite half a mile from the Crag.

"Well, did you see Teigue?" said his brother, whilst his nephews, scarcely able to smother their laughter, stood by. "Give me some wine," said the colonel. "I never was led such a dance in my life: the fellow carried me all round and round, till he brought me to the edge of the cliff, and then down he went into Hell-hole, telling me he'd be here in ten minutes: 'tis more than that now, but he's not come."

"Ho, ho ho! colonel, isn't he here? – Teigue never told a lie in his life: but, Mr Pratt, give me a drink and my dinner, and then good night to you all, for I'm tired; and that's the colonel's doing." A plate of food was ordered: it was placed by John, with fear and trembling, on the lawn under the window. Everyone kept on the watch, and the plate remained undisturbed for some time.

"Ah, Mr Pratt, will you starve poor Teigue? Make everyone go away from the windows, and Master Henry out of the tree, and Master Richard off the garden wall."

The eyes of the company were turned to the tree and the garden wall; the two boys' attention was occupied in getting down: the visitors were looking at them; and "Ho, ho ho! – good luck to you, Mr Pratt! – 'tis a good dinner, and there's the plate, ladies and gentlemen – goodbye to you, colonel – goodbye, Mr Bell! goodbye to you all!" – brought their attention back, when they saw the empty plate lying on the grass; and Teigue's voice was heard no more for that evening. Many visits were afterwards paid by Teigue; but never was he seen, nor was any discovery ever made of his person or character.

The Captain of the Pole-star

Sir Arthur Conan Doyle

[Being an extract from the journal of John McAlister Ray, student of medicine, kept by him during the six months' voyage in the Arctic Seas, of the steam-whaler *Pole-star*, of Dundee, Captain Nicholas Craigie.]

September 11th. Lat. 81° 40' N.; Long. 2° E. – Still lying-to amid enormous ice fields. The one which stretches away to the north of us, and to which our ice-anchor is attached, cannot be smaller than an English county. To the right and left unbroken sheets extend to the horizon. This morning the mate reported that there were signs of pack ice to the southward. Should this form of sufficient thickness to bar our return, we shall be in a position of danger, as the food, I hear, is already running somewhat short. It is late in the season and the nights are beginning to reappear. This morning I saw a star twinkling just over the fore-yard – the first since the beginning of May. There is considerable discontent among the crew, many of whom are anxious to get back home to be in time for the herring season, when labour always commands a high price upon the Scotch coast. As yet their displeasure is only signified by sullen countenances and black looks, but I heard from the second mate this afternoon that they contemplated sending a deputation to the Captain to explain their grievance. I much doubt how he will receive it, as he is a man of fierce temper, and very sensitive about anything approaching to an infringement of his rights. I shall venture after dinner to say a few words to him upon the subject. I have always found that he will tolerate from me what he would resent from any other member of the crew. Amsterdam Island, at the north-west corner of Spitzbergen, is visible upon our starboard quarter – a rugged line of volcanic rocks, intersected by white seams, which represent glaciers. It is curious to think that at the present moment there is probably no human being nearer to us than the Danish settlements in the south of Greenland – a good nine hundred miles as the crow flies. A captain takes a great responsibility upon himself when he risks his vessel under such circumstances. No whaler has ever remained in these latitudes till so advanced a period of the year.

9 P.M. I have spoken to Captain Craigie, and though the result has been hardly satisfactory, I am bound to say that he listened to what I had to say very quietly and even deferentially. When I had finished he put on that air of iron determination which I have frequently observed upon his face, and paced rapidly backwards and forwards across the narrow cabin for some minutes. At first I feared that I had seriously offended him, but he dispelled the idea by sitting down again, and putting his hand upon my arm with a gesture which almost amounted to a caress. There was a depth of tenderness too in his wild dark eyes which surprised me considerably. 'Look here, Doctor', he said, 'I'm sorry I ever took you – I am indeed – and I would give fifty pounds this minute to see you standing safe upon the Dundee quay. It's hit or miss with me this time. There are fish to the north of us. How dare you shake your head, sir, when I tell you I saw them blowing from the masthead!' – this in a sudden burst of fury, though I was not conscious of having shown any signs of doubt. 'Two and twenty fish in as many minutes as I am a living man, and not one under ten foot.* Now, Doctor, do you think I can leave the country when there is only one infernal strip of ice between me and my fortune. If it came on to blow from the north tomorrow we could fill the ship and be away before the frost could catch us. If it came on to blow from the south – well, I suppose, the men are paid for risking their lives, and as for myself it matters but little to me, for I have more to bind me to the other world than to this one. I confess that I am sorry for *you*, though. I wish I had old Angus Tait who was with me last voyage, for he was a man that would never be missed, and you – you said once that you were engaged, did you not?'

'Yes,' I answered, snapping the spring of the locket which hung from my watch-chain, and holding up the little vignette of Flora.

'Blast you!' he yelled, springing out of his seat, with his very beard

---

*A whale is measured among whalers not by the length of its body, but by the length of its whalebone.

bristling with passion. 'What is your happiness to me? What have I to do with her that you must dangle her photograph before my eyes?' I almost thought that he was about to strike me in the frenzy of his rage, but with another imprecation he dashed open the door of the cabin and rushed out upon deck, leaving me considerably astonished at his extraordinary violence. It is the first time that he has ever shown me anything but courtesy and kindness. I can hear him pacing excitedly up and down overhead as I write these lines.

I should like to give a sketch of the character of this man, but it seems presumptuous to attempt such a thing upon paper, when the idea in my own mind is at best a vague and uncertain once. Several times I have thought that I grasped the clue which might explain it, but only to be disappointed by his presenting himself in some new light which would upset all my conclusions. It may be that no human eye but my own shall ever rest upon these lines, yet as a psychological study I shall attempt to leave some record of Captain Nicholas Craigie.

A man's outer case generally gives some indication of the soul within. The Captain is tall and well formed, with dark, handsome face, and a curious way of twitching his limbs, which may arise from nervousness, or be simply an outcome of his excessive energy. His jaw and whole cast of countenance is manly and resolute, but the eyes are the distinctive feature of his face. They are of the very darkest hazel, bright and eager, with a singular mixture of recklessness in their expression, and of something else which I have sometimes thought was more allied with horror than any other emotion. Generally the former predominated, but on occasions, and more particularly when he was thoughtfully inclined, the look of fear would spread and deepen until it imparted a new character to his whole countenance. It is at these times that he is most subject to tempestuous fits of anger, and he seems to be aware of it, for I have known him lock himself up so that no one might approach him until his dark hour was passed. He sleeps badly, and I have heard him shouting during the night, but his room is some little distance from mine, and I could never distinguish the words which he said.

This is one phase of his character, and the most disagreeable one. It is only through my close association with him, thrown together as we are day after day, that I have observed it. Otherwise he is an agreeable companion, well read and entertaining, and as gallant a seaman as ever trod a deck. I shall not easily forget the way in which he handled the ship when we were caught by a gale among the loose ice at the beginning of April. I have never seen him so cheerful, and even hilarious, as he was that night as he paced backwards and forwards upon the bridge amid the flashing of the lightning and the howling of the wind. He has told me several times that the thought of death was a pleasant one to him, which is a sad thing for a young man to say; he cannot be much more than thirty, though his hair and moustache are already slightly grizzled. Some great sorrow must have overtaken him and blighted his whole life. Perhaps I should be the same if I lost my Flora – God knows! I think if it were not for her that I should care very little whether the wind blew from the north or the south tomorrow. There, I hear him come down the companion and he has locked himself up in his room, which shows that he is still in an amiable mood. And so to bed, as old Pepys would say, for the candle is burning down (we have to use them now since the nights are closing in), and the steward has turned in, so there are no hopes of another one.

September 12th. Calm clear day, and still lying in the same position What wind there is comes from the south-east, but it is very slight. Captain is in a better humour, and apologized to me at breakfast for his rudeness. He still looks somewhat *distrait*, however, and retains that wild look in his eyes which in a Highlander would mean that he was 'fey' – at least so our relief engineer remarked to me, and he has some reputation among the Celtic portion of our crew as a seer and expounder of omens.

It is strange that superstition should have obtained such mastery over this hard-headed and practical race. I could not have believed to what an extent it is carried had I not observed it for myself. We have had a perfect epidemic of it this voyage, until I have felt inclined to serve out rations of sedatives and nerve tonics with the Saturday allowance of grog. The first symptom of it was that shortly after leaving Shetland the men at the wheel used to complain that they heard plaintive cries and screams in the wake of the ship, as if something were following it and were unable to overtake it. This fiction has been kept up during the whole voyage, and on dark nights at the beginning of the seal-fishing it was only with great difficulty that men could be induced to do their spell. No doubt what they heard was either the creaking of the rudder-chains, or the cry of some passing sea-bird. I have been fetched out of bed several times to listen to it, but I need hardly say that I was never able to distinguish anything unnatural. The men, however, are so absurdly positive upon the subject that it is hopeless to argue with them. I mentioned the matter to the Captain once, but to my surprise he took it very gravely, and indeed appeared to be considerably disturbed by what I told him. I should have thought that he at least would have been above such vulgar delusions.

All this disquisition upon superstition leads me up to the fact that Mr Manson, our second mate, saw a ghost last night – or, at least, says that he did, which of course is the same thing. It is quite refreshing to have some new topic of conversation after the eternal routine of bears and whales which has served us for so many months. Manson swears the ship is haunted, and that he would not stay in her a day if he had any other place to go to. Indeed the fellow is honestly frightened, and I had to give him some chloral and bromide of potassium this morning to steady him down. He seemed quite indignant when I suggested that he had been having an extra glass the night before, and I was obliged to pacify him by keeping as grave a countenance as possible during his story, which he certainly narrated in a very straightforward and matter-of-fact way.

'I was on the bridge,' he said, 'about four bells in the middle watch, just when the night was at its darkest. There was a bit of a moon, but the clouds were blowing across it so that you couldn't see far from the ship. John McLeod, the harpooner, came aft from the foc'sle-head and reported a strange noise on the starboard bow. I went forrard and we both heard it, sometimes like a bairn crying and sometimes like a wench in pain. I've been seventeen years to the country and I never heard seal, old or young, make a sound like that. As we were standing there on the foc'sle-head the moon came out from behind a cloud, and we both saw a sort of white figure moving across the ice field in the same direction that we had heard the cries. We lost sight of it for a while, but it came back on the port bow, and we could just make it out like a shadow on the ice. I sent a hand aft for the rifles, and McLeod and I went down on to the pack, thinking that maybe it might be a bear. When we got on the ice I lost sight of McLeod, but I pushed on in the direction where I could still hear the cries. I followed them for a mile or maybe more, and then running round a hummock I came right on to the top of it standing and waiting for me seemingly. I don't know what it was. It wasn't a bear any way. It was tall and white and straight, and if it wasn't a man nor a woman, I'll stake my davy it was something worse. I made for the ship as hard as I could run, and precious glad I was to find myself aboard. I signed articles to do my duty by the ship, and on the ship I'll stay, but you don't catch me on the ice again after sundown.'

'That is his story given as far as I can in his own words. I fancy what he saw must, in spite of his denial, have been a young bear erect upon its hind legs, an attitude which they often assume when alarmed. In the uncertain light this would bear a resemblance to a human figure, especially to a man whose nerves were already somewhat shaken. Whatever it may have been, the occurrence is unfortunate, for it has produced a most unpleasant effect upon the crew. Their looks are more sullen than before and their discontent more open. The double grievance of being debarred from the herring fishing and of being detained in what they choose to call a haunted vessel, may lead them to do something rash. Even the harpooners, who are the oldest and steadiest among them, are joining in the general agitation.

Apart from this absurd outbreak of superstition, things are looking rather more cheerful. The pack which was forming to the south of us has partly cleared away, and the water is so warm as to lead me to believe that we are lying in one of those branches of the gulf-stream which run up between Greenland and Spitzbergen. There are numerous small Medusae and sealemons about the ship, with abundance of shrimps, so that there is every possibility of 'fish' being sighted. Indeed one was seen blowing about dinner-time, but in such a position that it was impossible for the boats to follow it.

September 13th. Had an interesting conversation with the chief mate Mr Milne upon the bridge. It seems that our Captain is as great an enigma to the seamen, and even to the owners of the vessel, as he has been to me. Mr Milne tells me that when the ship is paid off, upon returning from a voyage, Captain Craigie disappears, and is not seen again until the approach of another season, when he walks quietly into the office of the company, and asks whether his services will be required. He has no friend in Dundee, nor does anyone pretend to be acquainted with his early history. His position depends entirely upon his skill as a seaman, and the name for courage and coolness which he had earned in the capacity of mate, before being entrusted with a separate command. The unanimous opinion seems to be that he is not a Scotchman, and that his name is an assumed one. Mr Milne thinks that he has devoted himself to whaling simply for the reason that it is the most dangerous occupation which he could select, and that he courts death in every possible manner. He mentioned several instances of this, one of which is rather curious, if true. It seems that on one occasion he did not put in an appearance at the office, and a substitute had to be selected in his place. That was at the time of the last Russian and Turkish war. When he turned up again next spring he had a puckered wound in the side of his neck which he used to endeavour to conceal with his cravat. Whether the mate's inference that he had been engaged in the war is true or not I cannot say. It was certainly a strange coincidence.

The wind is veering round in an easterly direction, but is still very slight. I think the ice is lying closer than it did yesterday. As far as the eye can reach on every side there is one wide expanse of spotless white, only broken by an occasional rift or the dark shadow of a hummock. To the south there is the narrow lane of blue water which is our sole means of escape, and which is closing up every day. The Captain is taking a heavy responsibility upon himself. I hear that the tank of potatoes has been finished, and even the biscuits are running short, but he preserves the same impossible countenance and spends the greater part of the day at the crow's nest, sweeping the horizon with his glass. His manner is very variable, and he seems to avoid my society, but there has been no repetition of the violence which he showed the other night.

7.30 P.M. My deliberate opinion is that we are commanded by a madman. Nothing else can account for the extraordinary vagaries of Captain Craigie. It is fortunate that I have kept this journal of our voyage, as it will serve to justify us in case we have to put him under any sort of restraint, a step which I should only consent to as a last resource. Curiously enough it was he himself who suggested lunacy and not mere eccentricity as the secret of his strange conduct. He was standing upon the bridge about an hour ago, peering as usual through his glass, while I was walking up and down the quarterdeck. The majority of the men were below at their tea, for the watches have not been regularly kept of late. Tired of walking, I leaned against the bulwarks, and admired the mellow glow cast by the sinking sun upon the great ice fields which surround us. I was suddenly aroused from the reverie into which I had fallen by a hoarse voice at my elbow, and starting round I found that the Captain had descended and was standing by my side. He was staring out over the ice with an expression in which horror, surprise, something approaching to joy were contending for the mastery. In spite of the cold, great drops of perspiration were coursing down his forehead and he was evidently fearfully excited. His limbs twitched like those of a man upon the verge of an epileptic fit, and the lines about his mouth were drawn and hard.

'Look!' he gasped, seizing me by the wrist, but still keeping his eyes upon the distant ice, and moving his head slowly in a horizontal direction, as if following some object which was moving across the field of vision. 'Look! There, man, there! Between the hummocks! Now coming out from behind the far one! You see her, you *must* see her! There still! Flying from me, by God, flying from me – and gone!'

He uttered the last two words in a whisper of concentrated agony which shall never fade from my remembrance. Clinging to the ratlines he endeavoured to climb up upon the top of the bulwarks as if in the hope of obtaining a last glance at the departing object. His strength was not equal to the attempt, however, and he staggered back against the saloon skylights, where he leaned panting and exhausted. His face was so livid that I expected him to become unconscious, so lost no time leading him down the companion, and stretching him upon one of the sofas in the cabin. I then poured him out some brandy which I held to his lips, and which had a wonderful effect upon him, bringing the blood back into his white face and steadying his poor shaking limbs. He raised himself up upon his elbow, and looking round to see that we were alone, he beckoned to me to come and sit beside him.

'You saw it, didn't you?' he asked, still in the same subdued awesome tone so foreign to the nature of the man.

'No, I saw nothing.'

His head sank back again upon the cushions, 'No, he wouldn't without the glass,' he murmured. 'He couldn't. It was the glass that showed her to me, and then the eyes of love – the eyes of love. I say, Doc, don't let the steward in! He'll think I'm mad. Just bolt the door, will you!'

I rose and did what he had commanded.

He lay quiet for a little, lost in thought apparently, and then raised himself up upon his elbow again, and asked for some more brandy.

'You don't think I am, do you, Doc?' he asked as I was putting the bottle back into the after-locker. 'Tell me now, as man to man, do you think that I am mad?'

'I think you have something on your mind,' I answered, 'which is exciting you and doing you a good deal of harm.'

'Right there, lad!' he cried, his eyes sparkling from the effects of the brandy. 'Plenty on my mind – plenty! But I can work out the latitude and the longitude, and I can handle my sextant and manage my logarithms. You couldn't prove me mad in a court of law, could you, now?' It was curious to hear the man lying back and coolly arguing out the question of his own sanity.

'Perhaps not,' I said, 'but still I think you would be wise to get home as soon as you can and settle down to a quiet life for a while.'

'Get home, eh?' he muttered with a sneer upon his face. 'One word for me and two for yourself, lad. Settle down with Flora – pretty little Flora. Are bad dreams signs of madness?'

'Sometimes,' I answered.

'What else? what would be the first symptoms?'

'Pains in the head, noises in the ears, flashes before the eyes, delusions.'

'Ah! what about them?' he interrupted. 'What would you call a delusion?'

'Seeing a thing which is not there is a delusion.'

'But she *was* there!' he groaned to himself. 'She *was* there! and rising, he unbolted the door and walked with slow and uncertain steps to his own cabin, where I have no doubt that he will remain until tomorrow morning. His system seems to have received a terrible shock, whatever it may have been that he imagined himself to have seen. The man becomes a greater mystery every day, though I fear that the solution which he has himself suggested is the correct one, and that his reason is affected. I do not think that a guilty conscience has anything to do with his behaviour. The idea is a popular one among the officers, and, I believe, the crew; but I have seen nothing to support it. He has not the air of a guilty man, but of one who has had terrible usage at the hands of fortune, and who should be regarded as a martyr rather than a criminal.

The wind is veering round to the south tonight. God help us if it blocks that narrow pass which is our only road to safety! Situated as we are on the edge of the main Arctic pack, or the 'barrier', as it is called by the whalers, any wind from the north has the effect of shredding out the ice around us and allowing our escape, while a wind from the south blows up all the loose ice behind us and hems us in between two packs. God help us, I say again!

September 14th – Sunday, and a day of rest. My fears have been confirmed, and the thin strip of blue water has disappeared from the southward. Nothing but the great motionless ice fields around us, with their weird hummocks and fantastic pinnacles. There is a deathly silence over their wide expanse which is horrible. No lapping of the waves now, no cries of seagulls or straining of sails, but one deep universal silence in which the murmurs of the seamen, and the creak of their boots upon the white shining deck, seem discordant and out of place. Our only visitor was an Arctic fox, a rare animal upon the pack, though common enough upon the land. He did not come near the ship, however, but after surveying us from a distance fled rapidly across the ice. This was curious conduct, as they generally know nothing of man, and being of an inquisitive nature become so familiar that they are easily captured. Incredible as it may seem, even this little incident produced a bad effect upon the crew. 'Yon puir beastie kens mair, aye an' sees mair nor you nor me!' was the comment of one of the leading harpooners, and the others nodded their acquiescence. It is vain to attempt to argue against such puerile superstition. They have made up their minds that there is a curse upon the ship, and nothing will ever persuade them to the contrary.

The Captain remained in seclusion all day except for about half an hour in the afternoon, when he came out upon the quarterdeck. I observed that he kept his eye fixed upon the spot where the vision of yesterday had appeared, and was quite prepared for another outburst, but none such came. He did not seem to see me although I was standing close beside him. Divine service was read as usual by the chief engineer. It is a curious thing that in whaling vessels the Church of England Prayer-book is always employed, although there is never a member of that Church among either officers or crew. Our men are all Roman

Catholics or Presbyterians, the former predominating. Since a ritual is used which is foreign to both, neither can complain that the other is preferred to them, and they listen with all attention and devotion, so that the system has something to recommend it.

A glorious sunset, which made the great fields of ice look like a lake of blood. I have never seen a finer and at the same time more ghastly effect. Wind is veering round. If it will blow twenty-four hours from the north all will yet be well.

September 15th. Today is Flora's birthday. Dear lass! it is well that she cannot see her boy, as she used to call me, shut up among the ice fields with a crazy captain and a few weeks' provisions. No doubt she scans the shipping list in the *Scotsman* every morning to see if we are reported from Shetland. I have to set an example to the men and look cheery and unconcerned; but God knows my heart is very heavy at times.

The thermometer is at nineteen Fahrenheit today. There is but little wind, and what there is comes from an unfavourable quarter. Captain is in an excellent humour; I think he imagines he has seen some other omen or vision, poor fellow, during the night, for he came into my room early in the morning, and stooping down over my bunk whispered, 'It wasn't a delusion, Doc, it's all right!' After breakfast he asked me to find out how much food was left, which the second mate and I proceeded to do. It is even less than we had expected. Forward they have half a tank full of biscuits, three barrels of salt meat, and a very limited supply of coffee beans and sugar. In the after-hold and lockers there are a good many luxuries such as tinned salmon, soups, haricot mutton, etc., but they will go a very short way among a crew of fifty men. There are two barrels of flour in the store-room, and an unlimited supply of tobacco. Altogether there is about enough to keep the men on half rations for eighteen or twenty days – certainly not more. When we reported the state of things to the Captain, he ordered all hands to be piped, and addressed them from the quarterdeck. I never saw him to better advantage. With his tall, well-knit figure and dark animated face, he seemed a man born to command, and he discussed the situation in a cool sailor-like way which showed that while appreciating the danger he had an eye for every loophole of escape.

'My lads', he said, 'no doubt you think I brought you into this fix, if it is a fix, and maybe some of you feel bitter against me on account of it. But you must remember that for many a season no ship that comes to the country has brought in as much oil-money as the old *Pole-star*, and every one of you has had his share of it. You can leave your wives behind you in comfort while other poor fellows come back to find their lasses on the parish. If you have to thank me for the one you have to thank me for the other, and we may call it quits. We've tried a bold venture before this and succeeded, so now that we've tried one and failed we've no cause to cry out about it. If the worst comes to the worst, we can make the land across the ice, and lay in a stock of seals which will keep us alive until the spring. It won't come to that, though, for you'll see the Scotch coast again before three weeks are out. At present every man must go on half rations, share and share alike, and no favour to any. Keep up your hearts and you'll pull through this as you've pulled through many a danger before.' These few simple words of his had a wonderful effect upon the crew. His former unpopularity was forgotten, and the old harpooner whom I have already mentioned for his superstition, led off three cheers, which were heartily joined in by all hands.

September 16th. – The wind has veered round to the north during the night, and the ice shows some symptoms of opening out. The men are in a good humour in spite of the short allowance upon which they have been placed. Steam is kept up in the engine-room, that there may be no delay should an opportunity for escape present itself. The Captain is in exuberant spirits, though he still retains that wild 'fey' expression which I have already remarked upon. This burst of cheerfulness puzzles me more than his former gloom. I cannot understand it. I think I mentioned in an early part of this journal that one of his oddities is that he never permits any person to enter his cabin, but insists upon making his own bed, such as it is, and performing every other office for himself. To my surprise he handed me the key today and requested me to go down there and take the time by his chronometer while he measured the altitude of the sun at noon. It is a bare little room containing a washing-stand and a few books, but little else in the way of luxury, except some pietures upon the walls. The majority of these are small cheap oleographs, but there was one water-colour sketch of the head of a young lady which arrested my attention. It was evidently a portrait, and not one of those fancy types of female beauty which sailors particularly affect. No artist could have evolved from his own mind such a curious mixture of character and weakness. The languid, dreamy eyes with their drooping lashes, and the broad, low brow unruffled by thought or care, were in strong contrast with the clean-cut, prominent jaw, and the resolute set of the lower lip. Underneath it in one of the corners was written 'M. B., aet. 19.' That any one in the short space of nineteen years of existence could develop such strength of will as was stamped upon her face seemed to me at the time to be well-nigh incredible. She must have been an extraordinary woman. Her features have thrown such a glamour over me that though I had but a fleeting glance at them, I could, were I a draughtsman, reproduce them line for line upon this page of the journal. I wonder what part she has played in our Captain's life. He has hung her picture at the end of his berth so that his eyes continually rest upon it. Were he a less reserved man I should make some remark upon the subject. Of the other things in his cabin there was nothing worthy of mention – uniform coats, a camp stool, small looking-glass, tobacco box and numerous pipes, including an oriental hookah – which by-the-by gives some colour to Mr Milne's story about his participation in the war, though the connection may seem rather a distant one.

11.20 P.M. Captain just gone to bed after a long and interesting conversation on general topics. When he chooses he can be a most fascinating companion, being remarkably well read, and having the power of expressing his opinion forcibly without appearing to be dogmatic. I hate to have my intellectual toes trod upon. He spoke about the nature of the soul and sketched out the views of Aristotle and Plato upon the subject in a masterly manner. He seems to have a leaning for metempsychosis and the doctrines of Pythagoras. In discussing them we touched upon modern spiritualism, and I made some joking allusion to the impostures of Slade, upon which, to my surprise, he warned me most impressively against confusing the innocent with the guilty, and argued that it would be as logical to brand Christianity as an error, because Judas who professed that religion was a villain. He shortly afterwards bade me goodnight and retired to his room.

The wind is freshening up, and blows steadily from the north. The nights are as dark now as they are in England. I hope tomorrow may set us free from our frozen fetters.

September 17th. The Bogie again. Thank Heaven that I have strong nerves! The superstition of these poor fellows, and the circumstantial accounts which they give, with the utmost earnestness and self conviction, would horrify any man not accustomed to their ways. There are many versions of the matter, but the sum-total of them all is that something uncanny has been flitting round the ship all night, and that Sandie McDonald of Peterhead and 'lang' Peter Williamson of Shetland saw it, as also did Mr Milne on the bridge – so having three witnesses, they can make a better case of it than the second mate did. I spoke to Milne after breakfast and told him that he should be above such nonsense, and that as an officer he ought to set the men a better example. He shook his weatherbeaten head ominously, but answered with characteristic caution, 'Mebbe aye, mebbe na, Doctor,' he said; 'I didna ca' it a ghaist. I canna' say I preen my faith in sea bogles an' the like, though there's a mony as claims to ha' seen a' that and waur. I'm no easy feared, but may be your ain bluid would run a bit cauld, mun, if instead o' speerin' aboot it in daylicht ye were wi' me last night, an' seed an awfu' like shape, white an' gruesome, whiles here, whiles there, an' it greetin' and ca'ing in the darkness like a bit lambie that hae lost its mither. Ye would na' be sae ready to put it a' doon to auld wives' clavers then, I'm thinkin'.' I saw it was hopeless to reason with him, so contented myself with begging him as a personal favour to call me up the next time the spectre appeared – a request to which he acceded with many ejaculations expressive of his hopes that such an opportunity might never arise.

As I had hoped, the white desert behind us has become broken by many thin streaks of water which intersect it in all directions. Our latitude today was 80° 52' N., which shows that there is a strong southerly drift upon the pack. Should the wind continue favourable it will break up as rapidly as it formed. At present we can do nothing but smoke and wait and hope for the best. I am rapidly becoming a fatalist. When dealing with such uncertain factors as wind and ice a man can be nothing else. Perhaps it was the wind and sand of the Arabian deserts which gave the minds of the original followers of Mahomet their tendency to bow to kismet.

These spectral alarms have a very bad effect upon the Captain. I feared that it might excite his sensitive mind, and endeavoured to conceal the absurd story from him, but unfortunately he overheard one of the men making an allusion to it, and insisted upon being informed about it. As I half expected, it brought out all his latent lunacy in an exaggerated form. I can hardly believe that this is the same man who discoursed philosophy last night with the most critical acumen, and coolest judgement. He is pacing backwards and forwards upon the quarterdeck like a caged tiger, stopping now and again to throw out his hands with a yearning gesture, and stare impatiently out over the ice. He keeps up a continual mutter to himself, and once he called out, 'But a little time, love – but a little time!' Poor fellow, it is sad to see a gallant seaman and accomplished gentleman reduced to such a pass, and to think that imagination and delusion can cow a mind to which real danger was but the salt of life. Was ever a man in such a position as I, between a demented captain and a ghost-seeing mate? I sometimes think I am the only really sane man aboard the vessel – except perhaps the second engineer, who is a kind of ruminant and would care nothing for all the fiends in the Red Sea, so long as they would leave him alone and not disarrange his tools.

The ice is still opening rapidly, and there is every probability of our being able to make a start tomorrow morning. They will think I am inventing when I tell them at home all the strange things that have befallen me.

12 P.M. I have been a good deal startled, though I feel steadier now, thanks to a stiff glass of brandy. I am hardly myself yet however, as this handwriting will testify. The fact is that I have gone through a very strange experience, and am beginning to doubt whether I was justified in branding everyone on board as madmen, because they professed to have seen things which did not seem reasonable to my understanding. Pshaw! I am a fool to let such a trifle unnerve me, and yet coming as it does after all these alarms, it has an additional significance, for I cannot doubt either Mr Manson's story or that of the mate, now that I have experienced that which I used formerly to scoff at.

After all it was nothing very alarming – a mere sound, and that was all. I cannot expect that anyone reading this, if anyone ever should read it, will sympathize with my feelings, or realize the effect which it produced upon me at the time. Supper was over and I had gone on deck to have a quiet pipe before turning in. The night was very dark – so dark that standing under the quarter boat, I was unable to see the officer upon the bridge. I think I have already mentioned the extraordinary silence which prevails in these frozen seas. In other parts of the world, be they ever so barren, there is some slight vibration of the air – some faint hum, be it from the distant haunts of men, or from the leaves of the trees, or the wings of the birds, or even the faint rustle of the grass that covers the ground. One may not actively perceive the sound, and yet if it were withdrawn it would be missed. It is only here in these Arctic seas that stark, unfathomable stillness obtrudes itself upon you in all its gruesome reality. You find your tympanum straining to catch some little murmur and dwelling eagerly upon every accidental sound within the vessel. In this state I was leaning against the bulwarks when there arose from the ice almost directly underneath me, a cry, sharp and shrill, upon the silent air of the night, beginning, as it seemed to me, at a note such as prima donna never reached, and mounting from that ever higher and higher until it culminated in a long wail of agony, which might have been the last cry of a lost soul. The ghastly scream is still ringing in my ears. Grief, unutterable grief, seemed to be expressed in it and a great longing, and yet through it all there was an occasional wild note of exultation. It seemed to come from close beside me, and yet as I glared into the darkness I could make out nothing. I waited some little time, but without hearing any repetition of the sound, so I came below, more shaken than I have ever been in my life before. As I came down the companion I met Mr Milne coming up to relieve the watch. 'Weel, Doctor,' he said, 'may be that's auld wives' clavers tae? Did ye no hear it skirling? Maybe that's a supersteetion? what d'ye think o't noo?' I was obliged to apologize to the honest fellow, and acknowledge that I was as puzzled by it as he was. Perhaps tomorrow things may look different. At present I dare hardly write all that I think. Reading it again in days to come, when I have shaken off all these associations, I should despise myself for having been so weak.

September 18th. – Passed a restless and uneasy night still haunted by that strange sound. The Captain does not look as if he had had much repose either, for his face is haggard and his eyes bloodshot. I have not told him of my adventure of last night, nor shall I. He is already restless and excited, standing up, sitting down, and apparently utterly unable to keep still.

A fine lead appeared in the pack this morning, as I had expected, and we were able to ease off our ice-anchor, and steam about twelve miles in a west-sou'-westerly direction. We were then brought to a halt by a great floe as massive as any which we have left behind us. It bars our progress completely, so we can do nothing but anchor again and wait until it breaks up, which it will probably do within twenty-four hours, if the wind holds. Several bladder-nosed seals were seen swimming in the water, and one was shot, an immense creature more than eleven feet long. They are fierce, pugnacious animals, and are said to be more than a match for a bear. Fortunately they are slow and clumsy in their movements, so that there is little danger in attacking them upon the ice.

The Captain evidently does not think we have seen the last of our troubles, though why he should take a gloomy view of the situation is more than I can fathom, since everyone else on board considers that we have had a miraculous escape, and are sure now to reach the open sea.

'I suppose you think it's all right now, Doctor?' he said as we sat together after dinner.

'I hope so,' I answered.

'We mustn't be too sure – and yet no doubt you are right. We'll all be in the arms of our own true loves before long, lad, won't we? But we mustn't be too sure – we mustn't be too sure.'

He sat silent a little, swinging his leg thoughtfully backwards and forwards. 'Look here,' he continued. 'It's a dangerous place this, even at its best – a treacherous, dangerous place. I have known men cut off very suddenly in a land like this. A slip would do it sometimes – a single slip, and down you go through a crack and only a bubble on the green water to show where it was that you sank. It's a queer thing,' he continued with a nervous laugh, 'but all the years I've been in this country I never once thought of making a will – not that I have anything to leave in particular, but still when a man is exposed to danger he should have everything arranged and ready – don't you think so?'

'Certainly,' I answered, wondering what on earth he was driving at.

'He feels better for knowing it's all settled,' he went on. 'Now if anything should ever befall me, I hope that you will look after things for me. There is very little in the cabin, but such as it is I should like it to be sold, and the money divided in the same proportion as the oil-money among the crew. The chronometer I wish you to keep yourself as some slight remembrance of our voyage. Of course all this is a mere precaution, but I thought I would take the opportunity of speaking to you about it. I suppose I might rely upon you if there were any necessity?'

'Most assuredly,' I answered; 'and since you are taking this step, I may as well – '

'You! you!' he interrupted. '*You're* all right. What the devil is the matter with you? There, I didn't mean to be peppery, but I don't like to hear a young fellow, that has hardly began life, speculating about death. Go up on deck and get some fresh air into your lungs instead of talking nonsense in the cabin, and encouraging me to do the same.'

The more I think of this conversation of ours the less do I like it. Why should the man be settling his affairs at the very time when we seem to be emerging from all danger? There must be some method in his madness. Can it be that he contemplates suicide? I remember that upon one occasion he spoke in a deeply reverent manner of the heinousness of the crime of self-destruction. I shall keep my eye upon him however, and though I cannot obtrude upon the privacy of his cabin, I shall at least make a point of remaining on deck as long as he stays up.

Mr Milne pooh-poohs my fears, and says it is only the 'skipper's little way'. He himself takes a very rosy view of the situation. According to him we shall be out of the ice by the day after tomorrow, pass Jan Meyen two days after that, and sight Shetland in little more than a week. I hope he may not be too sanguine. His opinion may be fairly balanced against the gloomy precautions of the Captain, for he is an old and experienced seaman, and weights his words well before uttering them.

The long-impending catastrophe has come at last. I hardly know what to write about it. The Captain is gone. He may come back to us again alive, but I fear me – I fear me. It is now seven o'clock of the morning of the 19th of September. I have spent the whole night traversing the great ice-floe in front of us with a party of seamen in the hope of coming upon some trace of him, but in vain. I shall try to give some account of the circumstances which attended upon his disappearance. Should anyone ever chance to read the words which I put down, I trust they will remember that I do not write from conjecture or from hearsay, but that

I, a sane and educated man, am describing accurately what actually occurred before my very eyes. My inferences are my own but I shall be answerable for the facts.

The Captain remained in excellent spirits after the conversation which I have recorded. He appeared to be nervous and impatient however, frequently changing his position, and moving his limbs in an aimless choreic way which is characteristic of him at times. In a quarter of an hour he went upon deck seven times, only to descend after a few hurried paces. I followed him each time, for there was something about his face which confirmed my resolution of not letting him out of my sight. He seemed to observe the effect which his movements had produced, for he endeavoured by an over-done hilarity, laughing boisterously at the very smallest of jokes, to quiet my apprehensions.

After supper he went on to the poop once more, and I with him. The night was dark and very still, save for the melancholy soughing of the wind among the spars. A thick cloud was coming up from the northwest, and the ragged tentacles which it threw out in front of it were drifting across the face of the moon, which only shone now and again through a rift in the wrack. The Captain paced rapidly backwards and forwards, and then seeing me still dogging him he came across and hinted that he thought I should be better below – which I need hardly say had the effect of strengthening my resolution to remain on deck.

I think he forgot about my presence after this, for he stood silently leaning over the taffrail, and peering out across the great desert of snow, part of which lay in shadow, while part glittered mistily in the moonlight. Several times I could see by his movements that he was referring to his watch, and once he muttered a short sentence of which I could only catch the one word 'ready'. I confess to having felt an eerie feeling creeping over me as I watched the loom of his tall figure through the darkness, and noted how completely he fulfilled the idea of a man who is keeping a tryst. A tryst with whom? Some vague perception began to dawn upon me as I pieced one fact with another, but I was utterly unprepared for the sequel.

By the sudden intensity of his attitude I felt that he saw something. I crept up behind him. He was staring with an eager questioning gaze at what seemed to be a wreath of mist, blown swiftly in a line with the ship. It was a dim nebulous body devoid of shape, sometimes more, sometimes less apparent, as the light fell on it. The moon was dimmed in its brilliancy at the moment by a canopy of thinnest cloud, like the coating of an anemone.

'Coming, lass, coming,' cried the skipper, in a voice of unfathomable tenderness and compassion, like one who soothes a beloved one by some favour long looked for, and as pleasant to bestow as to receive.

What followed, happened in an instant. I had no power to interfere. He gave one spring to the top of the bulwarks, and another which took him on to the ice, almost to the feet of the pale misty figure. He held out his hands as if to clasp it, and so ran into the darkness with outstretched arms and loving words. I still stood rigid and motionless, straining my eyes after his retreating form, until his voice died away in the distance. I never thought to see him again, but at that moment the moon shone out brilliantly through a chink in the cloudy heaven, and illuminated the great field of ice. Then I saw his dark figure already a very long way off, running with prodigious speed across the frozen plain. That was the last glimpse which we caught of him – perhaps the last we ever shall. A party was organized to follow him, and I accompanied them, but the men's hearts were not in the work, and nothing was found. Another will be formed within a few hours. I can hardly believe I have not been dreaming, or suffering from some hideous nightmare as I write these things down.

7.30 P.M. – Just returned dead beat and utterly tired out from a second unsuccessful search for the Captain. The floe is of enormous extent, for though we have traversed at least twenty miles of its surface, there has been no sign of its coming to an end. The frost has been so severe of late that the overlying snow is frozen as hard as granite, otherwise we might have had the footsteps to guide us. The crew are anxious that we should cast off and steam round the floe and so to the southward, for the ice has opened up during the night, and the sea is visible upon the horizon. They argue that Captain Craigie is certainly dead, and that we are all risking our lives to no purpose by remaining when we have an opportunity of escape. Mr Milne and I have had the greatest difficulty in persuading them to wait until tomorrow night, and have been compelled to promise that we will not under any circumstances delay our departure longer than that. We propose therefore to take a few hours' sleep and then to start upon a final search.

September 20th, evening – I crossed the ice this morning with a party of men exploring the southern part of the floe, while Mr Milne went off in a northerly direction. We pushed on for ten or twelve miles without seeing a trace of any living thing except a single bird, which fluttered a great way over our heads, and which by its flight I should judge to have been a falcon. The southern extremity of the ice field tapered away into a long narrow spit which projected out into the sea. When we came to the base of this promontory, the men halted, but I begged them to continue to the extreme end of it that we might have the satisfaction of knowing that no possible chance had been neglected.

We had hardly gone a hundred yards before McDonald of Peterhead cried out that he saw something in front of us, and began to run. We all got a glimpse of it and ran too. At first it was only a vague darkness against the white ice, but as we raced along together it took the shape of a man, and eventually of the man of whom we were in search. He was lying face downwards upon a frozen bank. Many little crystals of ice and feathers of snow had drifted on to him as he lay, and sparkled upon his dark seaman's jacket. As we came up some wandering puff of wind caught these tiny flakes in its vortex, and they whirled up into the air, partially descended again, and then, caught once more in the current, sped rapidly away in the direction of the sea. To my eyes it seemed but a snow-drift, but many of my companions averred that it started up in the shape of a woman, stooped over the corpse and kissed it, and then hurried away across the floe. I have learned never to ridicule any man's opinion, however strange it may seem. Sure it is that Captain Nicholas Craigie had met with no painful end, for there was a bright smile upon his blue pinched features, and his hands were still outstretched as though grasping at the strange visitor which had summoned him away into the dim world that lies beyond the grave.

We buried him the same afternoon with the ship's ensign around him, and a thirty-two pound shot at his feet. I read the burial service, while the rough sailors wept like children, for there were many who owed much to his kind heart, and who showed now the affection which his strange ways had repelled during his lifetime. He went off the grating with a dull, sullen splash, and as I looked into the green water I saw him go down, down, down, until he was but a little flickering patch of white hanging upon the outskirts of eternal darkness. Then even that faded away and he was gone. There he shall lie, with his secret and his sorrows and his mystery all still buried in his breast, until that great day when the sea shall give up its dead, and Nicholas Craigie come out from among the ice with the smile upon his face, and his stiffened arms outstretched in greeting. I pray that his lot may be a happier one in that life than it has been in this.

I shall not continue my journal. Our road to home lies plain and clear before us, and the great ice field will soon be but a remembrance of the past. It will be some time before I get over the shock produced by recent events. When I began this record of our voyage I little thought of how I should be compelled to finish it. I am writing these final words in the lonely cabin, still starting at times and fancying I hear the quick nervous step of the dead man upon the deck above me. I entered his cabin tonight as was my duty, to make a list of his effects in order that they might be entered in the official log. All was as it had been upon my previous visit, save that the picture which I have described as having hung at the end of his bed had been cut out of its frame, as with a knife, and was gone. With this last link in a strange chain of evidence I close my diary of the voyage of the *Pole-star*.

[NOTE by Dr John McAlister Ray, senior. 'I have read over the strange events connected with the death of the Captain of the *Pole-star*, as narrated in the journal of my son. That everything occurred exactly as he describes it I have the fullest confidence, and, indeed, the most positive certainty, for I know him to be a strong-nerved and unimaginative man, with the strictest regard for veracity. Still, the story is, on the face of it, so vague and so improbable, that I was long opposed to its publication. Within the last few days, however, I have had independent testimony upon the subject which throws a new light upon it. I had run down to Edinburgh to attend a meeting of the British Medical Association, when I chanced to come across Dr P, an old college chum of mine, now practising at Saltash, in Devonshire. Upon my telling him of this experience of my son's, he declared to me that he was familiar with the man, and proceeded, to my no small surprise, to give me a description of him, which tallied remarkably well with that given in the journal, except that he depicted him as a younger man. According to his account, he had been engaged to a young lady of singular beauty residing upon the Cornish coast. During his absence at sea his betrothed had died under circumstances of peculiar horror.]

The Haunted Mill or The Ruined House

Jerome K. Jerome

Introduction

It was Christmas Eve.

I begin this way, because it is the proper, orthodox, respectable way to begin, and I have been brought up in a proper, orthodox, respectable way, and taught to always do the proper, orthodox, respectable thing; and the habit clings to me.

Of course, as a mere matter of information it is quite unnecessary to mention the date at all. The experienced reader knows it was Christmas Eve, without my telling him. It always is Christmas Eve, in a ghost story.

Christmas Eve is the ghosts' great gala night. On Christmas Eve they hold their annual fête. On Christmas Eve everybody in Ghostland who *is* anybody – or rather, speaking of ghosts, one should say, I suppose, every nobody who *is* any nobody – comes out to show himself or herself, to see and to be seen, to promenade about and display their winding-sheets and grave-clothes to each other; to criticize one another's style, and sneer at one another's complexion.

'Christmas Eve Parade,' as I expect they themselves term it, is a function, doubtless, eagerly prepared for and looked forward to throughout Ghostland, especially by the swagger set, such as the murdered Barons, the crime-stained Countesses, and the Earls who came over with the Conqueror, and assassinated their relatives, and died raving mad.

Hollow moans and fiendish grins are, one may be sure, energetically practised up. Blood-curdling shrieks and marrow-freezing gestures are probably rehearsed for weeks beforehand. Rusty chains and gory daggers are overhauled, and put into good working order; and sheets and shrouds, laid carefully by from the previous year's show, are taken down and shaken out, and mended, and aired. Oh, it is a stirring night in Ghostland, the night of December the twenty-fourth!

Ghosts never come out on Christmas night itself, you may have noticed. Christmas Eve, we suspect, has been too much for them; they are not used to excitement. For about a week after Christmas Eve, the gentlemen ghosts, no doubt, feel as if they were all head, and go about making solemn resolutions to themselves that they will stop in next Christmas Eve; while the lady spectres are contradictory and snappish, and liable to burst into tears and leave the room hurriedly on being spoken to, for no perceptible cause whatever.

Ghosts with no position to maintain – mere middle-class ghosts – occasionally, I believe, do a little haunting on off-nights: on Allhallows Eve, and at Midsummer; and some will even run up for a mere local event – to celebrate, for instance, the anniversary of the hanging of somebody's grandfather, or to prophesy a misfortune.

He does love prophesying a misfortune, does the average British ghost. Send him out to prognosticate trouble to somebody, and he is happy. Let him force his way into a peaceful home, and turn the whole house upside down by foretelling a funeral, or predicting a bankruptcy, or hinting at a coming disgrace, or some terrible disaster, about which nobody in their senses would want to know sooner than they could possibly help, and the prior knowledge of which can serve no useful purpose whatsoever, and he feels that he is combining duty with pleasure. He would never forgive himself if anybody in his family had a trouble and he had not been there for a couple of months beforehand, doing silly tricks on the lawn, or balancing himself on somebody's bed-rail.

Then there are, besides, the very young, or very conscientious ghosts with a lost will or an undiscovered number weighing heavy on their minds, who will haunt steadily all the year round; and also the fussy ghost, who is indignant at having been buried in the dustbin or in the village pond, and who never gives the parish a single night's quiet until somebody has paid for a first-class funeral for him.

But these are the exceptions. As I have said, the average orthodox ghost does his one turn a year, on Christmas Eve, and is satisfied.

Why on Christmas Eve, of all nights in the year, I never could myself understand. It is invariably one of the most dismal of nights to be out in – cold, muddy, and wet. And besides, at Christmas time, everybody has quite enough to put up with in the way of a houseful of living relations, without wanting the ghosts of any dead ones mooning about the place, I am sure.

There must be something ghostly in the air of Christmas – something about the close, muggy atmosphere that draws up the ghosts, like the dampness of the summer rains brings out the frogs and snails.

And not only do the ghosts themselves always walk on Christmas Eve, but live people always sit and talk about them on Christmas Eve. Whenever five or six English-speaking people meet round a fire on Christmas Eve, they start telling each other ghost stories. Nothing satisfies us on Christmas Eve but to hear each other tell authentic anecdotes about spectres. It is a genial, festive season, and we love to muse upon graves, and dead bodies, and murders, and blood.

There is a good deal of similarity about our ghostly experiences; but this of course is not our fault but the fault of the ghosts, who never will try any new performances, but always will keep steadily to the old, safe business. The consequence is that, when you have been at one Christmas Eve party, and heard six people relate their adventures with spirits, you do not require to hear any more ghost stories. To listen to any further ghost stories after that would be like sitting out two farcical comedies, or taking in two comic journals; the repetition would become wearisome.

There is always the young man who was, one year, spending the Christmas at a country house, and, on Christmas Eve, they put him to sleep in the west wing. Then in the middle of the night, the room door quietly opens and somebody – generally a lady in her nightdress – walks slowly in, and comes and sits on the bed. The young man thinks it must be one of the visitors, or some relative of the family, though he does not remember having previously seen her, who, unable to go to sleep, and feeling lonesome, all by herself, has come into his room for a chat. He has no idea it is a ghost: he is so unsuspicious. She does not speak, however; and, when he looks again, she is gone!

The young man relates the circumstance at the breakfast table next morning, and asks each of the ladies present if it were she who was the visitor. But they all assure him that it was not, and the host, who has grown deadly pale, begs him to say no more about the matter, which strikes the young man as a singularly strange request.

After breakfast the host takes the young man into a corner, and explains to him that what he saw was the ghost of a lady who had been murdered in that very bed, or who had murdered somebody else there – it does not really matter which: you can be a ghost by murdering somebody else or by being murdered yourself, whichever you prefer. The murdered ghost is, perhaps, the more popular; but, on the other hand, you can frighten people better if you are the murdered one, because then you can show your wounds and do groans.

Then there is the sceptical guest – it is always 'the guest' who gets let in for this sort of thing, by-the-by. A ghost never thinks much of his own family: it is 'the guest' he likes to haunt who after listening to the host's ghost story, on Christmas Eve, laughs at it, and says that he does not believe there are such things as ghosts at all; and that he will sleep in the haunted chamber that very night, if they will let him.

Everybody urges him not to be so reckless, but he persists in his foolhardiness, and goes up to the Yellow Chamber (or whatever colour the haunted room may be) with a light heart and a candle, and wishes them all good-night, and shuts the door.

Next morning he has got snow-white hair.

He does not tell anybody what he has seen: it is too awful.

There is also the plucky guest, who sees a ghost, and knows it is a ghost, and watches it, as it comes into the room and disappears through the wainscot, after which, as the ghost does not seem to be coming back, and there is nothing, consequently, to be gained by stopping awake, he goes to sleep.

He does not mention having seen the ghost to anybody, for fear of frightening them – some people are so nervous about ghosts, – but determines to wait for the next night, and see if the apparition appears again.

It does appear again, and, this time, he gets out of bed, dresses himself and does his hair, and follows it; and then discovers a secret passage leading from the bedroom down into the beer-cellar, – a passage which, no doubt, was not infrequently made use of in the bad old days of yore.

After him comes the young man who woke up with a strange sensation in the middle of the night, and found his rich bachelor uncle standing by his bedside. The rich uncle smiled a weird sort of smile and vanished. The young man immediately got up and looked at his watch. It had stopped at half-past four, he having forgotten to wind it.

He made enquiries the next day, and found that, strangely enough, his rich uncle, whose only nephew he was, had married a widow with eleven children at exactly a quarter to twelve, only two days ago. The young man does not attempt to explain the extraordinary circumstance. All he does is to vouch for the truth of his narrative.

And, to mention another case, there is the gentleman who is returning home late at night, from a Freemasons' dinner, and who, noticing a light issuing from a ruined abbey, creeps up, and looks through the keyhole. He sees the ghost of a 'grey sister' kissing the ghost of a brown monk, and is so inexpressibly shocked and frightened that he faints on the spot, and is discovered there the next morning, lying in a heap against the door, still speechless, and with his faithful latch-key clasped tightly in his hand.

All these things happen on Christmas Eve, they are all told of on Christmas Eve. For ghost stories to be told on any other evening than the evening of the twenty-fourth of December would be impossible in English society as at present regulated. Therefore, in introducing the sad but authentic ghost story that follows, I feel that it is unnecessary to inform the student of Anglo-Saxon literature that the date on which it was told and on which the incidents took place was – Christmas Eve.

Nevertheless, I do so.

The Haunted Mill

Well, you all know my brother-in-law, Mr Parkins (began Mr Coombes, taking the long clay pipe from his mouth, and putting it behind his ear: we did not know his brother-in-law, but we said we did, so as to save time), and you know of course that he once took a lease on an old mill in Surrey, and went to live there.

Now you must know that, years ago, this very mill had been occupied by a wicked old miser, who died there, leaving – so it was rumoured – all his money hidden somewhere about the place. Naturally enough, everyone who had since come to live at the mill had tried to find the treasure; but none had ever succeeded, and the local wiseacres said that nobody ever would, unless the ghost of the miserly miller should, one day, take a fancy to one of the tenants, and disclose to him the secret of the hiding-place.

My brother-in-law did not attach much importance to the story, regarding it as an old woman's tale, and, unlike his predecessors, made no attempt whatever to discover the hidden gold.

'Unless business was very different then from what it is now,' said my brother-in-law, 'I don't see how a miller could very well have saved anything, however much of a miser he might have been: at all events, not enough to make it worth the trouble of looking for it.'

Still, he could not altogether get rid of the idea of that treasure.

One night he went to bed. There was nothing very extraordinary about that, I admit. He often did go to bed of a night. What was remarkable, however, was that exactly as the clock of the village church chimed the last stroke of twelve, my brother-in-law woke up with a start, and felt himself quite unable to go to sleep again.

Joe (his Christian name was Joe) sat up in bed, and looked around.

At the foot of the bed something stood very still, wrapped in shadow.

It moved into the moonlight, and then my brother-in-law saw that it was the figure of a wizened little old man, in knee-breeches and a pigtail.

In an instant the story of the hidden treasure and the old miser flashed across his mind.

'He's come to show me where it's hid,' thought my brother-in-law; and he resolved that he would not spend all this money on himself; but would devote a small percentage of it towards doing good to others.

The apparition moved towards the door: my brother-in-law put on his trousers and followed it. The ghost went downstairs into the kitchen, glided over and stood in front of the hearth, sighed and disappeared.

Next morning, Joe had a couple of bricklayers in, and made them haul out the stove and pull down the chimney, while he stood behind with a potato-sack in which to put the gold.

They knocked down half the wall, and never found so much as a fourpenny bit. My brother-in-law did not know what to think.

The next night the old man appeared again, and led the way into the kitchen. This time, however, instead of going to the fireplace, it stood more in the middle of the room, and sighed there.

'Oh, I see what he means now,' said my brother-in-law to himself; 'it's under the floor. Why did the old idiot go and stand up against the stove, so as to make me think it was up the chimney?'

They spent the next day in taking up the kitchen floor; but the only thing they found was a three-pronged fork, and the handle of that was broken. On the third night, the ghost reappeared, quite unabashed, and for a third time made for the kitchen. Arrived there, it looked up at the ceiling and vanished.

'Umph! he don't seem to have learned much sense where he's been to,' muttered Joe, as he trotted back to bed; 'I should have thought he might have done that at first.'

Still, there seemed no doubt now where the treasure lay, and the first thing after breakfast they started pulling down the ceiling. They got every inch of ceiling down, and they took up the boards of the room above.

They discovered about as much treasure as you would expect to find in an empty quart pot.

On the fourth night, when the ghost appeared, as usual, my brother-in-law was so wild that he threw his boots at it; and the boots passed through the body, and broke a looking-glass.

On the fifth night, when Joe awoke, as he always did now at twelve, the ghost was standing in a dejected attitude, looking very miserable. There was an appealing look in its large sad eyes that quite touched my brother-in-law.

'After all,' he thought, 'perhaps the silly chap's doing his best. Maybe he has forgotten where he really did put it, and is trying to remember. I'll give him another chance.'

The ghost appeared grateful and delighted at seeing Joe prepare to follow him, and led the way into the attic, pointed to the ceiling, and vanished.

'Well, he's hit it this time, I do hope,' said my brother-in-law; and next day they set to work to take the roof off the place.

It took them three days to get the roof thoroughly off, and all they found was a bird's nest; after securing which they covered up the house with tarpaulins, to keep it dry.

You might have thought that would have cured the poor fellow of looking for treasure. But it didn't.

He said there must be something in it all, or the ghost would never keep on coming as it did; and that, having gone so far, he would go on to the end, and solve the mystery, cost what it might.

Night after night, he would get out of his bed and follow that spectral old fraud about the house. Each night, the old man would indicate a different place; and, on each following day, my brother-in-law would proceed to break up the mill at the point indicated, and look for the treasure. At the end of three weeks, there was not a room in the mill fit to live in. Every wall had been pulled down, every floor had been taken up, every ceiling had had a hole knocked in it. And then, as suddenly as they had begun, the ghost's visits ceased; and my brother-in-law was left to rebuild the place at his leisure.

What induced the old image to play such a silly trick upon a family man and a ratepayer? Ah! that's just what I cannot tell you.

Some said that the ghost of the wicked old man had done it to punish my brother-in-law for not believing in him at first; while others held that the apparition was probably that of some deceased local plumber and glazier, who would naturally take an interest in seeing a house knocked about and spoilt. But nobody knew anything for certain.

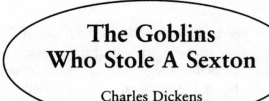

The Goblins Who Stole A Sexton

Charles Dickens

In an old abbey town, down in this part of the country, a long, long, while ago – so long, that the story must be a true one, because our great-grandfathers implicitly believed it – there officiated as sexton and grave-digger in the churchyard, one Gabriel Grub. It by no means follows that because a man is a sexton, and constantly surrounded by the emblems of mortality, therefore he should be a morose and melancholy nan; your undertakers are the merriest fellows in the world; and I once had the honour of being on intimate terms with a mute, who in private life, and off duty, was as comical and jocose a little fellow as ever chirped out a devil-may-care song, without a hitch in his memory, or drained off the contents of a good stiff glass without stopping for breath. But notwithstanding these precedents to the contrary, Gabriel Grub was an ill-conditioned, cross-grained, surly fellow – a morose and lonely man, who consorted with nobody but himself, and an old wicker bottle which fitted into his large deep waistcoat pocket – and who eyed each merry face, as it passed him by, with such a deep scowl of malice and ill-humour, as it was difficult to meet, without feeling something the worse for.

A little before twilight, one Christmas Eve, Gabriel shouldered his spade, lighted his lantern, and betook himself towards the old churchyard; for he had got a grave to finish by next morning, and, feeling very low, he thought it might raise his spirits, perhaps, if he went on with his work at once. As he went his way, up the ancient street, he saw the cheerful light of the blazing fires gleam through the old casements, and heard the loud laugh and the cheerful shouts of those who were assembled around them; he marked the bustling preparations for next day's cheer, and smelt the numerous savoury odours consequent thereupon, as they steamed up from the kitchen windows in clouds. All this was gall and wormwood to the heart of Gabriel Grub; and when groups of children bounded out of the houses, tripped across the road, and were met, before they could knock at the opposite door, by half a dozen curly-headed little rascals who crowded round them as they flocked upstairs to spend the evening in their Christmas games, Gabriel smiled grimly, and clutched the handle of his spade with a firmer grasp, as he thought of measles, scarletfever, thrush, whooping-cough, and a good many other sources of consolation besides.

In this happy frame of mind, Gabriel strode along: returning a short, sullen growl to the good-humoured greetings of such of his neighbours as now and then passed him: until he turned into the dark lane which led to the churchyard. Now, Gabriel had been looking forward to reaching the dark lane, because it was, generally speaking, a nice, gloomy, mournful place, into which the townspeople did not much care to go, except in broad daylight, and when the sun was shining; consequently, he was not a little indignant to hear a young urchin roaring out some jolly song about a merry Christmas, in this very sanctuary, which had been called Coffin Lane ever since the days of the old abbey, and the time of the shaven-headed monks. As Gabriel walked on, and the voice drew nearer, he found it proceeded from a small boy, who was hurrying along, to join one of the little parties in the old street, and who, partly to keep himself company, and partly to prepare himself for the occasion, was shouting out the song at the highest pitch of his lungs. So Gabriel waited until the boy came up, and then dodged him into a corner, and rapped him over the head with his lantern five or six times, to teach him to modulate his voice. And as the boy hurried away with his hand to his head, singing quite a different sort of tune, Gabriel Grub chuckled very heartily to himself, and entered the churchyard, locking the gate behind him.

He took off his coat, put down his lantern, and getting into the unfinished grave, worked at it for an hour or so, with right good will. But the earth was hardened with the frost, and it was no very easy matter to break it up, and shovel it out; and although there was a moon, it was a very young one, and shed little light upon the grave, which was in the shadow of the church. At any other time, these obstacles would have made Gabriel Grub very moody and miserable, but he was so well pleased with having stopped the small boy's singing, that he took little heed of the scanty progress he had made, and looked down into the grave, when he had finished work for the night, with grim satisfaction: murmuring as he gathered up his things:

> Brave lodgings for one, brave lodgings for one,
> A few feet of cold earth, when life is done;
> A stone at the head, a stone at the feet,
> A rich, juicy meal for the worms to eat;
> Rank grass over head, and damp clay around
> Brave lodgings for one, these, in holy ground!

'Ho! Ho!' laughed Gabriel Grub, as he sat himself down on a flat tombstone which was a favourite resting-place of his; and drew forth his wicker bottle. 'A coffin at Christmas! A Christmas Box. Ho! ho! ho!'

'Ho! ho! ho!' repeated a voice which sounded close behind him.

Gabriel paused, in some alarm, in the act of raising the wicker bottle to his lips: and looked round. The bottom of the oldest grave about him, was not more still and quiet, than the churchyard in the pale moonlight. The cold hoar frost glistened on the tombstones, and sparkled like rows of gems, among the stone carvings of the old church. The snow lay hard and crisp upon the ground; and spread over the thickly-strewn mounds of earth so white and smooth a cover that it seemed as if corpses lay there, hidden only by their winding sheets. Not the faintest rustle broke the profound tranquillity of the solemn scene. Sound itself appeared to be frozen up, all was so cold and still.

'It was the echoes,' said Gabriel Grub, raising the bottle to his lips again.

'It was *not*,' said a deep voice.

Gabriel started up, and stood rooted to the spot with astonishment and terror; for his eyes rested on a form that made his blood run cold.

Seated on an upright tombstone, close to him, was a strange unearthly figure, whom Gabriel felt at once, was no being of this world. His long fantastic legs which might have reached the ground, were cocked up, and crossed after a quaint, fantastic fashion; his sinewy arms were bare; and his hands rested on his knees. On his short round body, he wore a close covering, ornamented with small slashes; a short cloak dangled at his back; the collar was cut into curious peaks, which served the goblin in lieu of ruff or neckerchief; and his shoes curled at his toes into long points. On his head, he wore a broad-rimmed sugar-loaf hat, garnished with a single feather. The hat was covered with the white

frost; and the goblin looked as if he had sat on the same tombstone very comfortably, for two or three hundred years. He was sitting perfectly still; his tongue was put out, as if in derision; and he was grinning at Gabriel Grub with such a grin as only a goblin could call up.

'It was *not* the echoes,' said the goblin.

Gabriel Grub was paralysed, and could make no reply.

'What do you do here on Christmas Eve?' said the goblin sternly.

'I came to dig a grave, sir,' stammered Gabriel Grub.

'What man wanders among graves and churchyards on such a night as this?' cried the goblin.

'Gabriel Grub! Gabriel Grub!' screamed a wild chorus of voices that seemed to fill the churchyard. Gabriel looked fearfully round – nothing was to be seen.

'What have you got in that bottle?' said the goblin.

'Hollands, sir,' replied the sexton, trembling more than ever; for he had bought it of the smugglers, and he thought that perhaps his questioner might be in the excise department of the goblins.

'Who drinks Hollands alone, and in a churchyard, on such a night as this?' said the goblin.

'Gabriel Grub! Gabriel Grub!' exclaimed the wild voices again.

The goblin leered maliciously at the terrified sexton, and then raising his voice, exclaimed: 'And who, then, is our fair and lawful prize?'

To this inquiry the invisible chorus replied, in a strain that sounded like the voices of many choristers singing to the mighty swell of the old church organ – a strain that seemed borne to the sexton's ears upon a wild wind, and to die away as it passed onward; but the burden of the reply was still the same, 'Gabriel Grub! Gabriel Grub!'

The goblin grinned a broader grin than before, as he said, 'Well Gabriel, what do you say to this?'

The sexton gasped for breath.

'What do you think of this, Gabriel?' said the goblin, kicking up his feet in the air on either side of the tombstone, and looking at the turned-up points with as much complacency as if he had been contemplating the most fashionable pair of Wellingtons in all Bond Street.

'It's – it's - very curious sir,' replied the sexton, half dead with fright; 'very curious, and very pretty, but I think I'll go back and finish my work, sir, if you please.'

'Work!' said the goblin, 'what work?'

'The grave, sir; making the grave,' stammered the sexton.

'Oh, the grave, eh?' said the goblin. 'Who makes graves at a time when all other men are merry, and takes a pleasure in it?' Again the mysterious voices replied, 'Gabriel Grub! Gabriel Grub!'

'I'm afraid my friends want you Gabriel,' said the goblin, thrusting his tongue further into his cheek than ever – and a most astonishing tongue it was – 'I'm afraid my friends want you, Gabriel,' said the goblin.

'Under favour, sir,' replied the horror-stricken sexton, 'I don't think they can, sir; they don't know me, sir; I don't think the gentlemen have ever seen me, sir.'

'Oh yes they have,' replied the goblin; 'we know the man with the sulky face and grim scowl, that came down the street tonight, throwing his evil looks at the children, and grasping his burying spade the tighter. We know the man who struck the boy in the envious malice of his heart, because the boy could be merry, and he could not. We know him, we know him. '

Here, the goblin gave a loud shrill laugh, which the echoes returned twenty-fold: and throwing his legs up in the air, stood upon his head, or rather upon the very point of his sugar-loaf hat, on the narrow edge of the tombstone: whence he threw a somerset with extraordinary agility, right to the sexton's feet, at which he planted himself in the attitude in which tailors generally sit upon the shop-board.

'I – I – am afraid I must leave you, sir,' said the sexton, making an effort to move.

'Leave us!' said the goblin, 'Gabriel Grub going to leave us. Ho! ho! ho!'

As the goblin laughed, the sexton observed, for one instant, a brilliant illumination within the windows of the church, as if the whole building were lighted up; it disappeared, the organ pealed forth a lively air, and whole troops of goblins, the very counterpart of the first one, poured into the churchyard, and began playing at leap-frog with the tombstones: never stopping for an instant to take break, but 'overing' the highest among them, one after the other, with the most marvellous dexterity. The first goblin was a most astonishing leaper, and none of the others could come near him; even in the extremity of his terror the sexton could not help observing, that while his friends were content to leap over the common-sized gravestones, the first one took the family vaults, iron railing and all, with as much ease as if they had been so many street-posts.

At last the game reached to a most exciting pitch; the organ played quicker and quicker; and the goblins leaped faster and faster: coiling themselves up, rolling head over heels upon the ground, and bounding over the tombstones like footballs. The sexton's brain whirled round with the rapidity of the motion he beheld, and his legs reeled beneath him, as the spirits flew before his eyes: when the goblin king, suddenly darting towards him, laid his hand upon his collar, and sank with him through the earth.

When Gabriel Grub had had time to fetch his breath, which the rapidity of his descent had for the moment taken away, he found himself in what appeared to be a large cavern, surrounded on all sides by crowds of goblins, ugly and grim; in the centre of the room, on an elevated seat, was stationed his friend of the churchyard; and close beside him stood Gabriel Grub himself, without power of motion.

'Cold tonight,' said the king of the goblins, 'very cold. A glass of something warm, here!'

At this command, half a dozen officious goblins, with a perpetual smile upon their faces, whom Gabriel Grub imagined to be courtiers, on that account, hastily disappeared, and presently returned with a goblet of liquid fire, which they presented to the king.

'Ah !' cried the goblin, whose cheeks and throat were transparent, as he tossed down the flame, 'This warms one, indeed! Bring a bumper of the same, for Mr Grub.'

It was in vain for the unfortunate sexton to protest that he was not in the habit of taking anything warm at night; one of the goblins held him while another poured the blazing liquid down his throat; the whole assembled screeched with laughter as he coughed and choked, and wiped away the tears which gushed plentifully from his eyes, after swallowing the burning draught.

'And now,' said the king, fantastically poking the taper corner of his sugar-loaf hat into the sexton's eye, and thereby occasioning him the most exquisite pain: 'And now, show the man of misery and gloom, a few of the pictures from our own great storehouse!'

As the goblin said this, a thick cloud which obscured the remoter end of the cavern, rolled gradually away, and disclosed, apparently at a great distance, a small and scantily furnished, but neat and clean apartment. A crowd of little children were gathered round a bright fire, clinging to their mother's gown, and gambolling around her chair. The mother occasionally rose, and drew aside the window-curtain, as if to look for some expected object: a frugal meal was placed near the fire. A knock was heard at the door: the mother opened it, and the children crowded round her, and clapped their hands for joy, as their father entered. He was wet and weary, and shook the snow from his garments, as the children crowded round him, and seizing his cloak, hat, stick and gloves, with busy zeal, ran with them from the room. Then, as he sat down to his meal before the fire, the children climbed about his knee, and the mother sat by his side, and all seemed happiness and comfort.

But a change came upon the view, almost imperceptibly. The scene was altered to a small bedroom, where the fairest and youngest child lay dying; the roses had fled from his cheek, and the light from his eye; and even as the sexton looked upon him with an interest he had never felt or known before, he died. His young brothers and sisters crowded round his little bed, and seized his tiny hand, so cold and heavy; but they shrunk back from its touch, and looked with awe on his infant face; for calm and tranquil as it was, and sleeping in rest and peace as the beautiful child seemed to be, they saw that he was dead, and they knew that he was an Angel looking down upon, and blessing them, from a bright and happy Heaven.

Again the light cloud passed across the picture, and again the subject changed. The father and mother were old and helpless now, and the number of those about them was diminished more than half; but content and cheerfulness sat on every face, and beamed in every eye, as they crowded round the fireside, and told and listened to old stories of earlier and bygone days. Slowly and peacefully, the father sank into the grave, and soon after, the sharer of all his cares and troubles followed him to a place of rest. The few, who yet survived them, knelt by their tomb, and watered the green turf which covered it, with their tears; then rose, and turned away; sadly and mournfully, but not with bitter cries, or despairing lamentations, for they knew that they should one day meet again; and once more they mixed with the busy world, and their content and cheerfulness was restored. The cloud settled upon the picture and concealed it from the sexton's view.

'What do you think of *that*?' said the goblin, turning his large face towards Gabriel Grub.

Gabriel murmured out something about its being very pretty, and looked somewhat ashamed, as the goblin bent his fiery eyes upon him.

'*You* a miserable man!' said the goblin, in a tone of excessive contempt. 'You!' He appeared disposed to add more, but indignation choked his utterance, so he lifted up one of his very pliable legs, and flourishing it above his head a little, to insure his aim, administered a good sound kick to Gabriel Grub; immediately after which, all the goblins in waiting crowded round the wretched sexton, and kicked him without mercy: according to the established and invariable custom of courtiers upon earth, who kick whom royalty kicks, and hug whom royalty hugs.

'Show him some more!' said the king of the goblins.

At these words, the cloud was dispelled, and a rich and beautiful landscape was disclosed to view – there is just such another, to this day, within half a mile of the old abbey town. The sun shone from out the clear blue sky, the water sparkled beneath his rays, and the trees looked greener, and the flowers more gay, beneath his cheering influence. The water rippled on, with a pleasant sound; the trees rustled in the light wind that murmured among their leaves; the birds sang upon the boughs; and the lark carolled on high her welcome to the morning. Yes, it was morning; the bright, balmy morning of summer; the minutest leaf, the smallest blade of grass, was instinct with life. The ant crept forth to her daily toil, the butterfly fluttered and basked in the warm rays of the sun; myriads of insects spread their transparent wings, and revelled in their brief but happy existence. Man walked forth elated with the scene; and all was brightness and splendour.

'*You* a miserable man!' said the king of the goblins, in a more contemptuous tone than before. And again the king of the goblins gave his leg a flourish; again it descended on the shoulders of the sexton; and again the attendant goblins imitated the example of their chief.

Many a time the cloud went and came, and many a lesson it taught to Gabriel Grub, who, although his shoulders smarted with pain from the frequent applications of the goblins' feet, looked on with an interest that nothing could diminish. He saw that men who worked hard, and earned their scanty bread with lives of labour, were cheerful and happy; and that to the most ignorant, the sweet face of nature was a never-failing source of cheerfulness and joy. He saw those who had been delicately nurtured, and tenderly brought up, cheerful under privations, and superior to suffering that would have crushed many of a rougher grain, because they bore within their own bosoms the materials of happiness, contentment, and peace. He saw that women, the tenderest and most fragile of all God's creatures, were the oftenest superior to sorrow, adversity, and distress; and he saw that it was because they bore, in their own hearts, an inexhaustible well-spring of affection and devotion. Above all, he saw that men like himself, who snarled at the mirth and cheerfulness of others, were the foulest weeds on the fair surface of the earth; and setting all the good of the world against the evil, he came to the conclusion that it was a very decent and respectable sort of world after all. No sooner had he formed it, than the cloud which closed over the last picture, seemed to settle on his senses, and lull him to repose. One by one, the goblins faded from his sight; and as the last one disappeared, he sunk to sleep.

The day had broken when Gabriel Grub awoke, and found himself lying, at full length on the flat gravestone in the churchyard, with the wicker bottle lying empty by his side, and his coat, spade, and lantern, all well whitened by the last night's frost, scattered on the ground. The stone on which he had first seen the goblin seated, stood bolt upright before him, and the grave at which he had worked, the night before, was not far off. At first, he began to doubt the reality of his adventures, but the acute pain in his shoulders when he attempted to rise, assured him that the kicking of the goblins was certainly not ideal. He was staggered again, by observing no traces of footsteps in the snow on which the goblins had played leap-frog with the gravestones, but he speedily accounted for this circumstance when he remembered that, being spirits, they would leave no visible impression behind them. So, Gabriel Grub got on his feet as well as he could, for the pain in his back; and brushing the frost off his coat, put it on, and turned his face towards the town.

But he was an altered man, and he could not bear the thought of returning to a place where his repentance would be scoffed at, and his reformation disbelieved. He hesitated for a few moments; and then turned away to wander where he might, and seek his bread elsewhere.

The lantern, the spade, and the wicker bottle, were found, that day, in the churchyard. There were a great many speculations about the sexton's fate at first, but it was speedily determined that he had been carried away by the goblins; and there were not wanting some very credible witnesses who had distinctly seen him whisked through the air on the back of a chestnut horse blind of one eye, with the hindquarters of a lion, and the tail of a bear. At length all this was devoutly believed; and the new sexton used to exhibit to the curious, for a trifling emolument, a good-sized piece of the church weathercock which had been accidentally picked up by himself in the churchyard, a year or two afterwards.

Unfortunately, these stories were somewhat disturbed by the unlooked-for re-appearance of Gabriel Grub himself, some ten years afterwards, a ragged, contented, rheumatic old man. He told his story to the clergyman, and also to the mayor, and in course of time it began to be received, as a matter of history, in which form it has continued down to this very day. The believers in the weathercock tale, having misplaced their confidence once, were not easily prevailed upon to part with it again, so they looked as wise as they could, shrugged their shoulders, touched their foreheads, and murmured something about Gabriel Grub having drunk all the Hollands, and then fallen asleep on the flat tombstone; and they affected to explain what he supposed he had witnessed in the goblin's cavern, by saying that he had seen the world, and grown wiser. But this opinion, which was by no means a popular one at any time, gradually died off; and be the matter how it may, as Gabriel Grub was afflicted with rheumatism to the end of his days, this story has at least one moral, if it teach no better one – and that is, that if a man turn sulky and drink by himself at Christmas time, he may make up his mind to be not a bit the better for it, let the spirits be never so good, or let them be even as many degrees beyond proof, as those which Gabriel Grub saw in the goblin's cavern.

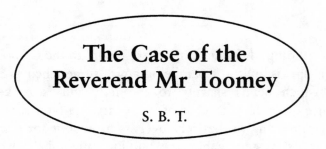

The Case of the Reverend Mr Toomey

S. B. T.

The time has come when the truth of this matter should be set on record.

I was six-and-twenty, sparkling with diplomas, full of science, when I joined my father in the Tyneside village of Cloughshaw; and the step to a partnership in the family practice was a crowning glory.

At Oxford I had found peace from the turmoil of an adolescent conscience under the direction of a Jesuit father. Later on, it is true, things went badly with me – to wit, when I came up to London and began to attend lectures at a famous medical school. It was not long before little matters which had been the subject of blushing confidences beneath the pale gleam of the half-seen ivory Christ furnished matter for ribald conversation in an atmosphere of tobacco and alcohol; and by the time the Royal College of Surgeons had gained in me an efficient member, the Catholic Church had practically lost a son.

Spring was melting into summer when I took possession of the rooms set apart for me in the wide rambling house that was my father's: earth was habited in new green; Easter smiled behind the tragedy of Holy Week.

On Good Friday morning I rode down the home side of the valley, across the wide, shallow river, and, bending to the left half-way up the opposite hill, followed the windings of a shady road as far as the park gates of Ridstowe Castle, a country house, the property of an ancient family by tradition faithful to the Old Religion. Upon the farther side of the house stands the Presbytery, where the family chaplain resides; his housekeeper it was whom my father had placed upon my list.

I committed my horse to a groom, for I had a purpose of assisting at the offices of the day, and walked the remaining hundred yards along a lane that shone with last night's downpour, past the prim little

Presbytery standing four-square upon its margin, to the Catholic chapel.

This chapel is built in a parallelogram of stone fencing, endlong to the lane, which bends sharply to the left; and is backed by an amphitheatre of green hills. One of them carries a faint scar, the work of pious feet, bearing to the right over its brow. But for a stone cross surmounting its western gable, the building might be a barn for its simplicity, if you should fail to note at the farther or eastward end the little rusty bell swinging in a crutch of masonry.

One side of this, I remember, was prolonged with an iron funnel, whence a thread of blue smoke went slenderly up.

The inside, as I found upon opening the door, matched well with this exterior. From the left, immediately within, came the warm gleam of candles, reflected from poor red hangings about the little temporary altar where, since the Mass of the day before, the sepulchred Sacrament had reposed. Rough benches accommodated a scanty congregation of simple folk, grey-headed many of them, tanned and wholesome, a few damsels of some pretension to gentility, a sprinkling of bright-eyed children. The high altar of rough sandstone faced me, stripped and cold, with its candles yet unlit. The priest at the Gospel side in a low harsh voice was reciting the Passion according to St John, while the people stood patiently and reverently, some telling their beads, some reading an English version of the narrative, some vaguely immersed in contemplation; the children striving for the most part with miniature jests to relieve the tedium of an unintelligible rite. I watched the officiant. A huge bulk of a redhaired, bull-throated personage, he stood there at the simple altar, his back from half to three-quarters towards me, leaning slightly forward over the missal, reading away for his life. His stature and vast proportions seemed to dwarf his environment, the oblong of his black chasuble to be but a patch upon the whiteness of the broad-stretched alb. Having finished the Passion, he turned and received his biretta from the server. I composed myself to an air of respectful attention.

It was not long, nor was it difficult to understand, the discourse that was roared from the altar-steps in tones of a trombone inflated with a zeal that is not according to knowledge: an orthodox exposition of the doctrine of Sacrifice; its terms crude, the application narrow. The gnawing of an empty stomach perhaps suggested to the preacher that much was yet to do before it might receive the solacement it craved, and he drew with welcome precipitancy to a close.

Meanwhile I had had time and a fair opportunity more exactly to observe him. At the base of a brow that retreated swiftly aloft bushy red tufts shadowed the caves in which smouldered two lacklustre eyes of indeterminate colour; a fat snub nose, with round distended nostrils, was mounted above an upper lip of portentous length; the mouth was wide and loose, the teeth jagged and discoloured; the chin and lower jaw were those of a prize-fighter. The accent which differentiated his speech I conjectured to be the strange resultant of Irish home influences modified by years spent at the Scot College under Italian professors, and subsequent residence in the North of England.

The ceremonies of the Mass of the Presanctified were resumed. Three audible grunts accompanied the triple genuflection with which the officiant in his stockinged feet led the way to pay reverence to the Crucifix lying cushioned before the Communion-rail. His offering for the Holy Places he deposited wrapped modestly in paper; and presently after, a little procession wended to the altar of repose.

I had never seen the ritual of the Church carried out with this extreme simplicity – the barest rubrical necessities, and no note of music to disguise the shuffling of heavy boots. Four grey-headed yeomen carried the simple canopy, whose bells tinkled warning of the priest's return bearing the Holy of Holies in a little fragrant cloud.

So strangely are common things transfigured by the touch of the great Mother Church. This dowdy little act of faith, by its very squalor of circumstance, moved me as nothing had had the power since the Pope's Mass, years before, and the silver trumpets. The rough features of the attendants were rigid with devout recollection; the priest's massive face was composed to a grave aspect of conscious responsibility, and his eyes were reverently fastened upon the swathed burden of the sepulchred Sacrament. A beam from a southern window lit up his cropped hair to a shining aureole.

Outside the chapel, while the people trailed heavily up the track to the top of the hill and disappeared one by one, I awaited his coming; and the last was hardly out of sight when, with a light coat drawn over his soutane, he issued. On seeing me he stretched out at once a cordial hand.

'I bid you welcome, sir,' he cried in his composite brogue. 'You'll be, I doubt not, Dr Moses, the younger of the name. Your respectable father gave me to understand that your advent was expected, and that you were of the Household of the Faith.'

'On Tuesday I arrived.' I answered. 'A most interesting little church you have here, and a charming corner of the world this, to live in. The building, snug between the hills, has a romantic air; hidden away, one might guess, from persecution in the good old times of prescription and the penal laws. Eighteenth century?'

'Bedad, sir, and you've mistaken entirely, though I don't say but it may have the air. Thirty years is the outside of its age; built by the gentleman who owns yon house and supports the mission. A great gentleman in London, but we see nothing of him here. He is proud of the church.'

'Why, as to its architectural pretensions –'

'Architecture! He boasts that it is the cheapest church in the land.'

'Ah, in that case it may be that he has foundation.'

'More than the building has, you'll agree, if you observed the walls. But you'll come into my house and let me offer you a little refreshment?'

We were at the door, and I followed him in. The room (he named it parlour) was such as I had expected to find it – poor, not with the clean, wholesome nakedness of St Francis' bride, but with the tawdriness of early-Victorian frippery. Set along two adjacent sides were half a dozen horsehair-covered chairs; a third wall was skirted by a sofa of uninviting exterior, from the vantage-ground of whose shining convexities a lace antimacassar perplexed the eye and set the teeth on edge. The centre of the scheme was a round mahogany table draped with a distressing entanglement of black ivy-leaves upon a scarlet ground. A gilt-framed mirror was based upon the mantel; below, an arrested rapid of coloured paper cloaked the empty grate.

'And there's my housekeeper, good woman: you'll be combining professional with religious duties, sir. I'll be right glad you should see her: I have faith in young men; for your science is not like mine, which can tell you little more than it could in the days of St Thomas Aquinas: and it's enough too, and be damned to it – we'll know the rest in good time. But this good woman of mine, Dr Moses,' he resumed anxiously, 'you'll do your best for her, sir? She's not as young as she was. She must be kept going – kept on, and on; be kept going, you understand, because I can't do without her – can't do without her.'

The speech ended with a silly quaver, and I stared at him. The bully host was eclipsed, and what emotion had wrought the change I could not understand; but, to my thinking, the man seemed afraid.

A lad brought in coffee and a light breakfast. After supplying me, he filled a vast beaker for himself and consumed it greedily, with infinite hoisting of eyebrow tufts and protrusion of heavy lips, with much puffing, and with noisy inarticulate expressions of satisfaction. He drank a second, and a third, sent the coffee-pot out to be refilled, and began upon the modest collation permitted in addition to the solitary full meal of a fast-day.

'It's a sore trial to a man of my physique, Dr Moses, is the law of fasting. I am grievously tempted whiles to seek dispensation, but there's that in me likes ill to be beaten.' I expressed sympathy. 'And now,' he continued, 'perhaps you would like to meet Mrs. Nolan – that keeps my house?'

The housekeeper I found to be a tall, dark Irishwoman, some fifty years of age, becomingly habited with strict regard to neatness in a dark gown set closely upon a spare figure, which apparently had yielded nothing of its spring and vigour to advancing years. Her iron-grey hair, parted in the mathematical middle, and drawn symmetrically to right and left over her ears, was surmounted by a decent cap. She was said to be suffering from an aneurysm, and my brief examination tended to confirm the theory. It was further evident that her nerves were in a strained, overwrought condition. There was an appearance of tension about the pallid face; her eyes were stretched to a weary watchfulness; the white lips were sucked in at the corners, as if to constrain them to immobility; her emaciated body leaned forward as if awaiting the signal of an invisible starter. The woman's manner was full of suppressions, of suspicions, of delayed hopes, of anticipated causes of terror.

When I questioned her as to her state of health her manner evinced indifference; it was that of one who is forced by a tactless companion to pursue a tasteless talk. I had even to reassure myself by a direct question whether there were anyone else in need of my services. Her sharp features became more pinched, her deep-set grey eyes lightened at me. Satisfied by her glance, she resumed her former demeanour as swiftly as on the instant she had left it, and lapsed into her previous condition of preoccupied civility. Having seen me at church –

'A Catholic?' she asked, with some animation.

'Of sorts.'

'Well, there is, maybe, hope for us yet,' she said, only half aloud; 'but I am getting an old woman.'

I took no pains to understand this comment on my answer; not every riddle is worth the riding.

'And what,' enquired her master upon my return to the parlour, 'might you think of her state of health?'

'I am but young to the trade, yet I cannot suffer your Reverence to rifle me of an opinion at such short notice.'

'That's well said – I will not press you. She is sixty, and I am forty; which, think you, has the better life?'

I smiled; it seemed a sufficient answer. His face clouded.

'There are other housekeepers,' I hinted.

'Who was denying it?' he cried roughly. 'And other priests, aye, and other doctors too; and what then?'

The tone of this reply reduced me to silence, and shortly after I took my leave.

The study into which on the occasion of my next visit he profusely welcomed me was a shade less dazzling than the parlour. On the shelves were ranged the standard books of theology, among them Gury's *Casus Conscientiae*, St Alphonsus' *Homo Apostolicus*, a copy of the *Summa*, Lingard's *History of England* in eight volumes, and the three spare tomes of a Mechlin Breviary. A large writing-table, supporting a crucifix and an image of Our Lady, and faced by a swivel chair, strove to suggest literary habits.

Upon the table, under the sheet of a local newspaper, peeped the shining segment of an iron ring.

My host followed me fussily, and gesticulated me into an easy chair. Seated, I found myself opposite the window, with the profile of the hearth and the length of the writing-table intervening. He turned to the latter to draw the swivel-chair nearer to me; there was an unevenness in his movements, and when his face came again into view it was dusky and the deepset little eyes glanced towards me apprehensively. I averted mine; sweeping the table as I turned to the view from the window; the steel was hidden.

I made a remark about the fishing-tackle, of which there was plenty. His face smoothed.

'You'll be a sportsman, sir?'

'I am no fisherman, father.'

'You like a more vigorous sport. You're a strong man, Dr Moses: a fine pair of shoulders you have on you, and your horse has need to be up to a heavy weight.'

'Twelve-stone-seven I rowed in the trials – for the University eight, you know – but I am in no sort of condition now.'

He fixed his eyes upon me watchfully.

'I am a strong man myself,' he said. 'Have you an arm to beat that?' And to my surprise he began to divest himself of his cassock and to roll up his shirt-sleeve. The childish display was accompanied by nothing of boastfulness; rather, as he gazed at the knotted muscles, his face clouded with profound dejection. In compliance with his request I exposed my arm for comparison. He paid me a compliment, and concluded, with a sigh, 'You're little more than a child to me.' It was the truth.

I paid a visit to Mrs. Nolan in her room. Hers was a case for which a doctor could do little; and after giving her some general advice I returned to the study. The priest was sitting in a brooding attitude before the paper Niagara, and seemed hardly aware of my entrance. The woman came in behind me.

'Just to bid your Reverence good-day.' And I offered a hand.

He hardly touched it, and turning to the housekeeper said in a husky voice, 'The lamp!'

The woman smothered an ejaculation, and her face was white as a leper's while she hurriedly guided me to the door.

Before I had descended the three little white steps it was abruptly closed.

This was the Tuesday in Easter week. On Wednesday I heard that Father Toomey's housekeeper was dead.

I waited a day, and received no summons. On Thursday I determined to call.

The man himself came to the door. He looked flabby and

frightened. His eyes were red, his great cheeks hung down, his shoulders were bowed; shame and defiance were mingled in his bearing.

'I saw who it was,' he said; 'and though I did not send for you, you are welcome. There is a woman here who has done what was necessary, but there must be a certificate. This way – follow me.'

He led upstairs to a darkened room, where the scent of flowers was heavy in the air, with the effluvia of burning wax. Six yellow flames stooped towards the open door.

The face was bare, and almost seemed that of a young woman. A holy-water stoup with an aspersory stood at the feet. 'I will send the woman up to you,' he said, 'in case you think it necessary to make any examination.'

When I descended I believed myself justified in certifying that the woman died from the rupture of an aneurysm.

Downstairs in the study the priest was sitting doubled up in his armchair, and his face wore a grey look of despair which, while it moved pity, kindled once again my curiosity as to the true relations of these persons; for that they were merely those of master and servant I could not pretend to believe. It was no business of mine – and yet, who could say?

'A great loss to you, Father Toomey. I condole with you very sincerely, believe me.' And I took his hand, which was limp and cold.

'You would say so,' he replied, 'if you knew all. Did you ever lose a mother?' he asked, looking up.

'My mother is living.'

'Mine is dead; you have just seen all that is left of her. But what is that – a mother? Most men live to see their mothers die; it is the order of Nature. But not while they have need of them – my God! – need of them. You wonder,' he went on, constraining his tone, 'how you came to find her here in the character of a housekeeper?'

'Tell me nothing more than you are disposed to say: I ask for no confidences.'

'Oh, it was simple: just a mother's pride – an Irish mother's pride – that has a son a priest. I must have a servant, and she must be there to see the glory – rest her soul! — that is how it began. And then – then, sir, came the need!'

'The need?'

'The need.' He steadied his gaze upon me as he spoke, leaning forward with his elbow on his knee and his great chin resting on the palm of his hand.

'It is not difficult to conceive that the loss of your mother's presence will be a bitter grief to you,' I began.

He laughed in my face, and the sound was not a merry one.

'My dear young man, we are two professional consolers; and we know too well the tricks of the trade to derive consolation from them. Also, allow me to say, you clean mistake the situation. If she that's gone had been related to me in any other degree of consanguinity, or in none, I'd be in just the same quandary. I will be frank with you, and you shall give me your professional word to observe my confidence; at present I can see but one way out of it – and that goes straight to Hell.'

I looked at him, and he meant it.

'Father Toomey,' I said, after a moment's reflection, 'you have given me a confidence which I would gladly have been dispensed from receiving – enough to make me very anxious about you, while it leaves me perfectly impotent to aid. I can imagine no motive for your saying so much unless a fancy that I may be able to help you; and that I will do very readily if you will show me how. But you must be good enough to tell me more. I am still too much in the dark to pretend to be of the slightest assistance. If you are willing to give me your full confidence I am ready to guard it.'

During this long exhortation he had grown distracted. I waited for an answer, but none came. Then rising abruptly, and stretching out his hand as I was preparing to leave him: 'The funeral,' he said, 'will be on Friday. Goodbye.'

'Come and see me on Friday,' he cried, as I mounted.

I nodded a promise.

Mr Toomey celebrated the Requiem Mass on the Friday with about as much show of emotion as if the intention were one of a batch. He aspersed the corpse with an air of conscious efficiency; and when it had been lowered into the grave, turned his back at once, doffed the sacred vestments, and returned to the house ravening. I found him swilling coffee at a vast rate.

His mood seemed uncommunicative, but I waited on. The man's

affairs were nothing to me: the less I knew of them, perhaps, the better; yet if he had need of my assistance, either as a doctor or as a fellow-creature, he should have his opportunity. Half an hour of his futile chatter wearied me; I remembered that there were patients, and rose to go.

'Goodbye, sir, and God bless you! It was a kind attention on your part to assist at the Mass today. And as to the matter I spoke to you about when last you were here – well, you'll please to forget it. I was not, perhaps, altogether myself at the time, and since then I have seen reason to believe that the affair is settled. The good woman that's gone, I have little doubt, has attained to her reward; she was a saint; and I know I can depend upon her making good use of her opportunities.'

He watched me away, with a confident smile upon his wide face.

For a fortnight I saw nothing of him. I had no professional call to his house, and the man himself, with his abrupt changes from morbid dread to a chuckling security – from what? – did not please me. There was something inhuman about him.

Then, on Thursday of the third week, as I was on the point to set out for my afternoon round, a telegram: 'At once; come without delay. – Toomey.'

Nothing less than a case of extreme necessity could excuse its peremptory tone. His confidence in heavenly intercession appeared to be intermittent.

'How is Father Toomey?' I asked of the lad who opened the door.

'Father Toomey is quite well,' he answered, 'thank you, sir.'

'The devil he is!' I thought; 'and that is a piece of impertinence on his part anyway, unless the new housekeeper is the patient.'

'Who is ill?' I asked.

'Nobody,' he replied.

'Is Father Toomey in?'

'He is in, sir: will you step forward?'

I stepped forward, opened the door of the study, and, without waiting to be announced, walked in.

'What brings you?' he asked, looking at me dully.

I showed him the telegram. 'You sent it?' I enquired.

'Aye, I sent it, and it's that has been troubling me – whether I had or no. I had an impression, but they are treacherous things.'

'Telegrams?'

'Impressions.'

'And now, perhaps, you will tell me what it is you want?'

'Want! Help it is I want, and shielding, and constraining, maybe; and strengthening to strive against it, and hope to win through with it, and a stout heart to give me courage; and where shall I look for them? I know of none for certain in the width and length of the land who can help me through. There was one: she is gone.'

'Let me, at least –'

'You must not interrupt me,' he hurried on, with an impetuous gesture. 'I have chosen to place confidence in you, and you must not fail me. You have a strong head and strong arms, if the call comes, and, I do believe, a strong heart; and it's of that above all there is need; for you must help me alone, and you must keep my secret. I am a priest, mind you; I love my office; I will live and die in the service of the altar.'

'My dear Father Toomey, I protest I have not the ghost of an idea what you are driving at, or what it is you want me to do; but it shall be done if it lies reasonably within my power.'

'Will you spend this night here?'

'You are very kind.'

'You will perhaps not say that tomorrow. I ask you as a favour; I beg you not to say no.'

'I will spend the night here.'

'Thank you – thank God! There is a saint above, and I do think there is no need, but I dare not watch by myself.' He turned his eyes upon me.

'You'll stay now?' he asked.

'I have patients.'

'Tomorrow for them?'

'Today.'

'What time will you be back?'

'Seven your dinner-hour?'

'It shall be. You'll not be late?'

'You may depend on me.'

We sat silent after dinner, smoking, thinking. I had learned the ugly story; the origin of his sufferings (but I am not to write his confession), the various forms of the recurrent horror, through which the mother had devoted herself to his service, his hopes for the future. And particularly he had shown me his spirits swinging between exultation and despair for the event of that cardinal night.

The long hand hid the short at the apex of the dial, the hammer rang upon the silver gong.

'The new day!' he cried. ''Tis good to have a friend at Court.'

My heart went forth to the man, and I stretched out my hand. There was no response. I looked. His face had fallen; the ray of exultation had deserted it, its ruddiness was fled, its lines gone smooth, its character all changed.

His voice when he spoke was another voice, thin and piping; I could scarcely realize that it came from the same throat. And he seemed to strive with a recalcitrant tongue; as a man strives in a dream to make his speech articulate, he babbled awhile before the vagrant syllables cohered into words – into a phrase:

'Mother – the lamp – is going down!'

His eyes were directed, not to the globe which lighted the room, but towards a spot on the wall to one side of it. They were silly and unfocussed, like machines out of gear, and the voice was the voice of a frightened child. The man's whole frame, too, had lost its tenseness and vigour, and had gone slack, like his face. His arms hung limply over the sides of the chair, the veins at the back of them all swollen. His knees leaned foolishly against each other, the feet apart; his tufted red eyebrows, raised ridiculously, showed the little doting eyes too large. I knew that his hope had failed him, that it rested with me to save the man from the dangers to which, while the trial should endure, he would be exposed. For years his mother's magnetic presence had been his safeguard, so that the means of forcible restraint, the chance glimpse of which some time before had surprised me, had been unnecessary. But tonight he was in strange hands, and when I looked at the herculean form opposed to me, and remembered that within a certain space it might be as animated by a wild beast – when I remembered that by my promise I was bound to worry through the trial alone, without aid from any other creature – I confess that my heart sank.

The further events of this night, as I am about to record them, I have no theory to explain. A theologian would be ready enough with his solution; but I am a man of science, and shall content myself with writing down the things I saw and heard.

Presently the clouded eyes cleared, the loose mouth took shape, the dangling knock-knee form was braced, and the person who sat there spoke.

The voice was the voice of a stranger – different from the childish falsetto which had whined of the failing light, quite another than the brassy roar in which the priest was accustomed to speak. This voice was round and full, and rich with musical modulations. The Reverend Mr Toomey talked habitually with an accent of blended provincialism; grammatically indeed, but with the pedantic syntax of a man whose ears had first been opened amongst the illiterate. The Voice spoke a language of noble literary form, articulated with a due consciousness of syllabic force and the distinction of vowel sounds. And the matter of the discourse offered a still more striking contrast. But my wits are too dull, my pen too clumsy to record the words that streamed from those gross lips during the hours of that wonderful night.

It was the speech of one to whom the events of the twilight past, to others matter of difficult conjecture, were of secure knowledge – the recurrence of ice-ages the incidents of a circling year. The secrets that scientists are feeling after he betrayed, as if by inadvertence, and apologized. History was unfolded, as by photographs thrown three hundred a minute onto a screen; the astonished hearer saw the world's events happen; smelt carnage, tasted blood; the music of pæans, the chuckle of successful diplomacy, sounded in his ears.

With fiery, luminous phrase he painted wonders of other worlds, as might have done a tout for some celestial Cook; every word convincing as a bullet, phrases that made the mind blink as at the bright shining of new horizons.

All literature was open, from the *Vedas* to the last sonnet of the last new minor poet. The speaker knew all philosophies with the intimacy of one who has watched (as one might watch under a microscope the activities of an anthill) great minds at work.

Hour after hour the wondrous golden speech flowed on, and held me hypnotized.

It was five o'clock, and the light of the young day crept through crevices in the shutters. There was a pause. Then the mouth opened again, and this time the Voice sang. At first a barbarous recitative, the long passages of monotone relieved by rare and vague inflections; the words articulate but unintelligible, and that not with the unintelligibility of a contemporary foreign speech, but with the doubtfulness of semi-bestial sounds indicative of simple emotions. The tone became purer, the intervals more justly defined; the scales were unfamiliar, but the melodies expressed the emotions of civilized life; and from the deepest recesses of my memory blurred reminiscences of the Greek classics came flitting forth in response. Great songs, caught from the dying breath of defunct races and vanished societies, hymned the elemental forces, Nature's springs.

Beneath the vaulting of a mediaeval choir black-robed Benedictines chanted the great paean of the Veiled Presence, *Lauda Sion Salvatorem*, and candles were red through incense fog. A puff of ribald parody extinguished them.

A certain fugue of Bach's in A, not printed in the ordinary collections, is familiar to me. That fugue the singer sang, all the twining phrases of it, in four distinct voices from his one mouth. While he sang I watched him, and this is what I am prepared to attest: that during the whole of that weird performance Mr Toomey's chest was *still*.

Of the paroxysm which he had warned me was customarily the last phase of the seizure, I had seen no sign. The means of restraint were to my hand, but I let the moment pass. A full chord from the one mouth, and then, in the pause of half a bar, the change came. The eyes became suffused and glared shiftily upon my face, the red shock of hair bristled erect, the yellow teeth were bare of the quivering updrawn lip, and with a snarl the Beast was upon me.

The blow with which I met the oncoming hardly checked it. The face where I had struck showed a hollow, but the creature's course was not stayed, nor did the burning eyes so much as blink; only the assailant modified his manner of attack. The hands, which had been stretched towards my neck, seized upon my left arm, which had struck, and, while the creature's head was recklessly exposed to my right hand, the fangs crunched through the rest of my left forearm and gnawed the bones.

The agony of this bestial attack multiplied my force. By a supreme effort I threw the grunting devil to the floor. He dragged me with him by his teeth still grimly fleshed, while with my free hand I strove to clutch his windpipe. In vain I stiffened my fingers upon the great throat; there was no sign of congestion about the face, the eyes burned with the same fire of undistracted cruelty, the heavy jawbone ground upon the lacerated limb as we rolled over and over in the stale light of the smoking lamp.

Upon our death-grapple broke in the tinkle of the bell from the little church, the first stroke of the morning Angelus. The Beast's teeth relaxed, and I fell round onto my back, lost for the moment to consciousness. The last strokes were still sounding when I recovered my senses and sprang up.

There upon the carpet lay the body of the Beast. From the widespread nostrils issued no breath; the eyes were open and glassy. I laid my hand upon the region of the heart; there was not the faintest flutter.

And the corpse of the man with whom not a hundred seconds before I had been at death-grips was stone cold. My fist had dented – not bruised – the face. That is, the man had been dead for hours.

But upon the fallen jaw my blood *was wet*.

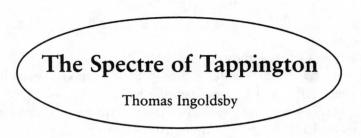

The Spectre of Tappington

Thomas Ingoldsby

'It is very odd, though; what can have become of them?' said Charles Seaforth, as he peeped under the valance of an old-fashioned bedstead, in an old-fashioned apartment of a still more old-fashioned manor house; "tis confoundedly odd, and I can't make it out at all. Why, Barney, where are they? – and where the d–l are you?'

No answer was returned to this appeal; and the lieutenant, who was, in the main, a reasonable person, – at least as reasonable a person as any young gentleman of twenty-two in 'the service' can fairly be expected to be, – cooled when he reflected that his servant could scarcely reply extempore to a summons which it was impossible he should hear.

An application to the bell was the considerate result; and the footsteps of as tight a lad as ever put pipe-clay to belt sounded along the gallery.

'Come in!' said his master. An ineffectual attempt upon the door reminded Mr Seaforth that he had locked himself in. 'By heaven! this is the oddest thing of all,' said he, as he turned the key and admitted Mr Maguire into his dormitory.

'Barney, where are my pantaloons?'

'Is it the breeches?' asked the valet, casting an inquiring eye round the apartment; 'is it the breeches, sir?'

'Yes; what have you done with them?'

'Sure then your honour had them on when you went to bed, and it's hereabout they'll be, I'll be bail'; and Barney lifted a fashionable tunic from a cane-backed arm chair, proceeding in his examination. But the search was in vain: there was the tunic aforesaid, – there was a smart-looking kerseymere waistcoat; but the most important article of all in a gentleman's wardrobe was still wanting.

'Where *can* they be?' asked the master, with a strong accent on the auxiliary verb.

'Sorrow a know I knows,' said the man.

'It *must* have been the devil, then, after all, who has been here and carried them off!' cried Seaforth, staring full into Barney's face.

Mr Maguire was not devoid of the superstition of his countrymen, still he looked as if he did not quite subscribe to the sequitur.

His master read incredulity in his countenance. 'Why, I tell you, Barney, I put them there, on that arm-chair, when I got into bed; and, by Heaven! I distinctly saw the ghost of the old fellow they told me of, come in at midnight, put on my pantaloons, and walk away with them.'

'May be so,' was the cautious reply.

'I thought, of course, it was a dream; but then, – where the d – I are the breeches?'

The question was more easily asked than answered. Barney renewed his search, while the lieutenant folded his arms, and, leaning against the toilet, sunk into a reverie.

'After all, it must be some trick of my laughter-loving cousins,' said Seaforth.

'Ah, then, the ladies!' chimed in Mr Maguire, though the observation was not addressed to him; 'and will it be Miss Caroline, or Miss Fanny, that's stole your honour's things?'

'I hardly know what to think of it,' pursued the bereaved lieutenant, still speaking in soliloquy, with his eye resting dubiously on the chamber-door. 'I locked myself in, that's certain, and – but there must be some other entrance to the room – pooh! I remember – the private staircase; how could I be such a fool?' and he crossed the chamber to where a low oaken doorcase was dimly visible in a distant corner. He paused before it. Nothing now interfered to screen it from observation; but it bore tokens of having been at some earlier period concealed by tapestry, remains of which yet clothed the walls on either side of the portal.

'This way they must have come,' said Seaforth; 'I wish with all my heart I had caught them!'

'Och! the kittens!' sighed Mr Barney Maguire.

But the mystery was yet as far from being solved as before. True, there *was* the 'other door'; but then that, too, on examination, was even more firmly secured than the one which opened on the gallery, – two heavy bolts on the inside effectually prevented any *coup de main* on the lieutenant's *bivouac* from that quarter. He was more puzzled than ever; nor did the minutest inspection of the walls and floor throw any light upon the subject! One thing only was clear, – the breeches were gone! 'It is *very* singular,' said the lieutenant.

Tappington (generally called Tapton) Everard is an antiquated but commodious manor-house in the eastern division of the county of Kent. A former proprietor had been High-sheriff in the days of Elizabeth, and many a dark and dismal tradition was yet extant of the licentiousness of his life, and the enormity of his offences. The Glen, which the keeper's daughter was seen to enter, but never known to quit, still frowns darkly as of yore; while an ineradicable bloodstain on the oaken stair yet bids defiance to the united energies of soap and sand. But it is with one particular apartment that a deed of more especial atrocity is said to be connected. A stranger guest – so runs the legend – arrived unexpectedly at the mansion of the 'Bad Sir Giles'. They met in apparent friendship; but the ill-concealed scowl on their master's brow told the domestics that the visit was not a welcome one; the banquet, however, was not spared; the wine-cup circulated freely – too freely, perhaps, for sounds of discord at length reached the ears of even the excluded serving-men as they were doing their best to imitate their betters in the lower hall. Alarmed, some of them ventured to approach the parlour; one, an old and favoured retainer of the house, went so far as to break in upon his master's privacy. Sir Giles, already high in oath, fiercely enjoined his absence, and he retired; not, however, before he had distinctly heard from the stranger's lips a menace that 'There was that within his pocket which could disprove the knight's right to issue that or any other command within the walls of Tapton.'

The intrusion, though momentary, seemed to have produced a beneficial effect; the voices of the disputants fell, and the conversation was carried on thenceforth in a more subdued tone, till, as evening closed in, the domestics, when summoned to attend with lights, found not only cordiality restored, but that a still deeper carouse was meditated. Fresh stoups, and from the choicest bins, were produced; nor was it till at a late, or rather early hour, that the revellers sought their chambers.

The one allotted to the stranger occupied the first floor of the eastern angle of the building, and had once been the favourite apartment of Sir Giles himself. Scandal ascribed this preference to the facility which a private staircase, communicating with the ground, had afforded him, in the old knight's time, of following his wicked courses unchecked by parental observation; a consideration which ceased to be of weight when the death of his father left him uncontrolled master of his estate and actions. From that period Sir Giles had established himself in what were called the 'state apartments'; and the 'oaken chamber' was rarely tenanted, save on occasions of extraordinary festivity, or when the yule log drew an unusually large accession of guests around the Christmas hearth.

On this eventful night it was prepared for the unknown visitor, who sought his couch heated and inflamed from his midnight orgies, and in the morning was found in his bed a swollen and blackened corpse. No marks of violence appeared upon the body; but the livid hue of the lips, and certain darkcolour spots visible on the skin, aroused suspicions which those who entertained them were too timid to express. Apoplexy, induced by the excesses of the preceding night, Sir Giles's confidential leech pronounced to be the cause of his sudden dissolution; the body was buried in peace; and though some shook their heads as they witnessed the haste with which the funeral rites were hurried on, none ventured to murmur. Other events arose to distract the attention of the retainers; men's minds became occupied by the stirring politics of the day, while the near approach of that formidable armada, so vainly arrogating to itself a title which the very elements joined with human valour to disprove, soon interfered to weaken, if not obliterate, all remembrance of the nameless stranger who had died within the walls of Tapton Everard.

Years rolled on: the 'Bad Sir Giles' had himself long since gone to his account, the last, as it was believed, of his immediate line; though a few of the older tenants were sometimes heard to speak of an elder brother, who had disappeared in early life, and never inherited the estate. Rumours, too, of his having left a son in foreign lands were at one time rife: but they died away, nothing occurring to support them: the property passed unchallenged to a collateral branch of the family, and the secret, if secret there were, was buried in Denton churchyard, in the lonely grave of the mysterious stranger. One circumstance alone occurred, after a long-intervening period, to revive the memory of these transactions. Some workmen employed in grubbing an old plantation, for the purpose of raising on its site a modern shrubbery, dug up, in the execution of their task, the milldewed remnants of what seemed to have been once a garment. On more minute inspection, enough remained of silken slashes and a coarse embroidery to identify the relics as having once formed part of a pair of trunk hose; while a few papers which fell from them, altogether illegible from damp and age, were by the unlearned rustics conveyed to the then owner of the estate.

Whether the squire was more successful in deciphering them was never known; he certainly never alluded to their contents; and little would have been thought of the matter but for the inconvenient memory of one old woman, who declared she heard her grandfather say that when the 'stranger guest' was poisoned, though all the rest of his clothes were there, his breeches, the supposed repository of the supposed documents, could never be found. The master of Tapton Everard smiled when he heard Dame Jones's hint of deeds which might impeach the validity of his own title in favour of some unknown descendant of some unknown heir; and the story was rarely alluded to, save by one or two miracle-mongers, who had heard that others had seen the ghost of old Sir Giles, in his night-cap, issue from the postern, enter the adjoining copse, and wring his shadowy hands in agony, as he seemed to search vainly for something hidden among the evergreens. The stranger's death-room had, of course, been occasionally haunted from the time of his decease; but the periods of visitation had latterly become very rare – even Mrs Botherby, the house-keeper, being forced to admit that, during her long sojourn at the manor, she had never 'met with anything worse than herself'; though, as the old lady afterwards added upon more mature reflection, 'I must say I think I saw the devil *once.*'

Such was the legend attached to Tapton Everard, and such the story which the lively Caroline Ingoldsby detailed to her equally mercurial cousin Charles Seaforth, lieutenant in the Hon. East India Company's second regiment of Bombay Fencibles, as arm-in-arm they promenaded a gallery decked with some dozen grim-looking ancestral portraits, and, among others, with that of the redoubted Sir Giles himself. The gallant commander had that very morning paid his first visit to the house of his maternal uncle, after an absence of several years passed with his regiment on the arid plains of Hindostan, whence he was now returned on a three years' furlough. He had gone out a boy – returned a man; but the impression made upon his youthful fancy by his favourite cousin remained unimpaired, and to Tapton he directed his steps, even before he sought the home of his widowed mother – comforting himself in this breach of filial decorum by the reflection that, as the manor was so little out of his way, it would be unkind to pass, as it were, the door of his relatives without just looking in for a few hours.

But he found his uncle as hospitable and his cousin more charming than ever; and the looks of one, and the requests of the other, soon precluded the possibility of refusing to lengthen the 'few hours' into a few days, though the house was at the moment full of visitors.

The Peterses were there from Ramsgate; and Mr, Mrs, and the two Miss Simpkinsons, from Bath, had come to pass a month with the family; and Tom Ingoldsby had brought down his college friend the Honourable Augustus Sucklethumbkin, with his groom and pointers, to take a fortnight's shooting. And then there was Mrs Ogleton, the rich young widow, with her large black eyes, who, people did say, was setting her cap at the young squire, though Mrs Botherby did not believe it; and, above all, there was Mademoiselle Pauline, her *femme de chambre* who '*mon-Dieu*'d' everything and everybody, and cried, '*Quel horreur!*' at Mrs Botherby's cap. In short, to use the last-named and much-respected lady's own expression, the house was 'choke-full' to the very attics – all, save the 'oaken chamber', which, as the lieutenant expressed a most magnanimous disregard of ghosts, was forthwith appropriated to his particular accommodation. Mr Maguire meanwhile was fain to share the apartment of Oliver Dobbs, the squire's own man: a jocular proposal of joint occupancy having been first indignantly rejected by 'Mademoiselle', though preferred with the 'laste taste in life' of Mr Barney's most insinuating brogue.

'Come, Charles, the urn is absolutely getting cold; your breakfast will be quite spoiled: what can have made you so idle?' Such was the morning salutation of Miss Ingoldsby to the *militaire* as he entered the breakfast-room half an hour after the latest of the party.

'A pretty gentleman, truly, to make an appointment with,' chimed in Miss Frances. 'What is become of our ramble to the rocks before breakfast?'

'Oh! the young men never think of keeping a promise now,' said Mrs Peters, a little ferret-faced woman with underdone eyes.

'When I was a young man,' said Mr Peters, 'I remember I always made a point of – '

'Pray how long ago was that?' asked Mr Simpkinson from Bath.

'Why, sir, when I married Mrs Peters, I was – let me see – I was –'

'Do pray hold your tongue, P, and eat your breakfast!' interrupted his better half, who had a mortal horror of chronological references; 'it's very rude to tease people with your family affairs.'

The lieutenant had by this time taken his seat in silence – a good-humoured nod, and a glance, half-smiling half-inquisitive, being the extent of his salutation. Smitten as he was, and in the immediate presence of her who had made so large a hole in his heart, his manner was evidently *distrait*, which the fair Caroline in her secret soul attributed to his being solely occupied by her *agrémens* – how would she have bridled had she known that they only shared his meditations with a pair of breeches!

Charles drank his coffee and spiked some half-dozen eggs, darting occasionally a penetrating glance at the ladies, in hope of detecting the supposed waggery by the evidence of some furtive smile or conscious look. But in vain; not a dimple moved indicative of roguery, nor did the slightest elevation of eyebrow rise confirmative in his suspicions. Hints and insinuations passed unheeded – more particular inquiries were out of the question: – the subject was unapproachable.

In the meantime, 'patent cords' were just the thing for a morning's ride; and, breakfast ended, away cantered the party over the downs, till, every faculty absorbed by the beauties, animate and inanimate, which surrounded him, Lieutenant Seaforth of the Bombay Fencibles bestowed no more thought on his breeches than if he had been born on the top of Ben Lomond.

Another night had passed away; the sun rose brilliantly, forming with his level beams a splendid rainbow in the far-off west, whither the heavy cloud, which for the last two hours had been pouring its waters on the earth, was now flying before him.

'Ah! then, and it's little good it'll be the claning of ye,' apostrophised Mr Barney Maguire, as he deposited, in front of his master's toilet, a pair of 'bran-new' jockey boots, one of Hoby's primest fits, which the lieutenant had purchased on his way through town. On that very morning had they come for the first time under the valet's depuriating hand, so little soiled, indeed, from the turfy ride of the preceding day, that a less scrupulous domestic might, perhaps, have considered the application of 'Warren's Matchless', or oxalic acid, altogether superfluous. Not so Barney: with the nicest care had he removed the slightest impurity from each polish surface, and there they stood, rejoicing in their sable radiance. No wonder a pang shot across Mr Maguire's breast, as he thought on the work now cut out for them, so different from the light labours of the day before; no wonder he murmured with a sigh, as the scarce-dried window-panes disclosed a road now inch-deep in mud, 'Ah! then, it's little good the claning of ye!' – for well had he learned in the hall below that eight miles of a stiff clay soil lay between the Manor and Bolsover Abbey, whose picturesque ruins, 'Like ancient Rome, majestic in decay' the party had determined to explore. The master had already commenced dressing, and the man was fitting straps upon a light pair of crane-necked spurs, when his hand was arrested by the old question, 'Barney, where are the breeches?'

They were nowhere to be found!

Mr Seaforth descended that morning, whip in hand, and equipped in a handsome green riding-frock, but no 'breeches and boots to match' were there: loose jean trousers, surmounting a pair of diminutive Wellingtons, embraced, somewhat incongruously, his nether man, *vice* the 'patent cords', returned, like yesterday's pantaloons, absent without leave. The 'top-boots' had a holiday.

'A fine morning after the rain,' said Mr Simpkinson from Bath.

'Just the thing for the 'ops', said Mr Peters. 'I remember when I was a boy –'

'Do hold your tongue, P,' said Mrs Peters, advice which that exemplary matron was in the constant habit of administering to 'her P', as she called him, whenever he prepared to vent his reminiscences. Her precise reason for this it would be difficult to determine, unless, indeed, the story be true which a little bird had whispered into Mrs Botherby's ear, Mr Peters, though now a wealthy man, had received a liberal education at a charity-school, and was apt to recur to the days of his muffin-cap and leathers. As usual, he took his wife's hint in good part, and 'paused in his reply'.

'A glorious day for the ruins!' said young Ingoldsby. 'But, Charles, what the deuce are you about? You don't mean to ride through our lanes in such toggery as that?'

'Lassy me!' said Miss Julia Simpkinson, 'won't you be very wet?'

'You had better take Tom's cab', quoth the squire.

But this proposition was at once overruled: Mrs Ogleton had already nailed the cab, a vehicle of all others the best adapted for a snug flirtation.

'Or drive Miss Julia in the phaeton?' No; that was the post of Mr Peters, who, indifferent as an equestrian, had acquired some fame as a whip while travelling through the midland counties for the firm of Bagshaw, Snivelby, and Ghrimes.

'Thank you, I shall ride with my cousins', said Charles, with as much *nonchalance* as he could assume – and he did so; Mr Ingoldsby, Mrs Peters, Mr Simpkinson from Bath, and his eldest daughter with her *album*, following in the family coach. The gentleman-commoner 'voted the affair d – d slow', and declined the party altogether in favour of the gamekeeper and a cigar. 'There was "no fun" in looking at old houses!' Mrs Simpkinson preferred a short *séjour* in the still-room with Mrs Botherby, who had promised to initiate her in that grand *arcanum*, the transmutation of gooseberry jam into Guava jelly.

'Did you ever seen an old abbey before, Mr Peters?'

'Yes, miss, a French one; we have got one at Ramsgate; he teaches the Miss Joneses to parley-voo, and is turned of sixty.'

Miss Simpkinson closed her album with an air of ineffable disdain.

Mr Simpkinson from Bath was a professed antiquary, and one of the first water; he was master of Gwillim's Heraldry, and Milles's *History of the Crusades*; knew every plate in the *Monasticon*; had written an essay on the origin and dignity of the office of overseer, and settled the date of a Queen Anne's farthing. An influential member of the Antiquarian Society, to whose 'Beauties of Bagnigge Wells' he had been a liberal subscriber, procured him a seat at the board of that learned body, since which happy epoch Sylvanus Urban had not a more indefatigable correspondent. His inaugural essay on the President's cocked hat was considered a miracle of erudition: and his account of the earliest application of gilding to gingerbread, a masterpiece of antiquarian research. His eldest daughter was of a kindred spirit: if her father's mantle had not fallen upon her, it was only because he had not thrown it off himself; she had caught hold of its tail, however, while it yet hung upon his honoured shoulders. To souls so congenial, what a sight was the magnificent ruin of Bolsover! its broken arches, its mouldering pinnacles, and the airy tracery of its half-demolished windows. The party were in raptures; Mr Simpkinson began to meditate an essay, and his daughter an ode: even Seaforth, as he gazed on these lonely relics of the olden time, was betrayed into a momentary forgetfulness of his love and losses; the widow's eye-glass turned from her *cicisbeo's* whiskers to the mantling ivy: Mrs Peters wiped her spectacles; and 'her P' supposed the central tower 'had once been the county jail'. The squire was a philosopher, and had been there often before, so he ordered out the cold tongue and chickens.

'Bolsover Priory,' said Mrs Simpkinson, with the air of a connoisseur, 'Bolsover Priory was founded in the reign of Henry the Sixth, about the beginning of the eleventh century. Hugh de Bolsover had accompanied that monarch to the Holy Land, in the expedition undertaken by way of penance for the murder of his young nephews in the Tower. Upon the dissolution of the monasteries, the veteran was enfeoffed in the lands and manor, to which he gave his own name of Bowlsover, or Bee-owls-over (by corruption Bolsover) – a Bee in chief, over three Owls, all proper, being the armorial ensigns borne by this distinguished crusader at the siege of Acre.'

'Ah! that was Sir Sidney Smith,' said Mr Peters; 'I've heard tell of him, and all about Mrs Partington, and –'

'P, be quiet, and don't expose yourself!' sharply interrupted his lady. P was silenced, and betook himself to the bottled stout.

'These lands,' continued the antiquary, 'were held in grand serjeantry by the presentation of three white owls and a pot of honey –'

'Lassy me! how nice!' said Miss Julia. Mr Peters licked his lips.

'Pray give me leave, my dear – owls and honey, whenever the king should come a rat-catching into this part of the country.'

'Rat-catching!' ejaculated the squire, pausing abruptly in the mastication of a drumstick.

'To be sure, my dear sir: don't you remember that rats once came under the forest laws – a minor species of venison? "Rats and mice, and such small deer," eh? – Shakespear, you know. Our ancestors ate rats ('The nasty fellows!' shuddered Miss Julia in a parenthesis); and owls, you know, are capital mousers –'

'I've seen a howl,' said Mr Peters; 'there's one in the Sohological Gardens – a little hook-nosed chap in a wig – only its feathers and –'

Poor P was destined never to finish a speech.

'Do be quiet!' cried the authoritative voice, and the would-be naturalist shrank into his shell, like a snail in the 'Sohological Gardens.'

'You should read Blount's *Jocular Tenures*, Mr Ingoldsby,' pursued Simpkinson. 'A learned man was Blount! Why, sir, his Royal Highness the Duke of York once paid a silver horse-shoe to Lord Ferrers –'

'I've heard of him,' broke in the incorrigible Peters; 'he was hanged at the old Bailey in a silk rope for shooting Dr Johnson.'

The antiquary vouchsafed no notice of the interruption; but, taking a pinch of snuff, continued his harangue.

'A silver horse-shoe, sir, which is due from every scion of royalty who rides across one of his manors; and if you look into the penny county histories, now publishing by an eminent friend of mine, you will find that Langhale in Co. Norf. was held by one Baldwin *per saltum sufflatum, et pettum*; that is, he was to come every Christmas into Westminster Hall, there to take a leap, cry hem! and –'

'Mr Simpkinson, a glass of sherry?' cried Tom Ingoldsby, hastily.

'Not any, thank you, sir. This Baldwin, surnamed *Le –*'

'Mrs Ogelton challenges you sir; she insists upon it,' said Tom, still more rapidly, at the same time filling a glass, and forcing it on the sçavant, who, thus arrested in the very crisis of his narrative, received and swallowed the potation as if it had been physic.

'What on earth has Miss Simpkinson discovered there?' continued Tom; 'something of interest. See how fast she is writing.'

The diversion was effectual: every one looked towards Miss Simpkinson, who, far too ethereal for 'creature comforts', was seated apart on the dilapidated remains of an altar-tomb, committing eagerly to paper something that had strongly impressed her: the air – the eye 'in a fine frenzy rolling', – all betokened that the divine *afflatus* was come. Her father rose, and stole silently towards her.

'What an old boar!' muttered young Ingoldsby; alluding, perhaps to a slice of brawn which he had just begun to operate upon, but which, from the celerity with which it disappeared, did not seem so very difficult of mastication.

But what had become of Seaforth and his fair Caroline all this while? Why, it so happened that they had been simultaneously stricken with the picturesque appearance of one of those high and pointed arches, which that eminent antiquary, Mr Horseley Curties, had described in his *Ancient Records* as 'a *Gothic* window of the *Saxon* order;' – and then the ivy clustered so thickly and so beautifully on the other side, that they went round to look at that; – and then their proximity deprived it of half its effect, and so they walked across to a little knoll, a hundred yards off, and in crossing a small ravine, they came to what in Ireland they call a 'bad step', and Charles had to carry his cousin over it; – and then, when they had to come back, she would not give him the trouble again for the world, so they followed a better but more circuitous route, and there were hedges and ditches in the way, and stiles to get over, and gates to get through; so that an hour or more had elapsed before they were able to rejoin the party.

'Lassy me!' said Miss Julia Simpkinson, 'how long you have been gone!'

And so they had. The remark was a very just as well as a very natural one. They were gone a long while, and a nice cosy chat they had; and what do you think it was all about, my dear miss?

'O, lassy me! love, no doubt, and the moon, and eyes, and nightingales, and –'

Stay, stay, my sweet young lady; do not let the fervour of your feelings run away with you! I do not pretend to say, indeed, that one or more of these pretty subjects might not have been introduced; but the most important and leading topic of the conference was – Lieutenant Seaforth's breeches.

'Caroline,' said Charles, 'I have had some very odd dreams since I have been at Tappington.'

'Dreams, have you?' smiled the young lady, arching her taper neck like a swan in pluming. 'Dreams have you?'

'Ay, dreams – or dream, perhaps, I should say; for, though repeated, it was still the same. And what do you imagine was its subject?'

'It is impossible for me to divine,' said the tongue; – 'I have not the least difficulty in guessing,' said the eye, as plainly as every eye spoke.

'I dreamt – of your great grandfather!'

There was a change in the glance – 'My great grandfather?'

'Yes, the old Sir Giles, or Sir John, you told me about the other day: he walked into my bedroom in his short cloak of Murray-coloured velvet, his long rapier, and his Raleigh-looking hat and feather, just as the picture represents him: but with one exception.'

'And what was that?'

'Why, his lower extremities, which were visible, were those of a skeleton.'

'Well.'

'Well, after taking a turn or two about the room, and looking round him with a wistful air, he came to the bed's foot, stared at me in a manner impossible to describe – and then he – he laid hold of my pantaloons; whipped his long bony legs into them in a twinkling; and strutting up to the glass, seemed to view himself in it with great complacency. I tried to speak, but in vain. The effort, however, seemed to excite his attention; for, wheeling about, he showed me the grimmest looking death's head you can well imagine, and with an indescribable grin strutted out of the room.'

'Absurd! Charles. How can you talk such nonsense?'

'But, Caroline – the breeches are really gone.'

On the following morning, contrary to his usual custom, Seaforth was the first person in the breakfast parlour. As no one else was present, he did precisely what nine young men out of ten so situated would have done; he walked up to the mantel-piece, established himself upon the rug, and subducting his coat-tails one under each arm, turned towards the fire that portion of the human frame which it is considered equally indecorous to present to a friend or an enemy. A serious, not to say anxious, expression was visible upon his good-humoured countenance, and his mouth was fast buttoning itself up for an incipient whistle, when little Flo, a tiny spaniel of the Blenheim breed – the pet object of Miss

Julia Simpkinson's affections, bounced out from beneath a sofa, and began to bark at – his pantaloons.

They were cleverly 'built' of a light grey mixture, a broad stripe of the most vivid scarlet traversing each seam in a perpendicular direction from hip to ankle – in short, the regimental costume of the Royal Bombay Fencibles. The animal, educated in the country, had never seen such a pair of breeches in her life – *Omne ignotum pro magnifico*! The scarlet streak, inflamed as it was by the rejection of the fire seemed to act on Flora's nerves as the same colour does on those of bulls and turkeys; she advanced at the *pas de charge*, and her vociferation, like her amazement, was unbounded. A sound kick from the disgusted officer changed its character, and induced a retreat at the very moment when the mistress of the pugnacious quadruped entered to the rescue.

'Lassy me! Flo! what *is* the matter?' cried the sympathising lady, with a scrutinising glance levelled at the gentleman.

It might as well have lighted on a feather bed. His air of imperturbable unconsciousness defied examination; and as he would not, and Flora could not expound, that injured individual was compelled to pocket up her wrongs. Others of the household soon dropped in, and clustered round the board dedicated to the most sociable of meals; the urn was paraded 'hissing hot', and the cups which 'cheer, but not inebriate', steamed redolent of Tyson and pekoe; muffins and marmalade, newspapers and Finnon haddies, left little room for observation on the character of Charles's warlike 'turnout'. At length a look from Caroline, followed by a smile that nearly ripened to a titter, caused him to turn abruptly and address his neighbour. It was Miss Simpkinson, who, deeply engaged in sipping her tea and turning over her album, seemed, like a female Chrononotonthologos, 'immersed in cogibundity of cogitation'. An interrogatory on the subject of her studies drew from her the confession that she was at the moment employed in putting the finishing touches to a poem inspired by the romantic shades of Bolsover. The entreaties of the company were of course urgent. Mr Peters, 'who liked verse', was especially persevering, and Sappho at length compliant. After a preparatory hem! and a glance at the mirror to ascertain that her look was sufficiently sentimental, the poetess began:

> There is a calm, a holy feeling,
> Vulgar minds can never know,
> O'er the bosom softly stealing –
> chasten'd grief, delicious woe!
> Oh! how sweet at even regaining
> Yon lone tower's sequester'd shade
> Sadly mute and uncomplaining –

– Yow! - yeough! – yeough! – yow! – yow! yelled a hapless sufferer from beneath the table – It was an unlucky hour for quadrupeds; and if 'ever dog will have his day', he could not have selected a more unpropitious one than this. Mrs. Ogleton, too, had a pet, – a favourite pug, – whose squab figure, black muzzle, and tortuosity of tail, that curled like a head of celery in a salad-bowl bespoke his Dutch extraction. Yow! yow! yow! continued the brute – a chorus in which Flo instantly joined. Sooth to say, pug had more reason to express his dissatisfaction than was given by the muse of Simpkinson; the other only barked for company. Scarcely had the poetess got through her first stanza, when Tom Ingoldsby, in the enthusiasm of the moment, became so lost in the material world, that, in his abstraction, he unwarily laid his hand on the cock of the urn. Quivering with emotion, he gave it such an unlucky twist, that the full stream of its scalding contents descended on the gingerbread hide of the unlucky Cupid. The confusion was complete; the whole economy of the table disarranged; the company broke up in most admired disorder; and 'Vulgar minds will never know', anything more of Miss Simpkinson's ode till they peruse it in some forthcoming Annual.

Seaforth profited by the confusion to take the delinquent who had caused this 'stramash' by the arm, and to lead him to the lawn, where he had a word or two for his private ear. The conference between the young gentlemen was neither brief in its duration nor unimportant in its result. The subject was what the lawyers call tripartite, embracing the information that Charles Seaforth was over head and ears in love with Tom Ingoldsby's sister; secondly, that the lady had referred him to 'papa' for his sanction; thirdly and lastly, his nightly visitations, and consequent bereavement. At the two first items Tom smiled auspiciously; at the last he burst out into an absolute guffaw.

'Steal your breeches! Miss Bailey over again, by Jove,' shouted Ingoldsby. 'But a gentleman, you say – and Sir Giles too. I am not sure, Charles, whether I ought not to call you out for aspersing the honour of the family.'

'Laugh as you will, Tom, be as incredulous as you please. One fact is incontestible – the breeches are gone! Look here – I am reduced to my regimentals; and if these go, to-morrow I must borrow of you!'

Rochefoucault says, there is something in the misfortunes of our very best friends that does not displease us; – assuredly we can, most of us, laugh at their petty inconveniences, till called upon to supply them. Tom composed his features on the instant, and replied with more gravity, as well as with an expletive, which, if my Lord Mayor had been within hearing, might have cost him five shillings.

'There is something very queer in this, after all. The clothes, you say, have positively disappeared. Somebody is playing you a trick; and, ten to one, your servant has a hand in it. By the way, I heard something yesterday of his kicking up a bobbery in the kitchen, and seeing a ghost, or something of that kind, himself. Depend upon it, Barney is in the plot.'

It now struck the lieutenant at once, that the usually buoyant spirits of his attendant had of late been materially sobered down, his loquacity obviously circumscribed, and that he, the said lieutenant, had actually rung his bell three several times that very morning before he could procure his attendance. Mr Maguire was forthwith summoned, and underwent a close examination. The 'bobbery' was easily explained. Mr Oliver Dobbs had hinted his disapprobation of a flirtation carrying on between the gentleman from Munster and the lady from the Rue St Honoré. Mademoiselle had boxed Mr Maguire's ears, and Mr Maguire had pulled Mademoiselle upon his knee, and the lady had *not* cried *Mon Dieu*! And Mr Oliver Dobbs said it was very wrong; and Mrs Botherby said it was 'scandalous', and what ought not to be clone in any moral kitchen; and Mr Maguire had got hold of the honourable Augustus Sucklethumbkin's powder-flask, and had put large pinches of the best double Dartford in Mr Dobb's tobacco-box; and Mr Dobbs's pipe had exploded, and set fire to Mrs Botherby's Sunday cap; – and Mr Maguire had put it out with the slop-basin, 'barring the wig'; – and then they were all so 'cantankerous', that Barney had gone to take a walk in the garden; and then – then Mr Barney had seen a ghost!

'A what? you blockhead!' asked Tom Ingoldsby.

'Sure then, and it's myself will tell your honour the rights of it,' said the ghost-seer. 'Myself and Miss Pauline, sir or Miss Pauline and myself, for the ladies comes first anyhow – we got tired of the hobstroppylous skrimmaging among the ould servants, that didn't know a joke when they seen one: and we went out to look at the comet – that the rory-bory alehouse, they calls him in this country, – and we walked upon the lawn – and divil of any alehouse there was there at all; and

Miss Pauline said it was because of the shrubbery maybe, and why wouldn't we see it better beyonst the trees? – and so we went to the trees, but sorrow a comet did meself see there, barring a big ghost instead of it.'

'A ghost? And what sort of a ghost, Barney?'

'Och, then, divil a lie I'll tell your honour. A tall ould gentleman he was, all in white, with a shovel on the shoulder of him, and a big torch in his fist, – though what he wanted with that it's meself can't tell, for his eyes were like gig-lamps, let along the moon and the comet, which wasn't there at all; and "Barney", says he to me – 'cause why knew me – "Barney," says he, "what is it you're doing with the *colleen* there, Barney?" – Divil a word did I say. Miss Pauline screeched, and cried murther in French, and ran off with herself; and of course meself was in a mighty hurry after the lady, and had no time to stop palavering with him any way; so I dispersed at once, and the ghost vanished in a flame of fire!'

Mr Maguire's account was received with avowed incredulity by both gentlemen; but Barney stuck to his text with unflinching pertinacity. A reference to Mademoiselle was suggested, but abandoned, as neither party had a taste for delicate investigations.

'I'll tell you what, Seaforth,' said Ingoldsby, after Barney had received his dismissal, 'that there is a trick here, is evident; and Barney's vision may possibly be a part of it. Whether he is most knave or fool, you best know. At all events, I will sit up with you to-night and see if I can convert my ancestor into a visiting acquaintance. Meanwhile your finger on your lip!'

'Twas now the very witching time of night,
When churchyards yawn, and graves give up their dead.

Gladly would I grace my tale with decent horror, and therefore I do beseech the "gentle reader" to believe, that if all the *succedanea* to this mysterious narrative are not in strict keeping, he will ascribe it only to the disgraceful innovations of modern degeneracy upon the sober and dignified habits of our ancestors. I can introduce him, it is true, into an old and high-roofed chamber, its walls covered on three sides with black oak wainscoting, adorned with carvings of fruit and flowers long anterior to those of Grinling Gibbons; the fourth side is clothed with a curious remnant of dingy tapestry, one elucidatory of some Scriptural history, but of which not even Mrs Botherby could determine. Mr Simpkinson, who had examined it carefully, inclined to believe the principal figure to be either Bathsheba, or Daniel in the lions' den; while Tom Ingoldsby decided in favour of the King of Bashan. All, however, was conjecture, tradition being silent on the subject. A lofty arched portal led into, and a little arched portal led out of, this apartment; they were opposite each other, and each possessed the security of massy bolts on its interior. The bedstead, too, was not one of yesterday, but manifestly coeval with days ere Seddons was, and when a good four-post 'article' was deemed worthy of being a royal bequest. The bed itself, with all the appurtenances of palliasse, mattresses, etc., was of far later date, and looked most incongruously comfortable; the casements, too, with their little diamond-shaped panes and iron binding, had given way to the modern heterodoxy of the sash-window. Nor was this all that conspired to ruin the costume, and render the room a meet haunt for such 'mixed spirits' only as could condescend to don at the same time an Elizabethan doublet and Bond Street inexpressibles.

With their green morocco slippers on a modern fender, in front of a disgracefully modern grate, sat two young gentlemen, clad in 'shawl pattern' dressing gowns and black silk stocks, much at variance with the high cane-backed chairs which supported them. A bunch of abomination, called a cigar, reeked in the left-hand corner of the mouth of one, and in the right-hand corner of the mouth of the other – an arrangement happily adapted for the escape of the noxious fumes up the chimney, without that unmerciful 'funking' each other, which a less scientific disposition of the weed would have induced. A small pembroke table filled up the intervening space between them, sustaining at each extremity, an elbow and a glass of toddy; – thus in 'lonely pensive contemplation' were the two worthies occupied, when the 'iron tongue of midnight had tolled twelve.'

'Ghost-time's come!' said Ingoldsby, taking from his waistcoat pocket a watch like a gold half-crown, and consulting it as though he suspected the turret-clock over the stables of mendacity.

'Hush!' said Charles; 'did I not hear a footstep?'

There was a pause: – there was a footstep – it sounded distinctly –

it reached the door – it hesitated, stopped, and passed on.

Tom darted across the room, threw open the door, and became aware of Mrs Botherby toddling to her chamber, at the other end of the gallery, after dosing one of the housemaids with an approved julep from the Countess of Kent's *Choice Manual*.

'Good night, sir!' said Mrs Botherby.

'Go to the d – l!' said the disappointed ghost-hunter.

An hour – two – rolled on, and still no spectral visitation; nor did aught intervene to make night hideous; and when the turret-clock sounded at length the hour of three, Ingoldsby, whose patience and grog were alike exhausted, sprang from his chair, saying:

'This is all infernal nonsense, my good fellow. Deuce of any ghost, shall we see to-night; it's long past the canonical hour. I'm off to bed; and as to your breeches, I'll insure them for the next twenty-four hours at least, at the price of the buckram.'

'Certainly. Oh! thankee – to be sure!' stammered Charles, rousing himself from a reverie, which had degenerated into an absolute snooze.

'Good-night, my boy! Bolt the door behind me; and defy the Pope, the Devil, and the Pretender!'

Seaforth followed his friend's advice, and the next morning came down to breakfast dressed in the habiliments of the preceding day. The charm was broken, the demon defeated; the light greys with the red stripe down the seams were yet *in rerum naturâ*, and adorned the person of their lawful proprietor.

Tom felicitated himself and his partner of the watch on the result of their vigilance; but there is a rustic adage which warns us against self-gratulation before we are quite 'out of the wood' – Seaforth was yet within its verge.

A rap at Tom Ingoldsby's door the following morning startled him as he was shaving; – he cut his chin.

'Come in, and be d – d to you.' said the martyr, pressing his thumb on the scarified epidermis. The door opened, and exhibited Mr Barney Maguire.

'Well, Barney, what is it?' quoth the sufferer, adopting the vernacular of his visitant.

'The master, sir –'

'Well, what does he want?'

'The loanst of a breeches, plase your honour.'

'Why, you don't mean to tell me – By Heaven, this is too good!' shouted Tom, bursting into a fit of uncontrollable laughter. 'Why, Barney, you don't mean to say the ghost has got them again!'

Mr Maguire did not respond to the young squire's risibility; the cast of his countenance was decidedly serious.

'Faith, then, it's gone they are, sure enough! Hasn't meself been looking over the bed, and under the bed, and *in* the bed, for the matter of that, and divil a ha'p'orth of breeches is there to the fore at all: I'm bothered entirely!'

'Hark'ee! Mr Barney,' said Tom, incautiously removing his thumb, and letting a crimson stream 'incarnadine the multitudinous' lather that plastered his throat, – 'this may be all very well with your master, but you don't humbug *me*, sir: – tell me instantly what have you done with the clothes?'

This abrupt transition from 'lively to severe' certainly took Maguire by surprise, and he seemed for an instant as much disconcerted as it is possible to disconcert an Irish gentleman's gentleman.

'Me? is it meself, then, that's the ghost to your honour's thinking?' said he, after a moment's pause, and with a slight shade of indignation in his tones: 'is it I would stale the master's things, – and what would I do with them?'

'That you best know: what your purpose is I can't guess, for I don't think you mean to "stale" them, as you call it; but that you are concerned in their disappearance, I am satisfied. Confound this blood! Give me a towel, Barney.'

Maguire acquitted himself of the commission. 'As I've a sowl, your honour,' said he solemnly, 'little it is meself knows of the matter: and after what I seen?'

'What you've seen! Why, what *have* you seen? Barney, I don't want to enquire into your flirtations; but don't suppose you can palm off your saucer eyes and gig-lamps upon me!'

'Then, as sure as your honour's standing there I saw him: and why wouldn't I, when Miss *Pauline* was to the fore as well as meself, and –'

'Get along with your nonsense – leave the room, sir!'

'But the master?' said Barney imploringly; 'and without a breeches

– sure he'll be catching cowld!'

'Take that, rascal!' replied Ingoldsby, throwing a pair of pantaloons at, rather than to, him: 'but don't suppose, sir, you shall carry on your tricks here with impunity; recollect there is such a thing as a tread-mill, and that my father is a country magistrate.'

Barney's eyes flashed fire, he stood erect, and was about to speak; but, mastering himself, not without an effort, he took up the garment, and left the room as perpendicular as a Quaker.

'Ingoldsby,' said Charles Seaforth, after breakfast, 'this is now past a joke; to-day is the last of my stay; for, not-withstanding the ties which detain me, common decency obliges me to visit home after so long an absence. I shall come to an immediate explanation with your father on the subject nearest my heart, and depart while I have a change of dress left. On his answer will my return depend! In the meantime tell me candidly, – I ask it in all seriousness and as a friend, – am I not a dupe to your well-known propensity to hoaxing? Have you not a hand in –'

'No, by heaven! Seaforth; I see what you mean: on my honour, I am as much mystified as yourself: and if your servant –'

'Not he: if there be a trick, he at least is not privy to it.'

'If there *be* a trick? Why, Charles, do you think –'

'I know not *what* to think, Tom. As surely as you are a living man, so surely did that spectral anatomy visit my room again last night, grin in my face, and walk away with my trousers; nor was I able to spring from my bed, or break the chain which seemed to bind me to my pillow.'

'Seaforth!' said Ingoldsby, after a short pause, 'I will – But hush! here are the girls and my father. – I will carry off the females, and leave you a clear field with the governor: carry your point with him, and we will talk about your breeches afterwards.'

Tom's diversion was successful; he carried off the ladies *en masse* to look at a remarkable specimen of the class *Dodecandria Monogynia* – which they could not find: – while Seaforth marched boldly up to the encounter, and carried 'the governor's' outworks by a *coup de main*. I shall not stop to describe the progress of the attack: suffice it that it was as successful as could have been wished, and that Seaforth was referred back again to the lady. The happy lover was off at a tangent; the botanical party was soon overtaken; and the arm of Caroline, whom a vain endeavour to spell out the Linnaeam name of a daffy-down-dilly had detained a little in the rear of the others, was soon firmly locked in his own.

"What was the world to them,
Its noise, its nonsense, and its 'breeches' all?"

Seaforth was in the seventh heaven; he retired to his room that night as happy as if no such thing as a goblin had ever been heard of, and personal chattels were as well fenced in by law as real property. Not so Tom Ingoldsby: the mystery, – for mystery there evidently was, – had not only piqued his curiosity, but ruffled his temper. The watch of the previous night had been unsuccessful, probably because it was undisguised. To-night he would 'ensconce himself' – not indeed 'behind the arras' – for the little that remained was, as we have seen, nailed to the wall, – but in a small closet which opened from one corner of the room, and, by leaving the door ajar, would give to its occupant a view of all that might pass in the apartment. Here did the young ghost-hunter take up a position, with a good stout sapling under his arm, a full half hour before Seaforth retired for the night. Not even his friend did he let into his confidence, fully determined that if his plan did not succeed, the failure should be attributed to himself alone.

At the usual hour of separation for the night, Tom saw, from his concealment, the lieutenant enter his room, and, after taking a few turns in it, with an expression so joyous as to betoken that his thoughts were mainly occupied by his approaching happiness, proceed slowly to disrobe himself. The coat, the waistcoat, the black silk stock, were gradually, discarded; the green morocco slippers were kicked off, and then – ay, and then – his countenance grew grave; it seemed to occur to him all at once that this was his last stake, – nay, that the very breeches he had on were not his own, – that to-morrow morning was his last, and that if he lost *them* – A glance showed that his mind was made up: he replaced the single button he had just subducted, and threw himself upon the bed in a state of transition – half chrysalis, half grub.

Wearily did Tom Ingoldsby watch the sleeper by the flickering light of the night-lamp, till the clock, striking one, induced him to increase the narrow opening which he had left for the purpose of observation.

The motion, slight as it was, seemed to attract Charles's attention; for he raised himself suddenly to a sitting posture, listened for a moment, and then stood upright upon the floor. Ingoldsby was on the point of discovering himself, when, the light, flashing full upon his friend's countenance, he perceived that, though his eyes were open, 'their sense was shut', – that he was yet under the influence of sleep. Seaforth advanced slowly to the toilet, lit his candle at the lamp that stood on it, then, going back to the bed's foot, appeared to search eagerly for something which he could not find. For a few moments he seemed restless and uneasy, walking round the apartment and examining the chairs, till, coming fully in front of a large swing-glass that flanked the dressing-table, he paused, as if contemplating his figure on it. He now returned towards the bed; put on his slippers, and, with cautious and stealthy steps, proceeded towards the little arched doorway that opened on the private staircase.

As he drew the bolt, Tom Ingoldsby emerged from his hiding-place; but the sleep-walker heard him not; he proceeded softly down stairs, followed at a due distance by his friend; opened the door which led out upon the gardens; and stood at once among the thickest of the scrubs, which there clustered round the base of a corner turret, and screened the postern from common observation. At this moment Ingoldsby had nearly spoiled all by making a false step: the sound attracted Seaforth's attention, – he paused and turned: and as the full moon shed her light directly upon his pale and troubled features, Tom marked, almost with dismay, the fixed and rayless appearance of his eyes:

> There was no speculation in those orbs
> That he did glare withal.

The perfect stillness preserved by his follower seemed to reassure him; he turned aside; and from the midst of a thickset laurustinus, drew forth a gardener's spade, shouldering which he proceeded with great rapidity into the midst of the shrubbery. Arrived at a certain point where the earth seemed to have been recently disturbed, he set himself heartily to the task of digging, till, having thrown up several shovelfuls of mould, he stopped, flung down his tool, and very composedly began to disencumber himself of his pantaloons.

Up to this moment Tom had watched him with a wary eye: he now advanced cautiously, and, as his friend was busily engaged in disentangling himself from his garment, made himself master of the spade. Seaforth, meanwhile, had accomplished his purpose: he stood for a moment with

His streamers waving in the wind,

occupied in carefully rolling up the small-clothes into as compact a form as possible, and all heedless of the breath of heaven, which might certainly be supposed, at such a moment, and in such a plight, to 'visit his frame too roughly'.

He was in the act of stooping low to deposit the pantaloons in the grave which he had been digging for them, when Tom Ingoldsby came close behind him, and with the flat side of the spade –

The shock was effectual; – never again was Lieutenant Seaforth known to act the part of a somnambulist. One by one, his breeches – his trousers – his pantaloons – his silk-net tights – his patent cords – his showy greys with the broad red stripe of the Bombay Fencibles were brought to light, – rescued from the grave in which they had been buried, like the strata of a Christmas pie; and, after having been well aired by Mrs Botherby, became once again effective.

The family, the ladies especially, laughed – the Peterses laughed – the Simpkinsons laughed – Barney Maguire cried 'Botheration!' and Ma'mselle Pauline, '*Mon Dieu!*'

Charles Seaforth, unable to face the quizzing which awaited him on all sides, started off two hours earlier than he had proposed: – he soon returned, however; and having, at his father-in-law's request, given up the occupation of Rajah-hunting and shooting Nabobs, led his blushing bride to the altar.

Mr Simpkinson from Bath did not attend the ceremony, being engaged at the Grand Junction Meeting of Sçavans, then congregating from all parts of the known world in the city of Dublin. His essay, demonstrating that the globe is a great custard, whipped into coagulation by whirlwinds, and cooked by electricity, – a little too much baked in the Isle of Portland, and a thought underdone about the Bog of

Allen, – was highly spoken of, and narrowly escaped obtaining a Bridgewater prize.

Miss Simpkinson and her sister acted as bridesmaids on the occasion; the former wrote an *epithalamium*, and the latter cried 'Lassy me!' at the clergyman's wig. – Some years have since rolled on; the union has been crowned with two or three tidy little offshoots from the family tree of whom Master Neddy is 'grandpapa's darling', and Mary-Anne mamma's particular 'Sock'. I shall only add, that Mr and Mrs Seaforth are living together quite as happily as two good-hearted, good-tempered bodies, very fond of each other, can possibly do: and, that since the day of his marriage Charles has shown no disposition to jump out of bed, or ramble out of doors o' nights – though, from his entire devotion to every wish and whim of his young wife, Tom insinuates that the fair Caroline does still occasionally take advantage of it so far as to 'slip on the breeches'.

The Hollow of the Three Hills

Nathaniel Hawthorne

In those strange old times, when fantastic dreams and madmen's reveries were realized among the actual circumstances of life, two persons met together at an appointed hour and place. One was a lady graceful in form and fair of feature, though pale and troubled and smitten with an untimely blight in what should have been the fullest bloom of her years; the other was an ancient and meanly-dressed woman, of ill-favored aspect, and so withered, shrunken, and decrepit, that even the space since she began to decay must have exceeded the ordinary term of human existence. In the spot where they encountered, no mortal could observe them. Three little hills stood near each other, and down in the midst of them sunk a hollow basin, almost mathematically circular, two or three hundred feet in breadth, and of such depth that a stately cedar might but just be visible above the sides. Dwarf pines were numerous upon the hills, and partly fringed the outer verge of the intermediate hollow, within which there was nothing but the brown grass of October, and here and there a tree trunk that had fallen long ago, and lay mouldering with no green successor from its roots. One of these masses of decaying wood, formerly a majestic oak, rested close beside a pool of green and sluggish water at the bottom of the basin. Such scenes as this (so gray tradition tells) were once the resort of the Power of Evil and his plighted subjects; and here, at midnight or on the dim verge of evening, they were said to stand round the mantling pool, disturbing its putrid waters in the performance of an impious baptismal rite. The chill beauty of an autumnal sunset was now gilding the three hill-tops, whence a paler tint stole down their sides into the hollow.

"Here is our pleasant meeting come to pass," said the aged crone, "according as thou hast desired. Say quickly what thou wouldst have of me, for there is but a short hour that we may tarry here."

As the old withered woman spoke, a smile glimmered on her

countenance, like lamplight on the wall of a sepulchre. The lady trembled, and cast her eyes upward to the verge of the basin, as if meditating to return with her purpose unaccomplished. But it was not so ordained.

"I am a stranger in this land, as you know," said she at length. "Whence I come it matters not; but I have left those behind me with whom my fate was intimately bound, and from whom I am cut off forever. There is a weight in my bosom that I cannot away with, and I have come hither to inquire of their welfare."

"And who is there by this green pool that can bring thee news from the ends of the earth?" cried the old woman, peering into the lady's face. "Not from my lips mayst thou hear these tidings; yet, be thou bold, and the daylight shall not pass away from yonder hill-top before thy wish be granted."

"I will do your bidding though I die," replied the lady desperately.

The old woman seated herself on the trunk of the fallen tree, threw aside the hood that shrouded her gray locks, and beckoned her companion to draw near.

"Kneel down," she said, "and lay your forehead on my knees."

She hesitated a moment, but the anxiety that had long been kindling burned fiercely up within her. As she knelt down, the border of her garment was dipped into the pool; she laid her forehead on the old woman's knees, and the latter drew a cloak about the lady's face, so that she was in darkness. Then she heard the muttered words of prayer, in the midst of which she started, and would have arisen.

"Let me flee – let me flee and hide myself, that they may not look upon me!" she cried. But, with returning recollection, she hushed herself, and was still as death.

For it seemed as if other voices – familiar in infancy, and unforgotten through many wanderings, and in all the vicissitudes of her heart and fortune – were mingling with the accents of the prayer. At first the words were faint and indistinct, not rendered so by distance, but rather resembling the dim pages of a book which we strive to read by an imperfect and gradually brightening light. In such a manner, as the prayer proceeded, did those voices strengthen upon the ear; till at length the petition ended, and the conversation of an aged man, and of a woman broken and decayed like himself, became distinctly audible to the lady as she knelt. But those strangers appeared not to stand in the hollow depth between the three hills. Their voices were encompassed and re-echoed by the walls of a chamber, the windows of which were rattling in the breeze; the regular vibration of a clock, the crackling of a fire, and the tinkling of the embers as they fell among the ashes, rendered the scene almost as vivid as if painted to the eye. By a melancholy hearth sat these two old people, the man calmly despondent, the woman querulous and tearful, and their words were all of sorrow. They spoke of a daughter, a wanderer they knew not where, bearing dishonour along with her, and leaving shame and affliction to bring their gray heads to the grave. They alluded also to other and more recent wo, but in the midst of their talk their voices seemed to melt into the sound of the wind sweeping mournfully among the autumn leaves; and when the lady lifted her eyes, there was she kneeling in the hollow between three hills.

"A weary and lonesome time yonder old couple have of it," remarked the old woman, smiling in the lady's face.

"And did you also hear them?" exclaimed she, a sense of intolerable humiliation triumphing over her agony and fear.

"Yea; and we have yet more to hear," replied the old woman. "Wherefore, cover thy face quickly."

Again the withered hag poured forth the monotonous words of a prayer that was not meant to be acceptable in heaven; and soon, in the pauses of her breath, strange murmurings began to thicken, gradually increasing so as to drown and overpower the charm by which they grew. Shrieks pierced through the obscurity of sound, and were succeeded by the singing of sweet female voices, which, in their turn, gave way to a wild roar of laughter, broken suddenly by groaning and sobs, forming altogether a ghastly confusion of terror and mourning and mirth. Chains were rattling, fierce and stern voices uttered threats, and the scourge resounded at their command. All these noises deepened and became substantial to the listener's ear, till she could distinguish every soft and dreamy accent of the love songs that died causelessly into funeral hymns. She shuddered at the unprovoked wrath which blazed up like the spontaneous kindling of flame, and she grew faint at the fearful merriment raging miserably around her. In the midst of this wild scene, where unbound passions jostled each other in a drunken career, there was one solemn voice of a man, and a manly and melodious voice it might once have been. He went to and fro continually, and his feet sounded upon the floor. In each member of that frenzied company, whose own burning thoughts had become their exclusive world, he sought an auditor for the story of his individual wrong, and interpreted their laughter and tears as his reward of scorn or pity. He spoke of woman's perfidy, of a wife who had broken her holiest vows, of a home and heart made desolate. Even as he went on, the shout, the laugh, the shriek, the sob, rose up in unison, till they changed into the hollow, fitful, and uneven sound of the wind, as it fought among the pine-trees on those three lonely hills. The lady looked up, and there was the withered woman smiling in her face.

"Couldst thou have thought there were such merry times in a mad-house?" inquired the latter.

"True, true," said the lady to herself; "there is mirth within its walls, but misery, misery without."

"Wouldst thou hear more?" demanded the old woman.

"There is one other voice I would fain listen to again," replied the lady faintly.

"Then, lay down thy head speedily upon my knees, that thou mayst get thee hence before the hour be past."

The golden skirts of day were yet lingering upon the hills, but deep shades obscured the hollow and the pool, as if sombre night were rising thence to overspread the world. Again that evil woman began to weave her spell. Long did it proceed unanswered, till the knelling of a bell stole in among the intervals of her words, like a clang that had travelled far over valley and rising ground, and was just ready to die in the air. The lady shook upon her companion's knees as she heard that boding sound. Stronger it grew and sadder, and deepened into the tone of a death bell, knelling dolefully from some ivy-mantled tower, and bearing tidings of mortality and wo to the cottage, to the hall, and to the solitary wayfarer, that all might weep for the doom appointed in turn to them. Then came a measured tread, passing slowly, slowly on, as of mourners with a coffin, their garments trailing on the ground, so that the ear could measure the length of their melancholy array. Before them went the priest, reading the burial service, while the leaves of his book were rustling in the breeze. And though no voice but his was heard to speak aloud, still there were revilings and anathemas, whispered but distinct, from women and from men, breathed against the daughter who had wrung the aged hearts of her parents – the wife who had betrayed the trusting fondness of her husband – the mother who had sinned against natural affection, and left her child to die. The sweeping sound of the funeral train faded away like a thin vapor, and the wind, that just before had seemed to shake the coffin pall, moaned sadly round the verge of the Hollow between three Hills. But when the old woman stirred the kneeling lady, she lifted not her head.

"Here has been a sweet hour's sport!" said the withered crone, chuckling to herself.

The Lady of Rosemount

Sir Thomas Graham Jackson

'And so, Charlton, you're going to spend part of the Long at Rosemount Abbey. I envy you. It's an awfully jolly old place, and you'll have a really good time.'

'Yes,' said Charlton, 'I am looking forward to it immensely. I have never seen it; you know it has only lately come to my uncle and they only moved into it last Christmas. I forgot that you knew it and had been there.'

'Oh! I don't know it very well,' said Edwards: 'I spent a few days there a year or two ago with the last owner. It will suit you down to the ground, for you are mad about old abbeys and ruins, and you'll find enough there to satisfy the whole Society of Antiquaries as well as yourself. When do you go?'

'Very soon. I must be at home for a week or so after we go down, and then I think my uncle will expect me at Rosemount. What are you going to do?'

'Well! I hardly know. Nothing very exciting. Perhaps take a short run abroad a little later. But I shall have to read part of the Long, for I am in for Greats next term. By the way, it is just possible I may be somewhere in your direction, for I have friends near Rosemount who want me to spend part of the vac. down there.'

'All right,' said Charlton, 'don't forget to come over and see me. I hope I may still be there. Meanwhile, *au revoir*, old man, and good luck to you.'

Charlton remained some time at his window looking on the quad of his college. Term at Oxford was just over and the men were rapidly going down. Hansoms were waiting at the gate, scouts and messengers were clattering down the staircases with portmanteaux and other paraphernalia proper to youth, and piling them on the cabs, friends were shaking hands, and bidding goodbye. In a few hours the college

311

would be empty, and solitude would descend upon it for four months, broken only by occasional visitors, native or transatlantic. The flight of the men would be followed by that of the Dons to all parts of Europe or beyond, the hive would be deserted, and the porter would reign supreme over a vast solitude, monarch of all he surveyed.

Charlton was not due to go down till the next morning. He dined in the junior common-room with three or four other men, the sole survivors of the crowd, and then retired to his rooms to finish his packing. That done, he sat on the window-seat looking into the quad. It was a brilliant night; the moonshine slept on the grass, and silvered the grey walls and mullioned windows opposite, while the chapel and hall were plunged in impenetrable shadow. Everything was as still as death; no sound from the outer world penetrated the enclosure, and for the busy hive of men within, there was now the silence of a desert. There is perhaps no place where silence and solitude can be more sensibly felt than the interior of an Oxford college in vacation time, and there was something in the scene that appealed to the temperament of the young man who regarded it.

Henry Charlton was an only child. His father had died when he was a lad, and his mother, broken down by grief, had forsworn society and lived a very retired life in the country. At Winchester and Oxford he naturally mixed with others and made acquaintances, but his home life was somewhat sombre and his society restricted. He grew up a self-contained, reserved lad, with few friendships, though those he formed were sincere and his attachments were strong. His temperament – poetical and tinged with melancholy – naturally inclined to romance, and from his early youth he delighted in antiquarian pursuits, heraldic lore, and legend. At school and college he revelled in the ancient architecture by which he was surrounded. His tastes even carried him further, into the region of psychical research, and the dubious revelations of spiritualism; though a certain wholesome vein of scepticism saved him from plunging deeply into those mazes, whether of truth or imposture. As he sat at his window, the familiar scene put on an air of romance. The silence sank into his soul; the windows where a friendly light was wont to shine through red curtains, inviting a visit, were now blind and dark; mystery enveloped the well-known walls; they seemed a place for the dead, no longer a habitation for living men, of whom he might be the last survivor. At last, rising from his seat, and half laughing at his own romantic fancies, Henry Charlton went to bed.

A few weeks later he descended from the train at the little country station of Brickhill, in Northamptonshire, and while the porter was collecting his traps on a hand-barrow, he looked out for the carriage that was to meet him.

'Hallo! Harry, here you are,' said a voice behind him, and turning round he was warmly greeted by his cousin, Charley Wilmot. A car was waiting, into which he and his belongings were packed, and in five minutes they were off, bowling along one of the wide Northamptonshire roads, with a generous expanse of greensward on each side between the hedges, and the hedgerow timber. The country was new to Henry Charlton, and he looked about him with interest. The estate of Rosemount had lately come unexpectedly by the death of a distant relation of his uncle, Sir Thomas Wilmot, and the family had hardly had time yet to settle down in their new home. His cousin Charles was full of the novelty of the situation, and the charms of the Abbey.

'I can tell you, it's a rattling old place,' said he, 'full of odd holes and corners, and there are the ruins of the church with all sorts of old things to be seen; but you'll have lots of time to look about and see it all, and here we are, and there's my dad waiting to welcome you at the hall-door.'

They had turned in at a lodge-gate, and passed up an avenue at the end of which Henry could see a hoary pile of stone gables, mullioned windows, massive chimneys, and a wide-arched portal, hospitably open, where Sir Thomas stood to welcome his nephew.

Some years had passed since Henry had seen his relatives, and he was glad to be with them again. A houseful of lively cousins rather younger than himself, had in former days afforded a welcome change from his own rather melancholy home, and he looked forward with pleasure to renewing the intimacy. His young cousin Charley was just at the end of his time at Eton, and was to go to university in October. The girls, Kate and Cissy, had shot up since he used to play with them in the nursery, and were now too old to be kissed. His uncle and aunt were as kind as ever, and after he had answered their enquiries about his mother, and given an account of his uneventful journey down, the whole party adjourned to the garden where tea awaited them under the trees, and then Henry for the first time saw something of the Abbey of Rosemount.

This ancient foundation, of Sanctus Egidius in Monte Rosarum, had been a Benedictine house, dating from the twelfth century, which at the Dissolution was granted to a royal favourite, who partly dismantled and partly converted it into a residence for himself. His descendants in the time of James I had pulled down a great part of the conventual buildings and substituted for the inconvenient cells of the monks a more comfortable structure in the style of that day. Many fragments of the Abbey, however, were incorporated into the later house. The refectory of the monks was kept, and formed the great hall of the mansion with its vaulted roof and traceried windows, in which there even remained some of the old storied glass. The Abbot's kitchen still furnished Sir Thomas's hospitable board, and among the offices and elsewhere were embedded parts of the domestic buildings. North of the refectory, according to the usual Benedictine plan, had been the cloister and beyond that the church, which lay at a slightly lower level, the lie of the ground inclining that way from the summit of the Mount of Roses on which the habitable part of the convent had been built. Of the cloister enough remained, though much broken and dilapidated, to show what it had been, but the greater part of the church was destroyed for the sake of its materials when the Jacobean house was built. A considerable part of the nave, however, was still standing, part of it even with its vaulted roof intact, and of the rest, enough of the lower part of the walls was left to show that the church had been of a fair size, though not on the scale of the larger establishments.

Henry Charlton, with the greedy eye of the born antiquary, took in the general scheme of the Abbey with his tea and buttered toast under the shade of the elms that bounded the lawn on that side of the house. But he had to control his impatience to visit the ruins, for after tea his cousins insisted on a game of tennis, which lasted till it was time to dress for dinner, and after dinner it was too late and too dark for exploration.

They dined in the great hall, once the monks' refectory, but not too large for modern comfort, the Abbey having been one of the smaller houses of the Order, and the number of the brotherhood limited. Henry was enchanted and could not restrain the expression of his enthusiasm.

'Ah!' said his aunt, 'I remember your mother told me you were crazy about architecture and antiquities. Well, you'll have your fill of them here. For my part. I often sigh for a little more modern convenience.'

'But my dear aunt,' said Henry, 'there is so much to make up for little inconveniences in living in this lovely old place that they might be forgotten.'

'Why, what do you know about housekeeping?' said his aunt. 'I should like you to hear Mrs Baldwin, the housekeeper, on the subject. How she toils up one staircase only to have to go down another. The house, she says, is made up of stairs that are not wanted, and crooked passages that might have been straight, and it took the maids a fortnight to learn their way to the food-store.'

'It's of no use, mother,' said Charles, 'you'll never convince him. He would like to have those old monks back again, and to be one of them himself with a greasy cowl on his head and sandals on his naked feet, and nothing to eat but herbs washed down with water.'

'No, no!' said Henry, laughing, 'I don't want them back, for I like my present company too well. But I confess I like to call up in imagination the men who built and lived in these old walls. I believe I shall dream of them tonight.'

'Well, Harry,' said his uncle, 'you may dream of them as much as you please, so long as you don't bring them back to turn us out. And you shall have every opportunity, for you are to sleep in a bit of the old convent that the abbey builders of the modern house spared; and who knows but that the ghost of its former occupant may not take you at your word and come back to revisit his old quarters.'

Harry laughed as they rose from table, and said he trusted his visitor would not treat him as an intruder.

The long summer day had enabled them to finish dinner by daylight, and there was still light enough for the old painted glass to be seen. It was very fragmentary, and not one of the pictures was perfect. In one of the lights they could make out part of a female figure richly dressed; she had been holding something that was broken away, and beside her was the lower half of an unmistakable demon, with hairy legs and cloven hoof. The legend below ran thus, the last word being imperfect:

QVALITER DIABOLVS TENTAVIT COMITISSAM ALI . . .

The next light was still more imperfect, but there was part of the same
female figure in violent action, with the fragment of a legend:

HIC COMITISSA TENTATA A DI . . .

Other parts evidently of the same story remained in the next window,
but they were too fragmentary to be understood. In one light was a piece
of a monk's figure and part of a legend:

HIC FRATER PAVLVS DAT COMI . . .

The last of all was tolerably perfect. It represented a female robed in
black, and holding in her hand a little model of a church. She was on her
knees prostrate before the Pope, who was seated and extended his hand
in the act of benediction. The legend below said:

HIC COMITISSA A PAPA ABSOLVTA EST

Henry was much interested and wanted to know the story of the sinful
Countess; but none of the party could tell him, and indeed, none of
them had till then paid much attention to the glass. Sir Thomas had once
made a slight attempt to trace the identity of the Countess, but with
little success, and had soon given up the search.

'There is an antiquarian problem for you to solve, Harry,' said he,
'but I don't know where you should look for the solution. The annals of
Rosemount are very imperfect. In those within my reach I could find
nothing bearing on the subject.'

'I am afraid, sir,' said Harry, 'if you failed I am not likely to
succeed, for I am only a very humble antiquary, and should not know
where to begin. It seems to me, however, that the story must have had
something to do with the history of the Abbey, and that its fortunes were
connected with the wicked Countess, or the monks would not have put
her story in their windows.'

'Well, then, there you have a clue to follow up,' said his uncle, 'and
now let us join the ladies.'

The room where Henry Charlton was to sleep was on the ground floor in one corner of the house, and looked out upon the cloister and the ruined abbey-church. It was, as his uncle had said, a relic of the domestic part of the Abbey, and when he had parted with his cousin Charley, who guided him thither, he looked round the apartment with the keenest interest. It was a fair-sized room, low-pitched, with a ceiling of massive black timbers, plastered between the joists. The wall was so thick that there was room for a little seat in the window recess on each side, which was reached by a step, for the window-sill was rather high above the floor. Opposite the window yawned a wide fireplace with dogs for wood-logs, and a heap of wood ashes lying on the hearth. The walls were panelled with oak up to the ceiling, and the floor, where not covered with rugs, was of the same material polished brightly. But for the toilet appliances of modern civilisation the room was unaltered from the time when the last brother of the convent left it, never to return. Henry tried to picture to himself his predecessor in the apartment; he imagined him sitting at the table, reading or writing, or on his knees in prayer; on his simple shelf would have been his few books and manuscripts, borrowed from the convent library, to which he had to return them when they met in chapter once a year, under severe penalty in case of loss or damage. As he lay on his bed Henry tried to imagine what his own thoughts would have been had he himself been that ghostly personage five centuries ago; he fancied himself in the choir of the great church; he heard the sonorous Gregorian chanting by a score of deep manly voices, ringing in the vaulted roof, and echoing through the aisles; he saw the embroidered vestments, the lights that shone clearer and brighter as the shades of evening wrapped arcade and triforium in gloom and mystery, and turned to blackness the storied windows that lately gleamed with the hues of the sapphire, the ruby and the emerald. Pleased with these fancies he lay awake till the clock struck twelve and then insensibly the vision faded and he fell asleep.

His sleep was not untroubled. Several times he half awoke, only to drop off again and resume the threat of a tiresome dream that puzzled and worried him but led to no conclusion. When morning came, he awoke in earnest, and tried to piece together the fragments he could remember, but made little of them. He seemed to have seen the monk sitting at the table as he had pictured him in imagination the evening before. The monk was not reading but turning over some little bottles which he took from a leather case, and he seemed to be waiting for someone or something. Then Henry in his dream fancied that someone did come and something did happen, but what it was he could not remember, and of the visitor he could recall nothing, except that he felt there was a personality present, but not so as to be seen and recognised; more an impression than a fact. He could remember, however, a hand stretched out towards the seated figure and the objects he was handling. More than this he could not distinctly recall, but the same figures recurred each time he fell asleep with slightly varied attitude, though with no greater distinctness. For the monk he could account by the thoughts that had been in his mind the night before, but for the incident in his dream, if so vague a matter could be called an incident, he could trace no suggestion in his own mind.

The bright summer morning and the merry party at breakfast soon drove the memory of the dream out of his head. After breakfast there were the horses and dogs to be seen, and the garden to be visited, and it was not till the afternoon that his cousins let him satisfy his longing to visit the ruins of the church and cloister. There they all went in a body. The cloister lawn was mown smoothly and well tended, and here and there barely rising above the greensward were the stones that marked the resting places of the brotherhood. Part of the cloister retained its traceried windows and vaulted roof, and on the walls were inscribed the names of abbots and monks whose bones lay beneath the pavement. At the end of the western walk a finely sculptured door led into the nave of the church, the oldest part of the building, built when the ruder Norman work was just melting into greater refinement. Henry was in raptures, and vowed that neither Fountains nor Rievaulx could show anything more perfect. The girls were delighted to find their favourite parts of the building appreciated, and led him from point to point, determined that he should miss nothing.

'And now,' said Cissy, 'you have to see the best bit of all, hasn't he, Kate? We don't show it to everybody for fear strangers might do mischief.'

So saying she pushed open a door in the side wall and led them into a chantry chapel built out between two of the great buttresses of the nave aisle. It was indeed a gem of architecture of the purest fourteenth-century Gothic and Henry stood entranced before its loveliness. The delicate traceries on wall and roof were carved with the finish of ivory, and though somewhat stained by weather, for the windows had lost their glass, had kept all their sharp precision. Part of the outer wall had given way, weeds and ivy had invaded and partly covered the floor, and a thick mass of vegetation was piled up under the windows against the masonry.

'What a pity to let this lovely place get into such a mess,' said Henry. 'I have never seen anything more beautiful.'

'Well,' said Charley, 'it wouldn't take long to clear all this rubbish away. Suppose we set to work and do it?'

So while the girls sat and looked on, the two men fetched some garden tools, and cut, hacked and pulled up the weeds and ivy and brambles, which they threw out by the breach in the wall, and soon made a partial clearance. Henry had begun on the mass that stood breast-high next the window, when a sudden exclamation made the others look at him. He was peering down into the mass of vegetation, of which he had removed the top layer, with an expression of amazement that drew the others to his side. Looking up at them out of the mass of ivy was a face, the face of a beautiful woman, her hair disposed in graceful masses, and bound by a slender coronet. It was evident that under the pile of vegetation was a tomb with an effigy that had long been hidden, and the very existence of which had been forgotten. When the rest of the vegetation had been cleared away there appeared an altar tomb on the top of which lay the alabaster figure of a woman. The sides bore escutcheons of heraldry and had evidently once been coloured. The figure was exquisitely modelled, the work of no mean sculptor; the hands were crossed on the breast, and the drapery magnificently composed. But with the head of the figure the artist had surpassed himself. It was a triumph of sculpture. The features were of perfect beauty, regular and classical, but there was something about it that went beyond beauty, something akin to life, something that seemed to respond to the gaze of the observer, and to attract him unconsciously whether he would or not. The group of discoverers hung over it in a sort of fascination for some minutes saying nothing. At last Kate, the elder girl, drew back with a slight shiver, and said,

'Oh! What is it, what is the matter with me, I feel as if there was something wrong; it is too beautiful; I don't like it; come away, Cissy,' and she drew her sister out of the chapel, in a sort of tremor.

Charley followed them, and Henry was left alone with his gaze still fixed on the lovely face. As he looked he seemed to read fresh meaning in the cold alabaster features. The mouth, though perfectly composed in rest, appeared to express a certain covert satire: the eyes were represented as open, and they seemed to regard him with a sort of amused curiosity. There was a kind of diablerie about the whole figure. It was a long time before he could remove his eyes from the face that seemed to understand and return his gaze, and it was not without a wrench that at last he turned away. The features of the image seemed to be burned into his brain, and to remain fixed there indelibly, whether pleasurably or not he could not decide, for mixed with a strange attraction and even fascination he was conscious of an undercurrent of terror, and even of aversion, as from something unclean. As he moved away, his eye caught an inscription in Gothic lettering round the edge of the slab on which the figure lay.

HIC JACET ALIANORA COMITISSA PECCATRIX
QVAE OBIT AÑO DÑI MCCCL CVIVS ANIMAE
MISEREATVR DEVS.

He copied the epitaph in his notebook, remarking that it differed from the usual formula, and then closing the door of the chantry he followed his cousins back to the house.

'Well, here you are at last,' said Lady Wilmot, as Charley and his sisters emerged on the lawn. 'What a time you have been in the ruins, and the tea is getting cold. And what have you done with Harry?'

'Oh, mother,' cried Cissy, 'we have had such an adventure. You know that little chantry chapel we are so fond of; well, we thought it wanted tidying up, and so we cleared away the weeds and rubbish, and what do you think we found? Why, the most lovely statue you ever saw, and we left Harry looking at it as if he had fallen in love with it and could not tear himself away.'

'By Jove!' said Charley, 'just like old Pygmalion, who fell in love with a statue and got Venus to bring it to life for him.'

'Don't talk so, Charley,' said Kate, 'I am sure I don't want this stone lady to come to life. There is something uncanny about her, I can't describe what, but I was very glad to get away from her.'

'Yes, mother,' said Cissy, 'Kate was quite frightened of the stone lady and dragged me away, just as I was longing to look at her, for you never saw anything so lovely in your life.'

'But there is one thing I noticed, father,' said Charley, 'that I think wants looking to. I noticed a bad crack in that fine vault over the chantry which looks dangerous, and I think Parsons should be sent to have a look at it.'

'Thank you, Charley,' said Sir Thomas, 'I should be sorry if anything happened to that part of the building, for archeologists tell me it's the most perfect thing of its kind in England. Parsons is busy on other matters for the next few days, but I will have it seen to next week. By the way, we shall have another visitor tonight. You remember Harry's college friend, Mr Edwards; I heard he was staying at the Johnstons and so I asked him to come here for a few days while Harry is with us, and here I think he comes across the lawn.'

Edwards had some previous acquaintance with the Wilmots, and was soon set down to tea with the rest, and engaged for lawn tennis afterwards, a game in which he had earned a great reputation.

Harry Charlton did not appear till the party were assembled in the drawing-room before dinner. On leaving the Abbey he was possessed by a disinclination for the lively society on the lawn. His nerves were in a strange flutter; he felt as if something unusual was impending, as if he had passed a barrier and shut the gate behind him, and had entered on a new life where strange experiences awaited him. He could not account for it. He tried to dismiss the finding of the statue as a mere antiquarian discovery, interesting both in history and in art; but it would not do. That face, with its enigmatical expression, haunted him, and would not be dismissed. He felt that this was not the end of the adventure; that in some mysterious way the dead woman of five centuries back had touched his life, and that more would come of it. To that something more he looked forward with the same indefinable mixture of attraction and repulsion which he had felt in the chapel while gazing at those pure alabaster features. He must be alone. He could not at present come back to the converse of ordinary life, and he set off on a swinging walk through field and woodland to try and steady his nerves, so as to meet his friends in the evening with composure. A good ten-mile stretch did something to restore him to his usual spirits. He was pleased to find his friend Edwards, of whose coming he had not been told, and when he took his place at the dinner table next to his aunt there was nothing unusual in his manner.

The conversation during dinner naturally turned on the discovery that had been made in the Abbey that afternoon. It was singular that so remarkable a work of art should have been forgotten, and been overlooked by the Northamptonshire Archæological Society, which had so many enthusiastic antiquaries in its ranks. There had been meetings of the society in the ruins, papers about them had been read and published, plans had been made and illustrations drawn of various parts of the building, including the chantry itself, but there was no mention or indication given of the monument either in the text or in the plates. Strange that no one should ever have thought of looking into that tangle of brambles by which it was concealed, till that very day.

'I must go first thing tomorrow,' said Sir Thomas, 'to see your wonderful discovery. The next thing will be to find out who this pretty lady was.'

'That I think I can tell you, sir,' said Henry, who now spoke for almost the first time, 'and I think it helps to solve the mystery of the sinful Countess in the painted windows opposite, which puzzled us last night.' All eyes were turned to the fragments of painted glass in the hall windows, as Henry continued.

'You see in the first window the devil is tempting the Countess ALI – , the rest of her name being lost. Well, on the tomb is an epitaph, which gives the missing part. She is the Countess Alianora; no further title is given. But whoever she was, the lady whose tomb we found is the same no doubt as the lady whose adventures were depicted in the windows.'

'Now I know,' broke in Kate, 'why I was frightened in the chapel. She was a wicked woman, and something told me so, and made me want to go away from her.'

'Well,' said Lady Wilmot, 'let us hope she mended her ways and ended her life well. You see, she went to Rome and was absolved by the Pope.'

'Yes, but I bet she did not get absolution for nothing,' said Charley. 'Just look at her in the last picture and you will see she has a church in her hand. Depend on it, she got her wicked deeds pardoned in return for her gifts to Rosemount Abbey; and I daresay she rebuilt a great part of it and among the rest her own chantry.'

'Charley,' said Edwards, 'you ought to be a lawyer; you make out such a good case for the prosecution.'

'At all events,' said Sir Thomas, 'Charley gives us a good lead for our research. I will look out the old deeds and try to find what connection, if any, there was between Rosemount Abbey and a Countess Alianora of some place unknown.'

The rest of the evening passed in the usual way. A few friends from neighbouring houses joined the party; there was a little impromptu dancing, and it was near midnight by the time they retired to rest. Henry had enjoyed himself like the rest, and forgot the adventure of the afternoon till he found himself once more alone in the monastic cell, looking out on the ruined Abbey. The recollection of his dream of the night before then for the first time recurred to him; he wondered whether it had any connection with his later experience in the chantry, but he could trace none whatever. The dream seemed merely one of those fanciful imaginings with which we are all familiar, devoid of any further meaning.

He was not, however, destined to repose quietly. This time his dream showed him the same monk; he recognised him by his coarse features and shaggy brows, but he was in the nave of a church and in the massive round pillars and severe architecture of the arches and triforium, Henry knew the nave of Rosemount Abbey, not as now, in ruins, but vaulted and entire. It was nearly dark, and the choir behind the pulpitum was wrapped in gloom, in the midst of which twinkled a few lights before the high altar and the various saintly shrines. The monk held something small in his hand, and was evidently, as on the night before, waiting for somebody or something. At last Henry was aware that somebody had indeed come. A shadowy figure draped in black moved swiftly out from behind a pillar and approached the monk. What the figure was he tried in vain to discover. All he could see was that just as had happened on the night before, a hand was stretched out and took something from the monk, which it promptly hid in the drapery with which the figure was covered. The hand, however, was more clearly seen this time. It was a woman's hand, white and delicate, and a jewel sparkled on her finger. The scene caused Henry a dull terror, as of some unknown calamity, or as of some crime that he had witnessed, and he woke with a start and found himself in a cold sweat.

He got up and paced his apartment to and fro, and then looked out of the window. It was brilliant moonlight, throwing strong shadows of the broken walls across the quiet cloister garth where the monks of old lay quietly sleeping till the last dread summons should awake them. The light fell full on the ancient nave walls

Where buttress and buttress alternately
Seemed framed of ebony and ivory

and the light touched with the magic of mystery the delicate traceries of the chantry where lay the Countess Alianora. Her face flashed upon his memory, with its enigmatical expression, half attracting, half repelling, and an irresistible desire impelled him to see her again. His window was open and the ground only a few feet below. He dressed himself hastily, and clambered out. Everything was still; all nature seemed asleep, not a breath of wind moved the trees or stirred the grass as he slowly passed along the cloister: his mind was in a strange state of nervous excitement; he was almost in a trance as he advanced into the nave where the shadows of column and arch fell black on the broken pavement. He paused a moment at the gate which led into the chantry, and then entered as if in a dream, for everything seemed to him unreal, and he himself a mere phantom. At last he stood beside the tomb and looked down on the lovely countenance which had bewitched him in the afternoon. The moonlight fell upon it, investing it with an unearthly mystery and charm. Its beauty was indescribable: never had he conceived anything so lovely. The strange semi-satirical expression of which he had been conscious in the afternoon had disappeared; nothing could be read in the features but sweetness and allurement. A passionate impulse seized him, and he bent down and kissed her on the lips. Was it fancy or was it real, that soft lips of warm life seemed to meet his own? He knew not: a delirious ecstasy transported him, the scene faded before his eyes and he sank on the floor in a swoon.

How long he lay he never knew. When he came to himself the moon had set, and he was in darkness. An indefinable terror seized him. He struggled to his feet, burst out of the Abbey, fled to his rooms, scrambling in through the window, and threw himself panting on his bed.

Henry Charlton was the last to appear next morning at the breakfast-table. He was pale and out of spirits, and roused himself with difficulty to take part in the discussion as to what was to be done that day. After breakfast he pleaded a headache, and retired with a book to the library, while the others betook themselves to various amusements or employments. The girls were in the garden where they found old Donald the gardener, whose life had been spent at Rosemount, and in whose eyes the garden was as much his as his master's, and perhaps more so.

'Yes, miss,' he was saying, 'the weeds do grow terrible this fine weather, and as you was saying it is time we cleaned up a bit in the old Abbey. But I see the young gentlemen has been doing a bit theirselves, chucking all them briars and rubbish out on the grass just as I had mown and tidied it.'

'Why Donald,' said Cissy, 'you ought to have thanked them, for the chapel was in an awful mess, and they have saved you some trouble.'

'Well, miss, I suppose they pleased theirselves, but that's not where I should have meddled, no, no!' and so saying he moved away.

'But why not there,' said Kate, 'why not there of all places?'

'Oh! I say nothing about it,' said Donald. 'Only folk do say that there's them there as don't like to be disturbed.'

'Indeed; what do they say in the village about it?'

'Oh! ay! I say nothing. I don't meddle with things above me. And I shan't tell ye any more, miss, it's not good for young women to know.'

'But do you know, Donald,' said Cissy, 'what we found there?'

'What did you find, miss? Not her? Oh, Lord! She was found once before, and no good come of it. There, don't ask me any more about it. It's not good for young women to know.' So saying Donald wheeled his barrow away into another part of the garden.

'Father,' said Kate, to Sir Thomas who now came up. 'Donald knows all about the tomb and the statue, and he won't tell us anything, except that the people think it unlucky to meddle with it. Have you ever heard of any superstition about it?'

'Nothing at all,' said he. 'I have just been down to look at your discovery. The statue is a wonderful piece of work. I have never seen anything finer either here or in Italy. But the chapel is in a bad way and part of the roof threatens to fall. I have just sent word to Parsons to come tomorrow morning and attend to it.'

They were joined presently by Edwards and Charley, and the day passed pleasantly enough, with the usual amusements of a country house in holiday time. Henry did not take much part with them. He was abstracted and inattentive, and altogether out of spirits. He had but a confused idea of what had happened the previous night, but there seemed still to linger on his lips that mystic, perhaps unhallowed kiss, and there still floated before his eyes the mocking enigma of that lovely countenance. He dreaded the approach of night, not knowing what it might bring, and did his best to divert his mind to other things, but without much success.

His friend Edwards was much concerned at the change in his behaviour, and asked Charley whether Henry had been upset in any way during his visit. He was assured that till yesterday afternoon Henry had been as happy and companionable as possible, and that it was only that morning that the change had come over him.

'But I can tell you one thing,' said Charley, 'I believe he was out of his room last night, for the flowerbeds show footmarks, and the creepers are torn outside his window, showing someone had been getting in and out, and there certainly has been no burglary in the house. Do you know whether he walks in his sleep?'

'I have never heard that he does,' said Edwards. 'We can't very well ask him whether anything is wrong, for he does not seem to invite enquiry, and has rather avoided us all day. But if it is a case of sleepwalking we might perhaps keep a look-out tonight to prevent his coming to mischief.'

'All right,' said Charley. 'My room is over his and looks out the same way. I'll try and keep awake till midnight, and will call you if I see anything of him.'

'That's well,' said Edwards, 'but we must be careful and not be seen, for it is dangerous to wake a somnambulist I believe.'

And so they departed to their several chambers.

The first part of the night passed peacefully enough with Henry. He had no dreams to trouble him, but towards midnight he began to turn uneasily in his bed, and to be oppressed by an uneasy feeling that he was not alone. He awoke to find the moon shining as brilliantly as on the previous night, and bringing into view every detail of the ancient buildings opposite. A dull sense of some sinister influence weighed upon him: someone was with him whom he could not see, whispering in his ear, 'You are mine, you are mine.' He could see no form, but to his mental vision was clearly visible the countenance of the figure in the chapel, now with the satirical, mocking expression more fully shown, and he felt himself drawn on he knew not whither. Again the mocking lips seemed to say, 'You are mine, you are mine.' Half unconsciously he rose from his bed, and advanced towards the window. A faintly visible form seemed to move before him, he saw the features of the countess more plainly, and without knowing how he got there he found himself outside the room in the cloister garth, and entering the shade of the cloister. Something impalpable glided on before him, turning on him the face that attracted him though it mocked him, and which he could not but follow, though with an increasing feeling of terror and dislike. Still on his ear fell the words 'You are mine, you are mine', and he was helpless to resist the spell that drew him on and on farther into the gloom of the ruined nave. And now the shape gathered consistency and he seemed to see the Countess Alianora standing facing him. On her features the same mocking smile, on her finger the jewel of his dream. 'You are mine,' she seemed to say, 'mine, mine, you sealed it with a kiss', and she outstretched her arms; but as she stood before him in her marvellous and unearthly beauty, a change came over her; her face sank into ghastly furrows, her limbs shrivelled, and as she advanced upon him, a mass of loathly corruption, and stretched out her horrible arms to embrace him, he uttered a dreadful scream as of a soul in torture, and sank fainting on the ground.

'Edwards, Edwards, come quick,' cried Charley, beating at his door. 'Harry is out of his room, and there is something with him, I don't know what it is, but hurry up or some mischief may happen.'

His friend was ready in a moment and the two crept cautiously downstairs, and as the readiest way, not to disturb the household, got out into the cloister through the window of Harry's room. They noticed on the way that his bed had been slept in, and was tossed about in disorder. They took the way out of the cloister by which Charley had seen Harry go, and had just reached the door that led into the nave when his unearthly scream of terror fell on their ears. They rushed into the church, crying, 'Harry, Harry, here we are, what is it, where are you?' and having no reply they searched as well as they could in the moonlight. They found him at last, stretched on the ground at the entrance to the fatal chantry chapel. At first they thought he was dead, but his pulse beat faintly, and they carried him out, still insensible, into the outer air. He showed some signs of life before long, but remained unconscious. The house was aroused and he was put to bed, and messengers were sent for the doctor. As they watched by his bedside, a thundering crash startled them; looking out of the window they saw a cloud of dust where the chantry had been, and next morning it was seen that the roof had fallen in, and destroyed it.

Harry Charlton lay many weeks with a brain fever. From his cries and ravings something was gathered of the horrors of that fatal night, but he would never be induced to tell the whole story after he recovered.

The fallen ruin was removed, and Sir Thomas hoped that the beautiful statue might have escaped. But strange to say, though every fragment of masonry was carefully examined and accounted for, no trace could be found of any alabaster figure nor of the tomb of the Comitissa Alianora.

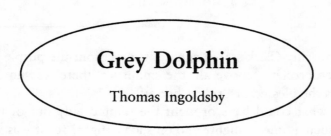

Grey Dolphin

Thomas Ingoldsby

'He won't – won't he? Then bring me my boots!' said the Baron.

Consternation was at its height in the castle of Shurland – a caitiff had dared to disobey the Baron! and – the Baron had called for his boots!

A thunderbolt in the great hall had been a *bagatelle* to it.

A few days before, a notable miracle had been wrought in the neighbourhood; and in those times miracles were not so common as they are now; no royal balloons, no steam, no railroads – while the few Saints who took the trouble to walk with their heads under their arms, or to pull the Devil by the nose – scarcely appeared above once in a century; so the affair made the greater sensation.

The clock had done striking twelve, and the Clerk of Chatham was untrussing his points preparatory to seeking his truckle-bed; a half-emptied tankard of mild ale stood at his elbow, the roasted crab yet floating on its surface. Midnight had surprised the worthy functionary while occupied in discussing it, and with his task yet unaccomplished. He meditated a mighty draft; one hand was fumbling with his tags, while the other was extended in the act of grasping the jorum, when a knock on the portal, solemn and sonorous, arrested his fingers. It was repeated thrice ere Emmanuel Saddleton had presence of mind sufficient to enquire who sought admission at that untimeous hour.

'Open! open! good Clerk of St Bridget's,' said a female voice, small, yet distinct and sweet – an excellent thing in woman.

The Clerk arose, crossed to the doorway, and undid the latchet.

On the threshold stood a lady of surpassing beauty: her robes were rich, and large, and full; and a diadem sparkling with gems that shed a halo around, crowned her brow: she beckoned the Clerk as he stood in astonishment before her.

'Emmanuel!' said the Lady; and her tones sounded like those of a silver flute. 'Emmanuel Saddleton, truss up your points, and follow me!'

The worthy Clerk stared aghast at the vision; the purple robe, the cymar, the coronet – above all, the smile; no, there was no mistaking her: it was the blessed St Bridget herself!

And what could have brought the sainted lady out of her warm shrine at such a time of night? and on such a night? for it was as dark as pitch, and, metaphorically speaking, 'rained cats and dogs'.

Emmanuel could not speak, so he looked the question.

'No matter for that,' said the Saint, answering to his thought. 'No matter for that, Emmanuel Saddleton; only follow me, and you'll see!'

The Clerk turned a wistful eye at the corner cupboard.

'Oh! never mind the lantern, Emmanuel: you'll not want it, but you may bring a mattock and a shovel.' As she spoke, the beautiful apparition held up her delicate hand. From the tip of each of her long taper fingers issued a lambent flame of such surpassing brilliancy as would have plunged a whole gas company into despair – it was a 'Hand of Glory', such a one as tradition tells us yet burns in Rochester Castle every St Mark's Eve. Many are the daring individuals who have watched in Gundulph's Tower, hoping to find it, and the treasure it guards – but none of them ever did.

'This way, Emmanuel!' and a flame of peculiar radiance streamed from her little finger as it pointed to the pathway leading to the churchyard.

Saddleton shouldered his tools, and followed in silence.

The cemetery of St Bridget's was some half-mile distant from the Clerk's domicile, and adjoined a chapel dedicated to that illustrious lady, who, after leading but a so-so life, had died in the odour of sanctity. Emmanuel Saddleton was fat and scant of breath, the mattock was heavy, and the Saint walked too fast for him: he paused to take second wind at the end of the first furlong.

'Emmanuel,' said the holy lady good-humouredly, for she heard him puffing; 'rest awhile, Emmanuel, and I'll tell you what I want with you.'

Her auditor wiped his brow with the back of his hand, and looked all attention and obedience.

'Emmanuel,' continued she, 'what did you and Father Fothergill, and the rest of you, mean yesterday by burying that drowned man so close to me? He died in mortal sin, Emmanuel; no shrift, no unction, no absolution; why, he might as well have been excommunicated. He plagues me with his grinning, and I can't have any peace in my shrine. You must howk him up again, Emmanuel!'

'To be sure, madam – my lady – that is, your holiness,' stammered Saddleton, trembling at the thought of the task assigned him. 'To be sure, your ladyship; only – that is –'

'Emmanuel,' said the Saint, 'you'll do my bidding; or it would be better you had!' and her eye changed from a dove's eye to that of a hawk, and a flash came from it as bright as the one from her little finger. The Clerk shook in his shoes; and, again dashing the cold perspiration from his brow, followed the footsteps of his mysterious guide.

The next morning all Chatham was in an uproar. The Clerk of St Bridget had found himself at home at day-break, seated in his own armchair, the fire out, and – the tankard of ale out too! Who had drunk it? – where had he been? –– how had he got home? – all was mystery! – he remembered 'a mass of things but nothing distinctly'; all was fog and fantasy. What he could clearly recollect was, that he had dug up the Grinning Sailor, and that the Saint had helped to throw him into the river again. All was thenceforth wonderment and devotion. Masses were sung, tapers were kindled, bells were tolled; the monks of St Romuald had a solemn procession, the abbot at their head, the sacristan at their tail, and the holy breeches of St Thomas à Becket in the centre; Father Fothergill brewed a XXX puncheon of holy water. The Road of Gillingham was deserted; the chapel of Rainham forsaken; everyone who had a soul to be saved, flocked with his offering to St Bridget's shrine, and Emmanuel Saddleton gathered more fees from the promiscuous piety of that one week than he had pocketed during the twelve preceding months.

Meanwhile the corpse of the ejected reprobate oscillated like a pendulum between Sheerness and Gillingham Reach. Now borne by the Medway into the Western Swale, now carried by the refluent tide back to the vicinity of its old quarters – it seemed as though the River-god and Neptune were amusing themselves with a game of subaqueous battledore, and had chosen this unfortunate carcass as a marine shuttlecock. For some time the alternation was kept up with great spirit, till Boreas, interfering in the shape of a stiffish 'Nor'-wester', drifted the bone (and flesh) of contention ashore on the Shurland domain, where it lay in all the majesty of mud. It was soon discovered by the retainers, and dragged from its ooze bed, grinning worse than ever. Tidings of the godsend were of course carried instantly to the castle, for the Baron was a very great man; and if a dun cow had flown across his property unannounced by the warder, the Baron would have kicked him, the said warder, from the topmost battlement into the bottommost ditch – a descent of peril, and one which 'Ludwig the Leaper', or the illustrious Trenck himself, might well have shrunk from encountering.

'An't please your lordship –' said Peter Periwinkle.

'No, villain! it does not please me!' roared the Baron.

His lordship was deeply engaged with a peck of Faversham oysters – he doted on shellfish, hated interruption at meals, and had not yet dispatched more than twenty dozen of the 'natives'.

'There's a body, my lord, washed ashore in the lower creek,' said the seneschal.

The Baron was going to throw the shells at his head; but paused in the act, and said with much dignity –

'Turn out the fellow's pockets!'

But the defunct had before been subjected to the double scrutiny of Father Fothergill and the Clerk of St Bridget's. It was ill gleaning after such hands; there was not a single maravedi.

We have already said that Sir Robert de Shurland, Lord of the Isle of Sheppey, and of many a fair manor on the mainland, was a man of worship. He had rights of freewarren, saccage and sockage, cuisage and jambage, fosse and fork, infang theofe and outfang theofe; and all waifs and strays belonged to him in fee simple.

'Turn out his pockets!' said the knight.

'An't please you, my lord, I must say as how they was turned-out afore, and the devil a rap's left.'

'Then bury the blackguard!'

'Please your lordship, he has been buried once.'

'Then bury him again, and be –!' The Baron bestowed a benediction.

The seneschal bowed low as he left the room, and the Baron went on with his oysters.

Scarcely ten dozen more had vanished when Periwinkle reappeared.

'An't please you, my lord, Father Fothergill says as how that it's the Grinning Sailor, and he won't bury him anyhow.'

'Oh! he won't – won't he?' said the Baron. Can it be wondered at that he called for his boots?

Sir Robert de Shurland, Lord of Shurland and Minister, Baron of Sheppey *in comitatu* Kent, was, as has been before hinted, a very great man. He was also a very little man; that is, he was relatively great, and relatively little – or physically little, and metaphorically great – like Sir Sidney Smith and the late Mr Bonaparte. To the frame of a dwarf he united the soul of a giant, and the valour of a gamecock. Then, for so small a man, his strength was prodigious; his fist would fell an ox, and his kick! – oh! his kick was tremendous, and when he had his boots on, would – to use an expression of his own, which he had picked up in the holy wars – would 'send a man from Jericho to June'. He was bull-necked and bandy-legged; his chest was broad and deep, his head large and uncommonly thick, his eyes a little bloodshot, and his nose *retroussé* with a remarkable red tip. Strictly speaking, the Baron could not be called handsome; but his *tout ensemble* was singularly impressive: and when he called for his boots, everybody trembled and dreaded the worst.

'Periwinkle,' said the Baron, as he encased his better leg, 'let the grave be twenty feet deep!'

'Your lordship's command is law.'

'And, Periwinkle' – Sir Robert stamped his left heel into its receptacle – 'and, Periwinkle, see that it be wide enough to hold not exceeding two!'

'Ye-ye-yes, my lord.'

'And, Periwinkle – tell Father Fothergill I would fain speak with his Reverence.'

'Ye-ye-yes, my lord.'

The Baron's beard was peaked; and his moustaches, stiff and stumpy, projected horizontally like those of a Tom Cat; he twirled the one, he stroked the other, he drew the buckle of his surcingle a thought tighter, and strode down the great staircase three steps at a stride.

The vassals were assembled in the great hall of Shurland Castle; every cheek was pale, every tongue was mute: expectation and perplexity were visible on every brow. What would his lordship do?

Were the recusant anybody else, gyves to the heels and hemp to the throat were but too good for him: but it was Father Fothergill who had said 'I won't'; and though the Baron was a very great man, the Pope was a greater, and the Pope was Father Fothergill's great friend – some people said he was his uncle.

Father Fothergill was busy in the refectory trying conclusions with a venison pasty, when he received the summons of his patron to attend him in the chapel cemetery. Of course he lost no time in obeying it, for obedience was the general rule in Shurland Castle. If anybody ever said, 'I won't', it was the exception; and, like all other exceptions, only proved the rule the stronger. The Father was a friar of the Augustine persuasion; a brotherhood which, having been planted in Kent soil some few centuries earlier, had taken very kindly to the soil, and overspread the county much as hops did some few centuries later. He was plump and portly, a little thick-winded, especially after dinner, stood five feet four in his sandals, and weighed hard upon eighteen stone. He was, moreover, a personage of singular piety; and the iron girdle, which, he said, he wore under his cassock to mortify withal, might have been well mistaken for the tyre of a cartwheel. When he arrived, Sir Robert was pacing up and down by the side of a newly opened grave.

'*Benedicite*! fair son!' (the Baron was as brown as a cigar).

'*Benedicite!*' said the Chaplain.

The Baron was too angry to stand upon compliment.

'Bury me that grinning caitiff there!' quoth he, pointing to the defunct.

'It may not be, fair son,' said the friar; 'he hath perished without absolution.'

'Bury the body!' roared Sir Robert.

'Water and earth alike reject him,' returned the Chaplain; 'holy St Bridget herself –'

'Bridget me no Bridgets! – do me thine office quickly, Sir Shaveling! or, by the Piper that played before Moses –' The oath was a fearful one; and whenever the Baron swore to do mischief, he was never known to perjure himself. He was playing with the hilt of his sword. 'Do me thine office, I say. Give him his passport to heaven.'

'He is already gone to hell!' stammered the Friar.

'Then do you go after him!' thundered the Lord of Shurland.

His sword half leaped from its scabbard. No! – the trenchant blade, that had cut Suleiman Ben Malek Ben Buckskin from helmet to chine, disdained to daub itself with the cerebellum of a miserable monk; it leaped back again; and as the Chaplain, scared at its flash, turned him in terror, the Baron gave him a kick! – one kick! – it was but one! – but such a one! Despite its obesity, up flew his holy body in an angle of forty-five degrees; then having reached its highest point of elevation, sunk headlong into the open grave that yawned to receive it. If the reverend gentleman had possessed such a thing as a neck, he had infallibly broken it! as he did not, he only dislocated his vertebrae – but that did quite as well. He was as dead as ditch-water!

'In with the other rascal!' said the Baron – and he was obeyed; for there he stood in his boots. Mattock and shovel made short work of it;. 20 feet of superincumbent mould pressed down alike the saint and the sinner. 'Now sing a requiem who list!' said the Baron, and his lordship went back to his oysters.

The vassals at Castle Shurland were astounded, or, as the Seneschal Hugh better expressed it, 'perfectly conglomerated', by this event. What! murder a monk in the odour of sanctity and on consecrated ground too! They trembled for the health of the Baron's soul. To the unsophisticated many it seemed that matters could not have been much worse had he shot a bishop's coachhorse – all looked for some signal judgment. The melancholy catastrophe of their neighbours at Canterbury was yet rife in their memories: not two centuries had elapsed since those miserable sinners had cut off the tail of the blessed Sir Thomas's mule. The tail of the mule, it was well known, had been forthwith affixed to that of the Mayor; and rumour said it had since been hereditary in the corporation. The least that could be expected was, that Sir Robert should have a friar tacked on to his for the term of his natural life! Some bolder spirits there were, 'tis true, who viewed the matter in various lights, according to their different temperaments and dispositions; for perfect unanimity existed not even in the good old times. The verderer, roistering Hob Roebuck, swore roundly, ' 'Twere as good a deed as eat to kick down the chapel as well as the monk.' Hob had stood there in a white sheet for kissing Giles Miller's daughter. On the other hand, Simpkin Agnew, the bell-ringer, doubted if the devil's cellar, which runs under the bottomless abyss, were quite deep enough for the delinquent, and speculated on the probability of a hole being dug in it for his especial accommodation. The philosophers and economists thought, with Saunders M'Bullock, the Baron's bagpiper, that a 'feckless monk more or less was nae great subject for a clamjamphry', especially as 'the supply considerably exceeded the demand'; while Malthouse, the taster, was arguing to Dame Martin that a murder now and then was a seasonable check to population, without which the Isle of Sheppey would in time be devoured, like a mouldy cheese, by inhabitants of its own producing. Meanwhile, the Baron ate his oysters and thought no more of the matter.

But this tranquillity of his lordship was not to last. A couple of Saints had been seriously offended; and we have all of us read at school that celestial minds are by no means insensible to the provocations of anger. There were those who expected that St Bridget would come in person, and have the friar up again, as she did the sailor: but perhaps her ladyship did not care to trust herself within the walls of Shurland Castle. To say the truth, it was scarcely a decent house for a female saint to be seen in. The Baron's gallantries, since he became a widower, had been but too notorious; and her own reputation was a little blown upon in the earlier days of her earthly pilgrimage: then things were so apt to be misrepresented – in short, she would leave the whole affair to St Austin, who, being a gentleman, could interfere with propriety, avenge her affront as well as his own, and leave no loop-hole for scandal. St Austin himself seems to have had his scruples, though of their precise nature it would be difficult to determine, for it were idle to suppose him at all afraid of the Baron's boots. Be this as it may, the mode which he adopted was at once prudent and efficacious. As an ecclesiastic, he could not well call the Baron out – had his boots been out of the question; so he resolved to have recourse to the law. Instead of Shurland Castle, therefore, he repaired forthwith to his own magnificent monastery, situated just without the walls of Canterbury, and presented himself in a vision to its abbot. No one who has ever visited that ancient city can fail to recollect the splendid gateway which terminates the vista of St Paul's Street, and stands there yet in all its pristine beauty. The tiny train of miniature artillery which now adorns its battlements is, it is true, an ornament of a later date; and is said to have been added some centuries after by a learned but jealous proprietor, for the purpose of shooting any wiser man than himself, who might chance to come that way. Tradition is silent as to any discharge having taken place, nor can the oldest inhabitant of modern days recollect any such occurrence. Here it was, in a handsome chamber, immediately over the lofty archway, that the Superior of the monastery lay buried in a brief slumber, snatched from his accustomed vigils. His mitre – for he was a mitred Abbot, and had a seat in parliament – rested on a table beside him; near it stood a silver wagon of Gascony wine, ready, no doubt, for the pious uses of the morrow. Fasting and watching had made him more than usually somnolent, than which nothing could have been better for the purpose of the Saint, who now appeared to him radiant in all the colours of the rainbow.

'Angel!' said the beatific vision. 'Anselm! are you not a pretty fellow to lie snoring there when your brethren are being knocked at head, and Mother Church herself is menaced? – It is a sin and a shame, Anselm!'

'What's the matter? – Who are you?' cried the Abbot, rubbing his eyes, which the celestial splendour of his visitor had set a-winking. 'Ave Maria. St Austin himself! Speak, *Beatissime*! what would you with the humblest of your votaries?'

'Anselm!' said the Saint, 'a brother of our order whose soul Heaven assoilzie! hath been foully murdered. He hath been ignominiously kicked to the death, Anselm; and there he lieth cheek-by-jowl with a wretched carcass, which our Sister Bridget has turned out of her cemetery for unseemly grinning. Arouse thee, Anselm!'

'Ay, so please you, *Sanctissime*!' said the Abbot. 'I will order forthwith that thirty masses be said, thirty *Paters*, and thirty *Aves*.'

'Thirty fools' heads!' Interrupted his patron, who was a little peppery.

'I will send for bell, book, and candle –'

'Send for an inkhorn, Anselm. Write me now a letter to his Holiness the Pope in good round terms, and another to the Coroner, and another to the Sheriff, and seize me the never-enough-to-be-anathematized villain who hath done this deed! Hang him as high as Haman, Anselm! – up with him! – down with his dwelling-place, root and branch, hearth-stone and roof-tree – down with it all, and sow the site with salt and sawdust!'

St Austin, it will be perceived, was a radical reformer.

'Marry will I,' quoth the Abbot, warming with the Saint's

eloquence; 'ay, marry will I, and that *instanter*. But there is one thing you have forgotten, most Beatified – the name of the culprit.'

'Robert de Shurland!'

'The Lord of Sheppey! Bless me!' said the Abbot, crossing himself; 'won't that be rather inconvenient? Sir Robert is a bold baron, and a powerful one; blows will come and go, and crowns will be cracked, and –'

'What is that to you, since yours will not be of the number?'

'Very true, *Beatissime!* – I will don me with speed, and do your bidding.'

'Do so, Anselm! – fail not to hang the Baron, burn his castle, confiscate his estate, and buy me two large wax candles for my own particular shrine out of your share of the property.'

With this solemn injunction the vision began to fade.

'One thing more!' cried the Abbot, grasping his rosary.

'What is that?' asked the Saint.

'O *Beate Augustine, ora pro nobis!*'

'Of course I shall,' said St Austin. '*Pax vobiscum!*' – and Abbot Anselm was left alone.

Within an hour all Canterbury was in commotion. A friar had been murdered – two friars – ten – twenty; a whole convent had been assaulted, sacked, burned – all the monks had been killed, and all the nuns had been kissed! Murder! fire! sacrilege! Never was city in such an uproar. From St George's Gate to St Dunstan's suburb, from the Donjon to the borough of Staplegate, it was noise and hubbub. 'Where was it?' 'When was it?' – 'How was it?' The Mayor caught up his chain, the Aldermen donned their furred gowns, the Town Clerk put on his spectacles. 'Who was he?' – 'What was he?' – 'Where was he?' – 'He should be hanged – he should be burned – he should be broiled – he should be fried – he should be scraped to death with red-hot oyster shells!' – 'Who was he?' – 'What was his name?'

The Abbot's Apparitor drew forth his roll and read aloud: 'Sir Robert de Shurland, Knight banneret, Baron of Shurland and Minster, and Lord of Sheppey.'

The Mayor put his chain in his pocket, the Aldermen took off their gowns, the Town Clerk put his pen behind his ear. It was a county business altogether: the Sheriff had better call out the *posse comitatus*.

While saints and sinners were thus leaguing against him, the Baron de Shurland was quietly eating his breakfast. He had passed a tranquil night, undisturbed by dreams of cowl or capuchin; nor was his appetite more affected than his conscience. On the contrary, he sat rather longer over his meal than usual: luncheon-time came, and he was ready as ever for his oysters; but scarcely had Dame Martin opened his first half-dozen when the warder's horn was heard from the barbican.

'Who the devil's that?' said Sir Robert. 'I'm not at home, Periwinkle. I hate to be disturbed at meals, and I won't be at home to anybody.'

'An't please your lordship,' answered the Seneschal, 'Paul Prior hath given notice that there is a body –'

'Another body!' roared the Baron. 'Am I to be everlastingly plagued with bodies? No time allowed me to swallow a morsel. Throw it into the moat!'

'So please you, my lord, it is a body of horse – and – and Paul says there is a still larger body of foot behind it; and he thinks, my lord – that is, he does not know, but he thinks – and we all think, my lord, that they are coming to – to besiege the castle!'

'Besiege the castle! Who? What? What for?'

'Paul says, my lord, that he can see the banner of St Austin, and the bleeding heart of Hamo de Crevecoeur, the Abbot's chief vassal; and there is John de Northwood, the sheriff, with his red cross engrailed; and Hever, and Leybourne, and Heaven knows how many more; and they are all coming on as fast as ever they can.'

'Periwinkle,' said the Baron, 'up with the drawbridge: down with the portcullis; bring me a cup of canary, and my nightcap. I won't be bothered with them. I shall go to bed.'

'To bed, my lord?' cried Periwinkle, with a look that seemed to say, 'He's crazy!'

At this moment the shrill tones of a trumpet were heard to sound thrice from the champaign. It was the signal for parley: the Baron changed his mind; instead of going to bed, he went to the ramparts.

'Well, rapscallions! and what now?' said the Baron.

A herald, two pursuivants and a trumpeter occupied the foreground of the scene; behind them, some three hundred paces off, upon a rising ground, was drawn up in battle-array the main body of the ecclesiastical forces.

'Hear you, Robert de Shurland, Knight, Baron of Shurland and Minster, and Lord of Sheppey, and know all men, by these present, that I do hereby attach you, the said Robert, of murder and sacrilege, now, or of late, done and committed by you, the said Robert, contrary to the peace of our Sovereign Lord the King, his crown and dignity: and I do hereby require and charge you, the said Robert, to forthwith surrender and gave up your own proper person, together with the castle of Shurland aforesaid, in order that the same may be duly dealt with according to law. And here standeth John de Northwood, Esquire, good man and true, sheriff of this his Majesty's most loyal county of Kent, to enforce the same, if need be, with his *posse comitatus* –'

'His what?' said the Baron.

'His *posse comitatus*, and –'

'Go to Bath!' said the Baron.

A defiance so contemptuous roused the ire of the adverse commanders. A volley of missiles rattled about the Baron's ears. Nightcaps avail little against contusions. He left the walls and retired to the great hall.

'Let them pelt away,' quoth the Baron: 'there are no windows to break, and they can't get in.' So he took his afternoon nap, and the siege went on.

Towards evening his lordship awoke, and grew tired of the din. Guy Pearson, too, had got a black eye from a brickbat, and the assailants were clambering over the outer wall. So the Baron called for his Sunday hauberk of Milan steel, and his great two-handed sword with the terrible name – it was the fashion in feudal times to give names to swords: King Arthur's was christened Excalibur; the Baron called his Tickletoby, and whenever he took it in hand it was no joke.

'Up with the portcullis! down with the bridge!' said Sir Robert; and out he sallied, followed by the *élite* of his retainers. Then there was a pretty-to-do. Heads flew one way – arms and legs another; round went Tickletoby; and, wherever it alighted, down came horse and man: the Baron excelled himself that day. All that he had done in Palestine faded in the comparison; he had fought for fun there, but now it was for life and lands. Away went John de Northwood; away went William of Hever, and Roger of Leybourne. Hamo de Crevecoeur, with the church vassals and the banner of St Austin, had been gone some time. The siege was raised, and the Lord of Sheppey was left alone in his glory.

But, brave as the Baron undoubtedly was, and total as had been the defeat of his enemies, it cannot be supposed that *La Stoccata* would be allowed to carry it away thus. It has before been hinted that Abbot Anselm had written to the Pope, and Boniface the Eighth piqued himself on his punctuality as a correspondent in all matters connected with Church discipline. He sent back an answer by return of post; and by it all Christian people were strictly enjoined to aid in exterminating the offender, on pain of the greater excommunication in this world, and a million of years of purgatory in the next. But then, again, Boniface the Eighth was rather at a discount in England just then. He had affronted Longshanks, as the royal lieges had nicknamed their monarch; and Longshanks had been rather sharp upon the clergy in consequence. If the Baron de Shurland could but get the King's pardon for what, in his cooler moments, he admitted to be a peccadillo, he might sniff at the Pope and bid him 'do his devilmost'.

Fortune, who, as the poet says, delights to favour the bold, stood his friend on this occasion. Edward had been for some time collecting a large force on the coast of Kent, to carry on his French wars for the recovery of Guienne; he was expected shortly to review it in person; but, then, the troops lay principally in cantonments about the mouth of the Thames, and his Majesty was to come down by water. What was to be done? – the royal barge was in sight, and John de Northwood and Hamo de Crevecoeur had broken up all the boats to boil their camp-kettles. A truly great mind is never without resources.

'Bring me my boots!' said the Baron.

They brought him his boots, and his dapple-gray steed along with them. Such a courser! all blood and bone, short-backed, broad-crested, and – but that he was a little ewe-necked – faultless in form and figure. The Baron sprang upon his back, and dashed at once into the river.

The barge which carried Edward Longshanks and his fortunes had by this time nearly reached the Nore; the stream was broad and the current strong, but Sir Robert and his steed were almost as broad, and a great deal stronger. After breasting the tide gallantly for a couple of miles, the knight was near enough to hail the steersman.

'What have we got here?' said the King. 'It's a mermaid,' said one. 'It's a grampus,' said another. 'It's the devil,' said a third. But they were all wrong; it was only Robert de Shurland. 'Gramercy,' said the King, 'that fellow was never born to be drowned!''

It has been said before that the Baron had fought in the Holy Wars; in fact, he had accompanied Longshanks, when only heir-apparent, in his expedition twenty-five years before, although his name is unaccountably omitted by Sir Harris Nicholas in his list of crusaders. He had been present at Acre when Amirand of Joppa stabbed the prince with a poisoned dagger, and had lent Princess Eleanor his own toothbrush after she had sucked out the venom from the wound. He had slain certain Saracens, contented himself with his own plunder, and never dunned the commissariat for arrears of pay. Of course he ranked high in Edward's good graces, and had received the honour of knighthood at his hands on the field of battle.

In one so circumstanced it cannot be supposed that such a trifle as the killing of a frowsy friar would be much resented, even had he not taken so bold a measure to obtain his pardon. His petition was granted, of course, as soon as asked; and so it would have been had the indictment drawn up by the Canterbury town-clerk, viz., 'That he, the said Robert de Shurland, etc., had then and there, with several, to wit, one thousand, pairs of boots, given sundry, to wit, two thousand kicks, and therewith and thereby killed divers, to wit, ten thousand, Austin Friars,' been true to the letter.

Thrice did the gallant gray circumnavigate the barge, while Robert de Winchelsey, the chancellor and archbishop to boot, was making out, albeit with great reluctance, the royal pardon. The interval was sufficiently long to enable his Majesty, who, gracious as he was, had always an eye to business, just to hint that the gratitude he felt towards the Baron was not unmixed with a lively sense of services to come; and that, if life were now spared him, common decency must oblige him to make himself useful. Before the archbishop, who had scalded his fingers with the wax in affixing the great seal, had time to take them out of his mouth, all was settled, and the Baron de Shurland had pledged himself to be forthwith in readiness, *cum suis*, to accompany his liege lord to Guienne.

With the royal pardon secured in his vest, boldly did his lordship turn again to the shore; and as boldly did his courser oppose his breadth of chest to the stream. It was a work of no common difficulty or danger;

a steed of less 'mettle and bone' had long since sunk in the effort; as it was, the Baron's boots were full of water, and Gray Dolphin's chamfrain more than once dipped beneath the wave. The convulsive snorts of the noble animal showed his distress; each instant they became more loud and frequent; when his hoof touched the strand, and 'the horse and his rider' stood once again in safety on the shore.

Rapidly dismounting, the Baron was loosening the girths of his demi-pique, to give the panting animal breath, when he was aware of as ugly an old woman as he had ever clapped eyes upon, peeping at him under the horse's belly.

'Make much of your steed, Robert Shurland! Make much of your steed!' cried the hag, shaking at him her long and bony finger. 'Groom to the hide, and corn to the manger! He has saved your life, Robert Shurland, for the nonce; but he shall yet be the means of your losing it for all that!'

The Baron stared: 'What's that you say, you old faggot?' He ran round by his horse's tail; the woman was gone!

The Baron paused; his great soul was not to be shaken by trifles; he looked around him, and solemnly ejaculated the word 'Humbug!' then, slinging the bridle across his arm, walked slowly on in the direction of the castle.

The appearance, and still more, the disappearance of the crone, had, however, made an impression; every step he took he became more thoughtful. ''Twould be deuced provoking, though, if he *should* break my neck after all.' He turned and gazed at Dolphin with the scrutinizing eye of a veterinary surgeon. 'I'll be shot if he is not groggy!' said the Baron.

With his lordship, like another great commander, 'Once to be in doubt, was once to be resolved': it would never do to go to the wars on a rickety prad. He dropped the rein, drew forth Tickletoby, and, as the enfranchised Dolphin, good easy horse, stretched out his ewe-neck to the herbage, struck off his head at a single blow. 'There, you lying old beldame!' said the Baron; 'now take him away to the knacker's.'

Three years were come and gone. King Edward's French wars were over; both parties having fought till they came to a standstill, shook hands, and the quarrel, as usual, was patched up by a royal marriage.

This happy event gave his Majesty leisure to turn his attention to Scotland, where things, through the intervention of William Wallace, were looking rather queerish. As his reconciliation with Philip now allowed of his fighting the Scotch in peace and quietness, the monarch lost no time in marching his long legs across the border, and the short ones of the Baron followed him, of course. At Falkirk, Tickletoby was in great request; and in the year following, we find a contemporary poet hinting at his master's prowess under the walls of Caerlaverock:

> Ovec eus fu achiminez
> Li beau Robert de Shurland
> Ki kant seoit sur le cheval
> Ne sembloit home ke someille

A quatrain which Mr Simpkinson translates,

> With them was marching
> The good Robert de Shurland,
> Who, when seated on horseback,
> Does not resemble a man asleep!

So thoroughly awake, indeed, does he seem to have proved himself, that the bard subsequently exclaims in an ecstasy of admiration,

> Si je estoie une pucelette
> Je li donrie ceur et cors
> Tant est de lu bons li recors.

> If I were a young maiden,
> I would give my heart and person,
> So great is his fame!

Fortunately the poet was a tough old monk of Exeter; since such a present to a nobleman, now in his grand climacteric, would hardly have been worth the carriage. With the reduction of this stronghold of the Maxwells seem to have concluded the Baron's military services; as on the very first day of the fourteenth century we find him once more landed on his native shore, and marching, with such of his retainers as the wars had left him towards the hospital shelter of Shurland Castle. It was then, upon that very beach, some hundred yards distant from high-water mark, that his eye fell upon something like an ugly old woman in a red cloak. She was seated on what seemed to be a large stone, in an interesting attitude, with her elbows resting upon her knees, and her chin upon her thumbs. The Baron started: the remembrance of his interview with a similar personage in the same place, some three years since, flashed upon his recollection. He rushed towards the spot, but the form was gone – nothing remained but the seat it had appeared to occupy. This, on examination, turned out to be no stone, but the whitened skull of a dead horse! A tender remembrance of the deceased Gray Dolphin shot a momentary pang into the Baron's bosom; he drew the back of his hand across his face; the thought of the hag's prediction in an instant rose, and banished all softer emotions. In utter contempt of his own weakness, yet with a tremor that deprived his redoubtable kick of half its wonted force, he spurned the relic with his foot. One word alone issued from his lips, elucidator of what was passing in his mind – it long remained imprinted on the memory of his faithful followers – that word was 'Gammon!' The skull bounded across the beach till it reached the very margin of the stream – one instant more and it would be engulfed for ever. At that moment a loud 'Ha! ha! ha!' was distinctly heard by the whole train to issue from its bleached and toothless jaws: it sank beneath the flood in a horse-laugh.

Meanwhile Sir Robert de Shurland felt an odd sort of sensation in his right foot. His boots had suffered in the wars. Great pains had been taken for their preservation. They had been 'soled' and 'heeled' more than once – had they been 'goloshed' their owner might have defied Fate! Well has it been said that 'there is no such thing as a trifle'. A nobleman's life depended upon a question of ninepence.

The Baron marched on; the uneasiness in his foot increased. He plucked off his boot – a horse's tooth was sticking in his great toe!

The result may be anticipated. Lame as he was, his lordship, with characteristic decision, would hobble on to Shurland; his walk increased the inflammation; a flagon of *aqua vitae* did not mend matters. He was in a high fever; he took to his bed. Next morning the toe presented the appearance of a Bedfordshire carrot; by dinner-time it had deepened to beetroot; and when Bargrave, the leech, at last sliced it off, the gangrene was too confirmed to admit of remedy. Dame Martin thought it high time to send for Miss Margaret, who, ever since her mother's death, had been living with her maternal aunt, the abbess, in the Ursuline convent at Greenwich. The young lady came, and with her came one Master Ingoldsby, her cousin-german by the mother's side; but the Baron was too far gone in the deadthraw to recognize either. He died as he lived, unconquered and unconquerable. His last words were – 'Tell the old hag she may go to –' Whither remains a secret. He expired without fully articulating the place of her destination.

But who and what was the crone who prophesied the catastrophe? Ay, 'that is the mystery of this wonderful history'. Some say it was Dame Fothergill, the late confessor's mamma; others, St Bridget herself; others thought it was nobody at all, but only a phantom conjured up by conscience. As we do not know, we decline giving an opinion.

And what became of the Clerk of Chatham? Mr Simpkinson avers that he lived to a good old age, and was at last hanged by Jack Cade, with his inkhorn about his neck, for 'setting boys copies'. In support of this he adduces his name 'Emmanuel', and refers to the historian Shakespeare. Mr Peters, on the contrary, considers this to be what he calls one of Mr Simpkinson's 'Anacreonisms', inasmuch as, at the introduction of Mr Cade's reform measure, the Clerk, if alive, would have been hard upon two hundred years old. The probability is that the unfortunate alluded to was his great-grandson.

Margaret Shurland in due course became Margaret Ingoldsby: her portrait still hangs in the gallery at Tappington. The features are handsome but shrewish, betraying, as it were, a touch of the old Baron's temperament; but we never could learn that she actually kicked her husband. She brought him a very pretty fortune in chains, owches, and Saracen ear-rings; the barony, being a male fief, reverted to the Crown.

In the abbey-church at Minster may yet be seen the tomb of a recumbent warrior, clad in the chain-mail of the thirteenth century. His hands are clasped in prayer; his legs, crossed in that position so prized by Templars in ancient, and tailors in modern days, bespeak him a soldier of the faith in Palestine. Close behind his dexter calf lies sculptured in bold relief a horse's head: and a respectable elderly lady, as she shows the monument, fails not to read her auditors a fine moral lesson on the sin of ingratitude, or to claim a sympathizing tear to the memory of poor 'Grey Dolphin'!

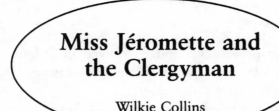

Miss Jéromette and the Clergyman

Wilkie Collins

My brother, the clergyman, looked over my shoulder before I was aware of him, and discovered that the volume which completely absorbed my attention was a collection of famous Trials, published in a new edition and in a popular form.

He laid his finger on the Trial which I happened to be reading at the moment. I looked up at him; his face startled me. He had turned pale. His eyes were fixed on the open page of the book with an expression which puzzled and alarmed me.

'My dear fellow,' I said, 'what in the world is the matter with you?'

He answered in an odd absent manner, still keeping his finger on the open page.

'I had almost forgotten,' he said. 'And this reminds me.'

'Reminds you of what?' I asked. 'You don't mean to say you know anything about the Trial?'

'I know this,' he said. 'The prisoner was guilty.'

'Guilty?' I repeated. 'Why, the man was acquitted by the jury, with the full approval of the judge! What can you possibly mean?'

'There are circumstances connected with that Trial,' my brother answered, 'which were never communicated to the judge or the jury – which were never so much as hinted or whispered in court. I know them – of my own knowledge, by my own personal experience. They are very sad, very strange, very terrible. I have mentioned them to no mortal creature. I have done my best to forget them. You – quite innocently – have brought them back to my mind. They oppress, they distress me. I wish I had found you reading any book in your library, except that book.'

My curiosity was now strongly excited. I spoke out plainly.

'Surely,' I suggested, 'you might tell your brother what you are unwilling to mention to persons less nearly related to you. We have followed different professions, and have lived in different countries, since we were boys at school. But you know you can trust me.'

He considered a little with himself.

'Yes,' he said. 'I know I can trust you.' He waited a moment; and then he surprised me by a strange question.

'Do you believe,' he asked, 'that the spirits of the dead can return to earth, and show themselves to the living?'

I answered cautiously – adopting as my own the words of a great English writer, touching the subject of ghosts.

'You ask me a question,' I said, 'which, after five thousand years, is yet undecided. On that account along, it is a question not to be trifled with.'

My reply seemed to satisfy him.

'Promise me,' he resumed, 'that you will keep what I tell you a secret as long as I live. After my death I care little what happens. Let the story of my strange experience be added to the published experience of those other men who have seen what I have seen, and who believe what I believe. The world will not be the worse, and may be the better, for knowing one day what I am now about to trust to your ear alone.'

My brother never again alluded to the narrative which he had confided to me, until the later time when I was sitting by his death-bed. He asked if I still remembered the story of Jéromette. 'Tell it to others,' he said, 'as I have told it to you.'

I repeat it, after his death – as nearly as I can in his own words.

II

On a fine summer evening, many years since, I left my chambers in the Temple, to meet a fellow-student, who had proposed to me a night's amusement in the public garden at Cremorne.

You were then on your way to India; and I had taken my degree at Oxford. I had sadly disappointed my father by choosing the Law as my profession, in preference to the Church. At that time, to own the truth, I had no serious intention of following any special vocation. I simply wanted an excuse for enjoying the pleasures of a London life. The study of the Law supplied me with that excuse. And I chose the Law as my profession accordingly.

On reaching the place at which we had arranged to meet, I found that my friend had not kept his appointment. After waiting vainly for ten minutes, my patience gave way, and I went into the Gardens by myself.

I took two or three turns round the platform devoted to the dancers, without discovering my fellow-student, and without seeing any other person with whom I happened to be acquainted at that time.

For some reason which I cannot now remember, I was not in my usual good spirits that evening. The noisy music jarred on my nerves, the sight of the gaping crowd round the platform irritated me, the blandishments of the painted ladies of the profession of pleasure saddened and disgusted me. I opened my cigar-case, and turned aside into one of the quiet by-walks of the Gardens.

A man who is habitually careful in choosing his cigar has this advantage over a man who is habitually careless. He can always count on smoking the best cigar in his case, down to the last. I was still absorbed in choosing my cigar, when I heard these words behind me – spoken in a foreign accent and in a woman's voice:

'Leave me directly, sir! I wish to have nothing to say to you.'

I turned round and discovered a little lady very simply and tastefully dressed, who looked both angry and alarmed as she rapidly passed me on her way to the more frequented part of the Gardens. A man (evidently the worse for the wine he had drunk in the course of the evening) was following her, and was pressing his tipsy attentions on her with the coarsest insolence of speech and manner. She was young and pretty, and she cast one entreating look at me as she went by, which it was not in manhood – perhaps I ought to say, in young-manhood – to resist.

I instantly stepped forward to protect her, careless whether I involved myself in a discreditable quarrel with a blackguard or not. As a matter of course, the fellow resented my interference, and my temper gave way. Fortunately for me, just as I lifted my hand to knock him down, a policeman appeared who had noticed that he was drunk, and who settled the dispute officially by turning him out of the Gardens.

I led her away from the crowd that had collected. She was evidently frightened – I felt her hand trembling on my arm – but she had one great merit: she made no fuss about it.

'If I can sit down for a few minutes,' she said in her pretty foreign accent, 'I shall soon be myself again, and I shall not trespass any further on your kindness. I thank you very much, sir, for taking care of me.'

We sat down on a bench in a retired part of the Gardens, near a little fountain. A row of lighted lamps ran round the outer rim of the basin. I could see her plainly.

I have said that she was 'a little lady'. I could not have described her more correctly in three words.

Her figure was slight and small: she was a well-made miniature of a woman from head to foot. Her hair and her eyes were both dark. The hair curled naturally; the expression of the eyes was quiet, and rather sad; the complexion, as I then saw it, very pale; the little mouth perfectly charming. I was especially attracted, I remember, by the carriage of her head; it was strikingly graceful and spirited; it distinguished her, little as she was and quiet as she was, among the thousands of other women in the Gardens, as a creature apart. Even the one marked defect in her – a slight 'cast' in the left eye – seemed to add, in some strange way, to the quaint attractiveness of her face. I have already spoken of the tasteful simplicity of her dress. I ought now to add that it was not made of any costly material, and that she wore no jewels or ornament of any sort. My little lady was not rich: even a man's eye could see that.

She was perfectly unembarrassed and unaffected. We fell as easily into talk as if we had been friends instead of strangers.

I asked how it was that she had no companion to take care of her. 'You are too young and too pretty,' I said in my blunt English way, 'to trust yourself alone in such a place as this.'

She took no notice of the compliment. She calmly put it away from her as if it had not reached her ears.

'I have no friend to take care of me,' she said simply. 'I was sad and sorry this evening, all by myself, and I thought I would go to the Gardens and hear the music, just to amuse me. It is not much to pay at the gate; only a shilling.'

'No friend to take care of you?' I repeated. 'Surely there must be one happy man who might have been here with you tonight?'

'What man do you mean?' she asked.

'The man,' I answered thoughtlessly, 'whom we call, in England, a sweetheart.'

I would have given worlds to have recalled those foolish words the moment they passed my lips. I felt that I had taken a vulgar liberty with her. Her face saddened; her eyes dropped to the ground. I begged her pardon.

'There is no need to beg my pardon,' she said. 'If you wish to know, sir – yes, I had once a sweetheart, as you call it in England. He has gone away and left me. No more of him, if you please. I am rested now. I will thank you again, and go home.'

She rose to leave me.

I was determined not to part with her in that way. I begged to be allowed to see her safely back to her own door. She hesitated. I took a man's unfair advantage of her, by appealing to her fears. I said, 'Suppose the blackguard who annoyed you should be waiting outside the gates?' That decided her. She took my arm. We went away together by the bank of the Thames, in the balmy summer night.

A walk of half an hour brought us to the house in which she lodged – a shabby little house in a by-street, inhabited evidently by very poor people.

She held out her hand at the door, and wished me goodnight. I was too much interested in her to consent to leave my little foreign lady without the hope of seeing her again. I asked permission to call on her the next day. We were standing under the light of the street-lamp. She studied my face with a grave and steady attention before she made any reply.

'Yes,' she said at last. 'I think I do know a gentleman when I see him. You may come, sir, if you please, and call upon me tomorrow.'

So we parted. So I entered – doubting nothing, foreboding nothing – on a scene in my life, which I now look back on with unfeigned repentance and regret.

III

I am speaking at this later time in the position of a clergyman, and in the character of a man of mature age. Remember that; and you will understand why I pass as rapidly as possible over the events of the next year of my life – why I say as little as I can of the errors and the delusions of my youth.

I called on her the next day. I repeated my visits during the days and weeks that followed, until the shabby little house in the by-street had become a second and (I say it with shame and self-reproach) a dearer home to me.

All of herself and her story which she thought fit to confide to me under these circumstances may be repeated to you in few words.

The name by which letters were addressed to her was 'Mademoiselle Jéromette'. Among the ignorant people of the house and the small tradesmen of the neighbourhood – who found her name not easy of pronunciation by the average English tongue – she was known by the friendly nickname of 'The French Miss'. When I knew her, she was resigned to her lonely life among strangers. Some years had elapsed since she had lost her parents, and had left France. Possessing a small, very small, income of her own, she added to it by colouring miniatures for the photographers. She had relatives still living in France; but she had long since ceased to correspond with them. 'Ask me nothing more about my family,' she used to say. 'I am as good as dead in my own country and among my own people.'

This was all – literally all – that she told me of herself. I have never discovered more of her sad story from that day to this.

She never mentioned her family name – never even told me what part of France she came from, or how long she had lived in England. That she was, by birth and breeding, a lady, I could entertain no doubt; her manners, her accomplishments, her ways of thinking and speaking, all proved it. Looking below the surface, her character showed itself in aspects not common among young women in these days. In her quiet way, she was an incurable fatalist, and a firm believer in the ghostly reality of apparitions from the dead. Then again, in the matter of money, she had strange views of her own. Whenever my purse was in my hand, she held me resolutely at a distance from first to last. She refused to move into better apartments; the shabby little house was clean inside, and the poor people who lived in it were kind to her – and that was enough. The most expensive present that she ever permitted me to offer her was a little enamelled ring, the plainest and cheapest thing of the kind in the jeweller's shop. In all her relations with me she was sincerity itself. On all occasions, and under all circumstances, she spoke her mind (as the phrase is) with the same uncompromising plainness.

'I like you,' she said to me; 'I respect you; I shall always be faithful to you while you are faithful to me. But my love has gone from me. There is another man who has taken it away with him, I know not where.'

Who was the other man?

She refused to tell me. She kept his rank and his name strict secrets from me. I never discovered how he had met with her, or why he had left her, or whether the guilt was his of making her an exile from her country and her friends. She despised herself for still loving him; but the passion was too strong for her – she owned it and lamented it with the frankness which was so pre-eminently a part of her character. More than this, she plainly told me, in the early days of our acquaintance, that she believed he would return to her. It might be tomorrow, or it might be years hence. Even if he failed to repent of his own cruel conduct, the man would still miss her, as something lost out of his life; and, sooner or later, he would come back.

'And will you receive him if he does come back?' I asked.

'I shall receive him,' she replied, 'against my own better judgment – in spite of my own firm persuasion that the day of his return to me will bring with it the darkest days of my life.'

I tried to remonstrate with her.

'You have a will of your own,' I said. 'Exert it, if he attempts to return to you.'

'I have no will of my own,' she answered quietly, 'where he is concerned. It is my misfortune to love him.' Her eyes rested for a moment on mine, with the utter self-abandonment of despair. 'We have said enough about this,' she added abruptly. 'Let us say no more.'

From that time we never spoke again of the unknown man. During the year that followed our first meeting, she heard nothing of him directly or indirectly. He might be living, or he might be dead. There came no word of him, or from him. I was fond enough of her to be satisfied with this – he never disturbed us.

IV

The year passed – and the end came. Not the end as you may have anticipated it, or as I might have foreboded it.

You remember the time when your letter from home informed you of the fatal termination of our mother's illness? It is the time of which I am now speaking. A few hours only before she breathed her last, she called me to her bedside, and desired that we might be left together alone. Reminding me that her death was near, she spoke of my prospects in life; she noticed my want of interest in the studies which were then supposed to be engaging my attention, and she ended by entreating me to reconsider my refusal to enter the Church.

'Your father's heart is set upon it,' she said. 'Do what I ask of you, my dear, and you will help to comfort him when I am gone.'

Her strength failed her: she could say no more. Could I refuse the last request she would ever make to me? I knelt at the bedside, and took her wasted hand in mine, and solemnly promised her the respect which a son owes to his mother's last wishes.

Having bound myself by this sacred engagement, I had no choice but to accept the sacrifice which it imperatively exacted from me. The time had come when I must tear myself free from all unworthy associations. No matter what the effort cost me, I must separate myself at once and for ever from the unhappy woman who was not, who never could be, my wife.

At the close of a dull foggy day I set forth with a heavy heart to say the words which were to part us for ever.

Her lodging was not far from the banks of the Thames. As I drew near the place the darkness was gathering, and the broad surface of the river was hidden from me in a chill white mist. I stood for a while, with my eyes fixed on the vaporous shroud that brooded over the knowing water – I stood, and asked myself in despair the one dreary question: 'What am I to say to her?'

The mist chilled me to the bones. I turned from the river-bank, and made my way to her lodgings hard by. 'It must be done!' I said to myself, as I took out my key and opened the house door.

She was not at her work, as usual, when I entered her little sitting-room. She was standing by the fire, with her head down, and with an open letter in her hand.

The instant she turned to meet me, I saw in her face that something was wrong. Her ordinary manner was the manner of an unusually placid and self-restrained person. Her temperament had little of the liveliness which we associate in England with the French nature. She was not ready with her laugh; and, in all my previous experience, I had never yet known her to cry. Now, for the first time, I saw the quiet face disturbed; I saw tears in the pretty brown eyes. She ran to meet me, and laid her hand on my breast, and burst into a passionate fit of weeping that shook me from head to foot.

Could she by any human possibility have heard of the coming change in my life? Was she aware, before I had opened my lips, of the hard necessity which had brought me to the house?

It was simply impossible; the thing could not be.

I waited until her first burst of emotion had worn itself out. Then I asked – with an uneasy conscience, with a sinking heart – what had happened to distress her.

She drew herself away from me, sighing heavily, and gave me the open letter which I had seen in her hand.

'Read that,' she said. 'And remember I told you what might happen when we first met.'

I read the letter.

It was signed in initials only; but the writer plainly revealed himself as the man who had deserted her. He had repented; he had returned to her. In proof of his penitence he was willing to do her the justice which he had hitherto refused – he was willing to marry her; on the condition that she would engage to keep the marriage a secret, so long as his parents lived. Submitting this proposal, he waited to know whether she would consent, on her side, to forgive and forget.

I gave her back the letter in silence. This unknown rival had done me the service of paving the way for our separation. In offering her the atonement of marriage, he had made it, on my part, a matter of duty to her, as well as to myself, to say the parting words. I felt this instantly. And yet, I hated him for helping me!

She took my hand, and led me to the sofa. We sat down, side by side. Her face was composed to a sad tranquillity. She was quiet; she was herself again.

'I have refused to see him,' she said, 'until I had first spoken to you. You have read his letter. What do you say?'

I could make but one answer. It was my duty to tell her what my own position was in the plainest terms. I did my duty – leaving her free to decide on the future for herself. Those sad words said, it was useless to prolong the wretchedness of our separation. I rose, and took her hand for the last time.

I see her again now, at that final moment, as plainly as if it had happened yesterday. She had been suffering from an affection of the throat; and she had a white silk handkerchief tied loosely round her neck. She wore a simple dress of purple merino, with a black-silk apron over it. Her face was deadly pale; her fingers felt icily cold as they closed round my hand.

'Promise me one thing,' I said, 'before I go. While I live, I am your friend – if I am nothing more. If you are ever in trouble, promise that you will let me know it.'

She started, and drew back from me as if I had struck her with a sudden terror.

'Strange!' she said, speaking to herself. 'He feels as I feel. He is afraid of what may happen to me, in my life to come.'

I attempted to reassure her. I tried to tell her what was indeed the truth – that I had only been thinking of the ordinary chances and changes of life, when I spoke.

She paid no heed to me; she came back and put her hands on my shoulders, and thoughtfully and sadly looked up in my face.

'My mind is not your mind in this matter,' she said. 'I once owned to you that I had my forebodings, when we first spoke of this man's return. I may tell you now, more than I told you then. I believe I shall die young, and die miserably. If I am right, have you interest enough still left in me to wish to hear of it?'

She paused, shuddering – and added these startling words:

'You shall hear of it.'

The tone of steady conviction in which she spoke alarmed and distressed me. My face showed her how deeply and how painfully I was affected.

'There, there!' she said, returning to her natural manner; 'don't take what I say too seriously. A poor girl who has led a lonely life like mine thinks strangely and talks strangely – sometimes. Yes; I give you my promise. If I am ever in trouble, I will let you know it. God bless you – you have been very kind to me – goodbye!'

A tear dropped on my face as she kissed me. The door closed

between us. The dark street received me.

It was raining heavily. I looked up at her window, through the drifting shower. The curtains were parted: she was standing in the gap, dimly lit by the lamp on the table behind her, waiting for our last look at each other. Slowly lifting her hand, she waved her farewell at the window, with the unsought native grace which had charmed me on the night when we first met. The curtains fell again – she disappeared – nothing was before me, nothing was round me, but the darkness and the night.

V

In two years from that time, I had redeemed the promise given to my mother on her deathbed. I had entered the Church.

My father's interest made my first step in my new profession an easy one. After serving my preliminary apprenticeship as a curate, I was appointed, before I was thirty years of age, to a living in the West of England.

My new benefice offered me every advantage that I could possibly desire – with the one exception of a sufficient income. Although my wants were few, and although I was still an unmarried man, I found it desirable, on many accounts, to add to my resources. Following the example of other young clergymen in my position, I determined to receive pupils who might stand in need of preparation for a career at the Universities. My relatives exerted themselves; and my good fortune still befriended me. I obtained two pupils to start with. A third would complete the number which I was at present prepared to receive. In course of time, this third pupil made his appearance, under circumstances sufficiently remarkable to merit being mentioned in detail.

It was the summer vacation; and my two pupils had gone home. Thanks to a neighbouring clergyman, who kindly undertook to perform my duties for me, I too obtained a fortnight's holiday, which I spent at my father's house in London.

During my sojourn in the metropolis, I was offered an opportunity of preaching in a church, made famous by the eloquence of one of the popular pulpit-orators of our time. In accepting the proposal, I felt naturally anxious to do my best, before the unusually large and unusually intelligent congregation which would be assembled to hear me.

At the period of which I am now speaking, all England had been startled by the discovery of a terrible crime, perpetrated under circumstances of extreme provocation. I chose this crime as the main subject of my sermon. Admitting that the best among us were frail mortal creatures subject to evil promptings and provocations like the worst among us, my object was to show how a Christian man may find his certain refuge from temptation in the safeguards of his religion. I dwelt minutely on the hardship of the Christian's first struggle to resist the evil influence – on the help which his Christianity inexhaustibly held out to him in the worst relapse of the weaker and viler part of his nature – on the steady and certain gain which was the ultimate reward of his faith and his firmness – and on the blessed sense of peace and happiness which accompanied the final triumph. Preaching to this effect, with the fervent conviction which I really felt, I may say for myself, at least, that I did no discredit to the choice which had placed me in the pulpit. I held the attention of my congregation, from the first word to the last.

While I was resting in the vestry on the conclusion of the service, a note was brought to me written in pencil. A member of my congregation – a gentleman – wished to see me, on a matter of considerable importance to himself. He would call on me at any place, and at any hour, which I might choose to appoint. If I wished to be satisfied of his respectability, he would beg leave to refer me to his father, with whose name I might possibly be acquainted.

The name given in the reference was undoubtedly familiar to me, as the name of a man of some celebrity and influence in the world of London. I sent back my card, appointing an hour for the visit of my correspondent on the afternoon of the next day.

VI

The stranger made his appearance punctually. I guessed him to be some two or three years younger than myself. He was undeniably handsome; his manners were the manners of a gentleman – and yet, without knowing why, I felt a strong dislike to him the moment he entered the room.

After the first preliminary words of politeness had been exchanged between us, my visitor informed me as follows of the object which he had in view.

'I believe you live in the country, sir?' he began.

'I live in the West of England,' I answered.

'Do you make a long stay in London?'

'No. I go back to my rectory tomorrow.'

'May I ask if you take pupils?'

'Yes.'

'Have you any vacancy?'

'I have one vacancy.'

'Would you object to let me go back with you tomorrow, as your pupil?'

The abruptness of the proposal took me by surprise. I hesitated.

In the first place (as I have already said), I disliked him. In the second place, he was too old to be a fit companion for my other two pupils – both lads in their teens. In the third place, he had asked me to receive him at least three weeks before the vacation came to an end. I had my own pursuits and amusements in prospect during that interval, and saw no reason why I should inconvenience myself by setting them aside.

He noticed my hesitation, and did not conceal from me that I had disappointed him.

'I have it very much at heart,' he said, 'to repair without delay the time that I have lost. My age is against me, I know. The truth is – I have wasted my opportunities since I left school, and I am anxious, honestly anxious, to mend my ways, before it is too late. I wish to prepare myself for one of the Universities – I wish to show, if I can, that I am not quite unworthy to inherit my father's famous name. You are the man to help me, if I can only persuade you to do it. I was struck by your sermon yesterday; and, if I may venture to make the confession in your presence, I took a strong liking to you. Will you see my father, before you decide to say No? He will be able to explain whatever may seem strange in my present application; and he will be happy to see you this afternoon, if you can spare the time. As to the question of terms, I am quite sure it can be settled to your entire satisfaction.'

He was evidently in earnest – gravely, vehemently in earnest. I unwillingly consented to see his father.

Our interview was a long one. All my questions were answered fully and frankly.

The young man had led an idle and desultory life. He was weary of it, and ashamed of it. His disposition was a peculiar one. He stood sorely in need of a guide, a teacher, and a friend, in whom he was disposed to confide. If I disappointed the hopes which he had centred in me, he would be discouraged, and he would relapse into the aimless and indolent existence of which he was now ashamed. Any terms for which I might stipulate were at my disposal if I would consent to receive him, for three months to begin with, on trial.

Still hesitating, I consulted my father and my friends.

They were all of opinion (and justly of opinion so far) that the new connection would be an excellent one for me. They all reproached me for taking a purely capricious dislike to a well-born and well-bred young man, and for permitting it to influence me, at the outset of my career, against my own interests. Pressed by these considerations, I allowed myself to be persuaded to give the new pupil a fair trial. He accompanied me, the next day, on my way back to the rectory.

VII

Let me be careful to do justice to a man whom I personally disliked. My senior pupil began well: he produced a decidedly favourable impression on the persons attached to my little household.

The women, especially, admired his beautiful light hair, his crisply curling beard, his delicate complexion, his clear blue eye, and his finely shaped hands and feet. Even the inveterate reserve in his manner, and the downcast, almost sullen, look which had prejudiced me against him, aroused a common feeling of romantic enthusiasm in my servants' hall. It was decided, on the high authority of the housekeeper herself, that 'the new gentleman' was in love – and, more interesting still, that he was the victim of an unhappy attachment which had driven him away from his friends and his home.

For myself, I tried hard, and tried vainly, to get over my first dislike to the senior pupil.

I could find no fault with him. All his habits were quiet and regular; and he devoted himself conscientiously to his reading. But, little by little, I became satisfied that his heart was not in his studies. More than this, I had my reasons for suspecting that he was concealing something from me, and that he felt painfully the reserve on his own part which he could not, or dared not, break through. There were moments when I almost doubted whether he had not chosen my remote country rectory, as a safe place of refuge from some person or persons of whom he stood in dread.

For example, his ordinary course of proceeding, in the matter of his correspondence, was, to say the least of it, strange.

He received no letters at my house. They waited for him at the village post-office. He invariably called for them himself, and invariably forbore to trust any of my servants with his own letters for the post. Again, when we were out walking together, I more than once caught him looking furtively over his shoulder, as if he suspected some person of following him, for some evil purpose. Being constitutionally a hater of mysteries, I determined, at an early stage of our intercourse, on making an effort to clear matters up. There might be just a chance of my winning the senior pupil's confidence, if I spoke to him while the last days of the summer vacation still left us alone together in the house.

'Excuse me for noticing it,' I said to him one morning, while we were engaged over our books – 'I cannot help observing that you appear to have some trouble on your mind. Is it indiscreet, on my part, to ask if I can be of any use to you?'

He changed colour – looked up at me quickly – looked down again at his book – struggled hard with some secret fear or secret reluctance that was in him – and suddenly burst out with this extraordinary question:

'I suppose you were in earnest when you preached that sermon in London?'

'I am astonished that you should doubt it,' I replied.

He paused again; struggled with himself again; and startled me by a second outbreak, even stranger than the first.

'I am one of the people you preached at in your sermon,' he said. 'That's the true reason why I asked you to take me for your pupil. Don't turn me out! When you talked to your congregation of tortured and tempted people, you talked of Me.'

I was so astonished by the confession, that I lost my presence of mind. For the moment, I was unable to answer him.

'Don't turn me out!' hc repeated. 'Help me against myself. I am telling you the truth. As God is my witness, I am telling you the truth!'

'Tell me the whole truth,' I said; 'and rely on my consoling and helping you – rely on my being your friend.'

In the fervour of the moment, I took his hand. It lay cold and still in mine: it mutely warned me that I had a sullen and a secret nature to deal with.

'There must be no concealment between us,' I resumed. 'You have entered my house, by your own confession, under false pretences. It is your duty to me, and your duty to yourself, to speak out.'

The man's inveterate reserve – cast off for the moment only – renewed its hold on him. He considered, carefully considered, his next words before he permitted them to pass his lips.

'A person is in the way of my prospects in life,' he began slowly, with his eyes cast down on his book. 'A person provokes me horribly. I feel dreadful temptations (like the man you spoke of in your sermon) when I am in the person's company. Teach me to resist temptation! I am afraid of myself, if I see the person again. You are the only man who can help me. Do it while you can.'

He stopped, and passed his handkerchief over his forehead.

'Will that do?' he asked – still with his eyes on his book.

'It will not do,' I answered. 'You are so far from really opening your heart to me, that you won't even let me know whether it is a man or a woman who stands in the way of your prospects in life. You use the word "person", over and over again – rather than say "he" or "she" when you speak of the provocation which is trying you. How can I help a man who has so little confidence in me as that?'

My reply evidently found him at the end of his resources. He tried, tried desperately, to say more than he had said yet. No! The words seemed to stick in his throat. Not one of them would pass his lips.

'Give me time,' he pleaded piteously. 'I can't bring myself to it, all at once. I mean well. Upon my soul, I mean well. But I am slow at this sort of thing. Wait till tomorrow.'

Tomorrow came – and again he put it off.

'One more day!' he said. 'You don't know how hard it is to speak plainly. I am half afraid; I am half ashamed. Give me one more day.'

I had hitherto only disliked him. Try as I might (and did) to make merciful allowance for his reserve, I began to despise him now.

VIII

The day of the deferred confession came, and brought an event with it, for which both he and I were alike unprepared. Would he really have confided in me but for that event? He must either have done it, or have abandoned the purpose which had led him into my house.

We met as usual at the breakfast-table. My housekeeper brought in my letters of the morning. To my surprise, instead of leaving the room again as usual, she walked round to the other side of the table, and laid a letter before my senior pupil – the first letter, since his residence with me, which had been delivered to him under my roof.

He started, and took up the letter. He looked at the address. A spasm of suppressed fury passed across his face; his breath came quickly; his hand trembled as it held the letter. So far, I said nothing. I waited to see whether he would open the envelope in my presence or not.

He was afraid to open it, in my presence. He got on his feet; he said, in tones so low that I could barely hear him: 'Please excuse me for a minute' – and left the room.

I waited for half an hour – for a quarter of an hour, after that – and then I sent to ask if he had forgotten his breakfast.

In a minute more, I heard his footstep in the hall. He opened the breakfast-room door, and stood on the threshold, with a small travelling-bag in his hand.

'I beg your pardon,' he said, still standing at the door. 'I must ask for leave of absence for a day or two. Business in London.'

'Can I be of any use?' I asked. 'I am afraid your letter has brought you bad news?'

'Yes,' he said shortly. 'Bad news. I have no time for breakfast.'

'Wait a few minutes,' I urged. 'Wait long enough to treat me like your friend – to tell me what your trouble is before you go.'

He made no reply. He stepped into the hall, and closed the door – then opened it again a little way, without showing himself.

'Business in London,' he repeated – as if he thought it highly important to inform me of the nature of his errand. The door closed for the second time. He was gone.

I went into my study, and carefully considered what had happened. The result of my reflections is easily described. I determined on discontinuing my relations with my senior pupil. In writing to his father (which I did, with all due courtesy and respect, by that day's post), I mentioned as my reason for arriving at this decision: First, that I had found it impossible to win the confidence of his son. Secondly, that his son had that morning suddenly and mysteriously left my house for London, and that I must decline accepting any further responsibility towards him, as the necessary consequence.

I had put my letter in the post-bag, and was beginning to feel a little easier after having written it, when my housekeeper appeared in the study, with a very grave face, and with something hidden apparently in her closed hand.

'Would you please look, sir, at what we have found in the gentleman's bedroom, since he went away this morning?'

I knew the housekeeper to possess a woman's full share of that amiable weakness of the sex which goes by the name of 'Curiosity'. I had also, in various indirect ways, become aware that my senior pupil's strange departure had largely increased the disposition among the women of my household to regard him as the victim of an unhappy attachment. The time was ripe, as it seemed to me, for checking any further gossip about him, and any renewed attempts at prying into his affairs in his absence.

'Your only business in my pupil's bedroom,' I said to the housekeeper, 'is to see that it is kept clean, and that it is properly aired. There must be no interference, if you please, with his letters, or his papers, or with anything else that he has left behind him. Put back directly whatever you may have found in his room.'

The housekeeper had her full share of a woman's temper as well as of a woman's curiosity. She listened to me with a rising colour, and a just perceptible toss of the head.

'Must I put it back, sir, on the floor, between the bed and the wall?' she enquired, with an ironical assumption of the humblest deference to my wishes. 'That's where the girl found it when she was sweeping the room. Anybody can see for themselves,' pursued the housekeeper indignantly, 'that the poor gentleman has gone away broken-hearted. And there, in my opinion, is the hussy who is the cause of it!'

With those words, she made me a low curtsy, and laid a small photographic portrait on the desk at which I was sitting.

I looked at the photograph.

In an instant, my heart was beating wildly – my head turned giddy – the housekeeper, the furniture, the walls of the room, all swayed and whirled round me.

The portrait that had been found in my senior pupil's bedroom was the portrait of Jéromette!

IX

I had sent the housekeeper out of my study. I was alone, with the photograph of the Frenchwoman on my desk.

There could surely be little doubt about the discovery that had burst upon me. The man who had stolen his way into my house, driven by the terror of a temptation that he dared not reveal, and the man who had been my unknown rival in the by-gone time, were one and the same!

Recovering self-possession enough to realize this plain truth, the inferences that followed forced their way into my mind as a matter of course. The unnamed person who was the obstacle to my pupil's prospects in life, the unnamed person in whose company he was assailed by temptations which made him tremble for himself, stood revealed to me now as being, in all human probability, no other than Jéromette. Had she bound him in the fetters of the marriage which he had himself proposed? Had she discovered his place of refuge in my house? And was the letter that had been delivered to him of her writing? Assuming these questions to be answered in the affirmative, what, in that case, was his 'business in London'? I remembered how he had spoken to me of his temptations, I recalled the expression that had crossed his face when he recognized the handwriting on the letter – and the conclusion that followed literally shook me to the soul. Ordering my horse to be saddled, I rode instantly to the railway-station.

The train by which he had travelled to London had reached the terminus nearly an hour since. The one useful course that I could take, by way of quieting the dreadful misgivings crowding one after another on my mind, was to telegraph to Jéromette at the address at which I had last seen her. I sent the subjoined message – prepaying the reply:

'If you are in any trouble, telegraph to me. I will be with you by the first train. Answer, in any case.'

There was nothing in the way of the immediate dispatch of my message. And yet the hours passed, and no answer was received. By the advice of the clerk, I sent a second telegram to the London office, requesting an explanation. The reply came back in these terms:

'Improvements in street. House pulled down. No trace of person named in telegram.'

I mounted my horse, and rode back slowly to the rectory.

'The day of his return to me will bring with it the darkest days of my life.' . . . 'I shall die young, and die miserably. Have you interest enough still left in me to wish to hear of it?' . . . 'You shall hear of it.' Those words were in my memory while I rode home in the cloudless moonlight night. They were so vividly present to me that I could hear again her pretty foreign accent, her quiet clear tones, as she spoke them. For the rest, the emotion of that memorable day had worn me out. The answer from the telegraph-office had struck me with a strange and stony despair. My mind was a blank. I had no thoughts. I had no tears.

I was about half-way on my road home, and I had just heard the clock of a village church strike ten, when I became conscious, little by little, of a chilly sensation slowly creeping through and through me to the bones. The warm balmy air of a summer night was abroad. It was the month of July. In the month of July, was it possible that any living creature (in good health) could feel cold? It was not possible – and yet, the chilly sensation still crept through and through me to the bones.

I looked up. I looked all round me.

My horse was walking along an open highroad. Neither trees nor waters were near me. On either side, the flat fields stretched away bright and broad in the moonlight.

I stopped my horse, and looked round me again.

Yes: I saw it. With my own eyes I saw it. A pillar of white mist – between five and six feet high, as well as I could judge – was moving beside me at the edge of the road, on my left hand. When I stopped, the white mist stopped. When I went on, the white mist went on. I pushed my horse to a trot – the pillar of mist was with me. I urged him to a gallop – the pillar of mist was with me. I stopped him again – the pillar of mist stood still.

The white colour of it was the white colour of the fog which I had seen over the river – on the night when I had gone to bid her farewell. And the chill which had then crept through me to the bones was the chill that was creeping through me now.

I went on again slowly. The white mist went on again slowly – with the clear bright night all round it.

I was awed rather than frightened. There was one moment, and one only, when the fear came to me that my reason might be shaken. I caught myself keeping time to the slow tramp of the horse's feet with the slow utterance of these words, repeated over and over again: 'Jéromette is dead. Jéromette is dead.' But my will was still my own: I was able to control myself, to impose silence on my own muttering lips. And I rode on quietly. And the pillar of mist went quietly with me.

My groom was waiting for my return at the rectory gate. I pointed to the mist, passing through the gate with me.

'Do you see anything there?' I said.

The man looked at me in astonishment.

I entered the rectory. The housekeeper met me in the hall. I pointed to the mist, entering with me.

'Do you see anything at my side?' I asked.

The housekeeper looked at me as the groom had looked at me.

'I am afraid you are not well, sir,' she said. 'Your colour is all gone – you are shivering. Let me get you a glass of wine.'

I went into my study, on the ground-floor, and took the chair at my desk. The photograph still lay where I had left it. The pillar of mist floated round the table, and stopped opposite to me, behind the photograph.

The housekeeper brought in the wine. I put the glass to my lips, and sat it down again. The chill of the mist was in the wine. There was no taste, no reviving spirit in it. The presence of the housekeeper oppressed me. My dog had followed her into the room. The presence of the animal oppressed me. I said to the woman, 'Leave me by myself, and take the dog with you.'

They went out, and left me alone in the room.

I sat looking at the pillar of mist, hovering opposite to me.

It lengthened slowly, until it reached to the ceiling. As it lengthened, it grew bright and luminous. A time passed, and a shadowy appearance showed itself in the centre of the light. Little by little, the shadowy appearance took the outline of a human form. Soft brown eyes, tender and melancholy, looked at me through the unearthly light in the mist. The head and the rest of the face broke next slowly on my view. Then the figure gradually revealed itself, moment by moment, downward and downward to the feet. She stood before me as I had last seen her, in her purple-merino dress, with the black-silk apron, with the white handkerchief tied loosely round her neck. She stood before me, in the gentle beauty that I remembered so well; and looked at me as she had looked when she gave me her last kiss – when her tears had dropped on my cheek.

I fell on my knees at the table. I stretched out my hands to her imploringly. I said, 'Speak to me – O, once again speak to me, Jéromette.'

Her eyes rested on me with a divine compassion in them. She lifted her hand, and pointed to the photograph on my desk, with a gesture which bade me turn the card. I turned it. The name of the man who had left my house that morning was inscribed on it, in her own handwriting.

I looked up at her again, when I had read it. She lifted her hand once more, and pointed to the handkerchief round her neck. As I looked at it, the fair white silk changed horribly in colour – the fair white silk became darkened and drenched in blood.

A moment more – and the vision of her began to grow dim. By slow degrees, the figure, then the face, faded back into the shadowy appearance that I had first seen. The luminous inner light died out in the white mist. The mist itself dropped slowly downwards – floated a moment in airy circles on the floor – vanished. Nothing was before me but the familiar wall of the room, and the photograph lying face downwards on my desk.

X

The next day, the newspapers reported the discovery of a murder in London. A Frenchwoman was the victim. She had been killed by a wound in the throat. The crime had been discovered between ten and eleven o'clock on the previous night.

I leave you to draw your conclusion from what I have related. My own faith in the reality of the apparition is immovable. I say, and believe, that Jéromette kept her word with me. She died young, and died miserably. And I heard of it from herself.

Take up the Trial again, and look at the circumstances that were revealed during the investigation in court. The motive for murdering her is there.

You will see that she did indeed marry him privately; that they lived together contentedly, until the fatal day when she discovered that his fancy had been caught by another woman; that violent quarrels took place between them, from that time to the time when my sermon showed him his own deadly hatred towards her, reflected in the case of another man; that she discovered his place of retreat in my house, and threatened him by letter with the public assertion of her conjugal rights; lastly, that a man, variously described by different witnesses, was seen leaving the door of her lodgings on the night of the murder. The Law – advancing no further than this – may have discovered circumstances of suspicion, but no certainty. The Law, in default of direct evidence to convict the prisoner, may have rightly decided in letting him go free.

But *I* persist in believing that the man was guilty. *I* declare that he, and he alone, was the murderer of Jéromette. And now, you know why.

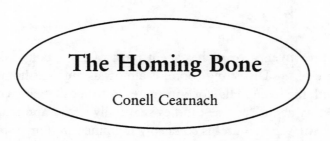

The Homing Bone

Conell Cearnach

Professor David Gillespie was a distinguished anatomist. It is scarcely necessary to add that he was a Scotsman; for has not a wise Providence ordained that the principal products of Caledonia shall be marine engineers, metaphysicians, and anatomists? Equally brilliant on what are technically known as the "hard" and "soft" parts of the human frame, he was particularly strong on the subject of the skeleton; and to hear him lecture on the petrous portion of the temporal bone was a revelation to the unsophisticated first-year student of medicine. In the lecture theatre he would stand at the rostrum, of a morning, and taking a bone for his text, he would hold forth for a full hour. Common "grinders" could point out foramina and muscle-insertions well enough for examination purposes; but their instruction was dry and uninteresting. In Gillespie's hands a bone became a thing of beauty. His lecture was not a lecture; it was not a sermon; it was an oration. He would wax eloquent as he went along, and his enthusiasm was infectious. Not infrequently, when his peroration closed with some apposite quotation from the poets, a spontaneous burst of applause went up from the crowded benches; and students, as they wended their way to pastures new, would remark to one another: "Man, but Gillespie's just great!"

Professor Gillespie came of Highland Gaelic stock; a stock which is far from materialistic; and his grandmother was reputed to have possessed the gift of "second sight." Many a time young Davy had shuddered as he listened, by the fire of the crofter's cottage, where he first saw the light, to the weird, uncanny tales of the Highlands; but five years' hard work at the Edinburgh School of Medicine had knocked the nonsense out of him in more ways than one. Now, at the age of fifty-four, one of the leading anatomists of Europe, he could afford to bestow an indulgent smile on the narrator of tales pertaining to the supernatural. A man who, for twenty years, has spent most of his waking hours in the atmosphere of the Dissecting-room, is almost as much at home with the dead as with the living. His stock-in-trade, so to speak, being corpses, the creepiest story about "corpse-candles" naturally leaves him unmoved. Yet the fear of the supernatural is so deeply ingrained in human beings, and the stories, heard in boyhood days, sink so deeply into the subliminal self, that the acquired scepticism of later years is, after all, the merest veneer, which may vanish in a moment; if only circumstances arise, in which a sufficiently strong appeal is made to those hereditary instincts and pre-historic beliefs that slumber beneath the surface.

So much, by way of preface to the secret history of the curious happenings which led to Gillespie's resignation of his Chair of Anatomy, and his retirement into private life; a step which astonished all who heard of it, for he was regarded as being but at the zenith of his powers. I now tell the tale as it was told to me by Cochrane, who heard it from the lips of Gillespie himself.

When the British Medical Association held its annual conference in Dublin, Gillespie was invited to preside over the Anatomical Section; and his address at the opening meeting of the section was as brilliant as might have been expected from one of his reputation. The conference over, Gillespie devoted his time to sightseeing. He spent a day visiting the Cathedrals, and, in the afternoon, he prowled about the quays and back streets of the city. Half an hour was given up to viewing the vaults of St. Michan's, with its celebrated mummies, and crossing over the Metal Bridge he wended his way through Cook Street, that home of undertakers, where every shop resounds to the stroke of the coffin-maker's hammer.

Having passed through this gruesome quarter, he wandered further afield, until he came upon the old church of St. Walburgh's. The ground about the church had long been closed to burials, and he found some workmen engaged in levelling the churchyard. The tombstones had been removed and arranged along the churchyard wall; for, since the inscriptions they bore were no longer legible, they had served their purpose, and were mere cumberers of the ground. During the levelling process some relics of mortality had become uncovered, and in one corner there lay a jumble of odd assortments of skulls and some large bones.

Gillespie's professional eye detected, amid the heap, a splendid specimen in a perfect state of preservation. It was a thigh-bone, or as an anatomist would more accurately describe it, a left femur; that of an adult man, for, by the trained eye, the sterner sex can be distinguished even in the bony structures. The Professor coveted the bone, and foresaw in it the material for an interesting and instructive paper. He had no qualms of conscience about securing it; only, in deference to any susceptibilities on the part of the Irish workmen, he did so quite unostentatiously, and walked away with the coveted femur concealed beneath his overcoat.

Arrived at his lodgings, he stowed it in his bedroom until after dinner; when he proceeded to brush away the adherent earth from the bone with a clothes-brush, and settled down to gloat over his treasure. From the great length of the femur, and the powerfully developed trochanters, he deduced the fact that the man who had owned it must have been an exceptionally tall and muscular individual; and the professor fell to wondering whether the said individual had been an Irishman, or one of the old Norse stock whose descendants among the Dubliners retain somewhat of the Viking characteristics. He sat in his dressing-gown until eleven o'clock, and strove to visualise the appearance which the owner of the bone must have presented in life; then he yawned sleepily, and dropping the femur into his portmanteau, lest he might forget it in his hurry to catch the morning boat, he tumbled into bed and fell fast asleep.

His sleep had not lasted for long when he was visited by a horribly vivid dream. In his dream he seemed to be awakened by a sound of knocking at his bedroom door. Before he had time to say "Come in!" the door opened, and four skeletons entered, carrying a coffin on their bony shoulders. They deposited their burden on two chairs beside his bed, and stood like waiting mutes. Suddenly the lid of the coffin flew open, and its occupant, a tall skeleton, sat up and pointed first at the professor, and then to its own lower limbs. Following the gesture, Gillespie looked and saw that the left femur was missing. Still sitting up in the coffin, the tall skeleton leaned forward towards the bed and clutched the professor by the throat with a vice-like grip of its bony fingers.

Gillespie gasped for breath, gave a strangled scream, and woke up in a fright. It took some little time for him to realise his surroundings. He sat up in bed to find his heart palpitating violently, his brow wet with perspiration, and about his scalp a curious sensation associated in the lay mind with the phenomenon known as "the hair standing on end." It was decidedly a novel experience for the professor, for he boasted that he never dreamed dreams, or that if he did, they were so unimportant, that his waking moments contained no recollection of them.

The explanation was perfectly simple, he told himself. During the conference his meals had been more irregular than they would have been at home. Some of the dinners, too, were more elaborate than those to which he was normally accustomed. Why, he wondered, could not a party of grave and learned scientists foregather without over-eating and over-drinking like a lot of schoolboys at a picnic? Then the material of his dream had been supplied by his afternoon saunter through that extraordinary street of coffin-shops, and the bone purloined from the churchyard completed the tale.

Yet, in that dark room, in the small hours of the morning there were stirrings of the hereditary fears – the fear of the dark and the fear of the dead; and he fell to moralising over the fact that Providence had for some reason or other seen fit to endow the human scalp with a set of "*erector pili*" or hair-raising muscles, and the further curious fact that that particular set of muscles could only be called into play by supernatural (or superstitious) terrors. Did not the pious Aeneas' hair stand on end at the apparition of his beloved dead wife, Creusa? But the professor's classics were decidedly rusty, and while attempting in vain to complete the line "*Obstupui, steteruntque comae*" – he fell asleep once more.

However, he was not destined to enjoy his resumed slumber for long. The ill dream was repeated with variations. Once more the door opened, the four skeletons entered, bearing a coffin which they placed on chairs by the bedside; but this time the lid did not fly open. Instead, the professor found his gaze directed by the bony forefingers of the skeletons to the name-plate on the coffin-lid; and, to his horror, he saw the name of the deceased was set forth as DAVID GILLESPIE.

While he still gazed in horror-stricken silence, a troupe of skeletons came crowding into the room, and circled round his bed in a dance of death, their bones rattling like castanets, and their grinning jaws gnashing as though chanting a hymn of hate. Closer and closer they circled, until one gigantic skeleton halted, and raising an enormous thighbone, aimed a stunning blow straight at the professor's head. Gillespie instinctively put up one arm to ward off the impending blow, and the effort awoke him.

This time he was indignant. He had refused several offers of hospitality from Dublin hosts, preferring to select quiet lodgings for himself. That was one of his idiosyncrasies; for he strongly objected to sitting up into the small hours, smoking and talking "shop"; and experience of many Medical Congresses had proved such dissipation to be the normal sequel to accepting the hospitality of professional colleagues. And now here he was faring no better, or rather worse. Confound it all! His digestion must be completely upset. If only he had strolled into the country, instead of through those unhealthy back streets adjoining the Liffey. His head felt decidedly queer, too, and he reflected that it was probably that queer feeling which had coloured the finale of his second nightmare. Could it be something more serious than indigestion?

Gillespie had read somewhere that Chinese physicians attached great importance to the prognostic interpretation of their patients' dreams. Did the curious variant by which he distinctly saw his own name inscribed on the coffin-lid portend a dangerous illness? Such gruesome visions reminded him of the creepy tales heard in his childhood days. His grandmother, who was popularly credited with "second sight," used to tell of how she had seen a coffin, with her husband's name on it, carried past in the moonlight, three days before he died.

One story recalled another. There were stirrings in the subliminal mind. As a boy he firmly believed in ghosts. Why exactly had he lost that belief? Like the Missionary, in one of Robert Louis Stevenson's fables, he began to think that after all there might be something in it. The French called ghosts "*revenants*," folk who came back. Came back for what? If he told his dream to any of the old wives in his native village they would roundly assert that the dead Irishman, or Dane, as the case might be, had come back for the femur that had been stolen from the churchyard. This introduced another train of thought; consecrated earth. Yes, the bones which had served him for purposes of lecturing for the past twenty years, were bones that had been taken from the dissecting-room, lacerated and bleached. They had never been interred; had never lain in consecrated earth. Should he, in deference to sentiment, restore the femur to the churchyard, after first making a neat sketch and recording the exact measurements?

Needless to say, Gillespie in his normal waking mood, and in broad daylight, would never have soliloquised in this strain; but, as I have already hinted, the dark brings back forgotten fears and scruples, and the professor was by no means in a normal mood. His thoughts were running on this long unused track for some minutes, when he dosed asleep again. But did he? For that is a question which no man living can answer – not even the intelligent reader. Gillespie stoutly denied that he did. Cochrane declared that he only dreamt that he did not; that, in point of fact, what followed was part of the same dream, and that it was a part of the dream to dream that he was awake.

Be that as it may, let us abide by Gillespie's version for the present. He was (let us premise) still awake, and following out this line of thought, when he heard a dull knocking sound in the room. It was a muffled tapping, repeated at regular intervals, and appeared to proceed from the closed portmanteau which lay on the floor close to the dressing-table. Although the room was quite dark, Gillespie instinctively glanced in the direction from which the sound proceeded, and as he did so he became aware of a faint, hazy luminosity of rectangular form. The luminosity increased in brilliance, until it became quite evidently the outline of the portmanteau, with a distinct view of its interior, as though it had been placed against a fluorescent screen, under the action of exceptional powerful Rontgen Rays; and the object which stood out most clearly, as in an actual skiagraph, was the purloined femur. So sharply was it defined that it appeared to impress a photograph of itself on Gillespie's brain; and then the fluorescence died away, and the room was plunged in darkness again.

By this time, the professor was (so he asserted to Cochrane) as wide awake as ever he had been in his life, his every sense strung to the highest pitch of expectation; but thenceforward he was obliged to depend solely upon his sense of hearing for information as to subsequent events. He distinctly heard, he alleged, a noise as of someone fumbling with the catch of the portmanteau; the click with which it opened; and a dull, thudding sound, as of someone walking in the room with a wooden leg or crutch. Next, his bedroom door swung ajar, and the someone or something stumped slowly down stairs and along the matting of the hall. The front door opened slightly – enough to send a current of air sweeping up the stairs and into the bedroom – and closed again noiselessly. All this time, Gillespie was mentally alert, and experienced no abnormal sensations, except for a tense feeling about the head, and a curious inability, or even unwillingness, to move or speak. Then came a blank in consciousness, and he remembered no more until he awoke to find it broad daylight.

A knock at his bedroom door heralded the arrival of no more supernatural a visitant than the maid-of-all-work with his boots and shaving-water. He rose with something of an effort, and the act of stooping for his boots and hot water caused his head to throb violently; while the singing in his ears almost deafened him. But, like Macbeth, the terrors of the night being gone, he felt himself a man again; and he was in a humour to explain his present, as well as past, experience in terms of materialistic philosophy. Dyspepsia; that was the explanation in a nutshell. Dyspepsia, coupled with a restless night.

Shaved and dressed, he hastened to complete his packing, and opened his portmanteau to stow away his shaving tackle and toilet brushes. As he opened it, he recollected with a smile how he had debated with himself in the watches of the night the advisability of returning the stolen bone to the churchyard; but he decided that such an action would be a concession to a temporary aberration of superstitious weakness; better keep it as a memento of his visit to Dublin.

Now if Professor Gillespie had been an untidy, unmethodical man, this story would not have been told; but the fact remains that nothing would do him but to empty the contents of the portmanteau on the floor, in order to pack away all his belongings neatly. And then it was that he made the discovery that caused him to abandon the idea of catching that day's boat, and sent him instead to consult Cochrane in Merrion Square. He discovered that the bone was missing!

It was only when he had thoroughly satisfied himself that it really was missing, by replacing the contents of the portmanteau, article by article, repeating the process several times, and making a thorough inventory of the objects in the room, that he decided that there was something wrong. Had he at his time of life begun to indulge in day-dreams, or was he the victim of hallucinations? He would have sworn in any court of law that he had conveyed the bone to his room the night before, brushed it clean, and placed it in his portmanteau. Was that waking experience on a par with the visions of the night? Was he taking leave of his senses?

He toyed with his breakfast, and informing his landlady that he had changed his mind, and intended to leave by the evening boat instead, he made a last desperate effort to regain his normal bearings. Mid-day found him once more standing in the churchyard of St. Walburgh's. The workmen were still engaged in levelling the surface, but one of their number was re-interring the heap of bones which had been laid aside in the corner. Only one portion of skull and a few long bones were left uncovered; and among the latter, in precisely the identical position which it occupied when Gillespie's eyes first lighted upon it, was the great left femur!

There was no mistaking it; for, apart from the size and abnormal development. it was as free from churchyard mould as though it had been freshly washed and dusted. Instead of throwing light on the subject, this only complicated matters still further. What was the meaning of it all? His head sang and throbbed so much that it was with difficulty that he made his way as far as his lodging.

In the afternoon he went to Cochrane's, and sent in his card. It had the opposite effect to that which he intended; for, instead of seeing him immediately, Cochrane kept him waiting until he had seen the last of his patients, hoping to settle down to a long chat on subjects arising out of the Conference.

When Gillespie's turn did eventually come, and he had finished relating his strange experiences, both in dreaming and waking states, Cochrane put to him a few questions, and set about a thorough examination. Every medical consultant has his own particular fad; and Cochrane's fad was blood-pressure. Once he adjusted the sphygmomanometer, and found that the professor's blood-pressure stood at 210, he cared nothing about reflexes or pupil-reaction. Blood-pressure explained everything, and in Cochrane's opinion the whole matter was simple.

Gillespie, like most anatomists and other specialists, had forgotten all he ever knew about the ordinary practice of medicine. He thought that, so long as he was oblivious to the flight of time, his arteries were in a similar state. As a matter of fact, they were prematurely senile and sclerosed from the routine of his life and the mental preoccupation which had caused him to neglect precautions suitable for a man of middle age. It was highly probable that the bursting of a small arteriole in the brain had given rise to the sensation of a "stroke," metamorphosed into a blow aimed at his head by the skeleton of his dream fancy.

The upshot of the consultation was that Gillespie was prevailed upon, under stress of warnings as to the serious consequences of disobedience, to resign his Chair of Anatomy and retire from public life. He took a quiet bungalow in his native air, and persevered in the gentle exercise treatment prescribed by Cochrane; but rest had come too late, for he was carried off by a severe stroke within seven months of his resignation; so that Cochrane's diagnosis was not very far wrong after all.

I first heard Cochrane tell this story at a clinical lecture on arteriosclerosis; but at the time he mentioned no names. It was since I qualified that I wormed the whole tale out of him, with full particulars, as well as he could remember them. Still, blood-pressure will not explain everything; and I firmly believe that Gillespie did remove the femur from the churchyard, and stow it in his portmanteau. To my mind, the only question that remains unanswered is this: "How did it find its way back again?"

The Ghost Ship

Richard Middleton

Fairfield is a little village lying near the Portsmouth Road about half-way between London and the sea. Strangers who find it by accident now and then, call it a pretty, old-fashioned place; we who live in it and call it home don't find anything very pretty about it, but we should be sorry to live anywhere else. Our minds have taken the shape of the inn and the church and the green, I suppose. At all events we never feel comfortable out of Fairfield.

Of course the Cockneys, with their vasty houses and noise-ridden streets, can call us rustics if they choose, but for all that Fairfield is a better place to live in than London. Doctor says that when he goes to London his mind is bruised with the weight of the houses, and he was a Cockney born. He had to live there himself when he was a little chap, but he knows better now. You gentlemen may laugh – perhaps some of you come from London way – but it seems to me that a witness like that is worth a gallon of arguments.

Dull? Well, you might find it dull, but I assure you that I've listened to all the London yarns you have spun to-night, and they're absolutely nothing to the things that happen at Fairfield. It's because of our way of thinking and minding our own business. If one of your Londoners were set down on the green of a Saturday night when the ghosts of the lads who died in the war keep tryst with the lasses who lie in the churchyard, he couldn't help being curious and interfering, and then the ghosts would go somewhere where it was quieter. But we just let them come and go and don't make any fuss, and in consequence Fairfield is the ghostliest place in all England. Why, I've seen a headless man sitting on the edge of the well in broad daylight, and the children playing about his feet as if he were their father. Take my word for it, spirits know when they are well off as much as human beings.

Still, I must admit that the thing I'm going to tell you about was queer even for our part of the world, where three packs of ghost-hounds hunt regularly during the season, and blacksmith's great-grandfather is busy all night shoeing the dead gentlemen's horses. Now that's a thing that wouldn't happen in London, because of their interfering ways, but blacksmith he lies up aloft and sleeps as quiet as a lamb. Once when he had a bad head he shouted down to them not to make so much noise, and in the morning he found an old guinea left on the anvil as an apology. He wears it on his watch-chain now. But I must get on with my story; if I start telling you about the queer happenings at Fairfield I'll never stop.

It all came of the great storm in the spring of '97, the year that we had two great storms. This was the first one, and I remember it very well, because I found in the morning that it had lifted the thatch of my pigsty into the widow's garden as clean as a boy's kite. When I looked over the hedge, widow – Tom Lamport's widow that was – was prodding for her nasturtiums with a daisy-grubber. After I had watched her for a little I went down to the Fox and Grapes to tell landlord what she had said to me. Landlord he laughed, being a married man and at ease with the sex. 'Come to that,' he said, 'the tempest has blowed something into my field. A kind of a ship I think it would be.'

I was surprised at that until he explained that it was only a ghost-ship and would do no hurt to the turnips. We argued that it had been blown up from the sea at Portsmouth, and then we talked of something else. There were two slates down at the parsonage and a big tree in Lumley's meadow. It was a rare storm.

I reckon the wind had blown our ghosts all over England. They were coming back for days afterwards with foundered horses and as footsore as possible, and they were so glad to get back to Fairfield that some of them walked up the street crying like little children. Squire said that his great grandfather's great-grandfather hadn't looked so dead-beat since the battle of Naseby, and he's an educated man.

What with one thing and another, I should think it was a week before we got straight again, and then one afternoon I met the landlord on the green and he had a worried face. 'I wish you'd come and have a look at that ship in my field,' he said to me; 'it seems to me it's leaning real hard on the turnips. I can't bear thinking what the missus will say when she sees it.'

I walked down the lane with him, and sure enough there was a ship in the middle of his field, but such a ship as no man had seen on the water for three hundred years, let alone in the middle of a turnip-field.

It was all painted black and covered with carvings, and there was a great bay window in the stern for all the world like the Squire's drawing-room. There was a crowd of little black cannon on deck and looking out of her port-holes, and she was anchored at each end to the hard ground.

I have seen the wonders of the world on picture-postcards, but I have never seen anything to equal that.

'She seems very solid for a ghost-ship,' I said, seeing the landlord was bothered.

'I should say it's a betwixt and between,' he answered, puzzling it over, 'but it's going to spoil a matter of fifty turnips, and missus she'll want it moved.' We went up to her and touched the side, and it was as hard as a real ship. 'Now there's folks in England would call that very curious,' he said.

Now I don't know much about ships, but I should think that that ghost-ship weighed a solid two hundred tons, and it seemed to me that she had come to stay, so that I felt sorry for landlord, who was a married man. 'All the horses in Fairfield won't move her out of my turnips,' he said, frowning at her.

Just then we heard a noise on her deck, and we looked up and saw that a man had come out of her front cabin and was looking down at us very peaceably. He was dressed in a black uniform set out with rusty gold lace, and he had a great cutlass by his side in a brass sheath. 'I'm Captain Bartholomew Roberts,' he said, in a gentleman's voice, 'put in for recruits. I seem to have brought her rather far up the harbour.'

'Harbour!' cried landlord; 'why, you're fifty miles from the sea.'

Captain Roberts didn't turn a hair. 'So much as that, is it?' he said coolly. 'Well, it's of no consequence.'

Landlord was a bit upset at this. 'I don't want to be unneighbourly,' he said, 'but I wish you hadn't brought your ship into my field. You see, my wife sets great store on these turnips.'

The captain took a pinch of snuff out of a fine gold box that he pulled out of his pocket, and dusted his fingers with a silk handkerchief in a very genteel fashion. 'I'm only here for a few months,' he said; 'but if a testimony of my esteem would pacify your good lady I should be content,' and with the words he loosed a great gold brooch from the neck of his coat and tossed it down to landlord.

Landlord blushed as red as a strawberry. 'I'm not denying she's fond of jewellery,' he said, 'but it's too much for half a sackful of turnips.' And indeed it was a handsome brooch.

The captain laughed. 'Tut, man,' he said, 'it's a forced sale, and you deserve a good price. Say no more about it;' and nodding good-day to us, he turned on his heel and went into the cabin. Landlord walked back up the lane like a man with a weight off his mind. 'That tempest has blowed me a bit of luck,' he said; 'the missus will be main pleased with that brooch. It's better than blacksmith's guinea, any day.'

Ninety-seven was Jubilee year, the year of the second Jubilee, you remember, and we had great doings at Fairfield, so that we hadn't much time to bother about the ghost-ship, though anyhow it isn't our way to meddle in things that don't concern us. Landlord, he saw his tenant once or twice when he was hoeing his turnips and passed the time of day, and landlord's wife wore her new brooch to church every Sunday. But we didn't mix much with the ghosts at any time, all except an idiot lad there was in the village, and he didn't know the difference between a man and a ghost, poor innocent! On Jubilee Day, however, somebody told Captain Roberts why the church bells were ringing, and he hoisted a flag and fired off his guns like a loyal Englishman. 'Tis true the guns were shotted, and one of the round shot knocked a hole in Farmer Johnstone's barn, but nobody thought much of that in such a season of rejoicing.

It wasn't till our celebrations were over that we noticed that anything was wrong in Fairfield. 'Twas shoemaker who told me first about it one morning at the Fox and Grapes. 'You know my great great-uncle?' he said to me.

'You mean Joshua, the quiet lad,' I answered knowing him well.

'Quiet!' said shoemaker indignantly. 'Quiet you call him, coming home at three o'clock every morning as drunk as a magistrate and waking up the whole house with his noise.'

'Why, it can't be Joshua!' I said, for I knew him for one of the most respectable young ghosts in the village.

'Joshua it is,' said shoemaker; 'and one of these nights he'll find himself out in the street if he isn't careful.'

This kind of talk shocked me, I can tell you, for I don't like to hear a man abusing his own family, and I could hardly believe that a steady youngster like Joshua had taken to drink. But just then in came butcher Aylwin in such a temper that he could hardly drink his beer. 'The young puppy! the young puppy!' he kept on saying; and it was some time before shoemaker and I found out that he was talking about his ancestor that fell at Senlac.

'Drink?' said shoemaker hopefully, for we all like company in our misfortunes, and butcher nodded grimly.

'The young noodle,' he said, emptying his tankard.

Well, after that I kept my ears open, and it was the same story all over the village. There was hardly a young man among all the ghosts of Fairfield who didn't roll home in the small hours of the morning the worse for liquor. I used to wake up in the night and hear them stumble past my house, singing outrageous songs. The worst of it was that we couldn't keep the scandal to ourselves, and the folk at Greenhill began to talk of 'sodden Fairfield' and taught their children to sing a song about us:

Sodden Fairfield, sodden Fairfield, has no use
    for bread-and-butter,
Rum for breakfast, rum for dinner, rum for tea, and
    rum for supper!

We are easy-going in our village, but we didn't like that.

Of course we soon found out where the young fellows went to get the drink, and landlord was terribly cut up that his tenant should have turned out so badly, but his wife wouldn't hear of parting with the brooch, so that he couldn't give the Captain notice to quit. But as time went on, things grew from bad to worse, and at all hours of the day you would see those young reprobates sleeping it off on the village green. Nearly every afternoon a ghost-wagon used to jolt down to the ship with a lading of rum, and though the older ghosts seemed inclined to give the Captain's hospitality the go-by, the youngsters were neither to hold nor to bind.

So one afternoon when I was taking my nap I heard a knock at the door, and there was parson looking very serious, like a man with a job before him that he didn't altogether relish. 'I'm going down to talk to the Captain about all this drunkenness in the village, and I want you to come with me,' he said straight out.

I can't say that I fancied the visit much myself, and I tried to hint to parson that as, after all, they were only a lot of ghosts, it didn't very much matter.

'Dead or alive, I'm responsible for their good conduct,' he said, 'and I'm going to do my duty and put a stop to this continued disorder. And you are coming with me, John Simmons.' So I went, parson being a persuasive kind of man.

We went down to the ship, and as we approached her I could see the Captain tasting the air on deck. When he saw parson he took off his hat very politely, and I can tell you that I was relieved to find that he had a proper respect for the cloth. Parson acknowledged his salute and spoke out stoutly enough. 'Sir, I should be glad to have a word with you.'

'Come on board, sir; come on board,' said the Captain, and I could tell by his voice that he knew why we were there. Parson and I climbed up an uneasy kind of ladder, and the Captain took us into the great cabin at the back of the ship, where the bay-window was. It was the most wonderful place you ever saw in your life, all full of gold and silver plate, swords with jewelled scabbards, carved oak chairs, and great chests that look as though they were bursting with guineas. Even parson was surprised, and he did not shake his head very hard when the Captain took down some silver cups and poured us out a drink of rum. I tasted mine, and I don't mind saying that it changed my view of things entirely. There was nothing betwixt and between about that rum, and I felt that it was ridiculous to blame the lads for drinking too much of stuff like that. It seemed to fill my veins with honey and fire.

Parson put the case squarely to the Captain, but I didn't listen much to what he said; I was busy sipping my drink and looking through the window at the fishes swimming to and fro over landlord's turnips. Just then it seemed the most natural thing in the world that they should be there, though afterwards, of course, I could see that that proved it was a ghost-ship.

But even then I thought it was queer when I saw a drowned sailor float by in the thin air with his hair and beard all full of bubbles. It was the first time I had seen anything quite like that at Fairfield.

All the time I was regarding the wonders of the deep parson was telling Captain Roberts how there was no peace or rest in the village owing to the curse of drunkenness, and what a bad example the youngsters were setting to the older ghosts. The Captain listened very attentively, and only put in a word now and then about boys being boys and young men sowing their wild oats. But when parson had finished his speech he filled up our silver cups and said to parson, with a flourish, 'I should be sorry to cause trouble anywhere where I have been made welcome, and you will be glad to hear that I put to sea tomorrow night. And now you must drink me a prosperous voyage.' So we all stood up and drank the toast with honour, and that noble rum was like hot oil in my veins.

After that Captain showed us some of the curiosities he had brought back from foreign parts, and we were greatly amazed, though afterwards I couldn't clearly remember what they were. And then I found myself walking across the turnips with parson, and I was telling him of the glories of the deep that I had seen through the window of the ship. He turned on me severely. 'If I were you, John Simmons,' he said, 'I should go straight home to bed.' He has a way of putting things that wouldn't occur to an ordinary man, has parson, and I did as he told me.

Well, next day it came on to blow, and it blew harder and harder, till about eight o'clock at night I heard a noise and looked out into the garden. I dare say you won't believe me, it seems a bit tall even to me, but the wind had lifted the thatch of my pigsty into the widow's garden a second time. I thought I wouldn't wait to hear what the widow had to say about it, so I went across the green to the Fox and Grapes, and the wind was so strong that I danced along on tip-toe like a girl at the fair. When I got to the inn landlord had to help me shut the door; it seemed as though a dozen goats were pushing against it to come in out of the storm.

'It's a powerful tempest,' he said, drawing the beer. 'I hear there's a chimney down at Hickory End.'

'It's a funny thing how these sailors know about the weather,' I answered. 'When Captain said he was going tonight, I was thinking it would take a capful of wind to carry the ship back to sea, but now here's more than a capful.'

'Ah, yes,' said landlord, 'it's to-night he goes true enough, and, mind you, though he treated me handsome over the rent, I'm not sure it's a loss to the village. I don't hold with gentrice who fetch their drink from London instead of helping local traders to get their living.'

'But you haven't got any rum like his,' I said, to draw him out.

His neck grew red above his collar, and I was afraid I'd gone too far; but after a while he got his breath with a grunt.

'John Simmons,' he said, 'if you've come down here this windy night to talk a lot of fool's talk, you've wasted a journey.'

Well, of course, then I had to smooth him down with praising his rum, and Heaven forgive me for swearing it was better than Captain's. For the like of that rum no living lips have tasted save mine and parson's. But somehow or other I brought landlord round, and presently we must have a glass of his best to prove its quality.

'Beat that if you can!' he cried, and we both raised our glasses to our mouths, only to stop half-way and look at each other in amaze. For the wind that had been howling outside like an outrageous dog had all of a sudden turned as melodious as the carol-boys of a Christmas Eve.

'Surely that's not my Martha,' whispered landlord; Martha being his great-aunt that lived in the loft overhead.

We went to the door, and the wind burst it open so that the handle was driven clean into the plaster of the wall. But we didn't think about that at the time; for over our heads, sailing very comfortably through the windy stars, was the ship that had passed the summer in landlord's field. Her portholes and her bay-window were blazing with lights, and there was a noise of singing and fiddling on her decks. 'He's gone,' shouted landlord above the storm, 'and he's taken half the village with him!' I could only nod in answer, not having lungs like bellows of leather.

In the morning we were able to measure the strength of the storm, and over and above my pigsty there was damage enough wrought in the village to keep us busy. True it is that the children had to break down no branches for the firing that autumn, since the wind had strewn the woods with more than they could carry away. Many of our ghosts were scattered abroad, but this time very few came back, all the young men having sailed with Captain; and not only ghosts, for a poor half-witted lad was missing, and we reckoned that he had stowed himself away or perhaps shipped as cabin-boy, not knowing any better.

What with the lamentations of the ghost-girls and the grumbling of families who had lost an ancestor, the village was upset for a while, and the funny thing was that it was the folk who had complained most of the carrying-on of the youngsters, who made most noise now that they were gone. I hadn't any sympathy with shoemaker or butcher, who ran about saying how much they missed their lads, but it made me grieve to hear the poor bereaved girls calling their lovers by name on the village green at nightfall. It didn't seem fair to me that they should have lost their men a second time, after giving up life in order to join them, as like as not. Still, not even a spirit can be sorry for ever, and after a few months we made up our mind that the folk who had sailed in the ship were never coming back, and we didn't talk about it any more.

And then one day, I dare say it would be a couple of years after, when the whole business was quite forgotten, who should come trapesing along the road from Portsmouth but the daft lad who had gone away with the ship, without waiting till he was dead to become a ghost. You never saw such a boy as that in all your life. He had a great rusty cutlass hanging to a string at his waist, and he was tattooed all over in fine colours, so that even his face looked like a girl's sampler. He had a handkerchief in his hand full of foreign shells and old-fashioned pieces of small money, very curious, and he walked up to the well outside his mother's house and drew himself a drink as if he had been nowhere in particular.

The worst of it was that he had come back as soft-headed as he went, and try as we might we couldn't get anything reasonable out of him. He talked a lot of gibberish about keelhauling and walking the plank and crimson murders – things which a decent sailor should know nothing about, so that it seemed to me that for all his manners Captain had been more of a pirate than a gentleman mariner. But to draw sense out of that boy was as hard as picking cherries off a crab-tree. One silly tale he had that he kept on drifting back to, and to hear him you would have thought that it was the only thing that happened to him in his life. 'We was at anchor,' he would say, 'off an island called the Basket of Flowers, and the sailors had caught a lot of parrots and we were teaching them to swear. Up and down the decks, up and down the decks, and the language they used was dreadful. Then we looked up and saw the masts of the Spanish ship outside the harbour. Outside the harbour they were, so we threw the parrots into the sea and sailed out to fight. And all the parrots were drownded in the sea and the language they used was dreadful.' That's the sort of boy he was, nothing but silly talk of parrots when we asked him about the fighting. And we never had a chance of teaching him better, for two days after he ran away again, and hasn't been seen since.

That's my story, and I assure you that things like that are happening in Fairfield all the time. The ship has never come back, but somehow as people grow older they seem to think that one of these windy nights she'll come sailing in over the hedges with all the lost ghosts on board. Well, when she comes, she'll be welcome. There's one ghost-lass that has never grown tired of waiting for her lad to return. Every night you'll see her out on the green, straining her poor eyes with looking for the mast-lights among the stars. A faithful lass you'd call her, and I'm thinking you'd be right.

Landlord's field wasn't a penny worse for the visit, but they do say that since then the turnips that have been grown in it have tasted of rum.

The Body Snatcher

Robert Louis Stevenson

Every night in the year, four of us sat in the small parlour of the *George* at Debenham – the undertaker, and the landlord, and Fettes, and myself. Sometimes there would be more; but blow high, blow low, come rain or snow or frost, we four would be each planted in his own particular armchair. Fettes was an old drunken Scotsman, a man of education obviously, and a man of some property, since he lived in idleness. He had come to Debenham years ago, while still young, and by a mere continuance of living had grown to be an adopted townsman. His blue camlet cloak was a local antiquity, like the church-spire. His place in the parlour at the *George*, his absence from church, his old, crapulous, disreputable vices, were all things of course in Debenham. He had some vague Radical opinions and some fleeting infidelities, which he would now and again set forth and emphasize with tottering slaps upon the table. He drank rum – five glasses regularly every evening; and for the greater portion of his nightly visit to the *George* sat, with his glass in his right hand, in a state of melancholy alcoholic saturation. We called him the Doctor, for he was supposed to have some special knowledge of medicine, and had been known upon a pinch, to set a fracture or reduce a dislocation; but, beyond these slight particulars, we had no knowledge of his character and antecedents.

One dark winter night – it had struck nine some time before the landlord joined us – there was a sick man in the *George*, a great neighbouring proprietor suddenly struck down with apoplexy on his way to Parliament; and the great man's still greater London doctor had been telegraphed to his bedside. It was the first time that such a thing had happened in Debenham, for the railway was but newly open, and we were all proportionately moved by the occurrence.

'He's come,' said the landlord, after he had filled and lighted his pipe.

'He?' said I. 'Who? – not the doctor?'

'Himself,' replied our host.

'What is his name?'

'Dr Macfarlane,' said the landlord.

Fettes was far through his third tumbler, stupidly fuddled, now nodding over, now staring mazily around him; but at the last word he seemed to awaken, and repeated the name 'Macfarlane' twice, quietly enough the first time, but with sudden emotion at the second.

'Yes,' said the landlord, 'that's his name, Doctor Wolfe Macfarlane.'

Fettes became instantly sober: his eyes awoke, his voice became clear, loud, and steady, his language forcible and earnest. We were all startled by the transformation, as if a man had risen from the dead.

'I beg your pardon,' he said, 'I am afraid I have not been paying much attention to your talk. Who is this Wolfe Macfarlane?' And then, when he had heard the landlord out, 'It cannot be, it cannot be,' he added; 'and yet I would like well to see him face to face.'

'Do you know him, Doctor?' asked the undertaker, with a gasp.

'God forbid!' was the reply. 'And yet the name is a strange one; it were too much to fancy two. Tell me, landlord, is he old?'

'Well,' said the host, 'he's not a young man, to be sure, and his hair is white; but he looks younger than you.'

'He is older, though; years older. But,' with a slap upon the table, 'it's the rum you see in my face – rum and sin. This man, perhaps, may have an easy conscience and a good digestion. Conscience! Hear me speak. You would think I was some good, old, decent Christian, would you not? But no, not I; I never canted. Voltaire might have canted if he'd stood in my shoes; but the brains' – with a rattling fillip on his bald head – 'the brains were clear and active, and I saw and made no deductions.'

'If you know this doctor,' I ventured to remark, after a somewhat awful pause, 'I should gather that you do not share the landlord's good opinion.'

Fettes paid no regard to me.

'Yes,' he said, with sudden decision, 'I must see him face to face.'

There was another pause, and then a door was closed rather sharply on the first floor, and a step was heard upon the stair.

'That's the doctor,' cried the landlord. 'Look sharp, and you can catch him.'

It was but two steps from the small parlour to the door of the old *George* inn; the wide oak staircase landed almost in the street; there was room for a Turkey rug and nothing more between the threshold and the last round of the descent; but this little space was every evening brilliantly lit up, not only by the light upon the stair and the great signal-lamp below the sign, but by the warm radiance of the bar-room window. The *George* thus brightly advertised itself to passers-by in the cold street. Fettes walked steadily to the spot, and we, who were hanging behind, beheld the two men meet, as one of them had phrased it, face to face. Dr Macfarlane was alert and vigorous. His white hair set off his pale and placid, although energetic, countenance. He was richly dressed in the finest of broadcloth and the whitest of linen, with a great gold watchchain, and studs and spectacles of the same precious material. He wore a broad-folded tie, white and speckled with lilac, and he carried on his arm a comfortable driving-coat of fur. There was no doubt but he became his years, breathing as he did, of wealth and consideration; and it was a surprising contrast to see our parlour sot – bald, dirty, pimpled, and robed in his old camlet cloak – confront him at the bottom of the stairs.

'Macfarlane!' he said somewhat loudly, more like a herald than a friend.

The great doctor pulled up short on the fourth step. as though the familiarity of the address surprised and somewhat shocked his dignity.

'Toddy Macfarlane!' repeated Fettes.

The London man almost staggered. He stared for the swiftest of seconds at the man before him, glanced behind him with a sort of scare, and then in a startled whisper, 'Fettes!' he said, 'you!'

'Ay,' said the other, 'me! Did you think I was dead too? We are not so easy shut of our acquaintance.'

'Hush, hush!' exclaimed the doctor. 'hush, hush! this meeting is so unexpected – I can see you are unmanned. I hardly knew you, I confess, at first; but I am overjoyed – overjoyed to have this opportunity. For the present it must be how-d'ye-do and goodbye in one, for my fly is waiting, and I must not fail the train; but you shall – let me see – yes – you shall give me your address, and you can count on early news of me.

We must do something for you, Fettes. I fear you are out at elbows; but we must see to that for auld lang syne, as once we sang at suppers.'

'Money!' cried Fettes; 'money from you! The money that I had from you is lying where I cast it in the rain.'

Dr Macfarlane had talked himself into some measure of superiority and confidence, but the uncommon energy of this refusal cast him back into his first confusion.

A horrible, ugly look came and went across his almost venerable countenance. 'My dear fellow,' he said, 'be it as you please; my last thought is to offend you. I would intrude on none. I will leave you my address, however – '

'I do not wish it – I do not wish to know the roof that shelters you,' interrupted the other. 'I heard your name; I feared it might be you; I wished to know if, after all, there were a God; I know now that there is none. Begone!'

He still stood in the middle of the rug, between the stair and the doorway; and the great London physician, in order to escape, would be forced to step to one side. It was plain that he hesitated before the thought of this humiliation. White as he was, there was a dangerous glitter in his spectacles; but while he still paused uncertain, he became aware that the driver of his fly was peering in from the street at this unusual scene and caught a glimpse at the same time of our little body from the parlour, huddled by the corner of the bar. The presence of so many witnesses decided him at once to flee. He crouched together, brushing on the wainscot, and made a dart like a serpent, striking for the door. But his tribulation was not yet entirely at an end, for even as he was passing Fettes clutched him by the arm and these words came in a whisper, and yet painfully distinct, 'Have you seen it again?'

The great rich London doctor cried out aloud with a sharp, throttling cry; he dashed his questioner across the open space, and, with his hands over his head, fled out of the door like a detected thief. Before it had occurred to one of us to make a movement, the fly was already rattling toward the station. The scene was over like a dream, but the dream had left proofs and traces of its passage. Next day the servant found the fine gold spectacles broken on the threshold, and that very night we were all standing breathless by the bar-room window, and Fettes at our side, sober, pale, and resolute in look.

'God protect us, Mr Fettes!' said the landlord, coming first into possession of his customary senses. 'What in the universe is all this? These are strange things you have been saying.'

Fettes turned toward us; he looked us each in succession in the face. 'See if you can hold your tongues,' said he. 'That man Macfarlane is not safe to cross; those that have done so already have repented it too late.'

And then, without so much as finishing his third glass, far less waiting for the other two, he bade us goodbye and went forth, under the lamp of the hotel, into the black night.

We three turned to our places in the parlour, with the big red fire and four clear candles; and as we recapitulated what had passed the first chill of our surprise soon changed into a glow of curiosity. We sat late; it was the latest session I have known in the old *George*. Each man, before we parted, had his theory that he was bound to prove; and none of us had any nearer business in this world than to track out the past of our condemned companion, and surprise the secret that he shared with the great London doctor. It is no great boast, but I believe I was a better hand at worming out a story than either of my fellows at the *George*; and perhaps there is now no other man alive who could narrate to you the following foul and unnatural events.

In his young days Fettes studied medicine in the schools of Edinburgh. He had talent of a kind, the talent that picks up swiftly what it hears and readily retails it for its own. He worked little at home; but he was civil, attentive, and intelligent in the presence of his masters. They soon picked him out as a lad who listened closely and remembered well; nay, strange as it seemed to me when I first heard it, he was in those days well favoured, and pleased by his exterior. There was, at that period, a certain extramural teacher of anatomy, whom I shall here designate by the letter K. His name was subsequently too well known. The man who bore it skulked through the streets of Edinburgh in disguise, while the mob that applauded at the execution of Burke called loudly for the blood of his employer. But Mr K– was then at the top of his vogue; he enjoyed a popularity due partly to his own talent and address, partly to the incapacity of his rival, the university professor. The students, at least, swore by his name, and Fettes believed himself, and was believed by others, to have laid the foundations of success when he had acquired the favour of this meteorically famous man. Mr K– was a *bon vivant* as well as an accomplished teacher; he liked a sly allusion no less than a careful preparation. In both capacities Fettes enjoyed and deserved his notice, and by the second year of his attendance he held the half-regular position of second demonstrator or sub-assistant in his class.

In this capacity, the charge of the theatre and lecture-room devolved in particular upon his shoulder. He had to answer for the cleanliness of the premises and the conduct of the other students, and it was a part of his duty to supply, receive, and divide the various subjects. It was with a view to this last – at that time very delicate – affair that he was lodged by Mr K– in the same wynd, and at last in the same building, with the dissecting-rooms. Here, after a night of turbulent pleasures, his hand still tottering, his sight still misty and confused, he would be called out of bed in the black hours before the winter dawn by the unclean and desperate interlopers who supplied the table. He would open the door to these men, since infamous throughout the land. He would help them with their tragic burthen, pay them their sordid price, and remain alone, when they were gone, with the unfriendly relics of humanity. From such a scene he would return to snatch another hour or two of slumber, to repair the abuses of the night, and refresh himself for the labours of the day.

Few lads could have been more insensible to the impressions of a life thus passed among the ensigns of mortality. His mind was closed against all general considerations. He was incapable of interest in the fate and fortunes of another, the slave of his own desires and low ambitions. Cold, light, and selfish in the last resort, he had that modicum of prudence, miscalled morality, which keeps a man from inconvenient drunkenness or punishable theft. He coveted, besides, a measure of consideration from his masters and his fellow-pupils, and he had no desire to fail conspicuously in the external parts of life. Thus he made it his pleasure to gain some distinction in his studies, and day after day rendered unimpeachable eye-service to his employer, Mr K– . For his day of work he indemnified himself by nights of roaring, blackguardly enjoyment; and when that balance had been struck, the organ that he called his conscience declared itself content.

The supply of subjects was a continual trouble to him as well as to his master. In that large and busy class, the raw material of the anatomists kept perpetually running out; and the business thus rendered necessary was not only unpleasant in itself, but threatened dangerous consequences to all who were concerned. It was the policy of Mr K– to ask no questions in his dealings with the trade. 'They bring the boy, and we pay the price,' he used to say, dwelling on the alliteration – *quid pro quo*. And, again, and somewhat profanely, 'Ask no questions,' he would tell his assistants, 'for conscience' sake.' There was no understanding that the subjects were provided by the crime of murder. Had that idea been broached to him in words, he would have recoiled in horror; but the lightness of his speech upon so grave a matter was, in itself, an offence against good manners, and a temptation to the men with whom he dealt. Fettes, for instance, had often remarked to himself upon the singular freshness of the bodies. He had been struck again and again by the hang-dog, abominable looks of the ruffians who came to him before the dawn; and, putting things together clearly in his private thoughts, he perhaps attributed a meaning too immoral and too categorical to the unguarded counsels of his master. He understood his duty, in short, to have three branches: to take what was brought, to pay the price, and to avert the eye from any evidence of crime.

One November morning this policy of silence was put sharply to the test. He had been awake all night with a racking toothache – pacing his room like a caged beast or throwing himself in fury on his bed – and had fallen at last into that profound, uneasy slumber that so often follows on a night of pain, when he was awakened by the third or fourth angry repetition of the concerted signal. There was a thin, bright moonshine: it was bitter cold, windy, and frosty; the town had not yet awakened, but an indefinable stir already preluded the noise and business of the day. The ghouls had come later than usual, and they seemed more than usually eager to be gone. Fettes, sick with sleep, lighted them upstairs. He heard their grumbling Irish voices through a dream; and as they stripped the sack from their sad merchandise he leaned dozing, with his shoulder propped against the wall; he had to shake himself to find the men their money. As he did so his eyes lighted on the dead face. He started; he took two steps nearer, with the candle raised.

'God Almighty!' he cried. 'That is Jane Galbraith!'

The men answered nothing, but they shuffled nearer the door.

'I know her, I tell you,' he continued. 'She was alive and hearty yesterday. It's impossible she can be dead; it's impossible you should have got this body fairly.'

'Sure, sir, you're mistaken entirely,' said one of the men.

But the other looked Fettes darkly in the eyes, and demanded the money on the spot.

It was impossible to misconceive the threat or to exaggerate the danger. The lad's heart failed him. He stammered some excuses, counted out the sum, and saw his hateful visitors depart. No sooner were they gone than he hastened to confirm his doubts. By a dozen unquestionable marks he identified the girl he had jested with the day before. He saw, with horror, marks upon her body that might well betoken violence. A panic seized him, and he took refuge in his room. There he reflected at length over the discovery that he had made; considered soberly the bearing of Mr K–'s instructions and the danger to himself of interference in so serious a business, and at last, in sore perplexity, determined to wait for the advice of his immediate superior, the class assistant.

This was a young doctor, Wolfe Macfarlane, a high favourite among all the reckless students, clever, dissipated, and unscrupulous to the last degree. He had travelled and studied abroad. His manners were agreeable and a little forward. He was an authority on the stage, skilful on the ice or the links with skate or golf-club; he dressed with nice audacity, and, to put the finishing touch upon his glory, he kept a gig and a strong trotting-horse. With Fettes he was on terms of intimacy; indeed their relative positions called for some community of life; and when subjects were scarce the pair would drive far into the country in Macfarlane's gig, visit and desecrate some lonely graveyard, and return before dawn with their booty to the door of the dissecting-room.

On that particular morning Macfarlane arrived somewhat earlier than his wont. Fettes heard him, and met him on the stairs, told him his story, and showed him the cause of his alarm. Macfarlane examined the marks on her body.

'Yea', he said with a nod, 'it looks fishy.'

'Well, what should I do?' asked Fettes.

'Do?' repeated the other. 'Do you want to do anything? Least said soonest mended, I should say.'

'Someone else might recognize her,' objected Fettes. 'She was as well known as the Castle Rock.'

'We'll hope not,' said Macfarlane, 'and if anybody does – well, you didn't, don't you see, and there's an end. The fact is, this has been going on too long. Stir up the mud, and you'll get K– into the most unholy trouble; you'll be in a shocking box yourself. So will I, if you come to that. I should like to know how any one of us would look, or what the devil we should have to say for ourselves, in any Christian witness-box. For me, you know there's one thing certain – that, practically speaking, all our subjects have been murdered.'

'Macfarlane!' cried Fettes.

'Come now!' sneered the other. 'As if you hadn't suspected it yourself!'

'Suspecting is one thing –'

'And proof another. Yes, I know; and I'm as sorry as you are this should have come here,' tapping the body with his cane. 'The next best thing for me is not to recognize it; and,' he added coolly, 'I don't. You may, if you please. I don't dictate, but I think a man of the world would do as I do; and I may add, I fancy that is what K– would look for at our hands. The question is, Why did he choose us two for his assistants? And I answer, because he didn't want old wives.'

This was the tone of all others to affect the mind of a lad like Fettes. He agreed to imitate Macfarlane. The body of the unfortunate girl was duly dissected, and no one remarked or appeared to recognize her.

One afternoon, when his day's work was over, Fettes dropped into a popular tavern and found Macfarlane sitting with a stranger. This was a small man, very pale and dark, with coal-black eyes. The cut of his features gave a promise of intellect and refinement which was but feebly realized in his manners, for he proved, upon a nearer acquaintance, coarse, vulgar, and stupid. He exercised, however, a very remarkable control over Macfarlane; issued orders like the Great Bashaw; became inflamed at the least discussion or delay, and commented rudely on the servility with which he was obeyed. This most offensive person took a fancy to Fettes on the spot, plied him with drinks, and honoured him with unusual confidences on his past career. If a tenth part of what he confessed were true, he was a very loathsome rogue; and the lad's vanity was tickled by the attention of so experienced a man.

'I'm a pretty bad fellow myself,' the stranger remarked, 'but Macfarlane is the boy –Toddy Macfarlane I call him. Toddy, order your friend another glass.' Or it might be, 'Toddy, you jump up and shut the door.' 'Toddy hates me,' he said again. 'Oh, yes, Toddy, you do!'

'Don't you call me that confounded name,' growled Macfarlane.

'Hear him! Did you ever see the lads play knife? He would like to do that all over my body,' remarked the stranger.

'We medicals have a better way than that,' said Fettes. 'When we dislike a dead friend of ours, we dissect him.'

Macfarlane looked up sharply, as though this jest was scarcely to his mind.

The afternoon passed. Gray, for that was the stranger's name, invited Fettes to join them at dinner, ordered a feast so sumptuous that the tavern was thrown in commotion, and when all was done commanded Macfarlane to settle the bill. It was late before they separated; the man Gray was incapably drunk. Macfarlane, sobered by his fury, chewed the cud of the money he had been forced to squander and the slights he had been obliged to swallow. Fettes, with various liquors singing in his head, returned home with devious footsteps and a mind entirely in abeyance. Next day Macfarlane was absent from the class, and Fettes smiled to himself as he imagined him still squiring the intolerable Gray from tavern to tavern. As soon as the hour of liberty had struck he posted from place to place in quest of his last night's companions. He could find them, however, nowhere; so returned early to his rooms, went early to bed, and slept the sleep of the just.

At four in the morning he was awakened by the well-known signal. Descending to the door, he was filled with astonishment to find Macfarlane with his gig, and in the gig one of those long and ghastly packages with which he was so well acquainted.

'What?' he cried. 'Have you been out alone? How did you manage?'

But Macfarlane silenced him roughly, bidding him turn to business. When they had got the body upstairs and laid it on the table, Macfarlane made at first as if he were going away. Then he paused and seemed to hesitate; and then, 'You had better look at the face,' said he, in tones of some constraint. 'You had better,' he repeated, as Fettes only stared at him in wonder.

'But where, and how, and when did you come by it?' cried the other.

'Look at the face,' was the only answer.

Fettes was staggered, strange doubts assailed him. He looked from the young doctor to the body, and then back again. At last, with a start, he did as he was bidden. He had almost expected the sight that met his eyes, and yet the shock was cruel. To see, fixed in the rigidity of death and naked on that coarse layer of sack-cloth, the man whom he had left well-clad and full of meat and sin upon the threshold of a tavern, awoke, even in the thoughtless Fettes, some of the terrors of the conscience. It was a *cras tibi* which re-echoed in his soul – that two whom he had known should have come to lie upon these icy tables. Yet these were only secondary thoughts. His first concern regarded Wolfe. Unprepared for a challenge so momentous, he knew not how to look his comrade in the face. He durst not meet his eye, and he had neither words nor voice at his command.

It was Macfarlane himself who made the first advance. He came up quietly behind and laid his hand gently but firmly on the other's shoulder.

'Richardson,' said he, 'may have the head.'

Now Richardson was a student who had long been anxious for that portion of the human subject to dissect. There was no answer, and the murderer resumed: 'Talking of business, you must pay me; your accounts, you see, must tally.'

Fettes found a voice, the ghost of his own: 'Pay you!' he cried, 'Pay you for that?'

'Why, yes, of course you must. By all means and on every possible account, you must,' returned the other. 'I dare not give it for nothing, you dare not take it for nothing; it would compromise us both. This is another case like Jane Galbraith's. The more things are wrong the more we must act as if all were right. Where does old K– keep his money?'

'There,' answered Fettes hoarsely, pointing to a cupboard in the corner.

'Give me the key, then,' said the other, calmly, holding out his hand.

There was an instant's hesitation, and the die was cast. Macfarlane could not suppress a nervous twitch, the infinitesimal mark of an immense relief, as he felt the key between his fingers. He opened the cupboard, brought out pen and ink and a paper-book that stood in one compartment, and separated from the funds in a drawer a sum suitable to the occasion.

'Now, look here,' he said, 'there is the payment made – first proof of your good faith: first step to your security. You have now to clinch it by a second. Enter the payment in your book, and then you for your part may defy the devil.'

The next few seconds were for Fettes an agony of thought; but in balancing his terrors it was the most immediate that triumphed. Any future difficulty seemed almost welcome if he could avoid a present quarrel with Macfarlane. He set down the candle which he had been carrying all the time, and with a steady hand entered the date, the nature, and the amount of the transaction.

'And now,' said Macfarlane, 'it's only fair that you should pocket the lucre. I've had my share already. By-the-by, when a man of the world falls into a bit of luck, has a few shillings extra in his pocket – I'm ashamed to speak of it, but there's a rule of conduct in the case. No treating, no purchase of expensive class-books, no squaring of old debts; borrow, don't lend.'

'Macfarlane,' began Fettes, still somewhat hoarsely, 'I have put my neck in a halter to oblige you.'

'To oblige me?' cried Wolfe. 'Oh, come! You did, as near as I can see the matter, what you downright had to do in self-defence. Suppose I got into trouble, where would you be? This second little matter flows clearly from the first. Mr Gray is the continuation of Miss Galbraith. You can't begin and then stop. If you begin, you must keep on beginning; that's the truth. No rest for the wicked.'

A horrible sense of blackness and the treachery of fate seized hold upon the soul of the unhappy student.

'My God!' he cried, 'but what have I done? and when did I begin? To be made a class assistant – in the name of reason, where's the harm in that? Service wanted the position; Service might have got it. Would *he* have been where *I* am now?'

'My dear fellow,' said Macfarlane, 'what a boy you are! What harm *has* come to you? What harm *can* come to you if you hold your tongue? Why, man, do you know what this life is? There are two squads of us –

the lions and the lambs. If you're a lamb, you'll come to lie upon these tables like Gray or Jane Galbraith; if you're a lion, you'll live and drive a horse like me, like K– , like all the world with any wit or courage. You're staggered at the first. But look at K– ! My dear fellow, you're clever, you have pluck. I like you, and K– likes you. You were born to lead the hunt; and I tell you, on my honour and my experience of life, three days from now you'll laugh at all these scarecrows like a high-school boy at a farce.'

And with that Macfarlane took his departure and drove off up the wynd in his gig to get under cover before daylight. Fettes was thus left alone with his regrets. He saw the miserable peril in which he stood involved. He saw, with inexpressible dismay, that there was no limit to his weakness, and that, from concession to concession, he had fallen from the arbiter of Macfarlane's destiny to his paid and helpless accomplice. He would have given the world to have been a little braver at the time, but it did not occur to him that he might still be brave. The secret of Jane Galbraith and the cursed entry in the day-book closed his mouth.

Hours passed; the class began to arrive; the members of the unhappy Gray were dealt out to one and to another, and received without remark. Richardson was made happy with the head; and before the hour of freedom rang Fettes trembled with exultation to perceive how far they had already gone toward safety.

For two days he continued to watch, with increasing joy, the dreadful process of disguise.

On the third day Macfarlane made his appearance. He had been ill, he said; but he made up for lost time by the energy with which he directed the students. To Richardson in particular he extended the most valuable assistance and advice, and that student, encouraged by the praise of the demonstrator, burned high with ambitious hopes, and saw the medal already in his grasp.

Before the week was out Macfarlane's prophecy had been fulfilled. Fettes had outlived his terrors and had forgotten his baseness. He began to plume himself upon his courage, and had so arranged the story in his mind that he could look back on these events with an unhealthy pride. Of his accomplice he saw but little. They met, of course, in the business of the class; they received their orders together from Mr K– . At times they had a word or two in private, and Macfarlane was from first to last particularly kind and jovial. But it was plain that he avoided any reference to their common secret; and even when Fettes whispered to him that he had cast in his lot with the lions and forsworn the lambs, he only signed to him smilingly to hold his peace.

At length an occasion arose which threw the pair once more into a closer union. Mr K– was again short of subjects; pupils were eager, and it was a part of this teacher's pretensions to be always well supplied. At the same time there came the news of a burial in the rustic graveyard of Glencorse. Time has little changed the place in question. It stood then, as now, upon a crossroad, out of call of human habitations, and buried fathom deep in the foliage of six cedar trees. The cries of the sheep upon the neighbouring hills, the streamlets upon either hand, one loudly singing among pebbles, the other dripping furtively from pond to pond, the stir of the wind in mountainous old flowering chestnuts, and once in seven days the voice of the bell and the old tunes of the preceptor, were the only sounds that disturbed the silence around the rural church. The Resurrection Man – to use a by-name of the period – was not to be deterred by any of the sanctities of customary piety. It was part of his trade to despise and desecrate the scrolls and trumpets of old tombs, the paths worn by the feet of worshippers and mourners, and the offerings and the inscriptions of bereaved affection. To rustic neighbourhoods, where love is more than commonly tenacious, and where some bonds of blood or fellowship unite the entire society of a parish, the body-snatcher, far from being repelled by natural respect, was attracted by the ease and safety of the task. To bodies that had been laid in earth, in joyful expectation of a far different awakening, there came that hasty, lamp-lit, terror-haunted resurrection of the spade and mattock. The coffin was forced, the cerements torn, and the melancholy relics, clad in sackcloth, after being rattled for hours on moonless by-ways, were at length exposed to uttermost indignities before a class of gaping boys.

Somewhat as two vultures may swoop upon a dying lamb, Fettes and Macfarlane were to be let loose upon a grave in that green and quiet resting-place. The wife of a farmer, a woman who had lived for sixty years, and been known for nothing but good butter and a godly conversation, was to be rooted from her grave at midnight and carried, dead and naked, to that far-away city that she had always honoured with her Sunday best; the place beside her family was to be empty till the crack of doom; her innocent and almost venerable members to be exposed to that last curiosity of the anatomist.

Late one afternoon the pair set forth, well wrapped in cloaks and furnished with a formidable bottle. It rained without remission – a cold, dense, lashing rain. Now and again there blew a puff of wind, but these sheets of falling water kept it down. Bottle and all, it was a sad and silent drive as far as Penicuik, where they were to spend the evening. They stopped once, to hide their implements in a thick bush not far from the churchyard, and once again at the Fisher's Tryst, to have a toast before the kitchen fire and vary their nips of whisky with a glass of ale. When they reached their journey's end the gig was housed, the horse was fed and comforted, and the two young doctors in a private room sat down to the best dinner and the best wine the house afforded. The lights, the fire, the beating rain upon the window, the cold, incongruous work that lay before them, added zest to their enjoyment of the meal. With every glass their cordiality increased. Soon Macfarlane handed a little pile of gold to his companion.

'A compliment,' he said. 'Between friends these little d–d accommodations ought to fly like pipe-lights.'

Fettes pocketed the money, and applauded the sentiment to the echo. 'You are a philosopher,' he cried. 'I was an ass till I knew you. You and K– between you, by the Lord Harry! but you'll make a man of me.'

'Of course we shall,' applauded Macfarlane. 'A man? I tell you, it required a man to back me up the other morning. There are some big, brawling, forty-year-old cowards who would have turned sick at the look of the d–d thing; but not you – you kept your head. I watched you.'

'Well, and why not?' Fettes thus vaunted himself. 'It was no affair of mine. There was nothing to gain on the one side but disturbance, and on the other I could count on your gratitude, don't you see?' And he slapped his pocket till the gold pieces rang.

Macfarlane somehow felt a certain touch of alarm at these unpleasant words. He may have regretted that he had taught his young companion so succcessfully, but he had no time to interfere, for the other noisily continued in this boastful strain:

'The great thing is not to be afraid. Now, between you and me, I don't want to hang – that's practical; but for all cant, Macfarlane, I was born with a contempt. Hell, God, Devil, right, wrong, sin, crime, and all the old gallery of curiosities – they may frighten boys, but men of the world, like you and me, despise them. Here's to the memory of Gray!'

It was by this time growing somewhat late. The gig, according to order, was brought round to the door with both lamps brightly shining, and the young men had to pay their bill and take the road. They announced that they were bound for Peebles, and drove in that direction till they were clear of the last house of the town; then, extinguishing the lamps, returned upon their course, and followed a by-road toward Glencorse. There was no sound but that of their own passage, and the incessant, strident pouring of the rain. It was pitch dark; here and there a white gate or a white stone in the wall guided them for a short space across the night; but for the most part it was at a foot pace, and almost groping, that they picked their way through that resonant blackness to their solemn and isolated destination. In the sunken woods that traverse the neighbourhood of the burying-ground the last glimmer failed them, and it became necessary to kindle a match and reillumine one of the lanterns of the gig. Thus, under the dripping trees, and environed by huge and moving shadows, they reached the scene of their unhallowed labours.

They were both experienced in such affairs, and powerful with the spade; and they had scarce been twenty minutes at their task before they were rewarded by a dull rattle on the coffin lid. At the same moment Macfarlane, having hurt his hand upon a stone, flung it carelessly above his head. The grave, in which they now stood almost to the shoulders, was close to the edge of the plateau of the graveyard; and the gig lamp had been propped, the better to illuminate their labours, against a tree, and on the immediate verge of the steep bank descending to the stream. Chance had taken a sure aim with the stone. Then came a clang of broken glass; night fell upon them; sounds alternately dull and ringing announced the bounding of the lantern down the bank, and its occasional collision with the trees. A stone or two, which it had dislodged in its descent, rattled behind it into the profundities of the glen; and then silence, like night, resumed its sway; and they might bend their hearing to its utmost pitch, but naught was to be heard except the rain, now marching to the wind, now steadily falling over miles of open country.

They were so nearly at an end of their abhorred task that they judged it wisest to complete it in the dark. The coffin was exhumed and broken open; the body inserted in the dripping sack and carried between them to the gig; one mounted to keep it in its place, and the other, taking the horse by the mouth, groped along by wall and bush until they reached the wider road by the Fisher's Tryst. Here was a faint, diffused radiancy, which they hailed like daylight; by that they pushed the horse to a good pace and began to rattle along merrily in the direction of the town.

They had both been wetted to the skin during their operations, and now, as the gig jumped among the deep ruts, the thing that stood propped between them fell now upon one and now upon the other. At every repetition of the horrid contact each instinctively repelled it with greater haste; and the process, natural although it was, began to tell upon the nerves of the companions. Macfarlane made some ill-favoured jest about the farmer's wife, but it came hollowly from his lips, and was allowed to drop in silence. Still their unnatural burthen bumped from side to side; and now the head would be laid, as if in confidence, upon their shoulders, and now the drenching sackcloth would flap icily about their faces. A creeping chill began to possess the soul of Fettes. He peered at the bundle, and it seemed somehow larger than at first. All over the countryside, and from every degree of distance, the farm dogs accompanied their passage with tragic ululations; and it grew and grew upon his mind that some unnatural miracle had been accomplished that some nameless change had befallen the dead body, and that it was in fear of their unholy burden that the dogs were howling.

'For God's sake,' said he, making a great effort to arrive at speech, 'for God's sake, let's have a light!'

Seemingly Macfarlane was affected in the same direction, for though he made no reply, he stopped the horse, passed the reins to his companion, got down, and proceeded to kindle the remaining lamp. They had by that time got no further than the cross-road down to Auchendinny. The rain still poured as though the deluge were returning, and it was no easy matter to make a light in such a world of wet and darkness. When at last the flickering blue flame had been transferred to the wick and began to expand and clarify, and shed a wide circle of misty brightness round the gig, it became possible for the two young men to see each other and the thing they had along with them. The rain had moulded the rough sacking to the outlines of the body underneath; the head was distinct from the trunk, the shoulders plainly modelled; something at once spectral and human riveted their eyes upon the ghastly comrade of their drive.

For some time Macfarlane stood motionless, holding up the lamp. A nameless dread was swathed, like a wet sheet, about the body, and tightened the white skin upon the face of Fettes; a fear that was meaningless, a horror of what could not be, kept mounting to his brain. Another beat of the watch, and he had spoken. But his comrade forestalled him.

'That is not a woman,' said Macfarlane, in a hushed voice.

'It was a woman when we put her in,' whispered Fettes.

'Hold that lamp,' said the other. 'I must see her face.'

And as Fettes took the lamp his companion untied the fastenings of the sack and drew down the cover from the head. The light fell very clear upon the dark, well-moulded features and smooth-shaven cheeks of a too familiar countenance, often beheld in dreams of both of these young men. A wild yell rang up into the night; each leaped from his own side into the roadway; the lamp fell, broke, and was extinguished; and the horse, terrified by this unusual commotion, bounded and went off toward Edinburgh at a gallop, bearing along with it, sole occupant of the gig, the body of the dead and long-dissected Gray.

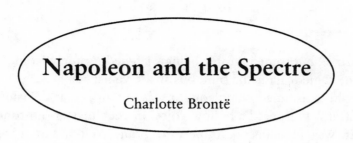

Napoleon and the Spectre

Charlotte Brontë

WELL, as I was saying, the Emperor got into bed.

'Chevalier,' says he to his valet, 'let down those window-curtains, and shut the casement before you leave the room.'

Chevalier did as he was told, and then, taking up his candlestick, departed.

In a few minutes the Emperor felt his pillow becoming rather hard, and he got up to shake it. As he did so a slight rushing noise was heard near the bed-head. His Majesty listened, but all was silent as he lay down again.

Scarcely had he settled into a peaceful attitude of repose, when he was disturbed by a sensation of thirst. Lifting himself on his elbow, he took a glass of lemonade from the small stand which was placed beside him. He refreshed himself by a deep draught. As he returned the goblet to its station a deep groan burst from a kind of closet in one corner of the apartment.

'Who's there?' cried the Emperor, seizing his pistols. 'Speak, or I'll blow your brains out.'

This threat produced no other effect than a short, sharp laugh, and a dead silence followed.

The Emperor started from his couch, and, hastily throwing on a *robe-de-chambre* which hung over the back of a chair, stepped courageously to the haunted closet. As he opened the door something rustled. He sprang forward sword in hand. No soul or even substance appeared, and the rustling, it was evident, proceeded from the falling of a cloak, which had been suspended by a peg from the door.

Half ashamed of himself he returned to bed.

Just as he was about once more to close his eyes, the light of the three wax tapers, which burned in a silver branch over the mantelpiece, was suddenly darkened. He looked up. A black, opaque shadow obscured it. Sweating with terror, the Emperor put out his hand to seize the bell-rope, but some invisible being snatched it rudely from his grasp, and at the same instant the ominous shade vanished.

'Pooh!' exclaimed Napoleon, 'it was but an ocular delusion.'

'Was it?' whispered a hollow voice, in deep mysterious tones, close to his ear. Was it a delusion, Emperor of France? No! all thou hast heard and seen is sad forewarning reality. Rise, lifter of the Eagle Standard! Awake, slayer of the Lily Sceptre! Follow me, Napoleon, and thou shalt see more.'

As the voice ceased, a form dawned on his astonished sight. It was that of a tall, thin man, dressed in a blue surtout edged with gold lace. It wore a black cravat very tightly round its neck, and confined by two little sticks placed behind each ear. The countenance was livid; the tongue protruded from between the teeth, and the eyes all glazed and bloodshot started with frightful prominence from their sockets.

'*Mon Dieu*!' exclaimed the Emperor, 'what do I see? Spectre, whence cometh thou?'

The apparition spoke not, but gliding forward beckoned Napoleon with uplifted finger to follow.

Controlled by a mysterious influence, which deprived him of the capability of either thinking or acting for himself, he obeyed in silence.

The solid wall of the apartment fell open as they approached, and, when both had passed through, it closed behind them with a noise like thunder.

They would now have been in total darkness had it not been for a dim light which shone round the ghost and revealed the damp walls of a long, vaulted passage. Down this they proceeded with mute rapidity. Ere long a cool, refreshing breeze, which rushed wailing up the vault and caused the Emperor to wrap his loose nightdress closer round, announced their approach to the open air.

This they soon reached, and Nap found himself in one of the principal streets of Paris.

'Worthy Spirit,' said he, shivering in the chill night air, 'permit me to return and put on some additional clothing. I will be with you again presently.'

'Forward,' replied his companion sternly.

He felt compelled, in spite of the rising indignation which almost choked him, to obey.

On they went through the deserted streets till they arrived at a lofty house built on the banks of the Seine. Here the Spectre stopped, the gates rolled back to receive them, and they entered a large marble hall which was part concealed by a curtain drawn across, through the half transparent folds of which a bright light might be seen burning with

dazzling lustre. A row of fine female figures, richly attired, stood before this screen. They wore on their heads garlands of the most beautiful flowers, but their faces were concealed by ghastly masks representing death's-heads.

'What is all this mummery?' cried the Emperor, making an effort to shake off the mental shackles by which he was so unwillingly restrained, 'Where am I, and why have I been brought here?'

'Silence,' said the guide, lolling out still further his black and bloody tongue. 'Silence, if thou wouldst escape instant death.'

The Emperor would have replied, his natural courage overcoming the temporary awe to which he had at first been subjected, but just then a strain of wild, supernatural music swelled behind the huge curtain, which waved to and fro, and bellied slowly out as if agitated by some internal commotion or battle of waving winds. At the same moment an overpowering mixture of the scents of moral corruption, blent with the richest Eastern odours, stole through the haunted hall.

A murmur of many voices was now heard at a distance, and something grasped his arm eagerly from behind.

He turned hastily round. His eyes met the well-known countenance of Marie Louise.

'What! are you in this infernal place, too?' said he. 'What has brought you here?'

'Will your Majesty permit me to ask the same question of yourself?' said the Empress, smiling.

He made no reply; astonishment prevented him.

No curtain now intervened between him and the light. It had been removed as if by magic, and a splendid chandelier appeared suspended over his head. Throngs of ladies, richly dressed, but without death's-head masks, stood round, and a due proportion of gay cavaliers was mingled with them. Music was still sounding, but it was seen to proceed from a band of mortal musicians stationed in an orchestra near at hand. The air was yet redolent of incense, but it was incense unblended with stench.

'*Mon Dieu*!' cried the Emperor, 'how is all this come about? Where in the world is Piche?'

'Piche?' replied the Empress. 'What does your Majesty mean? Had you not better leave the apartment and retire to rest?'

'Leave the apartment? Why, where am I?'

'In my private drawing-room, surrounded by a few particular persons of the Court whom I had invited this evening to a ball. You entered a few minutes since in your nightdress with your eyes fixed and wide open. I suppose from the astonishment you now testify that you were walking in your sleep.'

The Emperor immediately fell into a fit of catalepsy, in which he continued during the whole of that night and the greater part of the next day.

The Story of the Moor Road

E. and H. Heron

'The medical profession must always have its own peculiar offshoots,' said Mr Flaxman Low, 'some are trades, some mere hobbies, others, again, are allied subjects of a serious and profound nature. Now, as a student of psychical phenomena, I account myself only two degrees removed from the ordinary general practitioner.'

'How do you make that out?' returned Colonel Daimley, pushing the decanter of old port invitingly across the table.

'The nerve and brain specialist is the link between myself and the man you would send for if you had a touch of lumbago,' replied Low with a slight smile. 'Each division is but a higher grade of the same ladder – a step upwards into the unknown. I consider that I stand just one step above the specialist who makes a study of brain disease and insanity; he is at work on the disorders of the embodied spirit, while I deal with abnormal conditions of the free and detached spirit.'

Colonel Daimley laughed aloud.

'That won't do, Low ! No, no! First prove that your ghosts are sick.'

'Certainly,' replied Low gravely. 'A very small proportion of spirits return as apparitions after the death of the body. Hence we may conclude that a ghost is a spirit in an abnormal condition. Abnormal conditions of the body usually indicate disease; why not of the spirit also?'

'That sounds fair enough,' observed Lane Chaddam, the third man present. 'Has the Colonel told you of our spook?'

The Colonel shook his handsome grey head in some irritation.

'You haven't convinced me yet, Lane, that it is a spook,' he said drily. 'Human nature is at the bottom of most things in this world according to my opinion.'

'What spook is this?' asked Flaxman Low. 'I heard nothing of it when I was down with you last year.'

'It's a recent acquisition,' replied Lane Chaddam. 'I wish we were rid of it for my part.'

'Have you seen it?' asked Low as he relit his long pipe.

'Yes, and felt it!'

'What is it?'

'That's for you to say. He nearly broke my neck for me – that's all I can swear to.'

Low knew Chaddam well. He was a long-limbed, athletic young fellow, with a good show of cups in his rooms, and was one of the various short-distance runners mentioned in the Badminton as having done the hundred in level time, and not the sort of man whose neck is easy to break.

'How did it happen?' asked Flaxman Low.

'About a fortnight ago,' replied Chaddam, 'I was flight-shooting near the barn where the hounds killed the otter last year. When the light began to fail, I thought I would come home by the old quarry, and pot anything that showed itself. As I walked along the far bank of the burn, I saw a man on the near side standing on the patch of the sand below the reed and watching me. As I came nearer I heard him coughing; it sounded like a sick cow. He stood still as if waiting for me. I thought it odd, because amongst the meres and watermeadows down there one never meets a stranger.'

'Could you see him pretty clearly?'

'I saw his outline clearly, but not his face, because his back was toward the west. He was tall and jerry-built, so to speak, and had a little head no bigger than a child's, and he wore a fur cap with queer upstanding ears. When I came close, he suddenly slipped away; he jumped behind a big dyke, and I lost sight of him. But I didn't pay much attention; I had my gun, and I concluded it was a tramp.'

'Tramps don't follow men of your size,' observed Low with a smile.

'This fellow did, at any rate When I got across to the spot where he had been standing – the sand is soft there – I looked for his tracks. I knew he was bound to have a big foot of his own considering his height. But there were no footprints!'

'No footprints? You mean it was too dark for you to see them?' broke in Colonel Daimley.

'I am sure I should have seen them had there been any,' persisted Chaddam quietly. 'Besides, a man can't take a leap as he did without leaving a good hole behind him. The sand was perfectly smooth, because there had been a strong east wind all day. I looked about and seeing no marks, I went on to the top of the knoll above the quarry. After a bit I felt I was followed, though I couldn't see anyone. You remember the thorn bush that overhangs the quarry pool? I stopped there and bent over the edge of the cliff to see if there was anything in the pool. As I stooped I felt a point like a steel puncheon catch me in the small of the back. I kicked off from the quarry wall as well as I could, so as to avoid the broken rocks below, and I just managed to clear them, but I fell into the water with a flop that knocked the wind out of me. However, I held on to the gun, and, after a minute, I climbed to a ledge under the cliff and waited to see what my friend on top would do next. He waited, too. I couldn't see him, but I heard him – he coughed up there in the dusk, the most ghastly noise I ever heard. The Colonel laughs at me, but it was about as nasty a half-hour as I care to have. In the end, I swam out across the pool and got home.'

'I laugh at Lane,' said the Colonel, 'but all the same, it's a bad spot for a fall.'

'You say he struck you in the back?' asked Flaxman Low, turning to Chaddam.

'Yes, and his fingers were like a steel punch.'

'What does Mrs Daimley say to this affair?' went on Low presently.

'Not a word to my wife or Olivia, my dear Low!' exclaimed Colonel Daimley. 'It would frighten them needlessly; besides, there would be an infernal fuss if we wanted to go flighting or anything after dark. I only fear for them, as they often drive into Nerbury by the Moor Road, which passes close by the quarry.'

'Do they go in for their letters every evening as they used to do?'

'Just the same. And they won't take Stubbs with them, in spite of my advice.' The Colonel looked disconsolately at Low. 'Women are angels, bless them! but they are the dickens to deal with because they always want to know why?'

'And now, Low, what have you to say about it?' asked Chaddam.

'Have you told me all?'

'Yes. The only other thing is that Livy says she hears someone coughing in the spinney most nights.'

'If all is as you say, Chaddam – pardon me, but in cases like this imagination is apt to play an unsuspected part – I should think that you have come upon a unique experience. What you have told me is not to be explained upon the lines of any ordinary theory.'

After this they followed the ladies into the drawing-room where they found Mrs Daimley immersed in a novel as usual, and Livy looking pretty enough to account for the frequent presence of Lane Chaddam at Low Riddings. He was a distant cousin of the Colonel, and took advantage of his relationship to pay protracted visits to Northumberland.

Some years previous to the date of the above events, Colonel Daimley had bought and enlarged a substantial farmhouse which stood in a dip south of a lonely sweep of Northumbrian moors. It was a land of pale blue skies and far off fringes of black and ragged pine trees.

From the house a lane led over the wind-swept shoulder of the upland down to a hollow spanned by a railway bridge, then up again across the high levels of the moors until at length it lost itself in the outskirts of the little town of Nerbury. This Moor Road was peculiarly lonely: it approached but one cottage the whole way, and ran very nearly over the doorstep of that one – a deserted-looking slip of a place between the railway bridge and the quarry. Beyond the quarry stretched acres of marshland, meadows and reedy meres, all of which had been manipulated with such ability by the Colonel, that the duck shooting on his land was the envy of the neighbourhood.

In spite of its loneliness the Moor Road was much frequented by the Daimleys, who preferred it to the high road, which was uninteresting and much longer. Mrs Daimley and Olivia drove in of an evening to fetch their letters – being people with nothing on earth to do, they were naturally always in a hurry to get their letters – and they perpetually had parcels waiting for them at the station which required to be called for at all sorts of hours. Thus it will be seen that the fact of the quarry being haunted by Lane Chaddam's assailant, formed a very real danger to the inhabitants of Low Riddings.

At breakfast next day Livy said the tramp had been coughing in the spinney half the night.

'In what direction?' asked Flaxman Low.

Livy pointed to the window which looked on to the gate and the thick boundary hedge, the last still full of crisp ruddy leaves.

'You feel an interest in your tramp, Miss Daimley?'

'Of course, poor creature! I wanted to go out to look for him the other night, but they would not allow me.'

'That was before we knew he was so interesting,' said Chaddam. 'I promise we'll catch him for you next time he comes.'

And this was in fact the programme they tried to carry out, but although the coughing was heard in the spinney, no one even caught a glimpse of any living thing moving or hiding among the trees.

The next stage of the affair happened to be an experience of Livy's. In some excitement she told the assembled family at dinner that she had just seen the coughing tramp.

Lane Chaddam changed colour.

'You don't mean to say, Livy, that you went to search for him alone?' he exclaimed half-angrily.

Flaxman Low and the Colonel wisely went on eating oyster patties without taking any apparent notice of the girl's news.

'Why shouldn't I?' asked Livy quickly; 'but as it happens I saw him in Scully's cottage by the quarry this evening.'

'What ?' said Colonel Daimley, 'in Scully's cottage. I'll see to that.'

'Why? Are you all so prejudiced against my poor tramp!'

'On the contrary,' replied Flaxman Low, 'we all want to know what he's like.'

'So odd-looking! I was driving home alone from the post when, as I passed the quarry cottage, I heard the cough. You know it is quite unmistakable; I looked up at the window and there he was. I have never seen anybody in the least like him. His face is ghastly pale and perfectly hairless, and he has such a little head. He stared at me so threateningly that I whipped up Lorelie.'

'Were you frightened, then?'

'Not exactly, but he had such a wicked face that I drove away as fast as I could.'

'I understood that you had arranged to send Stubbs for the letters?' said Colonel Daimley with some annoyance. 'Why can't girls say what they mean?'

Livy made no reply, and after a pause Chaddam put a question.

'You must have passed along the Moor Road about seven o'clock?'

'Yes, it was after six when I left the Post Office,' replied Livy.

'Why ?'

'It was quite dark – how did you see the hairless man so plainly? I was round on the marshes all the evening, and I am quite certain there was no light at any time in Scully's cottage.'

'I don't remember whether there was any light behind him in the room,' returned Livy after a moment's consideration; 'I only know that I saw his head and face quite plainly.'

There was no more said on the subject at the time, though the Colonel forbade Livy to run any further risks by going alone on the Moor Road. After this the three men paraded the lane and lay in wait for the hairless tramp or ghost. On the second evening their watch was rewarded, when Chaddam came hurriedly into the smoking-room to say that the coughing could at that instant be heard in the hedge by the dining-room. It was still early, although the evening had closed in with clouds, and all outside was dark.

'I'll deal with him this time effectually!' exclaimed the Colonel. 'I'll slip out the back way, and lie in the hedge down the road by the field gate. You two must chivy him out to me, and when he comes along, I'll have him against the sky-line and give him a charge of No. 4 if he shows fight.'

The Colonel stole down the lane while the others beat the spinney and hedge. Flaxman Low was very much chagrined at being forced to deal with an interesting problem in this rough and ready fashion. However, he saw that on this occasion at least it would be useless to oppose the Colonel's notions. When he and Chaddam met after beating the hedge they saw a tall figure shamble away rapidly down the lane towards the Colonel's hiding-place.

They stood still and waited for developments, but the minutes followed each other in intense stillness. Then they went to find the Colonel.

'Hullo, Colonel, anything wrong?' asked Chaddam on nearing the field gate.

The Colonel straightened himself with the help of Chaddam's arm.

'Did you see him?' he whispered.

'We thought so. Why did you not fire?'

'Because,' said the Colonel in a husky voice, 'I had no gun!'

'But you took it with you?'

'Yes.'

Flaxman Low opened the lantern he carried, and as the light swept round in a wide circle, something glinted on the grass. It was the stock of the Colonel's gun. A little further off they came upon the Damascus barrels bent and twisted into a ball like so much fine wire. Presently the Colonel explained.

'I saw him coming and meant to meet him, but I seemed dazed – I couldn't move! The gun was snatched from me, and I made no resistance – I don't know why.' He took the gun-barrels and examined them slowly. 'I give in, Low, no human hand did that.'

During dinner Flaxman Low said abruptly: 'I suspect that you have lately had an earthquake down here.'

'How did you know?' asked Livy. 'Have you been to the quarry?'

Low said he had not.

'It was such a poor little earthquake that even the papers did not think it worth while to mention it!' went on Livy. 'We didn't feel any shock and in fact knew nothing about it until Dr Petterped told us.'

'You had a landslip though?' went on Low.

Livy opened her pretty eyes.

'But you know all about it,' she said. 'Yes, the landslip was just by the old quarry.'

'I should like to see the place to-morrow,' observed Low.

Next day, therefore, when the Colonel went off to the coverts with a couple of neighbours, whom he had invited to join him, Flaxman Low accompanied Chaddam to examine the scene of the landslip.

From the edge of the upland, looking across the hollow crowded with reedy pools they could see in the torn, reddish flank of the opposite slope the sharp tilt of the broken strata. To the right of this lay the old quarry, and about a hundred yards to the left the lonely house and the curving road.

Low descended into the hollow and spent a long time in the spongy ground between the back of the quarry and the lower edge of the newly-uncovered strata, using his little hammer freely, especially about one narrow black fissure, round which he sniffed and pottered in absorbed silence. Presently he called to Chaddam.

'There has been a slight explosion of gas – a rare gas, here,' he said. 'I hardly hoped to find traces of it, but it is unmistakable.'

'Very unmistakable,' agreed Chaddam, with a laugh. 'You'd have said so had you been here when it happened.'

'Ah, very satisfactory indeed. And that was a fortnight ago, you say?'

'Rather more now. It took place a couple of days before my fall into the quarry pool.'

'Anyone ill near by – at that cottage for instance?' asked Low, as he joined Chaddam.

'Why? Was the gas poisonous? There's a man in the Colonel's employ named Scully in that cottage, who has had pneumonia, but he was on the mend when the landslip occurred. Since then he has grown steadily worse.'

'Is there anyone with him?'

'Yes, the Daimleys sent for a woman to look after him. Scully's a very decent man. I often go in to see him.'

'And so does the hairless man apparently,' added Low.

'No, that's the queer part of it. Neither he nor the woman in charge have ever seen such a person as Livy described. I don't know what to think.'

'The first thing to be done is to get the man from here at once,' said Low decidedly. 'Let's go in and see him.'

They found Scully low and drowsy. The nurse shook her head at the two visitors in a despondent way.

'He grows weaker day by day,' she said.

'Get him away from here at once,' repeated Low, as they went out.

'We might have him up at Low Riddings, but he seems almost too weak to be moved,' replied Chaddam doubtfully.

'My dear fellow, it's his only chance of life.'

The Daimleys made arrangements for the reception of Scully, provided Dr Thomson of Nerbury gave his consent to the removal. In the afternoon, therefore, Chaddam bicycled into Nerbury to see the doctor on the subject.

'If I were you, Chaddam,' said Low before he started, 'I'd be back by daylight.'

Unfortunately Dr Thomson was on his rounds, and did not return until after dark, by which time it was too late to remove Scully that evening. After leaving the doctor's house Chaddam went to the station to inquire about a box from Mudie's. The books having arrived, he took out a couple of volumes for Mrs Daimley's present consumption, and was strapping them on in front of his bicycle, when it struck him that unless he went home by the Moor Road he would be late for dinner.

Accordingly he branched off into the bare track which led over the moors. The twilight had deepened into a fine, cold night, and a moon was swinging up into a pale, clear sky. The spread of heather, purple in the daytime, appeared jet black by moonlight, and across it he could see the white ribbon of road stretching ahead into the distance. The scents of the night were fresh in his nostrils, as he ran easily along the level with the breeze behind him.

He soon reached the incline past Scully's cottage. Well away to the left lay the quarry pool like a blotch of ink under its shadowing cliff. There was no light in the cottage, and it seemed even more deserted-looking than usual.

As Chaddam flashed under the bridge, he heard a cough, and glanced back over his shoulder.

A tall, loose-jointed form he had seen once before, was rearing itself up upon the railway bridge. There was something curiously unhuman about the lank outlines and the cant of the small head with its prick-eared cap showing out so clearly against the lighter sky behind.

When Chaddam looked again, he saw the thing on the bridge fling up its long arms and leap down on to the road some thirty feet below.

Then Chaddam rode. He began to think he had been a fool to come, and he counted that he was a good mile from home. At first he fancied he heard footfalls, then he fancied there were none. The hard road flew under him, all thoughts of economising his strength were lost, his single aim was to make the pace.

Suddenly his bicycle jerked violently, and he was shot over into the road. As he fell, he turned his head and was conscious of a little, bleached, bestial face, wet with fury, not ten yards behind!

He sprang to his feet, and ran up the road as he had never run before. He ran wonderfully, but he might as well have tried to race a cheetah. It was not a question of speed, the game was in the hands of this thing with the limbs of a starved Hercules, whose bony knees seemed to leap into its ghastly face at every stride. Chaddam topped the slope with a sickening sense of his powerlessness. Already he saw Low Riddings in the distance, and a dim light came creeping along the road towards him. Another frantic spurt, and he had almost reached the light, when a hand closed like a vice on his shoulder, and seemed to fasten on the flesh. He rushed blindly on towards the house. He saw the door-handle gleam, and in another second he had pitched head foremost on to the knotted matting in the hall.

When he recovered his senses, his first question was; 'Where is Low?'

'Didn't you meet him?' asked Livy. 'I – that is, we were anxious about you as you were so late, and I was just going to meet you when Mr Low came downstairs and insisted on going instead.'

Chaddam stood up.

'I must follow him.'

But as he spoke the front door opened, and Flaxman Low entered, and looked up at the clock.

'Eight-twenty,' he said. 'You're late, Chaddam.'

Afterwards in the smoking-room he gave an account of what he had seen.

'I saw Chaddam racing up the road with a tall figure behind him. It stretched out its hand and grasped his shoulder. The next instant it stopped short as if it had been shot. It seemed to reel back and collapse, and then limped off into the hedge like a disappointed dog.'

Chaddam stood up and began to take off his coat.

'Whatever the thing is, it is something out of the common. Look here!' he said, turning up his shirt sleeve over the point of his shoulder, where three singular marks were visible, irregularly placed as the fingers of a hand might fall. They were oblong in shape, about the size of a bean, and swollen in purple lumps well above the surface of the skin.

'Looks as if someone has been using a small cupping glass on you,' remarked the Colonel uneasily. 'What do you say to it, Low?'

'I say that since Chaddam has escaped with his life, I have only to congratulate him on what, in Europe certainly, is a unique adventure.'

The Colonel threw his cigar into the fire.

'Such adventures are too dangerous for my taste,' he said. 'This creature has on two occasions murderously attacked Lane Chaddam, and it would, no doubt, have attacked Livy if it had had the chance. We must leave this place at once, or we shall be murdered in our beds!'

'I don't think, Colonel, that you will be troubled with this mysterious visitant again,' replied Flaxman Low.

'Why not? Who or what is this horrible thing?'

'I believe it to be an Elemental Earth Spirit,' returned Low. 'No other solution fits the facts of the case.'

'What is an Elemental?' resumed the Colonel irritably. 'Remember, Low, I expect you to prove your theories so that a plain man may understand, if I am to stay on at Low Riddings.'

'Eastern occultists describe wandering tribes of earth spirits, evil intelligences, possessing spirit as distinct from soul – all inimical to man.'

'But how do you know that the thing on the Moor Road is an Elemental?'

'Because the points of resemblance are curiously remarkable. The occultists say that when these spirits materialise, they appear in grotesque and uncouth forms; secondly, that they are invariably bloodless and hairless; thirdly, they move with extraordinary rapidity, and leave no footprints; and, lastly, their agility and strength is superhuman. All these peculiarities have been observed in connection with the figure on the Moor Road.'

'I admit that no man I have ever met with,' commented Colonel Daimley, 'could jump uninjured from a height of 30 ft., race a bicycle, and twist up gun-barrels like so much soft paper. So, perhaps you're right. But can you tell me why or how it came here ?'

'My conclusions,' began Low, 'may seem to you far-fetched and ridiculous, but you must give them the benefit of the fact that they precisely account for the otherwise unaccountable features which mark this affair. I connect this appearance with the earthquake and the sick man.'

'What? Scully in league with the devil?' exclaimed the Colonel bluntly. 'Why, the man is too weak to leave his bed; besides, he is a short, thick-set fellow, entirely unlike our haunting friend.'

'You mistake me, Colonel,' said Low, in his quiet tones. 'These Elementals cannot take form without drawing upon the resources of the living. They absorb the vitality of any ailing person until it is exhausted, and the person dies.'

'Then they begin operations upon a fresh victim? A pleasant look-out to know we keep a well-attested vampire in the neighbourhood!'

'Vampires are a distinct race, with different methods; one being that the Elemental is a wanderer and goes far afield to search for a new victim.'

'But why should it want to kill me?' put in Chaddam.

'As I have told you, they are animated solely by a blind malignity to the human race, and you happened to be handy.'

'But the earthquake, Low; where is the connection there?' demanded the Colonel, with the air of a man who intends to corner his opponent.

Flaxman Low lit one cigar at the end of another before he replied.

'At this point,' he said, 'my own theories and observations and those of the old occultists overlap. The occultists held that some of these spirits are imprisoned in the interior of the earth, but may be set free in consequence of those shiftings and disturbances which take place during an earthquake. This in more modern language simply means that Elementals are in some manner connected with certain of the primary strata. Now, my own researches have led me to conclude that atmospheric influences are intimately associated with spiritual phenomena. Some gases appear to be productive of such phenomena. One of these is generated when certain of the primary formations are newly exposed to the common air.'

'This is almost beyond belief – I don't understand you,' said the Colonel.

'I am sorry that I cannot give you all the links in my chain of reasoning,' returned Low. 'Much is still obscure, but the evidence is sufficiently strong to convince me that in such a case of earthquake and landslip as has lately taken place here the phenomenon of an embodied Elemental might possibly be expected to follow, given the one necessary adjunct of a sick person in the near neighbourhood of the disturbance.'

'But when this brute got hold of me, why didn't it finish me off?' asked Chaddam. 'Or was it your coming that prevented it?'

Flaxman Low considered.

'No, I don't think I can flatter myself that my coming had anything to do with your escape. It was a near thing – how near you will understand when we hear further news of Scully in the morning.'

A servant entered the room at this moment.

'The woman has come up from the cottage, sir, to say that Scully is dead.'

'At what hour did he die?' asked Low.

'About ten minutes past eight, sir, she says.'

'The hour agrees exactly,' commented Low, when the man had left the room. 'The figure stopped and collapsed so suddenly that I believed something of this kind must have happened.'

'But surely this is a very unprecedented occurrence?'

'It is,' said Flaxman Low. 'Yet I can assure you that if you take the trouble to glance through the pages of the psychical periodicals you will find many statements at least as wonderful.'

'But are they true?'

Flaxman Low shrugged his shoulders.

'At any rate,' said he, 'we know this is.'

The Daimleys have spent many pleasant days at Low Riddings since then, but Chaddam – who has acquired a right to control Miss Livy's actions more or less – persists in his objection to any solitary expeditions to Nerbury along the Moor Road. For, although the figure has never been seen about Low Riddings since, some strange stories have lately appeared in the papers of a similar mysterious figure which has been met with more than once in the lonelier spots about North London. If it be true that this nameless wandering spirit, with the strength and activity of twenty men, still haunts our lonely roads, the sooner Mr Flaxman Low exorcises it the better.

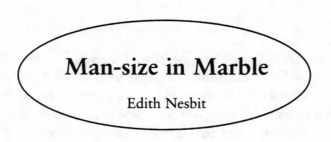

Man-size in Marble

Edith Nesbit

Although every word of this story is as true as despair, I do not expect people to believe it. Nowadays a 'rational explanation' is required before belief is possible. Let me, then, at once offer the 'rational explanation' which finds most favour among those who have heard the tale of my life's tragedy. It is held that we were 'under a delusion', Laura and I, on that 31st of October; and that this supposition places the whole matter on a satisfactory and believable basis. The reader can judge, when he, too, has heard my story, how far this is an 'explanation', and in what sense it is 'rational'. There were three who took part in this: Laura and I and another man. The other man still lives, and can speak to the truth of the least credible part of my story.

I never in my life knew what it was to have as much money as I required to supply the most ordinary needs – good colours, books, and cab-fares – and when we were married we knew quite well that we should only be able to live at all by 'strict punctuality and attention to business'. I used to paint in those days, and Laura used to write, and we felt sure we could keep the pot at least simmering. Living in town was out of the question, so we went to look for a cottage in the country, which should be at once sanitary and picturesque. So rarely do these two qualities meet in one cottage that our search was for some time quite fruitless. But when we got away from friends and house-agents, on our honeymoon, our wits grew clear again, and we knew a pretty cottage when at last we saw one.

It was at Brenzett – a little village set on a hill over against the southern marshes. We had gone there, from the seaside village where we were staying, to see the church, and two fields from the church we found this cottage. It stood quite by itself, about two miles from the village. It was a long, low building, with rooms sticking out in unexpected places. There was a bit of stonework – ivy-covered and moss-grown, just two old rooms, all that was left of a big house that had once stood there – and round this stonework the house had grown up. Stripped of its roses and jasmine it would have been hideous. As it stood it was charming, and after a brief examination we took it. It was absurdly cheap. There was a jolly old-fashioned garden, with grass paths, and no end of hollyhocks and sunflowers and big lilies. From the window you could see the marsh-pastures, and beyond them the blue, thin line of the sea.

We got a tall old peasant woman to do for us. Her face and figure were good, though her cooking was of the homeliest; but she understood all about gardening, and told us all the old names of the coppices and cornfields, and the stories of the smugglers and highwaymen, and, better still, of the 'things that walked', and of the 'sights' which met one in lonely glens of a starlight night. We soon came to leave all the domestic business to Mrs Dorman, and to use her legends in little magazine stories which brought in the jingling guinea.

We had three months of married happiness, and did not have a single quarrel. One October evening I had been down to smoke a pipe with the doctor – our only neighbour – a pleasant young Irishman. Laura had stayed at home to finish a comic sketch. I left her laughing over her own jokes, and came in to find her a crumpled heap of pale muslin, weeping on the window seat.

'Good heavens, my darling, what's the matter?' I cried, taking her in my arms. 'What is the matter? Do speak.'

'It's Mrs Dorman,' she sobbed.

'What has she done?' I enquired, immensely relieved.

'She says she must go before the end of the month, and she says her niece is ill; she's gone down to see her now, but I don't believe that's the reason, because her niece is always ill. I believe someone has been setting her against us. Her manner was so queer –'

'Never mind, Pussy,' I said; 'whatever you do, don't cry, or I shall have to cry too to keep you in countenance, and then you'll never respect your man again.'

'But you see,' she went on, 'it is really serious, because these village people are so sheepy, and if one won't do a thing you may be quite sure none of the others will. And I shall have to cook the dinners and wash up the hateful greasy plates; and you'll have to carry cans of water about and clean the boots and knives – and we shall never have any time for work or earn any money or anything.'

I represented to her that even if we had to perform these duties the day would still present some margin for other toils and recreations. But she refused to see the matter in any but the greyest light.

'I'll speak to Mrs Dorman when she comes back, and see if I can't come to terms with her,' I said. 'Perhaps she wants a rise. It will be all right. Let's walk up to the church.'

The church was a large and lonely one, and we loved to go there, especially upon bright nights. The path skirted a wood, cut through it once, and ran along the crest of the hill through two meadows, and round the churchyard wall, over which the old yews loomed in black masses of shadow.

This path, which was partly paved, was called 'the bierwalk', for it had long been the way by which the corpses had been carried to burial. The churchyard was richly treed, and was shaded by great elms which stood just outside and stretched their majestic arms in benediction over the happy dead. A large, low porch let one into the building by a Norman doorway and a heavy oak door studded with iron. Inside, the arches rose into darkness, and between them the reticulated windows, which stood out white in the moonlight. In the chancel, the windows were of rich glass, which showed in faint light their noble colouring, and made the black oak of the choir pews hardly more solid than the shadows. But on each side of the altar lay a grey marble figure of a knight in full plate armour lying upon a low slab, with hands held up in everlasting prayer, and these figures, oddly enough, were always to be seen if there was any glimmer of light in the church. Their names were lost, but the peasants told of them that they had been fierce and wicked men, marauders by land and sea, who had been the scourge of their time, and had been guilty of deeds so foul that the house they had lived in – the big house, by the way, that had stood on the site of our cottage – had been stricken by lightning and the vengeance of Heaven. But for all that, the gold of their heirs had bought them a place in the church. Looking at the bad, hard faces reproduced in the marble, this story was easily believed.

The church looked at its best and weirdest on that night, for the shadows of the yew trees fell through the windows upon the floor of the nave and touched the pillars with tattered shade. We sat down together without speaking, and watched the solemn beauty of the old church with some of the awe which inspired its early builders. We walked to the chancel and looked at the sleeping warriors. Then we rested some time on the stone seat in the porch, looking out over the stretch of quiet moonlit meadows, feeling in every fibre of our being the peace of the night and of our happy love; and came away at last with a sense that even scrubbing and black-leading were but small troubles at their worst.

Mrs Dorman had come back from the village, and I at once invited her to a tête-à-tête.

'Now, Mrs Dorman,' I said, when I had got her into my painting-room, 'what's all this about your not staying with us?'

'I should be glad to get away, sir, before the end of the month,' she answered, with her usual placid dignity.

'Have you any fault to find, Mrs Dorman?'

'None at all, sir: you and your lady have always been most kind, I'm sure –'

'Well, what is it? Are your wages not high enough?'

'No, sir, I gets quite enough.'

'Then why not stay?'

'I'd rather not' – with some hesitation – 'my niece is ill.'

'But your niece has been ill ever since we came. Can't you stay for another month?'

'No, sir, I'm bound to go by Thursday.'

And this was Monday!

'Well, I must say, I think you might have let us know before. There's no time now to get anyone else, and your mistress is not fit to do heavy housework. Can't you stay till next week?'

'I might be able to come back next week.'

'But why must you go this week?' I persisted. 'Come out with it.'

Mrs Dorman drew the little shawl, which she always wore, tightly across her bosom, as though she were cold. Then she said, with a sort of effort:

'They say, sir, as this was a big house in Catholic times, and there was a many deeds done here.'

The nature of the 'deeds' might be vaguely inferred from the inflection of Mrs Dorman's voice – which was enough to make one's blood run cold. I was glad that Laura was not in the room. She was always nervous, as highly strung natures are, and I felt that these tales about our house, told by this old peasant woman, with her impressive manner and contagious credulity, might have made our home less dear to my wife.

'Tell me all about it, Mrs Dorman,' I said; 'you needn't mind about telling me. I'm not like the young people who make fun of such things.'

Which was partly true.

'Well, sir' – she sank her voice – 'you may have seen in the church, beside the altar, two shapes.'

'You mean the effigies of the knights in armour,' I said cheerfully.

'I mean them two bodies, drawed out man-size in marble,' she returned, and I had to admit that her description was a thousand times more graphic than mine, to say nothing of a certain weird force and uncanniness about the phrase 'drawed out man-size in marble'.

'They do say, as on All Saints' Eve them two bodies sits up on their slabs, and gets off of them, and then walks down the aisle *in their marble*' – (another good phrase, Mrs Dorman) – 'and as the church clock strikes eleven they walks out of the church door, and over the graves, and along the bier-walk, and if it's a wet night there's the marks of their feet in the morning.'

'And where do they go?' I asked, rather fascinated.

'They comes back here to their home, sir, and if anyone meets them –'

'Well, what then?' I asked.

But no – not another word could I get from her, save that her niece was ill and she must go.

'Whatever you do, sir, lock the door early on All Saints' Eve, and make the cross-sign over the doorstep and on the windows.'

'But has anyone ever seen these things?' I persisted. 'Who was here last year?'

'No one, sir; the lady as owned the house only stayed here in summer, and she always went to London a full month afore the night. And I'm sorry to inconvenience you and your lady, but my niece is ill and I must go Thursday.'

I could have shaken her for her absurd reiteration of that obvious fiction, after she had told me her real reasons.

I did not tell Laura the legend of the shapes that 'walked in their marble', partly because a legend concerning our house might perhaps trouble my wife, and partly, I think, from some more occult reason. This was not quite the same to me as any other story, and I did not want to talk about it till the day was over. I had very soon ceased to think of the legend, however. I was painting a portrait of Laura, against the lattice window, and I could not think of much else. I had got a splendid background of yellow and grey sunset, and was working away with enthusiasm at her face. On Thursday, Mrs Dorman went. She relented, at parting, so far as to say:

'Don't you put yourself about too much, madam, and if there's any little thing I can do next week I'm sure I shan't mind.'

Thursday passed off pretty well. Friday came. It is about what happened on that Friday that this is written.

I got up early, I remember, and lighted the kitchen fire, and had just achieved a smoky success when my little wife came running down as sunny and sweet as the clear October morning itself. We prepared breakfast together, and found it very good fun. The housework was soon done, and when brushes and brooms and pails were quiet again the house was still indeed. It is wonderful what a difference one makes in a house. We really missed Mrs Dorman, quite apart from considerations concerning pots and pans. We spent the day in dusting our books and putting them straight, and dined on cold steak and coffee. Laura was, if possible, brighter and gayer and sweeter than usual, and I began to think that a little domestic toil was really good for her. We had never been so merry since we were married, and the walk we had that afternoon was, I think, the happiest time of all my life. When we had watched the deep scarlet clouds slowly pale into leaden grey against a pale green sky and saw the white mists curl up along the hedgerows in the distant marsh we came back to the house hand in hand.

'You are sad, my darling,' I said, half-jestingly, as we sat down together in our little parlour. I expected a disclaimer, for my own silence had been the silence of complete happiness. To my surprise she said:

'Yes, I think I am sad, or, rather, I am uneasy. I don't think I'm very well. I have shivered three or four times since we came in; and it is not cold, is it?'

'No,' I said, and hoped it was not a chill caught from the treacherous mists that roll up from the marshes in the dying night. No – she said, she did not think so. Then, after a silence, she spoke suddenly:

'Do you ever have presentiments of evil?'

'No,' I said, smiling, 'and I shouldn't believe in them if I had.'

'I do,' she went on, 'the night before my father died I knew it, though he was right away in the North of Scotland.' I did not answer in words.

She sat looking at the fire for some time in silence, gently stroking my hand. At last she sprang up, came behind me, and, drawing my head back, kissed me.

'There, it's over now,' she said. 'What a baby I am! Come, light the candles, and we'll have some of these new Rubinstein duets.'

And we spent a happy hour or two at the piano.

At about half-past ten I began to long for the good-night pipe, but Laura looked so white that I felt it would be brutal of me to fill our sitting-room with the fumes of strong cavendish.

'I'll take my pipe outside,' I said.

'Let me come, too.'

'No, sweetheart, not tonight; you're much too tired. I shan't be long. Get to bed, or I shall have an invalid to nurse tomorrow as well as the boots to clean.'

I kissed her and was turning to go when she flung her arms round my neck and held me as if she would never let me go again. I stroked her hair.

'Come, Pussy, you're over-tired. The housework has been too much for you.'

She loosened her clasp a little and drew a deep breath.

'No. We've been very happy today, Jack, haven't we? Don't stay out too long.'

'I won't, my dearie.'

I strolled out of the front door, leaving it unlatched. What a night it was! The jagged masses of heavy dark cloud were rolling at intervals from horizon to horizon, and thin white wreaths covered the stars. Through all the rush of the cloud river the moon swam, breasting the waves and disappearing again in the darkness.

I walked up and down, drinking in the beauty of the quiet earth and the changing sky. The night was absolutely silent. Nothing seemed to be abroad. There was no scurrying of rabbits, or twitter of the half-asleep birds. And though the clouds went sailing across the sky, the wind that drove them never came low enough to rustle the dead leaves in the woodland paths. Across the meadows I could see the church tower standing out black and grey against the sky. I walked there thinking over our three months of happiness.

I heard a bell-beat from the church. Eleven already! I turned to go in, but the night held me. I could not go back into our warm rooms yet. I would go up to the church.

I looked in at the low window as I went by. Laura was half lying on her chair in front of the fire. I could not see her face, only her little head showed dark against the pale blue wall. She was quite still. Asleep, no doubt. I walked slowly along the edge of the wood. A sound broke the stillness of the night, it was a rustling in the wood. I stopped and listened. The sound stopped too. I went on, and now distinctly heard another step than mine answer mine like an echo. It was a poacher or a wood-stealer, most likely, for these were not unknown in our Arcadia neighbourhood. But, whoever it was, he was a fool not to step more lightly. I turned into the wood and now the footstep seemed to come from the path I had just left. It must be an echo, I thought. The wood looked perfect in the moonlight. The large dying ferns and the brushwood showed where through thinning foliage the pale light came down. The tree trunks stood up like Gothic columns all around me: They reminded me of the church, and I turned into the bier-walk, and passed through the corpse-gate between the graves to the low porch.

I paused for a moment on the stone seat where Laura and I had watched the fading landscape. Then I noticed that the door of the church was open, and I blamed myself for having left it unlatched the other night. We were the only people who ever cared to come to the church except on Sundays, and I was vexed to think that through our carelessness the damp autumn airs had had a chance of getting in and injuring the old fabric. I went in. It will seem strange, perhaps, that I should have gone half-way up the aisle before I remembered with a sudden chill, followed by a sudden rush of self-contempt – that this was the very day and hour when, according to tradition, the 'shapes drawed out man-size in marble' began to walk.

Having thus remembered the legend, and remembered it with a shiver, of which I was ashamed, I could not do otherwise than walk up towards the altar, just to look at the figures – as I said to myself; really what I wanted was to assure myself, first, that I did not believe the legend, and secondly, that it was not true. I was rather glad that I had come. I thought now I could tell Mrs Dorman how vain her fancies were, and how peacefully the marble figures slept on through the ghastly hour. With my hands in my pockets I passed up the aisle. In the grey dim light the eastern end of the church looked larger than usual, and the arches above the two tombs looked larger too. The moon came out and showed me the reason. I stopped short, my heart gave a leap that nearly choked me, and then sank sickeningly.

The 'bodies drawed out man-size' were gone! and their marble slabs lay wide and bare in the vague moonlight that slanted through the east window.

Were they really gone, or was I mad? Clenching my nerves, I stooped and passed my hand over the smooth slabs and felt their flat unbroken surface. Had someone taken the things away? Was it some vile practical joke? I would make sure, anyway. In an instant I had made a torch of newspaper, which happened to be in my pocket, and, lighting it, held it high above my head. Its yellow glare illumined the dark arches and those slabs. The figures were gone. And I was alone in the church; or was I alone?

And then a horror seized me, a horror indefinable and indescribable – an overwhelming certainty of supreme and accomplished calamity. I flung down the torch and tore along the aisle and out through the porch, biting my lips as I ran to keep myself from shrieking aloud. Oh, was I mad – or what was this that possessed me? I leaped the churchyard wall and took the straight cut across the fields, led by the light from our windows. Just as I got over the first stile a dark figure seemed to spring out of the ground. Mad still with that certainty of misfortune, I made for the thing that stood in my path, shouting, 'Get out of the way, can't you!'

But my push met with a more vigorous resistance than I had expected. My arms were caught just above the elbow and held as in a vice, and the raw-boned Irish doctor actually shook me.

'Let me go, you fool,' I gasped. 'The marble figures have gone from the church; I tell you they've gone.'

He broke into a ringing laugh. 'I'll have to give you a draught tomorrow, I see. Ye've bin smoking too much and listening to old wives' tales.'

'I tell you, I've seen the bare slabs.'

'Well, come back with me. I'm going up to old Palmer's – his daughter's ill; we'll look in at the church and let me see the bare slabs.'

'You go, if you like,' I said, a little less frantic for his laughter; 'I'm going home to my wife.'

'Rubbish, man,' said he; 'd'ye think I'll permit of that? Are ye to go saying all yer life that ye've seen solid marble endowed with vitality, and me to go all me life saying ye were a coward? No, sir – ye shan't do ut.'

The night air – a human voice – and I think also the physical contact with this six feet of solid common sense, brought me back to my ordinary self, and the word 'coward' was a mental shower-bath.

'Come on, then.' I said sullenly; 'perhaps you're right.'

He still held my arm tightly. We got over the stile and back to the church. All was still as death. The place smelt very damp and earthly. We walked up the aisle. I am not ashamed to confess that I shut my eyes: I knew the figures would not be there. I heard Kelly strike a match.

'Here they are, ye see, right enough; ye've been dreaming or drinking, asking yer pardon for the imputation.'

I opened my eyes. By Kelly's expiring vesta I saw two shapes lying 'in their marble' on their slabs. I drew a deep breath.

'I'm awfully indebted to you,' I said. 'It must have been some trick of light, or I have been working rather hard, perhaps that's it. I was quite convinced they were gone.'

'I'm aware of that,' he answered rather grimly; 'ye'll have to be careful of that brain of yours, my friend, I assure ye.'

He was leaning over and looking at the right-hand figure, whose stony face was the most villainous and deadly in expression.

'By Jove,' he said, 'something has been afoot here – this hand is broken.'

And so it was. I was certain that it had been perfect the last time Laura and I had been there.

'Perhaps someone has tried to remove them,' said the young doctor.

'Come along,' I said, 'or my wife will be getting anxious. You'll come in and have a drop of whisky and drink confusion to ghosts and better sense to me.'

'I ought to go up to Palmer's, but it's so late now I'd best leave it till the morning,' he replied.

I think he fancied I needed him more than did Palmer's girl, so, discussing how such an illusion could have been possible, and deducing from this experience large generalities concerning ghostly apparitions, we walked up to our cottage. We saw, as we walked up the garden path, that bright light streamed out of the front door, and presently saw that the parlour door was open, too. Had she gone out?

'Come in,' I said, and Dr Kelly followed me into the parlour. It was all ablaze with candles, not only the wax ones, but at least a dozen guttering, glaring tallow dips, stuck in vases and ornaments in unlikely places. Light, I knew, was Laura's remedy for nervousness. Poor child! Why had I left her? Brute that I was.

We glanced round the room, and at first we did not see her. The window was open, and the draught set all the candles flaring one way. Her chair was empty and her handkerchief and book lay on the floor. I turned to the window. There, in the recess of the window, I saw her. Oh, my child, my love, had she gone to that window to watch for me? And what had come into the room behind her? To what had she turned with that look of frantic fear and horror? Oh, my little one, had she thought that it was I whose step she heard, and turned to meet – what'?

She had fallen back across a table in the window, and her body lay half on it, and half on the window-seat, and her head hung down over the table, the brown hair loosened and fallen to the carpet. Her lips were drawn back, and her eyes wide open. They saw nothing now. What had they seen last?

The doctor moved towards her, but I pushed him aside and sprang to her, caught her in my arms and cried:

'It's all right, Laura! I've got you safe, wife.'

She fell into my arms in a heap. I clasped her and kissed her, and called her by pet names, but I think I knew all the time that she was dead. Her hands were tightly clenched. In one of them she held something fast. When I was quite sure that she was dead, and that nothing mattered at all any more, I let him open her hand to see what she held.

It was a grey marble finger.

The Last of Squire Ennismore

Mrs. J. H. Riddell

"Did I see it myself? No, sir; I did not see it; and my father before me did not see it; nor his father before him, and he was Phil Regan, just the same as myself. But it is true, for all that; just as true as that you are looking at the very place where the whole thing happened. My great-grandfather (and he did not die till he was ninety-eight) used to tell, many and many's the time, how he met the stranger, night after night, walking lonesome-like about the sands where most of the wreckage came ashore."

"And the old house, then, stood behind that belt of Scotch firs?"

"Yes; and a fine house it was, too. Hearing so much talk about it when a boy, my father said, made him often feel as if he knew every room in the building, though it had all fallen to ruin before he was born. None of the family ever lived in it after the squire went away. Nobody else could be got to stop in the place. There used to be awful noises, as if something was being pitched from the top of the great staircase down in to the hall; and then there would be a sound as if a hundred people were clinking glasses and talking all together at once. And then it seemed as if barrels were rolling in the cellars; and there would be screeches, and howls, and laughing, fit to make your blood run cold. They say there is gold hid away in the cellars; but not one has ever ventured to find it. The very children won't come here to play; and when the men are plowing the field behind, nothing will make them stay in it, once the day begins to change. When the night is coming on, and the tide creeps in on the sand, more than one thinks he has seen mighty queer things on the shore."

"But what is it really they think they see? When I asked my landlord to tell me the story from beginning to end he said he could not remember it; and, at any rate, the whole rigmarole was nonsense, put together to please strangers."

"And what is he but a stranger himself? And how should he know the doings of real quality like the Ennismores? For they were gentry, every one of them – good old stock; and as for wickedness, you might have searched Ireland through and not found their match. It is a sure thing, though, that if Riley can't tell you the story, I can; for, as I said, my own people were in it, of a manner of speaking. So, if your honour will rest yourself off your feet, on that bit of a bank, I'll set down my creel and give you the whole pedigree of how Squire Ennismore went away from Ardwinsagh."

It was a lovely day, in the early part of June; and, as the Englishman cast himself on a low ridge of sand, he looked over Ardwinsagh Bay with a feeling of ineffable content. To his left lay the Purple Headland; to his right, a long range of breakers, that went straight out into the Atlantic till they were lost from sight; in front lay the Bay of Ardwinsagh, with its bluish-green water sparkling in the summer sunlight, and here and there breaking over some sunken rock, against which the waves spent themselves in foam.

"You see how the current is set, Sir? That is what makes it dangerous for them as doesn't know the coast, to bathe here at any time, or walk when the tide is flowing. Look how the sea is creeping in now, like a race-horse at the finish. It leaves that tongue of sand bars to the last, and then, before you could look round, it has you up to the middle. That is why I made bold to speak to you; for it is not alone on the account of Squire Ennismore the bay has a bad name. But it is about him and the old house you want to hear. The last mortal being that tried to live in it, my great-grandfather said, was a creature, by name Molly Leary; and she had neither kith nor kin, and begged for her bite and sup, sheltering herself at night in a turf cabin she had built at the back of a ditch. You may be sure she thought herself a made woman when the agent said, 'Yes: she might try if she could stop in the house; there was peat and bog-wood', he told her, 'and half-a-crown a week for the winter, and a golden guinea once Easter came', when the house was to be put in order for the family; and his wife gave Molly some warm clothes and a blanket or two; and she was well set up.

"You may be sure she didn't choose the worst room to sleep in; and for a while all went quiet, till one night she was wakened by feeling the bedstead lifted by the four corners and shaken like a carpet. It was a heavy four-post bedstead, with a solid top: and her life seemed to go out of her with the fear. If it had been a ship in a storm off the Headland, it couldn't have pitched worse and then, all of a sudden, it was dropped with such a bang as nearly drove the heart into her mouth.

"But that, she said, was nothing to the screaming and laughing, and hustling and rushing that filled the house. If a hundred people had been running hard along the passages and tumbling downstairs, they could not have made greater noise.

"Molly never was able to tell how she got clear of the place; but a man coming late home from Ballyclone Fair found the creature crouched under the old thorn there, with very little on her – saving your honour's presence. She had a bad fever, and talked about strange things, and never was the same woman after."

"But what was the beginning of all this? When did the house first get the name of being haunted?"

"After the old Squire went away: that was what I purposed telling you. He did not come here to live regularly till he had got well on in years. He was near seventy at the time I am talking about; but he held himself as upright as ever, and rode as hard as the youngest; and could have drunk a whole roomful under the table, and walked up to bed as unconcerned as you please at the dead of the night.

"He was a terrible man. You couldn't lay your tongue to a wickedness he had not been in the forefront of – drinking, duelling, gambling, – all manner of sins had been meat and drink to him since he was a boy almost. But at last he did something in London so bad, so beyond the beyond, that he thought he had best come home and live among people who did not know so much about his goings on as the English. It was said that he wanted to try and stay in this world for ever; and that he had got some secret drops that kept him well and hearty. There was something wonderful queer about him, anyhow.

"He could hold foot with the youngest; and he was strong, and had a fine fresh colour in his face; and his eyes were like a hawk's; and there was not a break in his voice – and him near upon threescore and ten!

"At last and at long last it came to be the March before he was seventy – the worst March ever known in all these parts – such blowing, sleeting, snowing, had not been experienced in the memory of man; when one blusterous night some foreign vessel went to bits on the

Purple Headland. They say it was an awful sound to hear the death-cry that went up high above the noise of the wind; and it was as bad a sight to see the shore there strewed with corpses of all sorts and sizes, from the little cabin-boy to the grizzled seaman.

"They never knew who they were or where they came from, but some of the men had crosses, and beads, and such like, so the priest said they belonged to him, and they were all buried deeply and decently in the chapel graveyard.

"There was not much wreckage of value drifted on shore. Most of what is lost about the head stays there; but one thing did come into the bay – a puncheon of brandy.

"The Squire claimed it; it was his right to have all that came on his land, and he owned this sea-shore from the head to the breakers – every foot – so, in course, he had the brandy; and there was sore illwill because he gave his men nothing, not even a glass of whiskey.

"Well, to make a long story short, that was the most wonderful liquor anybody ever tasted. The gentry came from far and near to take share, and it was cards and dice, and drinking and story-telling night after night – week in, week out. Even on Sundays, God forgive them! The officers would drive over from Ballyclone, and sit emptying tumbler after tumbler till Monday morning came, for it made beautiful punch.

"But all at once people quit coming – a word went round that the liquor was not all it ought to be. Nobody could say what ailed it, but it got about that in some way men found it did not suit them.

"For one thing, they were losing money very fast.

"They could not make head against the Squire's luck, and a hint was dropped the puncheon ought to have been towed out to sea, and sunk in fifty fathoms of water.

"It was getting to the end of April, and fine, warm weather for the time of year, when first one and then another, and then another still, began to take notice of a stranger who walked the shore alone at night. He was a dark man, the same colour as the drowned crew lying in the chapel graveyard, and had rings in his ears, and wore a strange kind of hat, and cut wonderful antics as he walked, and had an ambling sort of gait, curious to look at. Many tried to talk to him, but he only shook his head; so, as nobody could make out where he came from or what he wanted, they made sure he was the spirit of some poor wretch who was tossing about the Head, longing for a snug corner in holy ground.

"The priest went and tried to get some sense out of him.

" 'Is it Christian burial you're wanting?' " asked his reverence; but the creature only shook his head.

" 'Is it word sent to the wives and daughters you've left orphans and widows, you'd like?' But no; it wasn't that.

" 'Is it for sin committed you're doomed to walk this way? Would masses comfort ye? There's a heathen,' said his reverence; 'Did you ever hear tell of a Christian that shook his head when masses were mentioned?'

" 'Perhaps he doesn't understand English, Father', says one of the officers who was there; 'Try him with Latin.'

"No sooner said than done. The priest started off with such a string of *aves* and *paters* that the stranger fairly took to his heels and ran.

" 'He is an evil spirit', explained the priest, when he stopped, tired out, 'and I have exorcised him'.

"But next night my gentleman was back again, as unconcerned as ever.

" 'And he'll just have to stay,' said his reverence, 'for I've got lumbago in the small of my back, and pains in all my joints – never to speak of a hoarseness with standing there shouting; and I don't believe he understood a sentence I said.'

"Well, this went on for a while, and people got that frightened of the man, or appearance of a man, they would not go near the sand; till in the end, Squire Ennismore, who had always scoffed at the talk, took it into his head he would go down one night, and see into the rights of the matter. He, maybe, was feeling lonesome, because, as I told your honour before, people had left off coming to the house, and there was nobody for him to drink with.

"Out he goes, then, bold as brass; and there were a few followed him. The man came forward at sight of the Squire and took off his hat with a foreign flourish. Not to be behind in civility, the Squire lifted his.

" 'I have come, sir,' he said, speaking very loud, to try to make him understand, 'to know if you are looking for anything, and whether I can assist you to find it.'

"The man looked at the Squire as if he had taken the greatest liking to him, and took off his hat again.

" 'Is it the vessel that was wrecked you are distressed about?'

"There came no answer, only a mournful shake of the head.

" 'Well, I haven't your ship, you know; it went all to bits months ago; and, as for the sailors, they are snug and sound enough in consecrated ground.'

"The man stood and looked at the Squire with a queer sort of smile on his face.

" 'What do you want?' asked Mr Ennismore in a bit of a passion. 'If anything belonging to you went down with the vessel, it's about the Head you ought to be looking for it, not here – unless, indeed, it's after the brandy you're fretting!'

"Now, the Squire had tried him in English and French, and was now speaking a language you'd have thought nobody could understand; but, faith, it seemed natural as kissing to the stranger.

" 'Oh! That's where you are from, is it?' said the Squire. 'Why couldn't you have told me so at once? I can't give you the brandy, because it mostly is drunk; but come along, and you shall have as stiff a glass of punch as ever crossed your lips.' And without more to-do, off they went, as sociable as you please, jabbering together in some outlandish tongue that made moderate folks' jaws ache to hear it.

"That was the first night they conversed together, but it wasn't the last. The stranger must have been the height of good company, for the Squire never tired of him. Every evening, regularly, he came up to the house, always dressed the same, always smiling and polite, and then the Squire called for brandy and hot water, and they drank and played cards till cock-crow, talking and laughing into the small hours.

"This went on for weeks and weeks, nobody knowing where the man came from, or where he went; only two things the old housekeeper did know – that the puncheon was nearly empty, and that the Squire's flesh was wasting off him; and she felt so uneasy she went to the priest, but he could give her no manner of comfort.

"She got so concerned at last that she felt bound to listen at the dining-room door; but they always talked in that foreign gibberish, and whether it was blessing or cursing they were at she couldn't tell.

"Well, the upshot of it came one night in July on the eve of the Squire's birthday – there wasn't a drop of spirit left in the puncheon – no, not as much as would drown a fly. They had drunk the whole lot clean up – and the old woman stood trembling, expecting every minute to hear the bell ring for more brandy, for where was she to get more if they wanted any?

"All at once the Squire and the stranger came out into the hall. It was a full moon, and light as day.

" 'I'll go home with you to-night by way of a change', says the Squire.

" 'Will you so?' asked the other.

" 'That I will', answered the Squire.

" 'It is your own choice, you know.'

" 'Yes; it is my own choice; let us go.'

"So they went. And the housekeeper ran up to the window on the great staircase and watched the way they took. Her niece lived there as housemaid, and she came and watched, too; and, after a while, the butler as well. They all turned their faces this way, and looked after their master walking beside the strange man along these very sands. Well, they saw them walk on, and on, and on, and on, till the water took them to their knees, and then to their waists, and then to their arm-pits, and then to their throats and their heads; but long before that the women and the butler were running out on the shore as fast as they could, shouting for help."

"Well?" said the Englishman.

"Living or dead, Squire Ennismore never came back again. Next morning, when the tides ebbed again, one walking over the sand saw the print of a cloven foot – that he tracked to the water's edge. Then everybody knew where the Squire had gone, and with whom."

"And no more search was made?"

"Where would have been the use searching?"

"Not much, I suppose. It's a strange story, anyhow."

"But true, your honour – every word of it."

"Oh! I have no doubt of that," was the satisfactory reply.

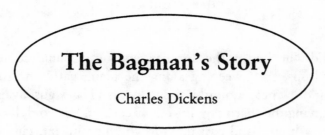

The Bagman's Story

Charles Dickens

'One winter's evening, about five o'clock, just as it began to grow dusk, a man in a gig might have been seen urging his tired horse along the road which leads across Marlborough Downs, in the direction of Bristol. I say he might have been seen, and I have no doubt he would have been, if anybody but a blind man had happened to pass that way; but the weather was so bad, and the night so cold and wet, that nothing was out but the water, and so the traveller jogged along in the middle of the road, lonesome and dreary enough. If any bagman of that day could have caught sight of the little neck-or-nothing sort of gig, with a clay-coloured body and red wheels, and the vixenish ill-tempered, fast-going bay mare, that looked like a cross between a butcher's horse and a two-penny post-office pony, he would have known at once, that this traveller could have been no other than Tom Smart, of the great house of Bilson and Slum, Cateaton Street, City. However, as there was no bagman to look on, nobody knew anything at all about the matter; and so Tom Smart and his clay-coloured gig with the red wheels, and the vixenish mare with the fast pace, went on together, keeping the secret among them: and nobody was a bit the wiser.

'There are many pleasanter places even in this dreary world, than Marlborough Downs when it blows hard; and if you throw in beside, a gloomy winter's evening, a miry and sloppy road, and a pelting fall of heavy rain, and try the effect, by way of experiment, in your own proper person, you will experience the full force of this observation.

'The wind blew – not up the road or down it, though that's bad enough, but sheer across it, sending the rain slanting down like the lines they used to rule in the copybooks at school, to make the boys slope well. For a moment it would die away, and the traveller would begin to delude himself into the belief that, exhausted with its previous fury, it had quietly lain itself down to rest, when, Whoo! he would hear it growling and whistling in the distance, and on it would come rushing over the hilltops, and sweeping along the plain, gathering sound and strength as it drew nearer, until it dashed with a heavy gust against horse and man, driving the sharp rain into their ears, and its cold damp breath into their very bones; and past them it would scour, far, far away, with a stunning roar, as if in ridicule of their weakness, and triumphant in the consciousness of its own strength and power.

'The bay mare splashed away, through the mud and water, with drooping ears; now and then tossing her head as if to express her disgust at this very ungentlemanly behaviour of the elements, but keeping a good pace notwithstanding, until a gust of wind, more furious than any that had yet assailed them, caused her to stop suddenly and plant her four feet firmly against the ground, to prevent her being blown over. It's a special mercy that she did this, for if she had been blown over, the vixenish mare was so light, and the gig was so light, and Tom Smart such a light weight into the bargain, that they must infallibly have all gone rolling over and over together, until they reached the confines of earth, or until the wind fell; and in either case the probability is, that neither the vixenish mare, nor the clay-coloured gig with the red wheels, nor Tom Smart, would ever have been fit for service again.

' "Well, damn my straps and whiskers," says Tom Smart (Tom sometimes had an unpleasant knack of swearing), "Damn my straps and whiskers," says Tom, "if this ain't pleasant, blow me!"

'You'll very likely ask me why, as Tom Smart had been pretty well blown already, he expressed this wish to be submitted to the same process again. I can't say – all I know is, that Tom Smart said so – or at least he always told my uncle he said so, and it's just the same thing.

' "Blow me," says Tom Smart; and the mare neighed as if she were precisely of the same opinion.

' "Cheer up, old girl," said Tom, patting the bay mare on the neck with the end of his whip. "It won't do pushing on, such a night as this; the first house we come to we'll put up at, so the faster you go the sooner it's over. Soho, old girl – gently – gently."

'Whether the vixenish mare was sufficiently well acquainted with the tones of Tom's voice to comprehend his meaning, or whether she found it colder standing still than moving on, of course I can't say. But I can say that Tom had no sooner finished speaking, than she pricked up her ears, and started forward at a speed which made the clay-coloured gig rattle till you would have supposed every one of the red spokes were going to fly out on the turf of Marlborough Downs; and even Tom, whip as he was, couldn't stop or check her pace, until she drew up, of her own accord, before a roadside inn on the right-hand side of the way, about half a quarter of a mile from the end of the Downs.

'Tom cast a hasty glance at the upper part of the house as he threw the reins to the hostler, and stuck the whip in the box. It was a strange old place, built of a kind of shingle, inlaid, as it were, with cross-beams, with gabled-topped windows projecting completely over the pathway, and a low door with a dark porch, and a couple of steep steps leading down into the house, instead of the modern fashion of a half a dozen ones leading up to it. It was a comfortable-looking place though, for there was a strong cheerful light in the bar-window, which shed a bright ray across the road, and even lighted up the hedges on the other side, and there was a red flickering light in the opposite window, one moment but faintly discernible, and the next gleaming strongly through the drawn curtains, which intimated that a rousing fire was blazing within. Marking these little evidences with the eye of an experienced traveller, Tom dismounted with as much agility as his half-frozen limbs would permit, and entered the house.

'In less than five minutes' time, Tom was ensconced in the room opposite the bar – the very room where he had imagined the fire blazing – before a substantial matter-of-fact roaring fire, composed of something short of a bushel of coals, and wood enough to make half a dozen decent gooseberry bushes, piled half way up the chimney, and roaring and crackling with a sound that of itself would have warmed the heart of any reasonable man. This was comfortable, but this was not all, for a smartly dressed girl, with a bright eye and a neat ankle, was laying a very clean white cloth on the table; and as Tom sat with his slippered feet on the fender, and his back to the open door, he saw a charming prospect of the bar reflected in the glass over the chimney-piece, with delightful rows of green bottles and gold labels, together with jars of pickles and preserves, and cheeses and boiled hams, and rounds of beef, arranged on shelves in the most tempting and delicious array. Well, this was comfortable too; but even this was not all – for in the bar, seated at tea at the nicest possible little table, drawn close up before the brightest possible little fire, was a buxom widow of somewhere about eight and forty or thereabouts, with a face as comfortable as the bar, who was evidently the landlady of the house, and the supreme ruler over all these agreeable possessions. There was only one drawback to the beauty of the whole picture, and that was a tall man – a very tall man – in a brown coat and bright basket buttons, and black whiskers, and wavy black hair, who was seated at tea with the widow, and who it required no great penetration to discover was in a fair way of persuading her to be a widow no longer, but to confer upon him the privilege of sitting down in that bar, for and during the whole remainder of the term of his natural life.

'Tom Smart was by no means of an irritable or envious disposition, but somehow or other the tall man with the brown coat and the bright basket buttons did rouse what little gall he had in his composition, and did make him feel extremely indignant: the more especially as he could now and then observe, from his seat before the glass, certain little affectionate familiarities passing between the tall man and the widow, which sufficiently denoted that the tall man was as high in favour as he was in size. Tom was fond of hot punch – I may venture to say he was very fond of hot punch – and after he had seen the vixenish mare well fed and well littered down, and had eaten every bit of the nice little hot dinner which the widow tossed up for him with her own hands, he just ordered a tumbler of it, by way of experiment. Now, if there was one thing in the whole range of domestic art, which the widow could manufacture better than another, it was this identical article; and the first tumbler was adapted to Tom Smart's taste with such peculiar nicety, that he ordered a second with the least possible delay. Hot punch is a pleasant thing, gentlemen – an extremely pleasant thing under any circumstances – but in that snug old parlour, before the roaring fire, with the wind blowing outside till every timber in the old house creaked again, Tom Smart found it perfectly delightful. He ordered another tumbler, and then another – I am not quite certain whether he didn't order another after that – but the more he drank of the hot punch, the more he thought of the tall man.

' "Confound his impudence !" said Tom to himself, "what business has he in that snug bar? Such an ugly villain too!" said Tom. "If the widow had any taste, she might surely pick up some better fellow than that." Here Tom's eye wandered from the glass on the chimney-piece, to the glass on the table; and as he felt himself becoming gradually sentimental, he emptied the fourth tumbler of punch and ordered a fifth.

'Tom Smart, gentlemen, had always been very much attached to the public line. It had long been his ambition to stand in a bar of his own, in a green coat, knee-cords, and tops. He had a great notion of taking the chair at convivial dinners, and he had often thought how well he could preside in a room of his own in the talking way, and what a capital example he could set to his customers in the drinking department. All these things passed rapidly through Tom's mind as he sat drinking the hot punch by the roaring fire, and he felt very justly and properly indignant that the tall man should be in a fair way of keeping such an excellent house, while he, Tom Smart, was as far off from it as ever. So, after deliberating over the two last tumblers, whether he hadn't a perfect right to pick a quarrel with the tall man for having contrived to get into the good graces of the buxom widow, Tom Smart at last arrived at the satisfactory conclusion that he was a very ill-used and persecuted individual, and had better go to bed.

'Up a wide and ancient staircase the smart girl preceded Tom, shading the chamber candle with her hand, to protect it from the currents of air which in such a rambling old place might have found plenty of room to disport themselves in, without blowing the candle out, but which did blow it out nevertheless; thus affording Tom's enemies an opportunity of asserting that it was he, and not the wind, who extinguished the candle, and that while he pretended to be blowing it a-light again, he was in fact kissing the girl. Be this as it may, another light was obtained, and Tom was conducted through a maze of rooms, and a labyrinth of passages, to the apartment which had been prepared for his reception, where the girl bade him good night, and left him alone.

'It was a good large room with big closets, and a bed which might have served for a whole boarding-school, to say nothing of a couple of oaken presses that would have held the baggage of a small army; but what struck Tom's fancy most was a strange, grim-looking high-backed chair, carved in the most fantastic manner, with a flowered damask cushion, and the round knobs at the bottom of the legs carefully tied up in red cloth, as if it had got the gout in its toes. Of any other queer chair,

Tom would only have thought it was a queer chair, and there would have been an end of the matter; but there was something about this particular chair, and yet he couldn't tell what it was, so odd and so unlike any other piece of furniture he had ever seen, that it seemed to fascinate him. He sat down before the fire, and stared at the old chair for half an hour;— Deuce take the chair, it was such a strange old thing, he couldn't take his eyes off it.

' "Well," said Tom, slowly undressing himself, and staring at the old chair all the while, which stood with a mysterious aspect by the bedside, "I never saw such a rum concern as that in my days. Very odd," said Tom, who had got rather sage with the hot punch, "Very odd." Tom shook his head with an air of profound wisdom, and looked at the chair again. He couldn't make anything of it though, so he got into bed, covered himself up warm, and fell asleep.

'In about half an hour, Tom woke up, with a start, from a confused dream of tall men and tumblers of punch: and the first object that presented itself to his waking imagination was the queer chair. ' "I won't look at it any more,' said Tom to himself, and he squeezed his eyelids together, and tried to persuade himself he was going to sleep again. No use; nothing but queer chairs danced before his eyes, kicking up their legs, jumping over each other's backs, and playing all kinds of antics.

' "I may as well see one real chair, as two or three complete sets of false ones," said Tom, bringing out his head from under the bed-clothes. There it was, plainly discernible by the light of the fire, looking as provoking as ever.

'Tom gazed at the chair; and, suddenly, as he looked at it, a most extraordinary change seemed to come over it. The carving of the back gradually assumed the lineaments and expression of an old shrivelled human face;the damask cushion became an antique, flapped waistcoat; the round knobs grew into a couple of feet, encased in red cloth slippers; and the old chair looked like a very ugly old man, of the previous century, with his arms a-kimbo. Tom sat up in bed, and rubbed his eyes to dispel the illusion. No. The chair was an ugly old gentleman; and what was more, he was winking at Tom Smart.

'Tom was naturally a headlong, careless sort of dog, and he had had five tumblers of hot punch into the bargain; so, although he was a little startled at first, he began to grow rather indignant when he saw the old gentleman winking and leering at him with such an impudent air. At length he resolved that he wouldn't stand it; and as the old face still kept winking away as fast as ever, Tom said, in a very angry tone:

' "What the devil are you winking at me for?"

' "Because I like it, Tom Smart," said the chair; or the old gentleman, whichever you like to call him. He stopped winking though, when Tom spoke, and began grinning like a superannuated monkey.

' "How do you know my name, old nut-cracker face!" inquired Tom Smart, rather staggered; – though he pretended to carry it off so well.

' "Come, come, Tom," said the old gentleman, "that's not the way to address solid Spanish Mahogany. Dam'me, you couldn't treat me with less respect if I was veneered." When the old gentleman said this, he looked so fierce that Tom began to grow frightened.

' "I didn't mean to treat you with any disrespect, sir," said Tom; in a much humbler tone than he had spoken in at first.

' "Well, well," said the old fellow, "perhaps not — perhaps not. Tom . . ."

' "Sir . . ."

' "I know everything about you, Tom; everything. You're very poor, Tom."

' "I certainly am," said Tom Smart. "But how came you to know that?"

' "Never mind that," said the old gentleman; "you're much too fond of punch, Tom."

'Tom Smart was just on the point of protesting that he hadn't tasted a drop since his last birthday, but when his eye encountered that of the old gentleman, he looked so knowing that Tom blushed, and was silent.

' "Tom," said the old gentleman, "the widow's a fine woman – remarkably fine woman – eh, Tom?" Here the old fellow screwed up his eyes, cocked up one of his wasted little legs, and looked altogether so unpleasantly amorous, that Tom was quite disgusted with the levity of his behaviour; – at his time of life, too!

' "I am her guardian, Tom," said the old gentleman.

' "Are you?" inquired Tom Smart.

' "I knew her mother, Tom," said the old fellow; "and her grandmother. She was very fond of me – made me this waistcoat, Tom."

' "Did she?" said Tom Smart.

' "And these shoes," said the old fellow, lifting up one of the red-cloth mufflers; "but don't mention it, Tom. I shouldn't like to have it known that she was so much attached to me. It might occasion some unpleasantness in the family." When the old rascal said this, he looked so extremely impertinent, that, as Tom Smart afterwards declared, he could have sat upon him without remorse.

' "I have been a great favourite among the women in my time, Tom," said the profligate old debaucher; "hundreds of fine women have sat in my lap for hours together. What do you think of that you dog, eh!" The old gentleman was proceeding to recount some other exploits of his youth, when he was seized with such a violent fit of creaking that he was unable to proceed.

' "Just served you right, old boy," thought Tom Smart; but he didn't say anything.

' "Ah!" said the old fellow, "I am a good deal troubled with this now. I am getting old, Tom, and have lost nearly all my rails. I have had an operation performed, too – a small piece let into my back – and I found it a severe trial, Tom."

' "I dare say you did, sir," said Tom Smart.

' "However", said the old gentleman, "that's not the point. Tom! I want you to marry the widow."

' "Me, sir!" said Tom.

' "You," said the old gentleman.

' "Bless your reverend locks," said Tom – (he had a few scattered horse-hairs left) – "bless your reverend locks, she wouldn't have me." And Tom sighed involuntarily, as he thought of the bar.

' "Wouldn't she?" said the old gentleman, firmly.

' "No, no," said Tom; "there's somebody else in the wind. A tall man – a confoundedly tall man – with black whiskers."

' "Tom," said the old gentleman, "she will never have him."

' "Won't she?" said Tom. "If you stood in the bar, old gentleman, you'd tell another story."

' "Pooh, pooh," said the old gentleman. "I know all about that."

' "About what?" said Tom.

' "About kissing behind the door, and all that sort of thing, Tom," said the old gentleman. And here he gave another impudent look which made Tom very wroth, because as you all know, gentlemen, to hear an old fellow, who ought to know better, talking about these things, is very unpleasant – nothing more so.

' "I know all about that, Tom," said the old gentleman. "I have seen it done very often in my time, Tom, between more people than I should like to mention to you; but it never came to anything after all."

' "You must have seen some queer things," said Tom, with an inquisitive look.

' "You may say that, Tom." replied the old fellow, with a very complicated wink. "I am the last of my family, Tom," said the old gentleman, with a melancholy sigh.

' "Was it a large one?" inquired Tom Smart.

' "There were twelve of us, Tom," said the old gentleman; "fine straight-backed, handsome fellows as you'd wish to see. None of your modern abortions – all with arms, and with a degree of polish, though I say it that should not, which would have done your heart good to behold."

' "And what's become of the others, sir?" asked Tom Smart.

'The old gentleman applied his elbow to his eye as he replied, "Gone, Tom, gone. We had hard service, Tom, and they hadn't all my constitution. They got rheumatic about the legs and arms, and went into kitchens and hospitals; and one of 'em, with long service and hard usage, positively lost his senses: – he got so crazy that he was obliged to be burnt. Shocking thing that, Tom."

' "Dreadful!" said Tom Smart.

'The old fellow paused for a few minutes, apparently struggling with his feelings of emotion, and then said:

' "However. Tom, I am wandering from the point. This tall man, Tom, is a rascally adventurer. The moment he married the widow, he would sell off all the furniture, and run away. What would be the consequence? She would be deserted and reduced to ruin, and I should catch my death of cold in some broker's shop."

' "Yes, but . . ."

' "Don't interrupt me," said the old gentleman. "Of you, Tom, I entertain a very different opinion; for I well know that if you once settled yourself in a public house, you would never leave it, as long as there was anything to drink within its walls."

' "I am very much obliged to you for your good opinion, sir," said Tom Smart.

' "Therefore," resumed the old gentleman, in a dictatorial tone; "you shall have her, and he shall not."

' "What is to prevent it?" said Tom Smart, eagerly.

' "This disclosure,' replied the old gentleman; "he is already married."

' "How can I prove it?" said Tom, starting half out of bed.

'The old gentleman untucked his arm from his side, and having pointed to one of the oaken presses, immediately replaced it in its old position.

' "He little thinks," said the old gentleman, "that in the right hand pocket of a pair of trousers in that press, he has left a letter, entreating him to return to his disconsolate wife, with six – mark me, Tom – six babes, and all of them small ones."

'As the old gentleman solemnly uttered these words, his features grew less and less distinct, and his figure more shadowy. A film came over Tom Smart's eyes. The old man seemed gradually blending into the chair, the damask waistcoat to resolve into a cushion, the red slippers to shrink into little red cloth bags. The light faded gently away, and Tom Smart fell back on his pillow, and dropped asleep.

'Morning aroused Tom from the lethargic slumber, into which he had fallen on the disappearance of the old man. He sat up in bed, and for some minutes vainly endeavoured to recall the events of the preceding night. Suddenly they rushed upon him. He looked at the chair: it was a fantastic and grim-looking piece of furniture, certainly, but it must have been a remarkably ingenious and lively imagination, that could have discovered any resemblance between it and an old man.

' "How are you, old boy?' said Tom. He was bolder in the daylight – most men are.

'The chair remained motionless, and spoke not a word.

' "Miserable morning," said Tom. No. The chair would not be drawn into conversation.

' "Which press did you point to? You can tell me that," said Tom. Devil a word, gentlemen, the chair would say.

' "It's not much trouble to open it, any how," said Tom, getting out of bed very deliberately. He walked up to one of the presses. The key was in the lock; he turned it, and opened the door. There was a pair of trousers there. He put his hand into the pocket, and drew forth the identical letter the old gentleman had described!

' "Queer sort of thing, this," said Tom Smart; looking first at the chair and then at the press, and then at the letter, and then at the chair again. "Very queer," said Tom. But, as there was nothing in either, to lessen the queerness, he thought he might as well dress himself, and settle the tall man's business at once just to put him out of his misery.

'Tom surveyed the rooms he passed through, on his way down stairs, with the scrutinising eye of a landlord; thinking it not impossible, that before long, they and their contents would be his property. The tall man was standing in the snug little bar, with his hands behind him quite at home. He grinned vacantly at Tom. A casual observer might have supposed he did it, only to show his white teeth; but Tom Smart thought that a consciousness of triumph was passing through the place where the tall man's mind would have been if he had had any. Tom laughed in his face; and summoned the landlady.

'"Good morning, madam," said Tom Smart closing the door of the little parlour as the widow entered.

'"Good morning, sir," said the widow. "What will you take for breakfast, sir?"

'Tom was thinking how he should open the case so he made no answer.

'"There's a very nice ham," said the widow, "and a beautiful cold larded fowl. Shall I send 'em in, sir?'

'These words roused Tom from his rejections. His admiration of the widow increased as she spoke. Thoughtful creature! Comfortable provider!

'"Who is that gentleman in the bar, madam?" inquired Tom.

'"His name is Jinkins, sir," said the widow, slightly blushing.

'"He's a tall man," said Tom.

'"He is a very fine man, sir,' replied the widow, "and a very nice gentleman."

'"Ah!" said Tom.

'"Is there anything more you want, sir?" inquired the widow, rather puzzled by Tom's manner.

'"Why, yes," said Tom. "My dear madam, will you have the kindness to sit down for one moment?"

'The widow looked much amazed, but she sat down, and Tom sat down too, close beside her. I don't know how it happened, gentlemen, – indeed my uncle used to tell me that Tom Smart said he didn't know how it happened either – but somehow or other the palm of Tom's hand fell upon the back of the widow's hand, and remained there while he spoke.

'"My dear ma'am," said Tom Smart – he had always a great notion of committing the amiable – "My dear ma'am, you deserve a very excellent husband; – you do indeed."

' "Lor, sir!" said the widow – as well she might: Tom's mode of commencing the conversation being rather unusual, not to say startling: the fact of his never having set eyes upon her before the previous night, being taken into consideration. ' "Lor, sir!"

' "I scorn to flatter, my dear ma'am," said Tom Smart. "You deserve a very admirable husband, and whoever he is, he'll be a very lucky man." As Tom said this his eye involuntarily wandered from the widow's face, to the comforts around him.

'The widow looked more puzzled than ever, and made an effort to rise. Tom gently pressed her hand, as if to detain her, and she kept her seat. Widows, gentlemen, are not usually timorous, as my uncle used to say.

' "I am sure I am very much obliged to you, sir, for your good opinion," said the buxom landlady, half laughing; "and if ever I marry again . . ."

' "If," said Tom Smart, looking very shrewdly out of the right-hand corner of his left eye. "If . . . "

' "Well," said the widow, laughing outright this time. "When I do, I hope I shall have as good a husband as you describe."

' "Jinkins to wit," said Tom.

' "Lor, sir!" exclaimed the widow.

' "Oh, don't tell me," said Tom, "I know him."

' "I am sure nobody who knows him, knows anything bad of him," said the widow, bridling up at the mysterious air with which Tom had spoken.

' "Hem!" said Tom Smart.

'The widow began to think it was high time to cry, so she took out her handkerchief, and inquired whether Tom wished to insult her: whether he thought it like a gentleman to take away the character of another gentleman behind his back: why, if he had got anything to say, he didn't say it to the man, like a man, instead of terrifying a poor weak woman in that way; and so forth.

' "I'll say it to him fast enough," said Tom, "only I want you to hear it first."

' "What is it?" inquired the widow, looking intently in Tom's countenance.

' "I'll astonish you," said Tom, putting his hand in his pocket.

' "If it is, that he wants money," said the widow, "I know that already, and you needn't trouble yourself."

' "Pooh, nonsense, that's nothing," said Tom Smart, "*I* want money. 'Tan't that."

' "Oh, dear, what can it be?" exclaimed the poor widow.

' "Don't be frightened," said Tom Smart. He slowly drew forth the letter, and unfolded it. "You won't scream?" said Tom, doubtfully.

' "No, no," replied the widow; "let me see it."

' "You won't go fainting away, or any of that nonsense?" said Tom.

' "No, no," returned the widow, hastily.

' "And don't run out, and blow him up," said Tom, "because I'll do all that for you; you had better not exert yourself."

' "Well, well," said the widow, "let me see it."

' "I will," replied Tom Smart; and, with these words, he placed the letter in the widow's hand.

'Gentlemen, I have heard my uncle say, that Tom Smart said, the widow's lamentations when she heard the disclosure would have pierced a heart of stone. Tom was certainly very tender-hearted, but they pierced his, to the very core. The widow rocked herself to and fro, and wrung her hands.

' "Oh, the deception and villainy of man!" said the widow.

' "Frightful, my dear ma'am; but compose yourself," said Tom Smart.

' "Oh, I can't compose myself," shrieked the widow. "I shall never find any one else I can love so much!"

' "Oh, yes you will, my dear soul," said Tom Smart, letting fall a shower of the largest sized tears, in pity for the widow's misfortunes. Tom Smart, in the energy of his compassion, had put his arm round the widow's waist; and the widow, in a passion of grief, had clasped Tom's hand. She looked up in Tom's face, and smiled through her tears. Tom looked down in her's, and smiled through his.

'I could never find out, gentlemen, whether Tom did or did not kiss the widow at that particular moment. He used to tell my uncle he didn't, but I have my doubts about it. Between ourselves, gentlemen, I rather think he did.

'At all events, Tom kicked the very tall man out at the front door half an hour after, and married the widow a month after. And he used to drive about the country, with the clay-coloured gig with red wheels, and the vixenish mare with the fast pace, till he gave up business many years afterwards, and went to France with his wife: and then the old house was pulled down.'

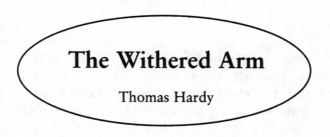

The Withered Arm

Thomas Hardy

I
A lorn milkmaid

It was an eighty-cow dairy, and the troop of milkers, regular and supernumerary, were all at work; for, though the time of year was as yet but early April, the feed lay entirely in water-meadows and the cows were 'in full pail'. The hour was about six in the evening and about three-fourths of the large, red rectangular animals having been finished off, there was opportunity for a little conversation.

'He brings home his bride tomorrow, I hear. They've come as far as Anglebury today.'

The voice seemed to proceed from the belly of the cow called Cherry, but the speaker was a milking-woman, whose face was buried in the flank of that motionless beast.

'Has anybody seen her?' said another.

There was a negative response from the first. 'Though they she's a rosy-cheeked, tisty-tosty little body enough,' she added; and as the milkmaid spoke she turned her face so that she could glance past her cow's tail to the other side of the barton, where a thin, faded woman of thirty milked somewhat apart from the rest.

'Years younger than he, they say,' continued the second, with also a glance of reflectiveness in the same direction.

'How old do you call him, then?'

'Thirty or so.'

'More like forty,' broke in an old milkman near, in a long white pinafore or 'wropper', and with the brim of his hat tied down, so that he looked like a woman. ' 'A was born before our Great Weir was builded, and I hadn't man's wages when I laved water there.'

The discussion waxed so warm that the purr of the milk-streams became jerky, till a voice from another cow's belly cried with authority,

'Now then, what the Turk do it matter to us about Farmer Lodge's age, or Farmer Lodge's new mis'ess? I shall have to pay him nine pound a year for the rent of every one of these milchers, whatever his age or hers. Get on with your work, or 'twill be dark before we have done. The evening is pinking in a'ready.' This speaker was the dairyman himself, by whom the milkmaids and men were employed.

Nothing more was said publicly about Farmer Lodge's wedding, but the first woman murmured under her cow to her next neighbour, "'Tis hard for *she*,' signifying the thin worn milkmaid aforesaid.

'Oh no,' said the second. 'He hasn't spoken to Rhoda Brook for years.'

When the milking was done they washed their pails and hung them on a many-forked stand made of the peeled limb of an oak-tree, set upright in the earth, and resembling a colossal antlered horn. The majority then dispersed in various directions homeward. The thin woman who had not spoken was joined by a boy of twelve or thereabout, and the twain went away up the field also.

Their course lay apart from that of the others, to a lonely spot high above the water-meads, and not far from the border of Egdon Heath, whose dark countenance was visible in the distance as they drew nigh to their home.

'They've just been saying down in barton that your father brings his young wife home from Anglebury tomorrow,' the woman observed. 'I shall want to send you for a few things to market, and you'll be pretty sure to meet 'em.'

'Yes, mother,' said the boy. 'Is father married, then?'

'Yes . . . You can give her a look, and tell me what she's like, if you do see her.'

'Yes, mother.'

'If she's dark or fair, and if she' tall – as tall as I. And if she seems like a woman who has ever worked for a living, or one that has been always well off, and has never done anything, and shows marks of the lady on her, as I expect she do.'

'Yes.'

They crept up the hill in the twilight, and entered the cottage. It was thatched and built of mud-walls, the surface of which had been washed by many rains into channels and depressions that left none of the original flat face visible; while here and there a rafter showed like a bone protruding through the skin.

She was kneeling down in the chimney-corner, before two pieces of turf laid together with the heather inwards, blowing at the red-hot ashes with her breath till the turves flamed. The radiance lit her pale cheek, and made her dark eyes, that had once been handsome, seem handsome anew. 'Yes,' she resumed, ' see if she is dark or fair, and if you can, notice if her hands are white; if not, see if they look as though she had ever done housework, or are milker's hands like mine.'

The boy again promised, inattentively this time, his mother not observing that he was cutting a notch with his pocket-knife in the beech-backed chair.

II
The young wife

The road from Anglebury to Holmstoke is in general level; but there is one place where a sharp ascent breaks its monotony. Farmers homeward-bound from the former market-town, who trot all the rest of the way, walk their horses up this short incline.

The next evening, while the sun was yet bright, a handsome new gig, with a lemon-coloured body and red wheels, was spinning westward along the level highway at the heels of a powerful mare. The driver was a yeoman in the prime of life, cleanly shaven like an actor, his face being toned to that bluish-vermilion hue which so often graces a thriving farmer's features when returning home after successful dealings in the town. Beside him sat a woman, many years his junior – almost, indeed, a girl. Her face too was fresh in colour, but it was of a totally different quality – soft and evanescent, like the light under a heap of rose-petals.

Few people travelled this way, for it was not a turnpike-road; and the long white riband of gravel that stretched before them was empty, save of one small scarce-moving speck, which presently resolved itself into the figure of a boy, who was creeping on at a snail's pace, and continually looking behind him – the heavy bundle he carried being some excuse for, if not the reason of, his dilatoriness. When the bouncing gig-party slowed at the bottom of the incline above mentioned, the pedestrian was only a few yards in front. Supporting the large bundle by putting one hand on his hip, he turned and looked straight at the farmer's wife as though he would read her through and through, pacing along abreast of the horse.

The low sun was full in her face, rendering every feature, shade, and contour distinct, from the curve of her little nostril to the colour of her eyes. The farmer, though he seemed annoyed at the boy's persistent presence, did not order him to get out of the way; and thus the lad preceded them, his hard gaze never leaving her, till they reached the top of the ascent, when the farmer trotted on with relief in his lineaments – having taken no outward notice of the boy whatever.

'How that poor lad stared at me!' said the young wife.

'Yes, dear; I saw that he did.'

'He is one of the village, I suppose?'

'One of the neighbourhood. I think he lives with his mother a mile or two off.'

'He knows who we are, no doubt?'

'Oh yes. You must expect to be stared at just at first, my pretty Gertrude.'

'I do, – though I think the poor boy may have looked at us in the hope we might relieve him of his heavy weight.'

'Oh no,' said her husband off-handedly. 'These country lads will carry a hundredweight once they get it on their backs; beside, his pack had more size than weight in it. Now, then, another mile and I shall be able to show you our house in the distance – if it is not too dark before we get there.' The wheels spun round, and particles flew from their periphery as before, till a white house of ample dimensions revealed itself, with farm-buildings and ricks at the back.

Meanwhile the boy had quickened his pace, and turning up a by-lane some mile and half short of the white farmstead, ascended towards the leaner pastures, and so on to the cottage of his mother.

She had reached home after her day's milking at the outlying dairy, and was washing cabbage at the doorway in the declining light. 'Hold up the net a moment,' she said, without preface, as the boy came up.

He flung down the bundle, held the edge of the cabbage-net, and as she filled its meshes with the dripping leaves she went on, 'Well, did you see her?'

'Yes; quite plain.'

'Is she ladylike?'

'Yes; and more. A lady complete.'

'Is she young?'

'Well, she's growed up, and her ways are quite a woman's.'

'Of course. What colour is her hair and face?'

'Her hair is lightish, and her face as homely as a live doll's.'

'Her eyes, then, are not dark like mine?'

'No – of a bluish turn, and her mouth is very nice and red; and when she smiles, her teeth show white.'

'Is she tall?' said the woman sharply.

'I couldn't see. She was sitting down.'

'Then do you go to Holmstoke church tomorrow morning: she's sure to be there. Go early and notice her walking in, and come home and tell me if she's taller than I.'

'Very well, mother. But why don't you go and see for yourself?'

'I go to see her! I wouldn't look up at her if she were to pass my window this instant. She was with Mr Lodge, of course. What did he say or do?'

'Just the same as usual.'

'Took no notice of you?'

'None.'

Next day the mother put a clean shirt on the boy, and started him off for Holmstoke church. He reached the ancient little pile when the door was just being opened, and he was the first to enter. Taking his seat by the font, he watched all the parishioners file in. The well-to-do Farmer Lodge came nearly last; and his young wife, who accompanied him, walked up the aisle with the shyness natural to a modest woman who had appeared thus for the first time. As all other eyes were fixed upon her, the youth's stare was not noticed now.

When he reached home his mother said 'Well?' before he had entered the room.

'She is not tall. She is rather short,' he replied.

'Ah!' said his mother, with satisfaction.

'But she's very pretty – very. In fact, she's lovely.' The youthful freshness of the yeoman's wife had evidently made an impression even on the somewhat hard nature of the boy.

'That's all I want to hear,' said his mother quickly. 'Now, spread the table-cloth. The hare you caught is very tender; but mind that nobody catches you. – You've never told me what sort of hands she had.'

'I have never seen 'em. She never took off her gloves.'

'What did she wear this morning?'

'A white bonnet and a silver-coloured gown. It whewed and whistled so loud when it rubbed against the pews that the lady coloured up more than ever for very shame at the noise, and pulled it in to keep it from touching; but when she pushed into her seat, it whewed more than ever. Mr Lodge, he seemed pleased, and his waistcoat stuck out, and his great golden seals hung like a lord's; but she seemed to wish her noisy gown anywhere but on her.'

'Not she! However, that will do now.'

These descriptions of the newly-married couple were continued from time to time by the boy at the mother's request, after any chance encounter he had had with them. But Rhoda Brook, though she might easily have seen young Mrs Lodge for herself by walking a couple of miles, would never attempt an excursion towards the quarter where the farmhouse lay. Neither did she, at the daily milking in the dairyman's yard on Lodge's outlying second farm, ever speak on the subject of the recent marriage. The dairyman, who rented the cows of Lodge, and knew perfectly the tall milkmaid's history, with manly kindliness always kept the gossip in the cow-barton from annoying Rhoda. But the atmosphere thereabout was full of the subject during the first days of Mrs Lodge's arrival; and from her boy's description and the casual words of the other milkers, Rhoda Brook could raise a mental image of the unconscious Mrs Lodge that was realistic as a photograph.

III
A vision

One night, two or three weeks after the bridal return, when the boy was gone to bed, Rhoda sat a long time over the turf ashes that she had raked out in front of her to extinguish them. She contemplated so intently the new wife, as presented to her in her mind's eye over the embers, that she forgot the lapse of time. At last, wearied with her day's work, she too retired.

But the figure which had occupied her so much during this and the previous days was not to be banished at night. For the first time Gertrude Lodge visited the supplanted woman in her dreams. Rhoda Brook dreamed – since her assertion that she really saw, before falling asleep, was not to be believed – that the young wife, in the pale silk dress and white bonnet, but with features shockingly distorted, and wrinkled as by age, was sitting upon her chest as she lay. The pressure of Mrs Lodge's person grew heavier; the blue eyes peered cruelly into her face; and then the figure thrust forward its left hand mockingly, so as to make the wedding-ring it wore glitter in Rhoda's eyes. Maddened mentally, and nearly suffocated by pressure, the sleeper struggled; the incubus, still regarding her, withdrew to the foot of the bed, only, however, to come forward by degrees, resume her seat, and flash her left hand as before.

Gasping for breath, Rhoda, in a last desperate effort, swung out her right hand, seized the confronting spectre by its obtrusive left arm, and whirled it backward to the floor, starting up herself as she did so with a low cry.

'Oh, merciful heaven!' she cried, sitting on the edge of the bed in a cold sweat, 'that was not a dream – she was here!'

She could feel her antagonist's arm within her grasp even now – the very flesh and bone of it, as it seemed. She looked on the floor whither she had whirled the spectre, but there was nothing to be seen.

Rhoda Brook slept no more that night, and when she went milking at the next dawn they noticed how pale and haggard she looked. The milk that she drew quivered into the pail; her hand had not calmed even yet, and still retained the feel of the arm. She came home to breakfast as wearily as if it had been supper-time.

'What was that noise in your chimmer, mother, last night?' said her son. 'You fell off the bed, surely?'

'Did you hear anything fall? At what time?'

'Just when the clock struck two.'

She could not explain, and when the meal was done went silently about her household work, the boy assisting her for he hated going afield on the farms, and she indulged his reluctance. Between eleven and twelve the garden-gate clicked, and she lifted her eyes to the window. At the bottom of the garden, within the gate, stood the woman of her vision. Rhoda seemed transfixed.

'Ah, she said she would come!' exclaimed the boy, also observing her.

'Said so – when? How does she know us?'

'I have seen and spoken to her. I talked to her yesterday.'

'I told you,' said the mother, flushing indignantly, 'never to speak to anybody in that house, or go near the place.'

'I did not speak to her till she spoke to me. And I did not go near the place. I met her in the road.'

'What did you tell her?'

'Nothing. She said, "Are you the poor boy who had to bring the heavy load from market?" And she looked at my boots, and said they would not keep my feet dry if it came on wet, because they were so cracked. I told her I lived with my mother, and we had enough to do to keep ourselves, and that's how it was; and she said then, "I'll come and bring you some better boots, and see your mother." She gives away things to other folks in the meads besides us.'

Mrs Lodge was by this time close to the door – not in her silk, as Rhoda had seen her in the bed-chamber, but in a morning hat, and gown of common light material, which became her better than silk. On her arm she carried a basket.

The impression remaining from the night's experience was still strong. Brook had almost expected to see the wrinkles, the scorn, and the cruelty on her visitor's face. She would have escaped an interview, had escape been possible. There was, however, no back-door to the cottage, and in an instant the boy had lifted the latch to Mrs Lodge's gentle knock.

'I see I have come to the right house,' said she, glancing at the lad, and smiling. 'But I was not sure till you opened the door.'

The figure and action were those of the phantom; but her voice was so indescribably sweet, her glance so winning, her smile so tender, so unlike that of Rhoda's midnight visitant, that the latter could hardly believe the evidence of her senses. She was truly glad that she had not hidden away in sheer aversion, as she had been inclined to do. In her basket Mrs Lodge brought the pair of boots that she had promised to the boy, and other useful articles.

At these proofs of a kindly feeling towards her and hers, Rhoda's heart reproached her bitterly. This innocent young thing should have her blessing and not her curse. When she left them a light seemed gone from the dwelling. Two days later she came again to know if the boots fitted; and less than a fortnight after that paid Rhoda another call. On this occasion the boy was absent.

'I walk a good deal,' said Mrs Lodge, 'and your house is the nearest outside our own parish. I hope you are well. You don't look quite well.'

Rhoda said she was well enough; and indeed, though the paler of the two, there was more of the strength that endures in her well-defined features and large frame, than in the soft-cheeked young woman before her. The conversation became quite confidential as regarded their powers and weaknesses; and when Mrs Lodge was leaving, Rhoda said, 'I hope you will find this air agree with you, madam, and not suffer from the damp of the water-meads.'

The younger one replied that there was not much doubt of it, her general health being usually good. 'Though, now you remind me,' she added, 'I have one little ailment which puzzles me. It is nothing serious, but I cannot make it out.'

She uncovered her left hand and arm; and their outline confronted Rhoda's gaze as the exact original of the limb she had beheld and seized in her dream. Upon the pink round surface of the arm were faint marks of an unhealthy colour, as if produced by a rough grasp. Rhoda's eyes became riveted on the discolorations; she fancied that she discerned in them the shape of her own four fingers.

'How did it happen?' she said mechanically.

'I cannot tell,' replied Mrs Lodge, shaking her head. 'One night when I was sound asleep, dreaming I was away in some strange place, a pain suddenly shot into my arm there, and was so keen as to awaken me. I must have struck it in the daytime, I suppose, though I don't remember doing so.' She added, laughing, 'I tell my dear husband that it looks just as if he had flown into a rage and struck me there. Oh, I daresay it will soon disappear.'

'Ha, ha! Yes . . . On what night did it come?'

Mrs Lodge considered, and said it would be a fortnight ago on the morrow. 'When I awoke I could not remember where I was,' she added, ''till the clock striking two reminded me.'

She had named the night and the hour of Rhoda's spectral encounter, and Brook felt like a guilty thing. The artless disclosure startled her; she did not reason on the freaks of coincidence; and all the scenery of that ghastly night returned with double vividness to her mind.

'Oh, can it be,' she said to herself, when her visitor had departed, 'that I exercise a malignant power over people against my own will?' She knew that she had been slyly called a witch since her fall; but never having understood why that particular stigma had been attached to her, it had passed disregarded. Could this be the explanation, and had such things as this ever happened before?

IV

A suggestion

The summer drew on, and Rhoda Brook almost dreaded to meet Mrs Lodge again, notwithstanding that her feeling for the young wife amounted wellnigh to affection. Something in her own individuality seemed to convict Rhoda of crime. Yet a fatality sometimes would direct the steps of the latter to the outskirts of Holmstoke whenever she left her house for any other purpose than her daily work; and hence it happened that their next encounter was out of doors. Rhoda could not avoid the subject which had so mystified her, and after the first few words she stammered, 'I hope your – arm is well again, ma'am?' She had perceived with consternation that Gertrude Lodge carried her left arm stiffly.

'No; it is not quite well. Indeed it is no better at all; it is rather worse. It pains me dreadfully sometimes.'

'Perhaps you had better go to a doctor, ma'am.'

She replied that she had already seen a doctor. Her husband had insisted upon her going to one. But the surgeon had not seemed to understand the afflicted limb at all; he had told her to bathe it in hot water, and she had bathed it, but the treatment had done no good.

'Will you let me see it?' said the milkwoman.

Mrs Lodge pushed up her sleeve and disclosed the place, which was a few inches above the wrist. As soon as Rhoda Brook saw it, she could hardly preserve her composure. There was nothing of the nature of a wound, but the arm at that point had a shrivelled look, and the outline of the four fingers appeared more distinct than at the former time. Moreover, she fancied that they were imprinted in precisely the relative position of her clutch upon the arm in the trance; the first finger towards Gertrude's wrist, and the fourth towards her elbow.

What the impress resembled seemed to have struck Gertrude herself since their last meeting. 'It looks almost like finger-marks,' she said; adding with a faint laugh, 'my husband says it is as if some witch, or the devil himself, had taken hold of me there, and blasted the flesh.'

Rhoda shivered. 'That's fancy,' she said hurriedly. 'I wouldn't mind it, if I were you.'

'I shouldn't so much mind it,' said the younger, with hesitation, 'if – if I hadn't a notion that it makes my husband – dislike me – no, love me less. Men think so much of personal appearance.'

'Some do – he for one.'

'Yes; and he was very proud of mine, at first.'

'Keep your arm covered from his sight.'

'Ah – he knows the disfigurement is there!' She tried to hide the tears that filled her eyes.

'Well, ma'am, I earnestly hope it will go away soon.'

And so the milkwoman's mind was chained anew to the subject by a horrid sort of spell as she returned home. The sense of having been guilty of an act of malignity increased, affect as she might to ridicule her superstition. In her secret heart Rhoda did not altogether object to a slight diminution of her successor's beauty, by whatever means it had come about; but she did not wish to inflict upon her physical pain. For though this pretty young woman had rendered impossible any reparation which Lodge might have made Rhoda for his past conduct, everything like resentment at the unconscious usurpation had quite passed away from the elder's mind.

If the sweet and kindly Gertrude Lodge only knew of the scene in the bed-chamber, what would she think? Not to inform her of it seemed treachery in the presence of her friendliness; but tell she could not of her own accord – neither could she devise a remedy.

She mused upon the matter the greater part of the night; and the next day, after the morning milking, set out to obtain another glimpse of Gertrude Lodge if she could, being held to her by a gruesome fascination. By watching the house from a distance the milkmaid was presently able to discern the farmer's wife in a ride she was taking alone – probably to join her husband in some distant field. Mrs Lodge perceived her, and cantered in her direction.

'Good morning, Rhoda!' Gertrude said, when she had come up. 'I was going to call.'

Rhoda noticed that Mrs Lodge held the rein with some difficulty.

'I hope – the bad arm,' said Rhoda.

'They tell me there is possibly one way by which I might be able to find out the cause, and so perhaps the cure, of it,' replied the other anxiously. 'It is by going to some clever man over in Egdon Heath. They did not know if he was still alive – and I cannot remember his name at this moment; but they said that you knew more of his movements than anybody else hereabout, and could tell me if he were still to be consulted. Dear me – what was his name? But you know.'

'Not Conjuror Trendle?' said her thin companion, turning pale.

'Trendle – yes. Is he alive?'

'I believe so,' said Rhoda, with reluctance.

'Why do you call him conjuror?'

'Well – they say – they used to say he was a – he had powers other folks have not.'

'Oh, how could my people be so superstitious as to recommend a man of that sort! I thought they meant some medical man. I shall think no more of him.'

Rhoda looked relieved, and Mrs Lodge rode on. The milkwoman had inwardly seen, from the moment she heard of her having been mentioned as a reference for this man, that there must exist a sarcastic feeling among the work-folk that a sorceress would know the whereabouts of the exorcist. They suspected her, then. A short time ago this would have given no concern to a woman of her common-sense. But she had a haunting reason to be superstitious now; and she had been seized with sudden dread that this Conjuror Trendle might name her as the malignant influence which was blasting the fair person of Gertrude, and so lead her friend to hate her for ever, and to treat her as some fiend in human shape.

But all was not over. Two days after, a shadow intruded into the window-pattern thrown on Rhoda Brook's floor by the afternoon sun. The woman opened the door at once, almost breathlessly.

'Are you alone?' said Gertrude. She seemed to be no less harassed and anxious than Brook herself.

'Yes,' said Rhoda.

'The place on my arm seems worse, and troubles me!' the young farmer's wife went on. 'It is so mysterious! I do hope it will not be a permanent blemish. I have again been thinking of what they said about Conjuror Trendle. I don't really believe in such men, but I should not mind just visiting him, from curiosity – though on no account must my husband know. Is it far to where he lives?'

'Yes – five miles,' said Rhoda backwardly. 'In the heart of Egdon.'

'Well, I should have to walk. Could not you go with me to show me the way – say tomorrow afternoon?'

'Oh, not I – that is,' the milkwoman murmured, with a start of dismay. Again the dread seized her that something to do with her fierce act in the dream might be revealed, and her character in the eyes of the most useful friend she had ever had be ruined irretrievably.

Mrs Lodge urged, and Rhoda finally assented, though with much misgiving. Sad as the journey would be to her, she could not conscientiously stand in the way of a possible remedy for her patron's strange affliction. It was agreed that, to escape suspicion of their mystic intent, they should meet at the edge of the heath, at the corner of a plantation which was visible from the spot where they now stood.

V
Conjuror Trendle

By the next afternoon Rhoda would have done anything to escape this inquiry. But she had promised to go. Moreover, there was a horrid fascination at times in becoming instrumental in throwing such possible light on her own character as would reveal her to be something greater in the occult world than she had ever herself suspected.

She started just before the time of day mentioned between them, and half an hour's brisk walking brought her to the south-eastern extension of the Egdon tract of country, where the fir plantation was. A slight figure, cloaked and veiled, was already there. Rhoda recognized, almost with a shudder, that Mrs Lodge bore her left arm in a sling.

They hardly spoke to each other, and immediately set out on their climb into the interior of this solemn country, which stood high above the rich alluvial soil they had left half an hour before. It was a long walk;

thick clouds made the atmosphere dark, though it was as yet only early afternoon; and the wind howled dismally over the hills of the heath – not improbably the same heath which had witnessed the agony of the Wessex King Ina, presented to after-ages as Lear. Gertrude Lodge talked most, Rhoda replying with monosyllabic preoccupation. She had a strange dislike to walking on the side of her companion where hung the afflicted arrn, moving round to the other when inadvertently near it. Much heather had been brushed by their feet when they descended upon a cart-track, beside which stood the house of the man they sought.

He did not profess his remedial practices openly, or care anything about their continuance, his direct interests being those of a dealer in furze, turf, 'sharp sand', and other local products. Indeed, he affected not to believe largely in his own powers, and when warts that had been shown him for cure miraculously disappeared – which it must be owned they infallibly did – he would say lightly, 'Oh, I only drink a glass of grog upon 'em – perhaps it's all chance,' and immediately turn the subject.

He was at home when they arrived, having in fact seen them descending into his valley. He was a grey-bearded man, with a reddish face, and he looked singularly at Rhoda the first moment he beheld her. Mrs Lodge told him her errand; and then with words of self-disparagement he examined her arm.

'Medicine can't cure it,' he said promptly. ''Tis the work of an enemy.'

Rhoda shrank into herself, and drew back.

'An enemy? What enemy?' asked Mrs Lodge.

He shook his head. 'That's best known to yourself,' he said. 'If you like I can show the person to you, though I shall not myself know who it is. I can do no more; and don't wish to do that.'

She pressed him; on which he told Rhoda to wait outside where she stood, and took Mrs Lodge into the room. It opened immediately from the door; and, as the latter remained ajar, Rhoda Brook could see the proceedings without taking part in them. He brought a tumbler from the dresser, nearly filled it with water, and fetching an egg, prepared it in some private way; after which he broke it on the edge of the glass, so that the white went in and the yolk remained. As it was getting gloomy, he took the glass and its contents to the window, and told Gertrude to watch them closely. They leant over the table together, and the milkwoman could see the opaline hue of the egg-fluid changing form as it sank in the water, but she was not near enough to define the shape that it assumed.

'Do you catch the likeness of any face or figure as you look?' demanded the conjuror of the young woman.

She murmured a reply, in tones so low as to be inaudible to Rhoda, and continued to gaze intently into the glass. Rhoda turned, and walked a few steps away.

When Mrs Lodge came out, and her face was met by the light, it appeared exceedingly pale – as pale as Rhoda's – against the sad dun shades of the upland's garniture. Trendle shut the door behind her, and they at once started homeward together. But Rhoda perceived that her companion had quite changed.

'Did he charge much?' she asked tentatively.

'Oh no – nothing. He would not take a farthing,' said Gertrude.

'And what did you see?' inquired Rhoda.

'Nothing I – care to speak of.' The constraint in her manner was remarkable; her face was so rigid as to wear an oldened aspect, faintly suggestive of the face in Rhoda's bed-chamber.

'Was it you who first proposed coming here?' Mrs Lodge suddenly inquired, after a long pause. 'How very odd, if you did!'

'No. But I am not sorry we have come, all things considered,' she replied. For the first time a sense of triumph possessed her, and she did not altogether deplore that the young thing at her side should learn that their lives had been antagonized by other influences than their own.

The subject was no more alluded to during the long and dreary walk home. But in some way or other a story was whispered about the many-dairied Swenn valley that winter that Mrs Lodge's gradual loss of the use of her left arm was owing to her being 'overlooked' by Rhoda Brook. The latter kept her own counsel about the incubus, but her face grew sadder and thinner; and in the spring she and her boy disappeared from the neighbourhood of Holmstoke.

VI

A second attempt

Half a dozen years passed away, and Mr and Mrs Lodge's married experience sank into prosiness, and worse. The farmer was usually gloomy and silent: the woman whom he had wooed for her grace and beauty was contorted and disfigured in the left limb; moreover, she had brought him no child, which rendered it likely that he would be the last of a family who had occupied that valley for some two hundred years. He thought of Rhoda Brook and her son; and feared this might be a judgment from heaven upon him.

The once blithe-hearted and enlightened Gertrude was changing into an irritable, superstitious woman, whose whole time was given to experimenting upon her ailment with every quack remedy she came across. She was honestly attached to her husband, and was ever secretly hoping against hope to win back his heart again by regaining some at least of her personal beauty. Hence it arose that her closet was lined with bottles, packets, and ointment-pots of every description – nay, bunches of mystic herbs, charms, and books of necromancy, which in her schoolgirl time she would have ridiculed as folly.

'Damned if you won't poison yourself with these apothecary messes and witch mixtures some time or other,' said her husband, when his eye chanced to fall upon the multitudinous array.

She did not reply, but turned her sad, soft glance upon him in such heart-swollen reproach that he looked sorry for his words, and added, 'I only meant it for your good, you know, Gertrude.'

'I'll clear out the whole lot, and destroy them,' said she huskily, 'and attempt such remedies no more!'

'You want somebody to cheer you,' he observed. 'I once thought of adopting a boy; but he is too old now. And he is gone away I don't know where.'

She guessed to whom he alluded; for Rhoda Brook's story had in the course of years become known to her; though not a word had ever passed between her husband and herself on the subject. Neither had she ever spoken to him of her visit to Conjuror Trendle, and of what was revealed to her, or she thought was revealed to her, by that solitary heath-man.

She was now five-and-twenty; but she seemed older. 'Six years of marriage, and only a few months of love,' she sometimes whispered to herself. And then she thought of the apparent cause, and said, with a tragic glance at her withering limb, 'If I could only again be as I was when he first saw me!'

She obediently destroyed her nostrums and charms; but there remained a hankering wish to try something else – some other sort of cure altogether. She had never revisited Trendle since she had been conducted to the house of the solitary by Rhoda against her will; but it now suddenly occurred to Gertrude that she would, in a last desperate effort at deliverance from this seeming curse, again seek out the man, if he yet lived. He was entitled to a certain credence, for the indistinct form he had raised in the glass had undoubtedly resembled the only woman in the world who – as she now knew, though not then – could have a reason for bearing her ill-will. The visit should be paid.

This time she went alone, though she nearly got lost on the heath, and roamed a considerable distance out of her way. Trendle's house was reached at last, however: he was not indoors, and instead of waiting at the cottage she went to where his bent figure was pointed out to her at work a long way off. Trendle remembered her, and laying down the handful of furze-roots which he was gathering and throwing into a heap, he offered to accompany her in her homeward direction, as the distance was considerable and the days were short. So they walked together, his head bowed nearly to the earth, and his form of a colour with it.

'You can send away warts and other excrescences, I know,' she said; 'why can't you send away this?' And the arm was uncovered.

'You think too much of my powers!' said Trendle; 'and I am old and weak now, too. No, no; it is too much for me to attempt in my own person. What have ye tried?'

She named to him some of the hundred medicaments and counterspells which she had adopted from time to time. He shook his head.

'Some were good enough,' he said approvingly; 'but not many of them for such as this. This is of the nature of a blight, not of the nature of a wound; and if you ever do throw it off, it will be all at once.'

'If I only could!'

'There is only one chance of doing it known to me. It has never failed in kindred afflictions, – that I can declare. But it is hard to carry out, and especially for a woman.'

'Tell me!' said she.

'You must touch with the limb the neck of a man who's been hanged.'

She started a little at the image he had raised.

'Before he's cold – just after he's cut down,' continued the conjuror impassively.

'How can that do good?'

'It will turn the blood and change the constitution. But, as I say, to do it is hard. You must get into jail, and wait for him when he's brought off the gallows. Lots have done it, though perhaps not such pretty women as you. I used to send dozens for skin complaints. But that was in former times. The last I sent was in '13 – near twenty years ago.'

He had no more to tell her; and, when he had put her into a straight track homeward, turned and left her, refusing all money as at first.

VII
A ride

The communication sank deep into Gertrude's mind. Her nature was rather a timid one; and probably of all remedies that the white wizard could have suggested there was not one which would have filled her with so much aversion as this, not to speak of the immense obstacles in the way of its adoption.

Casterbridge, the county-town, was a dozen or fifteen miles off; and though in those days, when men were executed for horse-stealing, arson, and burglary, an assize seldom passed without a hanging, it was not likely that she could get access to the body of the criminal unaided. And the fear of her husband's anger made her reluctant to breathe a word of Trendle's suggestion to him or to anybody about him.

She did nothing for months, and patiently bore her disfigurement as before. But her woman's nature, craving for renewed love, through the medium of renewed beauty (she was but twenty-five), was ever stimulating her to try what, at any rate, could hardly do her any harm. 'What came by a spell will go by a spell surely,' she would say. Whenever her imagination pictured the act she shrank in terror from the possibility of it: then the words of the conjuror, 'It will turn your blood,' were seen to be capable of a scientific no less than a ghastly interpretation; the mastering desire returned, and urged her on again.

There was at this time but one county paper, and that her husband only occasionally borrowed. But old-fashioned days had old-fashioned means, and news was extensively conveyed by word of mouth from market to market or from fair to fair; so that, whenever such an event as an execution was about to take place, few within a radius of twenty miles were ignorant of the coming sight; and, so far as Holmstoke was concerned, some enthusiasts had been known to walk all the way to Casterbridge and back in one day, solely to witness the spectacle. The next assizes were in March; and when Gertrude Lodge heard that they had been held, she inquired stealthily at the inn as to the result, as soon as she could find opportunity.

She was, however, too late. The time at which the sentences were to be carried out had arrived, and to make the journey and obtain admission at such short notice required at least her husband's assistance. She dared not tell him, for she had found by delicate experiment that these smouldering village beliefs made him furious if mentioned, partly because he half entertained them himself. It was therefore necessary to wait for another opportunity.

Her determination received a fillip from learning that two epileptic children had attended from this very village of Holmstoke many years before with beneficial results, though the experiment had been strongly condemned by the neighbouring clergy. April, May, June passed; and it is no overstatement to say that by the end of the last-named month Gertrude wellnigh longed for the death of a fellow-creature. Instead of her formal prayers each night, her unconscious prayer was, 'O Lord, hang some guilty or innocent person soon!'

This time she made earlier inquiries, and was altogether more systematic in her proceedings. Moreover, the season was summer, between the haymaking and the harvest, and in the leisure thus afforded her husband had been holiday-taking away from home.

The assizes were in July, and she went to the inn as before. There was to be one execution – only one – for arson.

Her greatest problem was not how to get to Casterbridge, but what means she should adopt for obtaining admission to the jail. Though access for such purposes had formerly never been denied, the custom had fallen into desuetude; and in contemplating her possible difficulties, she was again almost driven to fall back upon her husband. But, on sounding him about the assizes, he was so uncommunicative, so more than usually cold, that she did not proceed, and decided that whatever she did she would do alone.

Fortune, obdurate hitherto, showed her unexpected favour. On the Thursday before the Saturday fixed for the execution, Lodge remarked to her that he was going away from home for another day or two on business at a fair, and that he was sorry he could not take her with him.

She exhibited on this occasion so much readiness to stay at home that he looked at her in surprise. Time had been when she would have shown deep disappointment at the loss of such a jaunt. However, he lapsed into his usual taciturnity, and on the day named left Holmstoke.

It was now her turn. She at first had thought of driving, but on reflection held that driving would not do, since it would necessitate her keeping to the turnpike-road, and so increase by tenfold the risk of her ghastly errand being found out. She decided to ride, and avoid the beaten track, notwithstanding that in her husband's stables there was no animal just at present which by any stretch of imagination could be considered a lady's mount, in spite of his promise before marriage to always keep a mare for her. He had, however, many horses, fine ones of their kind; and among the rest was a serviceable creature, an equine Amazon, with a back as broad as a sofa, on which Gertrude had occasionally taken an airing when unwell. This horse she chose.

On Friday afternoon one of the men brought it round. She was dressed, and before going down looked at her shrivelled arm. 'Ah!' she said to it, 'if it had not been for you this terrible ordeal would have been saved me!'

When strapping up the bundle in which she carried a few articles of clothing, she took occasion to say to the servant, 'I take these in case I should not get back tonight from the person I am going to visit. Don't be alarmed if I am not in by ten, and close up the house as usual. I shall be at home tomorrow for certain.' She meant then to privately tell her husband: the deed accomplished was not like the deed projected. He would almost certainly forgive her.

And then the pretty palpitating Gertrude Lodge went from her husband's homestead; but though her goal was Casterbridge she did not take the direct route thither through Stickleford. Her cunning course at first was in precisely the opposite direction. As soon as she was out of sight, however, she turned to the left, by a road which led into Egdon, and on entering the heath wheeled round, and set out in the true course, due westerly. A more private way down the county could not be imagined; and as to direction, she had merely to keep her horse's head to a point a little to the right of the sun. She knew that she would light upon a furze-cutter or cottager of some sort from time to time, from whom she might correct her bearing.

Though the date was comparatively recent, Egdon was much less fragmentary in character than now. The attempts – successful and otherwise – at cultivation on the lower slopes, which intrude and break up the original heath into small detached heaths, had not been carried far: Enclosure Acts had not taken effect, and the banks and fences which now exclude the cattle of those villagers who formerly enjoyed rights of commonage thereon, and the carts of those who had turbary privileges which kept them in firing all the year round, were not erected. Gertrude therefore rode along with no other obstacles than the prickly furze-bushes, the mats of heather, the white water-courses, and the natural steeps and declivities of the ground.

Her horse was sure, if heavy-footed and slow, and though a draught animal, was easy-paced; had it been otherwise, she was not a woman who could have ventured to ride over such a bit of country with a half-dead arm. It was therefore nearly eight o'clock when she drew rein to breathe the mare on the last outlying high point of heath-land towards Casterbridge, previous to leaving Egdon for the cultivated valleys.

She halted before a pond, flanked by the ends of two hedges; a railing ran through the centre of the pond, dividing it in half. Over the railing she saw the low green country; over the green trees the roofs of the town; over the roofs a white flat façade, denoting the entrance to the county jail. On the roof of this front specks were moving about; they seemed to be workmen erecting something. Her flesh crept. She descended slowly, and was soon amid corn-fields and pastures. In another half-hour, when it was almost dusk, Gertrude reached the White Hart, the first inn of the town on that side.

Little surprise was excited by her arrival: farmers' wives rode on horseback then more than they do now; though, for that matter, Mrs Lodge was not imagined to be a wife at all; the inn-keeper supposed her some harum-skarum young woman who had come to attend 'hang-fair' next day. Neither her husband nor herself ever dealt in Casterbridge market, so that she was unknown. While dismounting she beheld a crowd of boys standing at the door of a harness-maker's shop just above the inn, looking inside it with deep interest.

'What is going on there?' she asked of the ostler.

'Making the rope for tomorrow.'

She throbbed responsively, and contracted her arm.

''Tis sold by the inch afterwards,' the man continued. 'I could get you a bit, miss, for nothing, if you'd like?'

She hastily repudiated any such wish, all the more from a curious creeping feeling that the condemned wretch's destiny was becoming interwoven with her own; and having engaged a room for the night, sat down to think.

Up to this time she had formed but the vaguest notions about her means of obtaining access to the prison. The words of the cunning-man returned to her mind. He had implied that she should use her beauty, impaired though it was, as a pass-key. In her inexperience she knew little about jail functionaries; she had heard of a high-sheriff and an under-sheriff, but dimly only. She knew, however, that there must be a hangman, and to the hangman she determined to apply.

VIII
A water-side hermit

At this date, and for several years after, there was a hangman to almost every jail. Gertrude found, on inquiry, that the Casterbridge official dwelt in a lonely cottage by a deep slow river flowing under the cliff on which the prison buildings were situate – the stream being the self-same one, though she did not know it, which watered the Stickleford and Holmstoke meads lower down in its course.

Having changed her dress, and before she had eaten or drunk – for she could not take her ease till she had ascertained some particulars – Gertrude pursued her way by a path along the water-side to the cottage indicated. Passing thus the outskirts of the jail, she discerned on the level roof over the gateway three rectangular lines against the sky, where the specks had been moving in her distant view; she recognized what the erection was, and passed quickly on. Another hundred yards brought her to the executioner's house, which a boy pointed out. It stood close to the same stream, and was hard by a weir, the waters of which emitted a steady roar.

While she stood hesitating the door opened, and an old man came forth shading a candle with one hand. Locking the door on the outside, he turned to a flight of wooden steps fixed against the end of the cottage, and began to ascend them, this being evidently the staircase to his bedroom. Gertrude hastened forward, but by the time she reached the foot of the ladder he was at the top. She called to him loudly enough to be heard above the roar of the weir; he looked down and said, 'What d'ye want here?'

'To speak to you a minute.'

The candle-light, such as it was, fell upon her imploring, pale, upturned face, and Davies (as the hangman was called) backed down the ladder. 'I was just going to bed,' he said; ' "Early to bed and early to rise," but I don't mind stopping a minute for such a one as you. Come into house.' He reopened the door, and preceded her to the room within.

The implements of his daily work, which was that of a jobbing gardener, stood in a corner, and seeing probably that she looked rural, he said, 'If you want me to undertake country work I can't come, for I never leave Casterbridge for gentle nor simple – not I. Though sometimes I make others leave,' he added formally.

'Yes, yes! That's it! Tomorrow!'

'Ah! I thought so. Well, what's the matter about that? 'Tis no use to come here about the knot – folks do come continually, but I tell 'em one knot is as merciful as another if ye keep it under the ear. Is the unfortunate man a relation; or, I should say, perhaps' (looking at her dress) 'a person who's been in your employ?'

'No. What time is the execution?'

'The same as usual – twelve o'clock, or as soon after as the London mail-coach gets in. We always wait for that, in case of a reprieve.'

'Oh – a reprieve – I hope not!' she said involuntarily.

'Well, – he, he! – as a matter of business, so do I! But still, if ever a young fellow deserved to be let off, this one does; only just turned eighteen, and only present by chance when the rick was fired. Howsomever, there's not much risk of it, as they are obliged to make an example of him, there having been so much destruction of property that way lately.'

'I mean,' she explained, 'that I want to touch him for a charm, a cure of an affliction, by the advice of a man who has proved the virtue of the remedy.'

'Oh yes, miss! Now I understand. I've had such people come in past years. But it didn't strike me that you looked of a sort to require blood-turning. What's the complaint? The wrong kind for this, I'll be bound.'

'My arm.' She reluctantly showed the withered skin.

'Ah! – 'tis all a-scram!' said the hangman, examining it.

'Yes,' said she.

'Well,' he continued with interest, 'that is the class o' subject, I'm bound to admit! I like the look of the place; it is truly as suitable for the cure as any I ever saw. 'Twas a knowing-man that sent 'ee, whoever he was.'

'You can contrive for me all that's necessary?' she said breathlessly.

'You should really have gone to the governor of the jail, and your doctor with 'ee, and given your name and address – that's how it used to be done, if I recollect. Still, perhaps, I can manage it for a trifling fee.'

'Oh, thank you! I would rather do it this way, as I should like it kept private.'

'Lover not to know, eh?'

'No – husband.'

'Ah! Very well. I'll get 'ee a touch of the corpse.'

'Where is it now?' she said, shuddering.

'It? – he, you mean; he's living yet. Just inside that little small winder up there in the glum.' He signified the jail on the cliff above.

She thought of her husband and her friends. 'Yes, of course,' she said; 'and how am I to proceed?'

He took her to the door. 'Now, do you be waiting at the little wicket in the wall, that you'll find up there in the lane, not later than one o'clock. I will open it from the inside, as I shan't come home to dinner till he's cut down. Good night. Be punctual; and if you don't want anybody to know 'ee, wear a veil. Ah – once I had such a daughter as you!'

She went away, and climbed the path above, to assure herself that she would be able to find the wicket next day. Its outline was soon visible to her – a narrow opening in the outer wall of the prison precincts. The steep was so great that, having reached the wicket, she stopped a moment to breathe; and, looking back upon the water-side cot, saw the hangman again ascending his outdoor staircase. He entered the loft or chamber to which it led, and in a few minutes extinguished his light.

The town clock struck ten, and she returned to the White Hart as she had come.

IX
A rencounter

It was one o'clock on Saturday. Gertrude Lodge, having been admitted to the jail as above described, was sitting in a waiting-room within the second gate, which stood under a classic archway of ashlar, then comparatively modern, and bearing the inscription, 'COUNTY JAIL: 1793.' This had been the façade she saw from the heath the day before. Near at hand was a passage to the roof on which the gallows stood.

The town was thronged, and the market suspended; but Gertrude had seen scarcely a soul. Having kept her room till the hour of the appointment, she had proceeded to the spot by a way which avoided the open space below the cliff where the spectators had gathered; but she could, even now, hear the multitudinous babble of their voices, out of which rose at intervals the hoarse croak of a single voice, uttering the words, 'Last dying speech and confession!' There had been no reprieve, and the execution was over; but the crowd still waited to see the body taken down.

Soon the persistent girl heard a trampling overhead, then a hand beckoned to her, and, following directions, she went out and crossed the inner paved court beyond the gatehouse, her knees trembling so that she could scarcely walk. One of her arms was out of its sleeve, and only covered by her shawl.

On the spot at which she had now arrived were two trestles, and before she could think of their purpose she heard heavy feet descending stairs somewhere at her back. Turn her head she would not, or could not, and, rigid in this position, she was conscious of a rough coffin passing her shoulder, borne by four men. It was open, and in it lay the body of a young man, wearing the smockfrock of a rustic, and fustian breeches. It had been thrown into the coffin so hastily that the skirt of the smockfrock was hanging over. The burden was temporarily deposited on the trestles.

By this time the young woman's state was such that a grey mist seemed to float before her eyes, on account of which, and the veil she wore, she could scarcely discern anything: it was as though she had nearly died, but was held up by a sort of galvanism.

'Now,' said a voice close at hand, and she was just conscious that it had been addressed to her.

By a last strenuous effort she advanced, at the same time hearing persons approaching behind her. She bared her poor curst arm; and Davies, uncovering the face of the corpse, took Gertrude's hand, and held it so that her arm lay across the dead man's neck, upon a line the colour of an unripe blackberry, which surrounded it.

Gertrude shrieked: 'the turn o' the blood,' predicted by the conjuror, had taken place. But at that moment a second shriek rent the air of the enclosure: it was not Gertrude's, and its effect upon her was to make her start round.

Immediately behind her stood Rhoda Brook, her face drawn, and her eyes red with weeping. Behind Rhoda stood her own husband; his countenance lined, his eyes dim, but without a tear.

'D–n you! what are you doing here?' he said hoarsely.

'Hussy – to come between us and our child now!' cried Rhoda. 'This is the meaning of what Satan showed me in the vision! You are like her at last!' And clutching the bare arm of the younger woman, she pulled her unresistingly back against the wall. Immediately Brook had loosened her hold the fragile young Gertrude slid down against the feet of her husband. When he lifted her up she was unconscious.

The mere sight of the twain had been enough to suggest to her that the dead young man was Rhoda's son. At that time the relative of an executed convict had the privilege of claiming the body for burial, if they chose to do so; and it was for this purpose that Lodge was awaiting the inquest with Rhoda. He had been summoned by her as soon as the young man was taken in the crime, and at different times since; and he had attended in court during the trial. This was the 'holiday' he had been indulging in of late. The two wretched parents had wished to avoid exposure; and hence had come themselves for the body, a wagon and sheet for its conveyance and covering being in waiting outside.

Gertrude's case was so serious that it was deemed advisable to call to her the surgeon who was at hand. She was taken out of the jail into the town; but she never reached home alive. Her delicate vitality, sapped perhaps by the paralysed arm, collapsed under the double shock that followed the severe strain, physical and mental, to which she had subjected herself during the previous twenty-four hours. Her blood had been 'turned' indeed – too far. Her death took place in the town three days after.

Her husband was never seen in Casterbridge again; once only in the old market-place at Anglebury, which he had so much frequented, and very seldom in public anywhere. Burdened at first with moodiness and remorse, he eventually changed for the better, and appeared as a chastened and thoughtful man. Soon after attending the funeral of his poor young wife he took steps towards giving up the farms in Holmstoke and the adjoining parish, and, having sold every head of his stock, he went away to Port-Bredy, at the other end of the county, living there in solitary lodgings till his death two years later of a painless decline. It was then found that he had bequeathed the whole of his not inconsiderable property to a reformatory for boys, subject to the payment of a small annuity to Rhoda Brook, if she could be found to claim it.

For some time she could not be found; but eventually she reappeared in her old parish, – absolutely refusing, however, to have anything to do with the provision made for her. Her monotonous milking at the dairy was resumed, and followed for many long years, till her form became bent, and her once abundant dark hair white and worn away at the forehead – perhaps by long pressure against the cows. Here, sometimes, those who knew her experiences would stand and observe her, and wonder what sombre thoughts were beating inside that impassive, wrinkled brow, to the rhythm of the alternating milkstreams.

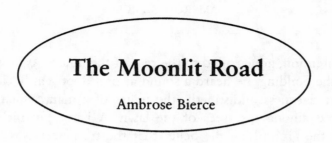

The Moonlit Road

Ambrose Bierce

I
STATEMENT OF JOEL HETMAN, JR.

I am the most unfortunate of men. Rich, respected, fairly well educated and of sound health – with many other advantages usually valued by those having them and coveted by those who have them not – I sometimes think that I should be less unhappy if they had been denied me, for then the contrast between my outer and my inner life would not be continually demanding a painful attention. In the stress of privation and the need of effort I might sometimes forget the sober secret ever baffling the conjecture that it compels.

I am the only child of Joel and Julia Hetman. The one was a well-to-do country gentleman, the other a beautiful and accomplished woman to whom he was passionately attached with what I now know to have been a jealous and exacting devotion. The family home was a few miles from Nashville, Tennessee, a large, irregularly built dwelling of no particular order of architecture, a little way off the road, in a park of trees and shrubbery.

At the time of which I write I was nineteen years old, a student at Yale. One day I received a telegram from my father of such urgency that in compliance with its unexplained demand I left at once for home. At the railway station in Nashville a distant relative awaited me to apprise me of the reason for my recall: my mother had been barbarously murdered – why and by whom none could conjecture, but the circumstances were these:

My father had gone to Nashville, intending to return the next afternoon. Something prevented his accomplishing the business in hand, so he returned on the same night, arriving just before the dawn. In his testimony before the coroner he explained that having no latchkey and not caring to disturb the sleeping servants, he had, with no clearly defined intention, gone round to the rear of the house. As he turned an angle of the building, he heard a sound as of a door gently closed, and saw in the darkness, indistinctly, the figure of a man, which instantly disappeared among the trees of the lawn. A hasty pursuit and brief search of the grounds in the belief that the trespasser was some one secretly visiting a servant proving fruitless, he entered at the unlocked door and mounted the stairs to my mother's chamber. Its door was open, and stepping into black darkness he fell headlong over some heavy object on the floor. I may spare myself the details; it was my poor mother, dead of strangulation by human hands.

Nothing had been taken from the house, the servants had heard no sound, and excepting those terrible finger-marks upon the dead woman's throat – dear God! that I might forget them! – no trace of the assassin was ever found.

I gave up my studies and remained with my father, who, naturally, was greatly changed. Always of a sedate, taciturn disposition, he now fell into so deep a dejection that nothing could hold his attention, yet anything – a footfall, the sudden closing of a door – aroused in him a fitful interest; one might have called it an apprehension. At any small surprise of the senses he would start visibly and sometimes turn pale, then relapse into a melancholy apathy deeper than before. I suppose he was what is called a "nervous wreck." As to me, I was younger then than now – there is much in that. Youth is Gilead, in which is balm for every wound. Ah, that I might again dwell in that enchanted land! Unacquainted with grief, I knew not how to appraise my bereavement; I could not rightly estimate the strength of the stroke.

One night, a few months after the dreadful event, my father and I walked home from the city. The full moon was about three hours above the eastern horizon; the entire countryside had the solemn stillness of a summer night; our footfalls and the ceaseless song of the katydids were the only sound aloof. Black shadows of bordering trees lay athwart the road, which, in the short reaches between, gleamed a ghostly white. As we approached the gate to our dwelling, whose front was in shadow, and in which no light shone, my father suddenly stopped and clutched my arm, saying, hardly above his breath:

"God! God! what is that?"

"I hear nothing," I replied.

"But see – see!" he said, pointing along the road, directly ahead.
I said: "Nothing is there. Come, father, let us go in – you are ill."

He had released my arm and was standing rigid and motionless in
the centre of the illuminated roadway, staring like one bereft of sense.
His face in the moonlight showed a pallor and fixity inexpressibly
distressing. I pulled gently at his sleeve, but he had forgotten my
existence. Presently he began to retire backward, step by step, never for
an instant removing his eyes from what he saw, or thought he saw. I
turned half round to follow, but stood irresolute. I do not recall any

feeling of fear, unless a sudden chill was its physical manifestation. It seemed as if an icy wind had touched my face and enfolded my body from head to foot; I could feel the stir of it in my hair.

At that moment my attention was drawn to a light that suddenly streamed from an upper window of the house: one of the servants, awakened by what mysterious premonition of evil who can say, and in obedience to an impulse that she was never able to name, had lit a lamp. When I turned to look for my father he was gone, and in all the years that have passed no whisper of his fate has come across the borderland of conjecture from the realm of the unknown.

II
STATEMENT OF CASPAR GRATTAN

To-day I am said to live; to-morrow, here in this room, will lie a senseless shape of clay that all too long was I. If anyone lift the cloth from the face of that unpleasant thing it will be in gratification of a mere morbid curiosity. Some, doubtless, will go further and inquire, "Who was he?" In this writing I supply the only answer that I am able to make – Caspar Grattan. Surely, that should be enough. The name has served my small need for more than twenty years of a life of unknown length. True, I gave it to myself, but lacking another I had the right. In this world one must have a name; it prevents confusion, even when it does not establish identity. Some, though, are known by numbers, which also seem inadequate distinctions.

One day, for illustration, I was passing along a street of a city, far from here, when I met two men in uniform, one of whom, half pausing and looking curiously into my face, said to his companion, "That man looks like 767." Something in the number seemed familiar and horrible. Moved by an uncontrollable impulse, I sprang into a side street and ran until I fell exhausted in a country lane.

I have never forgotten that number, and always it comes to memory attended by gibbering obscenity, peals of joyless laughter, the clang of iron doors. So I say a name, even if self-bestowed, is better than a number. In the register of the potter's field I shall soon have both. What wealth!

Of him who shall find this paper I must beg a little consideration.

It is not the history of my life; the knowledge to write that is denied me. This is only a record of broken and apparently unrelated memories, some of them as distinct and sequent as brilliant beads upon a thread, others remote and strange, having the character of crimson dreams with interspaces blank and black – witch-fires glowing still and red in a great desolation.

Standing upon the shore of eternity, I turn for a last look landward over the course by which I came. There are twenty years of footprints fairly distinct, the impressions of bleeding feet. They lead through poverty and pain, devious and unsure, as of one staggering beneath a burden –

Remote, unfriended, melancholy, slow.

Ah, the poet's prophecy of Me – how admirable, how dreadfully admirable!

Backward beyond the beginning of this *via dolorosa* – this epic of suffering with episodes of sin – I see nothing clearly; it comes out of a cloud. I know that it spans only twenty years, yet I am an old man.

One does not remember one's birth – one has to be told. But with me it was different; life came to me full-handed and dowered me with all my faculties and powers. Of a previous existence I know no more than others, for all have stammering intimations that may be memories and may be dreams. I know only that my first consciousness was of maturity in body and mind – a consciousness accepted without surprise or conjecture. I merely found myself walking in a forest, half-clad, footsore, unutterably weary and hungry. Seeing a farmhouse, I approached and asked for food, which was given me by one who inquired my name. I did not know, yet knew that all had names. Greatly embarrassed, I retreated, and night coming on, lay down in the forest and slept.

The next day I entered a large town which I shall not name. Nor shall I recount further incidents of the life that is now to end – a life of wandering, always and everywhere haunted by an overmastering sense of crime in punishment of wrong and of terror in punishment of crime. Let me see if I can reduce it to narrative.

I seem once to have lived near a great city, a prosperous planter, married to a woman whom I loved and distrusted. We had, it sometimes seems, one child, a youth of brilliant parts and promise. He is at all times a vague figure, never clearly drawn, frequently altogether out of the picture.

One luckless evening it occurred to me to test my wife's fidelity in a vulgar, commonplace way familiar to everyone who has acquaintance with the literature of fact and fiction. I went to the city, telling my wife that I should be absent until the following afternoon. But I returned before daybreak and went to the rear of the house, purposing to enter by a door with which I had secretly so tampered that it would seem to lock, yet not actually fasten. As I approached it, I heard it gently open and close, and saw a man steal away into the darkness. With murder in my heart, I sprang after him, but he had vanished without even the bad luck of identification. Sometimes now I cannot even persuade myself that it was a human being.

Crazed with jealousy and rage, blind and bestial with all the elemental passions of insulted manhood, I entered the house and sprang up the stairs to the door of my wife's chamber. It was closed, but having tampered with its lock also, I easily entered and despite the black darkness soon stood by the side of her bed. My groping hands told me that although disarranged it was unoccupied.

"She is below," I thought, "and terrified by my entrance has evaded me in the darkness of the hall."

With the purpose of seeking her I turned to leave the room, but took a wrong direction – the right one! My foot struck her, cowering in a corner of the room. Instantly my hands were at her throat, stifling a shriek, my knees were upon her struggling body; and there in the darkness, without a word of accusation or reproach, I strangled her till she died!

There ends the dream. I have related it in the past tense, but the present would be the fitter form, for again and again the sober tragedy reenacts itself in my consciousness – over and over I lay the plan, I suffer the confirmation, I redress the wrong. Then all is blank; and afterward the rains beat against the grimy window-panes, or the snows fall upon my scant attire, the wheels rattle in the squalid streets where my life lies in poverty and mean employment. If there is ever sunshine I do not recall it; if there are birds they do not sing.

There is another dream, another vision of the night. I stand among the shadows in a moonlit road. I am aware of another presence, but whose I cannot rightly determine. In the shadow of a great dwelling I catch the gleam of white garments; then the figure of a woman confronts me in the road – my murdered wife. There is death in the face; there are marks upon the throat. The eyes are fixed on mine with an infinite gravity which is not reproach, nor hate, nor menace, nor anything less terrible than recognition. Before this awful apparition I retreat in terror – a terror that is upon me as I write. I can no longer rightly shape the words. See! they –

Now I am calm, but truly there is no more to tell: the incident ends where it began – in darkness and in doubt.

Yes, I am again in control of myself: "the captain of my soul." But that is not respite; it is another stage and phase of expiation. My penance, constant in degree, is mutable in kind: one of its variants is tranquillity. After all, it is only a life-sentence. "To Hell for life" – that is a foolish penalty: the culprit chooses the duration of his punishment. To-day my term expires.

To each and all, the peace that was not mine.

III
STATEMENT OF THE LATE JULIA HETMAN, THROUGH THE MEDIUM BAYROLLES

I had retired early and fallen almost immediately into a peaceful sleep, from which I awoke with that indefinable sense of peril which is, I think, a common experience in that other, earlier life. Of its unmeaning character, too, I was entirely persuaded, yet that did not banish it. My husband, Joel Hetman, was away from home; the servants slept in another part of the house. But these were familiar conditions; they had never before distressed me. Nevertheless, the strange terror grew so insupportable that conquering my reluctance to move I sat up and lit the lamp at my bedside. Contrary to my expectation this gave me no relief; the light seemed rather an added danger, for I reflected that it would shine out under the door, disclosing my presence to whatever evil thing might lurk outside. You that are still in the flesh, subject to horrors of the imagination, think what a monstrous fear that must be which seeks in darkness security from malevolent existences of the night. That is to spring to close quarters with an unseen enemy – the strategy of despair!

Extinguishing the lamp I pulled the bedclothing about my head and lay trembling and silent, unable to shriek, forgetful to pray. In this pitiable state I must have lain for what you call hours – with us there are no hours, there is no time.

At last it came – a soft, irregular sound of footfalls on the stairs. They were slow, hesitant, uncertain, as of something that did not see its way; to my disordered reason all the more terrifying for that, as the approach of some blind and mindless malevolence to which is no appeal. I even thought that I must have left the hall lamp burning and the groping of this creature proved it a monster of the night. This was foolish and inconsistent with my previous dread of the light, but what would you have? Fear has no brains; it is an idiot. The dismal witness that it bears and the cowardly counsel that it whispers are unrelated. We know this well, we who have passed into the Realm of Terror, who skulk in eternal dusk among the scenes of our former lives, invisible even to ourselves and one another, yet hiding forlorn in lonely places; yearning for speech with our loved ones, yet dumb, and as fearful of them as they of us. Sometimes the disability is removed, the law suspended: by the deathless power of love or hate we break the spell – we are seen by those whom we would warn, console, or punish. What form we seem to them to bear we know not; we know only that we terrify even those whom we most wish to comfort, and from whom we most crave tenderness and sympathy.

Forgive, I pray you, this inconsequent digression by what was once a woman. You who consult us in this imperfect way – you do not understand. You ask foolish questions about things unknown and things forbidden. Much that we know and could impart in our speech is meaningless in yours. We must communicate with you through a stammering intelligence in that small fraction of our language that you yourselves can speak. You think that we are of another world. No, we have knowledge of no world but yours, though for us it holds no sunlight, no warmth, no music, no laughter, no song of birds, nor any companionship. O God! what a thing it is to be a ghost, cowering and shivering in an altered world, a prey to apprehension and despair!

No, I did not die of fright: the Thing turned and went away. I heard it go down the stairs, hurriedly, I thought, as if itself in sudden fear. Then I rose to call for help. Hardly had my shaking hand found the doorknob when – merciful heaven! – I heard it returning. Its footfalls as it remounted the stairs were rapid, heavy and loud; they shook the house. I fled to an angle of the wall and crouched upon the floor. I tried to pray. I tried to call the name of my dear husband. Then I heard the door thrown open. There was an interval of unconsciousness, and when I revived I felt a strangling clutch upon my throat – felt my arms feebly beating against something that bore me backward – felt my tongue thrusting itself from between my teeth! And then I passed into this life.

No, I have no knowledge of what it was. The sum of what we knew at death is the measure of what we know afterward of all that went before. Of this existence we know many things, but no new light falls upon any page of that; in memory is written all of it that we can read.

Here are no heights of truth overlooking the confused landscape of that dubitable domain. We still dwell in the Valley of the Shadow, lurk in its desolate places, peering from brambles and thickets at its mad, malign inhabitants. How should we have new knowledge of that fading past?

What I am about to relate happened on a night. We know when it is night, for then you retire to your houses and we can venture from our places of concealment to move unafraid about our old homes, to look in at the windows, even to enter and gaze upon your faces as you sleep. I had lingered long near the dwelling where I had been so cruelly changed to what I am, as we do while any that we love or hate remain. Vainly I had sought some method of manifestation, some way to make my continued existence and my great love and poignant pity understood by my husband and son. Always if they slept they would wake, or if in my desperation I dared approach them when they were awake, would turn toward me the terrible eyes of the living, frightening me by the glances that I sought from the purpose that I held.

On this night I had searched for them without success, fearing to find them; they were nowhere in the house, nor about the moonlit lawn. For, although the sun is lost to us forever, the moon, full-orbed or slender, remains to us. Sometimes it shines by night, sometimes by day, but always it rises and sets, as in that other life.

I left the lawn and moved in the white light and silence along the road, aimless and sorrowing. Suddenly I heard the voice of my poor husband in exclamations of astonishment, with that of my son in reassurance and dissuasion; and there by the shadow of a group of trees they stood – near, so near! Their faces were toward me, the eyes of the elder man fixed upon mine. He saw me – at last, at last, he saw me! In the consciousness of that, my terror fled as a cruel dream. The deathspell was broken: Love had conquered Law! Mad with exultation I shouted – I must have shouted, "He sees, he sees: he will understand!" Then, controlling myself, I moved forward, smiling and consciously beautiful, to offer myself to his arms, to comfort him with endearments, and, with my son's hand in mine, to speak words that should restore the broken bonds between the living and the dead.

Alas! alas! his face went white with fear, his eyes were as those of a hunted animal. He backed away from me, as I advanced, and at last turned and fled into the wood – whither, it is not given to me to know.

To my poor boy, left doubly desolate, I have never been able to impart a sense of my presence. Soon he, too, must pass to this Life Invisible and be lost to me forever.

Ghosts That Have Haunted Me

John Kendrick Bangs

If we could only get used to the idea that ghosts are perfectly harmless creatures, who are powerless to affect our well-being unless we assist them by giving way to our fears, we should enjoy the supernatural exceedingly, it seems to me. Coleridge, I think it was, was once asked by a lady if he believed in ghosts, and he replied, 'No, madame; I have seen too many of them.' Which is my case exactly. I have seen so many horrid visitants from other worlds that they hardly affect me at all, so far as the mere inspiration of terror is concerned. On the other hand, they interest me hugely; and while I must admit that I do experience all the purely physical sensations that come from horrific encounters of this nature, I can truly add in my own behalf that mentally I can rise above the physical impulse to run away, and, invariably standing my ground, I have gained much useful information concerning them. I am prepared to assert that if a thing with flashing green eyes, and clammy hands, and long, dripping strips of sea-weed in place of hair, should rise up out of the floor before me at this moment, 2 a.m., and nobody in the house but myself, with a fearful, nerve-destroying storm raging outside, I should without hesitation ask it to sit down and light a cigar and state its business – or, if it were of the female persuasion, to join me in a bottle of sarsparilla – although every physical manifestation of fear of which my poor body is capable would be present. I have had experiences in this line which, if I could get you to believe them, would convince you that I speak the truth. Knowing weak, suspicious human nature as I do, however, I do not hope ever to convince you – though it is none the less true – that on one occasion, in the spring of 1895, there was a spiritual manifestation in my library which nearly prostrated me physically, but which mentally I hugely enjoyed, because I was mentally strong enough to subdue my physical repugnance for the thing which suddenly and without any apparent reason materialised in my arm-chair.

I'm going to tell you about it briefly, though I warn you in advance that you will find it a great strain upon your confidence in my veracity. It may even shatter that confidence beyond repair; but I cannot help that. I hold that it is a man's duty in this life to give to the world the benefit of his experience. All that he sees he should set down exactly as he sees it, and so simply, withal, that to the dullest comprehension the moral involved shall be perfectly obvious. If he is a painter, and an auburn-haired maiden appears to him to have blue hair, he should paint her hair blue, and just so long as he sticks by his principles and is true to himself, he need not bother about what you may think of him. So it is with me. My scheme of living is based upon being true to myself. You may class me with Baron Munchausen if you choose; I shall not mind so long as I have the consolation of feeling, deep down in my heart, that I am a true realist, and diverge not from the paths of truth as truth manifests itself to me.

This intruder of whom I was just speaking, the one that took possession of my arm-chair in the spring of 1895, was about as horrible a spectre as I have ever had the pleasure to have haunt me. It was grotesque beyond description. Alongside of it the ordinary poster of the present day would seem to be as accurate in drawing as a bicycle map, and in its colouring it simply shrieked with discord.

If colour had tones which struck the ear, instead of appealing to the eye, the thing would have deafened me. It was about midnight when the manifestation first took shape. My family had long before retired, and I had just finished smoking a cigar – which was one of a thousand which my wife had bought for me at a Monday sale at one of the big department stores in New York. I don't remember the brand, but that is just as well – it was not a cigar to be advertised in a civilized piece of literature – but I do remember that they came in bundles of fifty, tied about with blue ribbon. The one I had been smoking tasted and burned as if it had been rolled by a Cuban insurrectionist while fleeing from a Spanish regiment through a morass, gathering its component parts as he ran. It had two distinct merits, however. No man could possible smoke too many of them, and they were economical, which is how the ever-helpful little madame came to get them for me, and I have no doubt they will some day prove very useful in removing insects from the rosebushes. They cost $3.99 a thousand on five days a week, but at the Monday sale they were marked down to $1.75, which is why my wife, to whom I had recently read a little lecture on economy, purchased them for me. Upon the evening in question I had been at work on this cigar for about two hours, and had smoked one side of it three-quarters of the way down to the end, when I concluded that I had smoked enough – for one day – so I rose up to cast the other side into the fire, which was flickering fitfully in my spacious fireplace. This done, I turned about, and there, fearful to see, sat this thing grinning at me from the depths of my chair. My hair not only stood on end, but tugged madly in an effort to get away. Four hairs – I can prove the statement if it be desired – did pull themselves loose from my scalp in their insane desire to rise above the terrors of the situation, and, flying upward, stuck like nails into the oak ceiling directly above my head, whence they had to be pulled the next morning with nippers by our hired man, who would no doubt testify to the truth of the occurrence as I have asserted it if he were still living, which, unfortunately, he is not. Like most hired men, he was subject to attacks of lethargy, from one of which he died last summer. He sank into a rest about weed-time, last June, and lingered quietly along for two months, and after several futile efforts to wake him up, we finally disposed of him to our town crematory for experimental purposes. I am told he burned very actively, and I believe it, for to my certain knowledge he was very dry, and not so green as some person who had previously employed him affected to think. A cold chill came over me as my eye rested upon the horrid visitor and noted the greenish depths of his eyes and the claw-like formation of his finger, and my flesh began to creep like an inch-worm. At one time I was conscious of eight separate corrugations on my back, and my arms goose-fleshed until they looked like one of those miniature plaster casts of the Alps which are so popular in Swiss summer resorts; but mentally I was not disturbed at all. My repugnance was entirely physical, and, to come to the point at once, I calmly offered the spectre a cigar, which it accepted, and demanded a light. I gave it, nonchalantly lighting the match upon the goose-fleshing of my wrist.

Now I admit that this was extraordinary and hardly credible, yet it happened exactly as I have set it down, and furthermore, I enjoyed the experience. For three hours the thing and I conversed, and not once during that time did my hair stop pulling away at my scalp, or the repugnance cease to run in great rolling waves up and down my back. If I wished to deceive you, I might add that pin-feathers began to grow from the goose-flesh, but that would be a lie, and lying and I are not friends, and, furthermore, this paper is not written to amaze, but to instruct.

Except for its personal appearance, this particular ghost was not very remarkable, and I do not at this time recall any of the details of our conversation beyond the point that my share of it was not particularly coherent, because of the discomfort attendant upon the fearful hairpulling process I was going through. I merely cite its coming to prove that, with all the outward visible signs of fear manifesting themselves in no uncertain manner, mentally I was cool enough to cope with the visitant, and sufficiently calm and at ease to light the match upon my wrist, perceiving for the first time, with an Edison-like ingenuity, one of the uses to which goose-flesh might be put, and knowing full well that if I tried to light it on the sole of my shoe I should have fallen to the ground, my knees being too shaky to admit of my standing on one leg even for an instant. Had I been mentally overcome, I should have tried to light the match on my foot, and fallen ignominiously to the floor then and there.

There was another ghost that I recall to prove my point, who was of very great use to me in the summer immediately following the spring of which I have just told you. You will possibly remember how that the summer of 1895 had rather more than its fair share of heat, and that the lovely Hudson River town in which I have the happiness to dwell appeared to be the headquarters of the temperature. The thermometers of the nation really seemed to take orders from Bronxdale, and properly enough, for our town is a born leader in respect to heat. Having no property to sell, I candidly admit that Bronxdale is not of an arctic nature in summer, except socially, perhaps. Socially, it is the coolest town on the Hudson; but we are at this moment not discussing cordiality, fraternal love, or the question raised by the Declaration of Independence as to whether all men are born equal. The warmth we have in hand is what the old lady called 'Fahrenheat,' and, from a thermometric point of view, Bronxdale, if I may be a trifle slangy, as I sometimes am, has heat to burn. There are mitigations of this heat, it is true, but they generally come along in winter.

I must claim, on behalf of my town, that never in all my experience have I known a summer so hot that it was not, sooner or later – by January, anyhow – followed by a cool spell. But in the summer of 1895 even the real-estate agents confessed that the cold wave announced by the weather bureau at Washington summered elsewhere – in the tropics, perhaps, but not at Bronxdale. One hardly dared take a bath in the morning for fear of being scalded by the fluid that flowed from the cold-water faucet – our reservoir is entirely unprotected by shade-trees, and in summer a favourite spot for young Waltons who like to catch bass already boiled – my neighbours and myself lived on cracked ice, ice-cream, and destructive cold drinks. I do not myself mind hot weather in the daytime, but hot nights are killing. I can't sleep. I toss about for hours, and then, for the sake of variety, I flop, but sleep cometh not. My debts double, and my income seems to sizzle away under the influence of a hot, sleepless night; and it was just here that a certain awful thing saved me from the insanity which is a certain result of parboiled insomnia.

It was about the 16th of July, which as I remember reading in an extra edition of the *Evening Bun*, got out to mention the fact, was the hottest 16th of July known in thirty-eight years. I had retired at half-past seven, after dining lightly upon a cold salmon and a gallon of iced tea – not because I was tired, but because I wanted to get down to first principles at once, and removed my clothing, and sort of spread myself over all the territory I could, which is a thing you can't do in a library, or even in a white-and-gold parlour. If man were constructed like a machine, as he really ought to be, to be strictly comfortable – a machine that could be taken apart like an eight-day clock – I should have taken myself apart, putting one section of myself on the roof, another part in the spare room, hanging a third on the clothes-line in the yard, and so on, leaving my head in the ice-box; but unfortunately we have to keep ourselves together in this life, hence I did the only thing one can do, and retired, and incidentally spread myself over some freshly baked bedclothing. There was some relief from the heat, but not much. I had been roasting, and while my sensations were somewhat like those which I imagine come to a planked shad when he first finds himself spread out over the plank, there was a mitigation. My temperature fell off from 167 to about 163, which is not quite enough to make a man absolutely content. Suddenly, however, I began to shiver. There was no breeze, but I began to shiver.

'It is getting cooler,' I thought, as the chill came on, and I rose and looked at the thermometer. It still registered the highest possible point, and the mercury was rebelliously trying to break through the top of the glass tube and take a stroll on the roof.

'That's queer,' I said to myself. 'It's as hot as ever, and yet I'm shivering. I wonder if my goose is cooked? I've certainly got a chill.'

I jumped back into bed and pulled the sheet up over me; but still I shivered. Then I pulled the blanket up, but the chill continued. I couldn't seem to get warm again. Then came the counterpane, and finally I had to put on my bath-robe – a fuzzy woollen affair, which in midwinter I had sometimes found too warm for comfort. Even then I was not sufficiently bundled up, so I called for an extra blanket, two afghans, and the hot-water bag.

Everybody in the house thought I had gone mad, and I wondered myself if perhaps I hadn't, when all of a sudden I perceived, off in the corner, the Awful Thing, and perceiving it, I knew all.

I was being haunted, and the physical repugnance of which I have spoken was on. The cold shiver, the invariable accompaniment of the ghostly visitant, had come, and I assure you I never was so glad of anything in my life. It has always been said of me by my critics that I am raw; I was afraid that after that night they would say I was half baked, and I would far rather be the one than the other; and it was the Awful Thing that saved me. Realizing this, I spoke to it gratefully.

'You are a heaven-born gift on a night like this,' said I, rising up and walking to its side. 'I am glad to be of service to you,' the Awful Thing replied, smiling at me so yellowly that I almost wished the author of the *Blue-Button of Cowardice* could have seen it.

'It's very good of you,' I put in.

'Not at all,' replied the Thing; 'you are the only man I know who doesn't think it necessary to prevaricate about ghosts every time he gets an order for a Christmas story. There have been more lies told about us than about any other class of things in existence, and we are getting a trifle tired of it. We may have lost our corporeal existence, but some of our sensitiveness still remains.'

'Well,' said I, rising and lighting the gas-logs – for I was on the very verge of congealment – 'I am sure I am pleased if you like my stories.'

'Oh, as for that, I don't think much of them,' said the Awful Thing, with a purple display of candour which amused me, although I cannot say that I relished it; 'but you never lie about us. You are not at all interesting, but you are truthful, and we spooks hate libellers. Just because one happens to be a thing is no reason why writers should libel it, and that's why I have always respected you. We regard you as a sort of spook Boswell. You may be dull and stupid, but you tell the truth, and when I saw you in imminent danger of becoming a mere grease spot, owing to the fearful heat, I decided to help you through. That's why I'm here. Go to sleep now. I'll stay here and keep you shivering until daylight anyhow. I'd stay longer, but we are always laid at sunrise.'

'Like an egg,' I said, sleepily.

'Tutt!' said the ghost. 'Go to sleep. If you talk I'll have to go.'

And so I dropped off to sleep as softly and as sweetly as a tired child. In the morning I awoke refreshed. The rest of my family were prostrated, but I was fresh. The Awful Thing was gone, and the room was warming up again; and if it had not been for the tinkling ice in my water-pitcher, I should have suspected it was all a dream. And so throughout the whole sizzling summer the friendly spectre stood by me and kept me cool, and I haven't a doubt that it was because of his good offices in keeping me shivering on those fearful August nights that I survived the season, and came to my work in the autumn as fit as a fiddle – so fit, indeed, that I have not written a poem since that has not struck me as being the very best of its kind, and if I can find a publisher who will take the risk of putting those poems out, I shall unequivocally and without hesitation acknowledge, as I do here, my debt of gratitude to my friends in the spirit world.

Manifestations of this nature, then, are harmful, as I have already observed, only when the person who is haunted yields to his physical impulses. Fought stubbornly inch by inch with the will, they can be subdued, and often they are a boon. I think I have proved both these points. It took me a long time to discover the facts, however, and my discovery came about in this way. It may perhaps interest you to know how I made it. I encountered at the English home of a wealthy friend at one time a 'presence' of an insulting turn of mind. It was at my friend

Jarley's little baronial hall, which he had rented from the Earl of Brokedale the year Mrs Jarley was presented at court. The Countess of Brokedale's social influence went with the château for a slightly increased rental, which was why the Jarleys took it. I was invited to spend a month with them, not so much because Jarley is fond or me as because Mrs Jarley had a sort of an idea that, as a writer, I might say something about their newly acquired glory in some American Sunday newspaper; and Jarley laughingly assigned to me the 'haunted chamber,' without at least one of which no baronial hall in the old country is considered worthy of the name.

'It will interest you more than any other,' Jarley said; 'and if it has a ghost, I imagine you will be able to subdue him.'

I gladly accepted the hospitality of my friend, and was delighted at his consideration in giving me the haunted chamber, where I might pursue my investigations into the subject of phantoms undisturbed. Deserting London, then, for a time, I ran down to Brokedale Hall, and took up my abode there with a half-dozen other guests. Jarley, as usual since his sudden 'gold-fall,' as Wilkins called it, did everything with a lavish hand. I believe a man could have got diamonds on toast if he had chosen to ask for them. However, this is apart from my story.

I had occupied the haunted chamber about two weeks before anything of importance occurred, and then it came – and a more unpleasant, ill-mannered spook never floated in the ether. He materialised about 3 a.m. and was unpleasantly sulphurous to one's perceptions. He sat upon the divan in my room, holding his knees in his hand, leering and scowling upon me as though I were the intruder, and not he.

'Who are you?' I asked, excitedly, as in the dying light of the log fire he loomed grimly up before me.

'None of your business,' he replied, insolently, showing his teeth as he spoke. 'On the other hand, who are you? This is my room, and not yours, and it is I who have the right to question. If you have any business here, well and good. If not, you will oblige me by removing yourself, for your presence is offensive to me.'

'I am a guest in the house,' I answered restraining my impulse to throw the ink-stand at him for his impudence. 'And this room has been set apart for my use by my host.'

'One of the servant's guests, I presume?' he said, insultingly, his lividly lavender-like lip upcurling into a haughty sneer, which was maddening to a self-respecting worm like myself.

I rose up from my bed, and picked up the poker to bat him over the head, but again I restrained myself. It will not do to quarrel, I thought. I will be courteous if he is not, thus giving a dead Englishman a lesson which wouldn't hurt some of the living.

'No,' I said, my voice tremulous with wrath – 'no; I am the guest of my friend Mr Jarley, an American, who –'

'Same thing,' observed the intruder, with a yellow sneer. 'Race of low-class animals, those Americans – only fit for gentlemen's stables, you know.'

This was too much. A ghost may insult me with impunity, but when he tackles my people he must look out for himself. I sprang forward with an ejaculation of wrath, and with all my strength struck at him with the poker, which I still held in my hand. If he had been anything but a ghost, he would have been split vertically from top to toe; but as it was, the poker passed harmlessly through his misty make-up, and rent a great gash two feet long in Jarley's divan. The yellow sneer faded from his lips, and a maddening blue smile took its place.

'Humph!' he observed, nonchalantly. 'What a useless ebullition, and what a vulgar display of temper! Really you are the most humorous insect I have yet encountered. From what part of the States do you come? I am truly interested to know in what kind of soil exotics of your peculiar kind are cultivated. Are you part of the fauna or the flora of your tropical States – or what?'

And then I realised the truth. There is no physical method of combating a ghost which can result in his discomfiture, so I resolved to try the intellectual. It was a mind-to-mind contest, and he was easy prey after I got going. I joined him in his blue smile, and began to talk about the English aristocracy; for I doubted not, from the spectre's manner, that he was or had been one of that class. He had about him that haughty lack of manners which bespoke the aristocrat. I waxed very eloquently when, as I say, I got my mind really going. I spoke of kings and queens and their uses in no uncertain phrases, of divine right, of dukes, earls, marquises – of all the pompous establishments of British royalty and nobility – with that contemptuously humorous tolerance of a necessary and somewhat amusing evil which we find in American comic papers. We had a battle royal for about one hour, and I must confess he was a foeman worthy of any man's steel, so long as I was reasonable in my arguments; but when I finally observed that it wouldn't be ten years before Barnum and Bailey's Greatest Show on Earth had the whole lot engaged for the New York circus season, stalking about the Madison Square Garden arena, with the Prince of Wales at the head beating a tomtom, he grew iridescent with wrath, and fled madly through the wainscoting of the room. It was purely a mental victory. All the physical possibilities of my being would have exhausted themselves futilely before him; but when I turned upon him the resources of my fancy, my imagination unrestrained, and held back by no sense of responsibility, he was as a child in my hands, obstreperous, but certain to be subdued. If it were not for Mrs Jarley's wrath – which, I admit, she tried to conceal – over the damage to her divan, I should now look back upon that visitation as the most agreeable haunting experience of my life; at any rate, it was at that time that I first learned how to handle ghosts, and since that time I have been able to overcome them without trouble – save in one instance, with which I shall close this chapter of my reminiscences, and which I give only to prove the necessity of observing strictly one point in dealing with spectres.

It happened last Christmas, in my own home. I had provided as a little surprise for my wife a complete new solid silver service marked with her initials. The tree had been prepared for the children, and all had retired save myself. I had lingered later than the others to put the silver service under the tree, where its happy recipient would find it when she went to the tree with the little ones the next morning. It made a magnificent display: the two dozen of each kind of spoon, the forks, the knives, the coffee-pot, water-urn, and all; the salvers, the vegetable-dishes, olive-forks, cheese-scoops, and other dazzling attributes of a complete service, not to go into details, presented a fairly scintillating picture which would have made me gasp if I had not, at the moment when my own breath began to catch, heard another gasp in the corner immediately behind me. Turning about quickly to see whence it came, I observed a dark figure in the pale light of the moon which streamed in through the window.

'Who are you?' I cried, starting back, the physical symptoms of a ghostly presence manifesting themselves as usual.

'I am the ghost of one long gone before,' was the reply, in sepulchral tones.

I breathed a sigh of relief, for I had for a moment feared it was a burglar.

'Oh!' I said. 'You gave me a start at first. I was afraid you were a material thing come to rob me.' Then turning towards the tree, I observed, with a wave of the hand, 'Fine lay out, eh?'

Beautiful,' he said hollowly. 'Yet not so beautiful as things I've seen in realms beyond your ken.'

And then he set about telling me of the beautiful gold and silver ware they used in the Elysian Fields, and I must confess Monte Cristo would have had a hard time, with Sindbad the Sailor to help, to surpass the picture of the royal magnificence the spectre drew. I stood enthralled until, even as he was talking, the clock struck three, when he rose up, and moving slowly across the floor, barely visible, murmured regretfully that he must be off, with which he faded away down the back stairs. I pulled my nerves, which were getting rather strained, together again, and went to bed.

Next morning every bit of that silver-ware was gone; and, what is more, three weeks later I found the ghost's picture in the Rogues' Gallery in New York as that of the cleverest sneak-thief in the country.

All of which, let me say to you, dear reader, in conclusion, proves that when you are dealing with ghosts you mustn't give up all your physical resources until you have definitely ascertained that the thing by which you are confronted, horrid or otherwise, is a ghost, and not an all too material rogue with a light step and a commodious jute bag for plunder concealed beneath his coat.

'How to tell a ghost?' you ask.

Well, as an eminent master of fiction frequently observes in his writings, 'that is another story,' which I shall hope some day to tell for your instruction and my own aggrandisement.